Darkness Blooms

Book II

The God Killers Trilogy

Written By:

Sean Gregory

Cover Art Hand-Painted by Libby Musacchio

Edited by:
RB Michaels & Laura Thompson - Writer's Journey Services

Proofread by:
Holly Hudson Jones

First Edition Printed 2025

For more information, visit: www.sean-gregory.com

Dedication

To those who are hurt

You are never alone

;

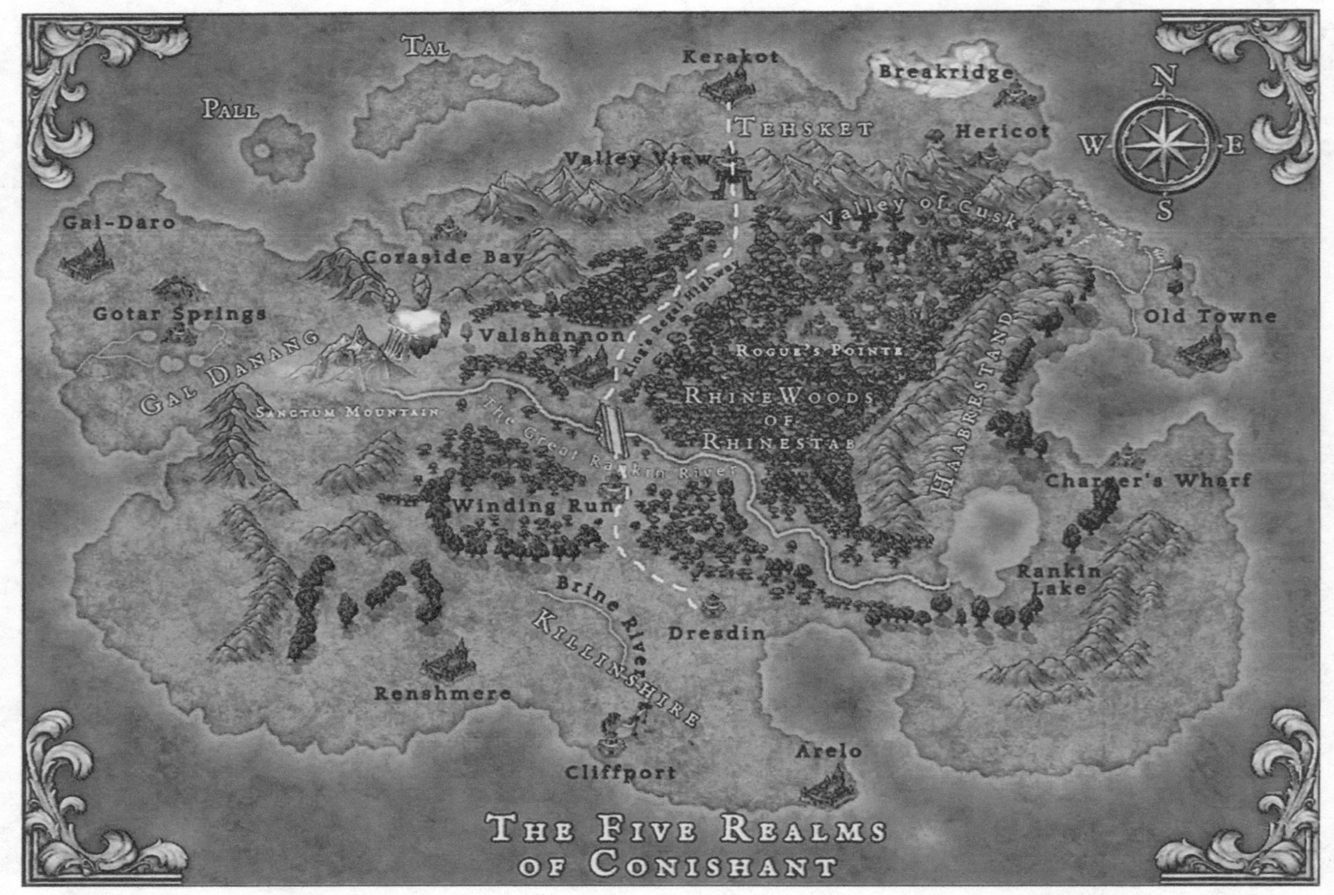

Tal
Kerakot
Breakridge
Pall
Tehsket
Hericot
Valley View
N E W S
Valley of Cusk
Gal-Daro
Coraside Bay
Old Towne
Gotar Springs
Valshannon
Rogue's Pointe
RhineWoods OF Rhinestab
Gal Danang
King's Regal Highway
Haabrestand
Sanctum Mountain
The Great Rankin River
Charger's Wharf
Winding Run
Rankin Lake
Brine River
Killinshire
Dresdin
Renshmere
Arelo
Cliffport
THE FIVE REALMS OF CONISHANT

Darkness
Blooms

The Queen

"**M**aybe I've been too soft on you, *Emissary*," the queen hissed, spit flying from her mouth in tiny droplets.

Krin winced at the delivery of her title, more accustomed to the whispered groans of her true name from the queen's lips than she was to the queen's disdain. Her head spun from the unexpected change in tone from last night's throes of passion to tonight's malicious verbal attack. Krin tried to hide her fear, but the monarch's ire rarely occurred without punishment. The queen could be ruthless when displeased by those she favored.

Krin had very different expectations of how tonight's events would progress. She eagerly anticipated another passionate night in the embrace of her sovereign. But that promise was lost now.

Krin didn't know whether the unmitigated rage or its catalyst frightened her more.

How did he survive?

As improbable as Krin joining the pantheon of gods, the *Harbinger* was alive—and here, in the queen's mansion. Shen suffered a devastating knife wound, a thirty-foot fall into the valley, *and* capture by the Cuska. Nobody survived the Cuska, especially in the condition she left him. It was too preposterous to believe. Legends were made of such feats.

That was the problem. Shen *was* a legend. One she'd underestimated.

Krin faced the very Cuska that should have finished the Harbinger. She'd only escaped the creature by sheer luck, a bit of fast action with her knife, and redirection toward the easy target of Shen's unconscious and dying body.

The Queen topped that news with the revelation that the Harbinger was here, in her mansion, and bedding the princess.

Even then, her majesty wasn't finished delivering bitter news. As if it were all somehow Krin's fault, the queen informed the emissary that the supposedly dead Harbinger murdered Captain Brogen of The Dark Guard of Killinshire less than a week after his presumed demise at the hands of the Cuska.

Krin sensed the final nail squeak through the wood that sealed her metaphorical coffin, or at least she hoped it was metaphorical. Her mouth went instantly dry from the news, all too aware of the queen's views on failure. Fueled by a torrent of emotions, the monarch's usual mask of civility showed cracks. Krin, more experienced than most with the queen's emotional undercurrents, waited for the queen's ruthlessness to show.

Krin swallowed back the panic-induced bile in her chest. She resisted the temptation to flee back into the dark streets of Kerakot. But she knew better. Krin wouldn't survive long on her own. The queen's network of spies and connections to the Guild ran too deep. Only the Harbinger could evade such a fate. A feat he'd achieved for over three decades.

No, Your Majesty, I won't run.

Instead, Krin faced the queen's venom. Krin stood tall at the glass-paneled doors onto the balcony, unwilling to display weakness. She steeled herself against the onslaught she knew was headed her way. Krin mourned the loss of the night's planned celebratory sessions of wanton passion. Her position as the Queen's favorite hung in precarious balance.

The Harbinger had one job. Die. But he didn't.

How is this possible? How did any of them survive?

The monarch paced her chambers, a caged lion only contained by its willingness to be so. The delicate teacup and saucer in her hands were belied by the tone of her posture.

The queen's silk nightgown floated behind her in wispy trails like mist in a breeze. The longest-standing ruler of Teshket passed before Krin as a light winter gust entered through the open balcony doors and pressed the delicate material into the elder woman's curves. The contours of her figure underneath drove Krin mad with desire, her conflicting emotions drawing beads of sweat on her brow. The hip-high slit spread open, revealing soft, smooth skin on the queen's thigh—too smooth for a woman of her age. Krin's mask of calm slipped into a lustful ache too raw to hide. She ogled the queen's feminine silhouette, and Krin's desire overcame her fear. Her cheeks flushed as memories of erotic nights overwhelmed her survival instincts.

The queen stood facing the enormous fireplace at the far end of the room. Dark shadows competed with the strong edge of firelight that flickered against the surfaces and decor. The shadows beyond the fire's reach encroached on Krin as if alive with the queen's anger, shattering the lustful fantasies against the dark energy. Dark energy that Krin knew was directed toward her. Krin turned her eyes away from the object of her desire, away from the memories, and once again considered escape through the open doors from which she had entered.

Beyond the walls of the mansion grounds, across the miles of city landscape below, Kerakot settled into the winter night. Specks of light swallowed by swaths of deep shadow stared back. Most of the city slept while night watchmen and civil servants greeted one another with routine familiarity, their voices carried along the wind from the dark streets.

Such was her distraction and desire to flee that Krin nearly missed the queen's words.

"One of his kind hasn't existed since that bastard at the bottom of the river," the queen whispered. She turned back to Krin, who struggled to hide her distraction, caught off guard by the queen's sudden motion.

One of whose kind? Krin wondered.

Krin masked her confusion, having learned long ago not to ask questions whose answers she didn't really want to know. Stupid questions were more often met with anger and violence.

Tension lingered in the air. The older woman raised her eyebrow, aware of Krin's inattention and expecting a response. Her mouth twisted into an accusatory smirk. The queen waited. Too late, Krin realized she was expected to ask the question. Krin knew better than to fall for the trap and remained silent rather than open the floodgates of extra abuse.

She's hungry for games. Or is this foreplay?

The queen leered at Krin over the rim of her teacup, the delicate porcelain hovering before her mouth. With graceful motions, she sipped her tea, eyes intent on Krin. Krin's body reacted to the gaze with desire, and her breath escaped in a gasp. Her mind burned with fear, while her body yearned. She fought the urge to drop to her knees before the queen's raw, sensual energy.

The queen continued, "*You* let him escape and come here." Her voice slid into a hiss. "You had one job—make sure The Harbinger never made it out of Rhinestab."

Pain exploded through Krin's temples, and she clutched her head in response. Powerful energy pressed against Krin's mind, familiar yet different from the psychic caress she'd grown addicted to. This pain was unlike the power she experienced when her goddess, Shamna, granted access to magic. This new sensation crushed her thoughts and overwhelmed her pain threshold. Her head throbbed, and she thought it might crack her skull.

Krin cried out in pain, collapsing to the floor, her feet kicking out in spasms. Terror seized her, certain the queen had no intention of ending the onslaught. Krin's vision blurred. Her body went rigid, and she was no longer in command of her own limbs.

The queen stood apathetic to Krin's plight, and the assassin trembled in pain. The queen's access to Shamna's magic was far greater than Krin ever understood.

"I-I'm s-sorry, your Majesty." Krin stammered, nearly biting off her own tongue. "I-I-I s-stabbed h-him with a poisoned blade. Rot root should have done the job. I-I-I p-punctured his lung and l-left him in the Valley of Cusk," she blurted. "W-when we fell into that cesspool, I was s-sure he c-couldn't survive. He was near death already. The Cuska s-should have f-finished him."

"Yet they didn't, and he survived," the queen hissed through clenched teeth. "Did it ever occur to you that rot root is native to that valley? The Cuska could easily have an antidote for it, Fool."

"W-why would t-they heal him?"

"Who knows why those nasty things do anything they do? And that is not the point, *Emissary*."

Krin convulsed as the seizure grew worse. Her teeth pierced her tongue, and the copper taste of blood filled her mouth. Saliva foamed around her lips.

The queen lessened her attack on Krin, and the seizure stopped, though the pain continued.

"H-he shouldn't have survived." Krin's words come in rapid succession, almost inaudible. "I-I b-barely escaped w-with my l-life.

Yet, I w-watched the C-cuska take h-him. He shou-shouldn't have survived."

The pressure in Krin's head subsided, and the headache faded into memory as quickly as it appeared.

"You repeat yourself. Of course, he shouldn't have survived." The queen turned back to the fireplace. "Because you should have slit his throat. Not given him a chance with a mere flesh wound."

The queen hurled her teacup into the flames of the fireplace. The shattered porcelain bounced against the stone walls inside, and pieces landed on the tile floor. The sound reverberated through the room. She spun on her heels and pointed at Krin.

"Results are what I pay you for, young lady. My special attention should have ensured your commitment to my commands."

The queen approached Krin, and the assassin shrank back.

"Your Majesty," Krin stammered. Panicked, her mind fumbled for a way out of her predicament. "I-I-I had to e-escape the Cuska. I was lucky to rec-cover when I did. The Cuska had already set its sights on Shen when I awoke. There was little time to react. I wounded the nasty creature enough to escape. It was obvious Shen was the easier target."

"Obvious? Obviously, you were wrong. From where I stand, you valued your life over your mission," the queen accused, ice in her tone. "Shamna blesses you with more magic than any other follower. Her gift to *me* is *you*. The Harbinger has none of these gifts, yet you couldn't get the job done. Either you held back, or the Harbinger is far more powerful than you, and you no longer have any usefulness." The queen paused. "Did you just use The Harbinger's true name?"

Krin nodded, "Yes, Your Majesty."

"Did he reveal his identity to you, Emissary?"

Krin shook her head. "No. I-I recognized him."

"Well, now, *that* is interesting. Who is he?"

"He killed my brother when we were kids."

Krin rolled onto her knees and pushed herself to her feet. If the queen intended to kill her, Krin resolved she wouldn't die like a dog. She lifted her chin and faced her death with courage. The queen stepped close and wrapped her hand around the back of Krin's neck. The softness of the caress sent shivers along Krin's spine as her body responded to the touch. The queen yanked Krin's hair with a forceful grip, exposing Krin's throat. Krin refused to flinch, and the queen smirked.

"No, it's more than that," the queen said, observing Krin's expression. "Is that the flicker of old flames long thought extinguished?"

"No," Krin said in defiance.

"He murdered your brother *and* jilted you? One would expect better motivation toward mission success. One would hope you'd stop at nothing to achieve your revenge."

The queen shoved Krin to the floor again and pressed the assassin's face against the cold tiles. She whispered into Krin's ear.

"Maybe your loyalties are not where they should be?"

"I assure you, my loyalties are to you," Krin growled, defiance building inside.

"Are they? I ask little of you, lover. Your life for my favor. Yet, instead of dead, that faithless man is here. In my house. Rubbing his peasant hands on *my* granddaughter. Who, along with her useless brother, never should have returned to Teshket."

The queen released Krin with a shove and turned from her. Krin rose and dusted herself off. She contemplated sliding a knife into the back of the queen's head. She shook with rage, but loyalty, lust, love, and fear stopped her. She pushed the thought aside.

"I never should have trusted you were capable. Or Brogen. That man was always too confident in himself. He'd grown too sure of his dominance. He never could learn from his mistakes. Pathetic, jealous fool."

The queen thumped her fist on the small table, and the force knocked the teapot onto the floor. It shattered, and shards slid along the puddle created by the pot's contents.

"Damn it! I will not let the Harbinger destroy everything we've built!" the queen hissed.

She wiped her hands with a tea towel and tossed it onto the ground over the puddle.

"And now, it seems, he's stolen the heart of my Jez." She bowed her head. "Just like I suspected, she's too much like her father. Unfit to rule. Too liberal in her heart."

"The Princess stole his heart too," Krin replied, her words laced with bitterness.

"Yes—most unfortunate. Are you jealous, Emissary?"

"I have no love for him, my queen."

The queen stared at Krin, silent. Krin sensed her expectations.

"What would you have me do?" Krin asked, contrite.

"Kill the son-of-a-bitch, foolish girl. It's what I hired you for." The queen turned her back on Krin. "Consider yourself permanently dismissed, Emissary."

Krin's heart sank at the words. With a wave of her hand, the queen dismissed Krin as if she were little more than a subject in the slums on the east side of Kerakot.

"But…"

"But what? Do you think I'm in love with you? You simply satisfied an urge. As skilled as you are in that department, it's hardly life-altering."

Krin struggled to hide her hurt. The queen smirked, pleased by Krin's reaction.

"Until that man is dead, you don't exist. Bring his head to me. Bring it and set it here. Preferably with a look of shock on his face."

"Yes, your Majesty. I will see to it today."

"No. It can't happen here. My Jez will tire of him soon enough, and he will leave. I will see to that."

"What about the princess and prince? Shall I dispose of them?" Krin asked.

The queen scowled at Krin. "Now? No. You've had your chance. Focus on the Harbinger. I will deal with my grandchildren after he leaves. I expected *you* to save *me* from that sorrow. Be ready when the Harbinger and his uncouth friend leave."

Krin's voice caught in her throat.

"Oh, speak up, Woman."

"Your Majesty, if what you fear of him is true…the Harbinger could be immortal."

A burst of wind knocked Krin to the ground. Krin gasped once again, stunned by the fervor of the expressed rage. The wind died, and the queen clicked her tongue.

"Have you reached the end of your usefulness?"

"N-no, your Majesty."

"Then prove it. Recruit your own team from the Guild if you must. Find a way. But kill the Harbinger when he leaves."

Krin stood tall, and her eyes flashed with bloodlust.

"Yes, your Majesty."

Krin remained calm as the queen approached. She stood so their noses touched. With a fury fueled by desire, the powerful ruler of Teshket pulled Krin close, their lips pressed together, tongues probing. Krin's body succumbed to the heat of passion. Every nerve ignited with pleasure, and the familiar lustful pressure on her mind washed away her fear. Her knees weakened and buckled. She fought to remain upright while she yearned to fall to the floor.

As quickly as it began, it ended, and the queen released her prey.

"And this?" the queen said. "This is over. It's clear that my favor is insufficient motivation for your success. You fight for your life, now, Krin. I'll find a new Emissary for Valshannon. And a new body for my bed. I'll have your chambers cleared and your things sent back to the Guild. You can return to the tower barracks."

Krin flinched at the queen's words, and her body tingled as fury welled up within her. She'd made a cardinal mistake in falling in love. Worse, she'd believed that love was reciprocal. As much as the loss of status devastated her, the realization that once again she'd fallen under the spell of unrequited love caused her chest to ache.

Why doesn't she love me?

The queen interrupted her thoughts with a raised eyebrow.

"I can feel the magic build in you, young lady. Do you think you stand a chance?"

Krin swallowed her anger, afraid of the queen's power. The tingling in her body dissipated, and she forced her retaliatory thoughts down.

"If you cannot take out the Harbinger, you'd better die in the attempt. Do not fail me again, *Assassin* Krin. I can give you pain far greater than that pleasure you crave."

"I won't fail you," Krin replied.

"No, I don't suppose you will. Your very life depends on it."

Krin swallowed bile and bowed. It had been four years since the queen demanded a bow from Krin.

The queen waited with mild amusement. Krin lingered for a scant second in the hope the queen would change her mind. But the woman tilted her head toward the balcony doors, and Krin's heart sank. Her life of luxury was over. Krin exited through the balcony door and steadied herself on the door frame.

The queen waited, impatient for the drama to reach its conclusion. Krin gathered herself and, without looking back, leapt over the handrail. Her cloak trailed behind as she disappeared into the night.

With long strides, the queen crossed the room, her thoughts of the woman who'd been her lover for countless nights tossed aside. She studied the antique hutch before her. The richly stained cherry adorned with bronze fixtures was one of the oldest items in her collection, dating back hundreds of years. She opened a set of small wooden doors at its center and pulled forth a wooden shelf.

A large glass orb on a gold stand shimmered with internal power. She placed her hand on the smooth glass surface, and a soft light emerged within the orb. The dark grey cloud inside swirled as the internal light pushed the grey aside.

"I am quite busy, my bride," a man said, his voice an almost metallic echo through the orb.

"I found him, husband," she said.

Sounds of a frenetic commotion emanated from inside the orb and echoed through the chambers. She rolled her eyes in exasperation.

"Who?" the man called from the orb.

"The baker," the queen replied with heavy sarcasm. "They named a cookie after you."

"What?" the man hundreds of miles away asked, confused.

"Nadur's nutsack. I found *the Harbinger*."

"Do you have to be so crass? You know how I hate that term."

"Harbinger?" she replied with a smirk.

"Some days I find you exhausting," the man replied.

The queen softened her tone. "Listen, Love, the Harbinger is *here*. He's in bed with our granddaughter right now. Worse, the stupid girl thinks she's in love with him."

"What? How in the nine hells did *they* end up together?" her husband exclaimed. "Can you handle him?"

The queen furrowed her brow in frustration.

"It's not clear," she said. "It's possible he's stronger than we realize."

"What makes you say that?"

"He killed two Cuska while injured and somehow escaped the Gathering."

"That's not possible!" the man exclaimed. "Nobody survives the Cuska."

"He has three periapts from that psychotic witch to prove it. Unless he runs around the valley stealing them while the bastards sleep, he's a real threat."

"This is terrible news, but what can I do about it from here?"

The queen held back a vitriolic outburst. She closed her eyes and took measured breaths before responding.

"Get here. Tonight," she finally responded.

"Not possible," the man replied. The queen gritted her teeth during a long pause. Her husband began again, his voice calm. "If he truly killed Cuska, maybe there's value in keeping him alive. What brought him to you? Isn't there still a bounty on his head?"

"He rescued the twins," she replied.

"Rescued them? From what?" her husband asked, shocked. "What happened? Are they okay? Rescued how?"

I wish you weren't so inattentive, she thought.

She never let her husband in on her plan. He never understood the tough choices peace in Conishant required of its rulers. The choices were key to everyone's survival. Her husband often failed to understand the relationship between politics, religion, and family.

"Brogen kidnapped them," she replied.

"I'm sorry?" her husband asked. "For what reason?"

"I don't know!" she snapped.

"Have you spoken with Brogen?"

"No. Nor will I. Nobody will, for that matter," she replied. "Brogen is dead."

"That explains it…" he mumbled. A long, uncomfortable silence settled over the conversation.

When he spoke again, her husband spoke with slow deliberation.

"You were right, my love. It appears the Harbinger is a greater threat. We should gather the others."

"It's too late," she replied. "At least now we know who he is…finally. I already have plans in the works. We will rid ourselves of him once and for all."

Another voice, its timbre a deep baritone, resonated from the orb. She recognized the man immediately and gasped.

"What if we can find a way to use the Harbinger? Maybe he'd be amenable to a truce and help us eliminate a few threats."

"Father? What are you doing there?" the queen asked.

"Do I answer to you, *Daughter*?" the man she called 'Father' demanded.

"Use him? How?" She struggled to hide her distaste for the idea.

"Offer him riches, a seat in your court, whatever it takes. If he's won the heart of your granddaughter, he could be made into a useful ally. Offer him a dukedom. Have a royal wedding," Father said.

"Or we do what we should have done when we first learned of his existence, and we kill him," the queen countered.

A rhythmic tap emanated from the orb, and the queen envisioned her husband with his nervous energy, the pen in his hand in full motion.

"I think she's right. We should rid ourselves of the problem before he becomes as powerful as the last one," her husband offered.

"This isn't a debate," Father retorted.

The queen and her husband grew quiet, each fearful of Father's ire.

"You miss the greater picture. There is use for this Harbinger. Make him an ally. Then leave him to me. You will not have him killed, is that understood?"

The queen clenched her jaw. "Yes, *Father*."

"Good. Now leave us alone. We have work to do. Surely you can handle this yourself."

The queen removed her hand from the orb, and the smoky cloud turned dark grey again. She slid the drawer back into the hutch and closed the doors with greater force than she intended.

With purposeful steps, she hurried to her desk, struck a match, and lit a small candle underneath a bronze spoon. The scent of old wax, burned and crusted on the bottom of the spoon, filled the air. She withdrew a quill pen from its holder, dipped it in the inkwell, and wrote two notes, her strokes aggressive and angry. Without a second glance, she rolled the papers and poured wax from the spoon onto the exposed edges. Pressing her signet ring into the wax, she sealed each note and left the small scrolls on the table. She stepped toward a lever on the wall by her door and, with aggression, pulled the lever. Somewhere in the mansion, a bell rang.

"I'll be damned if you'll stop my plans, *Father*. Maybe it's time you went away, too," she said aloud.

Chapter One

Journal Entry: 81

It's difficult to explain what I feel. For the first time, I've truly found peace in my soul. Knowing that I will be okay is an unfamiliar sensation. But this is where I find myself. And I'm content in this knowledge.

The mystery of who kidnapped the twins still needs resolution. But somehow, that's not what occupies my mind. For the first time, someone sees me for who I am. Multiple someones. And I feel complete. My closest friend knows my worst secrets. The woman I love accepts me for me, without restriction. Nothing about me remains hidden from those I love. I have new friends. I have true love.

I have openness, family.

They didn't leave me to die alone in the Valley of Cusk. They didn't assume I was dead and move on. Finding me meant more to them than their own lives.

They risked themselves despite my past.

They risked themselves for me.

Of all people, the girl loves me. And I her. There's no choice I wouldn't make for her.

Including choose life.

That's a recent development. Weight removed. I don't want to die anymore. Am I cured of those cursed thoughts? I hope so.

Maybe I never really wanted to die. I just thought it was the better option for everyone if I were gone. Now I can see it's not true. I can see how much it would hurt them.

It's difficult not to think this is all a dream. This can't be real.

But both my hearts beat for her. Both my eyes see her eyes when she looks at me. Both my ears hear her sighs when we touch.

This can't be a dream.

Please don't let this be a dream.

A Bitter Truth

Why is murder always the only viable solution to my problems? What the fuck do I do now?

Tamrin snores like he hasn't slept in months. I consider stuffing one of his furs into his gaping blowhole. It's not his fault. Krin's voice caught me off guard, though I'm not surprised she'd survived. My memory of events in the Valley of Cusk is tainted by fever. Besides, she'd always been a survivor. I am surprised at how relieved I am that she's alive. No one would blame me if I were bitter about it, but in a way, I kinda deserved what she did.

It's one debt I can finally relinquish.

The queen, on the other hand, shocks me. All the evidence pointed to an inside job. But nobody would have suspected a betrayal from within the genetic line. What I overheard was far worse than I had imagined.

It's always the ones that are supposedly love you the most that hurt you the worst.

How could we be this wrong?

The queen's voice echoes down the hall.

"Corvan, where have you been?" she demands.

Hearing her voice almost throws me into a rage. She's behind everything, and she knows I'm *the Harbinger.*

What the fuck?

I don't know how much time passes while I sit here listening to Tamrin snore. Normally I'd have punched him by now, but the events of the last several weeks replay in my mind. Our focus on Brogen caused tunnel vision.

Why didn't we discuss the potential outcomes of returning here?

I never considered that the queen would betray her own.

You are one cold-hearted bitch, Your Majesty.

It's my fault. Enthralled by Jesma, I forgot for a moment who I am. *The Harbinger of Death* should not be distracted by sex. As 'Quietius the Second,' I'm a distrustful murderer with a bounty on my head. Not a lovesick puppy. If I hadn't grown complacent and hadn't been thinking with my dick, I might not have forgotten how connected the Guild and the Crown are. I might have drawn a connection when Krin penetrated me with a shaft of her own.

Not smart, Shen. At this rate, the queen will piss on your dead corpse.

Tamrin rouses himself with a loud gasp for air that disturbs my thoughts. Blissful in his sleep and unaware of the danger down the hall, I grow impatient. Frustrated and hellbent on taking it out on someone, I rise to wake Tamrin, a task that is never pleasant but often fun. Waking him is like an ant pushing an elephant off a cliff. Especially when he sleeps with the mistaken perception that everyone he cares for is safe.

Well, we aren't safe, dumbass!

Tamrin rolls over onto his side and chomps something in his sleep. He looks so happy in bed.

Fuck you for sleeping soundly.

I know it's not his fault. And if I didn't need his attention, I'd hightail it out of this room and climb back into Jesma's bed.

Is it really too much to ask for a pleasant night with the woman I love, tangled in bed with me?

Tamrin doesn't think so. I envy his bliss.

I linger, caught between action and guilt over the necessity of Tamrin's involvement. He's the only person who can help me. There's no one else. Certainly not Jesma.

Jesma.

What am I going to tell her?

A poor grasp of the facts caused us to make bad choices. There was no reason to believe Brogen worked under any command other than that of the emperor. No one would believe two bitter enemies conspired in this way.

Surely Shamna wouldn't condone this behavior, would she? The acolytes preach that benevolent gods work good through those who believe in them. How is this 'good'?

I reach my hand inside my shirt and rub the handprint I know is there. Cool to the touch outside of my normal body temperature, Grankin pays me little heed at the moment. At least my 'god' doesn't try to convince me my beliefs are wrong. He proves to be inattentive until it suits him. I try to reach out to him, but there is no sense of connection.

Imagine that.

I'd feign offense, but I'm not built for existential crises. Besides, it's not like he could help from the river.

At least now I know where the threat against the twins originates. With the question of 'who' answered, I'm left with a bunch of 'whys'.

I know why the queen wants me dead. All of Conishant wants my head. Been that way for as long as I can remember. The power-brokers of Teshket have been at the top of the list since I reduced to cinders the heavy arm that exerts their will over the Five Realms.

But I've never threatened *her*. I've never threatened anyone in Teshket since that day. I never thought my death was still at the top of the queen's list.

She'll increase the bounty now that I've made matters worse and thwarted her twisted family murder-fest.

How in the nine hells do I tell the twins?

I must tell Tamrin before I forget any important details.

Sorry, big guy. I need you right now. This is too big to wait.

Mischievous joy flitters inside before I wake him. Tamrin doesn't respond to subtle gestures. With one hand hovering above his mouth and one close to his large, bulbous nose, I slap down hard and cut off his air supply. I wait. It doesn't take long. Tamrin startles, but I hold on. If I don't hold it long enough, he'll simply roll over and go right back to sleep.

Oh, no, you don't, big guy.

From an outsider's perspective, I look like I'm trying to kill him. Tamrin flails, and while he struggles to free himself, I hold on tight. When his giant meat-hook fist flies toward my head, I know he's finally awake. I've been here many times before and dodge his punch with a twist of my shoulders and a tilt of my head. I slap his forehead with my fingertips.

"Wake up, Dickhead."

He growls at me and kicks off the covers, an act that exposes his naked body.

"What the hell, Shen!" he coughs, ready to lift me from the ground and body slam me.

I hold a finger to his lips. He prepares to lay into me with a slew of curses, but when I don't remove my finger, he gets the message and sticks up his middle finger. I point to his bedroom door and then to my ear. He glances at the door with a squint and nods in understanding while he rubs sleep from his eyes.

"What is wrong with you?" he whispers.

"The queen killed her son," I blurt out in a hoarse whisper.

Might as well jump right in.

He blinks in rapid succession. "Say that again?"

"You heard me. Get dressed. That thing frightens me," I whisper and point to his pecker. "I'll fill you in while you do."

I rehash as much of the conversation as I can remember while he pulls on his pants, which, like mine, were washed while he slept. As with all manner of evil, the verbalization of the facts solidifies them into reality. As details spew from my mouth, Tamrin's expression darkens, and my sense of dread grows. He casts occasional sideways glances at the door, worried we might be overheard. By the time I finish, he sits contemplatively and stares at the wall.

No more than thirty minutes have elapsed since I stood outside the queen's door, though it feels much longer. Fully dressed, Tamrin sits on the edge of his bed. He hasn't said a word other than to repeat the details I relayed.

"It's a lot to take in," I admit.

He sighs, closes his eyes, and shakes his head.

"Shen, we gotta get you out of here," he whispers. "If the queen wants you dead, there's no escaping it here. We'd have to sleep in the same room, one of us always awake. She'd know we suspect something. How can we stop her?" He rises, and the bed squeaks.

I wince.

"I'll grab Jes, you grab Jez," he says, already in flight mode.

"And do what? We can't tell them this."

Tamrin's mouth falls open. "Are you daft? You must tell them! They must leave, or they'll be dead. There's no way they can stay here."

I shake my head.

Tamrin stands and places one hand on each shoulder.

"Listen, if they find out on their own that their grandmother wants them dead, the shock could be unrecoverable. And afterward, if they discover we knew…" he sighs, "there's no coming back from that. You might as well return to that monastery and take another vow of celibacy. She won't ever let you touch her again. Better if this news comes from us. At least that way we are present for them."

"First, I'm not making decisions based on whether she lets me touch her again. They *just* lost their father. Their mother is dead. All that's left is their grandparents, one of whom wants them dead. There's zero chance they'll accept the truth without proof. Not so soon and not here. Zero chance," I say.

"You don't know that. Sure, they've been through a lot. But they trust us."

"Tam, we have at most a month of history with them. I love Jesma. I even believe she loves me. But ours, all of ours, are still new relationships. It's possible we can't withstand this."

Neither of us speaks, lost in thought.

"Are you honestly willing to risk greater harm by not telling them? Is your faith in people that far gone?" he asks.

"This isn't about faith in people," I hiss. "Let's focus on getting them out of here first. Once we're safe, we tell them."

He points to the window. "Those guys were out there once already, and the queen's plan failed." The intensity of his gaze drives his point home. "She doesn't strike me as the type to leave another attempt to chance, so I would be shocked if she ever let them out of this mansion. Why kill them out there when she can do it here, out of sight? If her sole intent is to see them dead, we handed them right to her."

"I'm aware," I snarl. "Don't need you to tell me."

"I'm not laying a guilt trip, Pal," he says. "I'm trying to make you see reason."

I don't have any real counterarguments. Nobody conspires with their bitter enemy to murder their own family unless they intend to complete the task. The inclusion of Krin in the conspiracy only proves her resolve. We survived only because she underestimated the ability of the world to fuck anyone at any time. She also didn't recognize that I have loyal friendships throughout Rhinestab.

Underestimate me at your peril, bitch.

He interrupts my thoughts and says, "As long as we're around, she won't kill them in public. Or, at the very least, she'll have a much harder time."

"Poison has a way of sneaking past blades and war hammers," I reply.

Tamrin's face falls.

"She's not gonna let Jez and Jes walk out," he says.

"I know. She killed her son. Who does that?" I say.

"And you thought *your* mom was cruel," Tamrin says.

"I don't know what I think anymore," I whisper.

The faint light of morning peeks into the room from behind Tamrin's curtains. He opens them to reveal the double doors of the balcony beyond. Outside, the first sliver of the horizon is painted in bright hues of red and orange, colors that advance along the dark canvas of the vanishing night sky.

Overwhelmed with doubt, Tamrin hasn't spoken for a while. His only desire is to wake the twins and sneak out of Kerakot. He fondles his periapt of Fildeus, the wrinkles in his brow deep.

I want to find a way to fuck the queen's world and make her suffer. Today wasn't supposed to start out with more trauma drama. Today was supposed to be a light and joyful celebration. We survived the trials and tribulations of assassins, Grankin, spiderlyches, Cuska, and Captain Brogen of The Dark Guard.

"Krikhi's tits! I should be celebrating that the meanest bastard on my 'people to kill before I die' list is crossed out," I mumble.

Tamrin's jaw drops. I shrug in response. He doesn't acknowledge my comment further.

"Maybe she'll give up," Tamrin suggests, changing the subject. "*We* killed the infamous Captain of the Dark Guard, after all. That's a major coup. She must recognize that whatever she is up to has failed."

"Did anything in that conversation sound like she intends to let this go?" I ask.

"Maybe you remembered wrong," he says.

"Is this one of the stages of grief?" I ask.

He doesn't respond. I know he confronts the same dread I do.

It's not possible to express how tired I am of rage. If the previous three days taught me anything, it is that anger is exhausting, and it clouds my judgment.

Then again, so does a pretty girl.

But I don't want to live in anger and regret anymore. Already, my rage is back, and the only thought in my head at the moment is murder. We can't catch a break. When the truth is revealed, every bad event that happened to them since the day they set sail will take on new meaning. It will crush them.

"I can't continue like this, Tam. I'm tired. The powerful and rich play games with everyone's lives, and there's nothing we can do to stop it."

"Humans behave badly. People do evil things," he says.

"And the gods do nothing to stop them," I reply.

"Free will," he says.

"Free will is the shield people use to excuse the gods of their neglect and maintain their faith. I'm fine with free will. I'm not fine with gods who sit back and refuse to smite the ones who do evil in their names." I drop my shoulders in resignation. "We have to tell the twins. You're right. There's no other way."

"Then the decision is made. We tell them?" he replies.

I nod while watching the servants shovel snow from the mansion's circular carriageway below. With large shovels, they push the snow into small mounds at the farthest end of the drive. My thoughts drift through a habitual progression, and I turn to Tamrin.

"What if I kill her?" I whisper.

He doesn't respond. He stares at me, dumbfounded.

"Are you insane?" he whispers finally. His eyes dart all over the room.

"You think she's spying on us?" I ask.

He doesn't answer. His eyes bounce around, his body tense.

"She doesn't know we know," I say.

I pause.

"So what?" he responds.

"She won't avoid us. I stand next to her and kill her. Sure, I'll be hanged from the gallows, but she'll be dead, and our friends will no longer be at risk."

"Just like that?" he whispers, his eyes still darting about. "Kill the queen? In front of everyone?"

I shrug. "I kill her and run. I've spent thirty-five years on the run from the Guild. What's thirty-five more?"

"I'll tell them the truth before I let you go through with that," he says, his jaw tight.

We fall into silence once more, and I swing my arms back and forth restlessly.

"Okay, I'll go wake Jez. You go wake the spoiled prince," I say.

Tamrin shakes his head in consternation.

"What now?" I ask.

"Shen, he's not the same prince you met a month ago. In fact, I don't think he was ever the person you think he is."

"Fair enough," I say, my hands held in surrender. "It was a cheap shot. But you are right. We must tell them."

Tamrin gathers his gear, and we head for the chamber door to wake the twins. Before we exit his chambers, I scan the hallway. Already, a substantial amount of activity has begun on the main floor below. The residential hallway is empty in both directions, however. I shrug, and we head out.

We walk down the hall like we have every right to be here since we're in the open. I stand at Jesma's chamber door, and he stands across the hall at Jesmir's. We glance at each other, gather our courage, and he enters Jesmir's chambers without another word.

"Shamna be damned," I whisper out loud, and I make a quiet entry into Jesma's room. She sleeps, a naked leg protruding from the sheets. Silvery hair, still partially dyed red, cascades across the pillow, blocking her face. My chest aches with dread at the task fate has handed me, but my dick aches with yearning.

Fate is cruel. The gods are cruel. Life…is cruel.

I sit on the edge of the bed, careful not to disturb the sleeping beauty. She's beautiful, and all I can do is stare.

She's at peace.

How do I tell someone that their grandmother wants them dead?

Moments away from breaking her heart, I'm selfishly focused on my own worst fear.

What if she doesn't believe me and I lose her?

I stare at her peaceful expression. My eyes trace supple lips, the hooked nose, the soft curve of a delicate chin. With a melancholy smile, I stare at the puddle of drool on the pillow.

I brush my hand across her cheek and lose myself in the contrast of our skin together and consider the metaphor for how different our worlds are.

"I don't want to lose you," I whisper.

That's just like me. Everyone's world is about to be shattered, and all I can think about is what I will lose in the process. I was a fool to think the world would allow me to have this life. Regardless of her choice, I will be on the run again. The only question is whether it will be "me" or "us" who runs.

It's not about you. It's about her. Focus on her. Break this gently.

And accept the consequences.

Before I wake her, a soft knock on the door draws my attention from the sleeping naked beauty. I answer the knock. It's Tamrin. He simply shakes his head.

"You didn't tell him?"

"I couldn't. I couldn't even get the courage to wake him."

I step out of the room, and we stand in the hallway.

"I can't either," I say.

"Now what?" he says.

"Stay with Jes until he wakes," I say. "I'll stay here. Act normal but stay close."

"What do I say to him when he finds me in his room?" Tamrin says, skeptical.

"You're concerned about the spy. We maintain the story and refuse to leave either of them alone."

"It's not ideal, but at least keeps them safe till one of us grows a spine," he says.

I close the door and turn back to Jesma.

Chapter Two

Journal Entry: 83

It's delusional to think my issues vanished because I found happiness.

This amount of emotional trauma doesn't heal overnight. If only it were so easy to escape myself. Why do I allow my circumstances to control my state of mind?

Why can't I face emotional conflict the way Jesma does? She doesn't run away from the messy stuff.

Of course, she doesn't. She's always been secure in the knowledge that relationships won't disintegrate over minor conflicts. Everyone in her life sticks around.

I have abandonment issues—or Mommy issues—or Daddy issues. I can't help but think that I'm one screwup away from losing her. If I hide the truth from her, the damage could be irreparable. If I tell her the truth, I'm the bearer of the news. I'd be a constant reminder of her shattered life.

Either way, I lose.

This is the point where past 'me' would run away. It's my typical response. Fight or flight doesn't have to be life or death, does it? Flight works well to protect one's psyche.

Liar.

That's what I did with Krin when I took her brother's life. Look what that got me. The mere possibility of relationship strife presented itself, and I ran like the coward I am. Somehow, I convinced myself it was to protect Krin. But what I really did was run away from the consequences.

I should tell Jez what I learned.

No.

I must hold this one, even if the very existence of this secret could destroy all I've gained; I can't be the one to tell her.

I'll fight to protect her. I can compartmentalize and hide the secret where it can never get out. No sense in changing the narrative now.

Of course, I know I should confront this head-on. But I know I'm not going to. I can't be the one to break her. I can't be responsible for that. Sure, she's strong. But this is the ultimate betrayal.

At least I'm not alone in this. Tam always has my back.

Tam's a coward, too. We enable each other.

But what choice do we have?

Still, I have to do something. I have to get the twins out of here. Convince them to run away with me and Tam.

Or kill the queen.

But how?

I think I have a plan.

Jagged Bitter Pill

Jesma mumbles, but I can't make it out. We lay in bed one more time before breakfast. With her head on my chest, our naked bodies entwined, I stare at the cherubs painted inside the tray ceiling of her room, afraid to speak for fear I'll say the wrong thing and send her away.

"Is something on your mind?" she asks.

"Hmm?"

It's my classic stall tactic when I need time to formulate my response, or when I don't want to answer a question. She sits up and gives me an exasperated look.

"I asked if there's something on your mind?" she says, her eyes intent on mine.

"No, why?" I lie.

"You're really quiet. More so than usual. And you seem tense, distracted," she says.

"I'm not," I say.

"Then how about you answer the question?" she asks.

"I thought I just did."

Her earlier mumble comes back to mind, and I realize I missed something while I was stuck in my head.

"Not the question I asked, you didn't," she says.

"Well, okay," I say with a smile. "How about you ask it again and I'll answer."

She smirks and pushes me back into the pillows before she climbs on top of me.

"Do…" she kisses my neck, "you…," she kisses my cheek, "want…," she bites my earlobe, "to…," she kisses my forehead, "go…," she kisses my lips… "shopping?"

"For?" I ask, aroused by her playfulness.

"Clothes for tonight's dinner," she says and slaps my chest. The smack was louder than expected. "See, I knew you were distracted."

I lift her off me, careful not to hurt her injured leg, and sit up.

"I'm sorry, Jez. I am distracted," I say.

A little truth will help ease the pressure built up inside me.

"About?" she asks, concerned.

"I know we killed Brogen, and that much of the threat is gone. But I'm worried we don't have all the answers. Someone broke royal protocol. That means there's a traitor in the house of Teshket. We've been too wrapped up in celebration. But the real threat is still out there somewhere."

I brush her hair behind her ear.

"I don't know that it's safe here yet. What if we leave here and go somewhere for a while?" I ask.

"Leave here? We just spent a month on the run, in an endless fight to get back here. Grandmother's guards will protect us," she says.

I stare at my hands and pick at my cuticles.

"Hey. Talk to me," she says. "What has you so stressed? You're the best bodyguard a person could ask for. We are as safe here as anywhere."

She lies back and twists her legs into mine.

"Besides," she says, "name one place safer than wrapped in the protective embrace of *The Harbinger*."

She says the last part with a spooky voice and pinches my nipple.

"Ow!" I say, and we tussle in the sheets.

I must admit that at least one part of her argument is sound. As long as we remain here, in this room together, we are both safe. I pin her arms to the mattress and smile at her.

"Okay," I relent, still laying groundwork. "Listen. This spy must be close to the queen, maybe part of her inner circle. And I can't stay awake forever, and I like it when we *sleep* together. So, we must resolve this. Today."

"Right now?" she says, biting her lower lip.

I shake my head.

"No. Not right this *very* second," I say with a sly grin.

"Good," she says, "because I've got plans for right now. And don't think I didn't notice you still never answered my question."

I place my hand between her thighs. She takes a ragged breath.

"How's this for an answer?" I ask.

Jesma walks through the room naked. The sway of her hips hypnotizes me into a blissful fantasy. I should come clean with what I know, but the courage escapes me. Selfishly, I don't want this to end. Even with the threat of death, I'm happier than I've been in decades. The thought that I must deliberately hurt her is a bitter pill of guilt mixed within an elixir of pleasure. As difficult as that pill is to swallow, the curvature at the small of her back, the taper at her waist, the lines of her breasts, and that tawdry grin she flashed do one hell of a job of pushing that guilt aside. For better or worse, I choke it down.

She pours herself water from a pitcher and returns to sit next to me. I reach out for the cup. She pulls away and takes a long gulp before she hands it over. I reach for it a second time, and she pulls it away, laughing. I nudge her with my forearm, and she laughs again.

"Jerk," I say.

She takes another gulp and hands it to me. I accept the cup and devour its contents. When I hand over the empty vessel, she pouts.

"That's mean."

"That's the game," I laugh.

She places the cup on her nightstand and leans into me. I wrap my arm around her and close my eyes. We lay in silent bliss for a while. It's not until I feel the tears on my chest that I notice she's crying.

"Hey," I say with a stroke of her hair. "What's wrong?"

She sniffles and presses into me harder.

"This is the first time since my father died that I wasn't afraid for my life. We've been on the run for so long, I can't believe it's over."

She sobs for a few minutes. I hold her close and let her cry.

"I really miss him," she whispers.

An adrenal surge of guilt causes my stomach to flip, and my hearts beat faster.

"It'll all be okay," I lie.

"I know. It just hurts."

We lie there, she in her sorrow and me in my guilt, until Tamrin knocks on the door.

"Hey, you dressed?" he calls from the other side.

Jesma dries her eyes, grabs her robe, and walks to the door. Tamrin stands in the hall with Jesmir. Tamrin notices Jesma's swollen eyes. Before he speaks, he glances at me. I shake my head once. He bites his lower lip.

"You, okay, Jez?" he asks.

"I'll be okay." She spots Jesmir, who stands behind the giant tracker. "How are *you* holding up?"

"Same as you, it seems." He smirks, "Aside from the morning romp and the sack, that is. Some of us woke up alone."

"Hey!" she says, her cheeks flushed.

"Get dressed," Jesmir says. "I'm hungry and I don't want to play 'twenty questions' by myself."

Jesma sticks out her tongue at him and says, "Maybe I'll take my breakfast up here and spend the day naked."

"Gross," he says as she closes the door in his face.

"That'll teach him," she says.

"Wanna bet?" Jesmir calls back through the door.

I laugh despite myself.

We prepare to descend the grand staircase into the entryway. Thanks to the view from the top, I experience a very real sense of superiority. Within the comfort and ease of our collective relationships, I take in the splendor of the grand foyer from this perspective.

The large doors, twice as tall as Tamrin, reach nearly to our position at the top of the stairs. Over the foyer, at eye level from the second-floor landing, the massive chandelier with over one hundred gas-burning lanterns and thousands of precious stone crystals adds to the sense of scale. From this position, it's easy to feel the weight of your own importance. I imagine the queen, like last night, on a deliberate approach toward her lesser subjects, their eyes lifted toward her in awe.

I can imagine the allure of that power.

Our little foursome makes its grand appearance in the first-floor foyer, albeit with much less grace than her Majesty. I try not to think about how out of place I feel and focus instead on my role as Jesma's stabilizing crutch. Her limp is more pronounced today. She winces with each step.

"That bad?" I ask when we get to the bottom.

She shrugs and smiles. "I'm fine. Hurts less today than it did three days ago. But it still hurts to bend. As great as this morning was, I may have been overly exuberant."

I hold my hands up in defense. "That wasn't on me. I was gentle." I whisper. "Maybe we give it time." Then, concerned for her discomfort, I ask, "Still no healing?"

She answers, "I tried. I'm not sure why Ezra ignores my pleas."

What I want to say in response won't help, and she already knows my stance on prayers and gods, so I hold silent on the matter and instead help make the walk as easy as I can for her.

Once we land in the grand entry, I'm awed by how different it looks this time of day. Projected beams of colored light reflect on every surface. Ezra's rays through stained-glass windows of every shape and size scatter a kaleidoscope that decorates the hall with a brilliant mix of deep blues, soft yellows, and bright pastels.

The Crown must spend fortunes on the illuminated artwork, sculptures, and pottery displayed. The handcrafted wooden pedestals on which items rest are priceless. Intricate details in the tile and stonework that escaped my notice the night before catch my eye now. I'm both impressed and intimidated by the opulence.

This world couldn't be any further away from my homeless existence in the RhineWoods. Both physically and metaphorically.

Just ahead, a tall, frail man in a butler's uniform of black wool and leather greets us outside the dining hall. His short dark hair and deep-set eyes give him an almost skeletal appearance. His demeanor makes it clear that he doesn't see me as worthy of his presence, let alone the company of someone as elegant as Princess Jesma.

They call me Quietius the Second for a reason, asshole. Keep looking at me like that.

Tamrin glances at me, his jaw tight. He walks a fine line between playing cool and sweating daggers. I'd take the heat for his frayed nerves, but he is as duplicitous as I am now. He had the opportunity to tell Jesmir. He opted to hold his tongue. I tap my cheek with a finger, and he relaxes his jaw.

He has all the coolness of a rabid bakru.

Look who's talking, Captain Collected.

"Her Majesty requests you join her for breakfast in the atrium," the butler says, his tone laced with superiority. He eyes Tamrin and me with suspicion.

I offer him the same expression.

"Best keep your hands off the silver, Tam," I chide.

Tamrin, already stressed by guilt, glowers at me with a dirty look, which only tickles me with glee. I hide a smirk, and his cheeks flush.

"Seriously," I say to the butler, "You never know with us. Probably should lock up the porcelain, too."

The butler is not amused by my attitude any more than Tamrin is, but Jesma and Jesmir see the humor in it and giggle.

Jesma smacks my stomach with a playful backhand, and I flinch. "Come on, Smarty Arty. Atrium is through the dining hall," Jesma whispers to me. "Thank you, Corvan," she says to the butler.

"My pleasure, Your Highness," he says.

Corvan nods and turns to speak to a maid in a quiet tone. My adolescent tendencies win the day. I stick out my tongue at his back to be a dick, but Jesma yanks me along before Corvan can turn around and see me. She tilts her head toward the end of the dining hall as we enter. My false bravado catches in my throat, and my natural inferiority complex takes over.

The inadequacy of my presence here feels deliberate.

If ever a room was designed to make people feel small, the dining hall fits the bill. From the height of the ceiling to the three massive chandeliers that hang from it, every part of this room is scaled to impress.

Overhead, the tray ceiling rises too high to estimate its distance. Octagonal recesses lined with dark mahogany beams frame unique hand-painted murals. I can't imagine the scaffold work required to support the painters. Dark hand-carved wood, polished to a high shine, trims out the floor-to-ceiling windows and grand entryways.

Nice job on psychological warfare, Your Majesty.

On the longest wall across from us, between the large windows, hang three of the largest paintings I've ever seen. Each piece of artwork is held in place by thick cables wrapped in gold. The images look to be of former queens—most bear a striking resemblance to the current one. The matriarchal genetics of the Teshket royal line are strong.

The long table in the center of the room is surrounded by twenty chairs on each side. A team of white-gloved servants in pressed suits with perfectly coiffed hair places dinnerware at each chair. An older gentleman, dressed like Corvan, measures each utensil's placement with a ruler and adjusts its position. No one acknowledges our presence, though a few cast sideways glances at Tamrin and me.

"Grandmother is throwing a dinner party tonight," Jesma says, her eyes lit with excitement. "She wants to celebrate our safe return and reward your valiant efforts. She's invited dignitaries from all over Conishant."

Jesmir says, "I hope she invites some eligible single ladies."

Jesma looks back at him. "I'm sure Lady Verdant *and* Lady Parola will both be here."

Jesmir's expression sours. "I mean real ladies."

Jesma laughs. "On two occasions, our dear Jes was caught in full congress with one lady while dating the other. It was quite the scene the second time. Just wait. They'll fall all over themselves for him tonight, regardless."

She looks back at Jesmir. "And you'll probably torture them by giving some other lady your full attention tonight, I'm sure."

He shrugs. "They instigated the situation both times. They're insufferable."

Jesma stops at a pair of glass-paneled doors at the end farthest from where we entered. Jesmir leans over my shoulder and whispers in my ear.

"Her bark stings, but don't let it intimidate you," he says. "Grandmother comes across as hard, but she's a softy where my sister and I are concerned. Our father is…" he catches himself, "was her favorite, even though they disagreed on things quite often. Besides, since you already met her last night, this should be easy."

He gathers his poise, but the raw emotions crack through in his voice. Tamrin places a gentle hand on Jesmir's shoulder.

Jesmir pats Tamrin's hand. "Thanks, Tam."

"You are allowed to be emotional, Jes. Your grandmother will understand," Tamrin replies.

My personal discomfort grows inversely proportional to our proximity to the queen. The twins find relief in the moment. Meanwhile, I'm trying to keep myself from murdering their grandmother in front of them. I find it hard not to smile as I imagine the look of shock as I penetrate her with nine inches of Korund steel.

I'd love to give you nine inches and make it hurt, Your Majesty.

I remind myself that now is not the time. They have already witnessed one family member's murder. Besides, when I kill this bitch, I want to take my time. She doesn't deserve a quick death.

Jesmir inhales forcefully and adjusts his belt buckle to align correctly with the buttons on his coat. Jesma adjusts her dress. The sway the queen has over these two is significant, and the thought of breaking their hearts with the truth weighs on me.

Together, they are regal. With their expensive clothes, high cheekbones, blue eyes, and still-dyed silvery hair, they ready themselves. It occurs to me that royalty, though luxurious, might be its own kind of prison.

I stare at Jesma, enthralled for a moment. Her dress hugs her curves with not-so-subtle sexuality under a less subtle guise of wealth. Soft, purple fabrics adorned with pearls and hand-sewn flowers run in a loose spiral from her shoulder to her hip. Jemir's jacket, covered in polished brass buttons, tapers with his chiseled physique.

Meanwhile, in my tattered clothes, though washed and stitched in the scant few hours I slept, are even less appropriate than Tamrin's plethora of furs.

At least I had the time to bathe this morning.

Still self-conscious, I stand frozen. Bathed or not, I've been rode hard and put away wet. I should have taken Jesma's offer to shop for a new set of clothes. With a last glance back through the ornate dining hall toward my only escape from the embarrassment that looms, I swallow my pride.

The statuesque Jesma prepares to present her frumpy, homeless vagabond, orphaned murder-whore lover for breakfast. She attempts to put me at ease with a smile, but we both know this won't be easy. I'm certain she questions this decision.

A doorman opens the doors to the atrium, and Jesma steps through. Jesmir waves Tamrin and me forward. I'm caught unaware, lost in the rumination of my ruination, feet glued to the floor. The doorman raises an eyebrow. Though it's a brief hesitation, the queen notices, and I can see her delight in my self-consciousness.

As stunning as her appearance was last night, the queen is more radiant this morning. Atop her head of silver hair sits a crown of small white flowers. Diamonds speckle the crown's leaves and petals like dew. Her low-cut dress, soft and light, is made of fine silk. Between her breasts rests a periapt of Shamna constructed of gold and emeralds. If I weren't so wrapped up in my own discomfort, I'd roll my eyes at the show of faith. Instead, I bow and attempt to tame my bloody fantasy with a fake 'nervous peasant before the queen' routine.

She purses her lips, but I can tell it hides a sly smile. I don't think she buys my act.

Does she know I eavesdropped? Is it possible?

I pull out Jesma's chair and smile at her, my eyes on the hint of cleavage. Jesma catches my glance and raises an eyebrow. I wink at her as she takes a seat.

"Your Highness," I say with a smile.

"Thank you," Jesma says, with a blush.

"Have you two had a productive morning?" the queen asks. She smirks behind her teacup.

The large round cast iron table, painted white, boasts an intricate pattern of the symbol of Shamna Rocks, the negative spaces filled with stained glass. Yet another display of wealth and devout adoration for Shamna.

The walls of the atrium curve around us in a cozy arc that offers a wide view of the snow-covered grounds outside. Several sets of glass doors flanked by white stone alcoves that house marble statues of historical figures of Teshket form the curvature of the room. Beyond the lead glass panes, directly behind the queen, a stream winds through the garden and off the cliff past the garden wall. Several species of plants that I know not to be native to Teshket gather their meager dose of Ezra's rays within the warmth of the atrium—a sign of life within the cold stone, glass, and iron.

I point to a seat on the queen's right. "Your Majesty, may I sit next to you?" I ask.

She offers a polite nod and holds my gaze a little longer than is normal while I take my seat. I'm surprised at the sweat that forms on the back of my neck. I don't know the cause, but this old woman makes me more nervous than a pig in a slaughterhouse. I'm not used to subterfuge. If I want someone dead, they die. I don't hide my intent.

Could I be giving off murder vibes right now?

"Did you all sleep well?" she asks.

"Wonderfully, Grandmother," Jesma says. "Best night's sleep in weeks."

"Good," she says.

She extends her arm to the table. "Please, have some tea. Food is on the way. I'm sure some of you have worked up an appetite."

Jesma blushes.

Games.

I choose to engage.

"I wouldn't mind replenishing my energy reserves," I say. "Early morning exercise ravishes my appetite."

Tamrin snorts into his coffee cup. Jesma freezes with her mouth hung open. Jesmir directs his gaze toward his lap, though I see the grin on his face.

The queen blinks.

Take that, you murderous witch.

"Pray to Ezra, I haven't had yours poisoned," she says with a devious smile on her face. The playful tone of her statement is well-measured.

Clever.

"Grandmother!" Jesma exclaims.

"Oh, relax, Darling. Master Shen knows what game we play. And he seems well equipped to handle the heat."

"It wouldn't be the first time someone was displeased with my propensity to insert myself into someone else's…*Business*," I reply.

"We tend to cut off the *fingers* that touch things that don't belong to us in Teshket," the queen says with a smirk.

I grimace. Behind her grin lies plausible intent.

Our food arrives, and I welcome the distraction. Two servants deliver enormous platters to the center of the table. Regardless of the queen's playful tone, I wrestle with a twinge of indecision, unsure if her jest was a well-timed ploy to lower my guard. Poison would be the fastest and most effective way to be rid of all of us. I grimace at the plates of pastries, meats, cheeses, and breads.

"Is something wrong, Master Shen?" the Queen asks. "Would you prefer something more to your taste? I can have the Chef whip up some porridge if you like?"

"No, thank you. I can lower myself to eat these meager offerings," I bite back.

"Oh, you do have a wicked tongue. I may have to rethink my order to have you assassinated later." Her laugh and smile are genuine.

Jesma tries to hide her dismay with an awkward smile. Jesmir laughs along. I dismiss my fears and join in with Jesmir. Tamrin stuffs his face with food in an effort to hide his discomfort.

My stomach growls, and I remember that this woman has other plans for my demise. She intends to leave my death to Krin and her forthcoming band of murderers somewhere outside the mansion. I'm eternally grateful for that knowledge. Foolhardy or not, I eat.

It's the best food I've ever had. Wild boar bellies, so crispy and unctuous they melt in my mouth, force an undignified groan from my lips. Breads toasted to perfection, paired with the subtle sweetness of wild pear butter, complement the savory saltiness of the boar. A fruit juice I have never heard of, with a spicy tang and the subtle burn of liquor, becomes my favorite juice ever.

Tamrin and I shovel food into our mouths, clueless about our lack of decorum

While we eat, the conversation transitions from plans for the day to the night's festivities and finally into a more detailed account of the twins' ordeal and Tamrin's and my hand in their rescue.

The queen listens with great interest to the parts where Jesma and Jesmir describe my fight in the ring at Rogue's Pointe, battle with the Cuska, and our last stand against Brogen and his band of henchmen.

Now you know who protects the twins, Witch.

Chapter Three

Journal Entry: 88

I think Jesma suspects I've been less than forthcoming since our post-coital conversation. I fear the turmoil that I try to hide from my expression manifests in my body language.

Maybe if I'd deflected her question with a simple misdirection about my father, I could have explained away my tension.

I didn't because the truth about my father isn't my primary concern. That dragon waits in the shadows of the past, overwhelmed by the needs of the present.

How long must I continue like this?

A Tactical Game of Strategy

Breakfast in Teshket, even with royalty, is a brief affair. Teshket is a "heavy afternoon meal" society. The dinner party tonight is more about drinks, small plates, desserts, and being seen by important people. Our meal ends quickly, and the queen leads the way back through the dining hall, still engaged in our conversation.

"So, tell me, Master Shen, what kept you from a solid night's sleep?" She glances over her shoulder. "Besides the attention of my granddaughter."

I ignore the obvious attempt to get a rise out of me.

"My brain." I twirl a finger at my temple. "It has this uncanny refusal to fall silent. Your majesty, it was with no small amount of personal sacrifice that the princess and prince were returned home. I'm not in the habit of making sacrifices for nothing."

Jesma gasps, and I hold up a hand to stop her protestations.

"While Tamrin and I are very happy to return our friends home, and believe me, your majesty, they are now our friends, I'm also worried it could all be for nothing."

"How so?" the queen asks.

"Well, let's take your travel protocols. Would it be wrong to assume they are highly secretive?"

"They are one of Conishant's best-kept secrets, actually," she replies.

"Interesting. I know a few well-kept secrets myself." I allow the comment to hang. Tamrin tenses. "Some secrets are harder to maintain than others," I say. "Most tend to escape containment. Chatty folks aren't as aware of their surroundings as they think they are. Sometimes discussions are held under the misguided belief that the participants are alone. I've found that ears can be anywhere."

We enter the mansion's library, and my thoughts are interrupted by the splendor. Audacious spirals of white shelves line the circular room, stretching overhead the full three stories of the mansion. A continuous spiral staircase with a polished brass handrail rises at a gentle slope around the perimeter, following the spiral climb of the shelves. Clusters of leather chairs with gas lamps on reading tables fill the room. At the opposite end, a long couch in front of the tallest fireplace I've ever seen beckons with the promise of warmth and comfort.

"You think someone compromised our protocol?" the Queen asks.

"I don't think," I reply, distracted.

My eyes follow the curve of the stairs along the spiral of shelves. Filled with books of all types, sizes, and colors, the shelves and stairs climb up to a landing on the second and third floors, cantilevered high overhead. At the library's apex, a dome of windows reveals the sky above. Grey clouds pass overhead, a sign of more snow to come.

Windows, framed by bookshelves, break the continuous span of books with portals of natural light. I climb the stairs to the first of many windows, nestled between the shelves. The courtyard below buzzes with activity, more servants preparing the grounds for tonight's gala.

"Your Majesty," I say, continuing, "I know your protocol was compromised."

The queen leads the others to the enormous fireplace.

"How do you know this, Master Shen?"

I descend the stairs and head toward the mantel.

"How often are the protocols changed?" I ask, answering her question with one of my own.

"That is classified," the queen says. "Often enough."

"Interesting. Yet, with all the secrecy, Captain Brogen knew every detail of the protocol. He knew the signals, the location, even the pass phrase." I trace the carved figures of monsters and warriors within the stone mantel with my finger. "If the protocol is one of the best-kept secrets in all five realms, how could Brogen have that information?"

The queen takes a seat on the couch and appears to consider the question.

"I suppose, Master Shen, that what you are trying to say is that there must be a spy somewhere in my court. I assume *you* already know the answer to who the spy is. It should be obvious."

I withhold any reaction to her comment.

"Now, I'm not sure I follow, your Majesty."

"Oh, come now," she says. "You've demonstrated a very sharp mind. I don't imagine you would waste words. I assume you plan to reveal the culprit?"

Tamrin turns to study a marble bust on a pedestal in a not-so-subtle attempt to hide his panic. I return my gaze to the queen. Inept at subterfuge and courtly games, it's difficult to tell if her words have a double meaning. Before I respond, she continues.

"Have I given your intellect too much credit?" she asks. "Was it not Emissary Krin who attacked you?"

I condescend to her with alacrity. "That's not an unreasonable explanation."

"I'm glad you approve," the queen replies with equal condescension.

I tilt my head in acknowledgment and press on.

"About Krin. Don't you find it strange how she appeared? Odd that someone I have history with shows up like that. I can't explain it, but I feel like we haven't seen the last of her."

"Really?" Jesma asks, surprised.

The queen barely acknowledges my insinuation.

"After we fell into the valley, I don't remember much. I assume she is dead. But as my mother always said, 'Assumptions are the rocks where hides the viper that bites your ass.' She had a way with words."

I pull out Brogen's letter to the bandits who assaulted the twins. I stare at it before handing it to the queen. She reads it without reaction and lays it on the coffee table.

"You can keep that," I say. "I find the comment about identifying the Emissary most interesting. It's as if they didn't know who it was before, but by the time he wrote that note, they did. *'Eliminate and replace with our agent.' That* is quite telling."

"Telling how?" the queen asks.

"Oh, come now," I say, repeating her words back to her. "*You've* demonstrated a very sharp mind…"

Without so much as a glance at the others, I can sense the tension in their posture. I turn my back to her and stare at the fire.

"I'm sorry?" she scowls.

"Brogen didn't know the Emissary. Once he did, he decided to replace your agent with their own," I say. "Except they didn't replace her. Still, Krin betrayed us? Awfully odd coincidence."

I turn to face the queen again, "You appointed her…"

"You think I had a hand in this?" she says and feigns offense.

Let's dance, Queeny.

"Your majesty, I mean no offense. This is but an exchange of barbs, after all. I certainly do not imply you had a hand in this. My mother was awful, but even she'd never conspire to kill me. I apologize if that is how *you* heard it."

"It's unbecoming to apologize in the midst of a game, Master Shen. Play your hand," she says.

"Let me clarify." I point to her. "You think like a strategist." I hold my hand palm down, eye level. "From up here, you see all the big pieces and how they fit together. That's your role, Your Majesty. And while I would never assume you aren't a capable *tactician*," I lower my hand, palm up to below my waist, "you aren't accustomed to the view from the trenches. That's where I live."

She acquiesces in my point. "Astute observation," she says, throwing my words back at me.

I crack a smile at that.

"In the trenches, *we* think tactically. That requires us to make decisions on the fly, often with only partial evidence to guide us. We can't think too many moves ahead because we only see what's in front of us. It is through hindsight alone that we see deeper and catch glimpses of what you see from up here." I lift my hand high again. "In this case, the evidence on the ground points to a spy but offers no clue who. And while I admit that Krin's and my history clouded my perception, hindsight has cleared that cloud."

"I don't follow," the Queen says.

"Simple. There are two options. First, Krin is either Brogen's agent in the letter…or…Brogen's team didn't get to her in time to replace her, and she acted on someone else's accord."

The queen picks up the letter and reads it again.

"That's a good point," she says.

"Whether Brogen and Krin knew each other is impossible to say for certain. One's deader than Quietius and the other, well, could be anywhere." I glance around. "She could be in this mansion for all we know." I pause for effect. "But one thing is certain."

"What's that?" Jesmir asks, eager to hear where I'm headed.

"Your grandmother knows Krin," I say.

"Well, of course she does…did," Jesma says. "Krin was an Emissary. Grandmother appoints all emissaries."

"Follow along, Dear," the queen says to Jesma. "Your boy toy here noticed that I didn't flinch at the mention of Krin's name last night."

"Exactly. You didn't ask who she was. You didn't bring up a different emissary. You didn't suspect Brogen's plan to replace your appointee with his spy. None of that. Because she was, or is, a legitimate Emissary."

"She *was*," the queen replies. "You are correct. I appointed her. She's been in my employ for many years now. Her betrayal is quite upsetting. For the record, I am close to all of my Emissaries. They are hand-picked, and I remain in weekly contact with them."

"And she could very well have been the one who revealed the protocol. But if she's *your* agent, she wouldn't need to be replaced if she were working with Brogen."

"Then she couldn't be Brogen's agent," Jesma says. "And that leaves only one other possibility."

Oh, please say it, Jez.

"We definitely have a spy in the court, Grandmother."

Damnit.

"Thank Shamna that Shen showed up in the Rhine Woods when he did," Jesma says.

"Yes," the queen says, "thank Shamna for her love and luck. Those who pray to her are often blessed. The Eternal One looks out for my family for my sake." She makes a show of grateful relief and dabs her eyes with her napkin. "As for how Brogen received his intelligence, the sad truth is that secrets, no matter how protected, are, as you say, Master Shen, only a secret if the knowledge rests with one person. Unfortunately, a contingency plan with this level of complexity requires coordination with many folks. Since Captain Brogen is dead, we cannot question him to discover his source. That secret died with him."

"I'd like to help you find the spy," I say. "I consider the prince and princess friends. Any threat to them is a threat to me. I love your granddaughter, Your Majesty. I'll do whatever it takes to keep her safe."

The queen clears her throat.

"I appreciate your perspective and your willingness to serve the crown. I will consider your offer. But crown safety is the responsibility of the crown security forces. I will hand-pick my best guards to protect my grandchildren."

She rises from the couch.

"On the matter of love. I can see that you are both fond of each other, but love is too strong a word, young man. While it shouldn't come as a shock to you that I disapprove of anything more than a casual fling, my dear Jez and Jes are the products of their environment. I'm not so old or foolish to forbid whatever this is between you two, so long as it remains casual. Princesses love within their status. My son, their father, set an unacceptable precedent for them when he married a common girl."

"Grandmother!" Jesmir exclaims.

"It's no secret I wasn't happy with your father's choice. But I grew to love your mother as my own, as you well know. That doesn't change the way things are. One temporary lapse in the rules doesn't mean we throw out the rulebook. Your mother's death was a devastating loss. As is the loss of my son." A lone tear falls. "I don't know what I would have done if I lost you two as well. Now, let's put aside this foolish nonsense."

Wow, she's good.

Jesma and Jesmir eat up the show of emotion, fooled and blinded by their love for their grandmother.

A servant enters the room before I can reply and clears his throat. The queen turns to him and waves him over. The young man, barely in his teens, steps forward and hands over a sealed envelope. The queen raises an eyebrow, and the messenger bows. She waves him off, flaps the letter against her palm, and studies me.

The silence lingers long enough to become conspicuous.

She opens the letter, reads it, then looks back up at me, her face stone, before she returns to whatever is written on the paper. She folds the paper and holds it out to me. I take the letter while she speaks, my brow furrowed.

"You are a very interesting man, Master Shen. You seem to experience a lot that the rest of the world doesn't. You've survived, dare I say even thrived, during your encounters with Cuska. You've evaded a bounty that, to my knowledge, stands as the oldest and largest bounty in recorded history."

A loud crash from the other side of the library startles everyone. Tamrin stands at the base of the spiral stairs, his jaw agape.

"I'm so sorry, your majesty," he says. "I dropped my cup."

She purses her lips. "I think we are all aware of that, Master Tamrin. The timing suggests I said something to upset you."

The room falls silent except for the crackle of the fire, which seems to have grown too intense on my back as a very light draft appears in the room and feeds the fire. I step away from the heat a couple of steps and unfold the letter, uncertain where the draft came from.

"Grandmother? What do you mean?"

"Well, *The Harbinger*, of course. For all of Master Shen's accomplishments, there can only be one explanation. The object of your affection here must be the infamous Ghost of the RhineWood."

"Grandmother!" Jesma protests.

"Oh, don't give me that tone, young lady. You hardly know the man." She returns her attention to me. "I must admit, I have long been curious who *The Harbinger* is. I'll say this, Master Shen, you do not disappoint."

I read the letter.

That didn't take long.

The queen interrupts my thoughts.

"Do not insult my intelligence with a lie. After all, you've been so forthcoming thus far. I'm responsible for the safety and well-being of an entire nation. Don't you think I have spies all over Conishant to suit that purpose?"

I don't know how to respond.

She points to the letter. "Read it for the class."

I read the letter aloud.

"Your Majesty,

Rumors around Picaroon circles indicate the Harbinger has been identified. The Picaroon friend and folk hero, D'aonar, has been identified as The Harbinger. Spies within the Picaroon community indicated this to be Picaroon slang. As of now, no Picaroon we've questioned has offered up his true name. We've offered more money than any Picaroon has ever held and still have no takers. As you well know, they are loyal only to coin. Therefore, it is our assertion that his true identity is still a mystery.

We've sketched a profile of this person called D'aonar.

Description is dark-skinned, unshaven, with green eyes, dark locks, and a tattered cloak and bracers. Last seen in the companionship of a large man of presumed Haabrestand descent, a female,

pale skin, blue eyes, red hair, and a male, black hair,
pale skin, and blue eyes."

The second page of the letter contains a sketch of my face. The likeness is close enough to cause me trouble in public. I hold the picture up to my face with a big smile.

"Looks nothing like me," I say.

Tamrin's eyes open as wide as dinner plates. Jesma's hand goes to her mouth. Jesmir studies the sketch.

"Whoever drew that doesn't know what you look like at all," he quips.

I toss the pages onto the coffee table next to the letter from Brogen. The queen turns to her grandchildren.

"Associating with a known fugitive? Dying your hair? And participating in a diplomatic crisis by killing the Captain of Killinshire's Dark Guard? As Royals of the House of Teshket, you represent the crown. Really, my darlings, your behavior is uncouth. And you've created an international incident."

I have to hand it to her. The queen sure knows how to flip a table.

Shit.

An awkward silence hangs over the room. I exchange looks with Tamrin, Jesma, and Jesmir. The twins lock eyes, and Jesmir shakes his head.

"None of you have anything to say?" the queen quips, her tone lighter.

"Your Majesty…" I start.

She holds up her hand.

"I admit, I've often wondered who you were. No records of your origins exist. Wise choice to burn the tower and everything inside. The Guild Tower still bears the scars of your handiwork. For nearly three decades, that bounty has been on your head. And yet here you stand."

"Now tell me. Aside from the most gracious rescue of my grandchildren, why shouldn't I have you thrown into prison, or, as the bounty says, executed?"

"Grandmother! You wouldn't!" Jesma protests.

She ignores her granddaughter and remains focused on me.

"Really, Harbinger, I must admire the sack on you. Ballsy doesn't do justice to your presence here."

"Since the cards are on the table," I say, "yes. I am the infamous vigilante, assassin, murderer, rogue, and scoundrel."

I bow to her in my best impersonation of Picaroon flair.

"D'aonar, adopted son of Patrin, the Picaroon King, at your service, your Majesty. I believe that makes me a prince."

The queen's laugh is as genuine as any I've ever heard. "Well, you certainly have the Picaroon flair for drama. And you've eluded justice for thirty years. That's an impressive accomplishment."

Jesma faces her grandmother. "What will you do?"

"Right now, the world only knows that D'aonar is *The Harbinger*. The only people who know D'aonar and your lover here are one and the same, stand in this room. How long that secret will last, one can only guess. Especially since we now have a sketch of the infamous villain. As we've learned today, secrets are only secrets when one person knows the truth and the others who do are dead. Brogen's spy can attest to that."

The queen picks up the letter and walks over to stand next to me.

"How long do you think it will take for the rest of the world to put it all together?" she asks me.

"I don't know," I reply.

"I'd say not long. The bounty is fifty thousand now? That's a lot of motivation."

"But you're the one in charge of the bounty!" Jesmir exclaims.

She looks at her grandson with mild amusement and shakes her head.

"No, the Guild is," she says

"But you are Queen!" Jesmir cries.

"Yes. I am Queen. And the Guild is the Guild. We live in peaceful coexistence for mutual benefit. I can no more control the Guild than they can me, though so many believe otherwise. I can hardly influence it. But, in light of what you've done for the Crown, I will do what I can."

She holds the letter before me, the sketch of my face next to my actual one.

"My, but they did you justice," she says and tosses it into the fire.

"Why?" I ask.

"I like sporting chances," she says.

Like you gave your son? I'm so going to enjoy shoving my blade up your ass.

It's easy to have that sketch duplicated and sent throughout the Five Realms. She wasn't kidding when she said she didn't want our deaths to happen here. Placing my image in every tavern, inn, and town square would have been the easiest path. Whatever game she plays, she holds back. Something stays her hand.

Father!

An idea forms in my head, and I know I'm about to dance with fire. I reconsider the conversation she had with the man she called 'Father.' He had a suggestion for her. One, I'm sure she'll hate even more now. But one I can use to my advantage, one way or the other.

"Your Majesty? I may have a way to force the Guild to lift the bounty."

"Have you? Let's hear it," she replies.

"The Guild would never come after the queen's family...without your permission, of course..."

I let the last bit linger, as if I'm about to say more. When I don't elaborate, she replies.

"No, they would not. But my family is not the one they want," she says.

Oh, get ready for a surprise, lady.

"But if I were to marry Jesma, then *I* would be your family."

The blood rushes to her face. Her ears turn bright pink. But she maintains composure otherwise.

Jesma gasps, and I can't tell if it's shock, awe, joy, or anger.

When the queen responds, even I'm not prepared for the venom. "I'll have you executed first."

"Grandmother!" the twins yell in unison.

Now I'm under your skin. I'm going to wiggle around in here for a while.

The aftermath of my 'proposal' can only be described as utter chaos. The queen's voice echoes throughout the mansion. The background activity of the staff, once unnoticed, is now conspicuous in its silence.

Jesma stares at me, mouth agape.

Her Majesty's royal façade falters. "If you think for one second this will stop the Guild, let me assure you, any protection you think this will afford you is nonexistent."

Come at me!

I couldn't talk her into a confession. She's too smart for that. But if I anger her enough, she might reveal herself.

"Grandmother! I love him," Jesma says.

"No. You lust for him, like a horny teenager. There's a difference. You've trauma-bonded. That bond will not last once the trauma has cleared." She shakes her finger at us both. "And that trauma is cleared. Or very soon will be."

I touch Jesma's hand, and she grabs hold, her grip tight.

"Trauma bonds just compress time. They are not fake bonds," Jesma says.

"Time? What do you know of time?" The queen's voice rises in volume again. "You have no concept of time! You've known each other for how long? A week? Two? Three?"

"Long enough for me to see him for who he really is," Jesma whispers.

The queen shakes her head. "No, this will not happen. It was a mistake to allow these two to remain here. And it's a mistake to let whatever this is go on any longer. I offered you grace, *Harbinger*. No more."

"I will make arrangements at one of the more regal inns outside the mansion walls." She looks at Tamrin and me. "You can stay as long as they like. The crown will cover the costs. But your welcome in this house is at an end."

Jesma throws her teacup at the fireplace. It shatters against the stone interior, and the remnants of her tea hiss as it evaporates. Her face flushes with anger.

"No!" she says. "You always had a problem with Mother for her lack of birth status. Father is dead. Mother is dead. Aunt Fila is dead. You don't have much family left, Your Grace. You're too old to have another child. There is no one left in the direct line of succession except the two of us." She wiggles her finger between herself and her brother.

"You talk of time. If I've learned anything in the last four weeks, it's that time is short. The gods may have thousands of years, but we don't. Father thought he had time. *I* won't sacrifice the unknown sliver of time *I* have left to someone *you* force onto me. I know in my heart that I have found the person I want to spend life with."

"You don't know true love," she says. "You don't understand real sacrifice. You've lived a privileged, spoiled life of birthright, my dear daughter of my son. Yet you'd throw it away like it has no value. This union will not happen. And believe me, you don't have the leverage you think you do, *heir*."

The queen's face shakes with rage.

"Harbinger, accept my offer to leave the premises before my gratitude for your sacrifice is no longer sufficient to hold my ire. Now, if we are done with this foolishness, I have matters to address, and frivolous gestures are not on my agenda. Corvan will make the arrangements and see you both out before Ezra sets."

She turns to leave the room, stops, and faces us both.

"This matter is over. Make no mistake. I rule here. My word is law."

She leaves, her steps forceful. Jesma sighs. I begin to speak, but she rips her hand out of my grasp.

"Why?" she whispers. "Why did you put me in that position?" She presses a finger on my forehead and shoves. My head rocks back. "What is wrong inside that stupid head? That whatever it was…was stupid."

I can't do this.

"Jez, I have to tell you someth…"

She holds up her hand to cut me off.

"I don't want to hear it. I'll talk to her about making you leave the mansion, but I need some space." She storms out of the room, her exit dramatic despite her limp.

"You sure know how to win people over," Jesmir says over my shoulder. "I don't know what you're up to, but that was smooth, Shen, real smooth."

Jesmir pats my shoulder, snickers, and follows his sister out of the room.

Tamrin bumps me. "I don't know what your intent was either, but if it was to piss people off, I'd say you succeeded, Pal."

"I didn't really plan that."

"Obviously."

"I thought if I got the woman mad enough, she'd force Jez's hand, and maybe I could convince Jez to run away together. I tried to…shit, man, I have no idea what I hoped to accomplish."

"Well, I'll say this…you tipped your hand and made sure Jesma left the mansion all with one stroke," Tamrin says. "Now what? You know there's no way the queen doesn't kill you now, right?"

A maid enters with a broom and a pan to clean up the broken pieces of the teacup.

"I must go find Jez. I don't think I have a choice. I have to tell her the truth."

"Think she'll listen now?"

"I sure as hell hope so."

Chapter Four

Journal Entry: 91

Maybe I am crazy.

I spent my entire life with the truth of my identity hidden to protect those I love. Maybe I've fooled myself, sure. Maybe it was inevitable that the secret would get out.

Oh, fuck off, Shen. You always knew it would get out. There was never a maybe there. Deep down, you knew you couldn't hide forever. It's the reason you stayed in the RhineWoods for so long.

Why couldn't I just stay away from people?

Because I can't live without friends, though I've told myself otherwise my entire life.

I honestly hate being alone. Not alone, like I am now. But permanently alone. No camaraderie, no intimacy, no ties. That frightens me. For that reason, I kept those few friends in my life. Not for them. For me.

Fucking selfish bastard. That's what I am. If I truly cared about anyone but myself, I would have kept my distance from everyone. But no. Just had to have friends...

Well, there's little I can do about it now. Friends are what I have.

And they're all in danger for caring about me.

I should check in on Mistras and Cali.

But first, I must get us all out of Kerakot safely.

My initial plan backfired. How am I supposed to get them to leave now and not break the news to them that the person they love wants them dead?

I should burn this book...

All By Myself

The day is in shambles. Alone in the dark, I try to hatch a plan to get us out of Kerakot before that bitch in the mansion makes good on her threat. Jesma was so angry she wouldn't speak to me before we left. I don't understand why she's so bent out of shape. I didn't *actually* propose. I simply brought it up as a tactic to elicit a reaction from her grandmother.

Which worked in spectacular fashion, if I do say so myself.

Don't act so proud of yourself, Shen.

I guess I didn't consider the impact on Jesma. Of course, it set the queen off and forced Jesma to run to my defense. That was my intention.

Jesma's feelings never crossed my mind.

Way to go, Dumbass.

When Jesma stormed out of the mansion alone, I panicked and chased after her. She refused my company and instead asked for a guard to accompany her around the grounds. I think the guard thought she wanted protection from me, so he accepted her request and shoved me away. In a way, he was right.

The insufferable woman refused my apology and later my request to enter her chambers.

For her part, Queen Murder Whore made good on her promise to have Tamrin and me removed from the residence. At least the inn is nice. And it has a rooftop tavern. Tamrin and I had a few early drinks before we retired to our shared room, both exhausted from the lack of sleep.

After we rearranged the furniture to make it difficult for would-be assassins to reach us, we fell into fitful sleep.

Not long after Ezra set over the horizon, we received a visitor. After a lot of noise and effort, we opened our door and were greeted by a messenger with a letter from her Majesty.

It simply read, *"Your presence at tonight's festivities is expected. Use this letter and my seal as your invitation. You will arrive precisely at the rise of the second moon."*

The woman's a piece of work.

Carriages rush past us toward the mansion as Tamrin and I walk the long street to the main gate. The guard recognizes us, and I hold up the invitation. He nods us in, and we pass through the gate as dignitaries and the upper class of Teshket ride by, most not even giving us a second glance.

We arrive on time and are ushered in with raised eyebrows. Corvan gives us a disapproving look, and I'm immediately self-conscious. Music plays from the ballroom, and we make our way there.

"I don't like this," I say to Tamrin.

"Well, get drunk, make an ass of yourself, and get thrown out. That's always worked before," he replies with a smirk.

"Funny," I reply.

Jesma stands at the end of the room on a dais, looking as radiant as I've ever seen her. My heart leaps, and I make my way through the crowd. She presents her hand to me. I kiss it, but she's cold in her reaction. She still isn't happy with me, so we hardly speak. When she introduces me as 'the man who saved her and her brother, ' it stings.

The Queen seems pleased with the formality and lack of familiarity with which Jesma shuns any signs of affection toward me. When Jesma isn't looking, I make a quiet exit from the festivities.

One of the best uses of my skills is to easily escape a crowd.

Shun me? I'll show you.

The upper-class attendees show no desire to mingle with a vagabond like me, so it's easy to find myself ignored.

I wait until I blend into the background and slip out unnoticed before the formal dinner party begins. As a stress non-eater, I've lost my appetite anyway.

Tamrin's natural gregariousness appears to win over a few of the less formal royals, who seem to share his affinity for furs. He's having a good time, so I don't attempt to notify him either. If he's lucky, he may find a few commissions, so I let him be.

Jesmir, no surprise, is nowhere to be found after running off with one of the beautifully eligible young women. I assume he is likely engaged in some tryst somewhere. In his element, he's impressive.

I work my way up the stairs, confident that no eyes are on me, and sneak onto the residence floor. I enter Jesma's chambers. Her balcony overlooks the rear gardens, and it's a good place to hide and observe. I extinguish her lamps to ensure my presence on the balcony can remain undetected before stepping out into the brisk winter night. My cloak does little to fight off the cold, so I snatch a blanket from Jesma's bed.

The queen's grand party echoes throughout the mansion grounds below. Music, laughter, chatter—it's all there. It's best if I'm *not* there.

Frustrated and lonely, I lean over the balcony and look out over the city. The cold air stings my lungs a little—a sensation I sort of enjoy. My breath forms mist. It was my favorite part of cold air as a kid. I exhale a couple of heavy breaths to make the vapor thicker.

Out in the garden, gas torches, evenly spaced along the paths, illuminate pockets of the spindly bushes and flower beds, dormant for the winter. Guests meander in and out of the soft light, engrossed in drink and some level of planned debauchery.

Footprints throughout the snow-covered grounds tell the tale of wanderers whose paths reveal the difference between those who walk for pleasure and those who walk with purpose. Small paw prints from animals that live around us, wary of our presence, always on the move, intermingle with those of the human interlopers.

Boot prints mark a trail along the garden wall—a single pair, fresh. They follow the contour and disappear into the distance, where only the top of the wall is visible. Their proximity to the wall is suspicious, and I'm reminded that somewhere out there, Krin lurks, ready to strike. I trace the tracks until they are too difficult to see near the end of the grounds.

The curved wall surrounds the mansion grounds and follows along the natural contour of the hill on which the mansion sits. Beyond the wall, the city beckons. Stone-capped roofs sprawl for miles, a thin layer of new snow covering most of them. The rise and fall of roof peaks undulate in the distance, softened by the snowy blanket. Yellow dots, the light of lanterns and torches seen through windows, speckle the landscape. The natural moon glow of the twin moons, both full, reflects off the snow, and the up-close details appear as vibrant as if it were daytime.

At the farthest point of the city, to my right, almost blocked by the mansion's east wing, a tall, plain tower with few windows stands like a sentinel in the background of Kerakot. It might as well be a middle finger to me. I one-finger salute the Guild Tower back and smile. Even at night, the scars of the fire I started thirty years ago remain.

I haven't returned there since I wiped out the guild and set the tower ablaze.

"A lifetime ago, Shen," I whisper to myself.

Somewhere in those halls, Krin likely plots my demise

Maybe I should go set it on fire again.

I can't believe she's alive.

My thoughts drift to Krin. The events of our last encounter fill me with such sadness, it surprises me. The thought that she might have been dead hurt my soul more than I realized at the time. I still feel responsible for her pain. I don't love her in the romantic sense anymore, and I certainly don't harbor any delusions of reconciliation like I once did. But even in her absence, she played a significant role in my everyday life. The last thirty-five years were a quagmire of guilt over my hand in the death of her brother and the cowardly way I abandoned her. I don't hate her. I'm really not angry. It seemed just.

I'm angry about her betrayal of my friends. I'm furious over the revelation of her complicity. And I finally can absolve myself of that lingering guilt.

The sweet little thief I loved turns out to be a stone-cold liar. And a murderer.

Look who's talking, Hypocrite.

Laughter in the garden below draws my attention. Two lovers, arms entwined, stumble in the snow-covered grass, obviously drunk.

To the left and below Jesma's chambers sits the atrium, where we had breakfast. Its glass dome offers a clear view inside. People gather around the same table where we ate earlier. Men and women in formal attire, sit with drinks in hand, engaging in laughter and conversation. A woman's head sparkles as she moves—the royal crown atop the queen's head, reflecting the light from the lamps. This one is more like icicles instead of the dewy flowers from earlier.

She glances up as if sensing my gaze. We lock eyes, and hers narrow. A slight adrenal surge warns of danger, but I dismiss it. She'll come for me soon, either way. But not tonight. She turns, waves a servant over to her, and whispers in their ear. The servant bows and leaves the atrium.

Bring it on, bitch.

Prudence, however, tells me to find a new place to hang out.

In for a copper, in for a Realm Note.

My personal mantra tends to place me in some sticky predicaments. But it has also offered me many fortuitous advantages over my enemies. I take risks they'd never dream possible. Ones they'd never take themselves. The hallway outside Jesma's room is quiet. Surprisingly, no guards are posted up here. She seems to utterly lack an intrinsic fear of assassination. I exit Jesma's room and already know my destination.

The door to the queen's chambers looms at the end of the dimly lit hall. I sprint past the grand stairway, my body burning with effort once again. With no small amount of luck, I time the move well because just as I pass the stairs, the servant with whom the queen spoke appears in the crowd below. He's distracted, so he doesn't see me.

I grip the door handle. It's unlocked, so I slip into the darkness of the royal chambers. The only light in the room comes from the fireplace. I close the door and step to one side, my back against the wall, waiting. The servant's footsteps grow louder as they reach the top of the stairs and then fade as he makes his way toward Jesma's room.

Satisfied that I remain undetected, I snoop around the room. A small desk, its edges adorned with gold leaf flowers, its surfaces painted a light beige, the legs curved into a sweep outward, sits in the furthest corner of the room. I hurry over and rummage for anything that might incriminate the queen in her fuckery. Inside the first drawer lies a stack of stationery and a roll of twine. The second drawer hides a dagger, a strange key etched with Shamna's symbol like on a periapt, and a rolled-up scroll.

The wax seal on the scroll is already broken, so I unroll the paper and lay it on her desk. It is a map of Conishant, the continent on which I live. This one differs from the other maps I've seen. I carry the map over toward the fireplace to catch better light rather than risk discovery via the lamp on the desk.

A series of lines crosses over one another on the surface of Conishant. Each capital of the Five Realms is connected to the others. Off to the east, lines from each capital extend to an island far out into the southeastern sea. I've never seen these lines or that island on any map before. At one particular place, not far from a small town in Gal-Danang called Galbring, four of the lines intersect. A black dot on the map indicates the position. A voice in the back of my head tells me there is a meaning to the black dot, but I can't recall what my mind wants me to remember.

Heels click on the tile floors out in the hall. I move like a blur in the darkness, rolling the map as I go. With a flick, I tuck it back where I found it.

A tall hutch on the other side of the room catches my eye. The steps stop at the door, and the handle moves. I rush to the hutch and open the double doors. One side has a strange orb on a gold stand atop a sliding drawer. The other side houses dresses. I slide in between the gowns and pull the doors closed as the chamber doors open. Footsteps sound on the tile floor. I hold my breath in hopes the servant will leave without looking too closely.

The globe next to me glows with a faint, distant light. A dark grey cloud swirls inside, and I'm mesmerized by it. My curiosity gets the better of me, and I touch the globe. The faint glow grows steadily brighter within the cloud as the mist swirls outward toward me.

I gasp and rip my hand away.

The footsteps in the room stop, and through the gap between the doors, I see a shadow draw closer. I can sense the trepidation in the servant's approach.

"Hello?" a young male calls out.

I don't answer.

"If you're in there, come out. Guests aren't allowed in the residence, especially her majesty's chambers."

The footsteps draw closer.

"Look, I don't want to have to call the guards, but I will. You have to the count of three to come out."

I feel bad for the guy. He only wants to do his job. Too bad for him, bad days come with every job. I squat low. He counts, but I can hear him step closer still.

"One…, two…," he says.

It's a cardinal rule not to approach a place where you think someone may be hidden. Too bad he didn't go to the same school I did.

"thr…"

He never finishes the word. I burst from the armoire and tackle him up high at the shoulders. With a quick flip of my legs, my momentum carries me upward, and I spin around his torso. I twist my hips, land behind him with my arm around his throat, and yank him backward, his feet fighting to find purchase on the tile. Before he can cry out, I slam my fist into the back of his skull. He collapses, and I allow his weight to settle into my arms.

"Well, pal, you left me no choice," I say to the unconscious man. "And to prevent you from opening your mouth about this, I do apologize for the predicament I'm about to place you in."

One of the old lessons from the Guild comes back to me. The journeyman assassin in charge of my apprenticeship always said, "*It's not always necessary to kill a guard or servant. Folks who awaken in embarrassment are less likely to report the event that led to their embarrassment.*"

I drag the man to the queen's bed and lay him on the large carpet there. Careful not to rip his clothes, I strip him naked and toss the articles all over the room — the obvious sign someone undressed in the throes of passion. I rip the sheets apart on the bed and, with a grunt, toss the unconscious naked man face down, so he appears drunk.

"Sorry, but now, if anyone finds you, they'll never believe you," I whisper to him. For added measure, I slap him on his bare ass—hard. The handprint begins to swell and turn red. He stirs but falls back unconscious. He'll have a much harder time explaining that.

I close the queen's chamber doors and walk back to the armoire. The grey cloud in the globe swirls in a slow mist, like how it appeared when I first saw it. I reach out and touch the smooth glass again. The glow returns. The grey cloud spreads and envelopes me.

I'm surrounded by the mist, it's cool touch unsettling. The mist begins to fade. My gasp sticks in my throat.

Before me stands a tall tower. The roar of waves crashing against hidden seawalls surrounds me. I'm on a tiny island somewhere in the middle of the sea. The island is small. I can see the ocean in all directions, the landmass less than a few hundred yards wide, I'd guess. From my position, I notice I must be several hundred feet above the water's surface. Salt spray rises over the western shore with every crash of the waves below. I'm lost in the majesty of the undulating power of the sea and its assault on this tiny island and the stone tower ahead. It's unlike any place I've ever seen. A path around the island follows the edge of the steep cliff. I stare over the cliff, mesmerized by the violent display of foam and power.

Someone says from behind me, "Who are you?"

Turning, I find three people I don't recognize staring at me in shock.

"How did you get here?" the one in the middle asks, a well-dressed man, older, but much younger than his eyes suggest. His vest is low-cut, tailored to fit. His pants, tucked into his boots, have an expensive sheen to them.

"Where am I?" I ask.

"That depends on who you are? I do not recognize you."

"It's him!" a woman in furs with a large bow says. She stands almost seven feet tall. Her hair flows in the wind, wild and beautiful. There is a hunger in her eyes, like Tam's when he shapeshifts.

"It can't be," the man in the middle says. "How do you know?" His hair is perfectly styled and doesn't move in the breeze.

"Show us your periapt," the third one says, a woman from her shape. She has gills on her neck, webbed fingers, and is covered in fish scales. Around her head, an orb of water circles.

"I don't have one," I say. *"I do not worship the gods."*

"Why not?" the man asks.

"Because the gods are fake. Wreckless and uncaring."

"It is him," the man says. *"We must warn the others."*

"Who are you?" I demand.

The mists return as iron hands grip my shoulders. A force pulls me backward, firm but protective. I find myself in the royal chambers again, in apparent freefall. But my feet are on the ground. Hands on my shoulders catch my attention. I spin around, ready to fight.

Corvan holds his hands in surrender, his eyes wide in horror.

"What have you done?" Corvan asks, horrified. "You can't be here! She will have my head for this." He looks at the man on the bed and the clothes strewn throughout the room.

"You have no idea the trouble you've caused us. Get out of here, now!" he hisses.

I look at him, dumbstruck. "You aren't going to sound the alarm? Call out for the guards?"

He shakes his head violently. "You don't understand the danger you've put us all in. You must leave! Before her majesty finds out. If she does, we are all three dead men!"

I don't understand his game, but if Corvan's of the mindset that I can walk out of here, I'm not one to look a gift horse in the mouth.

With a final glance at the unconscious man on the bed, I shrug and point to the balcony.

"I'll see myself out, then?"

He holds his arm out toward the balcony doors. "The sooner the better, Shen-Zarl," he says.

Without further delay, I exit the balcony doors and close them behind me. The queen's chambers sit at the far south end of the mansion and offer the best views of the city. Hidden from both the front entrance of the mansion grounds and the party in the back garden, it's the perfect place for me to make a silent exit.

Far across the cityscape, a lone tower stands black against the shadows of the horizon. The darkened shadow is the tallest structure in all of Conishant. Like a black finger, it reaches to the sky, a darker shadow against the dark night.

The Guild Tower.

I flip it dual middle fingers for the second time and, with a quick motion, launch myself over the balcony rail and onto the grass below. Within a minute, I'm across the lawn and over the mansion walls, back into the city beyond.

It isn't until I am back at the inn with an ale in my hand that it occurs to me that Corvan used my full name.

"Shen?"

A distressed female voice invades my dreams. I recognize it, but can't quite place the owner. It comes from somewhere in the fog, wherever that is. From the mists in my mind, a rapid rhythmic pressure shakes my shoulder. I search for the source through the mist.

"Shen!" the voice calls. There's worry in the tone.

I open my eyes, and a face, lost in the shadows of reddish-silver hair, looms above. Jesma's blue eyes, moist from tears, startle me with their intensity. Beyond Jesma's dominance within my view, Tamrin stands, face furrowed with worry.

"What is it?" I ask through a yawn that I fight to stifle.

"Jes is missing," Jesma says.

"He's with some girl from the party. He walked off with her not long after the queen's entrance," I say as I sit up and rub my eyes. "You look worried. It's nothing."

"No, he always shows up for grandmother's toast. It's his favorite part of her parties," Jesma says.

Tamrin says, "No one has seen him since the party started, not Corvan, not the queen, not us."

"You brought this to your grandmother?" I ask.

"Of course I did," Jesma says, confused by my question.

"And?"

"She said the same thing you did. 'He's probably off with some lower court hussy.'" Jesma replies. "But he never leaves a party. He plays his role."

"Well, that was before…" I start and then stop myself.

Jesma bows her head, and I place a hand on her arm.

"Well, I saw him at the party," I say. "Just before I left, he had his arm locked with some spicy duchess or maybe even a courtesan. They wandered into the atrium, and that was the last I saw of him. But he looked safe to me."

"He takes the court events seriously. He doesn't disappear for the entirety of the event. Ever," Jesma counters.

A loud crash behind me causes me to grab Jesma and dive to the ground. Glass from a broken windowpane falls to the floor, and a loud thump overhead causes Tamrin to flinch. He glances toward the source of the thump and yanks a small crossbow bolt from where it is embedded in the ceiling.

"There's a note," he says, "wrapped around the shaft."

He unwraps the piece of scrolled paper and hands it to me.

Letter in hand, I walk toward a gas lamp on the night table, turn the knob, and flick the flint wheel. The flame comes to life with a *foomp*.

"What is it?" Jesma asks.

"A note from whoever has Jes is my guess," Tamrin says.

The note unravels easily enough. I read it aloud.

Harbinger,

Your precious prince is not the target. We will

make a trade. Your life for his. Come find us near

Trader's Pier. Come alone.

"It's not signed," I say.

"Who could this be?" she asks.

I glance at Tamrin. He doesn't move.

"What?" Jesma demands.

I shrug. "I don't know. But whoever it is, they're out there at the party."

I can't make myself tell her. She'll never believe me now, not after this morning.

"Let's tell Grandmother," she says.

I shake my head. "We don't know who she'll confide in. The spy is behind this. Maybe she'll enlist the wrong person's help."

"She's my grandmother. She should be informed that Jes is kidnapped…again."

"Jez, I don't have time to argue."

I point at the door to the room.

"Once I gather my gear, I'll disappear out that door. I reckon in less than five minutes from now, I'll be long gone and somewhere out into the city on a quest to save your brother, with or without your help. This is not open to discussion with your grandmother. I don't answer to her, and I never will. Take me as I am or let me go, Jez."

Tamrin's displeasure plays on his face.

I refuse to relent.

"What's it gonna be? Go with me or stay here? It's your choice. But I need you, for everyone's sake, not to mention this to anyone."

She glares at me. Her chest heaves with heavy breaths. Her face shakes with rage. It reminds me of her grandmother's reaction earlier. The likeness is chilling. But I stand my ground.

"Fine. But I'm coming with you. I'll keep it quiet, but not if you leave me here," she replies, teeth clenched.

Finally, I can get her out of here. I'll tell her the truth as soon as we get out of this damned city.

"I can live with that. But we do things my way."

"It's always your way, Shen. You never consult anyone. Ever."

She turns and walks to the door. When her hand touches the doorknob, she pauses and whispers, "I know there's something you're not telling me. You aren't that good at subterfuge, remember? What is it?" Her voice rises on the question.

I don't speak. I can't.

"When will this nightmare be over?" she asks as she leaves the room, her limp more pronounced than earlier.

"I don't have answers," I say. "I'm sorry, Jesma," I whisper.

Tamrin winces when the door closes.

"This will go badly when she learns the truth."

"That's a problem for future Shen to deal with. At least this gets her out of that house and away from that evil witch. If Jez comes with us, then at least I've accomplished that much."

"Agreed. Now what else have you held back?" Tamrin asks.

"Nothing you don't already know. It's definitely Krin," I reply.

"I thought as much. But how can you be sure?" he asks.

"Trader's Pier. She chose that place with purpose. It's where Krin and I first kissed."

"Well, you know I can't let you go after her alone," he says.

"No, old friend. I'll leave you two somewhere safe. You get her out of the city and meet us in Valley View. This note says I must go alone."

Tamrin pushes my shoulder.

"Not this time. I don't care what that note says. You can huff all you want about 'your way'. But from here on out, you and I are locked at the hip. Where you go, I go. This isn't a debate. I'll tie you up and strap you to my back. But I want your word, we stick together, Shen."

"Tam…"

"Don't 'Tam' me, Shen. If you're right, they intend to kill him anyway. Alone or together, the risk to him is the same. Together, we have a chance to rescue the poor guy. I won't let you trade yourself for him in a lose-lose proposition," he counters. "From now on, we stick together, no matter the cost. All of us."

He walks over to the window and stares out over the city.

"For the first time, these last few days, I saw you happy. You were different. Not brooding." He turns to look at me, his face streaked with tears. "For the last three days, I never once worried you'd kill yourself. I didn't realize how much that weighed on me till the burden was lifted. Now you decide you'll trade yourself for someone else without a second thought. It hasn't gone away, has it?"

My hearts ache when I look at him.

"Tam, this is not an attempt to kill myself. Jes is our friend. I don't intend to go quietly. This is a bunch of killers trained like me if Krin did what she was ordered. This is Guild Assassins. I'm the only one who knows their tactics. But I can't fight them if I'm worried about all of you. I have no intention of taking a blade to the throat."

Tamrin nods and wipes his eyes with the palms of his hands.

"Well, as you well know, we have no intention of letting you go in alone. So, let's bring them the fight of their lives. And let's not forget, when I'm mad, people die. And I'm really fucking mad right now, Shen."

I smile, knowing he's right. I'm surprised how relieved I am. "Okay. Then dress for cold combat. This will get ugly."

"It's like you don't even know me sometimes. Jackass."

I laugh.

"I love you, big guy."

"I know," he says.

Jesma peeks her head into the room. "Can we please get going?" Her voice cracks.

"Jez, we will get him back," I say. "I swear it."

"I know," she says, her voice soft. "You never quit."

I can't tell if she's sarcastic or hopeful, but either way, she isn't wrong.

I scribble on an empty page in my diary. This time it's not for me. After today, I refuse to hide in the shadows. Some people are unfit to rule. And once again, she's had her grandson kidnapped, this time as a ploy to draw me out. I want her to know that I know. I'm done shadowboxing this bitch. The last word written, I rip the page from the book. With quick fingers, I wrap it around the shaft of the crossbow bolt Krin used earlier.

I don't sign it. I don't even seal it. I don't care who finds it, as long as it's not the twins.

We sneak into the mansion through a side entrance. Jesma leads the way. She takes us to a servants' stairway up onto the residence floor. She enters her room, and I press my speed to the Queen's chambers. I lean the bolt against the Queen's chamber door. When she opens the door, it will fall in toward her.

The note simply says,

"Queen Rotten Crotch, I know your secrets. Get your house in order. The Harbinger comes for you."

Jesma dresses in the outfit we purchased for her in Valshannon. In her hands, she carries a package wrapped in brown parchment and tied with twine. Her eyes are swollen and red.

"You've been crying," I say.

"Of course I have."

She hands me the package as if it's the most precious item she owns. From her gentle smile and shoulder shrug, I assume it's a peace offering.

"No, *I* owe *you* an apology," I say.

"Damn right you do. This is a gift, not an apology. You don't deserve this. You did, but you don't, now. I had the royal seamstress make this for you." Her expression sours. "Before your stunt. Anyway, she's fast. I wanted you to wear it tonight at dinner, but you made me mad, and then you disappeared."

I want to defend myself, to remind her that *she* locked *me* out of *her* room, but I think better of it.

"But as always, you show up when it really counts." She places a soft hand on my chest. "So, I hope you like it."

She once again hits me with the compassion that made me love her in such quick order. I swallow my pride and open the gift. Inside the delicate paper lies a black wool cloak, nicer than any item I've ever owned outside of my old blades. I slide my hand under a fold. The lining is soft and warm.

"The outer cloak is gazard wool, and the lining is sheep's wool. And it has a hood. I thought that you'd only be comfortable if it were similar to what you already have. But I always thought you should have a hood. It won't protect you against stab wounds, but it will protect you against most cuts. Woven into the shell is Korund steel fiber."

The gift overwhelms me. The thoughtfulness and detail in the design are too exquisite for the likes of me.

"It should fit," Jesma says with kindness. "The royal seamstress has an eye for size."

I'm overcome with emotion. "Thank you," I whisper.

She nods. "If I ask you a question, will you tell me the truth?"

I nod before I know what she'll ask.

"Did you start a fight with Grandmother on purpose?"

My silence is all the confirmation she needs.

"Why?" she asks.

Pieces of truth can only help. I don't have to reveal who.

"Because I overheard talk this morning while I wandered the halls. I couldn't identify who spoke, but they discussed you and your brother. They said you were never supposed to make it back home."

"Who did you hear?" she asks.

"I never got a look at them."

I'm glad Tamrin is behind her because Jesma can't see his exasperated expression.

"We should tell Grandmother. She should hunt out this spy."

I shake my head. "We can't."

"Why not?" she asks.

"Because the other voice, I definitely recognized."

She freezes. "Who was it?"

My hearts pound with the force of my lies. I'm sure she can sense my deflection. I've said too much and consider pulling back, but it occurs to me she'll recognize the voice and never believe I didn't. I glance toward Tamrin, who encourages me with a nod.

Pieces of the truth.

"I don't know how it's possible, but I think it was Krin. It can only be someone I've met before. Someone close to the queen."

"What? That can't be possible. Emissaries don't betray the crown."

I shrug.

"I don't believe it. This doesn't happen," she whispers. "Why antagonize Grandmother? Why not enlist her help? It doesn't make sense."

I stare at the cloak to distract myself from her gaze. I swallow the twinge of self-recrimination that threatens to bubble out and press another small piece of truth into another lie.

"I hoped she'd anger you enough that you'd storm off, ready to run away, and then I could convince you to leave with me. I don't think she believes she's compromised, and I'm afraid she'll trust the wrong person."

That's sorta true, at least.

"Why didn't you say so?"

"Jez." I say, "Come on."

She blinks once.

"You did ask me to leave. I said 'no.'" She's quiet while she ponders our earlier conversation. "So instead, you used my affection as a weapon. I was a pawn? My emotions didn't matter? What about Jes?" she asks.

The hurt in her voice fuels my shame. I can't look at her. "Look at me, Shen."

It takes effort, but I do.

I'm a heel.

"I didn't intend to make you feel that way," I say, contrite. "I couldn't think beyond my immediate worries. It was a panic decision. At the time, I was willing to do anything to protect you. Even drive you away."

"It hurts to be used that way."

I nod again. "I was wrong. I'm sorry."

"I'm still mad at you. You're an asshole who hasn't had to consider others' feelings. Now you do."

She touches my cheek with the back of her hand.

"Your life isn't just about you anymore. You have a family of people who care about you. People you care about. Time to act like you are part of that family. That means you don't get to do whatever and hope for the best. Understood?"

I press my face into her hand.

"Yes, Your Highness. Understood."

"Good. There's one more thing," she says.

Tamrin and I exchange expressions that tell her we can't take much more. Jesma hands me a letter.

"This arrived today. It's addressed to you. That's an official seal on the wax," she says. "It's from Baron Bun-Marlon. I checked against the registry. Grandmother wasn't around, and Corvan brought it to me."

I take the letter and open it. It's not good news.

"Shit."

"What?" Tamrin asks.

I hand it to him and look at Jesma. "Seems we have a new pursuer. A Korund. The Baron sent this to warn us. They have pretty accurate descriptions of all of us."

"That's not all, is it?" she asks.

Tamrin hands her the letter.

"She's after the Harbinger, 'also known as D'aonar,'" Jesma gasps.

"Pick a crier, pick a bard, Picaroon, as they say," Tamrin quips.

The royal mansion is full of surprises. Jesma moves through the residential floor with the confidence of someone who has explored every nook as a child. With the sneakiness of a horny teenager, she navigates us to a dead-end hall, where hangs a large-framed canvas painted with a tower.

"I recognize that tower," I whisper.

Jesma holds a finger to her lips and scowls at me.

I study the image. The tower sits on an island barely larger than itself. The shoreline of this elevated island is one continuous cliff. A wave crashes against one side, the spray reaching the tower's upper floors. The structure appears ancient. In the foreground, rough waves give the impression of a storm. It's the same tower I saw when I touched the queen's strange little orb.

"Where is that?" I ask, the image of the orb in my mind.

"Grandmother never says. We asked her often when we were kids, but she always said that this painting had been here since before she was born and that she was never told."

Jesma turns to me and places a soft hand on my chest.

"You look handsome in that," she says as she brushes the shoulder of the new cloak. Butterflies flutter in my stomach.

I don't deserve you, Jez.

She turns back to the wall, removes a strange key from around her neck, and presses it into one of the many notches in the picture's frame. She turns it, and a wooden handle pops loose on the other side of the frame. She retrieves the key, places it back around her neck, and pulls on the handle.

I'm surprised at the smooth operation of the hidden door. It makes no sound. We step through and into a long tunnel. She pulls the door closed, and we stand in darkness. Even with my excellent night vision, it's too dark to see, and my eyes don't adjust as quickly as they would if even a small amount of light were present.

A series of intermittent squeaks echoes through the tunnel—the sound from a turned valve. The soft hiss from the flow of gas grows louder with each squeak. Jesma strikes what sounds like many flints at once, most far into the dark, echoey hall. A series of *foomps* precedes a trail of newly ignited flames along a copper line on the wall. The noise repeats in a pattern as tiny gas-fed torches come to life ahead. Jesma shifts into a light jog. She seems to ignore the hitch in her stride.

"Do we really have to run?" I ask, worried about her leg.

"This is the royal escape tunnel. We don't have long. There is a mechanism in the door. If we don't open the other door before that mechanism activates, the lights will go dark, and bells will chime upstairs."

"That's an odd function," Tam says.

"It signals when intruders enter from the other end. It works both ways. Engineers figured intruders wouldn't suspect a timer if they discovered the tunnel. Take too long, and it triggers the bells…and the guards. It's flawed logic, but no one has ever changed it. Now, let's hurry. Time is of the essence."

"Here, let me speed things up," Tamrin says, and he scoops her off her feet.

"Thanks, Tam," she says.

We increase our pace and reach the end of the hallway. Tamrin sets Jesma on her feet with the tenderness of a parent. Jesma pushes open another door. A frigid blast of winter air slams into us and freezes my breath to my nose hairs and mustache.

"That's colder than Quietius' nuts," Tamrin gasps.

Jesma turns and shuts off the gas valve at the end of the hall. The flames wick out, and the tunnel returns to darkness behind us.

"Interesting mechanism," I say.

"Teshket engineers are the best," she replies.

"Sure," I say.

"Better than Haabrestand's," Tamrin replies, with obvious envy in his voice.

The tunnel exits into a grove of trees. She turns and closes the hidden door. I glance up. We stand under the garden wall of the mansion, somewhere on the eastern side of the grounds. The Teshken sky sprawls above us, a blanket of grey clouds. Once the door closes, Jesma leans against a handle like the one she used to open the tunnel.

The handle slides into the stone face, and the door virtually disappears into the garden wall's lower foundation.

Jesma steps forward, and her leg buckles. I catch her before she drops to the ground. She adjusts her stance and gives me a thumbs-up.

"Okay. Now what?" she asks.

"Traders' Pier," I respond. "Let's move."

Krin, we're coming for you.

Interpersonal relationships are my biggest struggle. Next to Jesma, I still feel awkward. The lingering tension is difficult to withstand. Although I'll never fully understand why my actions upset her, I'm not confident my apology really smoothed anything over. She made it clear that I had hurt her feelings.

I *think* we are reconciled. Still, although she limps alongside me, determined as ever, I feel a distance. I don't know how to ease the tension. The best plan I can think of is rescuing Jesmir. Of course, I was going to do that anyway. But hopefully that is enough to clear the air.

It's a twisted thought, but the twins' dear old grandmother wasn't wrong. I am what I am—a hunter. I can deny it all I want, but this is what I'm built for.

Tamrin is a skilled tracker. And Fildeus knows, he's good at it. But this is more than simple tracking. What we do here now is hunt. Morbid. Macabre. Dirty.

I glance back at Jesma. Her face is steeled in determination. She and her brother have been through stark changes since the first day I met them.

I can't help but mourn the changes to come.

Midnight slips by, and we arrive at a new day. We hide within the shadows of an alley at Trader's Pier. Snow covers every flat surface. It's not ideal. Even the shadows offer little cover.

Krin's choice of location isn't accidental. She meant it as a message to me *and* Jesma. My ex-lover wants me to know she has Jesmir. Krin seems to have adjusted to the revelation that I survived the Cuska.

Against any other opponent, Krin's choice of location was a good plan.

Damn you, Krin, why are you forcing my hand?

Krin thinks she has the advantage here. She believes I'll show up alone out of my own belief in my superiority. Brogen shattered that illusion. I can't wait to see the look on her face when we show up prepared for her little ambush.

With a Guild bounty on my head, I've never underestimated my enemy. Well, with the possible exception of Brogen. Thank the Cursed Eight that fucking guy died. I know every tactic Krin's team uses. They've used them all in their efforts to capture or kill me for years. It's never been good enough, and it won't be now. Krin should have included that in her plan.

"Well, let's go ruin someone's day," I say.

"What's your plan for the 'come alone' expectation?" Tamrin asks.

"Fuck her."

"Good plan," Tamrin says with a smile.

Jesma gives me a wry smile. "Is that your plan or just your attitude?"

I pull out one of my knives. "The only thing I'm putting inside her is this. I'm gonna walk right through the front door, spank a few bottoms, tickle some insides with Brogen's sword, and rub their stunned faces with my nuts," I say with a smirk.

Tamrin grabs the periapt in his beard and whispers, "Pravé."

His expression turns serious. His usual continuous grin is lost in a cloud of total concentration. The whites of his eyes turn deep purple. I'm always fascinated by his gift.

"Okay, the coast is clear up ahead. There aren't many tracks at all." He turns his gaze to the roofs and windows. "No sign of lookouts."

Jesma is nervous but ready.

"I guess it's now or never," I say.

I point to a rundown building ahead on the left. Even thirty years later, I remember the details of this area. Many days of my youth were spent on the tail of random targets throughout Kerakot as a Guild apprentice—especially with Krin's brother.

"That ladder," I say as we approach. "Notice how the rungs have an inch of snow on them?"

"Yes," Jesma replies.

"It's undisturbed for several hours. The roof should be free of lookouts. That ladder is the only way up, if I remember correctly. From up there, we can observe the pier over the roof peak."

"No tellin' if there's anyone beyond my view on the other buildings till we get up there," Tamrin says.

"Guess you climb first, then, big guy," I reply.

"Yeah, I figured as much," he says.

Tamrin climbs the ladder until his head peeks over the roof's edge. He twists his body flat onto the roof and waves us up.

I look at Jesma. "Up you go, Princess." I smile.

"I'm still mad at you," she says.

"I know. But I figure once I put my hand on your butt, you'll swoon, and I'll be in the clear."

She snorts. "You're a jerk."

"Yeah, but I'm charming. So, let's go, pokey slow."

Please let this light banter be a sign.

She steps to the ladder and struggles to pull up onto the first rung, her leg stiff. I grab her waist and provide a boost. My hand presses on her ass to push her one more rung.

"Watch your fingers, pervert," she says.

"Hard to believe it was only four days ago I saw you naked for the first time."

"Actually, it was sixteen days ago," she says with a sideways glance.

I feel the blood rush to my face from the memory of that night in Valshannon when we accidentally saw each other naked. We'd only known each other for two days at the time and had developed no feelings yet.

"Oh yeah, I forgot." I feel my cheeks blush, grateful for my dark skin. Apparently, it's not enough.

"There's the Shen I first met. Timid around women," she winks.

"No, just around you," I say with a smile. "Now get up there. We have work to do."

She climbs as fast as she can. I follow behind and admire the view, my confidence in us returning.

Chapter Five

Journal Entry: 92

My history with Krin no longer holds the power over me it once did.

Or maybe it's better said that my history with Krin has changed. That's more appropriate. Either way, it's a relief. She's a bitch, and I'm absolved.

I beat myself up over her for decades. Guess I'm free of that guilt now.

Our history still influences me, for sure. But now, instead of guilt, it's rage. A firestorm of rage.

I'm going to murder that cunt when I get my hands on her.

I'm no longer enamored by our history, Krin. If you ever read this, you should know that. The romanticized version of our time together was a fraud. I don't know whether I always knew or if I was blind. Hindsight is a son-of-a-bitch, so it's impossible to say. Your brother tricked me. He fooled me into the mistaken belief that he was my friend.

Like your brother, you betrayed me, too.

I can't believe I held on to this guilt for so long. I can't believe I let you define my perception of myself.

Well, you've made it clear that we aren't friends. I'm not sure we ever were. Was our romance just another trap to lull me into the belief that your brother was my friend?

You've made my life a lie.

Actually, everyone has.

Even what I knew of my father was a lie.

What else don't I know about my life?

How much of me is based on lies?

Who the fuck am I?

Strange Events, Stranger Results

Merchant ships, their lanterns lit, sit anchored in the harbor. The docks are quiet, not abnormal for late winter nights, but this is different. The chilly ocean breeze sends drifts of snow in short bursts. The newest layer of icy powder is too dry to stick.

"There," Tamrin says.

He gestures across the road with his forehead. We peek over the peak of the roof and observe a water tower atop the pier's inspection station.

"You see him?" he asks.

"I do," I reply.

"I don't see anything," Jesma whispers.

"See the water tank on that building?"

"Yes."

"Trace the tank with your eyes. Pay attention to the shadows," I say.

She shakes her head. "I don't see anything."

I look at her. "It's not easy. He's a light bender. He can diffuse light to appear invisible. But the wind is too strong, and the snow's too cold, so he can't hold still. His shivers reveal his location, especially in the snow. Follow the tank's right edge. When you reach halfway, scan left. Wait for another breeze and observe the wisps of snow…he's not a ghost. He's solid…the illusion is visual. There, see?"

She squints her eyes, and I wait. A small clump of snow falls from a curved line. The wind blows, and more snow stacks against the veiled assassin's solid mass.

"Oh." She shifts to look at me. "How did you see that?"

"Well, I know what to look for. But whoever it is, they're good. I would have missed him if not for the snow. It's all Tam. He misses nothing."

"How?" she asks.

"He's lit up like Ezra in a dark room," Tamrin whispers. "I can see all the living things that are out in the open…and any tracks left behind. They're like beacons of bright color, thermal differences."

"I had no idea," she says.

"Fildeus is good to me," he replies with pride.

"Any others?" I ask.

Tamrin shakes his head. "If there are, they're inside. I can't see through walls." He stares at the inspection station's entry. "There are several sets of tracks that lead into and out of the station. That's to be expected. Unfortunately, I can't differentiate between assassin tracks and soldier tracks without a closer look."

"Be cooler if you could see through walls," Jesma says.

"Heh, yeah, it would," he replies.

"Well, at least we know where the lookout is. Let's go. I have an idea," I say.

I turn onto my back and slide along the slope of the roof. Tamrin and Jesma follow. Their boots scrape the shingles as they slide, and it's my turn to scowl. I descend the ladder in a slide, feet on the outside posts, hands loose but secure. Jesma follows with careful steps.

I step into the shadows and signal for them to follow me.

"Listen, you're a liability here. There's no way around this." I touch Jesma's shoulder. "Your limp will hinder us. Besides, you're the least stealthy person I know." I turn to Tamrin. "And, well, you're you."

He snickers. Jesma starts to protest, and I hold a finger to her lips. She scowls at me.

"I know you aren't gonna stand around and wait. Let's use your limp and lack of stealth as a distraction. Are you interested in a little role play?"

She blushes, and I have to stifle a laugh. Tamrin rolls his eyes.

"Kinda like that, but more as a victim. For a couple of minutes?"

She nods.

"That's the spirit. I promise I won't let anyone hurt you. That lookout won't leave their post, so our goal is to distract."

She nods again, but I can see she's frightened. I chose to ignore the obvious and focus on my instructions in the hopes it'll distract her from fear.

I hash out my plan, and both agree without question. Jesma has the highest risk of injury as the decoy, but it's our best option.

"Tam, you'll know when it's time."

"I always do."

Jesma and I sneak along a narrow road between some older homes, their windows dark. A pair of dock workers stumble past, too drunk to bundle themselves from the cold. They laugh as they trip and sway along, oblivious to the noise they make. I raise my hand in a half wave, a stranger's acknowledgment in the night. One lifts his chin toward us, continues his way, and shushes his partner so loudly that it carries throughout the street in both directions. This results in more laughter from them both.

"That works to our advantage," I say with gratitude.

The breeze picks up and whips the base of my cloak in the air. I tame it with a tug. Jesma's cloak buttons low, mitigating similar frustration.

We reach the intersection of the street that runs in front of Trader's Pier. Tamrin should be in his position by now. I scan around the corner. The snowfall is a little too heavy to see the water tower or any sign of the watcher.

"Okay, we're going right up that street," I say.

"I don't like the sound of this," she frowns.

"Well, we need the lookout's attention on us, so we need to cause a scene. When I give the signal, you run around this corner. Your limp should help sell it. When I catch you, you should slap me. Hard."

"I *do* like the sound of *that*."

"Still mad, huh?"

"Nothing a good slap won't cure," she says with a grin.

"Well, get it all out, will ya?" I laugh. "I'd like to go back to being friends again."

"Just friends?" she smirks.

It's my turn to blush.

"You offering?" I whisper.

"If you're interested, I'm offering," she replies.

"If you're offering, I'm interested," I smirk back.

She rolls her eyes, but I can tell we've moved on from this morning's drama, and it makes my hearts leap.

"Use what's left of your anger. I can take it. I need you to sell this. When I grab you, you must break away, slap me hard, and run back here. When I follow you, the lookout will watch, and if we're lucky, miss Tam's approach. The big guy will do the rest."

"Where do I go?"

"Right back here. This spot." I point to the ground.

She nods, frightened. I grab her shoulders.

"You've got this. Remember, you have to convince him I intend to hurt you."

"That's my brother in there. I know what's at stake."

"Good. Once you're back here, don't peek around the corner. We don't want to risk the scout catching on. Wait here till I come to get you. Then we'll go rescue Jes together."

"You promise?"

"I promise."

I pull the hood of my new cloak over my head, and she does the same.

"You run when you're ready."

She nods, her lower lip caught between her teeth.

Jesma's limp makes for good theater. She looks back, her fear only a partial act, and I step into the street. It's colder in the open than I anticipated. My cloak billows in the wind, and I suck up the blast of cold into my lungs. It burns.

The wide street provides ample space for traffic on heavy shipment days but offers no protection from the frigid breeze. This far north in Teshket, even early winter can turn harsh. This is one of those winters.

Jesma tumbles to the ground. It's so believable, I'm not sure it's fake. I grimace under the cowl of my hood and hope she's not hurt. With feigned malice, I advance, accelerating with each step, a hunter in proximity to his prey. I'm on a full-on jog when I reach her.

Jesma struggles to rise. Her boots slip on the icy cobblestones. Her stiff leg adds to the drama of the scene. I reach her without the use of my characteristic speed. The hood on my new cloak, coupled with the snowfall, hides my identifiable traits.

"No!" she cries. Her voice cracks.

She rises to her feet and breaks into a gimpish run. Her feet slip again, and she barely stays upright. She arrests her fall with an outstretched hand. Her awkward three-point stance places her in the ideal position for me to yank her by the hood of her cloak. With only enough force to convince the scout this is real, I pull her upright and spin her into my chest.

"Ow! Let me go!" she cries.

I grab her jaw and tilt her head back. "I'll never let you go, Janes. You're mine forever."

Damn, she's so beautiful.

"I hate you!" she yells. She spits in my face, which catches me off guard, and I almost falter. With a firm grip on her shoulders, I shake her. She tries to break free.

"You belong to me!" I shout. "You can't ever leave! I own you, my sweet Janes!"

I shake her again to sell my rage.

It backfires. Anticipating her slap, I never saw her knee. The explosive onslaught of pain is unreal. Instant fire ignites in my balls as she drives them back inside my body. I collapse to the ground in very real distress and cup my junk in tears.

"Bitch!" I yell, partly meaning it. A twinge of shame comes over me due to the venom with which I say the word. Hands still on my beanbag, I roll over onto my back and groan. The snow falls toward my face, streaks of white against a background of nighttime grey clouds. Tears streak my face and into my ears. Jesma's footsteps fade into the distance.

"Why?" I whimper.

I'd laugh if she hadn't caught me square. My beans throb, and I roll back onto my knees to vomit onto the snow-covered street. The pain is so intense I'm sure I'm about to shit myself.

It takes too long to recover, and I can't summon the motivation to back away from the vomit-stained snow. The stench of bile makes me want to hurl again, but the pain is too great.

Damn it, Jez, I don't think they're gonna come back!

Footsteps crunch in the snow toward me.

I remind myself to have a conversation with Jesma about role play and the preservation of future functionality.

With a grimace that borders on panic, I glance up at a dark shadow that approaches, its face hidden under a cowl. I recognize the black attire of a Guild Master Assassin. Soft black leather armor with the Guild Master chevron carved into the leatherwork, paired with tight, wool-lined pants and a black hooded blouse. Two short swords, or long knives, depending on one's perspective, cross their chest, hilts pointing downward.

"Well, you have bad timing," a female voice says.

I feel bad for her. As a Master, she shouldn't have fallen for this. Jesma's shot at my balls may have saved us some trouble.

"How's that?" I growl.

"I don't like rapists," she says.

"I'm no rapist," I groan, the pain still acute.

"Looks like someone thought otherwise," she counters, menace in her voice. Blades scrape against their hilts and sing a high-pitched note that hints of Korund steel.

I smile.

"What do you have to smile about? You're about to die," she says.

"What a shame," I say. "I think in another life, you and I could have been friends."

"We could never be friends," she says. "I don't like rapists."

"Me neither. Unfortunately, you're on the wrong side of the real fight, friend."

Grim satisfaction comes over me as the realization spreads across her smug expression.

"Shit," she curses.

Her blades move with expert precision. But her skill is not speed. It's deception. She never has a chance to land a strike.

I roll away from her blades and sweep her legs. She leaps over them and into the violent embrace of a hairy beast already in mid-flight toward her. With his long fangs and claws like iron, Tamrin's hunter form slams into the assassin while she is mid-air. The force of the impact carries them across the road, dark shadows lost in the driving snow. The Guild Master fights for her life, but Tamrin's massive jaws clamp onto her throat before she has a chance to scream. Both bodies land with a thud. Their momentum on the near-frictionless road sends them into a set of wooden stairs.

A blood trail stains the snow and road.

Tamrin rises from the dead assassin's body and lumbers toward me. When I can make out his expression, his crazed smile, fangs bloodied, and matted fur make me think of a demonic clown bear.

Twice his normal size and covered in snow-laden fur, he towers over me. If I didn't know him, I'd never believe that inside the beast was the kindest human I'd ever met.

I reach up to him. His large hand with its elongated fingernails, hardened and sharp, swallows my entire forearm. I groan as he helps me stand. I bend forward, hands on my knees, and catch my breath. The still-present pain in my groin has lessened to a dull throb.

I wince and straighten myself.

"She got you good," he says, his voice more like gravel than usual. "*That* was your plan?"

I shake my head and adjust myself.

"No. She was supposed to slap me. I told her to use her harbored anger to sell it."

"She must be angrier than you thought."

"You think?" I bite back.

He gestures over my shoulder. I make a show of the pain while I turn to address the woman I thought had forgiven me. Jesma limps up the road, shoulders slumped.

"I'm so sorry," she says, head bowed. "I got carried away."

"Yeah, you got carried away," I snap.

"Listen, you grabbed me pretty aggressively," she defends. "I got frightened."

"I went easy," I explain.

"You thought that was easy? When you shook me, it made me feel defenseless again. You're much stronger than I am, Shen. I also didn't expect you to forget how we met."

Shit. I didn't think of that.

She hugs herself, defensive. "It brought back those memories. Then it made me mad again." Her voice trembles, and she looks at me with sadness. "I wanted to slap you," she says.

"Why didn't you?" I blurt out, my voice an octave higher than I intended.

"I couldn't get my arms free," she snaps back, her ire rising again.

Tamrin covers a laugh with his massive claw. I sigh in recognition of the validity of her words.

"I'm really sorry, Jez. I didn't think about how this idea would affect you."

"Well, it worked. Regardless," she says.

"I'll say," Tamrin replies.

I look toward the pier, still feeling a bit like a heel. She touches my arm. Our eyes lock, and I smile.

"How are your…you know…beans," she says and reaches to touch my crotch.

I step back slightly, flinching. "They're mad at you right now. I'll have a conversation with them later, but right now, they don't want you anywhere near them."

"Well," Tamrin interrupts, "At least it doesn't look like we raised suspicion."

"I have no idea how we accomplished that," I say.

"Shamna's luck," Jesma says.

"We should get out of here. Guards could wander along any minute. And shadows or not, yours is ten feet tall," I say.

Tamrin turns to the body. "I'll take care of her. Count to a hundred. I'll be in position by then."

"Or I could sing the Hizeron anthem…that's about as long."

"No," he says. "No singing."

I smirk and clap him on the arm.

"Let's go rescue my brother," Jesma says.

I look back at the ground where I vomited.

"Remind me to come back here and rummage through the snow and vomit to find my balls when this is over," I joke.

She snorts, and I smile at the sound.

Jesma and I squat below the window of the inspection shack where we assume her brother is held captive. 'Shack' is a misnomer for a structure large enough to house twelve guards, six inspectors, and almost fifty customers.

We have no clue where those guards and inspectors are, but if they are also inside, things could get messy. Their presence would pose a much bigger problem. My hunch is the guards and inspectors are captives inside as well or been sent elsewhere…or they're dead. I'd be surprised if they were participants in the abduction of a prince.

Although I haven't been inside this facility in decades, I remember the layout quite well. Krin and I used to sneak in here at night and steal from the guards while they slept. We'd become quite good at it. If the inside hasn't changed, just beyond the front door is a large room with a long counter. A storage room will be on the right, and two barracks rooms to the rear. The ceiling, thirty feet high at least, will be hard to see this time of night. The rafters are perfect places to hide assassins accustomed to leaps from that high. Hopefully, the one skylight will provide enough illumination, but with the current cloud cover, I doubt it.

Poised under the forward-most window, we hear muffled voices of those inside.

"…will be here soon," Krin says.

I look back at Jesma. I don't think she recognizes the voice yet.

"Of course, he will. To kill you, *Emissary*," Jesmir says, defiant. His voice is hoarse, like he's been screaming.

Jesma grips my arm, her hand tight on my elbow. I glance back to comfort her, unprepared for what I see. Jesma shakes with rage. I hold my finger to my lip and signal her to stay put. She makes like she's about to argue, and I do my best to make it clear she needs to wait for my signal.

"Emissary? You believe that still? How in Shamna's bosom did you evade Brogen for so long?" Krin sounds incredulous.

"You're a traitor," Jesmir says.

Krin's laugh is cruel. A loud smack, followed by a grunt, echoes on the other side of the window.

"Oh, my dear prince. You have no idea how close you are to the real traitor, do you? It's a shame you won't live long enough to learn the truth. Sad to say, there's no rescue. When your precious Harbinger arrives, it will be too late."

There's a long pause before Krin speaks again. Part of me hopes Krin mentions the queen, so I hesitate.

"I hear you have no magic," she says. "Rumor is none of the Great Eight found enough favor in you to grant you powers. I thought it was because you were a spoiled brat. It never occurred to me that it is because you are stupid and weak."

"I'm neither," Jesmir replies.

"Come now. Surely you can reason out who betrayed you. Can you really not figure out the riddle? Give me one guess before you die."

"You're the one who's going to die," Jesmir says defiantly.

I have to admit, I really like his commitment.

"You think The Harbinger will arrive in time? Don't you see? This whole setup is for him. In fact, he could be outside right now."

"He won't be alone," Jesmir says.

"Oh, he better be. See, if he isn't, you die first. Now, where were we? Oh yeah, I was about to remove your ear."

With an intensity driven by years of self-hatred, my body tingles inside and out. I surge ahead and turn the corner to the front door, leaving Jesma behind. With all my strength, I kick the hinge side of the door. The door frame splinters with a loud boom as the barrier flies off the hinges and lands several feet inside.

Krin spins to face me. Jesmir, with a bloody grin on his face, is tied to a chair, his right eye black, cheek swollen, and lip split. There are cuts on his face and exposed arms.

"Uh oh," Jesmir coos. "Looks like someone's pissed."

Krin's grin is wicked and intense, her teeth bared. She holds Jesmir's ear in a tight grip, her knife held flat to his temple with the other hand.

"Hi, Honey," she says to me. "Rough day at work?"

"Yeah, Babe. Now fix me a fucking bakru pie."

She laughs. "How about some prince-ear soup instead?"

Her knife moves faster than I imagined it could.

Jesmir screams in pain. My wrist flicks, sending a knife aimed at her face, through the air. Instead of a direct impact with her eye socket, however, my blade passes through empty space.

Krin vanishes before it reaches its target.

My knife sticks into the wall behind the counter. Krin is gone, and a gasp escapes my lips.

She reappears inches from my face. Startled, I react with a punch to her nose. The reflexive response and my speed save me from another knife wound to the gut. She stumbles backward, and her stunned expression is both comical and gratifying. She vanishes again, and I spin around in search of her, in a panic.

"What the fuck was that?" I blurt, stunned.

"Shamna taught me some new magic, Lover," Krin's voice calls out from somewhere in the darkness above. I glance up at the rafters even though I know the low light and distance will hide bodies fully encased in black Guild attire.

Three more assassins drop from overhead.

"You didn't think I came alone, did you?" Krin calls.

I know all three of them by their reputations. There's no time to worry about how Krin vanished. These killers mean business.

Jesmir's screams of pain pierce the night. He rocks violently, his hands and legs constrained to the chair. I want to cut him free, but the assassin to my left, another Guild Master, lunges with two blades ready. He slices the air along the same lines I use in a dual-bladed fight.

Brogen's sword sings when I draw it from its sheath and deflect his blows. The speed at which I extract it causes the flexible Korund steel to ripple as it slices through the air. It strikes the blade of the assassin's left attack and deflects it wildly. His right blade comes toward me, and I use the pommel of the sword to jam the assassin's pressure point in his hand. The impact opens his grip, and the weapon falls to the ground. I kick it behind me through the door and into the snow outside.

With merciless speed, I drive him backward. A hatred-fueled snarl works its way out of my throat. The assassin dodges my blade and parries with his.

Another assassin attacks from behind, and I'm forced to split my attention. Both assassins are faster than I expected. They aren't Brogen-fast. They aren't even a match for me on an individual level. But they work with coordinated effort. Equally matched by skill, I loosen my joints and stumble like I'm drunk. Years at the drunken monastery kick in, and I wobble, throwing out a foot to the second attacker's midsection. She twists her hips and sidesteps my attack. But the move interrupts her attack long enough for me to dodge a counterattack by the first assassin by falling back on my ass and rolling out back onto my feet. I stumble first to my left and then my right, throwing off their expectations. I pretend to steady myself and reposition to keep them both in front of me.

Motion from the third assassin shimmers in my periphery. The glint of steel sailing through the air causes me to trip back again. With three sloppy stumbles, I'm positioned in front of Jesmir—his safety my primary concern.

The three assassins surround me, spread out in an arc, their expressions of frustration a secret pleasure for me. I step back, almost on top of the restrained prince. My eyes dart around in search of Krin.

The assassins move to attack in unison, and I realize I made a mistake with my position. If I lunge out of the way, Jesmir is at risk. I stumbled into a colossal tactical blunder. Using my foot, I shove Jesmir backward a couple of feet, the chair legs sending a screeching echo through the building. I use too much force, and he slams into the counter behind me with a grunt.

The assassins circle. I fling a knife at the one on the right, and she avoids it with a drop to the floor. It's enough to arrest her advance and buy me a precious second.

Fuck it. In for a gold, in for a realm note.

"I always like a good gang bang," I say. The female assassin pulls out a long, thin blade.

"Well," I say to the other two, "looks like she's got the length on you two…probably the girth too."

"Don't worry," the Guild Master says. "We've got plenty of girth to satisfy you."

My eyes dart back and forth, focused on the contraction of their muscles, twists of feet and hips, a sign of pending action. Inside, my body burns as I ready myself to move. Memories of torn muscles be damned; I intend to kill all of them.

My foot twists on its toes, ready to launch my offensive when a loud crash booms overhead. Chunks of shattered glass fall from the skylight as all eyes look up before shielding themselves from the shards. A massive dark shadow falls through the air. Snow billows through the new gap in the roof. My expression slides into a grin as Tamrin executes the most heroic entrance I've ever witnessed. The massive object, nearly as large as a Cuska, throws the body of the scout at the Guild Master while still falling to the ground.

Too surprised to react and too slow to recover, the assassin cries out as the full weight of the dead lookout pins him to the floor. His head impacts the floor with a thud that causes me to wince involuntarily. He loses consciousness as Tamrin lands next to me with a hard crash. The concussive impact shakes the entire structure at its foundation, and dust from the rafters joins the snowfall in a soft cloud.

"Well, that evens the odds a bit," I say with a smile.

Tamrin growls. His low rumble reverberates through the room. More dust from the rafters falls around us. A shadow appears in the doorway. A cloak blows in the wind, and I raise an eyebrow at Jesma, who stands with her knife ready.

"Never underestimate a determined survivor," I smile.

"And now, it's advantage good guys," Jesma says.

"Krin? Honey? You still with us?" I taunt.

"Oh, I'm here, Dear," Krin replies. Her voice doesn't come from the rafters this time.

The other two assassins exchange uneasy glances. Tamrin roars at them and flexes his muscles. I prepare for the female assassin on my right when another shadow appears in the doorway.

It happens so fast, I stand straight and curse. Like a ghost, Krin emerges from nowhere and wraps her arm around Jesma's chest. She pins Jesma's knife arm to her side and places a curved knife at Jesma's throat.

Jesmir thrashes against his restraints in protest. The legs of the chair thump on the hardwood floor.

"Isn't this sweet? You brought the other spoiled brat," Krin says. "I warned you to come alone, Honey."

"You know I'm oppositionally defiant, Sweetheart," I say.

"That's not a thing, Love," Krin admonishes.

"Emissary? You traitorous witch," Jesma growls.

"Come, your highness, join the party," Krin replies. She shoves Jesma forward, the knife held steady. As fast as Krin cut Jesmir's ear, I fear I might not be fast enough to save Jesma if I make any sudden moves.

The hatred I now harbor for this woman, one whom I've spent too much of my life drowning in a sea of guilt over, surprises me. Every inch of me wants to shred her to pieces.

"Krin, you're already dead. You just don't know it," I say.

"Oh, how you've overestimated your ability, Lover," Krin says. "I'm much stronger than I've ever been. Shamna blessed me with new magic."

"New magic or not, I intend to end you." My speed isn't my greatest asset. My tenacity is.

But Krin escaped earlier. I don't know how.

Is it possible she's faster than me?

My hearts nearly stop. Krin, with a satisfied smile on her face, knows she has the upper hand.

"You really are the spy," Jesma says.

Krin speaks directly to me over Jesma's shoulder. "I really thought you kept smarter company, Darling. No wonder you choose to live alone. For all their money and education, these royals really aren't all that bright."

I have to act. But I'm frozen. I have to stall.

"Why?" I ask.

"Why?" she replies. "I already told you. But also, for the money. Your bounty doubled overnight. I wonder what could have made it double. Did you piss anyone off recently? You must have done something really naughty."

Jesma's horrified expression shows she may know the answer. Now isn't the time for me to confirm what I believe she suspects.

I crouch, ready to lunge.

"Now, now. Think twice before you rely on that infamous speed of yours, Babe." Krin pushes Jesma a step closer. "You see, you aren't the only one with limitless ability anymore."

"Today we end *The Harbinger*," the assassin on my left says. "I thought it'd be a better fight. What a joke."

Tamrin shifts his weight.

"I agree, Tracker," Krin says to Tamrin. "Let's go ahead and get this party started. This dance starts with a song I'd like to call *'Shen's Tears of Fears'*. The theme is simple. Shen helplessly witnesses his ex-lover kill his current one. It has a nice melody that sounds like this," Krin says. She turns her gaze toward Jesma. Inside, I burn with pain, and I rush forward. Krin's forearm muscles twitch. Time seems to slow around me.

Desperation born of failure and fear drives my legs. The world blurs. I sprint at Krin, desperate to stop her blade. A thin, faint scarlet line forms on Jesma's neck. It's small, tiny, but the closer I get to her, the longer the line becomes.

"No!" Jesmir cries behind me.

I'm so close. If I can get there in time, I can stop this. The details of the world around me are lost in tunnel-vision focus. The assassin on my right moves to strike my exposed flank. But Jesma is my only concern.

Krin's knife traces a line that spreads. It's less than half an inch long, but it grows as I draw near. I can reach her. I know I can. Jesma's eyes fill with panic and tears. She tries to resist, which only quickens the draw of Krin's blade.

A shadow passes behind me, and I'm vaguely aware of a sting in my calf. I make a mental note to make the assassin who cut me pay. She drew blood somewhere below my knee, but my focus is on Jesma.

I'm so close. But I'm too slow. Krin's wrist twitches. I cry out while the knife continues to bite Jesma's skin, the line of blood growing too long.

"No! No! No!" I try to scream. But the words stop midstream. Jesmir emerges before me from thin air. I almost crash into him as he grabs Krin's wrist. Krin freezes in surprise.

Jesmir battles Krin in a test of strength, trying to pull the knife away from his sister's throat. He gains leverage and hip-checks Jesma to the side. Jesma falls, and I drop onto a slide, my body intercepting her impact with the ground. I catch Jesma in my arms, my vision blurred with tears.

Jesmir and Krin fight over the knife and fall through the front doorway. Blood on the side of Jesma's neck trickles toward her shoulder. Her head lands on my lap, and her eyes roll back.

I glance back at the chair where Jesmir should be tied. The ropes that once held him hang loose around the arms and legs, the chair otherwise empty. I turn my attention to Krin and Jesmir with the full expectation that Jesmir is dead. Behind me, Tamrin engages with the two assassins. My ears ring, and sounds turn hollow. The chaotic activity around me seems out of place. My brain struggles to keep up—my only thoughts on Jesma.

Jesmir and Krin crash onto the street, hard. Their bodies slide on the snow as they continue to struggle. Before I can act, Krin vanishes again, and Jesmir looks around in a panic, his face a mix of awe, confusion, and anger. Blood pours down his face from where his ear used to be.

Krin appears before me, ready to strike. We lock eyes. Before she can attack, one of her colleagues' bodies slams into her, propelled by supernatural force. The impact sends her sprawling. The assassin, thrown by Tamrin, rolls with his fall and sprints back into the fray. Krin looks at Tamrin and then back at me, panicked.

Tamrin howls in challenge. Krin vanishes again. Tamrin flexes his massive muscles. Spit flies from his mouth. His fangs drip with saliva. His eyes burn orange from beneath the thick fur on his face.

The two assassins strike in unison. Tamrin bats the woman with a swipe of his hand and catches her in the chest. The blow sends her sprawling backward onto the ground. The other assassin's sword lashes out, and Tamrin attempts to block with his long nails, but he's too slow. Before my friend can adjust his trajectory, the blade severs his pinky from his right hand. He howls with rage and pain.

The lady assassin recovers and lunges at him again, her blade poised for a thrust. I search for Krin but can't find her. Tamrin moves away from the lady assassin's attack with a big step back and finds himself against the wall.

A hand grips my forearm. Startled, I glance at the touch. It's Jesma. She stares up at me, alive.

"I'm fine. Go help Tam."

Relieved that Jesma's wound is superficial, I have no time to ponder how Jesmir somehow saved her. My brain resets back to the fight still taking place. I nod, and the fire inside burns. With all my strength and speed, I lunge at the male assassin who cut off Tamrin's finger.

The one who thought I'd be an easy kill.

The lady assassin flashes a signal to warn my target, but my body is on fire inside. I'm motivated to avenge. With a grunt, I collide with the unaware killer before he can register the signal from his accomplice.

Tamrin, now focused on a single attacker, advances. These assassins may work together, but they'll never be as attuned to one another the way Tamrin and I are. Tamrin, confident that my target will pose no threat to him, twists his massive frame out of my line of attack.

The assassin never saw what hit him. My shoulder impacts the small of his back. The force of my impact and the energy in my speed propel us forward. We collide with the edge of the counter, and I hear his ribs crack. With both hands, I drive the Korund steel sword through his body from behind and pin him to the wooden counter. His hair balled in my fist, I yank his head back and slam his face into the wooden countertop—repeatedly. I lose control.

"Fuck!" I slam his face and yank it back again. "You!" With more force, I slam his face again, teeth impacting the counter's edge. "And!" I yank him back and drive him forward again. "Your!…" slam… "Whore!…" slam… "Master!…" slam.

His skull gives way in my hand, and I slam again with a rage-filled scream.

"You piece of shit!" I yell with a final slam forward.

He stays there, motionless, his blood pooling on the counter, dripping on the floor. I spit on his shattered skull. Silence fills the air, and it becomes conspicuous. Turning, I face the room. Tamrin stands slack-jawed. His opponent's eyes, wide as teacups, stare at her colleague. I narrow my eyes at her, rip Brogen's sword from the dead assassin's body, and point it at her.

"You're next."

She looks to Tamrin, then back at me, and vanishes from the room the same way Krin did.

Panting, Tamrin stares at me. "You okay?"

"No," I reply. "The bitch got away."

"I wouldn't worry about her," he says.

I look at him and shake my head. "No, Krin."

"Fuck," Tamrin growls. He stares through the busted doorway. "We're in it, now."

"Yeah. We're in it now." I point at the assassin, still unconscious from Tamrin's entry. "Kill that one."

Tamrin heads over to the unconscious Guild Master pinned under the body of the lookout. I walk over to Jesma and help her stand.

"Umm, Shen?" Tamrin calls.

"What?" I reply, still agitated.

"We have a problem," he says.

"We have a lot of problems," I say.

"Well, add this to the list. That guy we knocked out got away," he says.

The unconscious assassin is nowhere to be found.

"Shit, His orders are to kill us or die in the attempt. If he returns a failure, his life is forfeit. Either he succeeds, or he dies. He'll be back. From here on out, no quarter."

Jesma surveys the room with her knife ready, her face a determined mask.

"Where did Krin go?" she asks.

"I don't know," I say.

"How did she do that?" Jesma says. "I've never witnessed that before."

"Me neither," I say, eyes searching the room. "But I think Jes did whatever it was, too."

"It all happened so fast," she says. "I wasn't sure what was real and what wasn't. Where's my brother?"

I nod through the doorway. Jesmir stands in the street, his head on a swivel, like a frightened bakru. His body shakes from shock and cold. Blood still flows from his missing ear. Tamrin walks outside and wraps the prince in a cloak he found in the barracks room.

"What happened?" Jesma asks.

Jesmir shakes his head, exhausted.

"Jes? How?" she asks.

"I…I…don't know," he stammers.

We guide him back to the lone chair. His clothes are soaked with blood, all his own. His face is pale from the pain and blood loss.

"We have to stop the bleeding," I say to Jesma.

Jesmir mumbles, but it's incoherent nonsense. "So dark…so bright…pushed…pulled."

Already in shock, I worry that at any moment he'll succumb, and we aren't equipped to help him.

"…just thought…reach you…save you…just wanted to reach you."

His head bobs. I'm not sure he's aware of us until he looks right at me and speaks directly to me.

"When Krin…started to cut her…" he grabs my arm. "I saw myself there. I could see myself there." He points to the open doorway. "The next thing I knew, I was there. Right where I wanted to be."

Jesma pleads with me to help him. I shake my head in alarm. I don't know what she expects me to do, but I can't help him.

"He's babbling," I reply. "I don't know what he means."

Jesma says, "Krin and that last assassin used the same magic."

I whisper, helpless. "I don't know what it is." I turn to Tamrin. "You?"

The big man shakes his head, his injured hand clutched to his chest. "I don't know what that was, but I don't like it."

Chapter Six

Journal Entry: 97

Just my luck. The gods want to throw new magic at me.

If they exist——and in light of recent events, I may have to think maybe they do——then they certainly have a twisted sense of humor. I hope they saw me dispatch that Guild Master. Hopefully, they enjoyed the show.

We're toys to them, oblivious playthings. It's obvious to me now.

So far, the only one who has a sense of humor that I can tell is Grankin. If he's actually a god. If I were to believe in a god, that dark and bitter little shit Grankin would be my flavor of coffee. I wonder if I asked him for powers, if he'd grant me some. Maybe give me a twelve-foot shlong so I could slap ole Queeny with it from across the room. Who am I kidding? If he were a god, he would be helpful. I guess he is, in his own weird way.

Gods do play favorites, that's for certain. Krin's new power is frightening. At first glance, it appears Jesmir somehow performed the same feat.

Has that son-of-a-bitch been holding out on us this whole time? Does he have a god?

No, he's an honest guy. For fuck's sake, he's a prince. If it were a god, he'd have told us. He wouldn't play games with his sister's life.

Does that mean he found a way to access magic on his own? Now, that would be something.

Wait...

If he can, then why can't the rest of us?

If I could learn how to do what Jesmir and Krin did, I could put some welts on dear old grandma's ass. I could eliminate her, and no one would know. Better yet, I could try to break her psyche.

Speaking of Queen Crusty Crotch, she should have found the note by now. Jesma hasn't brought up the bounty comment by Krin, either. Did she catch it?

I doubt it. Maybe I can trick Tam into bringing it up instead.

Escape

"The wound won't close," Jesma says. "I can't stop the bleeding."

"The salve isn't working?" I ask as a pit rises in my stomach.

"My prayers certainly aren't," she says, worried.

Jesma tries to stem the flow of blood, but the wound bleeds without mercy. Her hands shake as she holds a hard-packed ball of snow to his ear. The bleeding won't stop. Even her special salve from the jar does nothing to close the wound. Worse, we don't have Jesmir's ear to reattach either. Krin carried it with her wherever she disappeared to.

Adrenaline is the only thing that keeps Jesmir conscious. His breath comes in heaves. The sound is more animalistic than human.

I stand before him and put a hand on his shoulder.

"Your highness, look at me."

He doesn't respond. He squints like he searches for something far off; his gaze locked on a point through me. I look over my shoulder, but all that is there is a windowless wall. I turn back to him and wave a hand in front of his face.

"What are you looking at?" I ask.

He doesn't respond. Jesma glances at me from the corner of her eye.

Tamrin's presence behind me reminds me he is wounded, too. I stand and face him.

"Let me see your finger," I say, sure of what I'll find.

"It's okay," he grumbles. With a huff, I yank his hand toward me. "It hurts, and I'm sure gonna miss this pinky, but I'll be fine."

I study the wound only to notice a familiar, foul stench emanates from his skin. I hold it closer and sniff. Rank, the fermented stench causes me to grimace involuntarily.

"Hey, Jez," I call over my shoulder, Tamrin's bloody appendage still in my grasp.

"Yes?"

"Does Jes's wound smell strange to you?"

She's quiet, her face scrunched while she considers my question. "Now that you mention it? It kinda smells like licorice and rancid meat. I thought it was this place."

"Shit. I was afraid of that."

"What?" she asks.

Tam sniffs his finger. "Damnit!" he snarls.

I search for a lantern or any easily flammable object. Tamrin realizes what I'm looking for and aids in the search. He locates a lantern with oil in the barracks rooms.

"That'll have to do," I say.

We light the lantern, and Tam turns it as bright as it will go. It takes several minutes for the inside to reach a suitable temperature.

"You need help?" I ask.

"No, smartass. I think I got it." He opens the vein and sticks his finger inside. He grunts. The sizzle that precedes the scent of burned flesh as the flame cauterizes his wound is unnerving. He grits his teeth in response, and a low growl rumbles in his chest as he endures the pain. Jesmir's wound, more severe than Tamrin's, is not conducive to the direct use of the lantern. I search for an iron or solid metal rod to use.

"What is it?" Jesma asks in reference to the wounds.

"Rot root," I reply.

Jesma shakes her head. "That's an old legend."

"No, Jez, it's not. It grows along the edges of the Valley of Cusk. We passed a ton of it the other day. The sap smells like pickled licorice once it's cooked. An infected body smells like rotted meat at the wound. Krin's team must have soaked their blades in it."

"What do we do?"

"Well, first we cauterize the wounds. That at least works to stop the blood loss. Then we must keep the wounds clean, and I mean clean. Your prayers won't work, Jez. Somehow, the sap prevents magical healing. These two will have to heal the natural way, but the process is slowed. Could be months."

Tamrin wraps his hand in a cloth he pulled from his pack. Then he points at my calf.

"Looks like you could use some help, too."

I point to Jesma's neck.

"Looks like we all can."

"You'll need to keep it clean, Tam. Otherwise, infection can set in. And until the poison wears off, any new injuries will suffer the same fate."

Tamrin clenches his jaw. I carry the lantern over to Jesmir.

"This is the only way. The poison keeps the blood thin at the wound. We need to burn off what's on the surface. We can't do anything about the poison that's made it into our bloodstreams. That will have to wear off. Depending on how much, usually about a month."

"A month?" Tamrin asks in dismay.

"Yeah. And I know what you're thinking. Nothing can be done about it. Just don't let anyone draw blood."

"Just great. Of course, that Guild Master escaped," Tamrin retorts.

"I never thought that stuff really existed," Jesma says.

"The Guild pays top dollar for those who harvest the root. There are a few crazy enough, so their use of it here is either unsanctioned, or they really want us dead. It's expensive stuff. Someone is paying a lot of money to have you…me…us killed. A queen's ransom, I'd say."

Jesma doesn't react.

"Something on your mind?" I ask.

"You think someone hired Krin to have us killed that wasn't Brogen?"

"Us? I don't know. We know a spy is still out there. But with Brogen dead, it's hard to say," I lie. "It's me they want, now. You're the mechanism to draw me out."

That's right, Shen, maintain that lie.

"You're a shitty liar," she says, but returns to tend her brother.

My insides squirm under the guilt. I pull one of my knives from my belt and dip it in the lantern oil. I ignite the oil with the flame in the lantern and allow the knife to heat inside the glass. Tamrin hands me one of his smaller furs.

"You're gonna need this to grab that blade when it's hot."

"Thanks."

"It won't protect you long, so work quickly," he replies.

The oil on the knife burns off in a trail of black smoke after several minutes. I hold it to the fire until the knife glows a dull red. I wrap my hand in the fur and nod to Jesma.

"Take that bandage and salve off," I say.

Jesma complies with no argument. Jesmir still hasn't moved.

"Hold him still," I say. Tamrin steps behind Jesmir and wraps his arm around the prince. Jesmir's state is worse than I feared. When he doesn't react to Tamrin's clench, I grow concerned.

The knife glows a brighter red, still barely noticeable when I move it away from the lantern. The heat through the fur already warms my hand. With a quick motion, I apply the hot knife to Jesmir's ear. The skin and residual bits of Jesma's salve burn with a series of sizzling pops. The stench infiltrates my nostrils with immediate effect, and my gag reflex threatens to trigger. I resist the urge to step away and continue to press the blade hard against his wound. Jesmir doesn't register the pain, confirming my suspicions. The poor guy suffers from severe shock. His body has suspended all pain signals. We need to get out of here, but in his current state, we may be stuck.

This is not good.

Our little band of wounded warriors no longer bleeds. Wounds cauterized and Jesma's salve applied, our injuries will require regular attention—thanks to the rot-root spiked blades.

Jesmir sits catatonic, unwilling or incapable of speaking. With the bandage wrapped around his head, he looks like one of the many paintings I've seen of war. Tamrin, Jesma, and I huddle in a corner, away from the wind-blasted opening where the door used to be, and discuss our options while Jesmir sits, unaware of us.

"We've stayed too long," I say.

"I want to go back to the mansion," Jesma says.

I shake my head. Krin's words should have triggered some level of suspicion for her, but somehow, they didn't. If I hadn't heard it with my own ears, would I be equally as obtuse?

I must find a way to keep the twins away from their grandmother. Tamrin comes to the rescue with an answer.

"Krin abducted Jes right from the mansion grounds. Unless you plan to sit next to your grandmother's guards every minute of the day, the mansion offers no protection. It's obvious Krin wants Shen dead," he says. "And she's willing to kill you two to get to him."

"Krin said that we were closer to the traitor than we realized," I added.

Jesma's face drains of color.

"Whoever it is," she says, "must be very close to my family."

Welcome to the party, Lady!

"Too close to trust that dear old grandma won't entrust the wrong person with what we know," Tamrin says. "We need to find Krin and make her talk."

I'll make that swizzle slut scream until she admits who employed her.

Jesma eyes me critically. She jabs her thumb into her chest. "I heard what she said." She taps my chest with her finger. "You said it before. Someone wants all of us dead. Not just you. Us. She never intended to let Jesmir live tonight."

Jesma lifts her chin and shows the blistered and bloody burn on her neck.

"Nor me, for that matter."

She paces in front of the bar where the dead assassin's body lies in a pool of blood. She stares at him. I'm desperate for her to connect the dots. This is too much to keep in. I'm ready to blurt out what I heard, but Jesma speaks again.

"You're right. The mansion isn't safe. Someone uses their position with Grandmother to get our whereabouts. She can't help it if she doesn't know who to trust. Hell, we don't even know if we're the true targets. What if this whole kidnapping and murder of my father and aunt is all a small part of a bigger plan? What if we're the bait to get close to Grandmother? And I don't mean a spy. I think our best option is to stay away from the mansion and solve this on our own."

One crisis averted.

She touches my arm with a gentle hand.

"You've been my hero time and again."

"And you mine," I say with a smile.

"This time, we set out together. No heroes. The four of us. This little family we've made is all I trust."

She places her other hand on Tamrin's forearm.

"The day we met you two was the worst…and best day. I know it's been a very short amount of time, all things considered. But you are family to me. We stick together. Understood?"

"Does this mean you aren't angry anymore?" I ask.

"No, I'm still mad," Jesma replies. "But I realize you navigate relationships with the awareness of a toddler." She winks and says, "I guess I should expect you to trip on your dick a few times."

I can't help but laugh at that.

"You hear that, Tam? She said I have a big dick," I say.

Tamrin rolls his eyes. "Great Jez, as if his ego wasn't big enough. He'll have to walk through doors sideways now."

"Not with this big dick, I won't."

"Let's go find the son-of-a-bitch that hired Krin," Jesma says, slapping my arm.

"I like that idea," Tamrin says.

"I kinda like talking about how big—"

"Shut up!" Tamrin and Jesma say in unison.

I hold up my hands in surrender and toss my head toward Jesmir.

"What do we do about our boy here?" I ask, glancing over her shoulder at Jesmir. My mouth falls open. Jesma follows my gaze and lets out a stunned gasp. The chair is empty.

"Boo!" A loud voice echoes from behind me.

"What the ever-loving fuck!" Tamrin yells.

My reflexive fist stops inches from Jesmir's face. The prince stands behind us, expectant, eyes wide at how close my fist came to smashing his nose.

"How the hell did you get there?" I ask.

He shrugs and presses his hand to his ear, wincing in pain. "I'm not entirely sure, but I think…magic. Morze's tits, this hurts!"

"What do you mean, magic? And of course it hurts, your ear is gone," I say.

He looks confused as tears form in his eyes. I'm about to grab him to keep him from slipping back into shock when he continues speaking.

"Damn, this really hurts!" He breathes through the pain, gathers himself, and then looks at me again. "The first time, I definitely don't know how I did it. This time, I think I did it on purpose. But I'm not sure I understand *how* I did it."

"How, indeed," Jesma asks.

"I thought you were catatonic," I say.

"I don't think so. I just couldn't get out of my head." He closes his eyes and gathers his thoughts. "I can't explain it. There's this place I can step through. It's a bit scary." He looks at Jesma. "I couldn't stop thinking about how I got from there," he points at the chair, "to there." He points to where he saved his sister.

Jesma hugs him. "Which god did you pray to?" she asks, excitement in her voice. "Who answered your prayer?"

He shakes his head. "That's the thing. That's why I couldn't make myself speak. I…I don't know. I don't remember praying…at all."

"You had to pray to someone," she says. "Whose periapt do you have?"

He continues to shake his head, a bit frightened. "No one's. I don't even have Tam's spare Fildeus periapt. When Krin and her gang grabbed me, the stone was on the nightstand. I never had a chance to grab it."

He offers an apologetic shrug to Tamrin, who pats his shoulder with empathy.

"Besides, I'm not sure I even believed she'd answer me."

"What are you saying, Jes?" Jesma asks.

He takes a deep breath. "I'm saying I wanted to save you. I needed to save you. It looked like Shen couldn't, and I got so scared. Krin was so fast. Then this urge built inside..." He trails off, his eyes squeezed shut.

"What urge?" I ask.

His face covered in blood, head wrapped in a bandage, eyes wild, he says, "To move...so...I did."

My hands shake, and I clasp them behind my back. "You thought it, therefore you did it? That sounds a bit esoteric."

"I'd agree except that's how it went." He seems to ponder it, his face wincing in pain again. "Yeah. I *saw* myself there, next to Jez. Next thing I knew, there I was."

"And this time?" Jesma asks.

He glances at her, a sheepish smile on his lips. "I wanted to be next to you. To be part of whatever you guys were on about." He closes his eyes again.

I don't know what to make of his description, but there's no more time to talk about this here. He's mobile and responsive, and we need to move. My anxiety grows every second we linger.

"This is some new kind of magic," Tamrin says. "I'm not sure I like it."

I throw my hands up in frustrated confusion.

"Well, whatever it is, Jes here isn't the only one with it. What if I can't stop them?" I whisper.

It's what we are all thinking anyway. Someone had to say it.

Despite his pain, Jesmir engages us with surprising alacrity. One minute, I thought we'd have to carry him out of the station. The next, he behaves like he's invincible. I have little experience with trauma responses. My rescue habits always err more on the 'smash and run' than the 'rescue and mend' side of heroism. I fear another crash will come once this manic state ends, but he's currently better than the useless blob I thought he'd be.

The ruckus of battle somehow didn't draw the attention of roving patrols–another indication that a conspiracy exists. I look to the twins for any indication that these little signs will trigger their suspicions. Maybe I suffer from too much inside information, but neither of the twins seems to realize what that silence in the aftermath of this disturbance means.

Despite the absence of any alarm, it won't remain this quiet for long. Rather than delay our relocation to a point much farther away with further discourse, I rush everyone out the door. We cross the broad street and finally huddle up in a deserted alley between two dilapidated warehouses to formulate a plan.

It's too cold to stay in the streets, so a safe place to sleep is paramount. The snow continues to fall, now in clumps of flakes larger than they were mere minutes ago. This snowstorm is a heavy one.

Neither Tamrin nor I have any valuable contacts in Teshket.

"I have somewhere we can go," Jesmir offers.

"No," Jesma replies. "Not there."

"Look," he says to her, "Sure, he's a criminal. But he's a criminal with good intentions. And he's my friend."

"A friend who makes his living smuggling and selling goods on the black market. And let's not forget…information," she hisses. "I don't trust him."

"Because you never needed to," Jesmir says. "He's never once sold me out and more than once kept me safe. If anyone can get us out of Kerakot, it's him. You have no idea how extensive his network is. I know you *think* I'm reckless, but that's just perception."

"Going to Bengle's Row without telling the Royal Guard is by definition reckless," she retorts.

"Going without the Royal Guard does not mean I go without protection," he replies. "And Savis' thugs are far more dangerous bodyguards than the Royal Guard. They're like having ten Shen's." He adds, "…by comparison that is," when Jesma raises a skeptical eyebrow.

He continues. "If there are rumors of new magic, like say among the Assassins' Guild, Savis will know."

"Underworld activities do tend to cross-contaminate one another," I offer. My teeth chatter from the cold. "I'd like to get out of this snow," I add.

"Fine," Jesma relents with a sigh.

The slums of Kerakot are quiet tonight. So much so, the neighborhood feels deserted. I welcome the empty snow-laden streets, grateful for the cover. On two occasions, we encounter the Nightwatch. The first time, the guards were so cold and the snowfall so thick we avoided detection by default.

Jesmir, after several attempts to perform his new trick along the way, grows increasingly frustrated with repeated failures. His frustration turns reckless, which in turn frustrates me.

A second set of guards passes; their bodies dark shadows through the grey curtain of snow. Jesmir vanishes from beside us and reappears directly behind two members of the Nightwatch. Somehow, I expected this, likely a result of my frustration with him. Whatever triggered my alertness, it's little surprise when Jesmir appears right behind the patrol.

If not for my fast reflexes and quiet movement, we'd be in a fight right now. I sprint as soon as I notice him vanish and arrive a scant second after he reappears behind the two guards. With a tackle that would make Tamrin proud, I carry the wayward Prince, one hand over his mouth, into the alley across the street.

"What was that?" one guard says, turning to look behind him. "You feel that?"

"What?" the other says, her hand on her hilt.

I hold Jesmir still with a tight grip on his mouth.

They peer through the snow, but it's too heavy to see more than shadows.

"It's just your imagination, Gerard," the female guard says.

The pair continues without incident, and I release Jesmir, who shrugs as if it were a minor mistake.

"I get it, you have new powers. That doesn't bother me. Properly disciplined, it can only help us. I see the value in what you aim to master. But for fuck's sake, stop being reckless!" I hiss.

That none of us understands his new magic, least of all him, weighs on me. I've never been responsible for a toddler before. That he's accomplished magic without a periapt *has* piqued my curiosity, too.

Can the gods act through him without a periapt? If so, which god? Whoever it is, Jesmir wishes their identity to remain anonymous.

If that's even the answer.

"His house is just up ahead," Jesmir says. "The plain one on the right with the wooden bakru statues in the yard."

"*That* crappy house is your underworld friend's house?" Tamrin asks.

"Shamna's stones!" Jesma curses.

"If you're gonna swear, Jez, go for the gold," Jesmir replies.

She punches him in the shoulder and shakes her fist in pain.

"Hold up," I say. "You mean to tell me that the head of Kerakot's smuggling operation lives in a tiny house in the dodgy side of the city like some urban day-laborer? Did the bottom fall out on smuggled goods?"

Jesmir laughs.

"No. He likes to live 'understated'. At least on the outside," Jesmir says. "Easier to run things when constables think you're just a guy who runs a vegetable stand."

"He runs a vegetable stand?" I ask, incredulous.

"Three days a week," Jesmir replies.

"Must be some expensive vegetables," Tamrin mumbles.

Jesmir clicks his tongue and points at the house four doors to our left on the other side of the street.

"Let me go first. Then the three of you come through the door. Enter like you're expected. Don't knock, and don't linger. Just walk in."

"You sure about this?" Jesma asks.

"How do you think I snuck out of town to go to Bengle's Row all those times?"

He smiles. The bandage wrapped around his head, black eye, and swollen cheek detracts from the overall effect. In fact, it's downright creepy.

"How about we get out of this snow?" I suggest.

Jesmir nods.

"Right. I'll go over and give word you're coming. Wait three minutes after I'm gone and then come on in."

A large clump of snow lands on my eyelashes. I blink it away while I wave Jesmir on. Jesmir stares at the door and squints his eyes. His body is rigid for too long. I'm afraid he's frozen. He releases a heavy sigh and readjusts his position before he begins again. Without a sound, he vanishes. A gust of wind replaces him. We wait for him to reappear at the door.

A full minute goes by, and nothing happens.

Tamrin coughs conspicuously. The three of us exchange worried glances.

"Is it possible he may not come back?" Tamrin asks.

I punch him in the arm to shut him up and glance at Jesma, who stares at the house, chewing her inner cheek. Tamrin offers a quiet apology, and I glare at him.

A commotion breaks out inside the house. Shadows appear to tussle around in a frenzied burst of activity against the curtained windows. Muffled voices argue, and as suddenly as Jesmir vanished, the silent calm returns. With furtive glances, we hold a collective breath.

"Wait here," I say. "I'll flutter the curtain if it's safe."

I sprint, a blur of dark shadow, easily overlooked in the falling snow. Within seconds, I'm over the small fence and greeted by the three wooden bakru. Their frozen eyes stare at me in judgment. I refuse to meet their gaze and step into the house as Jesmir instructed.

The entry is small and narrow. Paint on the walls flecks in spots, exposing old, crumbled plaster. The surfaces and finishes of the handrail, balusters, and trim are old and worn, but well cared for. A set of stairs makes its way up into the dark upper floor several feet ahead. Ahead and to my right, warm light flickers through a plaster archway in slow waves caused by steady flames. The house's gas lamps, a sign that not everything in this house is modest, hold a constant flame, offering dim light.

A voice I don't recognize travels into the foyer from the room beyond the archway.

I step from the small foyer into the other room. Lit by a fireplace, Jesmir sits in one of four armchairs with a smirk. A blond man, not much older than his mid-forties, dressed in bedclothes and a nightcap, stands in the center of the room, bent toward Jesmir, and wags a finger in the prince's face.

The man is agitated.

"It's late, you spoiled prick. Too late for a trip. Now come back tomorrow."

"Look at me, Savis," Jesmir says and points to his head. "Do I look like someone who can walk out of here and wait a day for a more convenient time? Does this look like I'm after a night on the town?"

"Well, no. But since you won't tell me what happened, I can't really help. Anyone with the stones to do that to a royal is far scarier than anyone I've encountered. And *that* frightens *me*."

Jesmir glances my way, his smirk wider.

"Well, I have something scarier than those people," he says and nods in my direction.

The man stops and turns to face me.

"Who the hell are you?" the man asks.

"Umm," I begin, unsure what to say.

"He's with me, Savis. The others will be along any minute."

"What others?" the man named Savis asks.

"You'll see," Jesmir replies and sips a whiskey that I only just noticed.

If I believed in demons, I'd worry Jesmir was possessed. I've never seen this side of him.

Savis grumbles. "I don't suppose there's any chance I can interest you in a hike through the snow until a more reasonable hour is there?"

Jesmir rises from the chair and claps Savis on the back. "Not a chance, old friend. We need you."

Chapter Seven

Journal Entry: 99

Everything seems to have started with the death of the Tillions. If not for those bounty hunters, I'd never have been in a place to stumble onto the twins. If not for the twins, I'd not have run into Krin, Cuska, or Brogen. And without Brogen, I wouldn't have new questions about my father.

There's been little time to think about it. I'm not even sure what Brogen said is true. Brogen may have been a great fighter, but he was shit at shit-talk. We can't all sling insults with precision.

With Krin's new powers, I may not even be the baddest bully in the forest anymore. But at least I can devastate egos with a few well-chosen quips, and Brogen's dead.

I wish we could kill that fucker again.

Where the hell do I take these people to keep them safe? Jes seems to have a plan.

That's not all he has. He's an enigma. Where does his new ability come from? He hasn't told us who.

It bothers me because I don't know how to fight it.

Smugglers

This Savis fellow is quite hospitable now that he's accepted our presence. He offered Jesma his largest room, which she refused. She took the guest room, which put me in the guest room. It gave us some more alone time.

"Do you think you're out of the doghouse?" she asks as I enter the room.

I stand there, a little surprised, with a dumb look on my face.

"Umm, I…well…damn it, Jez, I thought you'd forgiven me," I say.

"Why, because we joked about the size of your manhood?" she smirked. "Let me tell you, it's going to take more than a simple apology and saving my brother to fix this," she says.

My jaw falls slack. I'm not sure what more I can offer. Ideas form in my head, but they all seem to be variations of the same thing. I'm neither suave nor debonair. Apologies are not in my skill set. I solve problems with violence—not very useful in this situation.

It's not like I have ever had to use conflict resolution to heal relationships. Whatever she needs from me, I don't know how to figure it out. I'm not even sure it's me she's mad at. If I were in her shoes, I'd be mad at the world and looking for someone to blame, somewhere to direct my rage. But I'm an angry bastard, so of course that's what I'd do. Jesma's not like me.

She's a peacemaker. She looks for gentle solutions to complex problems. Relationships matter to her.

Oh. Damn. She needs solace in what she has left.

I step toward her and take both of her hands in mine.

"I'm sorry. I put a wedge between you and your grandmother without any consideration for how you'd feel. I was trying to solve a problem through any means necessary. I should have considered the way it would hurt you. I'm trying to navigate this, but I've never been very good at it. It's a lame excuse, but I am sorry."

It's all I can think of to say.

Her eyes well up with tears, and she nods.

"That's much better," she replies. "Much better."

I pull her into my arms, and when our lips meet, I know she's forgiven me.

We did eventually sleep. Despite the events of the evening, we found peace in each other's touch. I can still taste her on my lips the next morning.

My bladder screams at me when I wake, but lying here next to her, it's hard to move. I can't take my eyes off her. For a princess, she is a mess when she sleeps. I'm not sure she'd like me seeing her like this, but it's like a window into her inner thoughts. Her arms sprawled, mouth slightly open, hair wild. There's little of the princess I know her to be and much of who she truly is in this state. It's adorable. A giggle escapes my lips when she snores herself awake.

"I'm not hungry for mint grass stew," she mumbles before she rolls over and falls back into a deep slumber. With a smile, I ease myself out of bed, careful not to disturb her. After an aggressive stretch, I step to the window and observe the street below. It's deserted. By the time Jesma and I fell asleep, the snowfall had increased into a total whiteout.

The timing is uncanny. There were no indications earlier today that a storm brewed anywhere near here.

Grateful for my inherent silence, I dress without worrying whether I'll wake her.

Downstairs, Savis moves about the well-appointed dining room.

"Well, good morning," he says with a warm smile. A little too warm for my tastes. I haven't pissed yet and need coffee.

"Morning," I grumble. I don't know this guy, but Jesmir very clearly trusts him. Repeatedly, if the stories told last night are to be believed.

"I've prepared some food. Help yourself." He indicates a spread of cured meats, cheeses, and a surprising amount of fresh fruit for this time of year. A long, thin loaf of bread, its end broken off, sits next to softened butter with a pool of honey on top. Next to all of that food is the only thing I care about, a silver pot.

"Is that coffee?" I ask.

"It is," he replies.

I've had the pleasure of a cup every morning since we left Hericot, nine days ago. I'm happy to see my luck continue.

I pour myself a cup and make my way into his piss room. The steam rises to meet my face in that distinct aroma while I void my bladder. "Imagine that," I mumble. "I return to Teshket and get to have coffee every single day."

"How's that?" Savis asks from the other room.

I don't respond and enjoy my only true vice. The warm liquid brings immediate satisfaction. I return to the dining area. Savis appears to be less angry than he was last night. Rather than broach the topic, I accept his good graces.

"I rarely find an opportunity to enjoy coffee. But ever since I crossed the Toerges, I've been fortunate to have a cup every morning."

He smiles. "Well, there's plenty. Drink your fill."

I tilt my head in gratitude.

"You maintain all of this with smuggling?" I ask as I move about the dining room. Unlike the foyer and the exterior of the house, the inside is immaculate. I realize the condition of the entry is a deliberate choice for those not invited beyond the stoop.

The table, a rich wood of a kind I've never seen, is polished to a high, flawless shine. The overhead chandelier reflects the light from the gas-fed lamps held there.

"I maintain the organization," he says. "All this is a mere bag of bakru nuggets. Maintenance costs less than acquisition. This table was my grandparents'."

I point up to the gas chandelier.

"Okay," he says, "some of this stuff is expensive."

"The exterior is a disguise, then?" I ask.

He laughs a quiet laugh.

"The Queen loves her taxes," he says. "Most people can't afford the cost of quality goods. What the Queen doesn't take, Shamna's acolytes take in as tithes, or as gambled promises of luck at the Shamna Rocks tables. To combat the poverty that results, I provide necessary services in support of the well-being of Teshket society. Especially here in Kerakot."

"So, you smuggle as a benevolent endeavor, not a profitable one? A real humanitarian?"

"Haha! I like you. You don't pull your punches. No, I would never pretend that I'm some benevolent philanthropist. I smuggle because it is lucrative." He spreads his hands, indicating everything in the room. "I am a profiteer, first. But I do not gouge my customers. I cover costs plus fifteen percent. And I pay taxes like everyone else. I tithe to Shamna, as my faith requires. I'm just very good at circumventing the inspection stations at city gates. And my customers know I can get anything they need."

I nod. "And that includes people?"

"That it does. Both ways." He takes a chunk of cheese and meat from the spread and pops it into his mouth. He talks while chewing. "Our rogue prince can attest to that. He's never missed an opportunity to sneak out to Bengle's Row."

"Rogue?"

Savis raises an eyebrow, confused. He opens his mouth to speak, thinks better of it, and waves the thought away. I want to ask what he intended to say, but I figure if he wanted to say it, he would have.

"He spends a lot of time in Bengle's Row?"

"There's a room there that is always empty in case of his arrival," Savis replies.

It's my turn to look confused, surprised that Jesmir, who seems incapable of defending himself, frequented the seedy streets of Bengle's Row.

Savis notices my confusion. "Its reputation is worse than its reality. Prince Jesmir is regarded as a bit of a celebrity in Bengle's Row. He plays well, spends well, and is a hell of a tipper. If harm befell him, that place would set itself on fire to locate the perpetrators. And everyone knows it."

Long arms wrap around me from behind. A soft face rests against my shoulder blade. "What's that?" Jesma whispers.

I turn to face her.

"Coffee. I almost can't remember what it's like to go without."

She giggles. "That's what I love about you. A good tumble in the hay and a cup of coffee, and you're all smiles again."

Savis bows to Jesma. "Your Highness," he says.

"Good morning," she replies and pours herself a cup.

Loud footsteps thunder from the stairs, followed by a bang as the front door opens with haste.

"Aw, damn." Tamrin's gruff voice booms in the narrow foyer. "There's two feet of snow out here."

"Winter moves fast in the northern realm," I call out.

He grumbles to himself and closes the door. The motion sends a blast of cold air through the house, and I fight a shiver. A minute later, Tamrin enters the room, covered in clumps of snow. He growls at me and snatches my coffee from my hand, consumes the contents like they're cold, and hands me the empty cup.

"You're…welcome?" I respond.

"We should get out of here," Tamrin replies. "I don't like sitting around."

"Someone's in a mood," I say.

He grabs a handful of morsels from the table and stuffs his face before he shows me his wounded hand. "Hurts like a son of a bitch. I hardly slept."

"Well, good morning to you anyway," Jesma offers. "Let's have a look at it."

He smiles, his cheeks reddened either from the cold or his embarrassment. My bet is both.

"I'm sorry, Jez. Good morning."

Savis raises an eyebrow. "You are all friends?"

Tamrin nods, "Good friends."

"Interesting. I thought you two were hired help," he says, wagging a finger between Tamrin and me.

"What gave you that impression?" Tamrin asks, his cheeks stuffed like a gorged bakru. He chomps another clump of meat and cheese into his mouth as Jesma leads him to a chair.

"The company you keep."

"I'm not in the habit of sleeping with hired help," Jesma replies.

Savis holds up his hands in defense. "I meant no offense. It explains the prince's behavior last night. He was a bit more…demanding."

Before we can continue the conversation, Jesmir appears in the archway.

"Savis, we need a quiet passage out of Kerakot. Not through the usual channels," the prince says.

"So right to business then?" Savis says with a frown.

Less than ten days ago, we crossed the Toerge Mountains, and it seemed winter had only just arrived. Now, Ezra barely creeps over the horizon at peak daylight. It's mid-morning, and the sky is still dark. The lack of light is usually an advantage, but the snow magnifies what little light there is. Even the shadows offer no protection from prying eyes. We have to assume the word is out about the missing royals again. Whether her majesty intends to send out search parties or not is anyone's guess. Still, I don't suspect she's going to be very happy when she learns her grandchildren left the castle.

Wish I could see the look on her face when she reads the note I left.

At least the snowfall stopped.

"The news of your disappearance is out," Savis says as he enters the front door.

That answers that.

"That didn't take long," Tamrin replies, dejected.

"There are patrols out all over the city. You're a conspicuous group," Savis says. "But, lucky for you, I have a plan."

He waves us along, and we follow him into the kitchen at the back of the house. Marble, hand-carved cabinets, brass and copper fixtures, and a dazzling display of pots, utensils, and dinnerware are on display behind glass doors and hanging from racks.

I raise an eyebrow, and Savis notices.

"Okay," he says, hands in mock surrender, "maybe I allow for a little decadence. But look at this place." He grabs hold of one countertop against the wall directly under the upstairs landing and rotates the entire corner.

"Well, that's handy," Tamrin says.

"No one would think to move a countertop in a kitchen such as this," Savis replies with a satisfied grin.

Behind the wall of cabinets hides a set of stairs that descends under the house.

"This," Savis says, his eyes on Jesmir, "is how I got you back into Kerakot that time you took too much of that Masicant Root."

Jesmir blushes. "That was a night."

Jesma gives him a stern look. "Masicant Root? Seriously?"

He shrugs. "Yeah, it was great. I never took it again, though."

"Yet," Jesma says, rolling her eyes.

Jesmir shrugs, noncommittal.

"Where does this lead?" I ask.

"That's a question, isn't it?" Savis says.

Jesmir snorts a laugh. "Everywhere."

Savis says. "You'll see. Let's get a move on. I have a special ride waiting for you, and we have a long walk. You're gonna like this one," he says to Jesmir. "But we don't have time to dilly-dally."

"How?" I ask. The hairs on my neck tingle.

"How what?" Savis asks.

"How did you arrange passage so quickly?" I ask suspiciously.

"This is what I do," he replies. "Trust me or don't. If you don't want to go this way, there's a door," he points toward the entry back into the dining area, "that way. You are welcome to walk right out of it and not look back."

"Shen," Jesmir says, "this is my friend."

Single file, we follow Savis into the hidden basement. I wait until I'm the last one left in the kitchen and take one last glance around. This is too easy. I don't like 'easy.' Easy makes me nervous.

"Savis," I call out.

"Yes?"

"If you betray us…"

"I'm well aware of the consequences. We may not know each other, but I recognize you aren't to be trifled with. You, sir, are more dangerous than most people I deal with."

I nod, still uneasy, and make my way into the unknown space below.

Either my eyes play tricks on me, or the basement is larger than the house above. Crates stacked in rows, six deep and three tall, fill the center of the room. On a far wall, barrels lay on their sides, stacked in racks on either side of a large door. A woman appears from around the back of one row, a basket in her arm.

"Desha," Savis says. "How's the schedule today?"

She glances at the four of us, curious. Savis nods for her to speak.

"We have an issue with the dwyer root," she replies. "It's not as potent as we were told. But I have Car…I have someone on it."

Savis nods. "Let me know if I need to step in?"

"I don't think that will be necessary. The mere threat seems to have worked. I sent samples across town."

Savis turns to Jesmir. "Our friend in Breakridge seems to have lost his touch."

Jesma gives Jesmir a shocked look.

Jesmir shrugs and turns back to Savis. "Is it still usable?"

Desha replies, "For cooking, yes. For medicine? Not at all. It's lost all of its moisture. Nothing to extract."

"You'll inform me as soon as it's resolved?" Savis says to the woman.

"Of course," she replies and walks toward a second stairway deeper into the cellar.

Savis indicates with a quick back and forth of his finger overhead, tracing a line across the full length of the ceiling.

"The houses on either side of me are mine too," he says. "The folks that live there, like Desha, live for free. Well, their rent is their silence. I pay them for their work."

Jesma grabs Jesmir's arm. "You knew about all this?"

"I know about the operation." Jesmir glances around the room.

"What's your role?" she asks.

"His highness is a supporter of the local poor," Savis says. "He brings to my attention the needs of the citizens of Teshket, and I see to their fulfillment."

"I don't take any money from it, Jez," Jesmir says.

"Not a copper," Savis replies. "His payment is my help, anytime he asks."

"As long as it's not interrupting your sleep," I reply.

Savis smiles and continues past the crates to the large door between the barrels. The door is unlocked and opens effortlessly. Dim orbs, like the ones in the sewers of Valshannon, light the way ahead. Before us, the longest set of stairs I've ever seen descends into the depths below Kerakot.

"This must have been an expensive endeavor," Tamrin says. His voice echoes in an endless song along the tunnel. We all wince.

"It was," Savis replies in a whisper. "Those lights aren't cheap. That's why they are spaced so far apart." He gives Tamrin a look. "While the tunnel was costly, it wasn't expensive enough that I spent the money to soundproof it. I'd recommend a whisper from now on. Sound travels far in these tunnels."

Tamrin clamps his mouth shut and taps his nose in acknowledgment.

We walk for what seems like hours through the underground passages. The lights, walls, and periodic splits in the tunnel lead to confusion, and I'm soon lost, left to trust where our smuggler guide leads.

The complex maze climbs stairs into other homes, through doors that connect one home to another in a series of hidden entries, and back into underground tunnels. Some homes are modest, while some belong to people of means. Others are little more than nearly dilapidated huts. We step from tunnels, cross rooms and halls, only to once again descend stairs.

I've lost track of time and grow claustrophobic in the underground. I yearn for the RhineWoods and its freedom. Savis' masterful planning and his ability to instill discretion through generosity are impressive. That he hasn't been discovered based on the number of people involved is a mystery.

"How is this possible?" Jesma asks.

"My great-grandmother and her brothers started these tunnels. Over one hundred years ago," he replies. "My grandmother and then my father continued to expand on them. When my folks passed, I finished the work. What you pass through is over a century of effort."

"But we've built sewers in that time. How have you avoided them?" she asks.

"The first sewer was built before my grandmother started these tunnels. That's how she got the idea. Her brother worked on the sewer construction."

We take the stairs without a word, our boots and heavy breathing the only break in the heavy silence. When we reach the bottom, the tunnel runs too far ahead to see its end.

"You'll understand if some secrets are kept," he replies.

At last, we step out of the tunnels and find ourselves in a study of some mansion. Dark-wood shelves, filled with books of all types and sizes, line the walls. Large windows allow the last of the waning light to grace the edges and cast shadows. The soft, warm gas lamps bathe the room in a cozy, warm yellow.

"Well, folks," Savis says. "That is the last of the tunnels. Please, make yourselves at home."

"Where are we?" Tamrin asks.

"Heal Hill," Savis replies.

"Whose mansion is this?" Jesma asks.

"I prefer not to say. This is the private study."

Heal Hill rests on the southwest border of Kerakot, just outside the city limits. It derives its moniker from the number of wealthy healers and potion makers who live here. A significant number of the wealthy spellcasters placed their mansions on this hill to have a view of the city away from the rest of Kerakot.

Savis holds a hand up to signal for us to stay put. He walks to the study doors and steps through. A startled scream echoes in the hall, followed by hushed whispers, muffled and undecipherable.

The door opens, and I prepare for a fight.

Savis raises an eyebrow.

"You really are wound tight, aren't you?"

"You would be too if you knew what we're up against," I say.

He glances around the room. "I suspected this was an escape mission," he replies in a hoarse whisper. "You can relax. The maid and butler are the only ones in the house. They know I only appear here if business is afoot. They'll leave us to it. We can wait it out here until nightfall. Though these houses are spread apart, the visibility is rather risky. The neighbors host a large party next door. Let's allow that to die out. I'd rather we weren't seen sneaking into the backwoods."

Tamrin groans. "We can't sit about. There are assassins after these two."

I give Tamrin a look that tells him to shut up.

"I see," Savis says. "Well, they won't find you here unless I hired them, which I didn't. Besides, this is more comfortable than a day out there in the frozen woods, don't you think?"

"You mean rather than spend the night?" I ask.

"Haha! You won't be spending the night. I have a special shipment headed out at first light, and we take a unique form of travel. I intend to place you on that vessel. We don't have much time to dawdle. Two days from now, you'll be in Gal-Danang. Rather than sit and freeze our asses off out there, I thought you'd like to be comfortable here till the party ends. Win-win. We'll take advantage of the cover of night from prying eyes next door."

"Sounds reasonable to me," Jesmir says. His body tenses, and his eyes grow vacant.

"Where are you trying to go?" I ask, the hair on my body standing on end. Every time he does this, my nerves grow tense, as if the air around me crackles as if it's in flux.

Before he can respond, he vanishes. A second later, he reappears in a chair, sitting with his legs crossed.

"This is better," he says.

I shake my head.

"That hardly seemed necessary," I whisper.

"I must practice," Jesmir says. "Why are you so glum?"

Jesmir's tone is combative. From the corner of my eye, I see Jesma's jaw tighten.

"I'm not glum, Jes," I reply. "I'm concerned you don't know enough about this new ability to be safe."

He stands and faces me, his brow twisted. "I don't know if you realize this, being our savior and all, but we haven't been safe since the day we hopped on that damn ship bound for Gal-Danang." He points to his bandage. "Not even in our own home. Do you think I care about safety anymore?"

"You should," I say.

"Are you worried about my safety? Or about your position as the toughest guy in Conishant?"

"Jesmir!" Jesma cries, dismayed.

"Bah!" Jesmir waves at us and plops back into his chair.

"I'm sorry," I say. "Did I miss something? What's with the attitude, *your highness*?" I emphasize the title with sarcasm.

"You know what?" Jesmir says. "I finally have more to offer than a shaky hand and a lucky shot with a crossbow. And I intend to use it. Last I checked, I'm a free person."

I go to speak, but he interrupts.

"No. All you see is some useless, weak, rich kid. I think you preferred it that way. The world is changing around you, and you don't like it."

"You don't know me well enough to make that judgment," I snap back, but he's not listening. I can tell he's shut me out, and all I want to do is punch him for being a prick.

"How about we all take a beat and get some rest? It's been a long day," Tamrin says, ever the peacemaker among friends.

I grab a chair and plop onto the soft leather. Jesma avoids her brother and kneels before Tamrin and taps his injured hand. Tamrin pats her shoulder and holds the bandaged appendage for her to inspect. She opens her pack, pulls out her salve jar, and works on replacing the bandage on his finger. They speak in soft tones, and Tamrin does his best to ease her tension.

Jesmir's words ring in my head. Deep down, I know that what Jesmir needs is grace, but his words pissed me off.

Am I mad because he said it or because there's truth in it?

I don't know the answer. And that bothers me. Thinking about it only makes me angrier, so I try to focus on something else. Thoughts working as they do, my mind drifts to the words of the Queen, which only worsens my tension. If I don't summon the courage to tell them both what I know, the damage could be irreparable. But now seems like the worst time.

This is why I live alone.

Jesma finishes with Tamrin and turns to her brother. He looks up at her with a blank expression, barely acknowledging her. She leans over him and pulls the bandage from his ear.

"Well," she says. "At least the bleeding has stopped." She caresses Jesmir's face. He pulls it away slowly.

"I need some sleep. Let's get this bandage changed, okay?" he mumbles, his face drawn.

She leans forward and kisses his cheek, and his shoulders slump. They touch foreheads, and I'm reminded of that first moment I saw them, when Jesma tended to his injuries in the glen deep in the RhineWoods. If anyone can get through to Jesmir, it's Jesma.

I'm in the gods-be-damned way.

While Jesma works to care for his wound, Jesmir closes his eyes and exhales slowly. Jesma pats his hand.

"Don't shut me out," she says. "Get some sleep."

She touches Jesmir's arm, and he looks at her and nods a weak apology. Jesma tends to my leg next.

"He's dealing with stuff," I offer to assuage her concerns, though I share them.

I don't think she's fooled, but she nods and says, "Yes, I know, Shen. If anyone understands him, it's me. He'll be alright, give it time."

Jesmir and I lock eyes, and I can see he's still angry. I know where that kind of anger leads, and my hearts race. I fear Jesmir's headed for a crash.

Chapter Eight

Journal Entry: 103

Is Jesmir's power a foreshadow of changes to come? It's just one more question that lingers in my mind.

It be my fucking luck that right when I find a reason to wake up in the morning, the world becomes more dangerous. I'll say this much, real or not, the gods have a fucking sense of irony. For all I know, I'm the butt of some divine joke. It makes sense why I'm the only unbeliever I've ever met.

There was a time I wished for it——people more powerful than myself. I yearned for just one person to be faster, better, and more skilled. I welcomed the day my soul could be dispatched from my body into the void of the nethers.

But now? Now that I have this family that I rely on, that relies on me. I feel different. Faced with this strange new power, I'm frightened.

For the first time, I'm afraid of death. Not the dying part. I'm fearful of what I'll miss out on. I'm afraid of how others will feel about *my absence and how they might be hurt by it. And I now know for certain that they would be.*

Who would have thought I'd care about that?

I guess I never believed this life was mine to hold. But it never occurred to me, once I had it, that it would be so short-lived.

I'm sure the Great Eight are tickled pink for a new way to torture me. How they love to see me squirm.

The Stream of Lies

Wind gusts lift the loose snow from the ground. The white curtain obscures our vision with sustained, frequent whiteouts. My nerves on edge, my mind plays tricks with every shadow. Tamrin, at least, prayed for true sight, evidenced by the purple hue in his eyes.

Our journey to the rendezvous with Savis' team drags through the night. Even with the cloak, it's bitterly cold out here. As the night wears on, time slips by. The endless winter darkness is held at bay by the blanket of stars in the sky and their reflection off the snow. The twin lunar orbs slip along, first following us, then leading us, the occasional view of their progression through the pines the only evidence that time passes.

The trees appear as little more than eerie shadows in the snowy micro-bursts, fading in and out of focus. The swirl of the snow-drifts in strange circular patterns distorts depth perception and threatens us with vertigo.

All things considered, we are well rested, and the trek itself doesn't tax us physically. Aside from the distance, cold, and visual distractions, the journey is effortless. Still, excluding the occasional comments from Savis, we walk in silence. Even Tamrin isn't immune to the doom-cloud that hangs over us. My thoughts center on Jesmir. I wonder if the same can be said of the others.

On more than one occasion, Jesmir stops, his face twisted in concentration, and vanishes, only to reappear some distance ahead. It's unsettling how often he does this. He waits for us to catch up, a satisfied smirk on his face, only to vanish again. Savis' body language changed after the third instance, a reaction I find odd. Jesma chastised him for his reckless behavior. Jesmir brushes off all attempts at reason with a flippant wave. Admittedly, with each attempt, he grows more proficient, each success taking less time than the previous attempt.

Part of me wants to sprint ahead and be there when he reappears, but the whole process is instantaneous. This time, he doesn't reappear as quickly. His absence drags on, and Jesma grows nervous. It's easy to get lost in this blizzard. When her glances grow frantic, my temper flares over his disregard for his sister's stress. Several minutes pass before his dark silhouette appears through the snow.

I grab his elbow and pull him aside. He rolls his shoulders back and pushes his chest forward.

"Can you give it a rest? Your sister is worried. And frankly, so am I."

"About what?" he says. It's the first real sign of his privileged upbringing showing through his usually friendly demeanor. I struggle to contain my own retaliatory aggression.

"She's worried that you don't know the consequences of this magic…or from where it comes," I say. "What if you end up lost in this blizzard?"

"Well, it's my ability. I intend to master it before we need it in an emergency. You saw what Krin could do. Yesterday could have turned into a worse tragedy than my loss of an ear."

I close my eyes and take a deep breath.

"All we ask is that you stop, for a moment. Stay close to us."

He shakes his head. "I aim to be as good as Krin by the time we run into her again."

He yanks his arm from my grip, turns, and vanishes again. I feel the air sucked away from me. It's a physical manifestation of the rising dread in my chest. Entrenched inside my thoughts, we arrive at the bank of Furkote Stream. Its sudden appearance catches me by surprise. The snowfall obscures a view of the slow-moving river's far bank. A gust of wind presses my cloak tight against my hip, the edges flapping in the wind.

"I haven't seen the Furkote in years," I say.

"I've never been here," Tamrin replies. "It's much less frightening than the Great Rankin."

"Well, it's slower and not as deep, so that helps," Jesmir says. "It runs into Coraside Bay, two hundred miles west."

"And follows the laws of physics," Tamrin says with obvious relief.

"And doesn't have river Gnomes," Jesma replies.

"Still not over your abduction by Grankin?" I tease.

Tamrin shivers under his heavy furs.

"I'm not," he says.

Savis steps between Tamrin and me.

"Grankin? You were abducted by the God of Time?" Savis asks. "That's got to be a story. I'd love to hear it sometime."

Tamrin and I exchange glances. Tamrin changes the subject. "This is still a wide stream. Too deep to walk across and too cold to swim. What's the plan?"

"Oh, we aren't crossing. We're gonna use the stream. Furkote is deep enough for shallow-bottom boats and barges to carry goods into Coraside Bay…and people."

Savis turns and walks downstream. The rest of us follow. I stare across the river, rubbing my chest involuntarily, my mind a thousand miles south.

"You coming?" Jesma calls.

I shiver and hurry to catch up.

We don't go far when Savis draws to a stop and raises his hand to halt the party. A gruff voice barks out from somewhere beyond the trees.

"You sure took your sweet ass time getting here."

The voice comes from within the blizzard. I can't locate the speaker.

"Well, since you work for me, I don't see what it matters," Savis calls out.

A group of five shadows step out from behind the surrounding trees.

"You didn't notice any tracks?" I mumble to Tamrin.

"Not at all," he replies, chagrined.

"You don't pay by the hour, chief," a man in leather armor and a heavy cloak says.

From the scars on his face and his slight limp, this man's seen some battles. Savis approaches, and the two clasp hands. Whatever the man's been through, his smile is genuine.

"Yes, but you are paid well. I'd say that an evening's delay is worth your time," Savis replies.

"Well, we can use the extra hands to get the lady on the water," the man says. He glances over Savis' shoulder.

"Royals?" he asks, his eyes narrowing.

Savis turns and looks at Jesma and Jesmir, then at me and Tamrin.

"And their bodyguards," he says. "It's classified. But I need you to get them to Coraside Bay on the quiet." He hands the man a small purse. "Eleven hundred Haabrestand gold. Another eleven hundred when they get to their destination."

The man nods.

"I'll see them safely there."

"Send word once you're done. I'll authorize the second payment via the usual channels," Savis says. He turns toward Jesmir, and they shake hands.

"You're in good hands with Cillian, here. He'll see you safely to Coraside. You owe me for this one, Your Highness…and I do mean more than gold."

Jesmir nods, "You know I'm good for it."

Savis turns to the rest of us.

"Well, folks, it's been fun. I've done what I can for you. It's up to you and Cillian's crew from here on out." Without another word, the smuggler walks back the way we came.

Cillian coughs to get our attention.

"Everyone pulls their weight. I'm not a luxury boat captain, and this isn't some love cruise. There isn't much for you to do, but what I tell you to do, you do quickly and without question." He looks at Jesma and Jesmir. "That includes royals. Follow me. Just a couple hundred yards this way."

This oughta be fun.

Jesma and Jesmir glance at Cillian, each a bit alarmed.

"You don't intend to steal the Queen's boat, do you?" Jesma asks, dismayed.

Cillian seems to ignore the question.

A large stone structure looms ahead, hidden within the evergreens. Two large iron doors take up the entire front facade. In the center where the doors meet, three separate locks—ornate disks with no noticeable keyholes—protrude like pointed bowls.

Moss grows on the slate roof, the irregular stones colored green and grey with time. Cillian steps up to the doors and removes an odd pendant. He presses it into a recess in the lower right of the door.

Loud clicks and grinding gears ring from within the doors. The three disks rotate until they align themselves. I recognize the symbol they create as the crest of the Teshket Crown—a lion's head surrounded by a set of Shamna Rocks.

I clench my jaw.

"This is a royal lock?" I ask. I prepare to release my blades.

Jesma turns to Cillian.

"I asked you a question," she demands.

Cillian directs two of his soldiers to open the doors. The doors open with little effort to reveal a massive, boat-shaped carriage. The wooden and steel structure stands over fifteen feet tall and rides on six wide wheels.

"Yes, your Highness, this is indeed the queen's river boat," Cillian says.

"How do you have access?" Jesmir demands.

Cillian laughs.

"How else would we smuggle you out of Teshket so easily?" Cillian says. "No one thinks twice when it appears you have the royal seal of approval."

"The queen gives you access to this?" I ask, incredulous.

Cillian laughs. "Oh, hell no. She'd behead me and my crew if she found out I was using it for personal gain. But since we travel with Royals, I don't think anyone will question this. Assuming the queen knows what you're up to, that is."

"We aren't…" Jesma starts, but Cillian stops her short.

"Look, I don't need the details. But my life and livelihood rely on my astute observational skills. I recognize royal blood when I see it."

He waits for us to react. When we don't, he continues.

"For your information, Savis has connections everywhere. Including within the royal guards. We only use this vessel for *special* occasions, like when a princess and a prince wish to leave the country in a hurry."

Tamrin steps forward and admires the vessel.

"What are you gonna pull that with?" he asks. "A dragon?"

Cillian smiles, "No, sir. With you."

"Ha!" Tam blurts.

Cillian's expression remains serious, even as he raises his eyebrows. He isn't joking.

"Look, I don't have any reason to take you anywhere. But," he points at Jesma and Jesmir, "Savis didn't lead you through his most profitable smuggling route for an adventure. You clearly don't want to be seen leaving. He risked his safety and livelihood to make it happen. So, I will be a good soldier and do the same."

He gestures behind us with a tilt of his head.

"The winds may have covered your approach, but the queen has the best trackers in Conishant. Snow drifts aren't going to cover your tracks from their sight." He points at the giant vessel. "That, on the other hand, will. Once we get on the water, there is no way they can track you. The nearest crossing is back on the Highland Road, back east, or the Timany bridge," he points west, "seventy miles that way. Should buy you a few days."

I look at Jesmir, an eyebrow raised. He shrugs.

Tamrin grumbles. "Let's quit yapping and pull this thing to the water."

Cillian laughs. "We use horses. You don't really need to help pull."

Three smugglers, their faces hidden behind scarves, appear from around the corner of the carriage house. Each leads two horses.

"Unlike you lot, we prefer not to walk everywhere."

Tamrin grumbles under his breath.

Calling this thing a carriage is a loose application of the term. While I've never sailed the oceans, I've seen the ships that do in the various ports along the coastlines of the realms. Their characteristic hull designs, with masts as tall as any building, are commonplace. The distinct scales, wide girth, and intricate carvings on this vessel are of Korund craftsmanship. It's definitely a boat, though it has wheels.

Gal-Danang, the peaceful nation of neutrality, is the greatest manufacturer of weapons of war.

Ironic.

The queen's carriage is a smaller version of the Korund ships. The most noticeable difference, aside from the size, between those ships and this carriage is the six large wheels that hold it a couple of feet off the ground. Large enough to house us, the guards, and the horses, the carriage moves with less effort than I expected. Cillian directs his crew to hitch the horses to this odd marvel of design.

I guess it's technically a carriage. It has wheels.

The carriage sits, wheels stuck in the muddy bed of the stream. One member of the crew, a female by her shape, climbs the hull with the help of handholds that run up the port side. She disappears over the wale, and moments later, chains clink against gears from inside. A ramp lowers onto the dock.

"Alright, people, let's get loaded up and on our way!" Cillian calls out.

We help guide the horses aboard and secure them in stables at the stern of the boat. Jesmir and I untie the lines from the cleats as the ramp raises, though I'm not sure why we even bothered tying the ship off with those wheels stuck. We toss the ropes up and scale the same handholds that Cillian's soldier did earlier. A loud thump, felt through the topside deck, signals that the ramp is secure.

Ten humans and six horses stand ready to make the slow, lazy journey downstream. Cillian shouts commands, and the crew cranks pulleys at the bow, midship, and stern. The deck echoes with movement beneath my feet. The sound carries over the water, and I can hear its echo through the trees.

In the center of the boat, carved into the deck, are symbols I recognize, wards like those on the trees in spiderlyche country.

"What are these?" I ask.

"There are things in the waters around Conishant you don't want to mess with," Cillian replies. "These ward them off."

I glance over the port side hull when the vessel shakes and more mechanical noises clang below deck. I step back as the top edges of the wheels rise over the wale. Water laps against the hull. The boat pitches and yaws with a lazy motion, released from the mud as the carriage becomes a boat. Two muscular women, one scarred from what appear to be battle wounds like Cillian's, push against the dock with large poles, and we break free of the stream's soft, shallow banks.

Within minutes, we float on a peaceful journey toward Coraside Bay. The horses whinny and neigh for a few minutes until they grow comfortable with the slight rocking motion.

I stand with Tamrin, amazed.

"You ever seen anything like this?" I ask.

He shakes his head. "I had no idea that Teshket was so innovative."

I shake my head. "I lived here the first seventeen years of my life. And never saw anything like this. This is Korund innovation. Still, it's impressive."

"A lot can happen in three decades," Tamrin chides.

"Who you tellin'?"

We step to the bow of the ship where Jesma and Jesmir stand, deep in a whispered conversation, their mannerisms heated. The boat makes a starboard turn up the middle of the stream.

"So begins the long journey to Coraside," I say as I approach them.

Jesmir rolls his eyes.

"Am I interrupting something?" I ask, aware that I am.

Jesmir turns to the bow and stares ahead.

Jesma addresses Jesmir, "Are you going to tell us what's eating at you?"

Jesmir stares at his sister, his jaw clenched. He shakes his head and walks away, frustrated. Tamrin stares after him.

Overhead, the moons make their way westward, ever closer to the horizon. Their light reflects off the water, and silver slivers shimmer on the tiny surface waves. The quiet river passes by the land in peaceful bliss. Jesma steps closer, and I wrap my arm around her, my eyes on the moons. She leans her head back against my shoulder.

If not for the burden of the secrets I keep from her, my concern for Jesmir, and the brevity of the journey ahead, I'd find comfort in the gesture. Instead, I close my eyes and fight back the tears that threaten to overtake me. We've been on the run for a full day now.

Yesterday, I awoke and overheard the queen and Krin discuss the death of all that I love.

I'm frustrated. Maybe Jesmir is, too. I know I need to give him a bit of leeway. He suffers more than the rest of us, his head wrapped in a bandage, a constant reminder of how close he came to death.

Tamrin's boots scrape the deck and grow more distant. He's always so intuitive. He's given us a moment of privacy.

"Shen?" Jesma says.

"Yes," I whisper.

"Something is eating you, too. Did something happen since yesterday morning? Besides the obvious with Jes." She pulls away and looks up at me. "I believe I know you well enough to leave you alone. But that isn't always the best way to handle a problem. Why don't you say what bothers you?"

"How can you know something bothers me. We haven't known each other that long. I'm a notorious brooder."

Her smile—sad, tender, and a bit self-assured, curls at the corners of her lips. "When you've made a decisive action, you don't hesitate. You don't mope. When you are sure of the path and of yourself, you act with confidence—so certain you have the only right answer. You're fearless in the moment."

She leans into my chest.

"But when you wrestle inside, it's written all over you. You wear your heart on your sleeve, Shen. You don't think you do, but you do."

I take a shuddering breath as I hold her tightly.

"Talk to me," she says.

"I can't. Not yet. Not here. But I will when we get off this boat."

"Promise?"

"Promise," I say, thankful to delay the inevitable.

I haven't left my position at the bow of the ship since Jesma left me to my thoughts. The moons prepare to leave my company, their edges touching the tops of the trees. Meanwhile, we chase them for reasons only Tamrin and I understand. The twins have misguided reasons for why we flee their home. No, not misguided. Just partially uninformed.

I don't know what to do next. We must escape the realm, but I have no clue what we should do once we get to Coraside Bay. Spies everywhere will be on the lookout for these two. Krin has effectively marked Jesmir. Prince or not, there aren't many young men in the company of a furry tracker, a silverish-red-haired traveler, and a man who fits the prevailing description of me.

The first moon touches the top of the trees. In the race to Coraside, we fall ever further behind our lunar guides, our speed at the mercy of the Furkote Stream.

My thoughts are interrupted by footsteps on the deck behind me.

"I think it's best if you spend the night in the main cabin," Cillian says.

"I'm fine up here," I reply.

"Well, it's my ship. And I want you off my bow," Cillian replies.

I turn to him, my expression blank. His face, hardened with time and experience, reveals nothing either. I'd guess he's ten years older than me, but he could be the same age. He reminds me of so many soldiers who found themselves incapable of blending into normal civilian life after a lifetime of adrenaline-fueled days and nights.

Neither of us flinches from the other's gaze. Opposite sides of the same coin. I can sense the tension within him. He raises an eyebrow, noticeable even in the dim moonlight.

I sigh. "I have no desire to fight, but I'm better off up here."

"This is not a request. On this vessel, I am Captain."

I smirk at him. "We both know you're no Captain. Let's not pretend there is some hierarchy I'm going to follow."

He shakes his head. "Look, it's clear you're no simple hired hand either. Obviously, you keep your own counsel and fear little. But whoever you are, I am charged with your safety. Savis asked this favor, and between you and me, I owe him more than this favor. He and I go back a long way. I am sure you can take care of yourself, but I can't guarantee your safety unless you do as I say."

I smirk. "I've used that line myself before."

He leans against the wale and crosses his arms, assessing how far he can push me. I answer him when I turn my back to him and continue to gaze downstream. The snow on the banks reflects the moon's light through the sparse pines on either bank. Visibility reaches deep into the forest, and I catch sight of a deer on the northern side. The tracks of small animals run in crisscross lines through the snow. Our slow pace through the landscape would be relaxing under other circumstances.

"So now what?" he asks.

"I guess you're free of your obligation," I reply with a sideways glance back over my shoulder.

He pushes himself from the wale. "Be that as it may, I have orders. So, I'll ask you to kindly step into the cabin. We can handle security from here."

"Unless you intend to physically force me down there, it's not happening," I reply.

We stare at each other for a long minute. His jaw clenches and releases repeatedly as he seems to consider that. Recognizing I will not obey, he turns abruptly and heads back to the stern of the boat. He gives orders to the hardened female from earlier. She looks my way and nods in response to his order.

Cillian looks back at me before he heads below deck. The smuggler walks over and leans into the same position Cillian once stood, eyes across the barge, focused on the port-side shore, her face stuck in a perpetual scowl. Her light armor, worn, dented, and dull, doesn't reflect any of the low moonlight. I can't tell whether her hair is short, long, or gone, hidden under her helm the way it is. At her side rests a short, straight sword, hilt positioned high near her ribcage. I note the unique hilt. Her expression is emotionless.

"You don't like orders, do you?" she says.

"Not really."

"He's only looking out for you."

"I appreciate that. But I don't like confined spaces." I turn back to the stream ahead without a word.

"I can understand that. You'll get no argument from me."

"You guys been together long?" I ask.

"Me and Cillian go back decades. Wet our metal side-by-side in many a fight."

"The others?"

"Nah. They're new. Savis sent them to work with us today. Usually just me and Cillian on this run. You guys must be important for him to risk using this route."

"Not really. We just paid well," I say.

She scoffs at my blatant lie.

Behind me and to my right, more boots scrape on the starboard side of the deck. I peek over my right shoulder. It's another one of the smugglers. He is younger than the rest. I don't remember his name, but he has all the appearance of a rookie. He leans against the port side wale and carves slivers of an apple with a throwing knife. He slides one into his mouth.

Great. More Babysitters.

Up ahead, the stream bends off to the left. The evergreens grow thicker, their trunks closer together. Other tree species appear in the mix. Little snowdrifts clump up as the wind blows through the thick trunks. Wispy clouds of snowflakes, driven across the stream by the winds, gather on the left bank. The slow, lazy stream threatens to lull me to sleep. I stifle a yawn. A male voice wakes me out of hypnosis.

"Harlan, right?" the young soldier with the apple says, striking up a conversation with the older woman.

"Yeah," she replies. Her tone is cold and disinterested.

"How'd you end up on this detail?" he asks.

"Cillian," she says.

"You guys work together long?" he asks.

I hear another set of footsteps behind me.

"A lifetime," she replies.

"You guys chew a lot of dirt together?" asks an unfamiliar voice that I assume belongs to the new set of feet. That one comes from my left, close to the woman named Harlan.

"Some," Harlan replies.

"Yeah, me and that youngster there, chewed lots of dirt together."

But he's a rookie.

"Good for you."

"Shame you weren't with us," the new voice says.

My hair stands up on end. Something is off.

Harlan snorts, "Yea? Why is that?"

"It'd just be better for everyone if you were."

Something in that one's tone triggers me into action. I chastise myself for my lack of awareness and spin around, my insides on fire. I block a throwing knife out of the air with my bracer. 'Apple Boy' is just finishing his follow-through when I send his knife sailing into the river. The seasoned veteran named Harlan clutches her throat as blood pours through her fingertips. She desperately fights to hold on to life. A short, curved blade held in the newcomer's hand drips with fresh blood. The older man faces me, his teeth bared. I recognize the hunger in his eyes–it's the bloodlust of a hunter who finally has his prey in sight.

In my periphery, I catch a quick glance of 'Apple Boy'. He draws two similarly curved blades. I recognize the knives immediately as the typical blades of the Killinshire Assassins' Guild.

Killinshire assassins? Here?

All motion freezes for an infinitesimal amount of time as the natural anticipation of battle fills the air with tension. Real killers don't hesitate, they prepare. I can see it in both of their eyes. The poor smuggler, Harlan, barely conscious, slips in her own blood and falls overboard. It's the moment we all waited for—the bell to start the fight. Before her body can splash into the water, three killers go into motion. My bracers block two strikes before I can spin out of the way and reach to draw my sword.

Damnit.

I hate that Ezra-be-damned sword. But it's all I have for close combat. And I left it in the cabin below.

Voices cry out below, followed by commotion and the clash of metal on metal. Both attackers smile. Tamrin's deep baritone sounds the alarm, followed by a curse, and I imagine the big guy stuck in a cramped space, unable to fight his way out. If I don't get down there, they could all die.

"That would be your friends dying," the younger one says with an air of triumph.

"You're next," the older one says.

My body tingles with an adrenaline surge that masks my inner fire as the two assassins come at me again, blades in motion. I sprint from the bow of the ship and propel myself forward. At the last moment, I drop into a slide while two sets of blades move with incredible speed toward my neck. I escape their sharp edges, but it's a close call between one blade and the tip of my nose.

I pass between the two men and twist around while sliding backward on my toes. My rear foot presses against the helm bulkhead, bringing my slide to a controlled stop. The assassins react in quick unison and spin to face me. Four blades glint in the moonlight, one still covered in blood. I release my broken blades from my bracers for the extra metal. The fractured edges barely pass my fists, but if I land a punch at the head or neck, their jagged edges could do some damage.

Fucking hell, if I could kill Brogen a second time, I would.

I reach to snatch two throwing knives from my belt, forgetting I'm down to one. I'm virtually weaponless against these two.

Well, I should have seen this coming. Fists and a tiny knife against four blades and two assassins.

The older one smiles at how screwed I am.

"You *should* be afraid," he says as they both attack. I push myself to the starboard side of the boat to remove my back from the bulkhead. Sandwiched between two trained killers intent on seeing me take my last breath isn't ideal either. The helm, elevated above the main deck, offers a narrow escape to the stern. Bootsteps overhead signal, I need to get beyond the helm before the younger assassin sprints across the hardtop and drops on top of me.

With a burst of speed, I backpedal between the wale and the helm and put some distance between me and the dynamic duo.

What I wouldn't give for Jesmir's skill right now.

In my panic, I move too fast and trip over a coiled rope on the deck. I roll backwards and, with all my core strength, throw my feet over my head to complete the roll and rise without leaving myself vulnerable. I barely slip past the helm before the younger killer appears above me. It's a shallow victory because I find myself once again with my back against a wall. Well, the door to a horse stall.

Behind me, the horses whinny at the screams and frenetic activity around them. One takes a panicked nip at me when I step too close. The distraction gives my opponents a chance to close in.

The helmsman, hidden until this moment, turns and faces me as if in slow motion. She falls backward when the young assassin drops from the hardtop, inches from her face, and lands on the deck. My body shivers as it dawns on me that my speed isn't granting me much of an advantage against these two.

I'm about to get a steel suppository up my ass if I don't figure a way out of this. Think.

My mind races over the possibility that I have somehow been egregiously ignorant of some key details about the people I've allowed to get close. If I survive this, it's time to reevaluate my decision-making paradigm.

"I've looked forward to this for a long time," the older one says as he lunges. His blades carve a crisscross pattern across my body. I dodge and weave his knife strikes, blocking some with my bracers in hopes that a deflection will open up an opportunity. I duck under his forward arm and drive a fist into his kidney. He gasps as the tiny remnant of steel from my broken bracer blade pierces his skin. It's merely a flesh wound, but it's enough.

It's not my best work, but drawing blood at least gives me hope.

"I know that seems like a little prick," I snarl, "but don't worry, I'm only teasing you with the tip for now."

The bite of steel nips my right triceps at the same instant that I deliver my little quip.

Son-of-a-bitch! Again? I scream inside.

Momentum carries me around the older assassin's backside as the younger assassin drives a knee into the back of my leg. My body drops, and my knee buckles. I allow myself to fall but twist sideways as I place my hand on the shoulder of my flanker and let my weight and energy drive him off balance.

The glint of a blade in an arc downward toward my shoulder causes me to cross my arms in its path. The block arrests the forward motion of the younger assassin's strike. I continue to rotate my body around while twisting my arms so I can lock his wrist in mine, redirecting my new forward momentum to yank the younger assassin between me and his partner. The motion catches both of them by surprise, and the older one is forced to redirect his blades to prevent a deadly strike to his colleague.

Drunken monks saved my ass again.

"Oh, so close," I say. "Don't hold back next time. Really. You almost had me."

I wobble backward on unsteady legs, and they attack again. My unpredictable motions are my only real defense right now. It's hard to keep track of the arms and legs coming at me. We exchange a series of attacks and counterattacks, and I notice their breath comes much heavier for them.

Damn, do I love the advantage of two hearts.

I'm barely faster than these two, but I'm still alive, much to their surprise. Unfortunately, it's not enough to prevent more cuts on my body. I'm bleeding in four places now, and the one on my face really pisses me off. I find solace in the fact that they've taken a few shots too.

From the corner of my eye, I spot the helmsman. She mutters something, her motions much slower than even the slower young assassin. I risk a glance while I dodge a new flurry of sharp metal. She seems to be at prayer.

Seriously! Prayer!

I realize there are two different teams on this boat, true smugglers and assassins disguised as smugglers. I have no idea how many of each there are. But from the sounds below, there's at least one more on the assassins' side.

I release a furious scream and push myself faster still. My body burns hot like I've broken into a fever. I recognize the sensation from when I fought the spiderlyches and tore a muscle, so I slow myself a little. The two assassins seem unfazed by my assault, and my frustration grows. I dodge several more knife strikes, but one blade cuts a second deep swath along my cheek.

I am not used to losing, and here I am in the same position as I was against Brogen. Torn muscles be damned. I *will* myself to move faster. Time slows, and my motions quicken with each effort. I block more knife strikes against my bracers. My fur-lined cloak, brand new, is torn in spots where assassin knives sliced, but I notice that in those places, I'm not injured.

The damage to the cloak pisses me off. I just got the goddamned thing. I'm going to shit on their faces when I kill them.

"This was a gift, you pricks," I snarl.

"I'll be sure to steal it when this is over," the older assassin says.

"When this is over, I'm going to desecrate your body," I say. "Do unspeakable things to it."

A knife comes at my face. I sidestep and throw a punch upward into the elbow of the arm holding it. The younger assassin cries out as the knife in his right hand flies from his grasp and into the icy stream. My knuckles scream in protest at the impact of hard bone on hard bone.

That hurt!

But it hurt him more. That sliver of my blade punctures the thin skin deep enough that I tether the tendon. He yanks away, his arm hanging at his side. We pause–they severely out of breath, me slightly winded. My two hearts beat harder than when I fought Brogen. Deep down, I know I need a weapon, but now one assassin has a handicap and lost a knife.

"Well, look at that," I say. "Three knives to one, now. What do you say we stop this nonsense? You've given a bit of effort, and I'm still here."

At this rate, these guys could wear me down. I'm stuck in defense and need to find a way to shift into offense.

What the fuck is happening to the world?

My chest pounds as both hearts threaten to burst through my ribcage. The only consolation to my present tiredness is that they seem to fight fatigue worse than I do. Labored though they are, my breaths come much easier to me than theirs.

The younger one, a little farther from me, holds one blade in front, angled back toward his elbow. The older one glares, his arms held down and slightly behind, blades ready. Each of us stands poised, our bodies covered in our own blood, our blades in each other's.

Minor cuts all over my body cry out in protest. The cold air stings the raw, exposed flesh. My blood drips from their blades, and my ego screams in protest. A low growl rumbles in my chest.

The younger one flexes, preparing to leap, his eyes locked on me.

I decide to beat him to it and press forward. Motion behind him causes me to freeze.

The young assassin is too focused on me to see it. Moonlight reflections twinkle behind the unaware killer as a giant hand made of water rises like a silent serpent over the wale.

"Behind you!" the older assassin calls out.

Too late to act, the younger assassin is caught by surprise as watery fingers snatch him from the deck. He screams in protest and fear as the massive liquid hand carries him overboard. His voice vanishes in a splash. The older one steps back as his partner's feet disappear over the side.

"Aw, I was beginning to like him," I say. "Looks like the three-some will have to be a twosome, sugar lips."

He moves so quickly that I have no time to react. With a twist of his waist, he throws his knife, and the blade flies toward the helmsman. With bitter regret, I stand helpless as it catches her in the neck. I retaliate and throw my last knife. It pierces the assassin's eye socket as he turns back to me. He stumbles backward and falls overboard, taking my last knife with him.

"Shit! That was my last fucking knife," I yell, stomping my feet.

The helmsman lies face-up on the deck, her blank eyes staring up at me, but she can't see me anymore. I feel bad for her. She never stood a chance.

I retrieve the knife from her neck and hurry to the lower level to rescue my friends. Tamrin and I collide as he makes his way up to me, and if not for my speed, he'd be impaled by the hooked Killinshire blade. Startled, we both laugh with nervous energy, thankful we didn't hurt each other with friendly weapons.

"Shen!"

"Tam!"

"Are you okay?" we both say in unison.

"Fine," we both say.

I hold up my hands.

"Are…"

"They're fine," Tam interrupts. "But Cillian is in a bad way."

I follow him back into the belly of the ship. Jesma sits with her hands on Cillian. Blood pours from his neck. He's stopped breathing.

Jesma fights back tears. Two more bodies decorate the cabin, one sprawled on a table, back arched awkwardly. From the looks of things, they were assassins, too.

"It couldn't heal him in time," Jesma whispers. "I tried."

Tamrin shakes his head in sorrow.

I kneel next to Jesma.

"There's nothing you could have done," Tamrin says to her quietly.

I look up at Jesmir, and his eyes are filled with rage.

"What?" I ask.

He barely makes a sound when he speaks.

"Savis betrayed us," he says. "It's the only explanation."

Tam puts his hand on my shoulder. "Cillian said that the team was handpicked by Savis."

"But this all happened on the fly," I reply. "How is that possible?"

Jesmir and I lock eyes. I open my mouth to speak, but my words are cut short by a jarring crunch, flying objects, and a violent tilting of the world. I come to a violent stop when my head impacts the wooden bulkhead.

As the world goes dark, it occurs to me, in all the commotion, no one is at the helm topside.

Chapter Nine

Journal Entry: 104

Life has a way of humbling us. We seem to survive purely by luck most times.

Trouble always finds me.

It's like I'm always in some pickle that needs unfucked. Some people are always behind, others ahead. Makes me think of my Picaroon pal. Patrin's always a step ahead of everyone.

What would he do in this situation?

Honestly, I have no clue. But he'd have figured this out already. Maybe I should find him.

Ram Shacked, Me Trashed, and Away We Go!

The waterline rises and falls on one side of my face. I choke on water as it enters my nostrils when I inhale. Distant voices call out amidst the high-pitched bell that rings inside my head. I struggle to lift my head as a violent cough threatens to pull more water into my lungs, my face half submerged. My body, twisted and uncomfortable, is pinned by a heavy object across my back. A hard edge of something digs into my sternum, causing sharp pain.

Water laps surfaces all around me. Flickering light from a small fire offers little solace from the darkness.

The voices grow louder, more distinct.

"Shen!"

It sounds like Jesmir.

"Shen, hold on. Don't move," he says.

"I can't move, asshole," I mumble, bubbling the water that invades my face.

I groan in discomfort. The heavy weight on my back shifts but doesn't relent. I'm too tired to fight.

Is it too much to ask for one full day of peace?

"We're digging you out, Buddy," Tamrin says.

"I'd appreciate it if you'd move a little faster," I mumble. "As much as it's nice to have some downtime, this is uncomfortable."

The scent of the stream would be soothing under normal circumstances, but I smell blood, too. The rise and fall of water against my face tickles, and I can do nothing about it. It occurs to me that Cillian said there were things in this water the boat was designed to protect us against. Frantic, I squirm in a panicked effort to escape, but whatever pins me digs deeper into my spine when I do.

The weight that holds me fast shifts again, and the pressure on my back and chest increases. It threatens to crush my lungs.

"Ow!" I cry out. "Whatever…you're…doing…stop!" I gasp between breaths.

"Hold on!" Tamrin calls out, and the commotion stops. "Listen, Pal. You're pinned in. If we don't move stuff, you'll never get out."

Nadur's nutsack!

"I'm so sick and tired of this! Can we please acknowledge that?" I grumble. "Get me the fuck outta here…please."

Tamrin laughs. "Atta boy. You must not be critically injured. Now, allow us to work. You suck up the discomfort, Buttercup."

"Asshole…Just get this shit off me!"

The commotion around me starts up again.

"Easy!" I cry out as the weight increases and knocks the air out of my lungs.

Whatever lies across my back shifts as Tamrin grunts with a last bit of effort. The pressure on my chest relents, and my lungs expand with a heave. Big hands grab me gently and roll me over. I gasp in another deep breath and grab hold of a big furry arm, my grip tight. Tamrin's big, bearded face fills my vision with dark, animalistic shadow, his expression contorted in concern.

"Where do you hurt?" he asks.

I rub the back of my head. "There's a lump. Other than that, I feel scattered spots of discomfort but no real pain now that you've finally got me free," I say.

The light from the fire grows a little more intense.

I cough, and the pressure hurts my head.

"We should get outta here," I say. I scrunch my face.

"What?" Tamrin asks. "You hurt somewhere else?"

"Yeah. In my nose."

"I don't see nothing," he replies.

"That's because it's your breath," I say.

"Dickhead," he laughs. "Let's grab what we can and get out before this whole thing is ablaze."

He offers me his hand and helps me sit up. Jesmir stands behind him, a smirk on his face.

"Where's Jez?" I demand, unable to hide my panic.

"She's outside," Tamrin replies. "She dug me out. Together, we got Jes and now you."

"Saved the best for last?" I quip.

"Something like that," Jesmir snorts.

I look at them both. "Thanks."

All around us, the contents of the cabin are piled at the front bulkhead. The flames seem to be localized to a small area where the lantern fell. Water trickles in from a crack in the hull.

I turn back to them both. "When we get out of this mess, all I want is a fucking Mistras' Ale and a week's rest…and none of you are invited."

"Who says we want to have a drink with you anyway?" Jesmir laughs.

"Fair enough," I say.

The boat is somehow intact, though it leans rather sharply on its port side. Other than the mess of dead bodies, shifted contents, and the giant crack in the hull from impact with a protruding rock on the southern banks, it's mostly in one piece.

Unfortunately, one horse was seriously injured, its leg broken in two places. Tamrin, miserable as it suffers, puts the animal out of its misery, blubbering like a baby as he soothes the mare into a forever sleep. As the horse passes, he thanks the animal for its service. After a quick prayer to Fildeus, he finds solace in his faith. Even as a hunter, taking an animal's life is a responsibility that Tamrin takes with grim care.

He returns to the group, his cheeks covered in frozen tears.

"Not fair for that girl to suffer," he blubbers.

The extraction of the other horses from the wrecked boat is a chore that requires all hands. Agitated horses become quite belligerent when freed from captivity. It takes an unbelievable amount of self-control to restrain myself from punching the big mare that belongs to Cillian as I try to get into the stall and put the lead on her. Eventually, she calms, and I lead her to safety.

The gangplank, thankfully, isn't ruined, and Jez and I can get that deployed enough to be useful. We grab saddles, bridles, and blankets. Jesmir leads the remaining horses from the boat to the trees, where he ties them off.

Tamrin searches the vessel for any supplies of value. By the time he returns, arms full of our gear and two spare packs filled with who knows what, the horses are saddled and ready. I attach Brogen's sword to the pommel of my saddle.

I search the bodies of the lower deck assassins and find two throwing knives that fit somewhat into my harness. I add to my armament another of the curved knives that the assassins carried.

Jesmir walks over to me and sticks out his hand. I accept his unspoken apology.

"I'm sorry I've been such a jerk," he says.

"You haven't been. I should have been more patient," I say. I look at his sister across the glen. "Listen, I understand. Believe me, I do. I'm struggling with my own issues and couldn't be bothered with yours. I'm sorry," I reply.

He smiles and claps my arm with a nod. I'm grateful he doesn't ask for more details.

To the east, the sky lightens up as Ezra starts to burn away the edges of the night. I pull myself up onto the saddle of the mare and turn her eastward.

"Where to?" Tam asks.

"Well, I'm not inclined to head where Savis intended. Someone betrayed us. The only people who knew our destination were Savis and Cillian. One of them made sure those assassins were there."

"Cillian's dead," Jesma says. "He died protecting us."

"That leaves Savis," I reply.

Jesmir closes his eyes, his face twisted in hurt.

"I can't believe it's Savis," he replies. "It makes no sense."

I have worse news. Those weren't Teshken assassins. They're from Killinshire." I shake my head. "We're on our own again. And I can't believe for a second that our destination isn't compromised. I say we head to ValleyView and back into Rhinestab to regroup. Our greatest advantage is that no one knows we're still alive, and Tam and I know the RhineWoods better than anyone."

I look to everyone for confirmation.

"I agree," Jesma says.

"It's as good a place to start as any," Jesmir says.

"I love ValleyView," Tamrin replies. "Let's get to it."

"Agreed," I reply and bump my horse on the sides, gently urging her forward. The queen likely knew our destination. She'd never suspect us of changing course. At least her assassins will have a hell of a time finding us. So long as the snowfall keeps up, that is.

With the twins focused on Savis' hand in our predicament, I have one more day to figure out how to tell them the truth.

As much as I've traveled Conishant, the southwestern wilderness of Teshket between the Furkote Stream and the Toerge Mountains is as unfamiliar to me as the furthest reaches of the oceans—that's to say, I know nothing of them. Until our recent visits to Hericot and Breakridge, my time in the northern realm was limited to the roads, Kerakot, the frozen tundra between Kerakot and the Temple of the Drunken Monks on the north coast, and the temple itself, where I spent several years. I've avoided Teshket since I left nearly thirty years ago. I haven't missed it. I don't love the cold. In fact, I abhor it.

Hemlocks and other pines grow in tight-knit clusters along the southern bank of the Furkote Stream. Heavy snowfall covers the trees in thick clumps of white. Brittle, needleless branches, intertwined with one another, block our passage in many places. Following a straight path is difficult.

The stream is the common trade route from Coraside Bay to Kerakot. As a result, there is no main trail for us to follow in this isolated woodland wilderness. What few trails exist within the woods are the work of a handful of wary travelers, like us, who wish to remain unseen.

Rolling hills covered with aging pines and firs mix with rocky terrain as the ground rises and falls in an endless series of snow-covered waves—foothills to the Toerge Mountains a few miles south. The frozen, rocky terrain forces us to dismount frequently. The snowpack crunches underfoot but offers some protection from the hazard-laden terrain. I can't imagine how much worse this would be without the snowpack.

The trees creak and moan against the wind like haunted wind chimes. Slight howls in the wind draw frightening parallels to the Valley of Cusk. The trees seem to breathe—like sentient sentinels, watching, lurking, waiting. I stifle a shudder, but the feeling lingers. Each moment that passes brings a growing sense that we aren't alone here. I imagine eyes on me, but when I turn and look, the dark shadows of trees obscured by driving snow slip into the distance.

Silent admonishment has become my frequent companion. Hard to imagine it was less than two weeks ago, I boasted a total absence of fear. Now I'm spooked by creaking trees in the wind. This is not who I am. I will not succumb to fear. Correction. I don't feel fear.

Keep telling yourself that.

I'm no longer sure we're headed eastward. A twinge of panic causes me to look around spastically.

What if we're already turned around?

Without a map and knowledge of the area, our only guide for direction is the stream far to our left. I confirm it's still there. The stream slips further into the distance as we go, and I realize it won't be long before its reassuring presence is lost.

"Maybe we should keep close to the stream," Tamrin says, his voice shaky.

"It turns hard north," Jesmir replies. "Keep the mountains to our right and we'll be fine."

"What mountains?" Jesma asks. "All I see are trees and snow."

I miss the Rhine Woods. The familiar paths, trails, trees, and sounds are home. Teshket, the Realm of my childhood, is more a stranger than a friend. Right now, it appears more foe than anything. I've always harbored a particular hostility toward the land here. Today, the feeling seems mutual.

As long as we keep heading east, we'll eventually run into the Highland Road and can turn south through the gap in the Toerges into Valley View.

A loud, rapid shudder of branches crashing startles us, which in turn startles the horses. Memories of a fevered flight through swamp and fog with a massive Cuska on my tail cause my mouth to go dry. I spot the final descent of a large, snow-covered branch crashing its weighted descent to the earth and breathe a sigh of relief.

"You okay?" Tamrin asks, concerned.

I nod. "Memories."

Tamrin giggles nervously. "Yeah, that was a bit too familiar."

A new gust of wind pushes the relentless snowfall into twisted clouds that obscure vision, once again making shadows of the trees. The shadows twist and bend as living beings. More unexpected movement to my left makes my skin crawl.

I write off these feelings as fatigue mixed with what I'm more certain is a concussion from my encounter with the boat's bulkhead.

Miles drift by in a relentless onslaught of infinite steps. The rocky terrain finally gives way to friendly, softer ground. After a brief rest and a quick meal of jerky and bread, we mount our horses, grateful to pick up our pace and get off our feet. I estimate that we've been on the move for a full day. Under normal circumstances, it wouldn't be an issue. But cold, combat-weary, shipwrecked, and spooked, we aren't at our best.

Cold nips at my bones, and my eyes water against the frigid gusts. The damage to my new cloak from the assassins' blades allows the wind to break through. It's not as warm inside this thing as it was before the events on the boat.

I curse the assassins…and Krin…and Queen Rotten Crotch.

"I'm gonna kill that bitch," I mumble, unaware I'm speaking loud enough to be heard.

"Who?" Jesma asks.

I wince. I'm not ready for this conversation.

"Krin," I finally reply, unsure if she believes me.

"We're never going to figure out who the real spy is, are we?" she says.

Thankfully, my hood covers my face from her view. I close my eyes in guilt. When I open them, I spot someone standing off to my left. After a quick glance, I realize it's not some*one* but some*thing*. A caribou watches us as we pass. I chastise my overactive mind for playing tricks on me and glance back to confirm it's a caribou.

I swear I saw a person a moment ago.

The creaking trees grow silent.

We all stop our horses.

"What the hell?" Jesma whispers.

The entire forest goes quiet for a moment. Even the wind seems to have stopped. The eerie silence blankets the entire forest, and the hairs on my neck rise. Tamrin grips his periapt and prays. His eyes glow purple, and I know he's using his true sight again. He looks at me and shakes his head.

"Nothing?" I ask.

"Nothing but animal tracks."

I turn back to look ahead. My horse bucks slightly. Something spooks her. More movement twitches in my periphery. When I look, it's just more shadows of trees, their branches swaying in the wind.

"How are the trees swaying without sound?" Jesmir whispers.

He searches overhead, but it's just a canopy of pines and grey clouds.

"Let's get moving," I say and spur my horse forward. The others follow, and just as the sound died, it returns.

"I don't like this," Jesma says.

I don't respond. We're all thinking it.

Jesma rides, head bowed, huddled against the driving wind. Another human-shaped form emerges in my periphery. When I look, it's just another caribou. Jesmir shakes his head at me.

"You saw it too?"

He nods. I want to chalk the vision up to exhaustion induced by environmental fatigue and circumstances, but I can't be sure if he saw it. Wiping freezing tears from my eyes, I see something to my right again. But a glance to confirm once again reveals nothing is there.

Once or twice, maybe, but three times?

I whistle over the wind to Tamrin, who looks up, snow collecting on his beard, ice on his mustache. He is the only one who doesn't look miserably cold. On days like today, I wish I were covered in hair like him. He kicks his horse forward and pulls alongside me.

"What's up?" he says.

I look around again but see nothing.

"I thought I saw something in the corner of my eye. Three times now. I can't shake this feeling."

I notice his eyes have returned to their normal brown.

"I thought I saw people a couple of times. But when I look, it's caribou. I haven't seen anything that I can't chalk up to imagination," he says. "But the creaking in the trees freaks me out. This place feels haunted."

I laugh nervously.

"Tam, I'd take that as a joke if you weren't such an avid believer in ghosts and spirits," I say. "It's more than visions. Jes and I are seeing the same thing you describe."

"Well, I'm not going to sugarcoat this. I'm freaked out." His stern expression lets me know he's not playing around. "Now isn't the time for you to pull your pranks. I don't think my heart could take you pretending to be possessed."

I shake my head, not even smiling at his reference to the practical jokes I play on him. "Not today," I reply. "I don't like this. You say you see people, and then it's caribou?"

He nods, but when I purse my lips, he frowns. I nod in confirmation.

"That can't be coincidence," I say. "Can it?"

He squishes his face in fright.

"I don't like this," he says. "What say we pick up the pace and get out of these Quietius be damned woods?" his voice shakes.

I pat his leg and allow his horse to fall back into position. He says something to Jesmir as they pass one another. I can't help but be concerned about the absurdity of our conversation. My eyes dart toward every perceived motion.

The sky is fully dark once again, the short day of winter passing. Another burst of cold, bitter wind cuts through the shredded sleeves of my cloak. I shiver in response. I curse the soul of the assassin who mutilated my only protection from winter's freezing embrace and pull the cloak tighter around me.

Asshole.

I knew my past was never as far behind as I hoped. It was a fool's belief that I'd get through life without being forced to face those memories. Foolish still that I allowed myself to think that Krin reentering my life could possibly be a good thing.

How could I be so stupid? I actually thought I still felt lingering love there.

I've grown too adept at fooling myself.

No sense dwelling on that. When she shows up, I'll have my hands full. Her magic is frightening. I know nothing about it. She will not be easy to fight when the time comes. I can't avoid her forever.

How did she dispatch a new set of killers after us so quickly? She must have returned to the Queen and informed her of her failure, or Savis, when he betrayed us, did.

But what hope could the second group have if the first group was the best of the Guild's lineup? Why send more, less-skilled fighters?

Except they weren't less skilled. They just weren't from Teshket.

Who the fuck were they?

Out of the corner of my eye, more shadows lurk through the trees, their numbers growing with every passing hour. Most times, I swear they're human. Flashes of red draw my gaze, and still, I only ever find caribou, huddling together, lurking, waiting. Their eyes, red like blood, watch us, as if in mourning. I squint through the snowfall and wait to see what they do.

"You see something?" Jesma asks.

"Tell me, Tam," I call out. "Have you ever seen caribou gather like this?"

"No," comes his brief reply.

My mare grows restless and bucks slightly. I pat her neck, and she calms, but I can tell it's temporary. Tamrin fidgets in his saddle. He shakes his head as his horse fidgets, too.

"What?" I say.

He looks distraught and swallows hard. "Shen," he begins, his voice quavering, "My true sight failed. I've been trying to get it back, but Fildeus won't answer my prayers."

My horse bucks backward again. The other horses tug against their reins. More caribou arrive. Jesma inches closer to me, nervous.

Just what we need—one more problem.

My vision blurs. We should sleep, but the caribou lurk, and none of us is keen on sitting still for long. We need to clear out of these woods. I fidget in my saddle, my nerves on edge. Tamrin tries to pray again and hangs his head when he receives no answer.

"Someone else must need her attention right now," he says again.

"Well, tell her it's important," I say, frustrated.

"It doesn't work that way, Shen," Tamrin replies.

"Of course it doesn't," I mumble. "Tell me again how the gods don't simply like to play fickle games with our lives."

Tamrin's true sight is the only skill we can trust to tell us the truth about what's out there. By his expression, I know he doesn't believe she'll answer his call. This sudden loss of magic and Jesmir's sudden appearance can't be a coincidence.

"Well, now what? These caribou aren't going to leave us alone, it seems," I say.

Jesma says, "They seem so sad."

"Could they be Kirwaq?" Jesmir asks, almost as if we should all know what that means.

Jesma shakes her head. "No. Those aren't real."

"What are we talking about here?" Tamrin asks.

"Maybe the caribou aren't caribou. What if they're Kirwaq?" Jesmir repeats. "I studied the ancient texts about them at university. Some texts say they've been in these woods for centuries."

Tamrin stares at Jesmir as if he speaks another language. "Who's Kirwaq?"

"You didn't think that was useful information hours ago?" I snap.

Jesmir ignores my question and answers Tamrin while he swivels his head to observe the caribou. "Not 'who.' What."

Tamrin furrows his brow. "Okay, what are Kirwaq?"

Jesmir turns to Tamrin and says, "Spirits of those that were lost in the snowstorms that come through here, doomed to walk the land in search of a way home. It's said that they appear when others are lost. Always hovering on the edges of your vision, and when you look, they disappear."

"That's convenient," Tamrin says.

Jesmir continues, "Well, not disappear. The text said that Kirwaq are shapeshifters, but that their eyes always glow red. It's the only way to identify them." He pauses, still swiveling his head back and forth.

"What the fuck are you doing?" I ask.

"If I remember correctly, the only way to see their true form is out of the corner of your eye."

Tamrin looks uncomfortable. "Are they dangerous?"

"Yes and no," Jesma says. "If they are Kirwaq, then we are proving the existence of ghosts. I read they can mess with your head. Cause you to get lost. Trap you in a never-ending circle until you freeze to death and become one of them."

"I don't like ghost stories," Tamrin groans.

"So, we could be lost?" Jesma asks.

"We aren't lost," I reply, sounding more confident than I am.

"We could be," Jesmir says.

"Let's settle this. I have an idea. Off your horse, your highness," I say as I dismount.

Jesmir dismounts, curious.

"Follow me," I say.

"Where?" he asks.

I wave for him to follow. We walk until Tamrin and Jesma are but shadows. I keep us close enough to the caribou that we can see them easily.

"Stand with me," I say when we're well away from the horses. "I don't want you to spook the horses. Look at me. But be ready to do whatever it is you do."

"What?" he questions.

"If those things are real…"

"The Kirwaqs?" he interrupts.

"Yes, the Kirwaqs," I reply, my tone harsh.

He nods.

"You say we can only see their true forms from the side?"

He nods.

"Fine. Position yourself so you can see one in your peripheral vision. Stay looking at me. But do that new thing you do and get next to them. Fast."

"I have to look where I'm going," he argues. "Attempts to go where I wasn't looking haven't worked."

"So, it's a line-of-sight thing?" I ask.

"I think so. I keep trying, but so far, it only works if I'm focused on the spot I want to be."

"But what about back at Savis' house?" I ask.

As he thinks about that, his face scrunches. "Okay…maybe it's a familiarity thing then?"

"Okay, let's forget about that for now. How quickly can you jump?" I ask.

"Jump? Like up?" he says.

"Oh, for fuck's sake, do the thing!" I hiss.

"Oh! Jump! I like it," he says.

I snap my fingers in his face several times. "Hey, are you with me? Focus. When you 'poof' into thin air, it's downright startling. But it's fast."

"Hence, not wanting to spook the horses," he says with a nod.

I grab his shoulders. "Morze's moist middle! Look at me."

The eerily creaking tree branches start up again. We lock eyes.

"Sorry, Shen. I'm spooked," he says.

"Don't look away from me," I say.

In the corner of my eye, I see the *alleged* Kirwaq, keeping its distance. It's human, of that I'm certain, though from here, peripheral vision is untrustworthy at best. I concentrate on the 'person' but keep my eyes on Jesmir's. I resist the urge to look over at the shadow. Red spots, right about where the eyes should be, stare out at us. They glow through the falling curtain of snow.

Jesmir maintains eye contact with me and concentrates.

"Can you see it?"

He nods very slowly.

"Good. Now, can you get close?"

His face contorts in frustration, and he shakes his head.

"What if you turn your head, look at my ear?"

He follows my instructions, locking his eyes on my ear.

"Can you get there now?"

He shakes his head. The shadow steps toward us. I let out a frustrated breath.

"Wait," he whispers, "I think I've got it."

I fight the smirk that tries to form on my face. The shadow with red eyes approaches us, and my hearts thump in my chest.

"The closer they get, the better chance I have," he whispers.

"Because a spot up close is easier to focus on?"

He nods.

Jesmir's eyes glow, the energy faint and blue. Tension forms in the air around us, like pressure squeezing me after a rainstorm passes. In my periphery, the 'person' approaches. Two more shadows appear behind the first one.

Jesmir's eyes glow brighter. He vanishes, and the pressure that was building disappears, taking the air in my lungs with it, and I realize I had held my breath. I keep my gaze forward, and the shadow remains. A new shadow appears against the others. I assume it's Jesmir, and I launch myself toward him, my body on fire. When I arrive, he stands before three large caribou—their eyes red like hot iron.

"What is this?" I ask.

"It's a caribou," Jesmir says. He strokes its face like it's his pet.

"I know that," I sigh. "What was it when you got here?" I ask.

"A caribou," he replies. The animal nuzzles him.

"It's super nice," Jesmir says, smiling.

"I don't like this," I mumble. The caribou nuzzles Jesmir's hand. I pull him away, and we head back to the others.

"Its eyes were red," he says.

I look back at the caribous still focused on us. The one in the middle cries out with a low resonant call. The sorrow in its sound sends chills down my spine. I'm no longer sure if it's the caribou or the cold.

"Let's get out of here as fast as we can," I say. "Caribou or Kirwaq, they creep me out."

We walk together back to our horses. I need a distraction.

"Will you tell me who your god is?" I ask Jesmir.

"That came out of nowhere," he replies.

"Jes, you have new magic. Frankly, it makes me nervous because you haven't talked about who you follow, like it's some big secret. Is there some new god we don't know about?"

He's quiet, and I realize he will not tell me. We walk a few feet.

Then he stops.

"Why do you care so much about what god I follow? You don't believe they exist anyway."

I shake my head. "That's not quite true. I don't believe they are what people say they are."

"What does the knowledge of who I follow do for that?" he asks.

"I don't know." I sigh. "Look. You have this new power. Tamrin's lost his. The quee…quick answer is that Fildeus dropped Tamrin and chose you."

That was a quick cover.

Jesmir considers my words. Then he says, "Here's the thing. I didn't."

"You didn't what?"

He puts his hand on my shoulder. He looks half mad.

"I didn't lie to you before. I never chose a god. I don't have a hidden periapt. My last periapt was the Fildeus one Tam gave me. I really did leave it behind on my nightstand. I never prayed for this to happen."

He appears to choose his next words carefully.

"I *will* it to happen, and it happens."

The caribou follow us relentlessly. I ponder Jesmir's words. Further questions got us nowhere. It's clear, he doesn't understand it any better than I do. If I hadn't been standing there—if I hadn't witnessed him blink out of existence without a prayer or a periapt—I don't know if I'd believe it. But I did, and he did, and I believe him. He didn't need a god to access whatever this power is. He wields it at will.

I look at Tamrin and say, "We need your magic. Maybe you don't need Fildeus?"

With a light flick, I spur my horse further forward, leaving the others behind. The caribous continue to stalk us, their numbers increasing as we go. Jesma nudges her horse beside mine. We ride side-by-side in silence for a while. I can sense she needs to talk, but I'm still reasoning through what Jesmir's admission means to Tamrin.

"You going to explain what you meant back there?" she asks.

"I'm still trying to figure it out," I say.

"Shen, what was all that back there? You two walk off without a word and come back with no explanation? That's not fair."

"I wanted Jes to use his new ability to get close to the caribou."

"The caribou, or the strange shadows that turn into caribou," she asks, her voice shaky.

"Both."

"And?"

"And nothing. They're just caribou. But their eyes *are* red. Like hot iron red."

She fidgets in the saddle.

"What is it?" I ask.

"Don't you understand? That's the Kirwaq. That's how they work. I can feel them calling. Can't you?"

The horses fidget underneath us. My mare rises on her hind legs slightly and stops. She resists any command to move forward as more caribou appear directly ahead. I barely keep her steady. Three caribou stand in our path. All thoughts of Jesmir's admission are pushed to the side. The presence of more caribou is a more pressing matter.

Tamrin pulls his horse to a halt. It neighs in protest as it eyes the strange creatures. Jesmir's and my horses pull against the reins, but we keep them under control. Jesma's horse bucks her off, and she lands on her back, releasing a billow of snow into the wind. I try to grab the horse's reins, but it flees.

"Nadur's balls!" I yell in panic.

Jesma's horse continues off into the blinding snow and vanishes beyond the haze.

Jesma, still on her back, holds her periapt in front of her and prays for divine protection.

"Guys?" Tamrin calls to us, a shake in his voice that forces us to pay attention. Tamrin looks at the ground and points south.

"What is it?" I ask.

"Look," he replies.

We all look at the ground he is pointing at.

"What? I don't see anything," Jez says.

"Exactly," Tamrin whispers. He looks up and points toward Jesma's horse and back at the pristine snow on the ground.

No tracks.

"Oh, damn," I say with a shiver.

The horses are spooked for a reason.

My eyelids get droopy, and I fight off sleep.

Chapter Ten

Journal Entry: 105

*J*ust two days ago, I was on top of the world—the happiest I'd ever
been.

> *A lot can happen in two days.*
> *Two days is a lot of time to think.*
> *Two days can feel like an eternity.*
> *Those two days can bite my ass.*

Trail of Fears

I don't know how long we've wandered through these trees. They all
look the same. We've eaten all of our food, but I don't remember eating. I don't remember sleeping either, but the moons passed over us
at least twice. We've also run out of water and are forced to pack our

canteens with snow. We store them inside our clothes, against our bodies, to allow the snow to melt, which makes us colder. Hypothermia must be a real danger by now.

The sightings of the Kirwaq continue, their presence growing more frightening. I'm not sure how much farther the road is, but I'd give anything for it to appear today. Jesma rides in front of me in my saddle, her body loose against me, her head drooping in sleep. I struggle to stay awake myself.

Tamrin startles himself awake, almost falling from his horse. Jesmir tied himself to the saddle with a rope, his body against the neck of his mare. I'm not sure how he manages to stay on, or why his horse hasn't bolted.

Meanwhile, the ever-present Kirwaq, for I'm certain they aren't just caribous, are never far from our sight. They lurk and wait, biding their time. Their numbers grow as we make our way through the forests. The river is long since out of sight, no longer there on our left. Its path is well north of our destination.

Ahead, through the snowfall, more caribou appear. They're close enough that I can see the snow gather on their fur—their proximity an opportunity to observe them in greater detail. I startle as one slips into my periphery from behind. Its form changes from humanoid to animal in a haze. The change no longer surprises me. I've grown accustomed to their presence. I don't even bother to look, knowing full well what I'll find.

Sometimes I catch some details of their humanoid faces and wish I hadn't. Their visages are blurred somehow, obscured as if through a veil. The true details are lost, unknowable. My mind struggles to make sense of their facelessness and their glowing eyes. In my head, I feel them urging us to follow them to safety, warning me that we'll go the wrong way if we leave them. But I can't trust it.

The others must feel it too. Their confusion and revulsion are written on their faces. Tamrin especially. He holds the reins of his horse in one hand, the periapt of Fildeus in the other, his eyes constantly focused ahead. His mouth moves in silent prayer that remains unanswered.

Jesma wakes herself, startled, and holds her periapt of Ezra tight in her hands, too. Her head hangs low; her body falls back against me.

She yawns, "You should sleep, love." She's asleep before she takes another breath.

I shake my head hard, forcing my eyes open, willing myself to stay awake.

Ahead, more dark forms lurk until we pass before they join the growing herd. I refuse to acknowledge them.

Jesma startles herself with a cry. I wrap my arm around her, worried. Her voice cracks, tears flowing.

"There's so much sorrow here," she cries. "It's overwhelming. We can't continue this way. We must break free of them."

I touch the side of her cheek, trying to reassure her, but she knows I'm as tired and confused as she is.

It's strange. I no longer feel the cold. The wind has less of an effect on me than it did. Consumed with overwhelming sadness, my only solace comes from knowing I'm not alone in a herd.

A soft, warm feeling begins in my chest, familiar, calling. I can't make out what it means, but it snaps me out of a dreamlike haze. I'm in a crowd of people, faceless and murmuring. Their macabre faces stare at me. My mind screams that we have to leave these creatures. But it's not my mind. It's not even my voice. But the voice is familiar.

Grankin? Is that you?

But he doesn't answer. There's just that familiar warm feeling where his handprint is. It's comforting to know it's there. Grankin is there for me. Is this what it is to have faith? My mind pushes against a different presence in my thoughts, and I feel a cloud lift. I stare into the face of one of the people in the crowd.

"Oh shit," I say. "Kirwaq."

The imaginary veil clears, and I cry out.

"What the hell!" I exclaim in horror.

The crowd comes to a halt. Twisted faces gape at me, red eyes lingering. But the faces don't hold their shape. Eye sockets slide along the cheeks of an elderly woman before me. Her face appears to melt, her skull no longer holding her features in place. Her nose turns sideways as if someone twisted it too far, as it sits offset from her mouth.

She gasps, trying to form words, but no sound comes. Her lips twist into an awkward vertical smile, away from her nose. The frightening transformation complete, the Kirwaq's mouth sits sideways under her drooping right eye. I look at the other members of the ghastly clans. Their features appear to have been through the same transformation—removed and replaced with random carelessness.

Misshapen claws, their nails long and sharp, extend from furs, like Tamrin's. The fingers flex like talons as the monsters turn away and resume their walk. Their feet, like hooves, leave behind wide, crescent-shaped tracks.

Just like caribou.

The Kirwaq make no move to attack, and my friends willingly follow along. Hundreds of them surround us now, the herd only parting to step around trees.

My hearts race, and I wish for the veil to return, to hide the horrors of their gaze from me. I wish I'd never seen what they are. I don't want to end up like them.

The horde presses against us as we wander aimlessly through the storm and forest. Their sideways mouths open and close—gaping maws, mindlessly trying to speak. The psionic assault, filled with continued supplication to follow them to safety, continues. But I see through their false warnings. To heed their words would leave us to suffer a similar fate—stuck some place between alive and dead. I can't let that happen. I push against calm malaise, against the illusion of warmth that removes the chill from my bones. I fight the sense of home that surrounds them and see it for what it is—a false promise of safety in their presence. With an aggressive kick, I spur my horse into Tamrin's and yank his reins from his hands. His horse startles, and he looks at me, his eyes clearing.

"They're luring us to our deaths!" I yell and point to Jesmir. "Grab his reins! Now!"

Tamrin shakes his head, refusing to relinquish control of his reins. He stares at me like I'm from another plane of existence. I shake Jesma, but she is equally lost. A quick glance back at Jesmir confirms that I alone know the truth. I try to snap Tamrin out of his trance, but he won't break free.

The old woman, the first to gaze at me, reaches up, and I recoil, afraid to allow her to touch my skin. I reach for my knife and swipe at her, and the entire herd moans a wailing cry that threatens to bring me to tears. So overwhelming is their sorrow that it threatens to overwhelm me. My friends cry out with the same horrifying voice, and I lament my inability to break them free.

Grankin's mark on my chest ignites with fire as I fight against the oppressive sorrow. Tears flow down my face. I want to succumb to the depression. Thoughts of death return. I'm so tired. The old woman tilts her head, her eyes on my chest.

Does she know?

My horse bucks, restless, and I decide that the best way to save my friends is to break free of this madness. If I escape, I can follow and formulate a plan before it's too late and my friends become one of these hideous things.

I can't lose my family, I lament.

With careful direction, I nudge the mare forward, pushing through the herd. The Kirwaq part only slightly, somehow allowing me to move forward. Behind me, the way back closes. The flanks are too hard to push through and tighten as I advance toward the front.

I don't know how long it takes, a mile, maybe two, before I can push through the crowd, their numbers so large and the terrain so hard. The sadness seems only to be kept at bay by the warmth of Grankin's sigil. Hours pass, but finally, I reach the lead position.

My jaw drops. The heat in my chest subsides into a warm, comforting sensation. The old woman Kirwaq stands next to me and points, her twisted maw trying to communicate. But I know what she's trying to say now.

And I couldn't have been more wrong.

"Are they smiling at us?" Jesmir asks.

"I think they are," Tamrin replies.

"How can you tell?" I ask, seeing them in their true form still.

"How many days do you think we were lost?" Tamrin asks.

Hell, we could have been lost for months for all we know.

"Maybe two?" I reply, keeping my thoughts to myself.

We stand at the edge of the forest, Highland Road a little over two hundred yards ahead. The blizzard, having finally relented, leaves behind a light snowfall, back beyond the tree line. The Kirwaq, no longer humanoid, are caribou once again. The older Kirwaq waves a solemn goodbye. I return her wave, and she turns back into the forest. With the frightening ordeal over, I see the Kirwaq with new eyes. We'd been led safely through the blizzard-obscured woods. Unable to communicate with us, projecting immense sorrow onto the world, the Kirwaq were saviors, not enemies.

"Jes, could your texts be wrong?" I ask.

"It seems plausible," he replies.

"I was about to start slaying them," I say, an ache in my chest and old guilt rising inside.

"But you didn't," Jesma replies.

"I don't think you'd have succeeded," Jesmir offers.

I shudder at the thought, anyway.

"Conishant is stranger and stranger to me, the longer I'm alive," I say.

Tamrin's big hand on my shoulder is both comforting and condescending. He says nothing and simply laughs at me.

We welcome the appearance of Highland Road. No longer lost, our proximity to Valley View lifts our spirits. Even though we are exhausted, we find the strength to push on. Rocky terrain, trees, and dark spirits fall away. We shed the weight of our close call with a fate worse than death placed on us. Jesma rides in the saddle in front of me still. This time, the feeling is peaceful. Her body presses against my chest, and we fall into the comfort of each other's company.

The topic of our flight from Kerakot was noticeably avoided. I'm content allowing specific thoughts to fade into the background and relish the sense of relief. The ordeal with the Kirwaq is behind us, regardless of their intent.

Ten miles farther north than we had hoped, we push to reach Valley View by evening. Ezra sits ready to touch the peaks of the Toerges. The traffic on the road is heavy in both directions. Lost in our own company, we don't acknowledge other travelers as we pass.

Highland Road changes names in Valley View, becoming The King's Regal Highway at the town square. But it still remains the major thoroughfare between Kerakot and Valshannon. I relax, happy to know that in a very short time, I will find myself back where I belong, deep within the RhineWoods. Ideally, we'd be through ValleyView already, but life has a distinct habit of altering plans.

Not that any of this can remotely be considered a plan.

Jesma weaves the mare through the fellow highway folk. More than a few travelers offer unfriendly glares at our temerity. I ignore them.

Day turns to evening by the time the lights of ValleyView appear over the horizon. With ValleyView in sight, we grow more eager to leave the long days behind us, the light ahead a beacon of respite.

By the time we reach the city limits, most of ValleyView has shut down for the night. Our timing isn't ideal, but the quiet streets afford us a better chance to identify eyes that may appear too curious. The downside is that our timing means the best rooms at ValleyView Inns will be occupied. We may not find a comfortable place to sleep.

Jesma urges us to visit the ValleyView royal house, located near the City Council District. Owned by the crown, accommodations there are readily available. But that comes at too steep a price—a message to the queen of our whereabouts. It's harder to argue the point and maintain the secret I hide from the twins, but we are short of suitable options.

I don't respond to her suggestion. Jesmir is the first to speak.

"Hey, Jez?"

Jesma turns to her brother, almost knocking me out of the saddle.

"I think it might not be such a good idea to stay in the manor."

"But it's late," she says. "I know we shouldn't, but I'm tired of the cold, and we won't find another place at this hour."

I am about to speak when she says, "But, honestly, I don't want to either. We don't know who we can trust or how deep this conspiracy goes."

Tamrin and I hide our relief and say nothing.

"Savis still shocks me," Jesmir says.

He points to a tiny street ahead on the left.

"At the end of that street, pressed against a high rock wall carved out of the mountain, we'll find a small inn. It's called 'The Vagabond.'"

"That sounds like the right place for me," I say.

Tamrin giggles. Jesma elbows me in the gut.

"Oof," I groan.

Jesmir continues, "When all else is filled, she usually has a room available. It's a bit out of the way, so most people forget or don't know she's there."

"That works for me," I chime in.

We all agree and head up the side street.

Lined with small estates–small by estate standards—I'm surprised to find this ratty inn located on the same street. Each estate is a couple of square acres wide. The further we ride, however, the smaller the estates become. By the end of the street, we reach a series of homes in desperate need of repair. Jesmir stops in front of a quaint three-story house that is older than I am. Paint peels from the slatted siding, and the windows are discolored with dirt or age…or both.

The warped wood on the porch bends upward at the front edge. The hitch post, grey and cracked from repeated changes in moisture and temperature, appears new compared to the home. We tie our horses to the post and snatch up our gear. Jesma stands empty-handed, her gear lost with her horse somewhere north in the frozen tundra. All she has left are the clothes on her back.

"We'll get you some clothes in the morning when the shops open," I say.

She laughs. "I've grown a bit used to wearing the same clothes for days on end lately."

I smile. "You're a seasoned adventurer now, Jez."

She tilts her head, demure and sweet.

"Thank you," she says.

Inside, we are greeted with a warm hearth close to the entrance. A portly woman approaches as we all rush to stand by the fire. She's dressed in a clean, well-kept dress that is a bit out of style but fits her properly.

"Welcome to The Vagabond Inn," she says.

"We're in need of rooms, Rita," Jesmir says.

Her eyes sparkle.

"Well, welcome back, Master Randal. I hardly recognized you." The woman's gaze settles on Jesma and then back to Jesmir. "Who are your companions?" she asks.

"I'd rather not say, if that is acceptable," Jesmir replies.

"It most certainly is," Rita answers back. "You are lucky. I have two rooms left. Each has two single beds. Will that suffice?"

"It will do nicely," Jesmir says.

Rita waddles behind a counter and grabs two keys off the wall. Next to the key rack is a wooden calendar with "Solstice Day" and the number "6" next to it. As the innkeeper passes the keys to Jesmir, I point to the calendar. Tamrin coughs.

"That can't be right, can it?" he asks.

"What's that?" Rita asks.

"Solstice is in six days?" Tamrin asks.

"Sure is," she says, eyeing him with curiosity.

"Nadur's balls," Jesma says. "Five days?"

I'm hit with a wave of exhaustion.

"Let's eat and then get some sleep," I say.

Our eyelids droopy, we sit in the main parlor. Hardly large enough to hold the three small tables that fill the room, we are the only ones seated at this late hour. Crammed into the space is a small couch by another rustic fireplace. The fire roars a little too hot, but after an unwelcome five days in the cold, we choose the table closest to the warm flames.

The innkeeper offers us a few meager bowls of stew and a loaf of day-old bread. We accept those eagerly, and Tamrin presses a silver piece into her hands.

"Oh no, too much," she says, her voice hard with age.

I smile. "This is better than we've had in days." Tamrin closes her fingers on the coin and pats her hand.

She leaves, heading to the back of the house, and comes back with a few pieces of leftover cake that are at least a couple of days older than the bread. We accept the cakes graciously. She heads back to the kitchen and returns with four mugs of ale.

Tamrin chugs his and grimaces with distaste. I take a tentative sip and mimic his expression. The ale is bitter and almost unpalatable. But it's alcohol, and any drink is a relief. Tamrin scarfs his slice of cake in fewer bites than I thought possible.

"Hungry?" I tease.

"Starved." He points at my cake, which I haven't touched. "You gonna eat that?"

I slide it across the table, and he snatches it from me. With the same wanton abandon, he devours mine. Jesma wraps her arms around her half-eaten remnant of cake and offers him a warning glare. Tamrin takes it in stride and pretends to reach over. Jesmir shakes his head at Tamrin, and we all break out in relieved laughter.

"I'll put an arrow in your eye if you even think about it," Jesmir says.

We all laugh harder at that, too hard.

It's the first genuine laughter since our ride from Breakridge to Kerakot, and it feels good.

I lay in bed with Jesma's head on my shoulder. She snores peacefully, lost in the dream world. It's a tight squeeze being in a twin, but she crashed, and I don't have it in me to disturb her. My mind won't allow me to sleep. Thoughts race through my head as I stare at the ceiling in the dark. The world outside is quiet, but my mind is a raucous parade.

My hearts pound and I'm certain they'll wake Jesma. But she sleeps, her silver hair a cascade of softness across my body.

My mind rattles on, and I don't know why. I can't pinpoint what keeps me awake, but the suspicion that I'm missing something won't relent.

Jesmir's words resound in my head.

"I didn't choose a god."

What does this mean?

This must be why sleep eludes me. Can the gods choose us without our knowledge?

That would piss me off.

They sure as hell never picked me.

But I still can't sleep, so either that isn't it, or I'm more jealous than I realized. That's my last thought before my body gives in to the exhaustion.

Chapter Eleven

Journal Entry: 107

Magic has always been an enigma. More so now than ever. The idea of magic consumes my thoughts.

Energy I'd rather spend on figuring out how to get my face between Jesma's thighs...

Focus, Shen.

Jesmir describes it in terms I understand. Still, I have more questions than answers. Where does it come from if not the gods? Do the similar sensations he describes mean my speed is magic?

That can't be. My body tingles and burns all the time. It didn't always burn. I remember a time when I was really young, when it didn't. I told my brother the day it first started. I remember that.

At least I think I do.

Who knows? I can never really trust memories.

There's this one memory I have where I drowned. In that memory, I'm about five years old, maybe six? I died. I think it was this recurring dream that eventually went away. So, who's to say any memory is real?

But this fire inside, as Jesmir called it, sounds so much like what I feel when I'm fighting or running.

If it's magic, it comes from somewhere. But it's always been the innate talent I have. I cast no spell. Sure, I can choose to be fast or slow. But I can't choose to be silent. I just am.

Magic, on the other hand, is controllable.

Isn't it?

While I can't make myself believe, I can't make my friends not believe.

Poor Tamrin. I see his faith go unanswered. Fildeus ignores his prayers now. No explanation. He says it's never happened for so long before. I've seen his prayers unanswered on occasion, but those moments are rare.

Jez's prayers have been answered every time she's prayed, except when she prayed for herself. In a way, that makes sense.

Everyone prays for their magic.

Except Jesmir.

I've objected to the gods my entire life. I've never taken the time to understand them. I hate them.

I wouldn't even let them pleasure me.

Well, maybe Ezra. Still, no. She'd probably fry my dick off for not worshipping her.

I'm a non-follower. I refuse to pay allegiance to gods who abandon their faithful, like Fildeus has Tam.

But now I have more profound questions. All because of Jesmir.

No.

All because of his and Jesma's words.

"It's like a fire burning inside."

That's something I do understand.

ValleyView

Jesma wakes me with an unintentional nudge as she attempts to extricate her limbs from mine. I struggle to open my eyes, unsure of the time of day. I fell asleep at some point in my endless thoughts, but it couldn't have been long because my eyes burn with exhaustion. With effort, I help untangle my legs from hers, my stiff body locked in protest. Our escape from Kerakot must have caught up with me because I slept hard.

Tamrin noticed the date on the innkeeper's calendar last night and pointed to the charcoal mark on the days. We spent almost an entire week trapped in the Teshket wilderness. Two days are accounted for. The other four are lost in the fog of the Kirwaqs' call.

It's horrifying to think about how close we came to oblivion—one we walked toward with willing abandon.

But that ordeal is over, and I prefer not to dwell on the memory or the faces of those who saved us.

Jesma leaves to bathe in the inn's bathhouse while I hunt down coffee. Just like the food and ale, the coffee is a watered-down, bitter version of coffee. Jesma returns, clothed, her hair still damp. I hand her a cup of coffee.

"Don't get your hopes up," I say.

"You either. The water is cold here."

I kiss her cheek and head off to remove the stench of five days in the wilderness from my sore and tired body.

When I return, our clothes sit on steam-heated drying racks near a furnace while we sit wrapped in blankets by a small fire. It's nearly evening by the time we are ready to make our way along the King's Regal Highway south into Rhinestab. We've slept for almost a full day.

Though the innkeeper's hospitality was warm and kind, her food and drink were not. She isn't much of a cook. At least the inn is warm. Last night's hunger-induced consumption of her leftover stew didn't settle the hunger in our bellies for long. Sleeping through breakfast didn't help our hunger either.

Rather than gorge our bellies on more tasteless old leftovers, we thank our host for her generosity and excuse ourselves from the premises. Jesmir suggests Toobee's Pub on our way out of Valley-View. Run by a lovely elderly couple, Toobee's is one of those places that most people frequent due to the elderly couple that runs it. It's the most popular place in ValleyView on account of the way the couple yells at each other. People come for the food but stay for the entertainment.

The streets of ValleyView are flooded with mid-evening activity. We reach Toobee's and choose a back corner table. We keep the twins with their faces obscured so that they won't be recognized by anyone who enters. Their hair, tied up under their hoods, hides the fading dye used to conceal their most identifiable connection to the royal line.

We'd no sooner taken our seats when a crowd filed in. Loud and agitated, several groups of folks search out tables and open seats at the bar.

"Ted! Move your ass!" Mrs. Toobee calls out. The elderly woman walks with a long pipe in her mouth. The smoke from the tobacco wafts into her pure white hair, the front bangs stained yellow from the nicotine.

"Te-e-ed! We got a crowd tonight!" she screams and enters a fit of deep-chested coughs.

When she doesn't get a response, she screams, "Te-ed!" We giggle as she somehow turns her husband's one-syllable name into two.

"Nadur's Nuts, Donna! I'm busy! What's all that racket?" Mr. Toobee yells as he busts out of the kitchen. "Ezra's Tits! What is all this?"

"Don't be crass, you horse's ass!" she yells. "It's customers! Get back there and start making plates!"

Old Mr. Toobee, his white hair a thin ghost of what it used to be the last time I saw him, turns back into the kitchen and mumbles under his breath.

"What?" Mrs. Toobee yells.

"I didn't say nothin'!" he yells from the kitchen.

Mrs. Toobee walks back to the kitchen, a cloud of tobacco smoke in her wake. Loud but muffled voices argue in the kitchen. Mrs. Toobee exits, armed with a tray of various meats, cheeses, and jams in one hand, a large loaf of bread tucked under her arm, and a large carafe of coffee in her other hand. She slams them onto our table.

"Eat up," she says, her voice gruff. "This is what we have today, so if ya don't like it, give the table to someone else."

I pour a coffee and take a sip. It's delicious and so much better than the dirty dishwasher we had earlier.

"Good to see you again, Mrs. Toobee," I say.

"Who the hell are you?" she asks. "How do you know my name?"

Tamrin snorts into his cup.

She glares at him.

"I say something funny?" she says.

Tamrin shakes his head in rapid, abrupt movements, his eyes wide with fear. She stares at each of us and stops at Jesmir for a little longer than the rest of us.

"I know you?" she says to him.

He shakes his head.

"I know you, ma'am," I say to her.

She studies me while she chews on the mouthpiece of her pipe.

"Do you, now? How do we know each other? You try to take me home one night or something?"

It's my turn to snort into my cup. Coffee splashes out from the force of my breath and up into my face. She smirks and clicks her false teeth sideways at me.

"Serves you right. Now, eat up. And if you need anything else, tough shit. This is what we have today." She blows a large cloud of smoke over us and storms away.

"Ted!" she yells on her way back toward the kitchen, drawing out the 'ed'.

"What?" Ted Toobee replies.

"We need more coffee!" Donna yells.

"Then make some, damn it! I'm busy!" he yells back.

I sip my coffee in silence.

"Well, at least she didn't recognize me," Jesmir says.

"Come here often?" I ask.

"Two or three times a year with father," he says.

He glances at Jesma, and I can see she fights back a sob. It's still raw for them. Aside from our night in Kerakot, they've had little time to grieve.

Tamrin focuses on an oddly dressed couple at the bar who engage in loud conversation. Two men in fluffy fur pants and coordinated vests, heads adorned with odd hats, stand at the bend in the bar closest to us. The one closest to us speaks with a loud voice and appears agitated.

"I'm tellin' ya, the Regal's shut down!" one exclaims.

His position at the bar offers me a clear view of his face. I must stare too long because he glances up and we make eye contact. I realize it could be a woman, but I'm not sure. Whoever he or she is, they look road weary.

"I just passed the spot when I hears screamin' behind me," the strangely dressed person says. "When I turn and look, all I saw is a massive netherstack, poison spillin' e'erywhere. Right there in the middle of the road. Kilt least five people. And two horses. Well, I wasn't waitin' 'round. I kicked Eldy inta a run and rode her straight here."

"Netherstacks? On the highway?" says the other, a long stocking cap on his head. His calm tone is irrelevant to his friend's panic. "You can't be serious."

"Corall," the first one says, "it killed a *lot* of people!"

"Only people netherstacks kill are those stupid enough to go near 'em," says Corall.

"Corall, nobody went near it. It just appeared. It didn't grow, it sprouted."

"I'm sure the king will figure it out."

"Don't you get it? They're sproutin' up everywhere! How can you not take this seriously? It blew one lady right off her feet!"

"You don't say. Off her feet? Well, then it must be serious. Speaking of feet," Carl says, raising a hand to grab Mrs. Toobee's attention. "You got pig's feet?"

Mrs. Toobee blows smoke in his face.

"What are you?" she says.

"Llama farmers," Corall replies.

Mrs. Toobee yells back, "Te-ed! One pig's foot!"

"Damn it, Donna! It's too early for pigs' feet! Tell 'em come back later!"

Mrs. Toobee shakes her head.

"Sorry. Have to grab some later. Get you something else?"

"Corall. Ya hear that? It's too early fer pig's feet," Pawlin groans. "It's gross."

"Look, if you're gonna go on about the netherstacks killin' folk and popping up outta nowhere, I'm gonna need to think. And I can't do that on an empty stomach. And I'm craving for pig's feet."

The two continue their discussion, but Tamrin and I have had our fill of the inane conversation. Our attention is drawn to another person in the tavern. Tamrin elbows me under the table.

"I noticed too," I reply, my eyes focused on my plate.

Jesma turns, and Tamrin stops her.

"Don't look," Tamrin says.

"What is it?" Jesma whispers.

"There's a Korund at the other end of the bar, trying to be sly," I reply.

"Not so sly if you both noticed," Jesmir says. "Especially since Korund stands out in ValleyView."

"That's why I said, '*trying* to be sly,'" I reply.

"Korund don't normally travel this way into Kerakot," Jesma says.

"No, they don't," Tamrin concedes. "But this one's going to great lengths to appear disinterested in us."

"The bounty, you think?" Jesma whispers.

"Could be," I reply, my eyes on Jesmir. "Korund bounty hunters aren't common, but I've heard of one or two over the years."

"You think this is the one the baron mentioned?" Jesmir asks.

"Odd coincidence, don't you think?" Jesma says. "We were lost for five days, and nobody knew we'd be here."

"What do you want to do?" Tamrin asks.

"Best we get on the road. We'll know soon enough if we're paranoid."

"I'd be happy with a little paranoia right now," Jesmir says.

"Me too," I reply.

We finish our meal. Tamrin pays the elderly woman, and we head out to our horses.

The Korund nods at us as we leave, a casual acknowledgement between two strangers.

Too casual.

I tend to eschew the belief that coincidences happen. As far as I'm concerned, a coincidence is nothing more than a connection that hasn't been identified yet. Savis and the assassins on the boat, Tamrin's loss and Jesmir's gain of magic, the Baron's letter, and a Korund in Toobee's Pub all fall into that category.

Maybe I'm jittery, but connected events are rarely a coincidence. Given time, relationships reveal themselves.

The four-beat rhythm of our horses' gaits against the long-worn, packed dirt of the King's Regal Highway echoes among the trees. Jesma smells lovely riding in the saddle with me, and my thoughts wander. The distraction of her body against mine isn't helping.

"Too bad we were both too tired last night," she whispers, and I clear my throat as blood rushes to my face.

"I can hear the smirk on your face, Princess," I say with a short laugh. "Should I assume the exaggerated motion in your hips is on purpose, then?"

"A bit hypocritical, don't you think? I can feel your lewd thoughts against my backside," she laughs.

"How about we pay attention to the road?" I reply, trying to distract myself from her excessive motion against my groin.

The foothills of the Toerges smooth into flatter terrain around midnight. The air, though still cool, is warmer than Teshket. The crisp wooded air brings on different memories of bakru, sunlight through trees, and the freedom of anonymity. I'm glad to be back in Rhinestab. The clear night sky brings on a sense of relief. Less than a mile ahead, the northern edge of my RhineWoods home beckons me.

Still a bit sleep deprived, we decide it's best to stay ahead of exhaustion while we can. We continue for a mile into the border of the RhineWoods before I guide us off the highway. Tamrin keeps a vigilant eye out for anyone following us, especially the emerald-scaled Korund. I don't believe we've seen the last of that one. Once we are far enough into the cloak of the forest for a fire to remain unseen from the road, we set up camp.

We split the watch in two this time. Tamrin and I take the first shift. Jesma and Jesmir, the second. Tamrin thought it essential to demonstrate that we see them as partners and not charges. With Jesmir's new magic, I couldn't argue with the logic. When our turn is over, Jesma and I exchange a brief moment of affection, and I settle in.

I'm asleep before my head comes to rest.

Morning arrived too soon. After a modest breakfast, we make our way back toward the highway, where travel is easier.

"You sure you don't want to stay in the cover of the trees?" Tamrin asks.

"You know I'd much rather do that," I reply. "But the road is faster."

We reach the King's Regal Highway.

"Something doesn't feel right," I say.

"You ever seen this road so quiet?" Tamrin asks. On a typical day, we'd pass hundreds of people by midday. Today, that's not the case. Behind us, the road is nearly deserted. Ahead, sporadic travelers, solemn or perturbed, depending on the person, head north back the way we came. "You can't go that way," a woman at the head of a small group of merchants says. "Road's closed."

"I'm sorry," I say, "How can the road be closed?"

"According to the folks behind me, a netherstack is blocking the highway." She turns and points at a man in a horse-drawn buggy.

"You folks headed into Valshannon?" he asks.

"No, around it," I reply.

"Through the Rhine Woods?" he says, surprised.

"I like the woods," I reply. "What's the problem here?"

He points south.

"We were all headed south, like you," he says, his voice shaky.

"Yeah," I reply.

"Well, *everyone* is turning around." The younger man looks at me, and I can tell he's upset. "A netherstack appeared out of nowhere, right in the middle of the road. It's poison rolls deep into the woods.

Everything it touched died. At least half an acre of trees is already dead."

He bows his head, and I can tell he's choked up.

"Happened yesterday. Apparently, many people were caught in the eruption," he says. "It's horrible."

By the expressions on my friends' faces, I know we all think the same thing.

"Those weird folks at the pub," Tamrin says.

"They weren't crazy," I reply.

I thank the man for his information and spur our mare into a canter. Tamrin and Jesmir follow close behind. The man yells out a warning, but we ignore him, knowing our path lies elsewhere.

We stand at the back of a crowd. Carriages, pressed against the tree line, sit empty as people mill about. Visible ahead, a dark plume rises above the treetops. My heart sinks. The noxious nether rises higher than any stack I've ever seen. The crowd is too large to see the stack itself.

"Well, I guess we should backtrack to the split and cut out for Rogue's Pointe," one man dressed in fine clothes, his fingers adorned with rings.

"If we go to Rogue's Pointe, we'll get murdered," the woman says. "We should head back to ValleyView and book a ferry to Coraside Bay."

"Marsha, that'll add five days to our trip," he replies in agitation. "This is mighty inconvenient."

"This is something," Tamrin says.

"It's definitely not good," I reply. "Next week is Festival. Most of these people are here for it."

Jesmir stands in the stirrups to peer over the top of the crowd. He points to the west. A group of people make their way through the trees.

"It's as good a plan as any," I say.

Jesmir leads us in that direction, and we steer our horses into the RhineWoods and away from crowds and the netherstack.

The woods are once again too quiet. It's as if some predator announced its presence and we are the only ones who didn't receive the message. I keep us close to the small crowd of people savvy enough to realize their numbers provide safety from bandits within the RhineWoods, out of curiosity. Regardless, everyone walks in stunned silence.

I push past the last of the crowd. A full day has passed since we first heard the rumor at Toobee's Pub.

"Why are we staying with the crowd?" Tamrin asks.

"I want to see how bad this is," I reply. "This is my home. If this is as bad as everyone is behaving, I need to know."

The others nod in agreement.

No warning could have prepared us for the scene ahead.

Precisely as the weirdos at Toobee's and the traveler on the highway said, a netherstack spews its black plume of death onto the highway. Slack-jawed, gripped with horror, I can only stare.

I don't dare move closer. Though we can't see the netherstack through the trees, fifty feet ahead, the emissions from the spike in the earth roll to a stop and settle on the ground like a black fog. Everywhere the noxious nether touches is stained with death. The oaks and maples within the nether's path already show signs of decay. The blackness climbs the trunks almost a full half foot above the top of the fog. In less than a day, these trees will die, and this part of the RhineWoods will have no sign of life.

Several large dark mounds rest within the circular border of the fog. I recognize them for what they are. Victims whose favor with Shamna is at an end, unlucky enough to be in the path of the netherstack when it formed. Their deaths were violent and sudden.

Death comes suddenly.

I've witnessed death. I've talked about death. I've caused death.

This is different. This is tragedy.

I look away and suppress the urge to vomit. Netherstacks are not new to me. Animals are their most common victims, too curious to understand the dangers presented by the fog. I know where most of the netherstacks exist within the RhineWoods, Gal-Danang, and Haabrestand.

Until now, I always assumed they occurred in remote locales–not close to civilization like this. The black fog, the way it dissolves the bodies of the dead, doesn't surprise me. I've seen many animal carcasses caught in the deadly mist.

I've never seen people caught this way. What is left of the bodies of the dead, reminders of our inherent fragility, crumbles and dissolves into nothingness before our eyes.

That happened a lot faster than it does with animals.

Something someone says catches my attention. I turn, looking for the source of the voice. He's an older gentleman, Teshken by his appearance.

"I'm sorry," I interrupt. "What did you say?"

Distraught but lucid, he nods to the cart closest to the netherstack. "I heard one of the folks up there. They cried, 'Why did he do this?'"

"Why did who do what?" I ask.

The man shrugs and says, "I don't know who. Some man is all I know. Stood in the middle of the road, did some magic, and this *thing* appeared."

"Suicide?" I ask. "Someone did this on purpose and killed themselves?"

That makes no sense.

"Who?" Jesma asks.

"No one knows," the man says. "I heard someone say a Killinfolk. Others said Picaroon. Someone else said it was one of the Great Eight."

One thing is sure. Once we stop the queen, I'm going to find out who did this.

And I'm going to kill them.

The grotesque image of the bodies as they disintegrated into the ground haunts me.

Those poor people.

Raw emotion causes my eyes to tear.

I never imagined the violence behind the formation of a netherstack. I've always regarded them like a fast-moving river, or a volcanic lava flow, or quicksand–always present but easy to avoid. We just passed through here weeks ago. This one appeared without warning. Those people never had a chance. And if the rumor is true, it was on purpose.

Why would someone deliberately cause netherstacks? Is someone trying to kill the world?

A sob escapes, and Jesma pats my leg.

Why the hell am I so emotional?

"Are you okay?" she asks.

I nod, though she can't see me.

"Your care for the suffering of others is why I love you," she whispers. I place my forehead against the crown of hers and take a shuddering breath to compose myself.

"If not for the delay by the Kirwaq," Tamrin says, "we could have been at that spot when the netherstack appeared."

I sigh in selfish relief that we weren't there when that thing appeared. That plume of darkness frightens me more than it ever did before. More than the death it caused. I can't help but think there's more there.

Crepuscular critters wake from their daytime slumber as the shadows of the RhineWoods lengthen into evening. The slow dimming of the light through the canopy brings back visions of the deadly fog as it rolls over the forest floor.

By force of will, I rip my thoughts away from the grisly scene and dismiss my brain's attempt to stay focused on those images, focusing instead on my friends and our destination.

Sarah's Vale, though it has the word 'vale' in it, is actually a glade. It's one of the most popular glades in RhineWoods because of its size. I often find myself here when I want a good look at the night sky.

By the time I arrived, it was already heavily populated. Thankfully, most groups opted to huddle close together, away from the dark tree line, due to the reputation of the RhineWoods in general. But the woods are my home. There's literally nowhere in Conishant I feel safer. And the closer I am to the trees, the safer I feel.

Not that danger frightens me. I think of the woods as my emotional safe place.

The team found a place well away from the larger cluster of campsites. I prefer the comfort that distance provides over the illusion of safety that proximity to others provides.

Jesma places stones in a circle for the fire pit. Tamrin gathers wood and kindling. Jesmir hunts food. Meanwhile, I tend the horses. The fire rolls along, and Jesma waves me over to sit next to her. I settle into a comfortable position when Jesmir stomps his way into the firelight with the carcass of a deer over his shoulders.

"I gotta tell ya," Jesmir says as he steps into the light, "this new power is amazing. I covered a lot of ground, and this guy never saw me coming. Got him with my knife."

The glint in his eyes doesn't hit as hard with that bandage on his head. I can't begrudge him, though. He's on a path of discovery. But the nagging suspicion that this could lead to trouble won't leave me. Something about this new ability eats at the back of my mind. I grow fearful of where it will lead. If we aren't careful, his recklessness could get one of us hurt.

"That's a twelve-point buck," Tamrin says with surprise.

Jesmir smiles with pride. "Yeah, it's the biggest deer I've ever bagged. My father would be gloating right now."

Jesma walks over to her brother and hugs him. "He'd be so proud of you."

"Umm, what are we supposed to do with this much meat?" Tamrin asks.

Jesmir looks at the crowd of campsites and shrugs. "Well, take what we need and give the rest to the other folks here in the vale, no?"

"We don't have time to make jerky, so it's better to share it," Tamrin agrees. "I'll go find a few folks and have them come take some. We don't want to cause a mad mob over here."

He lumbers toward the large camp of people in the middle of the glen. As my attention turns to Tamrin's retreat, a large body emerges from the darkness into the firelight. Jesma's gasp and Jesmir's warning call cause me to jump and draw the two curved knives I stole from the assassins. Jesmir draws his crossbow and aims it at the intruder's head.

"That's an impressive buck," the stranger says with a deep voice.

An impressively tall Korund steps into our camp. A long-bow string crosses between a pair of exposed breasts, the end of the bow peaking over one shoulder. Emerald scales cover the Korund's body from head to toe. Long, flowing red hair blows in the slight breeze. The Korund's hands rest on a pair of matched sword hilts, their long, slightly curved sheaths crossed at the waist. A traditional Korund skirt is the only visible article of clothing. The skirt's hem almost reaches the ground, while the slits on either side ride high enough to hint at more than is comfortable. The Korund's green scales reflect the dancing firelight in a flutter of sparkles along a muscular body and enhance the sense of motion.

"You're a hard man to find," the Korund says. "I've chased you all over Conishant."

I narrow my eyes.

"*You*," I say. "You were in Toobee's. Just who the fuck are you?"

"My name is Kara-Kar," the Korund says.

"Should that mean something to me?" I ask.

"I'd be surprised if it did," the Korund replies.

Kara-Kar glances at Jesmir's crossbow.

"First, could you point that somewhere else?" Kara-Kar whispers. "I've been looking for *you*, Harbinger, not your royal friends."

DARKNESS BLOOMS

Chapter Twelve

Journal Entry: 111

Is it too much to ask for the news of my identity to travel a little slower?

A lifetime spent building anonymity is lost.

How have I become so easily traceable?

Come to think of it…what are the odds that Krin happened to be the Emissary in Valshannon, or that I happened to escort the twins?

Why is this just occurring to me now?

Am I daft?

Fucking hell, I'm stupid!

Maybe Mom should have swallowed instead.

God of War No More

"**H**ave you now?" I reply. "Well, here I am. I don't recall ever tangling with a Korund, but I'm willing to give it a go."

Hands raised away from sword hilts, Kara-Kar acts surprised by my aggressive tone. Though slow to violence, preferring peaceful negotiation first, the Korund are fierce warriors, and though I'm aware of their culture, this one has stalked us for many miles, and I don't like the implication.

"In hindsight, maybe I should have approached you in Valley-View. Especially considering how you dispatched that bounty party a few weeks ago," Kara-Kar offers.

My skin tingles at the mention of the Tillions. Images of the butchered family at the hands of that mage and his minion flood back. I point a knife at our scaled stalker.

"Reminding me of how I failed to protect my friends is not the best place to start our conversation," I growl.

"I meant no offense," Kara-Kar replies, hands still up.

"You have a heartbeat to tell me why you are here before I skin you and sell your scales for ale," I reply.

"Shen," Jesma says, her hand on my arm. "I don't think this Korund means us harm."

The Korund nods toward Jesma. "Best you listen to Her Highness, D'aonar of the Picaroon."

My jaw clenches involuntarily. My eyes on the Korund, I address Jesma. "I'm liking this one less with each word."

Jesmir steps closer, his crossbow still pointed at the Korund's face.

"Easy, boys," Jesma says. "Let's not start an unintentional war between the Korund Council and Teshket."

Kara-Kar acknowledges Jesma with a slight tilt of the head.

Jesma points to the Korund's earrings.

"This is a Chieftain's Child," Jesma says.

Tamrin coughs conspicuously from behind me.

"Care to loop me in?" he asks.

"Kara-Kar is a chieftain's descendant. Those earrings signify lineage," Jesma replies.

"Yes, I am Chieftain's fourth child," Kara-Kar says.

"Why would the Korund Council track the Harbinger through two realms?" Jesma asks.

"Three, actually," Kara-Kar replies. "I started looking for you the last time you visited Chati Brinker."

"That was two seasons ago," I respond, eyes narrowed.

"Yes, the last Solstice Day," Kara-Kar replies. "I asked Chati to inform me if you returned. But you are a hard man to keep up with."

Still suspicious, I stand ready to strike. Jesma once again grips my arm. We exchange glances, and Jesma shakes her head. Her eyes plead with me to stand down. I exhale the tension built inside my chest and acquiesce to her request. With a huff, I sheath my knives and signal Jesmir to lower his crossbow. He does so with similar irritation.

"My chati tells me you two are close," Kara-Kar says.

"You and Brinker are kin?" I ask.

"Yes," the Korund replies.

"We've chewed some bones together, Brinker and I," I confirm. "How do you know about the bounty hunters and the Tillions?"

"I will answer that, but first I need you to confirm something for me," Kara-Kar says.

"Yes, I have a big dick. I like cold steel, hot coffee, and long walks in the woods. And I love bakru and their cute little bandit faces," I puff my cheeks, imitating the bakru face. "I don't know which of the two moons was dominant at my birth, but I suspect the smaller one, considering the violent course of my life."

My charm doesn't even elicit a smirk. While Korund aren't known for their sense of humor, I expected at least some acknowledgement.

"Having a big dick and being a dick aren't the same," Jesma hisses. "Read the situation, Shen."

"I see your reputation for glibness holds true," Kara-Kar says, unamused by my attitude.

"Usually right before I do the sticky work," I say. "It's like a rattlesnake's tail. A warning."

Kara-Kar appears unfazed by my threats. I'd expect nothing less from a member of the stoic tribes, but this one's unbending seriousness is on another level.

"Fight, or leave," I reply, too tired to continue the banter.

"Very well," Kara-Kar says and turns to leave.

Jesma calls out to the Korund while she glares at me. I shrug with feigned indifference.

"Forgive his brashness, Chieftain's Child. It's obvious you are here with a purpose other than violence, even if some people are too uncivilized to recognize it."

Kara-Kar nods at Jesma, a show of respect.

"That is partly true, Your Highness. I have a purpose. However, that purpose *is* violence. Just not against any of you."

A Korund *looking* for violence is unusual. It piques my curiosity, though it does little to ease my suspicion.

"You say you are in search of the Harbinger. Tell us why?" Jesma says.

"Well, for starters, I want to confirm rumors," Kara-Kar says and turns to address me. "Let me ask you this, Harbinger, which of the Great Eight is your patron?"

That gets my attention.

"Why don't you tell us what you're after?" I growl, my patience wearing thin.

"Fair enough."

"When you killed Brogen, you didn't just kill a man," Kara-Kar continues. "You killed a god. Killing a god is not possible—unless you are one."

"Well then, he's the one you want," I say, pointing at Jesmir. "He did the killing." The weight of the Korund's words doesn't register at first. Then it hits me. Did you just say we killed a god?"

"Do you mind if we cease hostility and sit?" the Korund asks. "It's been a long day already."

Jesma pulls me back to make room for the Korund to enter our camp.

"Hey, Tam? We keep enough of that venison for ourselves to share?" Jesma asks.

"We did, Jez," he replies.

Jesma pokes my arm. "Don't be rude. Let's sit and hear the Chieftain's Child out. If Kara-Kar wanted to kill us, a shot with that bow would have been much easier than walking into a jittery group with weapons sheathed."

In typical Korund fashion, Kara-Kar waits, aloof and quiet, for permission to remain. Curiosity and Jesma's logic are hard to resist.

"It seems you are invited to dinner," I reply and gesture toward a place to sit.

I sheath my knives and plop on the ground by the fire and wait for our visitor to speak. Kara-Kar takes a seat and remains non-threatening. Tamrin returns to help Jesmir butcher the deer.

"So, you've been following us? How did you know we'd come back through ValleyView?" Jesma asks.

"Not the question I would have led with," I mumble. Jesma casts a sideways glance, displeased. I roll my eyes.

"I didn't know. That was dumb luck," Kara-Kar replies.

"Or Shamna's luck," Jesma counters.

Kara-Kar regards Jesma with a look of surprise before turning back to address me. "*You* travel with believers?"

"If I didn't, I'd be alone," I reply.

"I'm sorry," Kara-Kar offers. "I assumed you traveled with those who view the world as you do."

I sit forward, eyes narrowed.

"Do we know each other?" I demand.

"No," Kara-Kar replies.

"Then how would you know my worldview? Did someone publish my inner monologue?" I ask.

"Nobody would be so crass as to unleash *that* on the world," Tam says with a grin.

Kara-Kar tenses and takes a slow, deliberate breath. The unusual outward display from a race known for stoic neutrality causes my skin to tingle. A current of anger flows underneath those emerald scales. Uncharacteristic of Korund as prayer is to me, the display heightens my caution. Kara-Kar releases a slow exhale and studies me, eyes intense.

"You are an 'unbeliever,'" Kara-Kar replies.

"How can you know that?"

"First, as an unbeliever, why do you travel with those who are believers?" Kara-Kar asks.

I glance at Jesma with a smirk.

"I can think of one reason."

Jesma doesn't laugh. I sigh.

"It's a source of discordance, but we accept each other as we are," Jesma replies. "And faith, or lack thereof, has never stopped anyone in this group from risking their lives to keep the others safe. We are family. Two of us have faith, one of us doesn't, and one of us hasn't decided."

"That's not true," Jesmir says from his position by the deer carcass. "I decided. We discussed this." He uses his knife to point at us. "If the eight walked into this glade right now and revealed themselves to me, I wouldn't follow them."

Kara-Kar regards Jesmir and Tamrin as they work together. The Korund addresses Jesma. "And you are amenable to unbelievers in your 'family'?"

"It makes no difference to me what they believe," Jesma says. "Real love and family don't care about that stuff. Now, we've talked enough about us. Why are you here?"

Kara-Kar takes a moment and says, "The tragedy of the netherstack on the highway had one unexpected benefit. It kept me in ValleyView one more night. You can imagine my shock when you walked through the door of Toobee's. I almost came to you then, but I was worried about spies."

"Spies?"

"D'aonar…you don't mind if I use your Picaroon name, do you?" Kara-Kar asks.

"Why the hell not? Seems you know everything."

"Fair enough. The gods have spies everywhere," Kara-Kar says.

"Why do the gods have spies?" Jesma asks.

"I *cannot* say at this moment," Kara-Kar replies.

"I think you'd better," I reply.

"If I could," Kara-Kar says, eyes focused on Jesma. "I would. And I intend to tell you everything I can. But at this moment, what I have to say is not safe to say in present company."

Kara-Kar stares at Tamrin. I don't like the implication, and my hand moves to the knives at my waist. Kara-Kar doesn't flinch and instead confirms my suspicions.

"At least not with them here," Kara-Kar says.

I stand and glare at the Korund with malice.

"I'd trust them over a stranger every fucking time, Chieftain's Child," I snarl. "Best you be on your way before I actually do skin you for your scales."

Sleep eludes me. Every sound in the darkness is a threat. Kara-Kar walked off after my not-so-friendly words, but the Korund's presence lingers in my mind. Jesma tried to convince Kara-Kar to stay, but I refused to listen to anyone who'd exclude those I trust from a conversation. Kara-Kar refused to explain the reasons for such a request. Jesma's attempts to convince me otherwise fell on deaf ears.

I didn't realize the price I'd pay was the cold shoulder and a night alone.

Jesma sleeps on the other side of the fire. I can't see her. The fire is too bright, relegating the background to relative blackness. Her snores are the only evidence she is there. I'd laugh, but those rumbles only remind me of the distance between us right now. This time, though, I refuse to relent. I'm angry too.

Jesmir stirs and rolls over, facing me. His eyes are open enough that the firelight reflects off the blue in them. I hope he doesn't wake. Since I'm awake and sleepless, I might as well let them rest.

What drove Kara-Kar's unwillingness to speak in front of Tamrin and Jesma? Why Jesmir and not them?

Regret tugs at me. A hot temper and rash conclusions lead to poor decisions. What harm would a quiet conversation with the Korund have done?

Jesma and Tamrin would have understood, I'm sure. They know I would have told them everything the Korund revealed, *and* I'd have information. Information is key. That's what Patrin preaches.

Damn it, stupid, stupid, stupid Shen.

The constellation known as Battling Bakru passes overhead. Visible most of the year in Teshket, this far south, the formation only appears during winter. I pull my cloak tighter around me to ward off the chill, though I'm not entirely sure it's physical.

Little critters move about throughout the trees. The nighttime symphony is less soothing in my current state. Even the presence of my favorite constellation and the bakru isn't enough to put my mind at rest. Something drove the Korund here, and I'm smart enough to reason that Kara-Kar had something important to say.

Regret sometimes makes stupid decisions worse.

What was so important that the Chieftain's Child chased me around Conishant for two seasons?

The fire fades, the flames visible as little trails of plasma. I stoke it and add more wood from Tamrin's healthy stack. The flames come back to life with pops and hisses. I look toward the last place I saw the Korund while I wait for the fire to bring warmth back to the camp.

I shake Jesmir enough to wake him, but don't wait for his acknowledgment. I'm several yards into the woods before he's fully awake. Behind me, one of the spent logs on the fire collapses with a loud crack. I turn and catch sight of Jesmir stoking the fire, his eyes on me. With a sizzle, floating embers rise into the night sky. Tamrin's snore stops as I disappear into the trees.

"Harbinger." Kara-Kar's deep voice rings out in the dark. I'm not surprised by the Korund's presence.

"Chieftain's Child," I reply and draw my knives.

Kara-Kar steps out of the shadows beyond a tree. What little moonlight makes it through the trees reflects off green scales in dim specs of radiance. The Korund draws both swords.

"You are after the bounty, then," I say with no inflection.

"I promise I am not," Kara-Kar says and steps before me. The Korund drives the tips of both swords into the ground, withdraws the bow, and drapes it, along with the quiver, onto the swords. Hands in the air, Kara-Kar takes several steps back and sits on the ground. The Korund grips the skirt material in a balled fist and kneels ten feet from the display of weapons.

I recognize the ritual of *'Qal-So'*.

So, Jesma was right. You aren't here for violence.

I wait until Kara-Kar bows.

Respect for the ritual is paramount here. I remove my knives from their sheaths and stab them in the ground next to Kara-Kar's swords. With the flick of my wrists, my throwing knives land next to the swords. I drive Brogen's sword into the ground at the center of the strange metal garden we've created. Kara-Kar's expression betrays no thoughts. I complete the ritual with the removal of my bracers and drop them to the ground.

Unarmed, I feel naked.

A slow twelve paces later, I squat. That's two farther than Kara-Kar from the weapons.

"Of course, you know the *Qal-So*," Kara-Kar says. "I should have known. Chati Brinker speaks highly of you."

"Let's be clear, I do not trust you. But it's possible I've been rather harsh. There's been little to trust of late," I reply. "Besides, I'm faster than you. I could run to Swill Street, drink four ales, and be back here with my weapons in my hand before you reached yours," I say with a smirk.

"Assuming you could get service," Kara-Kar says.

I raise my eyebrows with a slight smile.

"Fair enough."

"You'll hear me out?" Kara-Kar asks.

"I will," I reply. "If I don't like what I hear, I'll slice your throat and leave you here."

"I accept your terms," Kara-Kar says.

I can't help it. I actually like this Korund.

"Alright, Kara-Kar, tell me your story," I say. "And don't leave out the sexy stuff."

Kara-Kar doesn't laugh, and that causes me to snort. Korund are not known for their snark.

"Why not speak in front of everyone?" I ask.

"Because believers are never alone," Kara-Kar says. "The gods can hear everything around a believer."

"Come on," I say. "The gods are fake. They're grifters."

"You are partly correct. They are, as you say, grifters. But they are very real and very powerful."

"I'll bite. Say that's true. What does it have to do with me?" I ask.

Kara-Kar doesn't answer right away. A tear falls, and the Korund wipes it away. I've never seen a Korund show emotion, and the display surprises me.

Have I misjudged this one?

"I apologize for the uncouth display," Kara-Kar says. "It's hard to be a Korund and an unbeliever."

I gape wide at the admission.

"You don't worship Krikhi?" I ask.

"No."

"Why?" I ask.

"Short story? I lost my periapt in a fall from Sanctum Mountain a year ago. I broke my leg, shattered my hip, and lost eight scales in the process." Kara-Kar reveals a patch of green skin where scales are missing

"You fell from the top of Sanctum Mountain? That's quite a fall," I say.

"I wanted to know what was at the top. Krikhi always granted my prayers," Kara-Kar replies. "Never once had they failed me. When I was young, I discovered I could defy gravity in short bursts. It's my best magic. I believed myself favored. It took me nearly sixty years to master the skill enough to make it to the top of Sanctum Mountain."

"You don't look a day under seventy," I say.

Kara-Kar continues without reaction. "My periapt slipped from my grasp when I reached the top. I lost my footing trying to catch it. There are many rocks to hit on the way down the mountain."

The Korund's gaze intensifies.

"Have you ever felt your body catch fire on the inside?"

You have control. You can decide when to use it and when not to.

Grankin's words come back to me.

Kara-Kar's eyes ignite with a green glow of manic energy.

"You have felt it. I know you have."

Now it's Jesmir's voice in my head. *I didn't pray to any god.*

Kara-Kar continues. "My leg broke on the first impact, midway to the ground. I was so afraid. I knew I was in freefall, still several hundred feet in the air. In a panic, my body burned. I continued to fall, but I never landed. My body ignited with a fire more intense than any I've ever known. At first, I thought Krikhi had saved me. But this was different. I couldn't feel her presence." Kara-Kar leans toward me. "That was the day I lost my faith."

A low growl builds in the darkness beyond the trees. I lunge toward my weapons, unsure of what beast comes at us. Kara-Kar takes four steps toward me, grabs both swords, and faces the sound. The growl turns into a scream.

Tamrin steps out of the dark shadows. "Blasphemy!" he yells, his face contorted in rage.

"Tam…" I start.

Before I can stop him, Tamrin turns and crashes through the trees into the darkness of the Rhine Woods. Dumfounded, I chase after him.

Tamrin doesn't even try to hide his tracks, nor does he hide his presence. His massive body crashes through brush and snaps dried, frozen twigs. It takes no effort to follow him as he tears through the woods, his sobs loud and blubbery. I catch up to him with little effort.

"Go away, Shen," he growls. His voice quivers with heartache.

I follow him in silence.

"I can smell you, dumbass," he says as if he can read my thoughts. "You may be quiet, but you still have a scent."

"I bathed and washed my clothes," I whisper.

"You're downwind," he says as he chokes back another sob. "I can smell the lavender and vanilla. Now go away."

I make a mental note to remind myself of the obvious risks next time I bathe around Jesma. It's been so long since I used soap, I forgot how intense the scents can be. Not to mention how far downwind they can carry with a hunter like Tamrin. Then again, I wasn't trying to hide.

Tamrin runs out of steam and stumbles to a stop. He bends over, hands on his knees, his breath labored. His body shakes underneath his mismatched fur. He heaves, and I'm sure he's about to vomit. Instead, he breaks into ragged sobs. I step next to him and place my hand on his broad shoulder as he weeps.

I should have known he wasn't in a good place. Six days without an answered prayer from his patron, Fildeus, has broken him. His faith wasn't yet shattered. I know him. Until he overheard my conversation with Kara-Kar, he thought he'd simply lost Fildeus' favor.

You big dummy. Why did you follow me?

I kneel next to him and stare off into the shadows. I'm at peace in this place, where I feel more comfortable than anywhere else in the world. That realization causes me to shudder with guilt.

Throughout the woods, my favorite nighttime symphony plays out. Crickets, bakru, and even bats above the tree line sing their nightly song. I listen to the new life that begins when the day ends, ruminating on how different Tamrin and I are. It's a wonder we're friends. But thirty years is a long time, and he's never needed my emotional support. He's always been mine.

I'll sit here with my mouth shut, as long as you need, old friend.

Tamrin plops onto the ground next to me. I fall back and drop next to him, my chin on my knees. We sit in silence—two longtime friends—each other's port in the storm.

His sniffles turn into one big snort as he gathers himself, the tears spent, his sobs at their end. I pull my canteen and offer him some water. He shakes his head and reaches into a hidden pocket in his fur coat, then pulls out a metal flask. I recognize it immediately.

"You've had that on you this whole time?" I say, surprised.

"Of course."

"Why are you only breaking it out now?" I ask.

"Because I keep it for moments like this?" He opens it, takes a swig, and passes it to me. I take a swig. It burns and tastes like bakru piss. "You know as well as I do, if I'd opened it sooner, you'd have it gone in minutes."

"Ugh. Not if that's what you keep in it now. What the hell is that?"

"A new rice wine from Southern Haabrestand. I rather like it."

"That's swill, Tam. Your taste buds are off."

He shrugs and takes another swig, then holds it out for me. I snicker and relent. The second swig is worse than the first. I grimace, take a third, and hand it back. He drinks some more, closes the flask, and hides it away. His head hangs low, and another sob escapes.

"You know," I say, "The Korund could be wrong."

He snorts.

"You don't believe that."

"No. I don't. But I don't know for certain Kara-Kar's exactly right either."

"I don't understand why Fildeus has forsaken me," he says.

I can't offer any solace, so I remain mute.

"Do you remember what Grankin said?" I ask.

"That you're a smartass?" he replies.

I laugh and shake my head. "No. The other thing."

"About?"

"About me?"

Tamrin shakes his head. "Smartass is all I remember." He grabs a rock and throws it into the woods. It strikes a tree, and the loud clunk reverberates back at us.

"He said, *'You have control. You can decide when to use it and when not to.'* I didn't understand what he meant then. But I think I do now."

"Know what?"

"That my speed might be magic. You even said once that the feeling in my body is like the one you have when you use True Sight or transform form into your hunter physique."

He nods.

I continue to speak. "If my speed is magic, then I've always had magic without faith," I say.

"So?" he replies.

"Tam, you stupid oaf. When has my speed ever failed me?"

"When Brogen almost beat you."

"That's different. I was still fast. He was just…faster."

Tamrin chucks another rock. It lands in the darkness with a soft thud.

"You missed," I tease.

"I've hunted with Fildeus, Shen. I've been on two Wild Hunts with her. She's real. And my magic is stronger when I'm with her."

"True. And I acknowledge that. But maybe she's not a god."

"Of course she is. Her power is unmatched. She looks the same as she did the first day I met her when I was a teen. My dad and granddad say she's never changed since they've known her. She's at least older than my grandfather, and he lived to be ninety."

"Fair is fair. But still. Goddess or no goddess, your power may not be defined by her."

"But *I* am," he whispers. "Who am I without *her*?"

I have no words for that. But in one statement, he defined the largest chasm between us. Faith defines him. Absence of faith defines me.

He leans his massive head on my shoulder, and I pat his knee.

"We can sit here as long as you need, Buddy," I say.

"Hold me?" he says, and I can hear the smile in his voice.

"Sure…but that's as far as we go. Jez has a jealous streak, according to Jes."

"Well, I hate to say it, but I think I'm over you," he says.

"Damn. So, I won't be able to take advantage of your affections anymore to get you to do stuff you don't want to?"

"I wouldn't say that. You're still my best friend. No getting out of that," he laughs.

"You're going to be okay, Tam," I say. "I promise it will all be okay."

He nods, and I feel his body relax as he remains there, his massive head, filled with the weight of the world, on my shoulder. Selfishly, I know his words are hollow, and I'm struck with guilt. He's likely not 'over me' and I'm not sure he ever will be. I'm just grateful I'll always have at least one person who loves me and never stops.

I know it's unfair to him, but I can't imagine my life without his presence.

We break camp before dawn, intent on reaching the Great Rankin River before nightfall. Most of the folks in the center of Sarah's Glen still sleep. The few that stir speak in hushed tones. The tragedy of the netherstack is the dominant topic.

Kara-Kar's head towers over my mare's withers by a couple of feet. The Korund saddles them in silence while Tamrin gathers our gear and Jesma changes Jesmir's bandages.

"I can take care of the last saddle," I say. "Can you put out the embers?"

"Yes," is all Kara-Kar says, and walks over to the still glowing embers and spreads them out bare-handed.

Jesma and Jesmir lead the horses to our exit point and wait for the rest of us to join them.

"You don't have a horse," I comment to Kara.

"I don't need one," Kara-Kar says. "We travel south, no?"

"Correct."

"Then you won't ride hard enough to outpace me."

"Wanna bet?" I quip.

"Seems a pointless endeavor," Kara-Kar replies.

In the light of day, I notice that some scales on Kara-Kar's face are chipped, like a scar from impact against a hard object.

This Korund has seen combat. More than once.

Tamrin throws his gear onto his horse's back. Jesma mounts my mare and holds her hand out to me.

"Need a ride, my dear?" she asks.

"I think I'll walk beside," I reply and kiss her hand.

"Are you two promised?" Kara-Kar asks, with a slight lilt in the inflection.

"Does it matter?" Jesma asks in return.

"You are a royal," Kara-Kar says.

"A royal pain in the ass," I say.

"What is your point?" Jesma asks Kara while kicking my shoulder.

"I mean no disrespect, Your Highness, but shouldn't you be courted by someone of...," Kara-Kar begins.

"Be careful what you say, Chieftain's Child," Jesma says. Her eyes are on me as she responds to Kara-Kar's comment. "It will serve you well to remember that I do not answer to your opinions."

Kara-Kar bows with dignity. "Yes, Your Highness. I only meant I am surprised that the queen would allow such a union."

"My mother was a commoner. I have no reservations with D'aonar's status in this world. Or the next. We live in a free society."

"Yes, but we also bear the responsibility..."

Jesma interrupts the Korund. "You understand little of Teshket society if you think that matters to anyone *but* the queen. While we are on this subject, I do not recall soliciting your opinion."

Kara-Kar considers Jesma and says, "Understood, Your Highness."

Jesma offers Kara-Kar a curt nod. I follow with my head lowered, the Korund's words stinging more than I'd like.

"Let's get the day started, shall we?" I say in an effort to diffuse the tension.

"Where are we headed?" Kara-Kar says.

"You go where you like. We are headed to the Great Rankin River," I reply.

"And what do you intend to do when you get there?" Kara-Kar asks.

"We intend to jump in," I reply without looking back.

"I see," Kara-Kar replies and follows in silence.

We barely speak amongst ourselves the entire day. Tamrin, still lost in his emotional turmoil after last night, stares forward. I all but ignore the existence of the Korund. Normally, I couldn't care less what the Korund thinks of me or my relationship with Jesma, but the comments struck a nerve.

Maybe it's because I already feel out of place in Jesma's world. Maybe it's because I hate feeling judged. It could be that I like to ruffle feathers but don't like having my own mussed. Whatever the reason, when we reach the banks of the Great Rankin River, I look at Jesma with a smirk.

"Honey, let me help you from this horse," I say.

Jesma rolls her eyes but swings her leg over the saddle and presents her hips to me. I slide my hands along her thighs to her waist as she slides into my arms. Her sensual curves under her clothes, the width of her hips, cause a bit of arousal as her breasts press against my chest and our pelvises meet. Jesma stares me in the eyes with a tolerant expression while my hand slides around her lower back, and I pull her close, savoring the scent of her hair. Her breath brushes my neck, and the response in my groin is immediate.

"Thanks," she whispers.

"Anytime," I say with a smile.

I glance toward the emerald-green giant, and Jesma pats my chest and walks away. As much as I enjoyed the contact, I can't help but think I might have overplayed my hand a bit, and Jesma is a little disappointed in me.

An ironic thought, all things considered.

Kara-Kar raises an eyebrow. "I meant no offense."

I ignore the comment and turn to the river.

The roar of the Great Rankin and its gravity-defying flow is a welcome distraction from all the events of the last few days.

"Who'd have ever thought there'd be a day when I'd be happy to hop into this river?" Tamrin says.

"Life can change in an instant," I say with a finger snap.

The Crags and their wet, stony, treacherous crossing are many miles to our east, far beyond our view. We stand at the western bend, midway between the Sanctum Mountain and Valshannon, at the top of a plateau. Below, the water rushes toward us, its uphill climb much less of a mystery to me than it was a month ago.

"Wow, it really does flow uphill," Jesmir says, his eyes on the water kicking its foamy spray into the air.

I point southwest. "This bend curves southward for seven miles, then turns west again for four more. From there, it runs a pretty straight line into the Sanctum Mountain, forty or more miles westward. It straightens out just ahead. If we were standing there, we'd be able to see the tip of Sanctum Mountain over the horizon."

"We are going to cover almost fifty miles in half a day?" Jesmir says, incredulous.

"Not without help, we aren't," I reply.

"You were serious! You intend to jump in again?" Jesmir exclaims.

"Listen, this is no different than before," I reply. "We know what to expect. Unless Grankin plans to come escort us on land, we have no choice but to jump in."

"And if Grankin doesn't come?" Jesmir asks.

"Then it's been nice knowing you, Your Highness. I'm glad we met." I smile and bare my teeth.

"You're an ass," he replies.

"You humans aren't very nice to one another," Kara-Kar says.

"Do you plan to join us?" I ask. "Are you the rare Korund who can swim?"

"I cannot swim," Kara-Kar says. "But I am familiar enough with these waters."

"Well, that explains your reaction, or lack of one, when I said we'd be jumping in earlier. Grab your gear. Let's unsaddle these horses and let them roam. From here we go on foot."

The sounds of leather straps and buckles are drowned out by the rushing water of the Great Rankin. I'm curious how the Korund is familiar with these waters. Tamrin tosses the last saddle into a pile under a nearby oak and pats me on the back.

"Ready when you two are done with your pissing match," he says with a laugh.

"Sink or swim," I say to Kara-Kar. "We're going in. If I don't see you again, it's been…weird."

I turn to the river and sprint toward it at a leisurely pace.

"Bouldersplash!" I scream as I jump into the rushing waters of Grankin's domain.

Shit! I forgot it's winter. This water is fucking cold.

My balls pull back in retaliation.

Chapter Thirteen

Journal Entry: 114

"*U*nbeliever."

That's the term the Queen used, same as Kara-Kar. They both use the term as if it's a title and means something.

Yeah, dumbass, it means the joyless green giant might know something you don't.

Like the truth?

It's time to speak with the one person who has been around long enough to have answers——Grankin.

But that wily gnome loves his games. I don't think he'll answer my questions directly. God or not, I'll run him through with my sword if he doesn't.

Or die trying.

I don't know what to make of Kara-Kar. What lies behind the motivation to find me besides a shared disdain for the gods? That hardly seems enough. It's awfully convenient, too.

I'll keep my eye on the Korund. At least I know where to strike should death become a necessity.

Grankin Shmankin

The frigid blast from the water lasted longer than I expected. The heavy current tumbles me, and I smack my knee into a rather large rock as my head breaks the surface of the water. I cry out, which offers the river a chance to fill my gaping maw with water. I choke as I'm pulled back under. Frantic, I claw for the surface, but I'm disoriented.

What if I'm wrong and Grankin is completely at peace, or worse, entertained by the idea of us drowning?

The stones at the bottom of the river pass by in a blur. Aerated water obscures my vision with bubbles and reflected light. I lose sight of my friends and flail about to gain control of my body. A ball of limbs and tattered clothes, the river batters me like useless flotsam.

Time, measured solely by the steady increase in pressure on my chest, slips away quickly. The last bit of air escapes my lungs. I hold the emptiness in a death grip, my lungs desperate to gasp for air. With each tumble, the need to inhale grows. My chest burns, and my lungs threaten to expand.

I'm running out of time, or maybe I'm not. Maybe there is no time. The relativity of time in Grankin's realm is the only reliable constant, so forever could mean anything. Time is what Grankin decides it is, so it could be yesterday for all I know.

My head breaks the surface of the water, and I gasp for air in a desperate heave. My body rolls again, and I'm barely able to stop myself from inhaling more water.

Like a set of rocks from a manic Shamna acolyte's hands, I tumble and catch another glancing blow from a large underwater boulder. Its solid, smooth surface dislocates my shoulder. The pop muffled in the rushing water.

I scream, and again my last bit of air escapes in rapid bubbles. More water enters my mouth. My head bobs above water, and I spew the water and gasp for what air I can in yet another brief excursion on the surface.

I bounce on the rocky riverbed with an unreasonable amount of force and expel my life-saving air again.

Grankin better hope his balls can take the beating those rocks took.

My head pops above water again, and I take in yet another deep breath. I clench my fist, the one that still works, and think of how much damage I intend to do to the gnome's bulbous nose when I get a hold of him. It seemed a reasonable assumption that Grankin would appear, do his thing with the river, and allow us to get some answers.

Conspicuously absent, however, this magically moving mass of mystic water takes me to Shamna knows where, but my guess is oblivion. My muscles turn into mush, exhausted from the effort of fighting the current. I bounce off the bottom of the river again, and my back scrapes the smooth rocks as the current drags me along the bottom once more.

Darkness creeps into the edges of my vision as I drift into unconsciousness, no longer aware of my bearings. Long grass threatens to entangle my limbs. Freshwater fish gawk as I tumble past, their expressions oddly curious and aware. Some of the fish are too big for this river. For the briefest moment, I'm sure they see me as food, their mouths large enough to swallow me almost whole.

The rocky riverbed shimmers with color, surrounded by the black ring of fading awareness. The world turns grey, my oxygen spent, the pressure from my lungs to suck in air too intense to fight much longer.

A tug at my ankle startles me, and I spot a mass of grass. I'm pretty sure it grabbed me on purpose, but somehow the flow of water takes me further downstream. I'm pulled as if I'm on a rack, my foot caught in the firm, relentless grip of the grass. The blades stretch until I'm brought to a stop. The water flows by, and I've lost all will to fight.

Grankin, you'd better hope I never see you in the afterlife. I'll give you an eternity in hell if I do.

I can't hold my diaphragm anymore, and it involuntarily expands. The sensation of water in my lungs makes me flail. The last bit of fight left in me fades.

I don't want to die, not like this.

A fat little man swims up, his wily, bastard eyes locked on mine as if I'm in the wrong. He squints, those irises like the night sky filled with blinking stars in an expression of wondrous curiosity.

He glances at the reeds that have me tied up and shrugs.

This bastard intends to let me drown!

Instead, he pulls out a knife and severs the grass with a quick swipe. The river takes me again, and I'm carried downstream once more. My head breaks the surface, and the river calms down. I bob on the water's surface, releasing loud gasps, coughs, and several curses. My vision returns slowly, Ezra's bright light blinding me. Tingles build throughout my body as oxygen-starved nerves awaken from their near-permanent slumber.

The Great Rankin River carries me away from the one person I needed to find.

I cast about and search for my friends, whom I haven't seen since the foolish decision to jump into the river. Before I have a chance to breathe a sigh of relief that they didn't follow me, I catch sight of Tamrin's head. It breaks the surface several hundred yards upstream. He waves to me to show he is okay.

My body bounces off another rock, and the last thing I see of him is his face wincing.

The world goes black.

I call out to Grankin, and bubbles escape my lips. My voice is muffled and strange underwater.

Another impact knocks the last bit of air out of my lungs, the expulsion so violent I involuntarily suck in water again. My lungs fill with fluid. My chest burns. This wasn't supposed to happen, but I'm too tired to care.

Fuck you, Grankin. Get that Tome your damn self.

"Ezra's tits! What is wrong with you?" I scream at the miserable old gnome before me. The insufferable bastard doesn't even flinch at my outburst. Instead, he plays with the stupid goldfish that swims in his watery beard.

The top of Birdsong Waterrise appears just as it did in my vision when Grankin pulled me from the Cuska's spell. It's no less impressive in real life than it was in my dream. Misty cool spray fills the air as the Great Rankin River climbs the cliff face and splashes against the river landing at the plateau. It disappears into the cave beyond and roars back from the gaping maw of the mountain before it disappears into the Sanctum Mountain.

Every member of the party, including Kara-Kar, is accounted for. The Korund stands as if the recent ordeal were little more than an inconvenience. Tamrin looks on in shock, barely moving, in awe of the wondrous sight that few have seen in hundreds of years or more. Below us, the river rushes toward the Birdsong and lifts us, its gravity-defying climb mesmerizing. The slight hump of water as it rolls over the cliff edge shimmers in Ezra's light.

While Tamrin, Jesma, and Jesmir gape at the wonders of the Great Rankin River, I stand toe to toe with the short gnome dressed in white robes. I'm ready to punch him in his chubby nose like I promised myself I'd do before I nearly drowned. Grankin studies me with curious interest and shows no signs of anger, amusement, or frustration. He strokes his translucent beard, which squishes through his fingers, though he doesn't seem to notice. As his fingers pass through the fluid, the goldfish that lives there dodges his sausage fingers.

"Why?" I yell again. "Why did you do that?"

"I should ask you the same," he says.

"What?" I ask, dumbfounded.

"Why did you do that?" he asks.

"What the hell are you talking about?" I demand.

Tamrin's nervous cough behind me elicits a scowl, and I give him the finger. My friends shake their heads in slow unison. Kara-Kar looks surprised by my reaction. I couldn't give two shits about any of their warnings at the moment. I ignore the lot and point at Grankin.

"You nearly let us drown!"

Grankin shrugs. "Well, I wasn't foolish enough to jump into the water. Willingly and uninvited, I might add," he scorns. "All you needed to do was ask. I would have come and gotten you."

"Ask?" I spit out. "How was I supposed to do that?"

"My dear boy, you really must learn to pay attention," he says.

"I tried to tell him," Kara-Kar says, "but he didn't want to hear it."

"You what?" I say to the Korund.

"You made it clear my counsel was not required," Kara-Kar says.

"Wha…well…umm…you see…"

Words fail me, and I devolve into a series of sputters and grunts.

"I remember you being a little more well-spoken," Grankin says, the starlight in his irises twinkling in and out. It's difficult not to look deeper into those eyes. They threaten to pull me into his hypnotic spell, their vast depths so reminiscent of the night sky.

I shake my head. Violently.

"You preposterous asshole!" I yell.

Jesma gasps, "Shen!"

"Wow. I don't think I have ever had anyone speak to me that way," he says as he paces off the edge of the cliff.

"Wha…" I hear Tam say. I ignore him.

"Wait till I get my hands on you, then," I spit.

"Should I be worried?" Grankin asks.

With a sigh that indicates I will do nothing to him, I ask, "Why did you let us drown and then save us?"

Water drips from my clothes in a steady stream and pools at my feet. My lungs still hurt from the water they expelled and from my labored breaths. My pride hurts worse.

"Ah, that." He stands less than a foot away. Even with his short stature, he somehow looms. The deep black skies of his irises draw me in, and I feel myself grow smaller, in a metaphysical sense.

"I wasn't sure you wanted to be saved," he said. "But then you did something unexpected." He looks over at my friends and smiles. "He prayed. To me."

"I…I…what?" I stutter.

Tamrin doesn't even try to hide his smile. I hold up my hand as a signal to silence him before he speaks.

"Don't jump to conclusions," I say. "I did not pray."

"Oh, dear boy, but you did." Grankin spins and points to Tamrin. "I tell you, good man, that our friend here absolutely prayed to me."

Grankin approaches and pats my chest.

"Ask me how I know you did," he says. The handprint on my chest surges with heat. Of its own accord, my hand touches the spot.

"That's right," he says. "I am with you, all the time now. Every word you speak, every action you take. Every thought you have that invokes my name..." His comment lingers in the air. There's an implication there that's unsettling.

"I am everywhere you are," Grankin says. Anytime I want to be.

The gnome-god paces, his hands clasped behind his back. "I was there when you fought and beat the Cuska and when you bested Brogen." He turns and smirks, "I was there when you rediscovered what it is to love and be loved."

Jesma's face flushes a bright crimson against her pale skin. I feel the blood rush to my ears. I start to say something, but he raises his hands.

"No, it's not like that. Don't make it weird," Grankin laughs. "You haven't quite figured it out, have you?" he asks, disappointed. "I had hoped you'd be a little further in your understanding by now. I'm spoon-feeding you here."

I throw up my hands. "You speak in riddles, Grankin, and I'm in no mood."

Jesmir appears out of thin air in front of me and addresses the gnome.

"Oh, now isn't that something?" he says at Jesmir's sudden appearance. "Teleportation! I haven't seen that magic in thousands of years. Now you must tell me how you do that someday. I've never been able to figure it out."

"We need answers," Jesmir demands, ignoring Grankin's words. "I spent a lifetime praying to gods who never answered. Suddenly, I can do this. Why?"

"A lifetime, you say?" Grankin replies. "Can you really call thirty years a lifetime? I know fish older than you, young man."

"Please," Jesma says, "we have questions."

"What to do, what to do," Grankin ponders, stroking his beard again. He spins around. "I know! Let's fight!" His eyes and mouth are wide with excitement.

The handprint on my chest flares, and fresh pain assaults my senses. The suddenness of the onslaught drops me to my knees, exactly as when the handprint first appeared. An angry growl rumbles in my chest, and my hands shake as I ball my fists.

"You don't like that too much, do you?" Grankin asks. He mocks me, and my temper flashes like hot iron. I release it into the air with a scream, guttural and raw, as I stand and draw Brogen's sword. The gnome circles me, and I advance on the cocky little bastard, a grimace of pain on my face. My sword swipes across his beard. The tip passes through, and a significant drop of water falls to the rocky surface with a splash. The tip of his beard is lost in the saturated ground. Grankin doesn't flinch. He leans back enough to prevent my sword from cutting his flesh.

The goldfish in his beard shakes a fin at me in protest.

"Come and take your anger out on me, Shen-Zarl," the diminutive gnome-god taunts. I take the bait, too angry to think. We circle each other—antagonists in a fight I didn't start.

"I'm tired of the games, Grankin. You have no right to use us as pawns," I say.

"But don't I?" he asks. "You prayed to me to save you. Doesn't that give me some power over you?"

"I did not pray!" I scream and lunge for him.

He steps away from my strike, skipping as if we are two children playing a harmless game of tag. It won't be so harmless if I get my hands on him. He evades me by walking back out over the open air, skipping along the whole time. He's not particularly fast. But somehow, neither am I.

"Not so tough without that speed, are you?" Grankin sneers as he steps back onto the plateau.

"Tough? I'll show you tough," I snarl, but something is wrong. My motions feel sluggish. Grankin dodges my attack with ease.

"Something wrong?" Grankin asks, his lower lip in a pout.

I fling a throwing knife at him, and he turns aside, the metal sailing out over the cliff's edge into the river below.

No one can dodge my blades. How's he so fast?

"Do you *feel* different?" Grankin asks.

The clues click into place. My body doesn't tingle, but the handprint on my chest burns. I'm slower than I can ever remember being. I snap my gaze to Tamrin. His expression confirms my suspicion. This squat gnome with his short legs could never evade me, yet he does. With quick flicks, I move the tip of my sword with precision strikes, but I *feel* slow. Grankin spins around my blade with lazy steps. With little effort, he is inside my guard and grabs my tunic, his eyebrows bouncing. He pulls my face close to his and plants a kiss on my lips. He adds further insult when he spins around my hip and slaps my ass.

I stand straight up, eyes wide in shock, and let the tip of my sword fall to the ground. My chest burns where this little shit of a god emblazoned his knobby paw print. I resist the urge to touch it, unwilling to acknowledge its presence. The world pulls away, and my ears ring. The view over the valley below draws me in, and I walk to the edge. Far below and as far into the distance as I can see, the Great Rankin River rushes toward me in its mysterious climb uphill. Its mist fills the air with a damp fog. Its roar echoes in the hollow sounds beyond the ringing in my ears.

Where is my speed? There's no chance he's faster than me.

Pressure pulsates in my eardrums, sounds changing in a pattern that matches the beats of my hearts.

Whump-whump-whump.

My breath comes in rapid, shallow bursts. The world spins around me as my skin tingles in a strange new way. My fingers and toes go numb.

I turn toward Grankin, and odd sounds reach my ears. A boot on rocks. The swish of fabric. Familiar sounds come from beneath me and around me, much too close for my comfort. I look to find the source. The others observe, eyes wide.

"Still haven't caught on, have you?" Grankin asks.

I raise my sword and step toward him. My boot scrapes the ground, wet soles on damp and gravely earth. My pants swish as I step, a quiet swish almost drowned out by the river's noisy landing onto the plateau. Soft as it is, it might as well be a battle drum. It's as loud to me as any noise I've ever heard. Because, until now, I've never heard my own footsteps.

I stomp my foot on the ground. It thumps in time with the impact against the wet stone. A tiny splash carries over the roar of the flowing river.

Hands in the air, Grankin surrenders. I flick the end of my sword at his face.

"Easy, boy. I meant you no harm," the gnome says.

"What have you done?" I ask.

"Merely demonstrated a truth our Korund friend tried to explain. Experience is a better teacher than a lecture. The method is far more effective with you, dear boy."

He reaches past my blade and places his hand against my chest. Too confused to resist, I allow his tiny fingers, thick and calloused, to slip through the gap in my blouse. He places his hand where his imprint has been a constant reminder of my promise. The burning in my chest subsides. All I feel is the warmth of his skin against mine. He pulls his hand away and steps back, with a gentle smile on his face. Inside, my body vibrates, low and warm. It's a familiar sensation.

"Take a look," he says.

I pull my shirt open. His handprint has vanished, leaving no remnant.

He closes his eyes and then speaks. "I am Grankin, Wizard of Haabrestand Tower. I was nineteen years old when the others trapped me here. For eons, I've watched time slip by while I remained in this river, forced to witness lives pass." He gestures with an uplifted chin to the world behind me. "I've lost count of the years of my imprisonment. At least ten thousand circles around Ezra." He seems to consider that. "You'd think I'd know, since my specialty is time. 'God of Time.'" He scoffs at that moniker. "I'll let you in on a secret. I'm not a god. I am a human, as you are. All the gods are."

My sword falls from my hands.

He said it.

I look to the others, who appear as stunned as I am.

"Now, would you do me a favor? Please, please grab this goldfish from my beard? He's been stuck there for over nine hundred years, and it's driving me insane."

I exchange glances with the others. Tam shrugs. Despite the absurdity of this moment, I step forward and reach into the watery beard that no longer comes to a point since my sword cut it away. The goldfish swims away from me. Grankin giggles as my hand swishes around chasing the elusive swimmer. I pull my hand out, water dripping as I do. Grankin looks at me patiently but disappointed. With a flurry, I summon all the speed I can muster.

"Whoa!" says Grankin. He looks over at my friends. "See that?" he smirks.

I breathe a sigh of relief that my speed is not lost. The goldfish squirms in my hand. Grankin smiles.

"Oh, don't hurt him. I need a break. He never stops, and frankly, it itches."

We stare in utter amazement as the strange gnome scratches his beard like he's trying to satisfy a thousand-year itch.

"Oh, yeah. Ah, yes. That's better." His frantic activity comes to a stop. The goldfish wiggles in my hand, angry at the insult.

"Okay, you can put him back now," Grankin says.

"Uh, sure," I say, and I slide the fish back into his beard. The fish swims up the beard and nips the gnome on the chin.

"Yipes!" he shrieks. "Guess he didn't like that."

He reaches his hand to my chest again.

"May I?" he says. "I promise not to make it painful this time. I was rather cruel before. For that, I do apologize. One more demonstration, if you don't mind."

I hesitate, and he places his hand on my chest again. It's much less unpleasant the second time around. As he pulls his hand away, I look and see the slowing ebbing glow of his handprint has returned.

"Consider this my periapt," he says. After a slight pause, he adds, "If I were actually a god."

Once again, the handprint heats.

"Now, again, come get my fish."

I raise an eyebrow.

"It's okay, you'll soon understand."

I want this absurd exercise over with. I muster as much speed as I can, but I already know. The sounds my hand makes in his beard and the lack of that vibrational burning in my body, fueled by the fire in Grankin's mark, is all the proof I need.

The fish evades my clutches and slips through my fingers. The warm glow on my chest subsides, and I find myself speeding up, the pain in my chest replaced with the familiar fire in my body. I catch the fish with little effort this time.

Grankin and I stare into each other's eyes, my hand inside his beard. It's an awkward moment as the fish squirms. The gnome's gaze bears into me, willing me to understand.

"Come on," Grankin whispers. It's a plea.

"You can control me with this?" I say, touching my chest.

"That's one way to put it, but not quite accurate." He pauses, and I let his goldfish go, removing my hand from his beard.

"You can't control me?"

"Not in so many words. What if I told you that you weren't special? What if I said you were exactly like everyone else?"

"I'd say I never thought I was special."

"Come now," he said, "that's too easy." He looks over at Tamrin. "Why do you follow Fildeus?"

Tamrin walks over to stand next to us, frowning, with the twins close behind. Grankin waves his hands in a lazy, quick circle, and six stones erupt from the ground at different heights. He sits on the shortest one closest to him.

"Come, sit," he invites us.

Kara-Kar observes from just outside our circle.

"You too, my dear," he insists.

Grankin looks to Tamrin, waiting for an answer.

"Because faith is important. Faith is the currency that I pay Fildeus. She, in turn, makes me a better hunter and tracker," he says. "And because Fildeus answers my prayers. Most of the time, anyway."

Grankin turns to Jesma.

"Why do you follow Ezra?" he asks her, pointing to the necklace that hangs around her neck.

"Same reason," she says with a nod at Tam.

He looks at Jesmir. "And you? To whom do you pray?"

He squirms a bit. "No one."

Grankin laughs at that. "Oh, tell me you understand!" he exclaims.

Jesmir looks at his sister in discomfort. He nods.

"I think I do," he says. "I'm sorry. But if I'm right, you won't like it."

Grankin raises an eyebrow. "Now that is interesting. I believe maybe the young prince *does* understand."

My chest heats up again.

"You called this a periapt earlier," I say, and thumb my chest. "No, you called it 'my periapt.'"

He nods.

"It has an odd energy. When I thought all was lost, you made yourself known. In some pretty dire moments, I sensed your presence," I say, though I'm loath to admit it.

He nods. "And when you were drowning, I heard your *prayer*." He hangs his fingers in the air like quotes as he says the word 'prayer'.

"Because without the periapt, you can't hear my prayers."

He claps his hands. "That is what all of your friends understand that you never have. And now you do."

"Why did I pray?" I ask myself softly. "Because I knew."

"Knew what?" Jesma says.

"I knew he could hear me."

"Well done!" Grankin says. "That handprint of mine allows me to know where you are anytime, I want to know. It allows me to hear you, any time I want. It allows me to even communicate with you from anywhere."

I swallow hard.

"It does more than that," I say.

His eyes sparkle and his smile widens.

"Yes."

"It allows you to hurt me. Or to stop me from doing what I know I can do."

"Tada!" he says with a leap.

"You can affect me from anywhere," I whisper.

"Almost there. You have to accept a truth you've never accepted first," Grankin says.

"It's magic," I say. "All of it."

"Boy, is it ever," he says. "With that little charm of mine, I can limit your access to magic. I can do so much worse than that if I were of a different mind."

"You caused pain. You stole my abilities," I say, and my skin tingles with what that means.

"Come on a trip with me," Grankin says as he walks toward the cave at the top of Sanctum Mountain. "Have you ever wondered where the river goes once it comes up here?"

He doesn't check whether we follow. He knows we will. Stunned by his words, eager to learn more, my desperation to hear secret truths grows. This is simply a matter of logic. Pieces of a long-ruminated riddle, allowed to run rampant in my mind, fall into place.

Questions I've pondered for a lifetime are about to find answers I'm desperate to receive.

The roar of the river increases to a deafening crescendo as the penetration of the light lessens with each step deeper into the cave. The jagged walls, moist with humidity and spray from the turbulent waters, shimmer with reflected sunlight. Moss and mildew cling to the rocky surfaces and make our footing treacherous. Ezra disappears from view, and the growing darkness encroaches, our eyes adjusting slowly. Behind us, the cavern's opening grows smaller, so small I can block it with my thumb held at arm's length.

Grankin, barely illuminated, points toward the back of the cave. Before us is another cliff. I glance over the edge and can see only darkness shrouded in grey mists that rise toward us, the Great Rankin flowing *with* gravity on this cliff, into a dark void. The roar of this waterfall is louder inside this cavern than the waterrise outside.

"Fear not what you are about to experience," Grankin yells over the roar. "Take my hand," he says to Jesma, who does so without hesitation. "Now, come on, children, create a chain. Hold hands!" We line up, Grankin, Jesma, Tamrin, Jesmir. Jesmir raises an eyebrow at me, hand outstretched.

"Guess we're doing this," he says. I nod and smile a bit.

"Guess we're doing this," I reply and clasp his hand. I reach back to Kara-Kar, who grabs my hand without question.

Grankin yells out to us, "Remember, memories only fade with time. And time never ends." His smile is big. "Don't let go until I say it's safe, or you will be stuck in time, lost forever!"

He steps off the cliff and, as one group, we follow him into a terrifying freefall into the depths below.

Chapter Fourteen

Journal Entry: 116

Recurring dreams suck. I had one last night. I've never told anyone.

I run from something—or someone—until I stand at a great big bridge over a great big river. I'm about to get caught. Frightened, I hide under the bridge. The ground is slick, and I fall into the river. The river takes me. My hearts pounds so loudly I'm sure they'll give me away. But they don't. They never do.

Because I drowned. The sense of loss overwhelms me. My brother will be so lonely without me.

But none of it matters.

Because I'm dead.

But then my parents find me and pull me out of the river.

I haven't drowned. They save me.

It's such a stupid dream. My parents would have been glad to see me drown. I'm surprised they didn't think to drown me themselves.

The dream sticks with me always. But today in particular, I can't let it go.

There's Something About Grankin

They came for me in the middle of the night. I don't know how they found me. It was only a matter of time, anyway. If not for the minor spell I placed on the perimeter of the meadow, I would have no warning. This confrontation is long overdue. One can't push against the forces that hold a stranglehold on the world order and expect no pushback.

I reasoned with them.

I spoke out against them.

I've even fought them, pitting my power against theirs, losing ground with each confrontation.

Even with my small but loyal following, the power these eight wield is too strong, anchored by the faith of millions. The loss of my closest ally brought great pain. Thankfully, he was able to pass his magic onto me. I felt his suffering at their hands, tied together as we were by the symbols we emblazoned on each other and a love deeper than blood. But the Council of Tunia hunts my entire community. I don't know what has become of most of my friends, but their profound loss tells me they are all dead.

In my heart, I know the truth. The dastardly eight killed them all. Just as they did my dear husband, Troy.

No matter. Today is the day of reckoning. I thought I'd have more time to bring equal numbers to the fight. But it looks as if I'm on my own here. The Council is too powerful. Centuries of indoctrination filled humanity with the mistaken belief that these eight are the rightful rulers, the solutions to humanity's sorrows. Humankind chose faith over evidence, subjection over self-sovereignty.

"So, I guess this is it," I call across the meadow to the one who leads them. Shamna enters the clearing, hands out, inviting me to come to her. Her sheer dress billows in the breeze, its material pressed against the curves of her body. Her silver hair and bright blue eyes hide a dark, vile soul.

I will not become like them. I'll fight them to my last breath.

"We offered you a place among us, to help us shape the world and keep the peace. Instead, you enticed others to your misguided cause," she says.

"I offer truth, where you offer lies. You take from the world, giving pittance in return. For what? A false peace? To protect the world from itself?"

"You offer destruction!" yells Ezra, her yellow dress flaring outward in response to her anger.

"You hoard power and wealth," I spit.

Ezra glares at me, her hatred unmasked.

Shamna speaks, her voice resonant.

"Look around you. Look at the way we advanced the world. We've elevated humanity from clans and tribes. Wars are rare. From chaos, we created order. Cities thrive and grow under our gentle guidance."

"Gentle?" I spit out the word. "You steal life. Millennium after millennium, you steal the inherent gift of life only to re-grant it to those you deem worthy. You are no different than her.*"*

Their faces grow red with rage. I glance around at the slowly closing circle.

"Stop," I say. "Not one step closer."

I gather power within me, pulling from the energy I contain inside, ebbing my life as I do, peeling away years.

"Shamna," a voice behind me says, "wait."

Shamna peers over my shoulder as the group halts its advance, barely twenty feet from me in all directions. I turn to look at the speaker, recognizing her voice. Fildeus, her heavy furs clean and splendid, shifts in the breeze as she holds her hands up, a sign of peaceful approach.

"You don't know what it was like before," Fildeus says. "Rampant power, chaos, and destruction. Uncontrolled and untamed beings thirsting and searching for dominion over one another. We brought peace and prosperity to war-torn lands."

"At what cost?" I ask.

"No, to what benefit?" she asks. "We did not enter into this lightly. We labored and debated this decision. We stopped the worst of us."

"You think stopping one of you absolves all of you? You set the bar too low for yourselves," I counter.

"No. She was a symptom of the greater problem. Stopping her was only a minor step. Preventing a newer version of her from ever appearing absolves us. And that's why we must stop you."

"You think you save the world by limiting access to magic?" I ask. *"Humanity can govern itself. You speak of benevolence, prosperity, and peace, but leave many in poverty. You reward the faithful and punish the weak. You garner wealth and control lives with flippant glibness."* I point a finger at my chest. *"I bring a revelation to the world. I tell the truth. Gods aren't real."*

"You'll not be allowed to destroy everything we built!" Shamna growls. I face her.

She steps forward, and the others follow suit, the circle of mages pressing closer. I feel them closing in.

"I warn you. If you come any closer, I will act," I say.

They pause, barely ten feet from me.

"You have built a world of prisoners," I say as calmly as I can. It's imperative that I keep my cool. We've been battling for days now, each of us losing a little more of ourselves in each attack and counterattack. I can feel my body aging in response. My joints ache from the effort. There's no escape this time. Mutual destruction is the only way.

Shamna spreads her arms out.

"We have you outnumbered. You grow weaker with each move you make."

I laugh. It's a bitter one.

"Yes, but so do you. Each of you," I say as I spin in a slow circle, looking each of these so-called gods in the eyes. I want them to see that I am determined to fight to the death.

Returning to Shamna, those deep blue eyes ablaze with power, her shimmering hair cascading around her, I see why Hakaka loves her. Powerful, vain, beautiful. Everything a man of war and power would value.

"Yes, but our individual pools of energy are far greater than yours," Shamna says softly.

"Shamna," I say, *"I understand why you have done this. I see the reasons now. But that should have been temporary. You've taken this too far. All of you have. You've lost your way."*

"We can't stop now," Nadur says. "Chaos would ensue. For too long, mankind has lived this way. What you fail to comprehend is that the price of rampant magic is too high."

I turn to the well-dressed scholar of nature and science. He takes a small step forward, holding his hand out, a peace offering.

"No. The price of your protection is too high," I say. "You've taken the lives of far too many in the pursuit of peace, and how many more in your thirst to maintain power?"

I look at Quietius, his black hooded robe hiding his face. "Quietius, you have for so long hidden your face from the world, pretending to be the Lord of Death, preying on the faith of those who pray to you. Does it fulfill you to offer, in life, the promise of a peaceful transition to death that you never actually can deliver? Do you enjoy the corruption of your body that results from the consumption of life?"

Quietius lifts his hands to the cowl of his hood and removes it. His face is gaunt, skin rotting away, pieces of bone showing through. His leprosy has worsened through the years.

"Is the price you pay any different than the price paid by others? How is this better?" I ask.

"Enough!" Hakaka yells. "You will surrender now or perish. We've sacrificed much to prevent the world from destroying itself. You are a fool, and I can no longer suffer you. You will not be allowed to disturb the peace."

"Peace," I say with a laugh. "You, of all people, talk of peace?"

"Mankind must be allowed to purge itself. Before us, it was far worse. Without us, mankind would have seen to its own demise centuries ago."

"Why do we entertain this fool?" Ezra demands. "For twenty thousand years, we have governed this world." She steps toward me, her voice rising in volume and pitch. "You've barely survived two decades!"

A tickle travels up my neck. I summon my magic. Ezra's eyes glow pale yellow, and I know she is about to attack. Time slips into my control, and I pull myself forward to see her plan. She releases her spell, and I take three hurried steps backward. A spike of flame spins like a sideways tornado, rolling right over where I once stood. The heat singes my hair and heads straight toward Morze, who screams in surprise. Her eyes glow, and she rips moisture from the air, dousing the roiling column of fire.

"What are you doing, Ezra?" she yells.

"ENOUGH!" screams Shamna.

"You can't beat me," I say to them all.

"No, we can't," says Nadur. "We can't beat you. I've studied the source of your magic, but it eludes me. None of us can match you. We aren't here to beat you."

"What, then?" I ask. "My mind hasn't changed. I will not become one of you."

"No, Grankin. It is clear we cannot beat you. And it's clear we cannot reason with you. But we can't have you running free either," Morze says.

"So, what then?" I ask.

Too late, I realize I let them distract me. They clasp hands around me. How did I miss it?

Vanity. They used my vanity against me. I look at Quietius. He smirks. I realized I had fallen for his ruse. He played on my ego and compassion.

I'm a fool.

I push myself back in time, attempting to get out of the circle before it closes. But it's too late. I can't move back to safety without sacrificing myself. I've used too much of myself. I must stay alive. Fight another day, but how? There is nowhere for me to go. Beyond the trees, a rushing sound echoes. It originates from Rankin Lake, like rolling thunder, gaining volume as it draws closer. Over the trees, a massive wave looms forty feet high, ripping trees from their roots, washing them toward us.

I fight with time, gaining just enough foresight to dodge the debris hurtling toward me from all directions. Gathering the pockets of air from the turbulent waters, I pull the tiny bubbles close, combining them into a protective ball of air around myself. Too focused on saving my own life, I miss the moment the Great Eight Wizards vanish. The waves toss me about, and I bounce around in the air shield I struggle to maintain. My ears ring in protest as the water slams my protective ball against the earth and trees. The concussive sound compresses the giant air bubble and bursts my eardrums. Blood pours from my ears, muting all sound. I vomit from the disturbance to my equilibrium. The smell of stomach acid and bile fills the chamber.

The water carries me up hills and down, carving a shallow valley through the center of the RhineWoods. Trunks snap with loud cracks, their giant logs threatening to shatter my bubble.

I tumble for what seems like a century before the world goes black.

I wake in a dark cavern. Before me, a massive waterfall cascades from so high I can't see its origin. I cast a levitation spell to the top of the waterfall. In the distance, a bright white light beckons me. The long walk leads me through a massive cave. I stand at a great height above the land below. Before me, the landscape is unfamiliar. Where once a dense forest stood, a large river flows as far east as my eyes can see. The water somehow climbs a sheer cliff face to where I stand and heads into the cave from whence I came.

"That's a new one," I say to no one in particular.

I'm surprised to be alive. Somehow, I survived their attempts to kill me again. I laugh almost hysterically.

"You failed!" I yell over the valley.

"No, we didn't."

I recognize Quietius' voice behind me. I turn to face him. His skin has returned to normal, with no sign of the leprosy I'm so accustomed to seeing. He stands dressed in his dark robes.

"I still live," I say. "All you did was make me more determined."

"Yes," he says, "that's true. But you'll have to do it from the confines of this river."

"Says you," I reply, and jump from my perch into the river below. I pop to the surface and look at the waterfall. Levitate myself out of the water to the north bank and walk away. But something isn't right. I take another step, and the river is back in front of me. I turn and walk again. Before I've gone fifty paces, I find myself back to approaching the river.

Quietius appears before me. There is sorrow in his voice. "You can never leave the confines of this river. This is your prison now. This is where you can do the least harm."

I walk toward him, stopping a few feet from him. I don't know why I stop. Willing my feet forward, nothing happens. I am planted.

"What did you do?" I ask, incredulous.

"This was the only way," he says. "I'm sorry. You may go no further than the river's borders. This, at least, will give you the chance to get fresh air. But you can no longer influence the world."

He looks around. "I think we will call this the Great Rankin River. Fitting that Grankin should be imprisoned here."

He turns to leave, stopping for a moment.

"For the record, I do agree with you. There will be consequences for what we've done. Maybe not today. But someday, we will pay for our crimes." His voice drops to barely a whisper. "I never wanted this. We were supposed to be better than what we've become."

Quietius walks off into the distance and disappears into the northern Rhine Woods.

"What *was* that?" Jesma exclaims.

The volume of her voice startles me from a strange dream. When I recover from the confused fog in my head, I find we are treading water, our hands clasped together in a group. All around us, overhead and even below the surface, eerie green lights illuminate a massive cavern.

"I dreamed I was you," Jesmir says to Grankin.

"Wait, so did I," Tamrin adds.

"I won't ever get used to that," Kara-Kar says.

"Welcome to Memory Lake," Grankin says. He releases Jesma's hand and swims on his back toward a rocky shore where a strange house, complete with a door, windows, and a front porch, sits. Lanterns inside emit light through sheer curtains, where shadows of people move about.

Grankin continues to speak to us as we follow him out of the lake. "Deep within Sanctum Mountain, this reservoir gathers time's most precious resource—the history of humanity. Every person who has ever fallen into my river has memories locked away in here. Memories they themselves have long forgotten."

He waits for us to emerge from the lake, a sly smile on his face.

"Now that you've all been in the river, all your memories are stored here, too. As far back as maybe a decade or two before I was born, the history of Conishant is recorded. Barring any erroneous memories, that is."

"I discovered its secrets not long after I was trapped here. It was a strange consequence of the events you experienced alongside my magic. You can imagine my surprise when I learned its powers."

The roar of water echoes through the cavern. Ripples not caused by swimmers stretch toward us, their source hidden in the darkness beyond the strange green lights.

On closer inspection, the lights are strange luminescent insects that flitter along slow, lumbering paths like drunken fireflies that never go out. A pale cerulean glow lines the rock walls, caused by bioluminescent moss clinging to the stone. The moss climbs the rock walls in strange streaks like veins, circling around the great underground lake, climbing high above us, and fading into the distant cavern ceiling.

"So, that was your memory we just lived?" Jesma asks.

"That is *exactly* what you did," Grankin says.

The gnome turns and points to the house. "This is my home. I've been trapped in these waters a long time." He drifts off a bit as if we aren't there. "How many years? No, how many thousands? Is it nine? No, ten?" He counts on his fingers, then interrupts himself. "No matter. It's been a long time."

He points to Tamrin's beard. "You should remove that," he says.

Tamrin grips his periapt of Fildeus, his knuckles whitening. "Never," he says. Tears well in the big guy's eyes. His lower lip quivers. His eyes bounce from Grankin to me, and then to Jesma.

"After what we saw and what we've learned?" I whisper.

The pool of tears reflects the strange yellow glow of bug lights.

"Tam," I say, "Think about this. She can block you from your powers. She doesn't grant powers. She takes them."

Grankin closes the gap between himself and the giant man. The appearance of the massive framed, nearly seven-foot Tamrin next to the three-foot-tall and stout gnome would elicit hearty laughter if not for the levity.

"You see it, don't you?" Grankin says, not without compassion. "Fortunately, the moment you entered my river, they lost you. They know you are somewhere in my domain, but they don't know where. Just as they knew the first time you entered this realm. And they know they can't enter it without my permission. You are safe here."

I turn to the woman who, in the matter of a few weeks, has changed my world in so many ways. Eyes filled with tears, her hand clutching the periapt of Ezra around her neck.

"Jez, the gods lie to us. All of them. Generation after generation of lies." I turn back to Grankin. "That's what you wanted me to see. That's why you've shown up there, taking my ability away," I say.

"That's part of it, yes," he confirms. His eyes narrow as he waits for more. A gentle hand touches my arm now. It's Jesma. She weeps. In her hand lies her periapt, its chain still around her neck. Her hand trembles.

She looks at Grankin. "Why?" she asks.

"I believe that at one time they thought they were saving the world," Grankin says. "But now they are corrupted by the power. They are shells of the people they used to be."

Jesma then turns to her brother. "You believe this story?"

Jesmir bows his head and avoids her gaze. Jesma takes a shuddering breath, her eyes closed, tears falling down her cheeks. She hesitates, and as she clenches her jaw, she yanks the chain from her neck, the metal snapping.

"Take this from me," she says to Grankin. He accepts her necklace, his compassionate smile devoid of joy.

"It took me years to accept the truth as I learned it," he says to her. "I was only nineteen. I thought I understood the world, had all the answers. In hindsight, if I had taken my time, I could have made things right. But youth is wasted on the young and experience is wasted on the old."

"My whole life has been in the service of Fildeus," Tamrin says. He trembles as he speaks. "I *know* her. My experience with the gods differs from most people's. I've hunted alongside the Wild Huntress." He looks at me. "Who *am* I without her blessing?"

"You are far more powerful without her than with her," Grankin replies, holding his hand out for the periapt that hangs from the long beard of the giant man. "Fildeus doesn't grant you power. She withholds power that is rightfully yours."

"There's more to power than the doing," Tamrin says. "Power also comes from our bonds to others, not just within ourselves."

We lock eyes as he speaks, his pain resonating. He holds his hunting knife to his beard, takes a deep breath, and lets out a heavy moan. His anguish rings out through the cavern, low and sorrowful. My eyes tear at his heartbreak. I stumble backward from the burden of his pain, my own guilt for not recognizing its importance to him torturing me. With slow, deliberate cuts, he severs the periapt from his beard. When it's over, he drops the tangled knot of hair that contains the stone periapt that has been there as long as I've known him. When the stone lands, it shatters into pieces, and the shards scatter.

Tamrin drops the knife on the ground and walks off alone, into the darkened depths of Grankin's cave.

"So, what now?" I say, a lump forming in my throat.

"Well," Grankin says, his voice lighter, "First, we get some food and some rest. You've all been through a lot. My home is your home. We'll talk about how you are going to fulfill your promise…and kill another god in the process."

Jesma chokes.

"How in Ezra's light are we supposed to do that?" she asks.

"You've already taken the first step," Grankin replies. "Figure out how to control your power without their help, and you'll be halfway home." He levitates himself to be eye to eye with Jesma and places a hand on her chest. "It's all in here," he says.

"Now, let's eat. I'm famished," Grankin says and claps his hands. The door to the house opens. Two men walk out, laden with trays of food. I recognize one of them. His short stature, dark hair, and dark skin bring back memories of my first encounter with the gnome and his river.

Tamrin returns, his eyes red and swollen.

"Kairn?" Tamrin gasps.

The servant's face turns into a grimace. It's the mercenary who helped Tamrin track the twins two weeks ago.

"Ah, yes," Grankin says, "Kairn pays his penance for his hand in your plight through service to me." Grankin winks at us, "But don't worry. His sentence is a mere five hundred years. Then, if I am satisfied with his behavior and conversion, he will be set free into the world."

Kairn scowls at us and places the trays on the table.

"He's none too happy with the arrangement, but he really has no choice. The other, a paler man, about my size, and much older, sets two trays of food before us. He smiles and seems at ease here, unlike Kairn, who appears to resent his predicament.

"Karma's a bitch, huh?" I say to Kairn.

His scowl deepens, and he walks off in a huff.

"He's awfully touchy," I say. "Make better choices!" I yell after him.

"Please, eat and rest. We will bring wine and water out in a moment," the second man says.

Tamrin sulks at the water's edge, his knees pulled to his chest. I sit with him, tossing rocks into the water. The others, sensing he needs space, occupy themselves with the exploration of the cavern. Grankin provides a grand tour, explaining the various fauna and flora within the cavern.

"You really believe that was a memory?" Tamrin asks.

I throw another rock into the water.

"I have no reason to doubt it," I say.

He stares out over the water. He sniffles and wipes his nose on one of his furs.

"I don't know what to believe. That gnome is loopy. He could be making it up. It could be an illusion," Tamrin whispers.

"I assure you, it's no illusion," Grankin says from behind us.

"Go away," Tamrin snaps.

Grankin points to the enormous underground lake. "A side effect of the magic used to create the river and imprison me here is that the water seeps some magic from those who enter. Not much, but enough to capture memories. Every person who touches the waters gives a piece of their history to this lake. The longer a person is in the water, the farther back the memories go."

His voice carries a hypnotic timbre, "The water flows deep into an underground spring, back to refill Rankin Lake from below. Have you ever wondered what causes the plume in Rankin Lake?" Grankin asks.

"This lake and Rankin Lake feed each other?" I ask.

Grankin spreads his arms to the reservoir. "Rankin Lake feeds the Great Rankin River. The river feeds the Birdsong Waterrise, which in turn flows into the Memory Falls and feeds Memory Lake. Memory Lake feeds underground tributaries, which in turn sprout from deep under Rankin Lake and form the Fountain."

"This whole thing is one continuous loop powered by magic—the magic of memories. Time moves in continuous motion along that loop."

His voice trails off. For the first time, I see sorrow.

"It must be horrible to be stuck here for so long," Tamrin says.

Grankin pats Tamrin on the back. "I realize that what you've learned today hurts. If there were another way, I would try. But there isn't much time. The world is sick, but the poison comes from within. The signs are all over if you know what to look for."

"Netherstacks," I say, realizing what he means.

"Yes. You've all been in my waters twice…more for some, come to think of it. More than enough for me to get a sense of the people you are. I trust you will do what is right."

Grankin places his other hand on my shoulder.

"You are one seriously deranged soul, Shen-Zarl. But I like you," he says.

"You have a funny way of showing it," I reply.

"You hold a grudge," Grankin says. "I do too. I'm counting on that."

"I've done all I can to hold the history here, waiting for the day someone would have the courage to break the cycle. I couldn't tell you when we first met…no, not even then. You wouldn't have understood. Probably thought me crazy…" He slips into mumbling again. "Am I crazy? Who's to say what crazy is? I certainly don't. Or do I? Hmmm. Should ponder that more."

Tamrin and I glance sideways at each other.

"Where was I?" Grankin mumbles. "Oh! Right. I needed you to be ready to see the truth—to feel it."

"I didn't like it," Tamrin says. "It left me sad and angry."

"As I did at the time," Grankin says. "You saw my imprisonment through my eyes."

Grankin grows quiet.

The image of the Great Eight surrounding us replays in my mind. Eight wizards who fancied themselves gods. I recognized their visages from statues throughout the five realms. But it's their voices that ring in my head. The way the memory felt, even their voices were familiar, like I *knew* them.

"Powerful magic," I say. "It was like I knew them already."

"I'd say so," Grankin says.

What aren't you saying?

My breath catches in my chest. The corners of his mouth curl upward.

"That fucking bitch," I say out loud.

"They aren't ready to hear the truth, young man," Grankin says. "This burden you must carry, along with the other. The time will come. But not today."

"We've tangled with two of the eight already," I whisper.

"More, I'd say," Grankin replies. "At least one can no longer hurt us."

And another soon fucking will be.

Chapter Fifteen

Journal Entry: 120

Vindicated!

I'd celebrate the victory, except the revelation comes at a substantial cost. As if the truth of the Queen's hand in the twins' plight wasn't iniquitous enough. This newest revelation will lead to greater heartache.

Grankin's right. The twins aren't ready for this. I came to the realization on my own. How could they not notice what I did?

I can't say it aloud, but Queeny and I have a date with destiny. I don't enjoy torture, but I sure as hell will enjoy this. If the twins don't realize the truth soon, I'll beat the truth out of that lying witch.

A New Journey

Without explanation, Grankin refused to give us any more information about his memories or magic. Whether due to his obtuseness or some valid reason, I'm left with unanswered questions. He bid us goodnight, had his servants prepare us rooms in his strange house, and wandered off into the cavern.

We wake for breakfast alone. Grankin and his servants are nowhere to be found.

Jesma and Tamrin, left to reconcile the new realities of a faithless existence on their own terms, eat in silence. Bereft of the constant presence of protection, neither seems willing to talk.

Jesmir, unaffected by Grankin's revelations, steals concerned glances toward his sister. Attempts to engage her in conversation are fruitless. Headway with Tamrin is much the same. Uncomfortable in my inability to empathize with his sorrow, I try to remain quiet, but leaving one another to wallow isn't our style, so my silence is temporary.

"How are you holding up?" I ask.

"Fine," comes his curt reply, leaving little room for conversation.

"Well, since we aren't going to talk about you," I say, "can we talk about me?"

His sideways glance tells me I'm walking on thin ice, but I figure, *'fuck it'* if he won't talk about himself. I recognize the irony in that.

"I can't stop thinking about what Brogen said about my father."

That gets his attention.

"Damn, man, I forgot about that," he says.

"We've been a bit busy," I reply. "He's always been a villain in my story. What if that story is a lie? Who is he then?"

"You've never put forth the energy to understand him," Tamrin says. I startle at his abruptness.

"Nadur's balls, that's harsh," I say.

He continues, unfazed by my response. "Your only reference is from a child's perspective of memories—memories replayed, tainted by time and personal narrative."

I stare out at the lake and wonder if Grankin's comments about the memories contained within are true. Grankin returns and takes a seat next to me and stares out over the dark waters. Tiny waves lap against the rocks, while the ripples reflect the strange light sources throughout the cave.

"Many memories in this water," he says. "Many lifetimes, many secrets, many forgotten events. What a person could learn about themselves in that deep blackness. It could be enlightening. Or devastating, depending on your perspective."

He points at my head. "You've been in this river a few times now. I bet there's some juicy stuff up there hidden away and forgotten. But be careful. You may not like what you find. Our minds have ways of protecting us from ourselves."

I look back at the lake, but he nudges me. "Some other time. You have work to do." He points along the bank of Memory Lake. "A half mile that way, you'll come to the entrance of a tunnel. It forks a few times. The path is simple. Always stay to the left. When you come out, you'll be high enough to see Galbring."

Grankin looks to Kara-Kar. "Head there first." He drops a purse on the table. It jingles with the metal clinking of coins. "Here's enough gold to replace our lively assassin's blades and stock up on supplies. You'll need them for what lies ahead."

"What lies ahead?" Jesma asks.

"A better future, I hope. I never meant you harm, but I fear harm will come to you in the end. Your fates are intertwined with one another. I'm only realizing now how much. Human nature is remarkably complex. So much had to happen to bring you all here, together, at this time. You must discover the truth for yourselves. It's with no small amount of regret that I push you out into uncertainty. You take great risks at my behest. I assure you, it's for the best."

"What in Krikhi's bosom does that mean?" I ask.

He doesn't answer me. Instead, the strange god who isn't claps his hands, and the surface of Memory Lake froths and bubbles violently into a mound. We leap from our seats. A bulbous creature with large glass eyes rises from the depths of the lake. Strange metallic clangs and hisses echo from its body. Through its eyes, I can see inside the monster.

"What in Ezra's name is that?" Jesma asks.

"That, my friends, is the future," Grankin says. "My friends and I tinker with ideas. We call that the '*Metal Fish*'. It's a boat that goes underwater. This lake is too deep for my friends to swim. With this, we find all kinds of neat things down there. Like that pile of coins I just gave you."

"You have friends?" Kara-Kar asks, skeptical.

"Of course I do. Ten thousand years of people falling, jumping, and being tricked into my water world provides plenty of opportunity to meet a few people I actually like." He looks at me with a raised eyebrow. "*Some* not as much as others."

Loud clangs and bangs from the *Metal Fish* echo far throughout the cavern. A bearded man, short, with a bulbous nose and a round, squishy face, pops from behind a little round door. A full, white beard hangs from his face. Its texture is soft and well-groomed. The gnome's puffy cheeks and bushy eyebrows threaten to hide his eyes forever. He looks a lot like Grankin, except his beard is not made of water.

"River Gnomes are real!" Tamrin exclaims.

"Of course we're *real*," Grankin says. "I've been standing here the whole time."

"Well, sure, but you don't count," I say in Tamrin's defense.

"I most assuredly *do* count," Grankin snaps.

The gnome on the metal boat waves at us, his nubby sausage fingers too small for his hands.

"We all lived above once. But my people refused the gods. In this place, a smaller stature affords greater maneuverability. Caves and tunnels tend to be small and all."

He glances at me. "And speaking of long times. I've had my eyes on you for a very long time, Shen-Zarl. I've limited your exposure to just me. But yes, I have a large family of my own. The difference is, they are all here by choice, while I am not."

I nod and stick out my hand to him. He takes it and laughs.

"One last thing. Do you want me to remove that seal?" Grankin asks.

"It's not that I don't trust you," I say. "But I'm not sure I trust you."

Grankin nods. "No, no. I understand. Can't say I'm not sad. I've so very much enjoyed watching you these last few weeks. I'll miss the entertainment. Do me a favor, don't lose that dark wit. It's your crowning quality."

"I have to admit, I won't miss that burning sensation in my chest."

"Kinda like a venereal disease, huh?" he says, laughing.

"Something like that," I reply.

The stars swirl in the dark circles of his irises. His mouth turns downward. With a bit of melancholy, he touches his hand to my chest.

The warm feeling subsides. The sense of aloneness returns, and it occurs to me what Tamrin and Jesma must feel.

"I'll say I am disappointed. I've grown rather used to *your* presence, young man. Reminds me of days, long since gone, when I felt the presence of those I truly shared the world with." His eyes water, and he brushes the tears aside. "Now, go boldly and get my book."

"You *still* want your journal?" I ask.

"Journal. Funny choice of words. What is a journal really but a history of one's life that we've chosen not to share with others? Much like this river I live in," he says.

It's not a journal. *It's a historical account.*

I point to the lake. "You don't need a journal of your own, do you? Krikhi's tits, it's not *yours*."

Grankin taps the side of his nose and smiles. "See, you'll find the truth. Memories long since lost. Memories I never had a chance to discover," he says. "The truth. The emperor keeps it locked away. Don't forget your promise. Kill the emperor. But I believe you have all the motivation you need now. Happy hunting."

Without another word, the strange little gnome who controls time walks across the water as if its surface were solid. Tiny ripples spread from his feet in little rings. His friend waves, half-concealed within the belly of the *Metal Fish*. We stand in stunned silence as Grankin climbs aboard the metal beast and hugs the other gnome before descending into its hidden secrets.

The surface of the water churns, and the vessel slips below the water's surface, and the last bit of frothy water dissipates.

"Every time I come here, that Gnome shows me something different," Kara-Kar says.

"Maybe it's time you started telling us who you are," I reply.

"There will be plenty of time for that," Kara-Kar says. "For now, let's get out of here. I miss the open air."

"I'm with our bejeweled friend here," Jesmir says.

"Lead the way," I say to Kara-Kar.

I want you where I can see you.

The tunnels hidden within Sanctum Mountain meander upward and out for miles. The steady climb from the belly of the mountain taxes our muscles and stamina. My thighs burn at the point where the grade forces us to lean into the climb. Tamrin and Kara-Kar, much taller than any gnome, are forced to walk hunched.

"Ezra's Ass!" Tamrin bellows. I glance back, and he holds his head, wincing. "Remind me to give those gnomes a piece of my mind later."

"I don't think they expected normal-size folks like us to come through here," Kara-Kar says, the Korund's deep baritone resonating through the tunnel.

"You call yourself normal-sized?" Jesmir snorts.

"Yes. Do you think it is normal to be so short?" Kara-Kar replies without irony.

"Ha! There are more of us in the world than either of you," Jesmir says.

"Yes, Your Highness, that may be true. But it is not normal. Even many of your people, like Tamrin here, are taller than you are," Kara-Kar replies.

"Shorter people have a tendency to live longer," Jesma replies. "So maybe we are what humans should be."

"I'm far from human, Your Highness," Kara-Kar says.

"Are you? Did not Krikhi form you from humans?" Jesma asks.

"Might I remind you that I will live to be two hundred while you will pass before you reach a centennial celebration," Kara-Kar says with a frankness that stings.

"I don't care when I die as long as it's not in these tunnels," Tamrin growls.

Bug lights float ahead of us, a gift from Grankin. Their pale green glow reflects off the wet stone walls. Moisture puddles in low spots and gathers on the soles of our boots, making the journey more treacherous.

I grow bored with the conversation and start counting steps while the path climbs ever upward, grunting against the muscle strain. Tamrin calls for a break, and both he and Kara-Kar collapse on the ground. Tamrin stretches out along the length of the path with a groan.

"I'm sorry it's so tight, Tam," I say.

"Oh, it's nobody's fault but the gnomes'," he grumbles. "I just need to stretch a moment."

The bug lights return and hover beside us. The yellow glow illuminates moss in an alcove on the rock wall. Within the alcove, mushrooms grow. Their blue caps glow in the strange light.

"Well, look at that," I say. "Glowing mushrooms."

Jesma looks inside and gasps. "Those are Dynorphus Silas," she says, and picks the entire alcove clean. She places them in her medical pouch. "They could come in handy."

"What do they do?" I ask.

"They're natural pain killers, mood enhancers, and stress reducers. Dried, they are perfect for treating trauma. They also help the body produce blood after sustained blood loss. They're scarce and hard to find."

"Never heard of them."

"Let's hope we don't need them," she says. "They act as an energy booster too, but can mess with your mind a little if you aren't used to them."

"Have you eaten them?" I ask.

"Yes," she says. "Jes and I ate them as teens for fun."

Kara-Kar says, "I hate to interrupt an engaging conversation, but I hardly think this is the time for chatter. Can we please get out of this tunnel?"

"I'm with the Korund," Tamrin says. "I'd like to get fresh air."

"Okay, okay," I say, but glance at Jesma sideways, curious about the mushrooms and what truths they could reveal.

Over Jesma's shoulder, I notice Kara-Kar's mouth open as if to say something, only to think better of it. It's unusual behavior for a race known for speaking their minds.

"Something to say?" I ask.

"I'm curious. Do you really plan to kill the emperor?" Kara-Kar asks.

"I can't think of a reason why I shouldn't," I reply.

"On what basis does he deserve to die?" the Korund asks.

"On the basis that I never liked the fucker anyway," I say.

Kara-Kar scoffs. Tamrin snorts. I continue, "That son-of-a-bitch is a prick. He's a warmonger who values violence over compassion. He's too callous...and I abhor cruelty. Like every emperor before, he's a tyrant who seized power through violence and will lose it to violence at some point. All Killinshire emperors are the same."

Kara-Kar studies me, confused.

"What?" I ask.

"Your logic is that he values violence? That's an odd stance from *The Harbinger of Death*."

"I don't seek violence. Violence finds me," I reply. "The emperor sent Brogen after these two."

Kara-Kar blinks. "You think the emperor sent Brogen? Hardly. Brogen played a game with everyone. Brogen was always the one in control."

"How do you mean?" Jesmir asks, but Kara-Kar falls silent.

"Now's the time to speak up," I say.

"Never mind," the Korund replies and changes the subject. "Let's get out of these tunnels."

Tamrin pushes himself onto his feet, his body crouched once more.

"Yes, please," he says. "Let's get the hell out of here."

"Agreed," Jemsa replies.

Grunting, I pull myself out of a hole in the mountainside. I dust myself off and stand in awe. Ezra sets out over the Gal-Danang desert to the west. Her rays paint the sky in streaks of amber, orange, and yellow. Below, the vast Gal-Danang landscape stretches to the western horizon and spreads to the north and south. The gap-toothed terrain of lone mountain peaks, their tops long lost to volcanic eruption, spews smoke and steam into the atmosphere.

"It's so beautiful from here," Jesma says.

"This is my home," Kara-Kar says with pride. "No matter how often I run away, I'm always grateful to return."

Due west and midway between us and the distant horizon, the dark, noxious cloud that covers the Gal-Danang netherstacks in the desert basin spreads death in all directions. Beyond its black plumes, I can barely make out the town of Gal-Pot. To the south, Galbring rests, only a few miles from the netherstacks.

I point to Galbring, "That's our destination. Daylight's wasting. We don't want to get caught in the dark here. Let's take the route south around the netherstacks."

Tamrin says, "We can make Galbring by evening. He glances at Jesma. "It's going to be a hard hike with the leg, Jez."

She nods, "I'll manage," she says, and leads the descent from our perch on Sanctum Mountain into the desert below. I wait until everyone else starts their way down before I do. Jesmir slows to walk beside me. He seems anxious.

"Hey," he whispers, "Do you think it's true?"

I don't need clarification. The same thought is on my mind. "That the gods are human? I do. I hope Grankin's little book tells us something useful," I say.

"It's kill the Emperor and get the Tome, then?" he asks.

I smile, "Welcome to my life, Jes. Senseless sacrifice to protect those who can't protect themselves."

He says. "We're slaves to an idea. All of humanity."

I glance ahead at Tamrin, concerned for his state of mind.

Jesmir follows my gaze. He leans onto my side.

"Then let's kill some gods," I whisper.

"I know which one I'd like to start with," he says.

Jesmir holds his gaze forward. A shimmer of tears pools at his lower eyelids. Butterflies flutter in my stomach, anticipating his next words.

"It was her voice that triggered me," he says after another moment of silence.

"Shit, I'm sorry, Jes," I whisper.

"It makes me wonder if there ever was a spy…or if it's always been her," he mumbles through clenched teeth.

The tear breaks free, unable to hold back. It runs a trail from the corner of his eye to the corner of his mouth. He licks it away. Unsure how to react, I walk with him, shoulder to shoulder.

"Does Jez know?" I ask after another moment.

"I don't think so," he says.

"Should we…" I start, but he shakes his head.

"I don't know if she noticed. If she didn't, I can't even begin to formulate how to tell her," he says.

"You weren't surprised," Jesmir says. A statement, not a question.

I don't reply.

"You suspected her," he says, his voice a cracked whisper.

I close my eyes to emphasize the truth.

"I did," I admit. My chest aches at the revelation I've hidden from him.

"That's one fucked up burden you've been carrying," Jesmir whispers. "Leave it to me to tell Jes. This *can't* come from you."

Looks like the circle of secrets has a new member. I'd be lying if I said I wasn't relieved.

Thanks to the dry, cooler air of the high desert and open terrain, we cross the arid plains with little physical toll. Jesma, the exception, her leg still healing, struggles to keep pace. I walk beside her in support and help keep her mind off her brother, who's lost in melancholic disassociation. Jesmir, disinterested in further conversation, walks far ahead of the group. Jesma's attempts to pry into the cause of his attitude are unsuccessful.

"I don't know what's wrong," she says.

"Look at him," I reply. "His ear is missing. We trek through the desert on a near suicide mission. Meanwhile, he's worried about you. Frankly, you aren't yourself either."

"I suppose you're right," she says, though I sense she isn't satisfied.

A light breeze stirs, and tufts of sand float along the flat desert floor at knee height. We cover our faces from the small bits that escape higher and threaten to choke us.

Even at this distance, the netherstacks threaten. The width of the field makes them feel much closer. Their dark emissions rise into the atmosphere farther than I remember from my last visit. From this lower vantage point, the plumes block out the northwestern horizon. Ezra's lower half is hidden behind nether-plumes as she sets for the evening.

"Ezra moves quickly tonight," Tamrin says.

"That time of year," Kara-Kar replies. "We'd best pick up the pace. I don't want to be out here when the light dies."

I shudder with trepidation, my memory triggered by the urgency in their tone. "Me neither. There's more road to cover than there is daylight."

Without waiting for permission, the large Korund scoops Jesma off her feet and holds her close.

"I don't need you to carry me," Jesma protests.

"Have you been to Galbring at night since the Jandu arrived?" Kara-Kar asks.

Jesma looks back at me, concerned, and shakes her head.

"Jandu?" she asks.

"As I suspected," Kara-Kar replies. "Vile creatures, legless abominations. No one knows where they came from. They kill with glee and attack in packs. We need to move, and your injured leg holds us up."

"I'm not going to like this, am I?" Jesma asks.

"No, your Highness, you will not," Kara-Kar replies.

We kick into an aggressive jog. Desert terrain shifts from rocky white sand to black lava rock as we draw closer to Galbring. The change in footing is treacherous. Fissures, filled with hot lava below, emit heat and interrupt our stride with awkwardly timed hurdles.

Kara-Kar holds Jesma close but bears the weight easily.

Shimmering heatwaves blur the city ahead. We follow the path that weaves between them as much as we can in an attempt to avoid the fumes. Tamrin beads with sweat, and his breathing grows labored. The air temperature around the terrestrial cracks exacerbates our discomfort.

Ahead, Galbring beckons, a safe harbor from the dangers we know nightfall brings if we don't reach its borders in time. Surrounding the city, tall stone pillars, like sentinels, mark the point of safety. Korund priests from all clans emerge around the pillars, preparing to lock down Galbring. Ezra's light fades to dusk, and the lights about town ignite, illuminating the streets in preparation for the city's closure.

"We must hurry!" Kara-Kar yells, "Once the barrier is up, we cannot enter!"

"Ezra's tits, I'm not spending the night out here with those things!" Tamrin exclaims.

One of the Korund priests notices us and cries out an alarm.

"Hold!" the Korund calls, pointing.

Word passes along the protective perimeter of pillars, and the clusters of priests pause their ritual, audible from a few hundred yards away as we are. With one voice, they yell for us to hurry, many waving their arms in frantic encouragement. I run alongside Kara-Kar and reach for Jesma.

"You've done the hard work. I'm much faster than you'll ever be. Hand her over," I say.

Ezra disappears over the horizon. The sky turns from bright reds and yellows to the purple of dusk. From far in the darkness, a high-pitched scream carries over the desert, and my spine tingles. Return cries from multiple directions signal in response. Somewhere, not far away, a Jandu spotted us. I feel the blood drain from my face, and Kara-Kar nods.

"Okay, Harbinger, do your thing."

"Keep going!" I command Jesmir and Tamrin. They nod and sprint by.

Kara-Kar and I slow only long enough to transfer Jesma to my back. Jesma wraps her legs around my waist and her arms under my armpits. She cups my shoulders, my cloak tight in her balled fists. I wrap my hands around her thighs, less worried about her comfort than I am about her safety.

"Don't you fucking let go!" I yell.

"Don't you fucking drop me!" she returns.

My body reacts to my commands, and for the first time, I recognize the well of power as mine to command. Where it comes from, I cannot tell. The feeling of this revelation creates a strange euphoria. My body ignites like a massive furnace, endless energy that is mine to control. I break into a sprint, and the world blurs. Jesma gasps, and her legs and arms tighten around me. Ahead, Jesmir and Tamrin move much slower, and I pass them with little effort. I can't look back. They'll have to keep up the best they can for now.

The pillars approach quickly. Korund priests stand slack-jawed as I pass into the safe border of stones with my piggy-backed passenger. I stop just inside the pillars, set Jesma down, and turn to check on the others' progress.

The Korund priests scream in dismay. Two draw swords, long and curved, ready to fend off Jandu if necessary. The collective

Korund voice pushes my friends to sprint with all their might. Tamrin, the furthest back, slips further behind with every step.

More horrifying shrieks sound in the darkness, signaling the hunt is on. Jesmir and Kara-Kar cross between the pillars, both breathless. Jesma wraps her brother in a hug.

Behind Tamrin, a lone winged creature appears.

"He's not gonna make it," Jesma says, frightened.

The big guy is losing ground, and the Jandu gains on him. The distance between Tamrin and the Jandu is less than the distance between Tamrin and me. I bolt out to my friend, Korund priests crying out in dismay at my action.

"Get him, Shen!" Jesma cries out, her voice breaking.

Tamrin pumps his arms and legs as fast as he can, his face contorted in pain. He's at his limit. I feel my muscles threatening to tear again and slow my pace enough to keep myself from harm. Everything in me wants to push, but I'm of no use to Tamrin if my body can't function.

The Jandu is so close I can make out its pointed teeth. It's black eyes, matte orbs of evil, intent on Tamrin. It flies at incredible speed. I fight back the bile that rises in my throat at the sight of its entrails and spine dangling from where legs should be. Rotten flesh drips black ichor from the severed flesh as it flies. Long clawed hands reach out, so close to Tamrin I'm sure he can feel them.

Tamrin and I lock eyes. He's about to give up the chase and turn to fight.

"Roll!" I scream at the top of my lungs. But he's at a fissure and has to leap. He stumbles with the attempt and lands on the other side in a heap of fur, hair, sweat, and limbs. The expulsion of his breath is a sign he's knocked the wind out of himself with the fall. The Jandu dives, teeth ready to sink into my friend. Tamrin's face is contorted in concentration, and I know the Jandu has already begun its psionic attack. I leap over Tamrin, using his back as a step. Tamrin grunts from the force.

My curved Killinshire blades ready, I collide with the ghastly monster mid-air. Its severed spine whips forward like a tail underneath me and impacts my balls. I cry out in pain. The whipping action covers Tamrin in black blood, flung from the tip.

The Jandu's teeth strike at my face, so I wedge my blade into her maw. Her teeth clamp onto the metal, and I push the blade hard against her, hovering a few feet in the air. Her wings beat the air, and she starts to take us higher. With my other arm wrapped around her, I have little room to fight. I look down, and my stomach leaps. We're ten feet in the air already and still climbing. I grip my thighs under her arms and squeeze with all my might. One hand on the blade against her teeth, the other wrapped over her shoulder, I slice off her wing.

She screams and digs her claws into my arms, her long nails gouging my flesh. Fighting the pain, I hack at her until her right wing falls to the ground. The imbalance causes us to spiral toward the ground.

Angry, she screams again as we plummet to the hard black rock below. Aware of a missed opportunity, I rip the blade in her mouth, its curved edge severing the top of her head. The lower jaw falls slack, and I'm covered in blood. We hit the hard black rocks and tumble away from one another. My back cries out in protest.

Tamrin rises and runs to help me up.

"Get the fuck outta here," I growl. "I've got this."

He points over my shoulder.

"More."

A cry of dismay erupts from the crowd at the pillars. The Korund, unwilling to wait any longer, began their prayer.

"Okay," I say, "New plan. Run!"

Leaving the writhing Jandu to die, Tamrin and I haul ass toward the safety of the pillars.

"I could do without that experience," he says through gasping breaths.

"I had to smell her breath," I laugh, though it hurts to do so.

A few yards ahead, the twins cry out. More Jandu scream behind us. Tamrin tucks his chin and releases a terrifying growl to encourage himself for this last effort. A few feet from the pillars, we make diving leaps together and tumble just beyond the first two pillars.

The Korund prayer fades, and bright blue flashes ignite the sky around us. I turn to look at the source of the display of color. Two more Jandu crash into a barrier that wasn't there seconds before, the impact burning their flesh.

Kara-Kar extends a hand to each of us. We accept the offer, and the Korund yanks us off the ground. "I'll say this. You two make a crazy duo."

"You don't know the half of it," Tamrin says.

Jesma rushes to gather me into a tight embrace. I hold her close, and Tamrin grabs my shoulder.

"Thanks."

"No way I walk this life without you, big guy," I say.

"Remember that goes both ways, will ya?" he responds.

In that moment, I remember he still worries about me.

"Come on," Jesma says. "Let's get your wounds cared for and get you bathed."

We cross a black stone bridge over a fissure in the road and into the city proper. Orange light glows against the bridge wall. Lava flows beneath us, far below the surface of the earth. The lava flow moves in viscous waves. Dark splotches form and fade on its surface due to the interaction between cooler air and internal turbulence. I peek over the side, and a blast overheats my face. I pull back, my skin reddened temporarily.

"Surprising how much hotter it is over the edge," I comment.

"Korund scales, line the underbelly of the bridge. That is why we can walk on it," Kara-Kar replies. "Korund donate their scales in death for such use. No substance insulates from heat better than our scales."

"I've heard that sometimes these fissures overflow," Jesma says, a bit worried.

"Careful, Jez, if you look at them too long, they get mad and spew," Jesmir teases her.

"What?" she says.

I can't help it. The fear on her face causes me to laugh. She slaps my arm in response.

"What did I do?" I cry out.

"Encourage him," Jesma says.

We giggle at ourselves and step off the small bridge into the quaint Korund town.

"Jes," I call out. "Galbring has a well-known nightlife. Would I be reaching if I assumed you were very familiar with this place?" I ask.

He laughs. "You would not. I used to come here several times a year. But the nightlife is geared toward younger folk. I'm a bit aged out, I'm afraid."

"Galbring is known for more than its nightlife," Kara-Kar remarks, striking a defensive tone.

"How well do *you* know this place?" I ask.

"My Baba and I come here often since this is the home of Chati Brinker. But we head to the communal fires in the center of town. They haven't moved in ages, so I assume you know where they are," Kara-Kar says.

"*Chati* Brinker?" I say, surprised.

"Yes," Kara-Kar replies.

"That's an interesting coincidence since I head to him for new blades."

"I don't believe in coincidences," Kara-Kar replies.

"Communal fires are about a quarter mile ahead and around the bend, no?" I say, changing the subject. "I need rest and to tend these holes in my arms."

More high-pitched screams carry over the night air. Though nearby, they are dulled by the barrier that protects us. Still, Jesmir flinches.

"I forgot about the Jandu."

"You're safe in here," Tamrin replies. "That's what the pillars are for."

"What if the barrier fails?" Jesma asks.

"A slaughter. Many of us would not survive the night," Kara-Kar replies.

"Here's to Krikhi paying attention," Tamrin says and drinks from his flask.

"You really think she is?" I ask, spitting out the words without thought. Tamrin glares at me.

"Umm," I start, but Tamrin raises his hand.

"You've made your point," he says. "Let's not talk about it here."

"Let's get to the fires," Jesmir says in an attempt to diffuse the tension. "I'm chilly."

"That's fear, Your Highness," Kara-Kar says. "Not the cold." I snicker at Kara-Kar's words and realize our new companion is growing on me.

Chapter Sixteen

Journal Entry: 121

Sometimes the twins remind me of my brother and me. We were best friends, though we competed incessantly. I think about him a lot more often now. It's the presence of Jez and Jes, I know.

    I can't remember his face. It's been too many years.

    Death comes fast, time flies, and memories fade.

    No matter what Grankin says.

Pushing Boundaries

We huddle near one of twenty-five bonfires that offer respite from the desert chill. Korund and humans alike mingle through the crowd, most here for the nightlife that doesn't get going until midnight. Others are here for business or passing through like us, seeking a protected night's sleep away from the Jandu.

    The bonfires exist in the early hours before the invisible barrier can contain enough heat from the lava fissures.

"How does the dome keep heat in and allow the fumes out?" Jesma asks.

"Would that I knew myself," Kara-Kar replies. "I've never asked, but I believe it's porous. It doesn't keep the cold out so much as it slows its path, much like our scales."

A large Korund sporting long braids of deep ocean blue with scales of the clearest emeralds approaches, carrying five tankards. Jesmir ogles the Korund's breasts, which are much larger than any Korund I've ever seen. I kick him under the table, and he startles, his eyes shifting to Kara-Kar, whose breasts are significantly smaller.

Kara-Kar laughs. "We obviously don't see breasts the same as you do, your Highness."

The server stands uncomfortably close to Jesmir, and his face blushes.

"Welcome to Galbring. My name is Rilana. I shall be your host," the Korund says in a deep voice similar to Kara-Kar's. "Chieftain's Child, it is good to see you." Rilana studies the twins. "You two are from Teshket, no? Though your hair color is a bit dirty, your skin and eyes give you away."

"These are my friends," Kara-Kar says. "We are here to visit Brinker."

"You are in luck, Child of the Gal-Gohn. Your chati is scheduled to arrive tomorrow."

"Oh? I wasn't aware Chati had left," Kara-Kar says.

"Brinker traveled to Gal-Daro weeks ago to negotiate a new weapons treaty with the Royal Prince of Teshket. Word is the Teshket ship never arrived, but Brinker lingered in case the royals were delayed. Either way, your chati was due back last week but sent word of tomorrow's arrival," Rilana says.

The Korund host passes out the empty tankards, which we accept. Rilana then turns to Tamrin, his pale skin hidden under his heavy beard and long hair. Rilana raises an eyebrow.

"You are a handsome specimen," Rilana says. The Korund's eyes shimmer in the light from the bonfire. The only sign of emotion.

"Umm, thanks?" Tamrin says, his eyes wide with fear as if Rilana aimed a bow at him.

"Are you spoken for? I find I like the company of humans, especially large, handsome ones like you," our host asks.

"Umm, thank you," Tamrin stammers. "I'm afraid my heart belongs to another."

I laugh and slap Tamrin on the shoulder. "This one's mine, I'm afraid," I say.

Rilana bows to me. "Singularly?"

"For the moment, yes," I say and fight back a laugh. "He is a handsome specimen. And you," I say, "are stunning. I've never seen emeralds so pure before."

Rilana glances at Kara-Kar, and I realize what I've done.

"I meant no offense," I offer to Kara-Kar.

"I take none. Be at ease, Harbinger. It is as you say. Rilana's scales are exquisite."

"Thank you, Chieftain's Child," Rilana says and bows deeper than before. Rilana points toward a long shack behind us with the sweep of an emerald-scaled arm.

"Please enjoy some ale. Water barrels are also available on either side."

As Rilana turns to leave, shrieks fill the night. Humans scream, and the inexperienced cower in fear. High-pitched and angry, the sound carries from far out in the desert, the flat land providing little barrier to sound. Overhead, the milky streak of stars bathes the sky with color as far as the eye can see. A black shadow passes before the foam of light that splits the sky in two, wings and a strange tail that I know to be a fleshless spine. The shrieks continue, and I wonder if we'll ever find rest.

"Ah, you do not react as others," Rilana says to me.

"I have encountered the Jandu up close before today," I say.

"You aren't afraid, then?"

"I trust your priests. They've never let Galbring down," I reply.

"Krikhi's favor is indeed still upon us," Rilana responds with a bow.

"I'm not scared," Tamrin says with a crack in his voice.

"Oh, I bet you aren't," I laugh.

"The Jandu shriek, yet you may rest peacefully thanks to the dome that shields us. Some say the Jandu shriek over Krikhi's willingness to protect us. Jandu suffer from a hunger they cannot die from and cannot satiate. The longer they go unfed, the angrier they become. Fed Jandu are easier to slaughter. Hungry Jandu are a terrifying fight."

Rilana looks to the sky. "Occasionally, they fly overhead to instill fear, but they cannot get closer. Krikhi is good." Turning to look back at us, "The evening meal will be ready shortly. When the bell rings, help yourselves."

"Thank you, umm…," Jesma says.

"Rilana," the server replies.

"I am Jesma."

Rilana nods, "Pleased." With a bow toward Kara-Kar, Rilana sidles off back to help other guests. A group of Korund children blocks the path, and Rilana pushes them along with a gentle hand. The young children, scales not yet formed, jeer at our host as they run away, their rocky, coarse skin soft and glittery.

"I often wonder how Korund developed to become peaceful and friendly," Jesmir says. "Consider the raw power inherent to your race. You have unmatched talent in weapons technology. I'll never understand how such peaceful people chose to specialize in manufacturing weapons of war. It's an odd dichotomy, albeit a lucrative one."

Kara-Kar considers Jesmir's comment and takes some time to respond.

"We mastered what the land gave us the ability to master. Krikhi banded the tribes together for survival. Prior to her edicts, we warred as any people who focus on their differences rather than their similarities. It is a source of great pride in Gal-Danang that we foster harmony in our disharmony. We live in peace because she created the tribal council and the tribal elder rules of ascension."

"Do you fear what happens when the truth of the gods is revealed to the world?" Jesmir asks.

"Depends on which is more important to Gal-Danang," Jesma replies. "Freedom? Or safety?"

"Can one truly exist without the other?" Kara-Kar returns.

"I often wonder if both are a fallacy. People commit atrocities in the name of religion, safety, and freedom," I reply. I look to Jesma. "Even in the liberty-centric realm of Teshket."

Jesma furrows her brow, confused. Jesmir narrows his eyes in delicate warning.

A spicy aroma wafts over the camp. The communal food wagon rings its bell for mealtime, and the children run and scream like a pack of hyenas, ready to devour as much of the food as they are allowed. Jesma smiles at the children as they jockey for position in the food line, oblivious to the Jandu lurking in the darkness.

"Think you'll ever want children?" Jesma asks me.

The abrupt change in subject catches me off guard, and I answer without thought.

"Oh, hell no," I reply.

"You answered that fast," she replies, a scowl forming on her face.

Shit.

"I'm sorry. Knee-jerk reaction," I say. With my hand on hers, I look her in the eyes. "I've thought about it often. And I draw the same conclusion every time. I'd worry my past would catch up to me and put my family at risk. I'd become overprotective, which in turn would lead to impatience. And I have no parental role models when it comes to patience."

"You don't *know* you'd be a terrible parent," she says.

"We're about to make the targets on our backs much bigger," I reply.

Be gentle.

I pivot. "How about this? Ask me again when we get through this mess."

She nods like she understands, but I can see I've disappointed her.

"Jez, I'm sorry."

"At least you're honest," she whispers.

If only you knew how untrue that is.

"Let's grab some food," she says, changing the subject again.

The communal food line grows, and we step into the line. A ruby-scaled Korund approaches.

"Chieftain's Child, may I have a word?" the newcomer asks, eyes on Kara-Kar.

"You may," Kara-Kar replies and steps out of the line to speak in private. I've been around Korund enough to know that the discussion rapidly collapses and rides the edge of hostile by Korund standards. Kara-Kar nods, and the ruby-scaled Korund walks off and whispers in another Korund's ear. Kara-Kar returns to us.

"My apologies," Kara-Kar says. "Tribal business."

"I love Korund society," Jesmir says.

"We believe society means duty to all," Kara-Kar replies. "That necessitates equality and access. Even I am not immune to its requirements. The only difference between me and the other Korund around us is these earrings. I am required to wear them, or I wouldn't," Kara-Kar says and glances back at the ruby Korund.

"Problem?" I ask.

"No. Any Korund may approach me and place a request to the council. I am obligated to take that request to my baba, who will, in turn, take it to the Tribal Council."

"You are as obligated as we are," Jesmir says.

"Obligated? Yes, but that is where our similarities end. It is different between us and Teshket society," Kara-Kar replies. Jesmir tenses at the hostility in her words.

"Your society is about ownership. Who owns the business? Who owns the land? Who owns the labor? Teshken society consolidates power under a single ruler, accountable only to herself. Thankfully, your queen isn't as bad as the emperor. Ours is centered on community."

"I couldn't agree more," Jesmir says. "I hate how Teshken society is structured. Rhinestab comes close with their minimum wage standards, despite that, it's just another 'haves vs have-nots' arrangement."

"Yet you benefit from Teshket society, no?" Kara-Kar replies.

Jesmir's cheeks flush, and his jaw tightens.

"I was not given a choice in my birth status. Nor did I create the disparity in Teshket society. We are as trapped in it as everyone else. If I could tear it all down, I would. But I'd have to overthrow my grandmother."

"My brother continuously risks the ire of the queen in his efforts to help the less fortunate of our country," Jesma says. "Even if he takes advantage of his status with travel, and drink…among other things."

"I meant no offense," Kara-Kar replies.

"But didn't you?" Jesma demands. "You talk of Korund society, yet you question my relationship with 'a commoner' as you called him." She points at me. "Is he not worthy of me, regardless of his position in society? Let me ask you, Chieftain's Child. Are you free to marry a commoner in Korund society? Or are you required to marry another Chieftain's Child? I find your judgment of my relationship hypocritical to your supposed views."

"It seems we haven't started off very well, have we, Your Highness?" Kara-Kar says and grabs two trays from the buffet, handing one to Jesma.

"And whose fault is that?" Jesma replies, accepting the tray.

"I concede your point, Your Highness." Kara-Kar bows to Jesma with a slight nod.

I take a tray and exchange an awkward glance with Tamrin.

"As well you should," Jesma replies as she loads her tray with food.

"Damnit, that's hot."

Tamrin winces in pain as he sucks in air through his mouth and takes a big swig of ale from his mug. His cheeks are bright red from the heat. His mouth puckers, and he stares at the mug with disgust.

"Ugh," he says, "I don't remember food being so spicy in Gal-Danang. It's overwhelming."

"I hadn't noticed," I say, chewing a spicy piece of lizard tail. "The spices are strong, but not so hot I'd make a scene." I laugh at Tamrin as he takes another bite, winces, and drinks more ale and makes that disgusted face again.

"I think it's delicious," Jesma says. "But it is a bit overwhelming."

Tamrin hands me his tray.

"It's inedible," he says. He looks concerned. "It's like Fildeus granted my prayer for True Sight, but with my mouth." He downs his ale with a grimace and walks over to the alehouse for a refill.

He passes a gathering of Krikhi priests standing around a large barrel. Firelight flickers against the surface of a rolling sphere of water suspended in the air. It spins and grows until it is almost large enough for Tamrin to fit inside. The ball of water falls into the barrel, filling it to capacity.

"They make water out of thin air?" Jesma asks.

"In a sense. It never ceases to mesmerize me," Kara-Kar says.

"How do you suppose they do it?" Jesma asks, "Where does it come from?"

"I imagine it's a lot like morning dew," Tamrin replies, returning with an ale. His pallor has already returned.

"But they pray for it," Jesma replies. She looks at me. "I feel naked without my necklace. And strangely alone."

We've avoided the subject of abandoned faith long enough, it seems. Tamrin coughs and stares at his mug. Jesmir reaches across the table and grabs his sister's hand.

"Hey, it will be alright. It'll take time, but you'll figure it out."

I'm stunned by the way she glares at him. "You can't understand," she says, her voice bitter. "You never felt the presence of your god as they grant you power. You never received the internal warmth when Ezra responds and grants me the strength to help someone. You've never experienced the sense of purpose that knowledge and responsibility bring. The knowledge that one of the Great Eight has smiled on you. You don't understand how alone I feel."

Jesmir's expression turns dark. He yanks his hand from hers and rises from his seat.

"No, Jesma, I haven't. *Ever*." He turns to walk away, then steps back to her. "You're right. You were *always* special. The apple of father's eye. The one who reminded him of mother. The 'Blessed of Ezra'. No, I was *never* blessed with any of that. Not one of these gods," he waves his arms in the air and toward the priests who pray over another barrel, "not one, ever answered *my* prayers. No matter how much I wanted to believe. No matter how much I prayed, they didn't answer. A lifetime of futile effort. For what? For gods that pretend?" Spit flies from his lips. "That keeps the truth hidden? They made fools of us. Deal with it, like I have my entire life."

He looks at me and places a hand on my shoulder in solidarity. "Maybe see it from our perspective," he says.

Jesmir storms off, firing off one last comment over his shoulder. "The gods are fake. Welcome to my world, Jez."

Several faces turn our way, more than a few stunned by Jesmir's words of blasphemy.

Jesma rises to go after him, but he disappears into the darkness beyond the bonfire. She collapses back into her seat and covers her face with her hands. Her shoulders heave with silent sobs. Tamrin leans over and puts his arm around her, patting her shoulder as she weeps.

"He didn't mean to hurt you," he says. "We'll get through this together."

She falls into his furs, sobbing and nodding into his chest. This is the one area in which I'm of no use, so I go search for Jesmir.

I find Jesmir at the edge of the village, less than ten feet from one of the stone pillars that form the protective perimeter. I spot him as he throws rocks against the invisible barrier. Light blue rings spread out between the two pillars where the rocks make impact.

The rings carry upward in ripples and fade into nothingness.

"Hmm," I say, "I imagine the Korund kids have a blast with that."

He throws another rock. More rings float outward from the point of impact. He prepares for another throw, and I grab his arm. He spins and glares at me. I point out into the desert.

"Something is moving out there," I say. "See it?"

I hear footsteps behind me, heavy, deliberate.

"Jandu." The speaker's voice is deep and soft.

"Jes," I say, "I don't recommend throwing another one."

"No, you might be right," he replies, eyes on the darker shadow in the darkness.

"It can't enter," a Korund priest says, stepping from the shadows. "Nothing gets through the barrier but air. Even water and heat struggle to penetrate. You can throw your rock. All it will do is annoy the rest of us."

The ruby-covered priest stands almost eight feet tall and is covered in the translucent scales of youth.

The priest brushes one arm with the other hand, the scales flicking up and falling, a dazzling display of color even in the dim moonlight. It's a reflexive habit, like Tamrin rubbing his fur.

The priest holds out a hand. "I am Tatana, Low Priest of Galbring. How are you enjoying your stay?"

"The hospitality of Galbring has been fully satisfying," I reply.

Tatana nods, "Good to hear."

Outside the barrier, gravel shifts, the sound carrying to us. At the edge of the light, black claws dig into the ground, their shape growing more visible the closer they approach. Against the backdrop of blackness, a darker shadow grows. The claws rip at the ground, and the sinew of powerful forearms flexes and pulls the head of the Jandu into view. The Jandu twists its face toward us, its eyes black voids, dull and lifeless. It claws its way forward, sharp nails crunching on the dark rocky surface.

Tatana removes a slender rod from a holster and approaches the barrier.

"Ifa!" Tatana says with a voice like gravel. The end of the rod ignites with a soft yellow light, illuminating the approaching Jandu.

"Ugh!" Jesmir cries, "It's worse than I imagined!"

Tatana moves the light to keep the hideous monster in view. The Jandu drags itself with its arms, palms slamming onto the ground. A spray of sand and shattered rock explodes from the impacts. The dim light from the Korund wand penetrates the barrier and illuminates the monster's head. Though human-like, its facial features bear traces of a bat-like nose. Its ears point through long, wiry black hair. Straight, sharp teeth glint in the light, black liquid dripping from their tips. The tongue hangs from its mouth, so long that it almost touches the ground. It only has one wing, the other missing. I recognize this monster from before.

Jesmir grimaces and turns his head. I stare at the Jandu and pull my knife, still stained with its blood. The tongue pulls back into its mouth, and the Jandu screams. It draws close enough that the light from Tatana's rod glistens off the leathery skin of its one wing. The wing flaps, but doesn't lift the Jandu from the ground. Its naked breasts drag on the ground.

Jesmir gags as the Jandu turns and stalks the perimeter. Its lower body ripped away at the ribcage, the creature drags its intestines and rotted flesh behind. The base of its exposed spine protrudes like some grotesque tail.

"Why not come out and play?" the Jandu says, her voice like sand against my skin. "Release the barrier. We only want to talk."

Tatana says, "She can't hear us. The barrier absorbs our sound. But not hers. She can see us, however. And her psionic ability can penetrate only partially, but it can penetrate."

I feel pressure in my head as she speaks. There's the suggestion of a desire to obey. I take a step forward, and she turns to me.

"Yes, you. You are pretty. What is your name?"

"Don't answer," Tatana says. "She'll only use it to pressure you more."

I take another step toward her. The vile thing smiles, her teeth sharp yet pretty.

Such pretty teeth.

I want to reach out and touch them. I'm only slightly aware of Jesmir beside me.

"Yes, you," she says to Jesmir, her focus on him. "You can ask them to let down the barrier. Let's be friends."

"Duka!" Tatana says. Darkness returns the creature to the shadows beyond the barrier once more. Only the night sky and dim light from the pillar illuminate the Jandu. Tatana steps between us and the monster, drawing our attention.

"That is why we do not allow you to pass the barrier," Tatana says.

We both blink, and the brain fog clears.

"You felt it? The pressure to obey?" the priest asks.

"I did," I say. "I knew I shouldn't, but I also *wanted* to, needed to obey. I could resist it, though. I had no intention of stepping through the barrier."

"You couldn't if you wanted to. If you try to pass through the barrier, it will simply shock you and push you back. You could resist her because we improved the barrier. This latest iteration of the magic allows us to block some of the psychic pressure. Someday we hope to block it all." Tatana taps the rod on the barrier, causing the blue rings to ignite, and the creature shrieks, disturbed by the light. "The barrier reduces their powerful mind pull and prevents anyone or anything from passing. From the outside, the rings appear as bright as the sun. The Jandu hate the sun."

"No one can stop the barrier. It requires sunlight to dissipate," Tatana adds. "How about you two stay away from the village boundary?"

"I think that's a wonderful idea," I say.

"Yeah," Jesmir says, "me too."

We leave the priest and return to where Jesma and Tamrin are in deep conversation with Kara-Kar.

Just after the sun breaks the eastern horizon, we make our way to the breakfast line. Jesma and Jesmir still haven't spoken, and the tension between them makes me want to punch someone, and it isn't Jesma. Throughout the morning meal, she casts hopeful glances his way, but he ignores her and chooses instead to busy himself with maintenance on his crossbow, short bow, and arrows. Tamrin partakes of the meal after a quick discussion with the cook. His food looks bland, but at least he can eat.

He throws up his hands midway through the meal.

"Now I can't taste anything. What the hell is going on? It's as if Fildeus punishes me." He reaches for his beard only to realize he cut the periapt off a day ago.

"Bah!" he exclaims and storms over to get spices on his food. He returns, takes a seat, puts one bite in his mouth, and spits it out.

"Now what?" I ask.

"It's too spicy!" he cries.

"Why did you spice it, then?" Jesmir asks.

"Because it was bland before," he snarls.

He sulks while I finish my food.

"You humans are a temperamental lot," Kara-Kar says.

I look at Kara-Kar and wag my finger. "I'm looking for a fight today. So best not push it."

Kara-Kar finishes eating, rises, and bows.

"I think, for the sake of everyone's sanity, we should head out," Kara-Kar says.

Tamrin rises and grabs his gear. "Better than sitting around while Shen stuffs his face."

I grab a spicy pastry with pepper jelly and some sort of cheese and pop it in my mouth.

"Delicious," I say and lick my finger.

"Dick," Tamrin grumbles.

"That wasn't very nice," Jesma whispers.

"Everyone's on my nerves today," I say. "Don't add your name to the list."

She scowls at me, lifts her head high, and follows Tamrin.

Brinker's smithy shop is close by. We arrived in Galbring mid-month, the heaviest traffic time for Galbring's nightlife and tourism. Last night's revelry lasted well into the morning, but somehow folks bounced back as if none of them partook.

"Think you can refrain from breaking your weapons this time?" Jesmir says.

I shake my head, sufficiently chagrined. "You're a dick," I say.

He laughs heartily at that. Somehow, his joke eased my tension.

"Hey, Jes," I say to the prince with a hand on his arm. "Remember when you called me dense back in the Valley of Cusk?" I say.

"Yeah, you were," he replies.

"Well, don't make the same mistake."

"Huh?"

"Jesma's hurting…and lost. You are the only remaining constant in the life she's known. You know things she's yet to discover. Don't take the one safety net she has away from her."

He looks ahead at his sister. She walks alone, halfway between us and Tamrin, who is busy ogling the items for sale throughout the market of Galbring. Jesmir shakes his head.

"She didn't consider *my* feelings," he says.

"Any more than you did hers," I respond. "And her offense was unintentional. You took a strike at her weakest spot."

He stops and glares at me. "That's just it. It's always unintentional when your feelings are *never* considered. I'd rather she'd been intentional. Then at least I'd know she considered my suffering. Not dismissed it as unimportant or irrelevant."

His point is valid, and I consider it for a moment. "That is something I can understand. But she's lost everything now, too. Don't let another day go by without fixing it."

I give him a poke on the shoulder and wink before I rush to walk with Jesma.

We wonder at the intricate carvings of Krikhi's sigil, a volcano spewing magma at an anvil, that decorate the smithy structures. Every Korund in sight openly wears periapts—metal forgings of the symbol of Krikhi.

I used to think the Korund were a superstitious lot. Last night proved they have a good reason for their devout loyalty to Krikhi. It's a direct reflection of perceived protection. Even though it's based on a lie, I hide my disdain when in Gal-Danang. The gentle and friendly Korund may be slow to anger, but they never forget an offense.

Besides, I love their weapons too much to lose their friendship or get debarred. Activating my bracers, the remnants of the broken blades slide out. I frown.

"I'll offer to work it off," I mumble to myself.

"Sell the sword and all those knives," Jesma says. "I like you better when you fight with *your* blades."

I point to her. "That's a marvelous idea."

Chapter Seventeen

Journal Entry: 125

The distance between my old life and now is greater than the five weeks that divide the two. I'm in a constant state of vertigo. There have been too many changes for my comfort.

I don't fully trust Kara-Kar. It's too convenient how the Korund appeared in our lives. Kara-Kar hasn't been completely forthright with us. I'm sure of it.

Oh hell. What am I saying?

I don't trust Kara-Kar?

That's not true. I don't trust myself.

I Can't Believe It's Not Under

Brinker's shop is located on the same street as Korusite Furnace, famous as much for the Korund who work the furnace as for its product. Fueled by the lava river that fills the Galdinian Fault Line, Galbring is the primary melt source for Gal-Danang steels.

"I'm always amazed by this place," I say to Jesmir.

"Why is that?" he asks.

I point to the large black rock furnace that stands eighty feet tall and twenty feet square at its base. The lava-forged rocks that comprise the furnace's structure are blackened with age, soot, and iron. A massive plume of smoke rises from the center. Its large opening spews waves of heat through a bright orange-white glow.

"Korusite Furnace," I say. "Best metals in Conishant come from there."

"Korusite is the single largest supplier of all raw-block metal in Gal-Danang," Kara-Kar offers.

We stand in awe as the largest members of the Korund race fill crucibles suspended from chains with carefully measured chunks of ore. Four massive Korund, covered in thick sapphire scales, work the mechanisms close to the furnace. They pull and push the crucibles through the white flames.

"Only those with sapphire scales can work the furnace," I say to Jesma. "The Sapphire Korund scales are thicker than the rest of Korund society. That increases their tolerance to the furnace flames. It's a source of pride for the tribe."

I lean into Kara-Kar. "That's what I've been told anyway."

"You are well informed," Kara-Kar replies. "While all Korund scales offer great protection from the heat of Gal-Danang's fissures, sapphire is the better insulator. These Korund have the right combination of scales and size to handle the crucibles. The two you see here are Dovar and Latima, the most well-known Korund in all of Gal-Danang."

Jesma's eyes widen with wonder. Two master smelters on the extraction side step almost into the opening of the furnace. With heavy metal hooks, they pull out a crucible and pour its brightly molten contents into a large mold.

"It's amazing," Jesma says as the two similarly sized and scaled Korund on the other side quickly load the next crucible into the furnace.

Jesmir points to the recently filled mold and leans forward, addressing his sister.

"Watch this," Jesmir says.

Two shorter, thickly built Korund covered in diamonds slide a metal rod into rings on the mold's end closest to the furnace. They cry out with pride and drive the mold to the end of a set of tracks. The mold flips over at the end of the tracks and drops the large slat of glowing hot metal onto a set of rollers. They send the empty mold back in time for the next crucible while two more diamond-scaled Korund hurriedly push the glowing block through the opening of a dark stone building that stretches hundreds of feet along the street.

"That's it," Kara-Kar says, pointing to the furthest end of the building. "When it comes out over there, that block will somehow be in strips for making swords, or ship moldings, or plates for shields. Within that building, the raw block is reshaped into all kinds of raw stock. Only Chieftains and those who work the foundry are allowed."

"Reminds me of the waterworks at Winding Run," Tamrin says.

"No wonder Gal-Danang is so wealthy," Jesma quips.

"All right," I say, "enough tourism. Let's get to the smithy. I have an itch only new blades can scratch."

We cross to Brinker's shop. A wave of heat welcomes us, and Tamrin breaks into immediate sweat. Jesma blinks against the heat, and Jesmir huffs.

"Oh, it's too hot in here for me," Jesmir says. "I'm going to wait outside."

Jesma says nothing and stands beside me.

A young Korund apprentice by the name of Hadri welcomes us. I hand over Brogen's sword and the two Killinshire knives.

"I want to sell these for new blades."

Hadri inspects the blades with deft fingers. With a flick of the wrist, Hadri tosses the sword on its end and catches the blade to admire the hand-carved ruby shaped like the head of a snake embedded in the pommel.

"This is a Pathen," the apprentice smith says. "I see why you'd want to get rid of it."

"Besides my disdain for swords?" I reply. "It's too heavy. I prefer lighter, more flexible edges. And I'm a Brinker loyalist."

Hadri nods. "It is a bit much for your stature anyway." Hadri turns to Tamrin. "A bit too small for yours. A mid-sized weapon for you is as good as a book in the rain."

Tamrin snorts a laugh and points to his hammer. "I prefer blunt force, anyway," he smiles.

I point over the young Korund's shoulder to a Korund making a racket with a heavy hammer and a hot piece of metal. "Let your baba know I'm here," I say. In my hand, I hold five Rhinestab gold coins. I extend them out.

"Baba's not going to be happy you possess a Pathen," Hadri says.

"Wait till I explain why," I reply.

Hadri sets the sword on the counter and heads to the rear of the smithy shop, where a large ruby-scaled Korund brings the hammer onto a glowing workpiece. Sparks fly with each strike. Hadri leans in and speaks into the larger Korund's ear, who then delivers a final blow on the hot metal before dousing it in oil. The muscular Korund gives the younger smithy instructions, points to the metal in the oil, and passes over the hammer. Hadri nods and immediately gets to work on the piece while the larger one turns and glances at me with a raised eyebrow.

"I wondered when I'd see you again. Shen-sana," Brinker says and walks over to the counter. Eyeing Tamrin, the smithy offers a hand and says, "Tam-sana, I'd have thought you found better places to be than still consorting with this scoundrel." Tamrin snickers at the in-sult.

"Funny, I didn't know Korund had a sense of humor," I say. "Allow me to introduce our friend, Jesma."

"Your Highness," Brinker looks surprised. "I expected you in Gal-Daro. Where are your father and brother?"

"Umm…," she starts, but her eyes well with tears. Brinker rounds the counter and grips both of Jesma's shoulders with a tender caress. "Not here. It's clear something has happened. Let us talk else-where."

Jesma nods her head and chokes back tears. Brinker lingers a moment before turning to me.

"When did your association with Teshket royals begin?" Brinker asks. "And a Chieftain's Child? You've either moved up in the world, Shen-sana, or the world has fallen into the nine hells," Brinker says.

"Can't it be both?" I reply.

"That it can. Good for you, bad for the rest of us, then. What can I do for you?"

"I'm in need of new blades," I say, and lay my bracers on the counter next to the sword.

Brinker takes one, activates it, and plops it on the counter in disdain.

"How in Krikhi's name did you manage this?" Brinker asks, astounded. "These were some of my best works." The smithy sets the bracer on the counter and leans forward. Massive muscles bulge, and the Korund's scales ripple in response with a wave of reflected light.

I point to Brogen's sword. "That. The man who carried it used it to break my blades."

Brinker squints at me. "And what? Handed you his sword as contrition?"

"No. I took it from his dead body."

Brinker places a finger on the sword. "*This* sword broke *my* blades, and you killed the man wielding it for the crime? With what? Your bare hands?"

"You're partly right. I took the sword," I reply.

"Then who killed him?"

I point out the door at Jesmir. He's too distracted by the Korund at the Korusite Furnace to pay attention to us.

"Prince Jesmir? That Playboy killed the man who bested you? That's a tale I'd love to hear," Brinker says.

Brinker studies the two braces and the sword.

"It's a bit of an embarrassment that my blades broke at the hands of a Pathen. That one's skills have improved over the years, but not that much. There's more to this story. Still, I can't have word getting out that Pathen's blades are better than mine. The strongest blade is weaker than the reputation behind it."

"This blade isn't better," I say, almost defensively. "My opponent was. Mine were lodged in place at the moment of impact."

"Both of them?" Brinker says, incredulous.

"Both," I say.

"You were outfought by the wielder of this sword, and that wielder was killed by the prince?" Brinker points at Jesmir. "Shensana, you are either getting too old or you've finally located better fighters than you."

Jesmir enters the smithy shop and says, "It was a lucky shot."

"There is none luckier than those who think they are," Brinker says. "Shamna smiles on those who attribute their skill to her grace."

Nobody acknowledges Brinker's comment. The blacksmith taps the counter and says, "Give me till tomorrow. I will melt the sword to make your blades. The metal is good. As for payment, I'll take the pommel and mount it over my work table as a motivational factor. Adversity is the greatest teacher. So, pommel for the work…and you buy the ale tonight while you tell me the story of how this all happened." Brinker waves a hand in a circle around the entire group.

I stick out my hand. "Deal."

"Now get out of my shop so that I may work."

Jesma places a hand on my shoulder. "I would like a sword."

Brinker eyes Jesma, inspecting her. "Yes, you should. Especially traveling with these two." Brinker nods at Tamrin and me. "I think a rapier is the best choice for you. Can you use one?"

"I can, actually. It is my best weapon."

"Good. Let me see your hands," Brinker commands.

She places her hands in Brinker's, who inspects them. "Are you left-handed or right-handed?"

"I'm actually ambidextrous."

"Well, that's good. Place your hands against mine, heal to heal."

Jesma does. Jesma's fingers come to Brinker's first joint.

"Okay. Yours will be ready tomorrow morning as well."

"Now, meet me at my home at sundown. We will go to the visitor's tavern. There we will drink, and you will regale me with wild stories of how you all came to travel together."

Like most Korund homes, Brinker's is a single wall with a slanted roof and two posts. The stone wall holds a series of shelves, some tools for cooking, and a couple of minor smithing tools. Outside, in the open air, rests a stone with a small anvil and a small furnace. Two stone pillars support the front of the roof.

On the shelves sit a handful of bowls, a couple of tankards, and wood carvings of Brinker's spouse, Romori, and his child, Hadri.

Brinker's zatia of twenty-five years died in a tragic accident at Koru-site Furnace. Romori was one of the strongest sapphire Korund in Galbring. The couple had only one child before Romori's passing. I never knew Brinker's zatia. I would have liked to.

"Well met, friends," Brinker says as we approach. "Come, no sense in sitting around here. Let's head to the tavern."

As with all Korund towns, "buying your friend an ale" is a euphemism for what really happens—shared communal ale.

We arrive at the alehouse, which is really five small buildings that face a central courtyard. Each specializes in drinks from one realm. All five realms are represented in the alehouse. Octagonal communal tables fill the space between the taverns. More than half the tables are occupied by the time we arrive.

"Wow," Jesma says, "there are people from all over Conishant here."

"Always is," Jesmir says as he picks a table.

"The Tribal Council continues to woo dignitaries to buy weapons or ships from us. Or some of our other, more obscure exports. There's a lot of innovation going on in the world. Most come to witness our foundry operations," Brinker says. "Nothing inspires open purses like open demonstrations."

"You have a saying for everything," Jesma says with a gleam in her eye.

"A spoken word is like a caged bird. Once released, it won't return. Words without purpose are noise to the spirit. But that doesn't mean we can't use them well."

Brinker waves a young Korund server over—the server's scales lack the rigidity of adult Korund, indicating this one is a teenager.

"This is Tendar," Brinker says. "Please bring my friends and me some ale." The entire group orders from the Haabrestand house on Tamrin's insistence.

"It's unlike anything here," Tamrin says. "I've tried all their options over the years. This latest batch is the best."

We humor him. Tendar runs off to fulfill the order.

"Tell me the tale of how you are in one another's company."

Jesma relays the events of the last several weeks, starting with their departure from their home island of Pal. She breaks into tears when she reaches the death of her father at Brogen's hand. Brinker listens, in Korund fashion, with little reaction. I tell the story of the Cuska, the fight with Brogen, and the subsequent battle with Krin.

Brinker's eyes move about the party, while Kara-Kar finishes the story of how we ran into each other in Rhinestab. Kara-Kar leaves out the details of trailing us—an omission I find interesting. We offer no context for the *why's* and Brinker doesn't ask. Unwilling to interject into other people's ongoing business.

"Well, that is a tale. It seems the birds flew overhead, but the excrement landed clear. That is something."

We drink another round before the food bell rings. Tendar brings over a large bowl filled with some sort of rice dish and sets it in the center of the table. I salivate at the steamy dish. Tendar returns a few moments later with a covered stone container, five plates, and another bowl filled with a white sauce.

"Galina," Tendar says. "Have you ever had it?"

I shake my head along with the others.

"Ah, you are in for a delight," Tendar says and opens the stone container to hold it out to each of us. The server demonstrates by removing a piece of the flat, puffy bread and setting it on a plate. Tendar loads the rice mixture and the sauce next to the bread. Kara-Kar helps, and together the two Korund build plates for the rest of us. Tendar rips a piece of the puffy bread and uses it to pick up rice, swiping it through the sauce. With a glance at Tamrin, Tendar holds it in front of the big guy's mouth.

Tamrin takes a tentative bite and winces. Displeased, he drains his fourth mug of ale.

"Are you okay, Tam-sana?" Brinker asks, concerned.

Tamrin looks at me, uncertain.

Brinker, embarrassed, waves Tendar over.

"Please bring my large friend here a plate of unseasoned rice and more ale."

"It will be done," Tendar says and heads back to the food hall.

Brinker returns to the previous conversation. "Is it a safe assumption that you need to be on the move quickly?"

"It is," I reply. "Sooner the better."

Brinker turns to Kara-Kar. "And is this related to your recent activities, Chuto?"

"Yes, Chati," Kara-Kar replies.

"Then it appears I must get back to the forge. You need blades sooner rather than later." Brinker stands. "Come by before Ezra unlocks the barrier. I regret the brief visit, but circumstances have a way of making good on long-owed debts."

I nod, "We'll be there."

"Hmm," is Brinker's reply.

"Long-owed debts?" Jesma asks as Brinker leaves.

"I did a thing for him many years ago," I reply.

Jesmir raises an eyebrow in curiosity.

"Not *that* kind of thing," I say. "He wanted a special ore that only comes from the southern tip of Killinshire, and he needed it in a hurry. I made it there and back in six days without violence."

"You made a run from Galbring to Arelo in six days?" Kara-Kar asks.

"No," I reply.

"I was about to say, that is impressive," Kara-Kar replies. The Korund pauses and eyes me with suspicion, then asks, "Mind if I ask where you started from?"

"I thought you'd never ask. That was back before his armory was in Galbring."

"But his original shop was in Gal-Daro!" Kara exclaims.

"I'm wicked fast," I say with a smirk.

"Morze's bosom, these blades are absolutely gorgeous," I exclaim in a quiet tone.

The watered steel is covered with intricate waves, the sharp edges bright and clear.

"I modified your bracers with a new feature that will certainly come in handy." Brinker demonstrates with a flick of a thumb and a wrist twist that I mimic. The blade separates from the bracer and falls to the counter. "Easy blade detachment. If you ever find yourself lodged again, activate the release, and you can pull away. Then the metal can flex properly." Brinker winks, "Although it's better to not get lodged at all."

I snicker while I practice releasing both blades a few times. It takes only a few seconds longer to reinstall them. I laugh and give

Brinker a hug, which the giant Korund ignores and does not reciprocate.

"The alloy is a bit better, too," Brinker says with understated pride. "I added something to them to make them a bit less brittle, but they still maintain their strength. The edge will hold longer as a result. But it will take more work to sharpen."

"Master Brinker, you have done an amazing thing. I can't thank you enough," I say. "These improvements…I'm speechless."

"Would that it were true? It was nothing, really. After the firing of the blade, even Hadri could see how it could have been prevented."

Brinker lays a rolled leather case on the counter, unties the leather bindings, and rolls it out, revealing a set of six new throwing knives, identical in design to my previous ones, except with the same watered steel as my new bracer blades. The smithy swipes a hand over the collection.

"These are identical to what you had in all forms, but in appearance. You will not notice a difference when you throw them. But the edges will stay true longer."

"Six?" I say. "I only had four."

Brinker nods at Jesma. "Teach her to throw. Two are for her."

I pick up a knife and flip it in my hand. It's perfect. A familiar friend, long lost, has returned. Motion to my right catches my eye. Hadri approaches with a rapier in a sheath, accompanied by a beautifully crafted belt. "This is for you, Lady Jesma."

Jesma accepts it graciously. "Thank you." She pulls it from the sheath and spins on her toes, facing away from us. With the blade forward, she poses and pulls the thin metal to her face, inspecting the blade. The tip wiggles slightly from her motion, its springy flex visible. She takes a few practice swipes at the air and flicks the blade in well-practiced patterns. Tamrin raises an eyebrow, and we look at each other in stunned silence. She turns back to Brinker.

"This is wonderful. It's the most perfect blade I've ever held," she says with a big smile.

"I used what remained of the metal from that sword and added some material for flexibility. It will not break. Use it well."

Brinker turns back to me. "I hope that you are satisfied with the work. Now there is another matter." He points at Tamrin. "I haven't said anything till now, Tam-sana. But your beard is lighter than the last time I saw you. I thought little of it at first."

Tamrin stands tall. "I do not wish to offend you, so I will keep quiet."

Brinker nods, "Silence is the wall behind which wisdom hides. But as you travel with my chuto, the absence of certain adornments is now oddly conspicuous. And by your current discomfort, my assumption seems valid. While I disagree with Kara-Kar, I do not judge. But I want to be clear. Before you take irrevocable actions, take heed. The world will never be perfect. But some situations are far better than the alternatives."

"I am not sure what you mean," I reply.

"Safe journey. Be wise in deeds, not just words," Brinker says and walks away without further explanation.

Brinker slips out the back door of the shop. The silence becomes conspicuous. Tamrin fidgets behind me.

"Must everyone speak in riddles? What the hell was that?" I say.

Kara-Kar lays an open hand, palm up, on the counter. Emblazoned underneath the emerald scales is a mark similar to the one Grankin placed on me.

"Is that what I think it is?" I demand.

"I should have told you sooner," the Korund says.

"You knew about Grankin the whole time?" Jesmir hisses under his breath.

"Grankin pointed me to your trail," Kara-Kar replies. "I'm sorry I lied to you. It was a necessary ruse, one that goes against all we Korund believe. But I needed to be sure the royals weren't a trap. I've sacrificed much to find you, Harbinger. There is someone you should meet, and time is of the essence. If you'll follow me, there are things you must see, and we must be in position when the barrier ends if we are going to get where we need to in time."

"Where are we going?" I ask suspiciously.

"To see the others. They're anxious to meet you."

A stunned silence spreads over the group.

"Others?" Jesmir says, his voice quiet.

Kara-Kar smirks. It's unsettling.

"The Underground."

Chapter Eighteen

Journal Entry: 131

My blades are back! A part of me was missing. Don't judge me, but I value these blades more than my cock. They've done more for me than that thing ever did.

Well, until Jesma.

Still, I'm happy to feel like me again!

It's only a matter of time before a fight finds us, and I like my hands free to grapple in a fight. My blades are my security blanket. Little metal slivers of anger that I can project onto my enemies.

Besides, Krin is bound to show up, and I need to be at my best. She always finds me.

I wish I knew how...

Jandu Ja-boogey

Leaving Galbring, I make sure we stop by the supply depot and grab enough coffee for a few days. I forget the communal nature of Gal-

Danang when I'm not here. It's hard to hide my smile when I grab three pounds of the caffeinated nectar.

"No sexual favors for coffee, then?" Tamrin quips.

"Not for a while. And it's Gal-Danang coffee, dark as my heart and twice as bitter," I reply.

"Well, don't expect to be hoarding that all to yourself," Jesma says.

"I can think of a way you can earn some," I reply.

"Sorry, whoring yourself out for coffee is your thing. Tamrin warned me. Now, change your attitude, or what's in those bags won't be the only beans that get ground to dust," Jesma replies and skips ahead to talk with Kara-Kar.

"Have you ever thought about how much has changed since we met?" Jesmir asks from behind me.

"You mean like Shen being put in his place all the time?" Tamrin says with a laugh.

"There's that," Jesmir says, smiling.

"You've certainly changed," I say. "Do you miss the simpler life of leisure?"

He snorts, "Simpler? Far from it." He looks toward the sky. "In many ways, this is easier. I know what is expected of me with you guys. I never felt comfortable in my own skin until you and Tam."

"That surprises me," I say. "I thought all that privilege and wealth would be much easier."

"Oh, that part for sure is easier. Don't get me wrong, I miss a soft bed with bamboo sheets and clean clothes. But my life wasn't my own. It's all 'go here' and 'do this' and 'wear this' and 'meet these people' or 'marry this person'. Every moment is planned and controlled. No self-reliance allowed. It's why I snuck out."

He pulls out a small purse and jingles it. "You know that until we escaped Brogen, I never carried my own money? Every expenditure was controlled, measured, and scrutinized. Not for accounting purposes either. It was all measured on whether it was an appropriate purchase for 'a person of my title'. That's why I got hooked up with Savis. He made it easy for me to not need money."

He puts the purse back in his pocket.

"I hadn't thought of it like that," I said. "As someone who never had much, I assumed you were all much happier."

"I thought I was happy. But these last few weeks, while they've been the scariest of my life, they've been the best." He waves his hand at his bandaged ear. "Even with this, I feel alive, like I'm part of the world, not above it. I'm no longer an outsider watching from the window. And I've never had a true friend before."

He falls silent.

"Now you have two," Tamrin replies.

"Right," Jesmir says, smiling.

"I should say the same, ya know? My life is better for having you two in it, Jes," I add.

He punches my arm, and I laugh. "You just like sticking it to my sister."

"I'd like to stick it to your grandmother," I whisper and extend my blade. He turns pensive. "Sorry, Jes. I shouldn't have said that."

"No," he says as he taps the back of his head. "It's here. We didn't actually say it. But if she's who we think she is, there's no chance she's not the reason we are in this mess."

"What are you guys talking about?" Jesma asks as she falls back to eavesdrop on us.

Jesmir and I exchange glances, and I say, "Sticking it to you."

"Eww. Pigs," she says with a sour look.

Jesmir points to Kara-Kar, who is still several yards ahead of us. Tamrin pats my shoulder and hurries to catch our Korund escort.

"What do you think of that one?" Jesmir asks.

"I've never traveled with a Korund. Outside of my dealings with them in Gal-Danang, I've rarely encountered one. Then again, I lived in solitude for nearly thirty-five years."

"No, I mean, do you think Kara-Kar likes me?" he asks.

I laugh. "I'd pay to watch that!"

"Pervert," Jesma says.

The desert sands beneath our feet lighten as dark volcanic grains show signs of lighter silica-based sands mixing in. The transition from the volcanic region of Gal-Danang into the nomadic one signals that the terrain is about to change.

"Where do you think we're headed?" Jesma asks.

"I don't know," I reply. "But I trust Grankin, and that's saying something. By proxy, I guess we should trust anyone he trusts." I pause. "For now."

"Tam seems to like her," Jesma says.

The two larger members of our party walk together. Tamrin's voice carries back to us. He hasn't shut up for over an hour. Kara-Kar offers the new audience he needs for his embellished stories.

"Not as much as your brother, apparently," I jest.

"I'm not sure Kara-Kar's said a word," Jesma says. "Should we rescue Tamrin from himself?"

"Probably be a good idea," I say. "Let's catch up."

We hurry our pace and fall in step right behind the much taller pair.

"…and that's when I took hold of its tail and swung it around, smashing it against the guy's skull. He didn't call me an ape again after that."

"Are you telling the *tall 'tail' tale* again?" Jesma asks.

"Well, Kara-Kar's never heard it," Tamrin replies.

"Are you sure about that?" Jesma teases.

"Yes, I'm sure!"

Jesma says, "He will likely tell you that story again in about twenty minutes."

Kara-Kar replies, "Only true friends will tell you your face is dirty."

"Huh?" Jesma asks.

"One of my chati's proverbs. You speak honestly with one another. It is good to know. It means I can speak honestly."

Not sure what to say next, we fall silent. The desert transitions to the light sand and rocky plains. Sparse signs of desert foliage break up the landscape from the black rock and ash of the last several miles.

Kara-Kar points to a group of multi-colored tents. Several Korund wander about less than a quarter mile away.

"That is our destination," Kara-Kar says. "We will get food and take a rest."

"Which tribe is that?" Jesma asks.

"The Kalabali," Kara-Kar says. "Nomads. This is the Danadia Clan. The fiercest clan."

"I didn't know there were still nomadic tribes in Gal-Danang," Jesmir says.

"There are very few left. Most tribes surrendered the nomadic life, preferring settlements where commerce can thrive. Then the Jandu showed up. The Kalabali are the only Korund fighters in all

Gal-Danang. Warriors in the truest sense. They returned to the wilderness for the sake of the rest of us."

"Hold up," I say. "Fighters?"

"In every possible sense of the word," Kara-Kar says. "It was a difficult decision for the tribe. Only a very select few can join this clan. They are chosen from the Kalabali, those of the Jade Scales. And only after a rigorous test of their temperament are they selected for the physical tests. No lava-brains are allowed. Once selected, they must prove their courage and skill."

"Lava-brain?" Jesma asks.

"Hot-heads," I say.

"I didn't know there were hot-heads in Korund society," she says.

"Oh, there are. Chati Brinker is one. Bad temper that one," Kara-Kar says. "Chati is very angry at me for leaving the church. Didn't you notice this morning?"

"I can't imagine the scene if Brinker were happy," Jesma says sarcastically.

"Oh, it's quite the scandal," Kara-Kar says, missing the sarcasm. "Let's head up. They will have already spotted us and will be sending a scout to intercept."

Hefting a large shoulder pack, Kara-Kar sidles down the sand dune toward the Korund camp.

"Brinker was angry?" Jesma asks.

"Oh, very," I reply, in jest. "Enraged."

Tamrin taps my arm and points ahead of Kara-Kar. A large white Korund approaches from the camp. The Korund's stride is deliberate and powerful, proud. Two large swords, like Kara-Kar's, cross at the lighter scaled Korund's waist. The size of either sword would make them two-handed weapons for me, but in Korund's hands, they are barely even swords. The scout comes to a stop fifty feet ahead of us and waits.

We close the gap, and I realize the color of the Korund's scales are a mild green.

Just as Kara-Kar said—jade.

They appear dull and non-reflective, unlike Kara-Kar's. Covered in scratches and chips, I suspect this Korund has seen many battles.

"I have never seen Korund with such coloring," I say.

"Me neither," Jesmir replies.

Kara-Kar and the jade-scaled Korund stop within arm's length of one another. They stand motionless, like stone statues, facing each other. Kara-Kar raises a hand to the other's cheek and holds it there. It's a tender caress.

Tamrin and I exchange surprised glances, and we approach the pair.

"Kar," Kara-Kar says, "has it been so long? You look tired."

Kar places a hand on Kara-Kar's cheek, their arms pressed against each other.

"Kara, I have missed you," the jade Korund whispers. "Come, Zatia, tell me why you have brought strangers to my clan."

"Zatia?" Jesma asks.

"Korund, word for *spouse*," I whisper.

"Kara-Kar is married?" Jesma says.

"Yes, Your Highness, I am married. Hence, my name is Kara-Kar. This is my zatia Kar-Kara."

"Korund take each other's name and add it to their own," I say. "I should have known."

"Now that the pleasantries are out of the way, answer my question, Kara."

"I take them to Gal-So," Kara-Kar says. "To meet *her*."

"Well," the jade Korund replies, "Let's leave it at that. The Chief must be informed."

They drop their hands, and both turn to face us. "I am Kar-Kara, zatia of Kara-Kar. Welcome. We need to visit the Chief before we can get you settled."

"You have the same name?" Jesma asks, her brow furrowed in deep wrinkles.

"I am Kara," Kara-Kar says. "This is Kar. If it makes things easier, you may call me Kara."

"That doesn't lead to confusion at all," Jesmir mumbles under his breath.

"I don't see why it would," Kar-Kara says. "But if it helps, call me Kar."

"Well met, Kar," I say to the jade Korund.

"Well met," Kar replies. "Let's move. We can use an extra set of hands to finish setting the perimeter."

Kar leads the way into the campsite. Twelve large tents, evenly spaced in perfect rows, outline a central square, their openings facing east. Over fifty Korund are busy securing lines and pulling tall tents taut. Each tent bears the Krikhi's emblem, the iron anvil hovering over an erupting volcano. A trio working together at the corner tent stops to observe us, one with a raised brow.

Kar leads us to the back of the camp, where others work together to set up a food wagon surrounded by small folding chairs in a large clearing in the center of the camp. Toward the rear of the grid of tents, four smaller wagons with five camels rest in the sand. The Korund camels each sport a single hump and are coated in jade scales as well.

Kar pauses at the entrance to the rearmost tent and emits three clicks of the tongue. The sound is replicated from inside, and Kar steps into the tent, motioning us to follow. Four lanterns on stakes illuminate the interior. Sparsely furnished, the tent contains a cot, a table, and a folding chair. Two more jade Korund stand at the table, bent over a stack of maps. One wears an odd gauntlet on one hand. The other carries two swords, like Kar and Kara. The two new Korund stare at us, expectant.

Kar bows. Kara does not.

"Chief," Kar begins, "I have travelers in need of shelter for the night."

The Chief exchanges glances with the other Korund, then points to a spot on one of the maps. The other nods and leaves the tent, eyeing us on the way out.

The Chief waits until the flap of the tent falls before acknowledging us.

"Chieftain's Child? I assume you have an explanation for why you traveled all this way and brought outsiders to my camp?"

"Chief, we travel southwest to Gal-So. We will not make it before nightfall."

"No, I'd dare say you wouldn't make it at all. You are many days' ride from Gal-So. You have horses, I assume?" the chief asks.

"We do not," Kara replies.

"Many days indeed," the chief replies.

"We request shelter and an escort from you or help arranging for us to meet with other clans along our journey in order to get through the Jandu-infested lands," Kara says.

The chief eyes us. "Why do you travel with outsiders?"

Kara steps forward. "Chief, these are trusted friends of my chati. I would not impose on you, otherwise. They are the reason we head to Gal-So."

Something about how Kara repeats Gal-So piques my interest. The chief circles the table and leans against it, facing us. I can't tell whether it's out of anger or curiosity. I risk the offense and approach.

"Chief, my friends and I…"

The chief interrupts me with a raised hand. I flinch in surprise at my ready compliance.

"Well, that's never happened before," Tamrin says under his breath as if he read my mind.

Jesmir giggles, which draws a look from the chief.

"They head to Gal-So? With you? Are you certain of their intent?" the chief asks.

"Yes, Chief."

The chief's eyes scan each of us and come to rest on the twins with scrutiny.

"Who are you?" the Korund asks them. "You do not appear to be warriors like your companions."

The chief rises from the table and approaches Jesmir.

"What happened to your head?"

"A battle wound," Jesmir replies honestly.

"Curious." Turning to Tamrin, the chief assesses my large friend. The Korund's shoulders are over Tamrin's head, and I've never seen the big man look so small. Nodding with approval, the chief turns to me. We lock eyes, but as with all things Korund, I can't get a read from him.

"If I had to guess, I'd say you were from Killinshire. The features are hidden beneath the beard, but you have Killin-blood in you. And violence in your heart. But you don't carry yourself as Killinshire raised. Where are you from?"

"Teshket," I say.

"No. You aren't," the chief replies.

My head ticks involuntarily. It's uncharacteristically rude to a Korund to call anyone a liar. The chief bends down, standing less than a foot in front of my face. Massive not only in height, but in frame, the jade-scaled warrior towers over me. Kara and Kar exchange uneasy glances. At any other time, under any other circumstances, I would punch a person in the nose for the encroachment.

Don't push me, pal. Don't.

"You may have spent time in Teshket, maybe even grown up there. But you aren't Teshken."

"I was born in Teshket. My parents are dead, but I recently learned they were from Killinshire. I may have Killinblood, but I am Teshken." I take a step closer. "For over thirty years, I've made my home in Rhinestab."

I turn to the twins. "These two are from the royal line of Teshket. They were under my charge for a while. Now we choose to travel together as friends." I tilt my head. "Does that satisfy your curiosity, *Chief*?"

The chief turns from me and addresses Jesma. She smiles softly but confidently. "Why do you go to Gal-So?"

"For answers," she replies.

"You have questions?" the chief asks. Jesma nods. "Good. Questions are always good. Shows humility."

To Jesmir, the chief asks, "Do you enjoy this life?"

"Huh?" Jesmir says.

"Do you like the hard life? Traveling dangerous roads, with…" the chief casts a sideways glance at me, "dangerous companions?"

Jesmir smiles, his expression particularly roguish.

"It's been interesting to say the least," he says.

"You sure you wouldn't be happy back at the palace or castle or wherever you spend your days?" the chief asks.

"I wouldn't change a thing," Jesmir replies. "And frankly, who I travel with is my business."

"It was. Until you walked into my camp," the chief says, squatting eye level with Jesmir. The prince shrugs as if the chief's words are simply a matter of circumstance. I can't hide my smirk.

The chief addresses Tamrin. "Why do you travel to Gal-So?"

"Same as them. To find answers," Tamrin says.

"Why?"

"Because a piece of me has been taken. And I want to know why."

The chief stands up. "A piece of you was taken? Very interesting choice of words."

"Well, since you travel with a Chieftain's Child, I will assume you are honest folk. You are all welcome to stay with us. But we offer no free rides. We do not function like those in cities and villages. Here everyone works. That includes you," the chief says.

Covering the space with two strides, the chief walks back to the table and sits in the chair on the other side.

"Kar will hand out work assignments." With an underhand wave, the meeting is over. "Welcome to the Kalabali Clan."

Kara and Kar hold the tent flaps open for us as we start to leave.

"One more thing," the Chief says.

We stop and face him.

"Have you ever heard of the Fellowship of the Hand?"

I shake my head.

"Which god do you worship?" the chief asks.

I narrow my eyes at him. "Interesting folk, gods, so full of mystery."

The chief's head tilt is the first sign of any personality. "You prefer not to say? Interesting. I'd like you to ride with me tonight. Get some rest. You're going to need it."

"However I can be of service," I say and exit the tent.

Jesma raises her arms to me in question. I shake my head.

"I don't know. But apparently, I have night duty with the Chief."

Kara turns to look at me, about to speak, and thinks better of it.

Is Kara worried about me?

The western desert sky fades from bright reds into the deep purples and blacks to the east. The bright streak of stars to the west glows as the brightest of them force their presence through the fading light of Ezra. As far as the horizon in all directions, endless waves of desert sand stretch, growing cold as the night falls.

Eight Kalabali Korund and I stand at the camp's protective pillars—smaller versions of those around Galbring, but no less effective. The stacks of stones stand eight feet tall, a few inches taller than the Korund in our troop. It's a strange and somber group. It's unlike Korund to show such emotion, and the feeling makes me uneasy.

Ezra's tits. Am I frightened?

Pushing aside doubt, I focus on the companions I find myself mixed with. I feel absurd amidst these giant warriors. The shortest one is a whole foot taller than I am. The gender neutrality of Korund society took a while to get used to when I was younger. This Korund, like Kara, stands next to me, small, scaled breasts exposed. Equality in all things, each Korund is armed with swords identical to those carried by Kara and Kar, similarly crossed at the waist. Each wears a small pack filled with what I assume to be supplies.

Jesma approaches with a similar pack in her hands. It looks much larger against her more diminutive stature, and I realize small is relative. She holds it out for me to slip on, then reaches around me and pulls two straps around my waist and ties them together.

"These will hold it tight to your body. Apparently, you won't need what's in it unless you're hurt. Then," she nods to the squad, "one of them will be the one to use what's in it."

I nod and look into her eyes. She's frightened and her eyes mist. I pull her close, and she holds me tight, her embrace hard.

"Don't leave me," she says.

"I'll be fine," I say. "Think of it as a night with friends doing what friends do. Other than Brogen, nothing in this world can raise a welt on my fanny."

"Don't try to make me laugh," she says. She looks into my eyes again. "I love you, Shen-Zarl of Ditherun. Remember that. You remember that and return safely in the morning."

I hold a strand of her hair between my fingers. "I will."

She nods and pushes herself away from me.

"Now go. Before I change my mind and strap you to a cot, safe inside the barrier."

I blow a kiss and turn to face the squad. Eight pairs of eyes stare at me, unblinking.

The chief sizes me up and says, "Where is your weapon?"

"Chief, I am a weapon. Don't worry about me."

"I don't know if you understand the danger…"

I raise my hand to interrupt the chief. "I understand the danger."

"You must carry your weight. No liabilities here. Understood?"

"I've understood that my entire life, Chief."

Watch and learn, jagoff.

Once again, the voice of my mother rings in my head.

Be an asset, not a liability.

The deep bass of the chief's voice rings out in command, and Eight Korund, plus one *Harbinger of Death*, march into the desert beyond the protective pillars of the camp as night falls on Gal-Danang. Behind me, Korund priests begin their nightly prayer to close the barrier, the only protection between them and the Jandu that I know will come.

We march less than a mile when the first screech sounds.

The responses from the other Jandu come from all around. Blades pulled from sheaths ring in preparation as the eight Korund warriors draw their swords. The warriors spread out in a circle, backs to the center. The chief points to a spot where I slip into position on the Korund leader's right.

"Jandu send scouts in search of prey and signal others when one is located." The chief looks at me without emotion. "They found us. They're close. Always seven. Depending on how spread apart the scouts are, we may get all seven at once, or we may be in for a long night as the rest trickle in. If we don't deal with the scouts quickly, many more will come."

"How many more?" I ask.

"Too many," the chief replies.

"How many warriors have you lost?"

"Nine this season," the chief says, glancing at me. "All fine warriors. There's a real chance you may die tonight, stranger."

"I've chased death every day of my life. Quietius shuns me. Someday, maybe he won't. But so far, that bastard has always escaped my clutches. It seems that my death lies somewhere in the future."

"You hunt death?"

"I don't hunt death, I *am* death, Chief."

The concussive strobe of wings displacing air approaches from the darkness. A chill travels my spine when a loud, high-pitched shriek rings out, shattering the silence of the desert night. The pitch hurts my ears, increasing with the proximity of the source.

Eight voices cry out in unison, "Ifa!".

Green light bursts forth from sixteen swords, much like Priest Tatana's rod did in Galbring. Bathed in green light, the entire circle stands ready. The eerie glow casts shadows that provide far less comfort than I expected.

Across the barrier between shadow and light, clawed hands break into the green haze, aimed at me. Black poison drips from their long, bent tips. The Jandu, her arms outstretched, is two feet from my face before it registers that I'm its target. Teeth bared, she screams, and I flinch, reflexive muscle memory taking over. My arm snaps in a circular motion, my bracer slapping her hands away as I slip around the winged demon. Her forked tongue trails low from her gaping mouth. My body igniting with magical energy, I spin to keep her in my sight, trusting the others to have my back. The Jandu's eyes widen in surprise as I slip away from her grasp with ease.

Adrenaline surges, and my skin tingles. The new sensation of euphoric delight fills me with wonder, and I think about how I could get used to the feeling. Elated over the familiarity of my preferred weapons, I laugh with glee. I charge at the Jandu as she chooses a new target, everyone's backs still to the center. I catch her, and her screams startle everyone when I sever a wing from her body. My new blades experience no resistance in the action.

"That's gotta sting," I taunt.

Imbalanced and angry, she spins sideways, exposing her chest. I grimace at the way her intestines hang. Thick, black ichor drips from my blade. The severed wing lies at my feet, twitching as the nerves release their final bit of life.

I admire the blade. "Brinker, you outdid yourself!" I yell into the night.

That's right, I did that.

The Jandu faces me and tries to right herself from her lopsided flight, but the chief's sword severs her head, and she falls to the ground, lifeless. I study the face covered in blackened skin. Grey hair crinkled and dry from age—or death—falls about her face. Her teeth, sharpened to fine needles, drip poison. Her eyes, black as the darkest night, are devoid of any reflection.

A chorus of screeches echoes from the darkness in every direction. I ready myself, expectant.

"They're not so tough," I laugh.

"Well, Stranger, I hope your words are true. Because Jandu are telepathic. The others are on the way." The chief winks at me. "And they come for *you* now."

"I'm sorry?" I say. "Why me?"

"They seek revenge. You drew blood first. That one marked you, so you are their target. And our bait."

I flick the dark blood from my blade. "Bring it on."

"Kalabali! On the stranger!"

A loud guttural cheer booms from the deep chests of the Korund squad. They surround me as a unit, the circle tighter. I have no room to step outside their protective flanks.

"This isn't necessary," I say. "Let them through."

The chief's grin does little to put me at ease. "They won't need to get through to get you. Ready yourself, stranger. Nightmares come."

The chief's words cause me to wonder if I've underestimated the Jandu. I swallow hard, double-check my knives, and cycle my blades with nervous energy.

I don't know what to expect.

The rhythmic beat of wings comes from every direction, like we've stepped into a lair full of bats. The closer the sound draws, the more nervous I become. The beating turns into a rhythm pressing on my ears and into my head. A flash of bright light sears inside my mind, and my vision blurs. Pain erupts in my temples with the intensity of metal spikes. It's the worst pain I've ever experienced.

I cry out and fall to my knees. Voices, both familiar and unfamiliar, call out, as mixed and jumbled as their messages. Pressure builds in my head like it wants to explode. I fall to the ground, knees tucked in, my hands on my head, and beg for the pain to stop.

My pants grow warm as my bladder gives way. Slowly, the pressure subsides, and the world falls silent. The sounds of battle, blades against flesh, warriors' battle cries, grunts of effort, and vile screams of malicious intent fade away. The migraine relents, and I open my eyes.

My first thought is the smell. Coppery scent fills the air, as familiar to me as the scent of coffee.

Blood. I smell so much blood.

I push myself from my fetal position onto my knees. Before me lies a bloody scene of anguish and hate. Bodies lie strewn across a vast battlefield. I recognize the northern plains of Killinshire. Human and Korund lie dead, limbs severed, bodies pierced, backs broken. Mixed in with the familiar forms are dark, vile things, some like Jandu, others unfamiliar but just as frightening. Dark fog rolls over the carnage, seeping from their wounds.

Motion within the field draws my attention. Creatures, black as the darkest night, crawl from under the bodies, that same black fog rolling off them like some deadly emission. Some creatures I recognize as Jandu, others as spiderlyches, and still others are unlike anything I've seen. Thin creatures with wiry muscles and elongated limbs, strange dogs with six legs and two heads…too many variations to comprehend, search for human and Korund survivors, slaughtering any they find.

A flash of bright light bursts from the background, blinding and sudden. From within the light, a woman approaches. She moves with grace and subtle power. The dark things bow to her, their action reverent. Immediately familiar, the woman's dark skin, darker than mine, shines with radiant energy. Her brown eyes consider me with compassion, even love. I know her, and my body tenses with anger.

"Mother?" I say. Years of anguish and hatred rush to the surface of my thoughts.

She approaches me as if the years haven't passed. She stands before me, and her face turns hard, lines of age forming.

"Child of Killinshire," she says to me.

From somewhere in the distance, a voice calls out, "Stranger! You must resist!" but I can barely hear it.

My mother holds out her hand, offering to help me stand.

"Come with me," she says. "I only ever meant to prepare you. Come help me save the world."

"I don't understand," I whisper. "What is this?"

"We are not the enemy, child of Killinshire. We've come to keep the world safe. Those who hold you within their circle are the true enemy. Help us so we may set you free."

My mother screams and arches as if she's been struck from behind, her body bending backward. A green haze intrudes on the white light and black fog. My mother's voice changes, replaced by something less beautiful, more vile.

"They lie to you, warrior prince. Even that vile Hakaka lied to you."

"Hakaka?" I ask, confused.

The battlefield fades away, and I find myself on the ground, surrounded by active battle. A Korund warrior stands above me, swords ready. Beside me, a Jandu's severed head stares at me, dead.

I can't reconcile what I witnessed with the new reality before me. Another headache begins to take hold, and I grip my head again. A new voice speaks.

"*You* are a rightful heir to the throne of Killinshire, child. *They* keep you from your true place. They *all* do. Even your princess lies to you."

"No! Lies!" I cry out.

Another burst of green light flashes around me, a bright streak that cuts a line toward another Jandu's head from behind. I raise my forearms to block the strike with my bracers. The dark shadow of the Jandu moves from the strike, and the sword jars my forearms with its impact.

"See, child, they lured you here to kill you!" Again, the voice is laced with venom.

"Don't listen, Stranger! They lie to you!" the chief calls out.

"No, Killinchild, *they* lie. Kill them. Kill them all, and we can set you free. They were sent by the Hateful Eight. Sent to hold you in chains like the others. Sent to prevent knowledge of the truth."

"But why?" I ask.

"They prefer you subdued. They refuse to let you rise to your true power."

A loud battle cry breaks through the noise in my mind. The Jandu before me shrieks in pain as a sword cleaves her in two. Both halves fall to the ground.

My vision clears, and I spot another Korund warrior on the ground, eyes gouged out, lifeless. It's the shorter one who stood next to me as we left the camp. "Help us! Then we can help you. Kill the warriors who seek to harm us! We only wish to be left alone. But they hunt us. Kill them, and we will show you the truth. Please!"

The fearful plea overwhelms my emotions, and I pity the Jandu.

Why can't I help end their suffering? Why was my mother here?

Memories of the woman who left me to the guild cause anger and spite to boil over. She hated me, shunned me, and sold me to the guild. Old wounds open my mind, and I observe the scene before me. Korund warriors fight for their lives. Jandu attack in numbers far greater than ours. The battlefield before me fills me with rage.

Another Korund falls at my feet but rolls out of the fall and recovers quickly. A Jandu seizes the opportunity and breaks the circles. This one, a male, dives in toward me.

"Hello, little one. You are so handsome. Won't you come with us? There is freedom and power here."

What is this? Why do they stop to speak with me?

The green light around me fades into a softer, more natural light. A beautiful woman floats before me, her eyes bright, her smile wide. Supple lips spread wide to reveal perfect teeth. She's happy to see me. My mother smiles, and I feel the pressure in my head recede to a dull ache. I breathe a sigh of relief at the reprieve.

"Are you really my mother?" I ask.

"I am your heart's desire," she says. "I wish you peace, child."

"Peace? I will never know peace," I say. "I'm not meant for peace."

"With me, you shall know peace, my beautiful boy. Come. Let me take away the pain."

She holds out her hand, and I reach for it. She leads me toward the light behind her. Her face draws close, and she means to kiss me on the forehead.

But she sold you, reviled you, hated you.

"No!" I cry out.

I pull away from the woman, and she pouts.

"Why do you resist?" she says.

"I don't trust you," I reply.

She frowns, and her face contorts with rage, and I remember our mutual hatred for one another. That hatred builds, and I fuel it, hellbent on vengeance. The form shimmers and fades, replaced by a man's torso, black and rotten. Leathery wings flap, and the Jandu hovers before me. His entrails and spine sway beneath him, dragging behind.

He screams with rage, and his long black tongue tries to probe toward my mouth. My body reacts instinctively, and I strike. My blade severs his tongue, and he falls back, frightened. Two bright streaks of green light flash behind the Jandu. Both of the monster's wings fall to the ground.

The severed torso lands on the ground, writhing in pain. He hurls foul curses at me. He claws the ground in an attempt to drag himself toward me, intent on death. Repulsed, I sever his head with my blades.

"Why do you hurt us?" a new voice asks in dismay.

"It's my nature," I reply. "I am death."

"Oh, child, why do you hate yourself so?"

"I don't hate myself."

"But you do. You loathe who you are. You loathe what you might become. You loathe your father. You are half him, Emperor's child."

"You know my father?"

"We know all things."

"How?"

"Because she's never left you. She's always been here."

"Who?"

"Don't you know? Isn't that the question you most seek to answer?"

"No."

"No?"

"No."

"Then ask the question you most want answered. I am sure we can help."

Hovering before me, another Jandu smiles, the teeth hideous and pointed. Her hair flows in the breeze of her wings. Our eyes lock, and I know the pressure in my head comes from her.

"No!" I scream.

I punch forward with both fists. My blades pierce the Jandu's face, her eyes wide with horror. I rip my arms apart, and my new blades slice the top of her head from the lower jaw. The Jandu falls to the ground.

The pressure in my head ceases. I retract my blades and press my palms against my eyes. I gasp for air.

"Stranger!" the chief calls.

Covered in black blood, I offer a thumbs-up. The chief, also covered in blood, nods in acknowledgment.

"I'm thinking," I call back.

"Thinking and fighting are not mutually exclusive tasks," the chief says, with no hint of malice.

"Sure," I mumble, "Why not?"

Another scream echoes, carried in the desert breeze.

"How many more of these things are there?" I lament, throwing my hands up.

"Many," a Korund warrior replies.

"That was a rhetorical question," I mumble under my breath.

Behind me, voices rise in triumph. Korund voices. Another hideous half-body flies into the circle of light cast by the collection of glowing swords. The pressure on my head begins again, but I am ready for it this time.

Instinctively, I fling four knives from my belt in rapid succession as the dark form enters the green light behind the chief.

The hideous beast never saw my blades. The chief's eyes track the flight of my knives through the air. Before the chief can react, the Jandu's arms fall to her side, and her wings sag. Her momentum carries her through the space between us, and she crashes to the ground. I rip my knives from her face and clean them in the desert sand.

The battle rages for hours. I grow tired, but still the Jandu come. The pressure on my head lessens as the night goes on, each attempt to trick me less subtle and more obvious. I lose count of the numbers we've slain. Nearly every Korund has injuries. Two lie dead. Each of us is covered in black blood.

Over the horizon, a dim light pushes against the night sky. The Jandu cry out in anguish and flee from the coming dawn. The Korund warriors cheer in victory. I bend over, exhausted from the mental assaults.

The chief nods in satisfaction and turns to me.

"You've survived, Stranger." The chief inspects the carnage. "This is the largest attack we've seen. Their numbers grow."

"Then I guess we have work to do," I reply.

"Who are you, Stranger?" the chief asks, this time with genuine interest.

"I go by many names. Most know me as the Harbinger."

"Rhinestab is home?"

"No, I say," looking around, "My home currently resides in your camp, hopefully sleeping soundly and not sitting worrying about me."

The chief nods and says, "Where your heart currently lies. That is the answer of a man truly blessed." Hand outstretched, the chief adds, "Well met. My name is Vanian."

"Folks call me Shen," I reply.

The Jandu bodies burn in a pile of black ichor and decayed flesh. Rancid smoke fills the air, and even upwind, the smell is nauseating. Dawn has come.

"We burn the bodies, so they do not return," Vanian says. "Their deaths are temporary otherwise."

Once the pyre of bodies is ablaze, we stand in silent vigil until the pile is reduced to embers. The Jandu bodies fade into burning embers, and the Korund squad gathers their dead. Two of the warriors were lost in the battle. The Korund remove large cloths from their packs and create makeshift litters with their scabbards. Chief Vanian and I take the rear.

"Walk by my side, Shen," Vanian commands, and we hang back as the squad begins the long march back to camp.

"I wish to ask you a question," Vanian says. "One you may not want to answer."

"Go ahead," I say. "If I don't like the question, I will not answer."

"Do you trust in the gods?"

"No."

"So easily answered?" Vanian asks in surprise.

"Why wouldn't I answer truthfully?" I reply.

"How have you survived all these years?"

"Did I not *just* demonstrate that?"

"Yes, but that is not what I mean. It's curious the gods haven't sent their soldiers to kill you," Vanian clarifies.

I hold up my fists. "Who says they haven't? Truth is, until recently, no one ever existed who could beat me." I look at my hands. "And still that man is dead." Visions of Brogen and his sword at my throat come rushing back. "What's your point?"

"The gods will never allow you to survive. You threaten the way of things."

"I couldn't care less what gods think. Whatever their opinion, the feeling is mutual," I reply. "The Great Eight have never looked after me. Everything I have done has been on my own."

"Everything?" he questions.

Well, no, that's not true, is it?

"No. That's a lie," I whisper. "The gods help no one. People do."

We walk in silence.

"The Gods aren't real," I say.

"They are as real as you and me," Vanian says. "But your sentiment is shared," Vanian says, "By me and by Kara-Kar. By all of us within this clan."

"Say that again?"

"I can say little else. You wish to go to Gal-So. You are a man of evidence and action. We can use a man like you in our ranks."

"Who's *we*?"

"That's for Kara-Kar to decide when to tell you. For now, the Kalabali will see you safely out of this Jandu-infested desert. In Gal-So, you will find the answers you seek. In the meantime, it is good to have you in our ranks. You fight well."

Vanian picks up his pace to catch up to the rest of the squad, who are now several yards ahead. I jog to keep up.

"What else don't I know?" I whisper.

"A great many things, I'd imagine," Vanian says, no jest in the comment.

I shake my head. "Relevant to this conversation, I mean."

"Magic resides in all humanity," the chief says and thumps my chest with a heavy hand, "In here. Inherent in our genes. Each of us possesses a deep well of it. But it is finite. Even for the gods."

"They aren't gods," I reiterate.

"No, Stranger, they are not," Vanian says. "Do your friends believe as you do?"

"They didn't. But they do now. At least in part."

The chief considers that. "Let us get you to Gal-So. There is a woman there you should meet."

Already the temperature rises. We've been out in the desert wilderness the entire night. White tents beckon to us from ahead. Tall stone markers, the sentinels of the camp, are a welcome sight. I yawn, the adrenaline of battle long faded. My thoughts float between the chief's words, a nice nap, and Jesma's naked body pressed against mine.

Chapter Nineteen

Journal Entry: 132

The Kalabali no longer call me "Stranger." They've given me a name.

"Karsifa"
I'm told it means "sufferer."
Just what I need. Another nickname.
Just once, I'd like a name with some humor in it or a nice double entendre, like "Lord Long Blade" or "The Poker".
I don't know what I expected out of the humorless Korund.
Not that they don't have a point. The Jandu are relentless pursuers, and I'm a glutton for punishment.
They call to me—even in the daylight, while I sleep. They taunt me with lies. But I suspect that within every lie there is an element of truth. There's consistency in their words. Den after relentless den, they tell the same story.
Either their telepathy allows them to read my thoughts, or they are all somehow connected like one giant hive mind.

Every night the Jandu arrive—and every night I draw first blood. The Korund can fight like hell, but they cannot beat me to the first contact. They stopped trying two nights ago.

For six straight nights, I open myself to their psychic onslaught.

I wish I could say it is easier each time, but it isn't. They know things. Things they can't possibly know. But I have to find out how deep that knowledge goes.

Nightmares are a recent phenomenon for me. I wake up screaming.

Yet I still draw first blood.
Hence the name. Karsija.
But the Jandu call me something else.
Child of Killinshire.
Emperor's Child.
I'm not sure they lie. The mystery of my past haunts me more each day.
Nothing haunts me like the words of these Jandu.
But they must lie. I'm no child of Killinshire.

Confronted

The dry desert, with its soft, loose sands, gives way to the semi-arid diversity dominated by cacti and other spiny plants that conserve water.

"Karsija," Vanian calls from the peak of a rocky outcrop.

"Chief."

"It's been an honor to have you in our ranks, Karsija. I hate to lose you. But your destiny lies elsewhere."

Vanian points to the horizon.

"Just over the horizon is Gal-So. Twenty miles. Kara-Kar will take you to meet a woman. Her name is Anastaja. I believe you will find her…interesting. She's certainly going to have an interest in you." The chief turns to Tamrin. "All of you, actually. Don't fret over the Jandu. You have plenty of time to reach Gal-So."

"I'd prefer not to spend the night in the desert," Tamrin says.

"Chicken shit," I say with a grin.

"That shouldn't be a problem," Vanian replies, unamused.

"Hence, no humor in the nickname," I mumble.

Vanian has grown accustomed to ignoring me. The chief continues, pointing southeast to a dark mound near the horizon. "That's a recent netherstack formation. It first appeared six months ago…and that one, to the southwest, formed early last season. We think they are boundary markers. Jandu never cross the line between those two."

"I'm sorry?" I say.

Vanian sweeps an arm along the sky.

"This place used to be a safe place for us to camp, to regroup and recover undisturbed by Jandu. It gave us a chance to honor those we lost before we return to the fight. The Jandu never came here back in those days." Vanian turns and nods to the southwest stack. "Then that one appeared. We lost four warriors the night we heard them form. My eldest child witnessed the formation. I lost a piece of me that day when my eldest died. Not long before that netherstack formed, a wagon passed by our camp. It headed to where that stack now sits."

Vanian points to the southwest stacks.

"Those stacks appeared the next day. My child said it destroyed the wagon. We believed all occupants were lost."

"We witnessed the same carnage in Rhinestab," I say.

Head bowed, Vanian says, "The loss of life is always tragic. The same night after these stacks formed, the Jandu arrived here. Four of my warriors died, including my eldest. Coincidences are merely events that evidence hasn't yet connected. This was always a safe space. Since those netherstacks arrived, it is a battlefield."

"The netherstacks and the Jandu are connected?" Jesma asks.

Vanian looks out over the southern horizon. I'm struck by the sorrow reflected in the Korund's face. "They might be. I sent word to the other tribes, and they've confirmed similar suspicions."

The chief turns to me. "Something is wrong with the world, Karsija. I can feel it in my scales. The gods seem powerless to stop it. Or they don't care. Neither bodes well for Conishant."

"Maybe, in your hunt for the gods, you can have them answer this riddle first. The Jandu increase in numbers. No matter what we do, they spread. It's only a matter of time before they outnumber us. I fear what will happen when that day comes."

"I don't know what I can do," I say.

"I don't suspect you do. But take this information to Anastaja." Vanian hands me a folded piece of paper with a wax seal on it. "Give her this. It's everything I told you, but with the details of which clans confirmed my suspicions and where they patrol. Maybe she can find a pattern."

I accept the note.

"I'll add it to the list of things I am responsible for," I say with sarcasm.

"I know you will," Vanian says without irony.

Tamrin snorts in an attempt to resist a laugh. I scowl.

"Welcome to Gal-So."

"I've actually never been here," Jesmir says.

"Its only difference from any other city in Gal-Danang is its status as a border town," Kara replies. "As such, we have a large immigrant population, predominantly Killinfolk. Refugees who no longer wish to live under the emperor's rule."

"How does *that* work?" Jesma asks. "Killinfolk aren't known for their peaceful coexistence with others. They can't even get along with themselves."

"Be careful of your bias, your Highness," Kara says. "Not all who share blood ties share worldviews. Those who live here flee the emperor's violence and oppression. They strive to adopt a more peaceful existence here. There are occasional issues, but the refugees here are people who wish for a better life. They are torn between what they were and what they wish to be."

"Wouldn't they have more in common with Rhinestab?" Jesma asks.

"Yes, and that commonality includes a deep-seated mistrust and hatred for one another. Rhinestab is a staunch ally to Teshket, and though friendly to Killinshire, that northern alliance doesn't come without its prejudices. Here, they live peacefully and thrive. Gal-So's climate is similar to Killinshire's. The refugees can farm food and build the housing they are used to."

"I hate Killinfolk," I say.

"That's an interesting statement, considering," Kara says with a stern tone. "You'd best stay away from the settlement then, Karsija. Gal-So leadership doesn't tolerate violence here if that is your intent."

"Good luck stopping me," I say without thinking. "I apologize, Chieftain's Child. Rest assured, I have no plans to start trouble. Now, let's find this Anastaja."

Kara leads the way through Gal-So. We encounter many Korund from every tribe along the way. Even a few Kalabali. This surprises me, considering I never encountered that tribe until recently. Every Korund we pass inclines their head toward Kara. Another Korund, scales of diamond, some yellow and others so clear the light refracts with incredible radiance like stars in the sky, approaches. I notice this one wears earrings similar to Kara's. The two clasp hands, whisper into one another's ear something we can't hear, and continue on their way.

"That was a Chieftain's Child of the Wata Tribe," Kara says. "My baba has business with that tribe. I may leave you after we meet Anastaja."

We pass through the communal center and into a residential neighborhood. Traditional open-air-style homes line the streets. One structure stands out. Nestled between two lean-to homes rests a Teshken-style house. The high-peaked, steep-sloped, slate-shingled roof stands out like a sunflower in a field of daisies.

Along the roofline, ornate latticework carved into shapes reminiscent of the symbols emblazoned into the trees surrounding spiderlyche country, adorns the house. If I had to guess, the home is protected.

A large front stoop with wide steps from the street leads to a curved door, also emblazoned with the same symbols on the roof.

Kara turns to address us. "I must warn you. Anastaja is very old, but she is keen. Some believe she is a seer. Others think that she transcends time. Anastaja has lived in Gal-So for nearly forty years.

She is well-respected here and protected. Where she came from, no one knows, but based on the house, we assume Teshket. But she calls Gal-So home. Do not offend her, or all Gal-So will fall upon you."

Kara's eyes wander the street with conspicuous intent. I follow the Korund's gaze and notice that several of the Korund homes are occupied, their occupants equally conspicuous in their return gaze.

"She's even more respected among the underground. Mind your manners. She doesn't tolerate rudeness. And mind your behavior. Those who protect her will do so to the death."

"Hear that? That means you," Tamrin says, poking my shoulder.

"Fucking hell, Tam. I'm not gonna run through her house and call her names."

He snickers.

"Just mind your manners," he says.

You'll be lucky if I don't insult her with my first word, dickhead.

"Let's get this party started," I say instead.

Kara knocks with a gentle rap, which, for a Korund, sounds like the queen's guards serving a warrant.

"Who is it?"

The aged voice is calm and friendly.

"It's Chieftain's Child Kara, Anastaja," the Korund says.

"Kara? Is it really you?" asks the woman inside with a hint of surprise in her voice.

Soft, slow footsteps cause the floorboards beyond the door to creak. The door opens, and an elderly woman smiles at us from inside. Her stylish dress hangs loosely and flows with her motion. It's clear it once fit her well, but she'd lost weight since acquiring it. Her hair is almost pure white. Her dark skin, as chocolate as mine, is etched with wrinkles from age. If I didn't know better, I'd think she was a hundred years old.

No fucking way.

But I do know better.

I know all too well how old she is. I know more about her than anyone standing on this stoop. Her green eyes lock with mine. I study the locks in her hair, unchanged except for their color. The long scar along her left cheek and chipped front tooth that looks like a fang are as familiar to me as the RhineWoods.

I stare at the fang that I always thought she'd bite me with when she became angry.

"What the fuck is this? A joke?" I snarl, my temper flaring, blades extending.

Four pairs of eyes turn to me in complete shock at my reaction. Motion behind me triggers my fight reflex as Korund protectors rush from their homes, swords drawn.

"Shen?" Tamrin gasps.

The old woman's eyes pool with tears, and she raises her hand to stop the guards who surround us. When she speaks, it's all the confirmation I require.

"Shen-Zarl? Is it really you?"

Forty years of anger and hatred raise bile in my throat. My mother steps from the doorway, her eyes misted with tears. I clench my jaw so tight my teeth grind, and a small chip of a molar breaks free in my mouth with a crack. With an involuntary reflex, I retract and extend my blades in a frenetic rhythm, their deadly tips pointed to the ground. My body shakes with decades of pent-up anger, hurt, and anguish.

The woman doesn't flinch. Her eyes remain locked on mine.

A flurry of activity breaks out behind me, and my friends turn ready to fight. My mother steps closer, standing a few inches before me, her body erect, her posture proud. But her face is filled with sorrow.

"Oh, my boy, I've missed you. I've hoped you were still alive all these years," she says.

She reaches for my face. I raise my hands, the blades retracting, and grab her wrists. She doesn't react. She simply allows me to hold her arms in place. The tension on the porch and in the street is thick like a netherfog.

Kara steps to intervene, towering over my mother and me, menacing and stunned.

"No, Kara. This must play out," the woman says.

Her words don't register. Her tone doesn't coincide with my emotions. My body trembles.

"Anastaja, I cannot let him harm you," Kara warns.

"I'd like to see you stop me," I snarl, spit flying from my mouth onto my mother's face.

"He won't hurt me," she says. Her eyes never leave mine. "My son could never hurt me. No matter how angry he is."

Jesma's gasp startles me.

My mother doesn't press me, nor does she attempt to break free. I hold her wrists in an iron grip, and she allows me to keep them locked. I can't control myself, and I squeeze. She winces from the pain but holds my gaze. There's no fear in her eyes. No anger in her posture. No reprimand in her expression. She simply stares at me with compassion.

"This woman sold me and abandoned me," I say to them. To her, I say, "You hated me for things I couldn't control—punished me for every little infraction. You never came back, never told me where you went. You just took the money from the guild and left," I say.

More than Krin. More than gods. More than the Guild. More than assassins, bounty hunters, or the entire writhing nest of Conishant. You are the genesis of every hurt and betrayal I've ever experienced.

"This is your mother?" Tamrin asks.

I should kill you where you stand.

My body shakes with rage and decades of open wounds.

I should kill you.

But I can't.

Decades of hurt return.

It's pain I can't face.

I release the woman who so easily sent me away.

My body burns, the world blurs.

And I run.

The jagged sandstone boulder on which I sit digs into my ass. The discomfort doesn't compare to the discomfort in my soul. A mile away, Gal-So settles into nighttime silence.

Childish though my behavior might be, it's justified. Forty-one years since I last saw my mother, and with but a moment in her presence, I diminished myself into an insolent child again. Mages, assassins, all manner of undead, soldiers of fortune, Cuska, and a damn god couldn't hurt me the way the sight of *her* did.

Everything spins out of control, and I feel small.

I argue with myself.

You can't sit here forever.

Watch me.

No, you must face this.

But I don't want to.

At least go for a walk. You think more clearly when you walk.

I'll think better when you shut up and stop telling me what to do.

You know I'm you, right?

No, you're an asshole.

Then kill me.

I've tried, but you just won't die.

I'm like a bad case of fleas that way.

Fuck off.

You fuck off.

I hate myself for being right, but when I'm right, I'm right.

When all else fails, I lose myself in curiosity. Pissed at my ability to talk myself into and out of shit, I slide off the boulder and make my way back to town.

The streets are quiet. What noise exists does so in the low rumble of quiet conversations in the communal center of town, several blocks away. In an aimless wander, I meander through the streets. Korund families sleep in the open air in their homes. It's too much exposure for my taste.

I miss home. I miss the solitude of the RhineWoods, the freedom of not caring. The lack of responsibility.

I don't notice the shift in the architecture until I'm several blocks deep. The refugee camp is less a camp and an actual neighborhood. I'd never been in a Korund settlement that included permanent residents of another realm. In my imagination, I pictured dilapidated or slapped-together homes made of scraps. I imagined poverty and filth.

What I discover is quite the opposite. The neighborhood of refugees is organized, well planned, and clean. I walk through the dark streets among the wood-framed houses covered in stucco and plaster. The single-story homes are identical to one another, each with a wooden stairway that leads to the roof. Everyone seems to have closed themselves in for the night, shuttered away from the world. Slivers of light shine through a few wooden shutters.

Compelled to investigate, I pick a dark house and climb the stairs to the roof. Thin, wispy clouds overhead allow the light from the twin moons to reveal the secrets hidden at the top of the home.

Long wooden boxes, elevated to waist height, hold treasures of lettuce heads, onions, garlic, and other alliums whose names I can't recall. Another box holds leafy stalks that can only be carrots, beets, or turnips. I glance across the small space between houses and notice the next-door house is outfitted with identical boxes. I leap the gap and investigate the small gardens there. Other vegetables grow here— potatoes, beans, and squashes.

I hop from house to house and find tomatoes, berries, grapes, and strange vegetables I've never seen with bulbous heads and stringy flowers. I lean over the front of a house and look out over the organized rows and columns of homes. It's a sea of gardens on flat single-story roofs.

The Killinfolk of Gal-So maximized their use of space by growing their food on their roofs. I pull a strawberry from one of the plants and taste it. It's sweet and I mumble with delighted surprise.

"May I help you?" a man asks behind me.

His appearance startles me as I hadn't noticed him there.

I turn with as peaceful a posture as I can muster. A tall man, thin as a rail, eyes filled with mild curiosity, observes me with friendly curiosity. He's older than I am, at least five years or so. Shirtless, in tattered pants and sandals, he waits, expectant. His thin and wiry muscles reflect a life of toil. His aquiline nose and his angular cheeks remind me of my father and Brogen. His hair is grey and very short on his scalp, unlike mine, which is typical of Killinfolk who've served in the emperor's army.

"I'm sorry. I'm trespassing," I reply. "I was curious what was here. I had no right."

"You are new here? A refugee?" he asks.

"No, I'm from Teshket," I reply.

"Haha, sure you are. And I'm the Teshken queen. You don't have to hide here. We're all refugees. This is a safe place."

"I'm sorry, but you're mistaken. I grew up in Teshket and now spend my days in Rhinestab. I've never lived in Killinshire. And I'm not a refugee."

"That may be true, but your blood is Killinfolk, sure as I'm standing here."

Child of Killinshire.

"Why are you refugees?" I ask.

"Do you know much about Killinshire?" he asks.

"I know enough to be offended when you say my blood is Killinfolk."

He closes his eyes. My words hurt him.

"That is a shame. We are a great people. But I understand your distaste. Killinshire is an aggressive land that worships rugged individualism. A society bred to value the virtues of combat, exceptionalism, and aggressive capitalism tends to leave a distaste toward its citizens. Many of us, however, wish for different and emigrate to the other realms."

His eyes reflect the moonlight, and he smiles.

"You've known great violence, a true child of the Emperor."

There it is again.

"That obvious, huh?" I say.

He snickers.

"Come, it is dinner time. Join me," he says.

"Why?" I ask.

He raises an eyebrow. "Because you are here, we have food, and you seem lost. Be found and break bread with my wife and me. Come." He signals for me to follow. We descend the stairs to his small, one-room home. His wife, her hair in long locks like mine, places food on the table. She furrows her brow when we enter.

"This is my wife, Jilliana," he says.

"Welcome," Jillianna says, her eyes narrowed on her husband.

"I'm sorry," I say, self-conscious. "I should go."

"Nonsense," the man says, and he smiles at his wife.

She sighs and waves towards a small table. "Please, join us. My husband obviously invited you, and we rarely have visitors."

"Sit, eat," the old man says. "My name is Brill." The home is cozy but cramped. Above a small hearth rest a couple of books and a small chest. The fire inside burns low. In the back, where Jilliana stands, is a meal preparation area with a tiny stove. In the corner furthest from us sits a bed that barely fits two atop a stand with drawers. Besides the table and four chairs, where she invited me to sit, there is a modest shelf with a few books and pots on it.

I sit at the table with my back to the door in awkward silence. Jilliana hands a basket of bread across the table.

"Thank you," I say.

Her eyes sparkle as she smiles. "Welcome, stranger. Do you have a name?"

I have so many.

I nod. "My name is Shen. Shen-Zarl."

"Ah, Shen-Zarl. *That* is a fine name. That's a Killinspeak name. Did you know that?" Brill asks. "Do you know what it means?"

"It's just a name," I say.

"It's so much more. Zarl means *'God's Bane'*. And Shen means *'Beloved'*. Interesting name, Shen-Zarl. Your parents had a certain view of the world, or a wicked sense of humor, I think."

"My parents were ruthless tyrants," I say.

"Did you lose them when you were young?" Jilliana asks.

"Yes," I say.

"The eyes of a child miss things that memories cannot explain. I'm sorry your parents aren't alive to help you through the cloud," Jilliana says. "Too heavy a topic for dinner. Where have you come from, Shen-Zarl?"

"It's Shen. Just Shen," I say.

"Shen, then. What brings you to Gal-So?" she asks.

"I came to meet someone. I don't like who they turned out to be."

"They didn't meet your expectations?" Jillianna asks.

"In a manner, I guess," I reply.

"Everyone has a story," Brill says. "No one is who they seem…or make themselves out to be."

Jillian ladles soup into my bowl. The aroma triggers a memory of my brother. I tear a piece of my bread and dip it in the bowl. The memory floods back, and the ache in my chest stops me.

"What is this?" I ask.

"Chicory Soup," Brill replies. "It's a staple back home. Do you like it?"

"It tastes like my childhood," I reply in a whisper, and the tears fall.

The couple offers me a place to rest. It's a kind gesture and unexpected from Killinfolk. I politely decline the offer. It's time to face what I've spent the evening avoiding. My friends are bound to worry—if they haven't started already. By now, Tamrin is trying to track me. Too bad for him, I made sure his efforts would occupy him for hours.

I'm not ready to face the villain in my story. Procrastination gets the better of me. My circuitous route through town starts as a delay of the inevitable. After an hour of wandering, I'm lost. Lost in a strange city, I'm left to my thoughts, and it's not long before guilt takes hold. The twins are still very much in danger, and I stormed off like a prepubescent preteen.

My cowardice is on display now. I've always wanted to confront my mother, dreamed about it. Here, the opportunity is presented, and I ran.

Her reaction when she recognized me was unexpected. Hers was the expression of a mother overjoyed, relieved…one of love.

But that's *not* how I remember her. Other kids' mothers doted on them, cared for them, loved them. Mine offered none of those things.

Yet somehow, I feel guilty. *Why?*

She hated *me*, blamed *me* for everything, the loss of my brother especially. I've spent a lifetime wrestling with that.

Which is worse? My experience? Or the twins? They've spent a lifetime convinced of their grandmother's love. Jesma is still unaware of the danger that looms over her head.

Lost in my own thoughts, I stumble into the communal commons. Relieved to have found something mildly familiar, I push through the crowd to find an alehouse. Korund mingle, almost shoulder to shoulder, in Korund style revelry—deep philosophical conversations on topics of technology, the nature of man, or the benefits of Korund society on the greater world—all while they drink their thick Korund ale. An occasional group of Killinshire refugees appears through the crowd as I weave through the throng of large, scaled bodies, and we nod at each other. Strange to think of them as kin. A thrum of deep voices rumbles against my eardrums in waves of pressure.

Every Korund I pass acknowledges my presence with a nod or a brisk "Be at peace, friend." The constant polite acknowledgements are exhausting. I pull my hood over my head to hide, eyes focused on the ground as I walk. My view becomes scaled calves and feet.

A pair of giant green Korund feet steps into my path. The scales are dulled but still reflect light. The brown skirt hem that hangs inches from the ground is indistinguishable from the hundreds of others I've already passed. The embroidered edge sways between the shoeless feet. I excuse myself without glancing up and sidestep. The pair of feet sidesteps with me, blocking my way again. I raise my gaze to address the obstacle. Kara-Kar stares down, frowning.

"Where have you been, Karsija? We've searched for you for hours."

"It's none of your business where I've been, Chieftain's Child. Now, if you'll excuse me…"

Kara places a firm hand on my shoulder. The force in that grip makes it clear I'm expected to comply. I glance at Kara's hand and back at those bright green eyes. Kara's expression softens in an uncharacteristic show of emotion. I scowl in response.

"If you wish to keep that hand…"

Kara's frown deepens.

"Will you walk with me, Karsija?"

"I'm in no mood," I say.

"I understand. And I understand why you feel that way.

"You understand little of me, Chieftain's Child."

"Enjoy an ale with me. If you don't like what I have to say, I'll leave you be and tell no one we ran into each other."

I do not reply.

Kara's hair blows in the breeze, red locks flowing to one side. The Korund continues, "Anastaja explained much to us after you left. Though she left out many details, I'd say your anger is justified. I empathize with you, Karsija."

I don't respond.

"My people like you. Chati Brinker's friendship is hard to achieve. Grankin's affinity toward you testifies to your character. And my zatia, Kar, said no human is respected more by the Kalabali. With all these character witnesses, I'd be honored to call you a friend. So, please, *friend*, walk with me."

I shudder with a ragged breath. I'm exhausted.

"She told you?" I ask.

"She told *us*, yes."

"Fine," I say in resignation. "Let's fucking drink."

Kara spins me around, and we head back the way I came.

"I wish to tell you a story. Maybe it will help, maybe it won't. But I think I should tell it either way."

We navigate through the crowd, Kara's hand firm on my shoulder. The presence of a Chieftain's Child elicits a different reaction from the other Korund than my previous interaction with the crowd. The crowd acknowledges my escort and barely takes notice of my presence. We stop in front of the Haabrestand Alehouse.

"Well, slap my ass and call me Jumbo!" a familiar voice calls out. "Shen! What are you doing in Gal-So?"

Mistras, my dear friend and owner of my favorite tavern, runs from the rear of the shack, his hand extended. Of all the people I expected to see, he was not on the list. His black eyes crinkle with delight. Sweat drips from his shoulder-length dark hair. His clothes are dirty and moist with sweat.

"Mistras? Are you a sight for sore eyes?" I say and hug the guy with more emotion than I thought possible.

Mistras stands awkwardly and doesn't hug me back right away.

"Well, umm, uh…" he stutters and then embraces me. "Hell, Shen. You miss me that much?"

I release him and punch him with a playful tap on the arm.

"Yeah. I guess I did. What are you doing here?"

"Well, my latest batch of Mistras Reserve is so popular that people asked me to start brewing enough to ship! I delivered ten barrels here."

"Why didn't you hire someone?" I ask.

"Well, Cali wanted to get out of Winding Run for a while. See some of Conishant before she gets too far along."

"Cali's here?" I say. "Where?"

A light tap on my shoulder causes me to turn around. Cali stands there with a big smile on her face. She wraps her arms around me, her embrace tight. I can't help it; I hug her back.

"Cali!" I exclaim. "Let me get a look at you!"

"Hi, Uncle Shen!" Cali exclaims and releases me.

I push her back to look at her. Though she looks no different than she did a month ago, the swell in her belly has grown more noticeable.

"Uncle?" Kara asks.

"That's what I call him. He rescued me from kidnappers when I was four. Ever since then, he and my dad are like brothers. Hence, I call him 'Uncle'."

"You are a beloved man, Karsija," Kara says.

Cali makes a funny face.

"Why do you call him Karsija?" Cali asks.

"It's a joke," I say.

"No. It's an honor. Korund gives names to those whom they wish to honor, not as a joke."

Kara looks at Cali.

"Your uncle likes to suffer for the sake of others. My zatia's clan gave him the name."

"Enough about me," I say. "You have a baby bump!"

Cali touches her belly. "I know. It's really going to happen."

"Well, I am sure glad to see you."

"Alright, Cal, back to work. I want to get on the road," Mistras says.

"So soon?" I ask.

"You know those lazy bastards at the inn won't do a thing if I'm not there. I've been gone two days already. Time to go home."

"One for the road?" I plead.

"Well. Okay, but just one," Mistras says.

"Barkeep! Four Mistras' Reserves, please!" I yell. I turn to Kara and say, "I can't believe they have Mistras' Reserve in Gal-So. The day is brighter."

"You're a strange man, Karsija. I can't wait to know you better," Kara says.

"Careful what you wish for," I say, and savor the dark maltiness of my favorite ale. I didn't realize how much I missed it until this moment. "This is the longest I've gone without your witch's brew, Mistras. Thank you."

Cali raises her mug and says, "To my favorite uncle."

The sentiment almost makes me cry.

We finish our ales., Mistras and Cali say goodbye. Kara orders another ale, and I order two. We leave my friends and the communal space behind, mugs in hand.

My mood is lightened by the appearance of Mistras and Cali. Their unexpected reappearance leaves me longing to be where they are. Even though Winding Run has a strict policy on how to gain residency status, I lose myself in the fantasy of Jesma and me settling close by.

Maybe we could build a cottage in the woods.

That would be a wonderful life.

Who am I kidding? Me as a husband and dad?

That life can't happen for me.

But why not?

I don't have a good answer.

Kara leads me along a residential street. A few Korund, still awake, relax in their homes, most in quiet conversation. Those who notice the chieftain's child nod to Kara as we pass. Kara walks in silence for a long while. The Korund's stride pushes mine to its limit, and my shins ache. Kara notices and slows the pace to accommodate mine. I finish the first ale and set the mug on one of the little tables common throughout Gal-So.

Kara doesn't speak for a long while. It's of little consequence to me since I'm in no hurry. My second ale is still full, and I get to avoid my past a little longer. When the gentle giant finally speaks, it startles me.

"I never wanted to be Chieftain's Child," Kara says.

Korund don't express their innermost thoughts to strangers, so I'm surprised.

"When our sitting Chieftain was elevated to the Tribal Council, my baba, Latisi, became the eldest of the tribe and stepped into the role without question. The impact on my life was immediate. I went from a freedom-loving wild child to Chieftain's Child overnight. With it came responsibilities I never wanted."

"I can imagine the burden," I say.

"My baba's, Latisi and Zuta were compatible. But when Baba Zuta passed, life grew…difficult. Zuta died at one hundred and eighty years old, not much older than Latisi is now. Latisi wasn't ready to manage four children alone. And while we as Korund don't recognize gender as you do, we do recognize the hormonal differences that can impact relationships, no matter how strong those relations are."

"Latisi struggled, especially with a youngest child whose willfulness outmatched his late zatia's. Zuta knew how to handle me. Latisi struggled. Then Latisi became Chief."

Kara points to an empty home. "Let's sit here."

I follow Kara to a large bench covered with brightly colored pillows.

"This is my eldest siti, Hamal's place. Hamal lives here part-time but is currently in Gal-Daro on council business," Kara says, and sits on the large bench.

I ease myself onto the far side.

"You hate being Chieftain's Child?"

"Most days."

"The change must have been hard."

"It was. Is. Especially since I've learned the truth."

I wait for Kara to continue.

"Now that I know you are Anastaja's child, it occurs to me you've *never* been a man of faith."

"I've never hidden my disdain. Gods are no more useful to me than bakru shit."

"Your lack of faith makes you powerful."

"It seems so."

"I ran away from home when my baba became Chieftain."

I suck in air through my teeth, and Kara smiles.

"You are very well acquainted with our customs. I like that about you."

"How did your family receive that?" I ask.

"As anticipated. It took almost a decade for Latisi to recover from the disgrace. An undisciplined Korund child is frowned upon, ostracized." Kara pauses. "We can't fight our nature, though. I'm more undisciplined than most. Certainly, less disciplined than my sitis. I never wanted to be tied down in Gal-Danang."

Again, Kara shows uncharacteristic emotion and falls quiet. With a half pint of Mistras' Reserve remaining, I can be patient.

"I met a man. He was powerful, beautiful, and human. Max demonstrated great skill with fire magic. I was enthralled. He introduced me to people. Wonderful people who became my new family. They were eager for me to discover some truth they couldn't simply share. One day, I grew impatient, and I asked what they weren't telling me."

"It took many years for them to share their stories. When they finally revealed their belief that the gods are frauds, I took offense."

I sit straight.

"You mentioned 'the underground' back in Galbring," I whisper.

"Max was my introduction to them. He offered to show me how to access magic power without the gods. But his beliefs angered me. As Korund, we don't often express our rage. It's a useless emotion. But I've always been a firebrand. I raged. And I left him in that rage."

The muscles in Kara's jaw tighten, and the bulge creates a wave of reflected light. For the first time in my life, I witness tears form in a Korund's eyes.

"I loved him. I couldn't stay away long."

Tears glisten against the small scales on the Korund's cheeks. I can't look away from the glittering trail of vulnerability. The atmosphere grows uncomfortable in the presence of Kara's pain.

"I returned to find his home reduced to ash. His body was charred beyond recognition. I found the others burned. All dead. It appeared Max had lost control of his magic."

Kara's gaze burns into my soul with anger and bitter sorrow. My resistance to Kara's presence melts away.

"It was no accident. Max never practiced magic at home. He was too cognizant of others. They were murdered. Whoever killed them didn't know Max's rule."

Kara wipes away tears. The stoic resolve returns.

"When we first met, Max introduced me to Anastaja. That's where I was headed when I lost my faith on Sanctum Mountain. At that moment, I knew Max had been right. That fall changed my mind. I never had the chance to tell him."

"Your story didn't make sense before," I say. "On the mountain. Now it does."

Kara stares across the street, eyes distant.

"For a Korund, you sure are emotional," I say with a smile.

Kara scoffs but remains quiet.

"If I'd listened to him, maybe they'd all be alive. I blame myself. It's irrational logic, but it's ever-present."

I roll my sleeve, remove my left bracer, and turn my arm palm up to reveal my self-inflicted wounds. With a gentle hand, Kara traces the deep remnants of my suicide attempts, all eight of them. The Korund's fingers follow the long ones that run the length of my inner forearm.

"How did you survive these?" Kara whispers.

"Fucking healers," I say. "They show up at the wrong time. Every time. It's almost enough to make one believe the gods care. Except if they really did, they'd have let me die."

Kara reaches out and places a hand on my cheek.

"It's good that you are alive, Karsija," Kara says. "We need you here."

"Well, ask me now if I'm glad every attempt failed."

"Are you?"

"More than anything. I would never have fallen in love if any one of these had succeeded. Kara, I only show you this so that you know you are not alone. I know where blaming yourself leads."

"I appreciate you, Karsija," Kara says. "That name is an uncanny coincidence."

We both laugh, and it's the first Korund laugh I've ever heard. Eons could pass, and I know I'll never forget the sound. It resonates against Kara's scales like wind chimes. The sound draws attention from several passing Korund. More than one looks aghast that a Chieftain's child would display such behavior.

We settle into silence, and Kara smiles at me. With her pointed teeth in the dark, it looks sinister, but rather than shudder, I laugh again, which makes Kara laugh once more.

"Max introduced you to my mother?" I ask after we take control of ourselves.

"Yes. After I found their bodies, I came here. Anastaja told me about this growing underground of 'unbelievers', as she called them. She told me the gods sent death squads out to eradicate them. Hundreds have died over the last three decades, including my friends."

"And you joined them," I say.

"Not at first. I needed to reconcile with my Korund family. After a few years, I was welcomed back. Latisi gave me these." Kara flicks the earrings at me.

"A year later, I met Kar. When we met, I told Kar about Max. Since we were courting, I revealed every detail."

"Kar was very patient and told me that everything we do comes from the Great Eight. But Kar also said the gods' influence comes at a cost. I realized then that I'd found a partner who saw the world as I do."

"The underground seeks to end the reign of the gods. They claim dominion over luck, earth, water, life, death, animals, and until recently, war."

"I'm still a little confused by that," I say.

"Karsija, you and your friends proved the gods don't just bleed like all living beings. You've proven we don't need them. And that we can kill them when you killed Hakaka."

"I'm sorry? I don't know how you mean."

"Don't you? Were you not there? In Grankin's memories?"

My mind revisits the memory. God's surrounding Grankin—Nadur, Morze, Ezra, Quietius, Fildeus, Krikhi, Shamna, and Hakaka. *Nadur's nutsack. He was there too!*

"Brogen," I whisper, my voice caught in my throat. "I'm so stupid. That's what you meant when we first met. I've been focused on the queen and *her* presence in Grankin's memories."

"The Queen?" Kara asks. "Of Teshket?"

Should I trust you?

Nothing this Korund has done since joining our party has shown malicious intent. Yet, Kara's presence hasn't been without suspicion, but now that suspicion I harbored has receded, wiped away by her sincerity.

If not now, when?

"Kara, I haven't trusted you, even after Grankin. For that, I am sorry. What I'm about to reveal is known by only three. As far as I am aware, Jesma still hasn't reasoned this out, and I've been terrified to tell her."

"We don't keep our own secrets," Kara says, understanding my point. "But we also do not gossip. Your burdens are mine now."

I laugh at that. "Fair enough."

"What of the queen?"

"She was there, too. I heard her voice."

"Krikhi's tits," Kara whispers.

I can't help but smile at that. Kara regards me with concern. "Does the prince know?"

"He does."

Through clenched teeth, Kara takes in a tight breath. "This is a heavy burden, Karsija."

Kara stands.

"I know this is hard to accept, but I believe that Conishant needs the Harbinger of Death right now. My destiny lies with you."

The Korund extends a hand.

"Come. It's time you grew up and put away a child's memory. Your mother wishes to tell you her story, if you are ready to listen."

My hearts race and my adrenaline surges. I take a deep breath. It does nothing to assuage my anxiety. But I have no choice. I *need* to know.

"I'm ready," I reply. "Take me to my mother. It's about time I find out who the hell I really am. Time to lay everything out in the open."

Chapter Twenty

Journal Entry: 134

Fucking Hakaka.

I wish I could go back and kill Brogen again.

Shamna and Hakaka conspired to kill Jesma and Jesmir. If I didn't already distrust the gods, this would be the blade in the back of the neck for any faith I carried. Jesmir is already burdened with the knowledge. Did none of the others notice Hakaka was Brogen?

We can't hide this from Jesma any longer.

But there's another question I don't dare contemplate aloud.

What if we are all wrong and the gods are actually gods? Is Hakaka really dead?

And what would that make the princess?

Could it be I stuck metal in one god and my rod in another?

That would explain why she can drive me insane in bed.

Grow up, man.

Past Presented Future

My throat constricts so tight I can't swallow. The small, out-of-place house with answers to too many questions appears no different than it did hours ago when I first saw it. Still, somehow, its presence now intimidates me. Anxiety prevents me from taking the last few steps that will place me at the door. My hands shake, something they haven't done since I killed Krin's brother. Everything that happened in my life after my mother sold me is a direct result of that choice.

Everybody has a story.

What if my mother's story is too hard to hear?

What if it breaks me?

"Everything over the last five weeks should have broken you, Dumbass," I say aloud.

"What's that, Karsija?" Kara asks.

"Nothing," I mumble. "Just talking to myself."

"Need I worry about your sanity?"

I turn to look at Kara and smile. "I worry about my sanity."

"What purpose would that serve? It won't change your behavior," Kara asks.

"You're not as different from other Korund as you think, Kara."

The door creaks, and my stomach flutters. The woman whom I vilified for decades stands surrounded by dim lantern lights, her silhouette a diminutive presence in the doorway. This old, frail, tiny shadow is the demon in my story. The one person I most needed to accept me, who instead sent me away, waits.

Is it possible she's as frightened as I am?

The sad smile on her face brings back other memories. I recognize that smile. *But how can I?* She never smiled.

But she did. A memory emerges of the day after my brother died. I cried myself to sleep. When I woke, she was there. She smiled, this *same* smile, born from pain. A smile caused by someone else's suffering. A smile that told me more about my mother than I cared to notice.

A smile that, today, breaks me.

"Mom," I say as I fall into her arms.

"My sweet boy," she whispers. "I'm sorry. I'm sorry for the hand life dealt you. I'm sorry I forced you to play it as it was dealt."

We weep as we slowly sink to the floor.

Ezra sets. My mother and I talk. Ezra rises. Still, we talk. Four decades of anger, loss, and suffering flow. We open old wounds and gently tend to them. The process leaves me emotionally, mentally, and physically drained. Somewhere in all that, my head found my mother's lap. Her hands found my hair. And sometime after the light came into the windows, I slept.

It's strange to wake to the gentle hands that stroke my hair. I'm a fifty-three-year-old killer. A killer who cried himself to sleep on his mommy's lap.

I push myself upright and rub my eyes. My mother never moved. We sit alone in her small home. The voices of my friends, deep in conversation, travel through the front windows from where they sit on the porch. I'm grateful to them for their compassionate gift of this private time with my mother.

"Shen-Zarl," she says, her voice threatening to break again, "May I offer a word of advice?"

"You could offer me anything and I'd be grateful," I reply.

She touches the side of my face with the back of her hand.

"You shouldn't hide the truth from your friends," she says.

"I know," I reply. "Wait. How?"

She smiles, this time it's one of secrets and the patience of a teacher toward a student.

"We've always known who they are," she says. It's no secret if you pay attention. The only one without a public persona is Quietius. You need to tell them."

"He knows," I reply, "But how do I tell her?"

She adjusts herself and pats my hand.

"All the more reason to tell her."

My mother shifts in her seat. "I have more to tell you."

"More?"

"We always believed your father was the first of his kind. He discovered *his* truth when you were born. It frightened him. You were too young to remember, but when you were four years old, we fled Killinshire. He'd been discovered."

Vague memories of a dream come back to me—of a river—of hiding.

"The emperor put a bounty on your father's head. Your father and Brogen were very close. Kindred spirits. Equal in all things, strong, skilled warriors. Brogen wanted your father to become the ruler of Killinshire. But your father refused."

You are the rightful ruler of Killinshire.

The words of the Jandu.

My mother leans back in her seat, her face twisted in pain. I rise to help her, but she stops me.

"No, no. It's the pain of old age," she says with a smile. She studies me with care. "I never thought I'd see you again. Not a day has passed that I haven't thought about you. I always imagined you out in the world doing great things. I never believed the guild could hold you forever."

"I haven't been doing great things," I say with sadness. "I spend most of my days hiding away in Rhinestab."

She grins. "You are *'The Harbinger.'*"

"I am."

"Then you are a great many things," she says. "The stories of your deeds sound so much like your father."

I bite my lip, afraid to ask the question.

"You want to know why he left?" she asks.

I nod, and my emotions make me feel small again.

"Brogen's spies found us. That vile man couldn't let your father go. Or wouldn't. That same night that he killed the spies, he came home, gathered his things, and left."

I fall back onto the couch. My hearts pound so hard I can feel them in my ears.

"Why didn't you tell us?" I ask. "Why did you leave Bren and me in the dark?"

She closes her eyes, and another small tear falls. When she opens them, I see a sign of the woman I feared. It flashes and then fades.

"I wanted him to take us with him. But he insisted he would return. He planned to reveal Brogen's plan to the emperor. But we didn't know who Brogen was back then, or that he'd been named Captain of the Dark Guard. I only know that your father never returned."

"You had such a temper as a young boy. I don't know if you remember. You'd take it out on other kids, and your powers grew daily. We lived in constant fear of discovery. Your inability to control your *silence* placed you at risk, especially then. I made you wear a bell, remember? To keep everyone from noticing how silent you were."

"I thought, all this time, that you made me wear it to keep me from scaring you. I remember when you dropped the stew."

"I remember that, too. I didn't know how else to keep you safe. The bell was all I could afford. You were a handful," she says with a smile. "I couldn't help but love you for it."

"Boy, you tested me every chance you had. Bren was the only one who could talk sense into you. When he died, I feared the worst. You were out of control. I couldn't lose you to Brogen, too."

She bows her head, and more tears flow.

"Your father was supposed to teach you, guide you. He was supposed to show you how to access your magic. And most importantly, how to shut it off."

She reaches into her pocket and pulls out a letter.

"I've held on to this. I've read it three times. Once, when it came. Once, after I sent you away. And yesterday, after you ran."

She hands it to me.

"It was meant for you. It's from your father."

My hands shake again, and my nose stings as I fight back the urge to cry again. My vision blurs from the tears that threaten. I take the letter. She stands, her shadow hovering over me, and kisses my forehead. Without another word, she leaves the room.

Dear Liana,

I don't have much time. Things are worse than when we left. Brogen is no longer just another warrior making his way through the ranks. The son-of-a-bitch IS the rank. He is Captain of the Dark Guard, the Emperor's favorite.

There's little chance I can get to the emperor now. Even with my speed and silence, Brogen has always been faster. I've only bested him through tenacity and skill. But it's been far too long since I've fought anyone of his caliber. I fear my greatest advantage is lost to time.

I know why Brogen wanted me to be the emperor instead of taking the title for himself all those years ago. I'm right about the world, love. Seeing him in the Captain's Armor here confirmed it.

Brogen is the image of Hakaka in the Battle of Hizeron. He is the man in the paintings. We always wondered what happens when gods fight. Where do they go?

This raises the question that I must answer. If the gods are not who they say they are, then who are they? What if they walk among us, hiding in plain sight?

It's too much to fathom. But I must know for sure. I go to confront the man who hunts us. I know I'm right. I don't know if I'm strong enough to kill him anymore. I aim to expose him. If he is Hakaka...

I know life with me wasn't easy. I should have told you about Brogen's plan before we married. Certainly, before the boys were born. I'm sorry to leave the burden on you, my love.

Bren will be fine. He's a strong boy, mentally tough, compassionate, and intelligent. He shows no sign of magic. It may still come. Just watch over him.

Shen, I fear, will be a different story. He's faster than I was at his age. It's frightening. I don't know how it is that he does what he does so easily. He's stronger than I was at that age. Maybe it's that weird heartbeat. Who knows? He'll require a heavy hand in my absence. You must be both hard and gentle with him. I don't know how to guide you.

When he's of age, give him this letter. He needs to understand his place in the world. He must gain control of his anger before it rules him. It will be hard for both of you. Especially since I leave you with nothing but these words.

If he becomes too much to handle, contact the Assassin's Guild in Teshket. They are best equipped to fight Killinshire warriors. Better the Guild teach him discipline and how to fight rather than be left to the streets. It's for his own good...and yours.

Teach him to be an asset to the world, not a liability. Help him do good where evil prevails.

Tell our sons nothing of the truth until it's time.

Maybe this letter is wasted words, and I'll return home to teach them myself.

But I have little faith in that, my dear Liana.

I wish I had been a better husband to you. I wish I hadn't taken this foolhardy journey.

With a devoted heart, I love you, woman of Killinshire.

Yours forever,
Degan

"Liana. Degan."

I say their names aloud for the first time.

I never knew their names. I reread the letter, careful to keep my tears off the paper that is nearly as old as I am.

Everything I understood was a lie.

My mother stands in the entryway between rooms, her cheeks wet with tears.

"He loved you boys so much," she says.

"Why do I remember everything so differently?"

"A child sees from a child's perspective." She sits next to me, taking my hand once again. Her hands are cold, almost icy. The skin is wrinkled, and her veins show through in reddish-brown streaks. Little brown freckles cover her skin.

"You look so much like your father now. It's like he's here in the room."

She smiles and touches my cheek.

"When it was obvious your father would never return, I had to do as he asked. It hurt me to be so hard on you. I just wanted to hold you and hug you every minute."

She strokes my hair and tugs my chin to face her.

"I'm sorry, I never told you why I sent you away. I was afraid you'd talk, that you'd reveal too much. That it would be used against you. I feared Brogen would find you."

"Funny," I say. "I hated him my whole life. He represented the vilest evil. He was at the top of my kill list for a very long time."

"And according to Kara, you killed him. Is that true?"

I snort a light laugh.

"Almost. Jesmir dealt the death blow. I only put him in a vulnerable position."

"You know what that means? Don't you?" she asks.

I nod.

"I killed a god. I killed Hakaka."

She smiles, and questions formulate in my mind.

"So why an underground network?" I ask her.

She pats my knee.

"In due time, Shen-Zarl. First, let's invite your friends in. It is late. You all need some rest."

The day waxes and wanes. Stories are exchanged, new memories are unlocked, and old memories are redefined in retellings by my mother. Laughter happens, and on one occasion, Kara loses that stoic immobility again, and everyone bears witness to the beauty of the Korund's laughter.

Jesmir is smitten by the green giant and takes to calling Kara "a green goddess" when the Korund isn't in the room.

"It's kinda cute the way he's following Kara around now," Jesma whispers when neither of them is within earshot.

Later that evening, my mother and I sit on the front porch and talk about many things. We share memories of my father and my brother. She tells me about her favorite foods, and I share a few of my less sinister adventures. As we share, I see my mother as the person she is and not the monster I believed. With each laugh, tear, and story, my adult mind resets my childish memories. Somewhere along the way, my heart spills out, and I grip her hand as tightly as her frail bones will allow.

"I'm sorry. I thought the worst of you," I finally say, tears flowing again.

"You were a child. There was little chance for you to think otherwise. You're here now. That's all that matters to me," she says.

We fall into a comfortable silence, and she falls asleep on my shoulder. Pedestrians pass, nodding silent acknowledgements at me or each other. Most glance our way with curiosity, likely due to their beloved Anastaja resting her head on a strange man's shoulder. I remain with her until morning.

Dawn arrives, and Mom's small house resonates with jovial footsteps and voices. I rise and stretch. Mom extends her hands out, and I help her up.

Breakfast is a mix of Korund and Killinshire fare. All I care about is coffee, and somehow, Mom has plenty.

Tamrin storms off once again, his complaints over tastes and smells still the topic of his ire. Whatever ails him, it lingers.

After so many days of turmoil, these days are a welcome respite. At some point in the day, I crash. When I wake, everyone is occupied with another lazy afternoon on the front porch. Many townspeople wave to Anastaja, happy to see her. She waves back and always asks about loved ones or some event she was aware of that meant something to the person passing.

I'm chewing a slice of salt bread when we revisit the topic of the underground.

"The gods have everyone convinced the only way to access magic is through them. They use the periapts as the conduit. We now know that is not true. What we also know is that those who carry the periapts are incapable of using magic without prayers," Kara says.

Mom adds, "Every child in Conishant is indoctrinated with this belief. Most never question it. Those who do only question it due to trauma. For me, it was your father's insistence that this was the case. For your father, it came at a young age."

She pats my knee.

"For you, dear boy, it came as no surprise because you were never indoctrinated into faith. Thank your father for that."

"Are you saying I have magic?"

"Like your father," she says.

I only just learned I have control of some of it," I say.

"Unfortunately, you've been left feral for so long, I think that full control will be difficult. You've grown too used to it bleeding out continuously."

"And my lack of magic against the Kirwaq?" Tamrin asks.

"Simple answer? Fildeus blocked your access," Mom replies.

"How do they do this?" Jesma asks.

"That's the question we've been trying to answer. As far as why? We assume it's about control. It's *that* control that *we* resist. Self-discovery, self-actualization, and self-fulfillment are concepts to cherish. To do so in a community and be allowed to use our gifts to help one another is a noble cause. Our purpose is to build a large enough gathering of unbelievers that we can take on one of the gods, find them, and learn the truth."

"So where is everyone?" Jesmir asks.

"Well, Your Highness," Mom says, choking back tears. "I'm afraid most are dead. We don't know how they find us. Every time we build an advanced team powerful enough to do the job, someone finds them. I never discovered who or how."

"The last group were my friends," Kara says.

"What's the plan?" I ask.

"We grab a god."

"How?" I ask.

"Well, you are the fastest living being in Conishant now that Hakaka is dead," Mom says.

"No," I say and point at Jesmir. "He is."

"Really?" Mom asks Jesmir.

"I wouldn't say that. I can cross the distance in an instant, but it's not speed. At least not how I understand speed."

"Oh…you are a bender!" my mom exclaims. "You bend the world to your will. Place two points together and step between them. Not many of you in the world," Mom says with a whisper.

"Well," I say, and draw out the 'l' sound. "That's not true. We know of two more."

"That can't be," she says, dismayed.

"A murdering emissary named Krin. And an assassin she hired."

"Well, that is bad news. The only benders I knew were very favored by Shamna. All practitioners of luck." She winks at Jesmir. "Except you, of course."

I exchange a knowing look with Jesmir.

"What?" Jesma asks.

My mother gives me a knowing look.

It's time.

I frown at Tamrin. He reads my face immediately. Jesmir grabs my arm, and we exchange glances.

"Jez," Jesmir says, "We need a drink. There's something I must tell you."

❧❦❧

Jesma takes the news as expected. Eyes filled with tears, lips quivering, her balled fists shake. "How long have you known?"

"Since that first night in Teshket," I whisper.

"And you said nothing?" she demands.

I have no idea how to respond, so I remain quiet.

Jesma slaps me across the face.

My mother gasps.

"Jez," Jesmir says, "He was in a tough place."

"He was protecting himself," she spits. "And when did you discover my grandmother and Shamna are one and the same? The next day?"

I shake my head.

"No," I reply, "I only realized it after Grankin's memory."

"But you didn't tell me." Jesma turns to Tamrin. "Did you know?"

Tamrin's inability to bluff dooms him before he can speak.

"I told him not to tell you," Jesmir says. "I wanted to give you time to figure it out or tell you myself."

"Everyone knew except me?" she says. "Let me guess. The *little girl* couldn't handle the truth. Is that it?"

"No, that's not it at all," I say and stand and reach for her.

"Don't touch me, you bastard. Don't ever touch me again."

Jesma turns and storms off the porch into the crowd of passing Korund.

333

Jesmir stares after her in shock.

Kara says, "I'll stay with her. She won't get far, and she won't be unprotected."

"I'd better go too," Jesmir says.

"Great. The two people I'm trying to protect are going to storm off unprotected."

Jesmir retorts, "We aren't your *charges* anymore, Shen. When are you going to realize we are a team? It's not Shen, *the Great and Mighty Harbinger*, against the world, protecting two helpless royals. It's *all* of us, working together, fighting for a common purpose. You aren't a 'lone hero' anymore, Asshole. You're part of a team. A team that loves you."

He steps off the porch and turns back to me, his expression softened.

"I know you know that. Don't worry. She does, too," he adds.

Jesmir disappears into the crowd, followed by Kara. I stand at the top of the porch staring after them.

"We knew it wasn't going to go well," Tamrin says. "It didn't matter when we told them. At least now they know the truth."

"It's little consolation," I say.

"Sit, Son," my mom says. "They'll be back. They need time."

Chapter Twenty-One

Journal Entry: 134

Forty years of anger and angst washed away in a single day, only to have turmoil with Jez.

A lifetime of perceived neglect doesn't vanish overnight. Wounds don't heal that way, even psychological ones.

Still, hate-fueled emotions toward my mother no longer fester within open wounds. I see my mother through new eyes. My readiness to forgive her surprises me. Certainly, the healing process will take time. I know this. But after all these years of bitterness toward her and my father, I feel relief.

Anger is now sorrow. Sorrow over the lost years. Sorrow over the torture I put myself through. Sorrow over misguided memories.

There's a new ache too, a hollowness. I never understood the energy required to hold on to those negative emotions. And now that I'm forced to relinquish my stranglehold on them, they are free to evaporate into the nether. As they leave, they take with them my sense of self.

I don't know who I am without the constant loathing.

I know it should be replaced with a sense of pride. Pride in who my mother is.

Courageous, selfless, filled with sadness and joy, love and duty, pain, and loss, my mother is a human, like any other. She is a whole person who is much more than the angry memories of a twelve-year-old boy who hadn't evolved beyond the misplaced anger of his youth.

And my father? He made the ultimate sacrifice to protect his family.

I'm going to nurture this new truth.

I'm going to give it the proper care it deserves.

I'm going to fill the void with a new sense of self. A new purpose.

I'll make you both proud.

I'm going to take vengeance on those who stole our lives.

Hidden Message

In the hours since the twins stormed off, I sat on the porch waiting for their return, eyes on every non-Korund who passed. Of all the Korund towns, Gal-So is the most segregated. Never one to look a gift horse in the mouth, the lack of diversity in this neighborhood makes any non-Korund easy to spot. Very few humans have passed by.

Tamrin brought back a jug of Mistras' Reserve. We share it as we wait for the twins and Kara to return. My mother sits beside me, refusing to leave my side for a second.

There's a unique comfort in her presence.

Tamrin rises from his chair and stretches.

"I'm so hungry. But everything tastes like shit. Smells are off, too," he says.

My mother asks, "Why do you think that is, Master Tam?" my mother asks.

"I'm down with some ailment," Tamrin replies. "My body tingles everywhere like a mild fever."

I glance at him, but Mom speaks before I do.

She considers his words before asking, "Have you used your magic since you removed your periapt?"

"No. I haven't," he admits.

"When you consumed your magic before, did it affect your other senses?"

"It enhanced my hearing and sense of smell. When it's active, I can differentiate the smallest vibrations in the wind," Tamrin replies.

"What is it you call it? True Sight?"

"It's what my dad called it."

"Strange choice. It seems to limit your understanding, no?" she asks.

"How so?"

"Names are important. We name everything to better understand our world, or to control it. Your father called your magic True Sight. And maybe for him, that's all it was. But for you, it is so much more than sight, is it not?"

Tamrin scrunches his face, trying to understand her words. I put it together before he does.

"Tam?" I say. "If you named it, would you choose 'True Sight'?"

"No," he replies after some thought. "I would call it knowing or something."

"Sensing?" I offer.

"Yeah, like true sensing."

His grin grows until it's as wide as his face. He kisses my mother's cheeks with glee.

"You're a genius," he says to her.

He sniffs the air and sticks out his tongue. He winces and retracts it as if he tasted offal.

"Ugh, even the air tastes overwhelming."

"Try to differentiate your perceptions. Isolate each one. Don't allow every impulse to overwhelm your senses. Pick one, and focus," she suggests.

He sucks in air through his mouth with slow deliberation. His face twists in distaste, but he forces himself to endure the discomfort. His expression changes from agony to curiosity.

Tamrin loses himself in experimentation. My heart leaps when I see the happy expression that is his hallmark return.

"What is it?" I ask.

"I can taste the venison cooking a few doors down," he says and points to a Korund home where a spit turns in the fire. He leans forward and kisses my mother on the cheek. "Anastaja! You fixed me! My taste buds are off because I didn't know I was using magic."

"Which explains the fever," I say.

He smacks his head and laughs.

"I thought I was dying or something."

She smiles, "And now you know the answer. Don't you?"

Tamrin laughs his deep laugh, bends down, and kisses my mother on both cheeks again.

"Anastaja, you are a genius." He turns to me. "Buddy, I'm off to get some of that venison and maybe go drain the alehouse of every drop of Mistras' Reserve! You wanna tag along?"

I shake my head, lift the jug, and pat my mom's hand. "I'd like to be here when Jez returns."

"You want to go look for her? I can track her for you."

As much as I want to, I know she needs time. If she ever returns. I shake my head and wave him off.

"I'll be back soon. Don't wait up," he says.

Tamrin trots down the street, his large body bouncing like he's off to play with friends. "Hi! I'm Tamrin Salzar of Haabrestand. This venison smells delicious. Do you mind if I join you for dinner?"

"Of course not," a deep, Korund voice booms. "A stranger is a friend I haven't met yet! Come, have a seat!"

"Well," I say to my mother, "He's gone for the night."

"Well, don't fret, Child."

"I'm fifty-three, Mom."

"And I'm eighty-seven. You're a child to me. Anyway, someone waits for you. I think you two should talk privately."

A break in the crowd reveals a stunning woman, her silvery hair cascading off her shoulders, crystal blue eyes sparkling. My breath catches. Jesma stands across the street on the edge of the throng of pedestrians, eyes locked on me. From her posture, I think she's been there for quite a while. I offer a half-wave, unsure. She doesn't acknowledge the wave but crosses the street.

I rise to greet her. She stops at the first step onto the porch.

"I'm sorry I didn't tell you sooner. Please believe me. I wanted to," I say. "It was the hardest thing I've ever had to do."

"You didn't tell me because you were afraid I wouldn't believe you when I found out. Is that what you are going to tell me?" she asks.

I nod.

"And I was afraid I'd lose you," I whisper.

"I'm allowed to be mad at you. If every time we disagree, you think I'm going to leave, this isn't going to work out well for either of us. You know that's not healthy, right?"

I nod. "I'm trying, Jez. But you did say not to ever touch you again."

"Fair enough. I shouldn't have said that. I meant it in the moment, but it was wrong. I understand that everyone has left you in your life. Except for Tamrin, of course."

"And Mistras and Cali," I say.

"See? That's three people, then. I guess not everyone has abandoned you, have they? I don't know Mistras and Cali. But I know you and I know Tam."

"And I know you," I say.

"Then give me the benefit of trust, even if I lash out. Show me that you know me. That's not a request."

"Understood," I say and risk a smile.

Jesma climbs the stairs, passes me, and sits on the bench where my mother was. I sit next to her, and she leans her head on my shoulder.

"I should have known Grandmother was behind this," she says. "She never liked my mother. And Father was always on edge around her. He feared her in a way he feared no one else. Jes and I talked about it once, but we never asked him. Now I wish we had."

"I'm sorry that this is happening," I say.

"You thought your family was cruel," she says with irony. "Being a royal is a royal pain in the ass." She lifts her head and looks at me. "Even after everything, I still didn't believe any of you."

"What changed?" I ask.

"Three truths dawned on me. First, she should have known we were missing. Father sends a message every time he arrives at his destination. In all the frantic attempts to escape, through all the constant danger, there was never any real time to think. I forgot about his letters until today. Second, and this is going to sound strange, I think I heard grandmother's voice in Grankin's memory."

I look at her and frown.

"I did, too, but it was your brother who confirmed it. I wasn't sure until that moment. Her voice is the reason I overlooked Brogen. I mean, I noticed. But it didn't register. All I could think about was how I now had to tell you two horrible truths about your grandmother."

"That leads me to my last point. And this one is something that always struck me about Grandmother. She looks good for her age. I always thought that."

"Well, I have one other for you," I say.

"What's that?"

"I looked. Your grandmother wears pretty, revealing clothing, draws the eyes, if you catch my drift."

"Gross," Jesma groans.

"Sorry, but that's not the point. That morning, at breakfast, I observed her jewelry. Do you know what I didn't notice?"

Jesma shakes her head, nose scrunched at the thought of my observation of Queen Grandma's cleavage.

"A periapt. Shouldn't the Teshken queen to display her allegiance to Shamna prominently?"

"No, she never has. Grandmother always said, 'Shamna protects me as Queen. A periapt is of little use in my 'day-to-day'."

"Strange answer."

Jesma chews the side of her cheek. "What do we do now?"

"I think we do what Grankin wants. We get his Tome. Whatever is in that Tome, Grankin wants the world to know. That's his point, isn't it?"

"Agreed."

"We should head out tonight," I say.

"No. Let's head out tomorrow. It's time for angry make-up sex," she says.

"Oh, is it?"

Jesma tilts her head.

"And it's gonna be rough on you, Harbinger. You have much to apologize for, and I intend to take it out of your flesh," she smirks.

"What if your brother comes along?"

"He's engaged in his own style of angry sex."

"With whom?" I say, shocked.

Jesma doesn't reply. Her grin is my only clue.

"Nooooo."

"They had a bit to drink, started flirting, and took off into the woods together. He yelled back, 'Don't wait up.' I don't think they plan on coming back tonight."

I stand and offer my hand.

"Then, how about you make good on your promise and punish me for my crimes?"

She smirks.

"Just remember. You have it coming," she says.

I laugh, and she leads me off the porch, around the back of the house, and deep into a section of the woods out of sight from the world.

The knock on the door startles me awake. My mother speaks in hushed tones, but I can tell from her pace that something is wrong.

The front door closes, and she crosses over to me.

"Shen," she whispers, "wake up."

"What is it?" I ask.

"Death squad."

"I'm sorry?" I say.

She pulls me upright.

"We just received word. A death squad from the gods approaches, looking for unbelievers."

I jump from the couch and grab my clothes. I kick Tamrin, who sleeps on the floor next to me. He startles but doesn't wake. I kick him harder than I intend, but it works.

"What the hell?" he groans, gripping his thigh.

"Wake the twins," I say. "We have trouble."

Leaving my mother is hard. Our hands entwined, the bond impossible to break, she pushes me backward off the porch with slow steps. Her gaze continues to arouse new memories. So many times, as a child, she looked at me as she does now. Memories tainted by my own bias are now cleansed by the truth, shored by the evidence of the last few days. These revelations give birth to a new style of guilt, one I know I can heal from in time. In that, there is a new peace.

But that peace is secondary to the urgency we have now.

"Life has been an unfair toss of Shamna's Rocks," Mom says. "We rolled the dreaded five as a family. I should have told you the truth then. Your father wanted me to tell you. But he wasn't there to guide me, and I reacted out of fear."

I fight back more tears, exhausted from the emotional turmoil. Even the process to heal is tiresome.

"Now, this is important," Mom says. "You must not have any periapts on you." She looks around at the rest of the group. "None of you can carry them. If you do, then every attempt to use magic will notify the eight. They sense us through those symbols. One other thing. If anyone uses magic against you and they are believers, assuming they will be, the Eight will know."

"Seven," I remind her.

She smiles, but it's a reprimand. My hearts beats with love. "Every encounter, from here on, is a beacon to them."

"You three, especially," Mom says to Tamrin, Jesma, and Jesmir.

"*That's* how Brogen found us," Tamrin says.

"And Krin," I say.

"Unfortunately, it's not a two-way street. You can't reverse track them with a periapt. So don't think you can outsmart them," Mom says.

"Can we trust Grankin?" I ask.

She laughs, a soft laugh. "You can trust Grankin in that he's not one of them. The gnome has his own agenda. But, yes, you can trust he means *you* no harm. Grankin's stuck in the river because he exposed the Great Eight ten millennia ago."

"You know him?" I ask.

Mom releases my hands and looks at me, confused. "You don't remember?"

"Remember what?" I say.

"Grankin saved you when we fled Killinshire for Teshket. You were barely four years old. You ran to the river and fell in. He didn't tell you?" She's genuinely surprised by this.

"That gnome isn't very forthcoming with information," I say, frustrated.

"Ask him directly. *If* you see him again," Mom says. "It's not much to tell. A minor event in your life. But still. Odd, he didn't mention it."

"I'll choke it out of him," I say.

"Now, that's the sort of temper that got you into trouble as a boy. You've always overreacted," she says, her voice tender. She reaches and pulls my face to hers, kisses my cheeks, and pats my cheek. "Be more thoughtful, less reactionary. One of these days, that temper will cause you great pain if you're not careful."

She addresses the group.

"Get out of here. It's best we aren't seen together, better you aren't found at all. Finish the mission Grankin tasked you with. Uncover the truth. If you're able, I'd like to see the Tome before you take it to Grankin. But if not, try to record what you can. We should have a say in how we live our lives."

I hand Mom my father's letter.

"No. That is for you."

"Keep it. You can give it to me when I return."

She smiles at that. I kiss her forehead, slow to pull away.

"I love you," she says. "I always have."

"I know that now. I love you, Mom."

It isn't easy to reconcile hope in the future with the work we must do now. My whole life is one long fight against depression. Angst is the hallmark of my inner monologue. In a matter of weeks, that version of myself evaporated, leaving behind mere remnants of an ancient past I hardly recognize. Suicidal inclinations, once a constant companion, are now little more than somebody I used to know. Revelations and time severed all sense of common connection. Until now, I assumed happiness was never mine to grasp.

Though there is more trauma to come, I face it secure in the happiness that surrounds me. Against all odds, I've not only found family—I've found purpose.

With high spirits, we flee our pursuers and embark on a mission of great importance.

Free the world? I guess this is what we're doing now.

But the Dastardly Seven don't play fair. Never content to allow a joyful moment to go untainted, the darkness in my soul hasn't vanished. It's manifested itself. Like a virus, it spreads and is transferred to someone else. As the days roll on, the twins, each in their own way, carry the burden of despair that once was my domain.

The journey south to the capital city of Killinshire is arduous. We will cross the great Killinshire Plains. There's nowhere to hide for hundreds of miles. Once there, we will be exposed. For now, we rest in the relative safety of the last bit of wooded terrain. We push ourselves to stay ahead of our pursuers, hiding from the world by avoiding familiar roads and trails.

I don't know how the gods found out about us. I trust that the wards in Mom's home do the job of keeping her safe.

Idle minds dwell on dark thoughts. Three days of travel so far without incident. We hunt. We eat. We walk. We sleep. Boredom sets in when nothing happens. Nobody mentions that when they retell stories—the boring parts of wild adventures are where the real trouble lies. In those moments, one must deal with oneself.

When days pass and every moment is as uneventful as the last, even good friends fall silent. And in that silence, the mind lays its traps.

Every evening, it's the same ritual. We set up camp. Jesma wanders off without a word. Jesmir and Kara hunt. Tamrin and I gather wood for a fire. Tamrin skins and butchers the kill. And Jesma returns just in time to eat.

Each time Jesma returns, she's a little less light and a little more darkness. My darkness has taken root and bloomed inside her. Any attempt to pull her out is met with resistance. We've all tried. Each night she rolls into her blanket and falls asleep, her back to the rest of us.

Tonight is no different. Jesma sets her bedroll while the fire crackles and tiny sparks float on waves of heat like fireflies sent into the atmosphere. She avoids eye contact and instead follows the rising embers as they vanish against the backdrop of stars in the night sky. The twin moons straddle the streaks of bright stars across the eastern sky, the smaller one soon to pass the bigger as it does every night. Happy as I am to know the truth about my parents, I'm saddened by the brooding of the woman I love. At a loss, I toss pebbles into the flames—a mindless activity to fill the uncomfortable void. Sometimes the residual oil or dust ignites in a brief flash of color.

Jesma wanders off again, her form fading into the darkness beyond the fire. She made it clear that my company was unwelcome. I thought we were in a good place after our evening in Gal-So. Now I realize that was more for her than it was for us. She used our sexual escapade as a distraction before the storm to come.

Jesmir seems to have made peace with his new reality.

"You've improved quite a bit with your magic," I say to him.

He tosses an acorn into the fire.

"Yeah, it's easier with each attempt. I can almost do it without thinking now." He pauses. "But it hurts like hell."

"Now that I understand my abilities a little, I can say it will never not hurt like hell. The more aggressive you are, the worse it hurts. You get used to it, though. I always thought it was muscle strain or something related to physics or speed. Now I know—using our powers hurts—it takes a physical toll. It's nothing permanent, as far as I can tell, though."

"I hope not," Jesmir says.

"It always feels like I'm losing something," Kara adds. "Like somehow, a piece of me is left behind or consumed."

"Interesting perspective," I say.

"I miss Fildeus," Tamrin says.

I grunt. Jesmir sighs. Kara pats Tamrin's shoulder.

"Look, I'm not saying I want her back. But I've thought about this. Remember how you hurt yourself against the spiderlyches? And then again against the Cuska?" he says. "What if the gods limit our access only so that we don't overreact and harm ourselves? Maybe the gods understand something we don't."

"I'm sure they do. I just think it's something less benevolent than keeping us safe from ourselves. It doesn't make what they're doing right," I say.

"Doesn't make my point any less valid," Tamrin counters. "It takes a lot of concentration on my part to control the way my senses activate. It didn't used to be that way. It was easier with help. That's all I'm saying."

"You seek reasons to bring Fildeus back into your life," Kara says.

"Maybe," Tamrin replies. "This isn't easy."

"Well," I say, "I don't need that kind of help. And I don't want it."

Jesma reappears in the circle. Two finger-wide red streaks mar her face.

"My leg is healed," she says, her tone flat.

"How?" Jesmir asks.

"I healed it," she says.

"What's this?" I ask, running two fingers down my cheek.

She ignores my comment and doesn't speak. Instead, she walks over to Jesmir with her pouch. She removes the bandage from his ear.

"It still isn't healed," she says. "Let me try something."

She places her hand on his ear and closes her eyes. Her mouth moves, but no words come out. When she opens her eyes, they glow light blue. She frowns at Jesmir's ear and removes her hand. Her eyes return to normal.

"It's definitely still infected with rot root," she says. "I can't heal your wound. It wants to heal. It just can't."

She stomps to where she laid her bedroll and throws herself onto it. In a huff, she wraps herself in her blanket, turns her back to us, and falls asleep.

Don't disappear on me, Jez. Not now.

I want to talk about the streaks on her face, but Kara places a hand on my shoulder.

"Give her time," Kara whispers. "It took me time, too. It's different for us than it is for you. And she has more to deal with than the loss of Ezra."

I know Kara's right, of course. But it does little to assuage my worry. And the marks of the 'blood right' on her cheek worry me more.

What did you do, Jez?

Chapter Twenty-Two

Journal Entry: 135

Kara's friends are all dead. We haven't spoken about it since the Korund shared the story. Too much has happened. But now the god's killers pursue us.

It never occurred to me that a lack of religious faith would be a death sentence. Who cares if a handful of folks don't want to pay homage to some unseen deity? What could it matter to them?

Unless it does matter? I can't think of any reason it should.

The question is, who stood to gain when Kara's friends were killed? If bounties on the heads of unbelievers are real, what if the bounty on my head didn't come from the Guild?

The Plain Truth

Jesmir shakes with anxiety. We stand on the edge of a cliff, both literal and figurative. Renshmere, the capital of Killinshire, looms dark and malicious, several days' journey ahead. Pressed against the

Black Sea, its dark stone walls encompass the tightly packed structures of homes and imperial buildings. Jagged spikes, reminiscent of the view of netherstacks from the plateau on Sanctum Mountain, send a message of warning to all who travel into the city.

"Strangers beware," I say aloud.

"Even this far away, that city oppresses," Tamrin says. "Must we really go there?"

"I want to know the truth," Jesma whispers. It's the first words she's said since she couldn't heal Jesmir two days ago.

"Then let's go find it," I reply.

She doesn't respond.

Jesmir's teeth grind. The crackle in his jaw sounds like he chews sand. "Are you up for this?" I ask him.

He gives me a curt nod. Jesma glows at the city, her face flushed.

"Our father died in this realm," Jesma says. "I know Brogen is dead, but his death is a hollow consolation. I don't imagine the death of the emperor will offer any additional solace. Brogen conspired with the queen, and I aim to find out why."

Her switch from the use of 'Grandmother' to 'the queen' and the venom in her inflection are new. Dark circles under her eyes hollow out her appearance.

"I want to burn this entire realm to the ground," she says.

Tamrin and I exchange uneasy glances. I'm frightened for her. Whatever happens on her solitary walks, I intend to find out tonight.

"We don't have to do this. We can turn back. Hide from the world," I say. It's a pointless request. I know she'd never agree. But here at this moment, I'd give up the world for her.

"No. We move forward," Jesma says. "This ends when they are all dead."

Along the Killinshire plains, a herd of antelope runs by in frantic flight from a pride of wraith-lions hot on their tails. I wonder what would happen if the antelope pressed the attack instead of running. They outnumber the lions ten to one. But nature always ensures that hunters and prey live out their roles. Life and death seem predetermined by genetic superiority.

The wraith-lions vanish in a whisp of smoke and reappear on the last antelope. Two of the predators subdue their prey in a tumble of grass and dust. Others reappear at the feast, and the pride tears into the flesh with savage aggression.

The similarity to our current plight makes me wonder if we each charge straight into our own pride of wraith-lions.

"*They* did this to us, the emperor and the queen. And I want to know why," Jesma adds. "Better or worse, we take this to the end."

"It is as you see there, playing out in the plains," Tamrin says. "The prey must get lucky every time, the hunter only once. The hunter never stops, and the prey grows tired."

"We are both hunter and prey," Jesma says. "If we don't hunt, we wait for death."

"Your analogy is sound, Master Tracker," Kara says and glances at Jesma. "I agree with the princess. We must fight this fight. The gods are fickle, indiscriminate killers. For reasons we do not understand, they use us to bend the world to their will. Within *that* city, the emperor holds the answers. Many more will die by the hands of these gods if we don't stop them."

"Can we stop calling them gods?" Jesma blurts. "If they're anything, they're evil. Gods can't be evil. Gods are supposed to be the antithesis of evil."

"Well, I don't want to call them the 'Great Seven,'" Tamrin says. "That's for sure."

"Fine. Call them 'The Seven,'" I say, bored with the conversation.

"Call them dead," Jesma says.

"Fine," I say, "The Dead Seven." I step onto the trail into the plains below. "Come. There's work to do."

The great plains of Killinshire spread east, west, and south, far beyond the horizons. Gusts of wind push the tall fescue in waves of alternating green. Patches of acacia trees break the continuous fields of fescue with bark and long limbs. Occasional patches of elephant grass, prime hiding spaces for predators, keep us vigilant. The extra hours of sunlight this far south allow us to cover more ground each day.

Renshmere still looms a full day's walk. A pride of wraithlions rests under a cluster of acacias, some watching us warily. I'm certain they view us with hungry curiosity. We give them a wide berth, but they seem content to let us pass.

"I feel like a snack," Jesmir says.

"They're more afraid of us than we are of them," Tamrin says with a giggle.

"That's just something parents tell their kids to keep them calm," Jesmir mumbles.

Twilight approaches, and I point to a small group of three acacias that appear unoccupied with a clear view for miles in all directions. It's a perfect place to spend the night.

"Jez," I say, "don't wander too far off, please? This is Killinshire. Everything here wants to kill us or thinks we want to kill it. That includes people. The emperor has instilled a 'kill or be killed' mentality here. Even the snakes take heed. Murder isn't even a crime unless the victim is a member of the emperor's army."

"I'll be fine," she says and wanders off once more.

"I've got her," Tamrin says, his eyes a reassuring pale purple.

"Thanks."

We decide not to risk a fire this far out in the open. The cloud cover is heavy, making visibility difficult in the dark. Although winter is in full bloom in Teshket, the cold has barely reached this far south, so a fire is unnecessary.

I chew a piece of jerky in silence, drink water from my canteen, and settle with my back against the trunk of the largest of the three trees. Kara walks the perimeter around the trees, eyes vigilant. The night drags on, and we each take turns napping, rest less easily found in this violent land.

Jesma still hasn't returned, and I grow nervous.

"Umm, guys," Tamrin whispers.

"Is Jez in trouble?" I ask, rising to my feet.

"No," he says, "but we may be. I count twelve unfriendlies, four hundred yards north of us."

I climb the tree like a spider monkey, a surge of speed aiding my progress into an elevated position. Tamrin stands to my left, fifteen feet below.

"Animals or people?" I whisper.

"People," he replies and slides his hammer from his back. The giant warhead thumps on the ground, and he poises himself in his usual stance. I would not want to be in the way of that thing when it moves.

"They are definitely not friendly."

"How can you tell that in the dark?" Kara asks and stands off to my right, both swords drawn.

"Because friendlies don't crouch low like predators the way these folks are." He points both arms outward. "Some moved to flank us on both sides. Six ahead, three on each side."

"Tam, do a quick scan all around. Find Jez. Make sure she's safe. And make sure we aren't being flanked from another direction."

"Naders Nuts," he says. "Eight more coming from the south. Twenty total."

"I'm going up," Kara-Kar says, and the Korund rises into the air.

"Jez?" I ask.

"No sign. But her trail runs between the group of eight and the three that flank on the right."

"Go find her, Tam," I say. "We got these assholes."

"Will do."

Tamrin takes off on Jesma's trail.

"Jes, got your crossbow ready?"

"Bet your ass, I do," he whispers.

"Good. Don't hesitate. I'll take the six ahead of us. You take out the eight to the south. Kara, if you can hear me, snag the three that flank from the left."

A light bird whistle, too deep for any bird I know, signals that the Korund heard me. I can't see a thing in this dark night, and my hair stands on end. I wish we had fire magic, but none of us do.

I'd give anything for some light.

As if someone read my mind, bright yellow light flares bright against my eyes, which had adjusted to the near-total darkness. Temporarily blinded, I block my eyes from a sudden burst of flame headed right at my position.

"Shit!" I cry out and jump, blindly, from my perch. Unable to judge my distance, I hit the ground hard, and my legs collapse. I fall into a heap with a grunt.

"Harbinger? Are you okay?" Kara calls down.

"I'm fine," I mumble and crawl away from the trees.

My body burns with energy, and I sprint out into the darkness away from the flames and toward the six attackers. No longer hiding, the assailants' footsteps sound in all directions. I pinpoint the advancing raiders for a flanking position in the direction Tamrin headed.

I've lost track of Jesmir already, but trust he can carry himself now. Another fireball aimed toward Kara engulfs the green-scaled warrior. Kara drops amidst three hostiles. The Korund's battle cry carries for miles in a low rumble that rattles my bones.

"Fire against a Korund? Good luck with that, assholes," I whisper.

Footsteps behind me signal danger. I dive to my right, spinning out of the way of a heavy sword. The blade strikes the ground where I stood only a second prior.

Soundless, I vanish again into the darkness, far from the tree.

"Damn," the attacker curses.

I target the voice with a knife and throw my first new blade. I'm rewarded with a cry of pain and use the sound as a beacon. With my new blades hidden inside my bracers, I accelerate and tackle the assailant with a stiff shoulder. Punching with both fists into his abdomen, I knock the wind out of him. Both blades trigger, and he screams with pain. He's close enough now. I can see his eyes, wide in horror. I twist my wrists and press my hands toward his hips, my blades shredding his insides.

"Harbinger!" Kara calls. "I can use some help!"

"I'm not diddling myself over here!" I yell.

The body of my attacker falls, and I run toward Kara's voice, but something trips me as I go.

"Not so fast," a new attacker says. "*Harbinger?* It's my lucky day. Let's see if you're as good as they say."

A tall, wiry man, his skin much darker than mine, rises from the ground. He holds a spear that is as tall as he is.

"You're about to find out," I respond with a grin.

Screams ring out from Jesmir's last known position, but I don't recognize any of them.

"Find him!" another voice rings out.

A memory of lions on antelope comes to mind, and I suppress a giggle.

Jesmir is our very own wraith-lion.

My opponent never takes his eyes off me. His spear swipes the air so fast I almost can't get out of the way in time. I dodge, and his foot comes toward my face. His anticipation of my move is almost dead accurate.

A boot knife glints in the firelight as it passes too close to my eye for comfort, its tip nicking my cheek.

"So close," the new attacker taunts. "Looks like today I will elevate the ranks. If I kill you, the emperor will surely make me the new Captain of the Dark Guard."

"I wouldn't bet my life on that," I say. "I killed Captain Brogen. You really think you are better than him?"

"I heard the story. You had help. There's no help for you here."

News really does travel fast.

The spearhead whistles as he swings at my midsection. I dodge and swipe at the shaft with my blade.

I laugh at the shocked gasp that escapes his lips when my blade shears the tip off his weapon. Before I can make a snide comment, he spins the spear, and I almost don't notice the second blade on the other end. I raise my bracers in time to block his strike two inches from my face. The clash of steel-on-steel rings like a high-pitched temple bell.

I swipe my other blade upward to shear it away like the other, but he twists away before my blade can catch the wooden shaft. The spear spins around his body and comes straight at my abdomen. I side-step and strike at it with my blade again, but he snaps his hips, and the wooden shaft slams into my rib cage with a crack that forces me to absorb the blow. I recognize the move too late to prevent the bite of metal against my skin as he yanks the spear back.

"That stings," he says, my blood on his blade. The wound is only a surface cut, thanks to my reflexive shift sideways. He follows through with a high spin kick, directed at my head.

I counter with a punch to his calcaneal tendon, the crack against my fist more painful for him than it is for me. His initial grunt of pain transitions into a cry when I return the favor of metal to skin. I duck under the weakened attack, my blade slicing his tendon clean. I flick a knife into his other leg.

His ankle buckles, and my knife catches his thigh below the hip. He grunts again but doesn't fall, which catches me by surprise. He bears his weight on the damaged hip and remains upright. He throws his spear at me. Off balance, his spear flies off the mark, and instead of my chest, it pierces through my cloak. The sharp blade nearly catches my leg.

Even off balance, he's strong, and the throw has enough power that his spear yanks my cloak and causes me to stumble to the ground.

Krikhi's tits, this guy is fast!

As I fall, I wrap my arm around the shaft and slam my other blade against the wooden pole. The steel sings as it slices the shaft in two. Still falling, I grunt on impact with the ground. Even though the spear's shaft is shortened, the blade pierces the dirt, and thanks to my cloak, I struggle to stand.

His dark shadow hobbles toward me, the other end of the broken spear shaft poised to strike, its splintered wood aimed at my face.

I fling a knife at his face.

"Hey, scumbag," Tamrin's voice rings out. My knife strikes a hard object with a thud that sounds far more violent than I ever thought a knife could sound. The dark shadow of my attacker vanishes in a blur with a bone-shattering crunch. My attacker's silhouette is replaced by another when Tamrin's giant wooden war hammer slams into the side of my attacker's head.

My attacker's body lands in a heap, lifeless, in the darkness beyond.

"You gonna lie there all night, or we gonna kill these bastards?" he taunts.

"Give me a hand, would ya, Dickhead?" I raise my hand out.

"I already did. Twice," he retorts. "I got the third one too."

He yanks me to my feet.

"I'd like my knife back."

"What knife?" Tamrin asks.

"The one stuck in your hammer."

He rips the blade from his hammer and hands it to me.

"Help Jes," I order, pointing in Jesmir's last known direction. I sprint to help Kara, who is now surrounded by seven attackers. Dark forms, backlit by the conflagration that consumes the grove of acacias, surround Kara. The Korund's left arm hangs limp, one sword lost somewhere.

I sprint with a furious yell, hoping to draw the attention of as many attackers as possible. Four turn to address the new threat. One's eyes glow a pale yellow.

Magic user.

My internal fire burns with fury. I fling my last three knives, and they streak through the air. Their blued steel is impossible to see in the dark, and I tell myself to thank Brinker for the change.

"Light's out!" I yell the moment one of my blades strikes the magic user's eye. His final jet of flame heads in my direction. Weakened by his death, it passes by harmlessly.

Another attacker falls, my blade lodged in her neck. Her hand grasps her throat, blood spewing onto her fellow attacker. She gasps in panic and collapses in a gurgling heap. The third knife strikes the attacker closest to Kara in his spine. He falls to his knees. Kara swipes the blade in a backhanded arc and severs his head. With my focus on the last attacker to face me, I leap.

My final opponent struggles to block my attacks, blades cutting his body's supportive tendons. He still stands when I turn my back on him and face what remains of the horde of killers that press Kara. The dead man collapses with a thump behind me, and Kara's remaining attacker looks around for help.

"How great was that?" I ask. "Did he collapse like a pile of loose bricks?"

The last assailant holds two heavy axes in her hands. She throws one at me, and I step out of the way.

"You missed," I growl. She can't be more than fifteen years old. Too young to be in a fight to the death.

"I'll give you one chance to run," I say.

"The gods will make me one of them after I kill you," she snarls.

If I hadn't already witnessed one person move faster than I expected, her response would have caught me by surprise. With a sneer, she lunges at me and spins so that her axe approaches my neck in a wide arc. It should be the wrong weapon for her petite frame, but the power in her strikes sends me stumbling backward in stunned evasion. Her blades move like she has small, fast weapons. I block with my bracers, and the shock causes my wrists and elbows to ache with the energy.

We exchange strikes. The handles of her axes must be Korund steel, and my blades bounce off them with loud clangs.

She presses, and I dodge. A body falls behind me, and I know someone has died, but I can't chance a glance. This teenage attacker is too relentless to take my attention off her.

"You blaspheme the gods," she says, eyes on fire, magical energy burning through her.

I kick at her legs, and she blocks with her shins. I'm stunned by the power in her block.

We pause, assessing one another. A tall shadow rises behind her. Kara's blade slices through the air, and the attacker's eyes go wide with shock.

"Too bad you won't live to learn from your mistake, Kid," I say as both halves of her body fall to the ground.

"Behind you!" Kara yells.

I drop into a spin kick. My shin catches another attacker in the legs. She screams in surprise. My body burns hotter, and I push harder. My other boot reaches her head before she hits the ground, and her neck snaps from the impact of my kick.

Kara faces off against one final attacker. I step beside the green giant.

"You okay?" I ask.

"It'll heal. He broke my shoulder." Kara points to a large dead man with a hammer next to him, larger than Tamrin's.

"He hit you with *that*?" I exclaim, knowing that the hammer would have killed me on impact.

"Yeah."

We both face the last of the gods' kill squad.

"Remind me never to piss you off," I quip. "What's it gonna be?" I ask the final attacker.

He moves to hold his hand in surrender. I notice the periapt tattooed on the palm of his hand. The ground rumbles beneath us, and roots wrap around Kara and me. It happens so quickly that we are tangled before either of us can react. The strong, thick roots wrap around us and tighten. The air escapes our lungs. My ribs pop, and I know they're broken. Kara flexes against the pressure, but it's no use.

"Nice of you to choose to camp under a tree," he says. "Makes my life easier. With everyone else dead, I get credit as the one who kills the Harbinger."

He steps forward. "Did you know that the bounty on your head is now four hundred thousand gold? It was only a matter of time before the number reached so high that entire armies would come after you. But the Great Eight wants you dead by their hands. So here we are."

He looks around at his people.

"Anyone else out there?" he calls out.

No responses come.

He laughs a hearty, genuine laugh.

"You killed them all." He laughs again. "Twenty of us. That's twenty thousand gold apiece you've saved me."

He bows.

"From the bottom of my heart, thank you. Shamna smiles on me."

"Shamna…can lick…bakru shit," I reply.

His expression darkens at my blasphemy.

"Who leads your tiny band of heretics?" he asks. "You vermin pop up like cockroaches. The gods keep you safe. Why can't you see that?"

"The gods can…cut their tongues on my…scaled tits," Kara replies, laughing, though her words come in gasps.

"Tell me, who is the leader of your tribe of blasphemers?" the mage demands, his face twisted in rage.

With my last bit of breath, I squeak out an answer.

"Your mom."

The roots squeeze tighter around my chest and choke out my cry. Another rib pops, and this time, sharp pain seizes my chest, and blood rises into my throat. The light of the fire grows dim. The last thing I see is a dark shadow, sultry, moving with deliberate grace, a wraith in the night. She's the most beautiful and violent creature I've ever seen.

And I'm saddened by her presence. My heart breaks as she approaches the magic user from behind. Jesma's face illuminates in the light from the burning trees. Her eyes are wild and as black as the night sky.

She reaches around the mage's head and places her hand on his face. She bares her teeth like a demon.

The man screams in agony. His body shakes with tremors.

Jesma, what have you done?

My last thought is one of terror. Images I can't identify carry me into darkness.

"Easy there," Tamrin says.

Bright sky causes me to blink against the pain in my eyes. Tamrin helps me sit upright, his hand on my back. Kara sits next to me, cross-legged, eyes closed, meditating.

I look around, trying to gain my bearings. What was a beautiful grove of ancient life now stands as little more than charred fossils. It takes a moment for me to register that the pain in my chest is more memory than actual.

I take a shuddering breath and search for the twins, but they aren't around. Dark images invade my consciousness, and I cringe. Tamrin wrinkles his brow in concern.

"How do you feel?" Tamrin asks.

"I'm not sure," I say. "Where's the demon?"

"The what?" Tamrin asks.

"He means the princess," Kara says in a soft voice.

"No," I say. "Something else was here."

Tamrin shakes his head and points to the still-burning trees.

"There was no demon," Kara says. "What you saw was your love. She's discovered how to unheal."

My heart aches from the Korund's words.

Tamrin pulls me to my feet. Kara's expression portrays the same turmoil I feel.

"Good to see you back."

"Those roots broke my ribs," I say.

"Same," Kara offers. "Although I was fortunate enough not to have died from my injuries. Your lungs collapsed."

Kara stares back at the trees, a move which draws my gaze to the baleful female form that passes in front of the dying flames. Jesma paces the scorched earth alone. With her arms wrapped tight around herself, she stops, and I think she glances our way but does not approach.

"I fear the princess may suffer ill effects from her actions," Kara says.

"What actions?"

The silence is uncomfortable. Tamrin shifts his feet.

"Spit it out," I say.

"She's not quite…*herself*. It took some effort to convince her to heal you both," Tamrin says. He looks at me with sadness. "*You* almost didn't make it. If she'd resisted much longer, we'd be burying you right now."

"It's hard to say if it was reluctance due to fear…or disdain," Kara adds. "She was manic."

Jesma, her arms still crossed, back to us, stares at the blackened acacia trees.

Darkness blooms for us all.

"I don't like these changes, Shen," Tamrin says.

We hang back, the others walking several hundred yards ahead.

"I'm inclined to agree. Jez killed with a touch."

"I saw." He bites his cheeks. "It was the most terrifying thing I've ever seen. I tended four corpses with bolts in their necks. Jes is a hell of a shot, but those were taken in the dark. I don't know how he did it. No idea how he could even see them. Worse were the other bodies. It looked like they'd been leeched of their souls." He falls silent.

"Guess they really don't need us anymore," I say.

"That's what you take out of this?" Tamrin says.

"No. I'm…no. Sorry. I've never been through so many emotional ups and downs. Jez has been different since Gal-So. I think I know what she's been up to on her nightly disappearances," I say.

"That night when she returned with the blood rite on her face," Tamrin acknowledges.

We stand in the darkness, each lost in our thoughts. Filled with trepidation, all I can think about is my next conversation with Jesma. Relationship or not, this new dynamic could have lasting effects on how we work together as a party. Unresolved issues will fester.

"Not to change the subject, but how did that death squad know where to find us?" he asks.

"I have no idea. Time to go through our stuff and make sure there are no periapts hidden amongst us," I say.

"Think there are more?" Tamrin asks.

"You can count on it," I say.

Jesmir turns to face us and vanishes. He instantly appears next to me.

"Ezra's tits, don't do that!" I exclaim.

"Sorry," he says.

"I think we should get rest," he says

"I can use a break," I reply.

Kara and I sit in silence while the others sleep. Sounds of the daily struggle over life and death carry over the wide-open plains. We opt to stagger our shifts this time. Stifling a yawn, I wake Tamrin and curl into my cloak for the night.

Sleep arrives slowly. My dreams are fitful, filled with images of nether, demons, and a strange goddess with three black heads.

Jesmir wakes me with a nudge much sooner than I hoped.

"I'm worried about Jez," he whispers. "I can't get through to her."

He says no more than that and saunters off to catch a final few hours of sleep.

What am I supposed to do about it, Jes?

Jesma sits on the opposite side of camp, facing Ezra's slow rise, her back to me.

Go talk to her, Dumbass.

The will to approach her is difficult to muster. I pace, my gaze on her. It's possible she's fallen asleep in a seated position. She hasn't moved for almost an hour. With a deep breath, I summon the courage and make my way over.

"Mind if I join you?" I whisper.

She doesn't react to my presence or respond to my question.

I sit next to her. She tenses.

The silence fills the space between us with a physical quality. In my mind, I envision a barrier between us, impenetrable and solid. Streaks of clouds reflect colors from Ezra's rays across the lightening sky. To the west, the last of the deep purples of dawn fades away.

Rather than bring peace, the new day brings dread. Foreboding blankets any hope in the future.

The long shadows of our bodies on the brown grass shorten with time. Behind us, Tamrin's low familiar rumble is the only sound. Even Jesma's breathing is soundless. Try as I might, I can't think of any words to break the ice. Closed off as she is, any words risk pushing her further away. The thought of her, lost inside herself forever, is more than I can bear.

Every part of me screams to rip her out of wherever she's allowed herself to go, but I am unsure if the desire is for her sake or mine. The power she demonstrated last night must affect her in ways I cannot fathom. This isn't the first life she's taken. But her first was much like mine. Reflexive.

My first kill is a distant memory, but I still remember the feeling…the horror and remorse. I remember I was afraid of what it said about me. I remember I didn't want to hurt anyone. I remember exactly how it happened. It went much like the man Jesma killed in Breakridge.

My second victim was different.

Exactly like Jesma's.

"I remember the first time I deliberately chose to take a life," I say.

She flinches at my voice.

"I never told anyone about it. I mean, I guess I kinda did back in Valshannon. But not really."

I dig in the dry grass in front of me with a throwing knife, a mindless activity.

"I was thirteen years old. She was fourteen. It was my second time being called into the Culling Ritual. My first time was like yours. I was a reluctant participant. The second time, while I didn't want to be a part of it, was the first time I understood the stakes. I almost died the first time. The second time was different."

I continue to fling dirt out onto the grass. With each pass, the little trench grows deeper. The scratching sound turns rhythmic, and I stop, annoyed by the predictability of it.

"She was one of four girls in our class of twelve. Everyone was afraid of her after her first match. She came out with ruthless aggression. It was animalistic. Everyone thought she'd be the last one standing after her first culling."

"I remember her face. The glee in her expression, the blood-lust in her eyes. It was obvious what I needed to do. Her aggression still caught me by surprise. But it also made me angry. And I didn't want to see her unleashed onto the world. She enjoyed killing too much."

"Death still frightened me back then. But, in a moment of clarity, I knew death couldn't be avoided. Quietius always came. I unleashed violence on her that I never knew was in me. There was no place on her that wasn't cut. My knife was so sharp that my final strike nearly decapitated her. The smell of blood filled the air. There was so much of it."

I turn to Jesma, but I don't touch her.

"I cried myself to sleep that night. The guilt overwhelmed me. All I thought about was the look on her face when she realized what it's like to face someone who wanted her dead. She saw what her first victim saw, and it frightened her. But I was committed. It took me years to get over that guilt."

She turns to me, and I tilt back, surprised by her expression.

"You think I feel guilty?" she asks, incredulous.

I don't know how to respond.

"I don't. He was going to kill you and Kara, and then Tamrin, Jes, and me, if he could. I knew I could stop him…and that nothing could stop me."

She turns back to the wilderness.

"I felt like a *god*."

I swallow. This is not what I expected.

"Jez," I start, but she interrupts me.

"Don't, Shen. Don't act like you understand. Do you know what I was doing the past three nights? Well, you wouldn't."

"I saw the blood, Jez. What you did to that mage? I may not be the smartest person in Conishant, but I can follow clues."

She looks at me with a frown.

"You think less of me, don't you?" she asks.

This time, I don't hold back my touch. I grab her face with both hands and pull it close to me. She tenses, but I don't relent.

"You could never diminish in my eyes, Jez. I don't think less of you. I'm trying to tell you I know what you are going through. And you can say you don't feel guilty, but I know you. It will hit, and when it does, I'm here. But I am concerned. You went into the woods three nights in a row specifically to discover this magic."

"I know. And I'm ashamed by it," she says.

"Who was your first victim?" I ask.

"It wasn't a who. It was a what."

I look at her in dismay.

"Please tell me you didn't kill a bakru," I whisper.

"Ezra's sake, no!"

I let out a sigh of relief. "Oh, good. I love Bakru."

"I know. I'd never hurt something you love. It was rattlesnakes," she whispers.

I try not to laugh, but I fail.

"That's all? I thought so much worse."

Her eyes well with tears. "I'm so angry," she says, and her voice shudders. "Grandmother killed my father, her *son*. She's never been truthful. Which makes my whole world a lie. Can you unders…?" She stops and covers her mouth with both hands in shock.

"Oh, Shen," she says. "I'm so sorry. I wasn't thinking."

I pull her close.

"Of course I understand. Your life fell apart."

I hold her close, and she releases her emotions.

"You helped my horrible life fall into place while yours fell apart around you. If anyone is allowed to be angry and bitter, it's you. Just don't shut *me* out, Jez. You pulled me out of hell. Don't recede into your own."

She lays her head on my shoulder and sobs quietly.

"I don't feel bad about killing those people," she whispers. "I feel bad because I enjoyed killing them. They deserved it."

"I can understand *that*," I reply.

"But what it made me realize is worse." She lifts her head and holds my gaze.

"After we get the Tome and kill the Emperor, I want you to do me a favor."

"Anything," I say.

"Help me find a reason not to kill my grandmother. She can't be allowed to continue, but killing her is not an option. There must be a better way."

Besides the one that says she's an evil bitch with a god complex?

Chapter Twenty-Three

Journal Entry: 138

The closer we are to Renshmere, the louder the words of the Jandu repeat in my head.

"Child of Killinshire."

"Emperor's son."

The refugee couple said the same thing.

My mother's confirmation that I'm Killinfolk doesn't make the news any easier to accept. I want to scream against it. I want to deny it—make it not true. I don't wish to share kinship with Brogen. I've never met a person from Killinshire I didn't want to kill.

Killin-born.

Fuck.

I'm no better than they are.

Violence is in my blood. It's who I am. There was no escaping my destiny.

"Child of Killinshire."

And now, Jesma is just like me.

Hive of Villainy

It takes two more days to reach the capital city of Killinshire.

Renshmere looms before us like a cancer, a dark mass against an otherwise stunning landscape. The black waters of the southern sea beyond lose their attraction from this vantage point, tainted by the presence of the blood-stained jagged walls that surround the violent city. Built of dark granite from deep in the emperor's mines, covered in centuries of dirt and blood, the walls pulse with baleful energy.

Regardless of the danger, the city draws us in, pulling us toward impending doom, unwilling to relinquish us from whatever fate awaits beyond its hard, bloodthirsty border. The discernible gloom over us deepens as the dark city grows larger and fills our field of view.

Collectively, we've grown tired of this trip, weary of each other, and exhausted by Killinshire. Empathy wears thin, and tempers are short. The oppressive nature of this realm seeps into our pores, infecting our minds. Though I know it's a foolish thought, I imagine Killinshire as a living being, breathing with bad energy.

Jesmir takes the lead. His shoulders slumped, and his back hunched, he pushes himself to continue. His boot scuffs the road, and he faceplants into the dirt.

"Damnit!" he yells. He rolls over onto his back and stares blankly at the sky.

"I remember the first time I walked a dusty road," I mumble as I yank him upright by his vest with little compassion. "Let's go, Your Highness."

"Hey," Jesma snaps, unhappy with how I handled her brother. "Be nice."

I throw my hands in the air.

"Sorry," I retort.

But I'm not. I'm too tired to care about anyone's feelings, and I don't want to be anywhere near this shithole city. Every visit leaves me with nothing but troubled thoughts. This time, armed with the knowledge of my lineage and why my parents fled, only makes me hate this place more.

We are all on edge. Me more than anyone. I know what they do not; there's no chance we can break into the Emperor's compound without a massive fight. Only an invitation can get a person inside. There are only two ways to get that invitation. Both come with considerable risk.

"We should formulate a plan," Kara suggests as if reading my thoughts.

Only Kara seems unaffected by the gloom and doom mood that settles over the rest of the party. It's impossible to tell what the Korund's state of mind is.

"There is no plan," I say. "We get invited in and we trash the place once inside."

"What?" Jesma says. "We're going to waltz in and start a fight? Are you daft?"

I point ahead at the black walls. We are close enough for details to form.

"Do you see the lighter shapes about a quarter of the way down the wall?" I ask, my tone hard.

The others squint and stare at the spots in question. I wait.

"I don't…," Jesma interrupts herself with a gasp. "Are those bodies?"

"Barbaric," Kara says.

"Those are the remains of the family and friends of the last person to challenge the emperor. As unfriendly as your experience in Killinshire has been, you've never experienced anything like Renshmere."

I glare at the group. "Turn around now if you don't want to go. But I'm going in there. This was never going to be easy. Reconcile that now. Once we cross into that city, there's no going back."

I leave them to decide for themselves. But I have every intention of seeing this through.

I stop cold, the city gate mere yards ahead. Two groups of five guards dressed in black armor, dented from years of combat, stand on either side of the opening. They laugh and joke among themselves, selecting victims to terrorize at random. Everyone presses close as I stare at the high archway.

Grateful they chose to go forward with me, I whisper.

"I need you to trust me on this one," I say. "No plan will work. Follow my lead, act as I do…and for the love of bakru, don't fucking interfere with anything that happens in this city unless you want to fight."

I hesitate to enter.

"What is it?" Jesma asks.

"I haven't been through these gates in almost a decade," I say.

"It's a city like any other," Kara says.

Tamrin grips my shoulder.

"You aren't going through this alone," he says.

"This has been a long, strange trip," Jesma says, her tone softer. "For all of us. We're in this together, no matter how much the last few days may indicate otherwise."

Jesmir bumps my shoulder, and I stumble at the unexpected force applied.

"Walk much?" he jokes.

Even Kara snickers. Our behavior draws the attention of the group of guards on the left. They approach, their swagger indicative of most bullies. Jesma tenses.

"Teshken scum," the leader says, his armor dented more than the others. "What brings your kind to Killinshire? Looking to start something?"

He grabs Jesma's arm, and Tamrin growls. Jesma winces at his grip but holds her head high.

"Unhand me," Jesma replies, her tone curt.

"Here to surrender? Let me help you. Come inside the shack. We can work out terms," he says, his eyes roaming her body.

The other guards snicker. Kara places a large hand on the guard's shoulder.

"Wouldn't you rather have a piece of something stronger?" Kara says.

The guard removes his hand from Jesma and smirks at Kara.

"Well, look what we have here. A Chieftain's spawn. Always wanted a piece of royal ass."

Jesmir punches the guard in the mouth. The guard staggers back. Tamrin and Jesma draw their weapons, which triggers the guards to draw theirs. The crowd separates from the commotion, eager to avoid the fray.

"Well, let's get this over with," Tamrin says.

I hold my hands to stop my friends. The guard's eyes are wide, and his jaw is clenched. Jesma stares at him, smirking.

"You see," Jesma says, "It's not nice to touch folks who don't wish to be touched. Now, my friends here have the shortest tempers of anyone you've ever met. And this one," she indicates toward me with a head tilt, "enjoys nothing more than eating the flesh of…what is it you call them, honey?"

"Killintwerps," I reply, baring my teeth.

"You've heard of the man, I'm sure. My honey goes by many names."

Jesma's position is awkwardly close to the guard. I peek around to find her hand resting near the guard leader's groin. The dark steel of a throwing knife is visible in the folds, its tip between the guard's scrotum and inner thigh.

I laugh.

"Oh my," I say to the others. "She's got the fucker right where she wants him."

"Who are you?" one of the other guards asks. The other set of five guards approaches, weapons drawn.

I'm in motion before anyone realizes. One guard falls to the ground unconscious, and my bracer blades hover at the throats of two others before anyone knows I've moved. The two guards freeze in panic. The others glance around and begin shouting orders at each other.

"You've heard of *The Harbinger*," Jesma whispers.

The words pass through the crowd in hushed whispers, equal parts fear and awe.

"It's the Harbinger," the gathering crowd says.

The two guards, with my blades at their throats, swallow hard.

"I wouldn't do that," I warn. "It won't take but the slightest motion for these blades to slice you clean." I address Jesma, "Honey? What's the play here?"

Kara chimes in, "As a Chieftain's Child, I'm inclined toward non-violence and de-escalation of international hostilities."

The guard leader lets out a sigh of relief.

"However," Kara continues, "these men are rude. As is the custom here, I believe we should kill 'em all. Let Quietius sort them out. Seems like a proper diplomatic response when low guards fail to exercise caution."

"Two to one odds hardly seem fair," Tamrin says. "Or fun."

The guard smirks.

"Should we wait for more Killintwerps to show up? Even the odds," Tamrin growls. "I'm willing to wait if you are."

The guard leader's smirk fades, and his face pales. He says, "Listen, no one informed us that a delegation was en route. Ours is an ancient rivalry. We were just playin' around. Let's not start a war over it."

"I'm hungry. Am I free to kill these two or not?"

Jesma considers my request and shakes her head. "No. I think today, cooler heads will prevail." She withdraws her knife and holds it to the guard's face. "Now, what is your name?" she asks the leader.

"Marshall, ma'am," he replies, equal parts respect and disdain.

"I think you and your men will escort us safely to the emperor's gate."

He glances around, uncertain, but the other guards all nod their heads, eager not to experience whatever hell our little band of five seems capable of unleashing.

"We can spare four of our ranks to do that," he says.

"Good," Jesma replies. "And you will be one of them. Any harm falls on us, you die first. Sound good?"

He swallows hard. "No harm will befall you prior to the Citadel gates. What happens afterwards is out of my hands."

"That is all I ask," she replies and draws a small cut on the guard's cheek. "Never touch me again."

I retract my blades, leaving slight cuts on the two guards' necks trickling blood.

"Damn. This city stinks," I say, wrinkling my nose in distaste.

"That should have been my first clue," Kara says.

"Clue to what?" Jesmir asks.

"That this is Shen's homeland," Kara replies.

Tamrin's laugh brings us a lot of attention, but it doesn't stop him.

"The Korund's got jokes, now," I say to the two guards whose necks I nicked. "I was really hoping for a reason to kill you all," I whisper.

The fear on their faces is delightful.

We aren't fifty feet into the city when a body flies out of a door and into the street. Arms and legs flail, attempting to correct the trajectory of the ejected body to no avail. The person, scruffy and dressed in tattered clothes, lands with a thud on the muddy road. The expulsion of air, audible to everyone within twenty feet, causes a collective groan followed by vicious laughter. The man gasps for breath with high-pitched and desperate wheezes. A tall, thin woman, her black hair in two long braids, steps out of the house, a deep scowl on her face. The man on the ground rolls onto his back and fights for air.

He raises his hands defensively to the woman as if to ward her off.

The woman, her hands gripping two dull kitchen knives, growls, "Fight me, Petro. Fight or die."

Petro shakes his head, his cheeks flapping, his words rushed. "Honey, I will not fight you, ever," he replies.

"You should have thought of that before you turned down a chance to fight for the Regent's position. I will not stay married to a coward."

The woman steps toward Petro, and Jesma tries to push past me, but I block her way before she can interfere.

"He said he has no desire to fight you," Jesma warns from behind me.

The woman walks into the street and raises one knife. She addresses Jesma and says, "Then maybe you can die in his place, Teshket whore."

Jesma scowls and counters the woman's threat with, "Or you can die where you stand."

The woman laughs until the guard leader steps in front of her. The crowd grows, the newcomers cheering for bloodshed. Kara moves to protect Jesma, and the Killinshire woman casts a sideways glance.

"Mind your business, Korund," the woman says.

"I intend to," Kara replies. "And this Teshken is my friend and under my protection, which *makes* her my business. *You* are not my friend, or my business. I only ask that you not make me an enemy."

Kara's muscles flex, sending a ripple of clicks along emerald scales, and a wave of reflected light ripples with brilliant color. The man on the ground catches his breath and stands.

Petro finds his courage and says, "This is none of your business, Teshken. Nor is it yours, Korund. This is between me and my wife."

Jesma's gaze alternates between the two Killinfolk, and she lowers her rapier.

"Fine. You two wish to kill each other. Do it," Jesma replies.

"Not so fast," the woman says. "You made the challenge. I accept, Blondie."

Jesmir appears behind the woman and places a blade to her throat.

"That's my sister." He nicks her neck with the tip. "Consider that a gift from Teshket. Next time you address a Royal, I suggest you use the proper courtesy."

Jesmir vanishes and reappears next to Jesma. The guard leader looks around at the crowd and raises his arms in warning.

"Now listen up. These people are under the protection of the emperor. If you wish to challenge the emperor and decide a different fate for them, this is Challenge Week. You are free to head to the gates and make your challenge known."

The crowd falls into quiet mumbles.

Challenge Week. What a lucky break!

The woman touches the blood that forms on her neck. She sucks it off her finger with a smirk.

"I meant no disrespect to the emperor," the woman says. Her eyes dart around the crowd. A few try to egg her into a challenge, but the woman refuses to acknowledge the crowd. Taunts of "boo" rumble through the audience.

"Look who's a coward now, love," the husband says. She scowls at him but doesn't respond.

The husband pushes past Jesma and Jesmir and stands before his wife. He holds out his hand to her.

"What do you say we go inside and forgive one another?"

The woman takes his hand but never takes her eyes off Jesma. The couple disappears into their home and closes the door behind them.

Kara turns and says, "Killinshire hasn't evolved beyond alpha dog pack mentality. I'll never understand this place."

"Rugged individualism and glory are the only currency they care about here," I say. "It's run amok for so long that no one remembers its original intent. And the Emperor does little to change it. In fact, his policies only encourage the behavior."

"Can we go do what we came here to do and get the hell out of here?" Jesmir asks. "I don't want to spend any more time in this shithole than I have to."

The Citadel, built against the port-side docks, sits behind another set of walls, only half as high as the city walls. The emperor, his cabinet, and his family, plus twenty thousand members of The Dark Guard, reside within this inner circle. In my lifetime, there has been only one emperor. The current ruler is the longest-standing emperor of the last two hundred years.

Or so the legend goes.

A loud bell rings from somewhere in the city.

"It's the challenger's bell!" someone calls out.

Cheers and jeers echo throughout the streets in an uproar that carries for miles.

"What does that mean?" Jesma asks.

"Hey!" I call out to a woman who rushes past. "Is that the first or the second bell?"

"What, you just arrive? It's the second. First was yesterday."

I bow my head.

"What is it?" Jesma asks.

"It's the execution bell," I say.

"Someone is about to be executed?" Kara asks, appalled.

"A lot of someone's," the guard replies. "There was a challenger yesterday. Time to learn who was victorious."

"I'd say they failed if they are about to be executed," Jesmir says.

I shake my head.

"That's not how it works. Anyone can challenge the emperor at any time during challenge week. If they succeed, they become the new Emperor."

"And if they fail?" Jesma asks.

"The outcome for the loser is death. Whether challenger or Emperor. But that was decided yesterday."

"Then who is being executed today?" Tamrin asks.

"The family of the loser. The victor eliminates any potential vengeance seekers to deter more challengers." I turn to the guard. "How many days left?"

"Today is the final day. Tomorrow, the Dark Guard will protect whoever is Emperor until next year.

"That's appalling," Jesma says in dismay.

"It's worse than you think," I say. "The family of the loser is executed to three generations in every direction, from grandparents to grandchildren. That includes every descendant of the grandparents of the loser. Aunts, uncles, cousins, all slaughtered. Today's death toll could be in the hundreds."

"We have to stop this," Jesma says.

"We can't, Jez. It's Killinshire law. It's the only thing that deters a massive war inside the country." I spread my arms and spin in place. "Look around you. Do any of these people look like they care about anyone but themselves?"

The crowd rushes toward the front gates of the Citadel.

"Can't we stop it?" Jesmir asks.

"Well, yes, we can. But you won't like how."

"How?" Kara asks.

"One of us has to challenge the current winner."

"One of us?" Jesmir says.

"Technically? Yes," I say.

"No. Not one of us," Jesma replies. "You mean you."

"Gotta be native to Killinshire to be Emperor."

"You can't," she says.

"It's why we're here," I say.

"*This* was the plan all along?" she hisses.

"It was one option," I reply.

Tamrin steps toward me and grabs my blouse in his massive fist.

"You could have told us," he says.

"I know."

"And we can't help you?" Jesmir asks.

"Nope. The fight is one-on-one."

Tamrin grips my cloak with both hands and pulls my face into his. "What's the other option?"

I slap Tamrin's hand several times in rapid succession. "Not the cloak! Not the cloak! Let go, sheesh."

He shakes me like a toddler.

"You should have told me, you selfish asshole!"

"What do you want? I'm Killinfolk. We're selfish by nature."

"Agh!" he yells and lets go with a shove.

"What then?" Jesmir demands.

"We hurry to the gallows and issue the challenge before the executions begin," I say.

Seven people stand, hooded at the gallows, nooses around their necks.

"Hear the bells for whom they toll!" a hooded executioner calls from the deck of the wooden gallows. "The following traitors are to be executed per the emperor's command! These souls have been found guilty of treason against the emperor, of sowing a weak blood-line, and for an inability to defend their right to positions of leader-ship."

He reads from a book as he paces across the platform in front of seven hooded and bound people.

"The first one will reveal the loser of the challenge," I say.

"Wait, you mean nobody knows?" Kara says.

"Nobody," a woman behind us says. "It's a surprise! I hope we get a new one. If it's a new one, we get to celebrate all week. Im-agine a week-long celebration! Won't it be glorious? My mother says the last one was spectacular, but that was long before I was born."

Jesma struggles to hide her dismay.

"Shh, old bat," a man says from behind and whacks the woman in the back of the head. "No one wants to hear you ramble on."

"This is disturbing," Jesmir mumbles under his breath.

"Are you ready, Killinshire?" the executioner calls.

"We are ready!" the entire crowd yells in unison. The cheers ring throughout the city in a wave that fades into the distance.

"No, you really aren't," I say with a smirk, my eyes on Tamrin. He raises a fist, threatening to punch me.

"The first to be executed is...First Son, Prince Veran!"

The sudden burst of cheers is so loud that my ears ring with immediate effect. The woman next to me cries out in joy. She dances and bounces into me. She spins, her voice raised in a high-pitched scream, and she hops onto my chest, her legs wrapped around my waist. I try to push her away, but she grabs my face and kisses me. Her tongue tries to get through my lips while I struggle to throw her off.

The guards, in a panic, rip the woman from me. She screams in delight until she realizes they intend to toss her like a rag doll. The crowd around us laughs at the scene as it plays out. The guards toss the woman on her ass. She hits her head on a cart and falls unconscious.

The crowd around us cheers.

The executioner continues to reveal the traitors about to be hanged, and with each reveal, an enthusiastic cheer resounds. The condemned shake and fight against their restraints as the executioner reveals each remaining member of the former emperor's family.

"We have a new emperor!" people yell throughout the crowd.

The executioner's voice is drowned out by the cheers. Four loud drums echo from beneath the gallows. The crowd falls silent, and the executioner continues.

"By the laws of the great Hakaka, Patron God of Killinshire, Lord of Valor, God of War, you are sentenced to death for the crime of Descendancy from a Loser!"

More cheers erupt. The executioner waves his hands to silence the crowd.

"Pursuant to the law, you can be saved. But only by one who is willing to replace your blood with the blood of others. I offer a chance for mercy to the crowd! Does anyone wish to save this family by replacing it with their own?"

I step forward, and the guards step away in shock.

"Why don't you tell the emperor to get fucked!" I yell. "Tell his chicken shit ass to come out here and fight me."

The great hall of the Citadel continues the motif of the dark walls of the city, the polar opposite of the queen's manor in Teshket. Where the queen decorates with taste and a fabulous display of wealth, the Citadel's halls are bare, adorned only with weapons of war and depictions of battles long since lost in history.

There is no artistic expression. There are no priceless relics. There are no tables, chairs, or stained glass. The black stone and dark mortar walls glisten with darkened highlights, illuminated by failing candlelight. What few windows exist are tiny slivers that a child couldn't fit through.

Where Teshket intimidates with its success, Killinshire intimidates with fear and violence.

My friends walk behind me, allowed to enter as witnesses to my success or failure. I am permitted to have witnesses for my challenge to ensure that my fight is fair. The rule is five witnesses. Most challengers do not take members of their family with them in the vain hope that their family will never be found. But family is always found. Killinfolk show no loyalty to their neighbors. Killinfolk crave the execution spectacle.

But I have no family. My family is dead as far as anyone knows. That will come as quite a shock to the new emperor should I lose. Since my mom is long hidden, she is safe.

"This place is depressing," Jesma whispers.

"That it is," I say. "If I win, we can liven it up a bit."

"I'm not inclined to let you win a challenge, Shen-Zarl. Especially after you told me to 'get fucked,'" a familiar voice yells out from deep within the hall. "As for you, Your Highness, I agree. This place needs some sprucing up. Please do share your ideas, Princess Jesma. Though I do think your taste rather boring compared to mine."

The acoustics within the hall make it difficult to discern the source of the voice. It doesn't matter whether or not I can see the speaker. I'd know that voice anywhere. And I can't believe my ears.

"You have *got* to be shitting me," I yell with a smile on my face. My voice booms off the walls.

"Shitting you?" the man says. "When have I ever lied to you, D'aonar?"

"Every chance you can," I reply. "How about you show your face so I can smack that shit-eating grin I know you're hiding, you son-of-a-bitch!"

Laughter echoes from several places in the hall. Picaroons emerge from every corner and surround us, each with a big smile. A beautiful brunette, with an undue amount of exposed cleavage and a slit in her skirt that rises so high it's clear she's not wearing undergarments, sidles up to me.

"D'aonar, now will you have me? I am a princess now, too. And I can do things to you that would make your Teshken girl blush."

The tip of her tongue passes over her lips as she circles me, grabs my ass, and laughs, before she kisses my cheek.

"Reena," I say. "As much as I find your charms to be the most alluring of all Picaroon, they do not outshine my love for Princess Jesma."

Reena pouts, her full lower lip protruding. She caresses my face and turns to Jesma. "Surely she isn't afraid of the challenge."

Reena wraps her hand around my neck and yanks me to her, her lips locking onto mine, her hips grinding against my hips. I push her away gently, so as not to offend.

"Nope," I say. "I am hers. And she is mine."

Reena looks at Jesma. "You can't blame a girl for trying."

"Wanna bet?" Jesma says, her eyes cold.

"Reena! Leave our D'aonar alone. He is here to challenge me!" Patrin says as he steps from the shadows. We each spread our arms in the usual Picaroon greeting, big smiles on our faces. The embrace is warm, genuine, and filled with laughter. We exchange kisses and step away, arms out to our sides, fingers open, palms out.

Patrin breaks into laughter.

"Did you really come to challenge me?" he asks, feigned hurt on his face.

"Of course!" I say. "To claim the throne for your house! But you beat me to it and ruined the surprise. If allowed, I withdraw my challenge."

"Well, I'll have to check the laws." He glances around the hall, pondering. "Oh, who am I kidding? Of course! Send word the challenge is withdrawn on the basis of family ties. Let the executions move forward!"

"No!" Jesma cries.

Patrin's face alights with joy.

"Oh, what a lovely gift it would have been, D'aonar! I'm sorry to ruin the surprise." Patrin laughs with a hearty belly shake.

"Well, since you're sorry for ruining my surprise, in the custom of the family, make it up to me!" I say.

"Of course! As long as it's not something I don't want to give, it's done," he says.

"Stay the executions."

The entire hall goes silent.

"Why do you ask for that?" he says, surprised.

"Because I ask it of him," Jesma says.

"D'aonar, have you sworn fealty to the Teshken crown?" Patrin asks. He glances at Jesma and back at me, a full-toothed smile on display. "Oh, I see! You are betrothed to the Princess!" he exclaims.

Reena cries out in dismay. Patrin warns her with a glance.

"You have already bought a day with your challenge," Patrin says. "We can discuss these matters later, if you like. There is time. But first…we party. I am Emperor after all."

His smile contains a hint of warning.

The party lasts well into the night. Food, drink, music, voices, and the raucous energy of dance fill the dining hall long after Ezra slips behind the veil of the night sky. Tamrin flirts with one of Patrin's sons, and it isn't long before the two of them are lost in their own little world of drink and merriment. Jesma plays with my hair and rubs my inner thigh, her eyes on Reena, who casts lascivious glances my way. I squirm like a worm on a hook. This will be a long night.

Jesmir's laughter draws our attention. He dances with some of the unmarried women of Patrin's clan–the only eligible bachelor in our group. He's the new shiny toy for the Picaroon men and women to play with. Kara watches on with interest.

Reena's eyes narrow, and the corner of her mouth curls. Patrin's daughter unties her blouse to expose her cleavage more than it already was, her ample breasts nearly fully exposed, winks at Jesma, and lurches toward Jesmir, hips swaying with deliberate sexuality.

Jesma goes to rise, and I place a hand on her arm to hold her steady. I turn to Patrin.

"Ariki, please tell me that my prince is safe from any obligations. He doesn't know our ways and is likely to find himself in trouble."

Patrin laughs a good-natured laugh.

"Relax and enjoy the party, D'aonar. The family has been warned not to trick, steal, or trap the young prince. As Emperor of Killinshire, I cannot afford an inter-realm incident on the first day. Next week, however, all bets are off," he says with a wink.

"Not ever, Ariki," I say. "Please," I add.

"A favor then?"

Shit. I fell into the trap.

"A small favor," I say.

"I'm not sure this constitutes a small favor," he says with a gleam in his eye.

"Per the rules: A request from a *family* member whose intent is to negate an activity that incurs no risk or loss to the current business of the requestee is, by definition, a small favor and…"

He waves his hand in annoyance. "Shall be granted without malice or chicanery, under the protection of familial ties and honored in perpetuity…yes, yes. I know the rule. I wrote that damn rule."

Patrin leans into me. "Sometimes I wonder if I made a mistake taking you into my family." He winks. "You learn too quickly and are too shrewd. But I have a strange affinity for you, D'aonar. I love you like I love myself." He wiggles a finger at my chest. "It's like a part of me is in you, and there aren't many through the years where that was true."

He laughs and winks again.

"But, you do not know what business I have and whether the prince's usefulness impacts my current business."

I raise my eyebrow at Patrin and do not speak. He knows I am within my rights. But if I say the wrong thing, I could negate them.

Arguing that he couldn't possibly have current business, by Picaroon law, means I would admit to the possibility that current business exists. To Picaroon's, any argument for or against an idea by definition gives the argument merit, and, by the rules, means whatever 'it' is, must exist.

I raise my chalice and say instead, "It is a pleasure to see you doing so well."

"Ah, you have become so skilled in our ways, D'aonar. I'm almost compelled to ask you to stay and be here with me as my counselor. Better yet. Take the position of Captain of the Dark Guard. Some would say it's your right…as my son. But, as we agreed, I will let you roam your world. Please tell me, have you brought me something?"

"Now, Ariki, you know damn well that I had no idea you were here. There is no way I could have anticipated the duty of a gift today."

"Yet here is where we find ourselves!" he says with a smile.

"Yet here I am," I say, conceding his point. I pull out the coin that hangs from the gold chain he gave me and dangle it in front of him. "I could just give this back," I say.

"Yes, you could. But you won't. I know you better than you know yourself, lad."

I snicker. Turning to Jesma, I lean in and whisper in her ear.

"I'll get you another one. I promise," I say to her.

"Another what?" she asks.

I take one of her knives from her belt and hand it, handle first, to Patrin.

"Ariki Patrin, please accept this duty from your son and his family. This is a Korund blade, forged by Brinker directly in the fires of Galbring."

His eyes grow wide, and he takes the knife with a delicate hand, like I've given him the greatest gift in the world. He admires the edges, the watermarks, and the handle. He whistles with pleasure and surprise. A few heads turn his way.

"This, my son, is a great gift! I accept your duty as your father and cast my blessing on you."

He turns and throws the knife at a wooden shield that hangs on the wall. It hits the center of the shield with surprising precision.

"Haha! Korund steel. From Brinker, no less. Come! Let us drink a toast to good days ahead."

Almost everyone has passed out or wandered to find a private place to enjoy the company of one or more fellow partiers in naked bliss.

Patrin, Jesma, and I sit together, our conversation drifting into peaceful silence. Sloppy drunk, Jesma slurs a comment and falls over face-first on the table, passed out.

Patrin and I, nearly as intoxicated, point and laugh. He signals me to draw close.

"Tell me, D'aonar," he slurs, his feet on another chair, his head leaning toward me. "You really came to challenge the emperor?"

"I didn't come here to play footsies," I slur back.

"This is indeed a surprise. Had I known, I would have left his demise to you!"

Jesma's slides from her chair onto the floor. Patrin and I laugh again.

"We are the last two standing," he exclaims in drunken triumph.

"Here's to us," I cheer, and drink the last of my wine.

"Seriously," he says. "Why didn't you tell me?"

"It only just came up," I say.

"Ah, you say that! But you had to know somewhere in your soul that this was what you wanted! No one wakes up one day and says, 'I think I'll be Emperor of Killinshire today.'"

I lean forward with a smirk.

"No one?" I ask. "Are you telling me you didn't catch wind that Brogen was dead less than a few weeks ago and seize an opportunity? You didn't think to yourself that the emperor, without his most trusted ally, is weakened?"

He points his finger at me. Gold rings on his knuckles sparkle in the candlelight.

"Back at you, my son," he says with his signature smile. "What is it you were after, I wonder?" he says. He leans back.

"Glory. Power. Wealth," I say.

He shakes his head.

"You care for none of these things. You are sloppy drunk, young man, if you think I'll fall for that. No. I think you have something else you are after. What could it be?"

He taps his chin.

"Revenge, maybe?" he says.

"For what?" I reply.

"For your father?" Patrin says with a smirk.

I blink.

"Haha! See. I know so much more about you than you give me credit for."

"I got my revenge," I say. "*I* killed Brogen."

"Did you? I have it on good authority that he was killed with a bolt to the neck. From a crossbow." He spins his head around as if looking for something. "Now I know I saw that prince somewhere. If I recall, *he* had a crossbow. Where is he, I wonder?"

"Seducing your daughter," I say.

"Oh, if only that were true. Imagine a Teshket-Killinshire child, tied between the two nations more than *you* are, old friend."

"Where do you get your information?" I say with a laugh. "For the record, I *can* use a crosh…crost…crosthbow."

"But your prince is the one who carries it. I'm not saying you lie. If he were the one to make the shot, he could never have gotten that shot off on his own. No. You probably put that vile man in a compromised position. But the kill shot came from the prince. I'd stake my title as Picaroon King on it."

"Again, how?" I ask.

"I'm the King of Information!" He throws out his arms, and wine flies from his goblet. He refills his cup. "Information, as you well know, is king."

He sits and places his hand on mine.

"Take you, for instance. Now I know you didn't know I'd be here. If you did, I'd be offended that you challenged me. But I also know you didn't come here to *be* Emperor. So, I ask myself, 'What would possibly drive the Harbinger nearly seven hundred miles, from Breakridge, through Gal-Danang, into Killinshire, to challenge the emperor?' Wanna know what I think?"

"If you're willing to share," I slur.

His knowledge of our path is one more testament to his network of spies. I wonder if he knows about my mother, and my hearts race a bit.

"Guess," he says.

"Revenge," I reply.

"Nice try. I think it's something else entirely. Could it be this?"

He pulls a book out from behind his back and sets it on the table. It is covered with strange signs and sigils.

"What is that?" I ask, fighting to keep the shock from my face.

"It's called a book, dummy. And don't play coy with me. I know you better than you know yourself. You've always had a bit of me in you. I found this in the emperor's…correction…*my* room. It's an interesting book. Hard to open. Most people couldn't open it. It required some special items. There isn't much I don't have."

"You read it?" I say, surprised.

"In its entirety. Last night and this morning."

I ogle the book and consider a snatch-and-grab. I'm fast enough to rip it from the table. But that would insult my friend and go against Picaroon custom.

"Yes. That is what I am after. I'm in need of that Tome," I say. "That is why I am here."

"That is interesting. I wasn't sure. You gave that up so easily. Why?"

"Because I cannot insult you by stealing it. Which I could have easily accomplished."

"Of this I have no doubt," he says. "I appreciate the honesty. For that, I am willing to give it to you. You must know something about its contents."

"A history of the gods," I say.

"That is exactly what it is," he says. "A priceless relic if I were to guess."

"What is your price?" I ask. There is no way he'd simply hand it over, so I know this will cost.

"A major favor," he says.

"I am not a killer for hire," I say.

"Oh, but I think you *are*, especially for this death. Something tells me you'd take this contract for less. In fact, I believe you are *very* willing to kill for this book."

My chest hurts from the stunned realization that Patrin played a very long game to get me to kill for him. My jaw tightens, and his eyes sparkle with glee. He outsmarted me. He's always been several moves ahead of me. I wish I knew how.

"Who could you want dead so badly that you'd play such a long game?" I ask.

"The Teshket Queen."

I bolt upright.

"The terms are set?" I say.

"Do that for me. Accomplish that, Harbinger. And this Tome is yours."

"Deal," I say.

"Deal," he replies, eyes sparkling with glee.

I smirk.

"Why do you smirk like you've won?" he asks.

"Because the Tome costs me nothing," I reply.

"How so?" Patrin asks, his brows furrowed.

"Because I'd have killed her for free. I already planned to kill her. Now I get paid to do it."

Patrin laughs a deep belly laugh.

"Oh, D'aonar, you never fail to please me! Well done, my son. Well done."

Chapter Twenty-Four

Journal Entry: 141

That Patrin found a way to enlist me in murder for hire is of little surprise. This has been his ultimate ambition since our first encounter. He seems not to care that I had already intended to kill the queen. For me, this fact frees me from the guilt that killing for gold would leave behind.

Patrin's appearance in Killinshire, on the other hand, was a shock. "Emperor Patrin" may take me a lifetime to unravel. Patrin, the Picaroon King. Patrin, Emperor of Killinshire.

What's next? Patrin, Supreme Ruler of Conishant? Patrin, Lord of Gods?

That would be funny. Teach those bastards a lesson.

But what if we do succeed in killing the queen? Then what?

How does this play into whatever plan Patrin has?

I wish I knew why he wants the queen dead. Too late to ask now, though. I'm busy playing swashbuckler on the high seas.

Come Sail Away with Me

A loud roar echoes outside the Citadel walls. It starts as a quiet chant, and by the time we stand at the gate, it sounds like the whole of Renshmere is about to lose its mind.

"Ring the bell! Ring the bell! Ring the bell!"

"Why do they want the bell rung?" Kara asks. "Seems a silly request."

"It's a euphemism," I say. "They want to know if the challenger lived or died."

"Umm," says Tamrin. "Isn't that going to be a problem?"

"I must admit," Patrin says, a chalice of wine in his hands. "We didn't consider that one of us is supposed to be dead." He's dressed in a silk robe, open in the front, and nothing more.

"Aren't you cold?" I ask him.

"This is a brisk morning," he says. "Good for the blood. Now, about our problem. If you walk out those doors, they will assume you won. We can't have that. Besides, no Emperor has shown their face in a millennium, at least."

"What do we do?" Jesmir says. "We can't stay here forever."

"Oh, but how I wish that you could!" Patrin says with a laugh. "Unfortunately, you have work to do. But what kind of Emperor would I be if I didn't already have a plan?"

Patrin points toward the Citadel proper. His finger traces a line up the building until it reaches a thin post that towers over the roofline. A small flag blows in the wind.

"That, dear friends, is the mast to my new Flag Ship."

His smirk is twice as big this time.

"It came with the title. Call me Emperor Patrin, Admiral of Killinshire. It's best if you leave by sea. My ship is as fast as any. You'll be in Teshket in seven days if you sail the coast."

"I am no sailor," I say with a scowl.

"Well, it's a good thing my family is," he says. "What better way to get around the seas than with Picaroons at the helm!"

Incredulous, I say, "You're sailors, too?"

"See, my boy, this is why you must come around more often. There is much for you to learn. I think, after you have your Tome, you should come and stay. Maybe marry your princess here…or one of mine." He winks.

Patrin turns with a dramatic flair and throws his chalice to the ground. His robe flies open and blows in the wind. He stands with his naked body exposed, his hands raised high. The rings on his fingers and the silk robe were at odds with his nonchalant nudity. Jesma looks away in disgust. Patrin calls out with a loud booming voice that echoes off every stone surface.

"Family! Prepare to sail. All able-bodied sailors report to the Famoza. You sail at Ezra's peak."

"I don't like this," Tamrin says as we stand on the deck of the Famoza.

"Sailing?" I say.

He scowls. "Come on, Man. Don't play coy with me."

"You don't find it strange that he seems to know everything and yet has no idea we already planned on confronting the queen?" Kara says.

The Picaroon sailors load the ship with stores. Enough for a ten-day trip in the event we are waylaid by storms. They wheel large wagons with crates of dried meat, fruits, and breads. Barrels arrive next, filled with wine and spirits. In a flurry of Picaroon efficiency, the ship is ready to sail. Too soon for my comfort.

"I think I changed my mind," I say.

"About?" Jesma asks.

"The boat," Tamrin scoffs. "Mister 'I'm not afraid of anything' hates boats." He slaps my back, and I stumble forward.

"I'd think that a boat would be right up your alley the way you scale trees," Jesmir says and points to a Picaroon in a full climb up the pilot ladder.

"Different when it's on the water," I grumble.

"I don't know who they think is going to drink all of that," Tamrin says, pointing at the last of the barrels. "But we sure will give it one hell of a try." His eyes sparkle with delight.

"Tam," I say, "I am not sure what Patrin's game is, but he's up to something. This business of playing Emperor is odd, even for him. Picaroons don't plant roots. We do this job. We get the Tome. That's it."

Tamrin studies me, concerned.

"Since when don't you trust Patrin?" he says.

"I've never trusted Patrin. That's why he and I get along. He knows I don't trust him. He boxed me in on this one. He boxed *us* in. I want to know why."

I turn and address the group.

"In the meantime, we don't need any new liabilities. No business. No games. No gambling. No trading. And no drinking on this ship. We keep our wits about us."

With a resigned sigh, he nods.

"Okay, Shen. Okay. But that's Mistras' Reserve in those barrels there." He winks. "Think you can resist its call?"

The last barrel disappears into the hold, and I can almost hear it call my name.

"Why do you think Patrin loads barrels of *Mistras' Reserve* onto the ship while we stand here? Let's go find the twins and issue the same warning to our party-prone prince."

"They're at the bow," Kara says. "They seem upset."

Jesmir holds his sister close, her face buried in his shoulder. His chin rests on her head as he stares out over the sea.

"The last time they were at sea started this whole ordeal," I say. "This can't be easy on them."

I cross the deck and head toward the twins. I remind myself to be compassionate to the emotional siblings.

The captain gives the command, and thirty-three Picaroons head below deck. Those above retract the mooring lines as the dock crew releases them. Back at the shore, four capstans spin cranks to warp the ship clear of the dock. From below us, oars splash into the water while a drummer beats a rhythm that reverberates underfoot. The ship releases from the warp, and we begin the push out of the harbor into the open sea.

We stand at the stern of the Famoza as Renshmere slips away. Jesma leans into me and pats my chest. I put an arm around her.

"You okay?" I ask.

"I'm fine," she says. "Jes and I needed a moment to grieve."

The Famoza is a couple of ship lengths from the docks when a loud boom travels across the water from somewhere inside the Killinshire capital city. Startled by the sound, we run to the stern as a group. Tamrin leans over the wale and searches for the source. The topside sailors hurry over and surround us, their bodies huddled tight. Almost immediately, screams and cries of dismay travel the distance over the water.

"What the hell was that?" a sailor exclaims.

"I don't know," Jesmir responds. "But it can't be good."

We scan the city for signs of what caused the noise.

"There," I point out.

Toward the eastern side of town, opposite The Citadel, a plume of smoke rises above the roofs of the smaller homes in the area. It behaves unlike any smoke I've seen. The upward plume oozes out in a dome before it falls back to the ground in a slow roll like a mushroom.

The adrenal response in my body causes my skin to tingle and my hearts to race. I recognize the behavior of neither.

"No," I say. "Not another one."

Kara-Kar stands in shock.

"Is that what I think it is?" Tamrin asks, his voice shaking.

Dismayed cries echo among the crew, and the deck vibrates with the thrum of rushing boot stomps until every member of the crew crowds around us.

"Netherstacks," I whisper. "Another one just appeared."

"They appear with greater frequency," Jesmir says. "What does it mean?"

No one has an answer.

The black waters of the southern sea are calm, the winds mild. I don't know how this ship can move with such low winds. The surface of the water, even close to shore, is like glass. The oars of the ship and the wake behind it create more motion in the inky black surface than the wind. Still, somehow, the Picaroon's prove to be as adept at the helm of this massive galleon as they are at horsemanship.

More than mere sailors, Picaroons are masters of the sea. Some say the first pirates were Picaroons tired of wandering Conishant. The crew finds the wind with little effort, and the full sails overhead fill with a loud snap as the fabric stretches taut. The ship keels slightly and heads west along the southern shore of Killinshire. Renshmere grows smaller with each passing wave as I struggle to find a footing on the rocking, sloped deck.

It doesn't take long for my lack of seamanship to betray me. My stomach flips with each wave. By the time we round the southwestern shores of Conishant and leave Killinshire behind, I'm ready to vomit. Out over the horizon, the skies turn bright red.

"Strong weather ahead," the captain says from behind me. I lean over the wale and vomit the last bit of my lunch into the ocean. "If we keep the wind, we should beat it and make this an easy trip north. We'll ride with the Great Western Current. There's a risk of encounters, but it's the fastest way north. Pray for clear skies. We may make Coraside Bay a day early."

"I'd like that," I say. "Sooner I can get off this thing, the better."

"Stop looking down," the captain says. He grabs my shoulders and turns me toward the bow. "Look at the horizon straight ahead," he says. He applies pressure to my left shoulder, and I step toward the center of the ship. "Stand here, eyes on the horizon. When you feel better, take ten steps forward. Keep your eyes on the horizon. Work your way forward only when you feel up to it. Before you know it, you'll be at the bow of the ship, and your sea legs will grow under you."

He hits my canteen with his knuckles. "And stay hydrated. Avoid the booze. You ain't up for it." He laughs and barks out orders to some of the deckhands.

A series of "Aye, Aye, Captain!" responses sound out from around the deck. Jesmir appears beside me. I can't tell whether he walked up or appeared. I'm too focused on the horizon to pay attention.

"Had no idea you weren't a fan of the sea," Jesmir says.

"I'm not so sick I won't throw you overboard," I say. Another wave of nausea starts, and I look down despite what I was told.

"Chin up, sailor," Jesmir warns. He points to the horizon. "See how it rises and falls? When you look down, your mind expects to see that, but it can't. Meanwhile, your body feels it. That's the reason you're sick. It takes time to develop that reflex. The horizon keeps your mind from fooling your body."

We stand there for a few minutes, and the nausea subsides.

"Follow me," he says, and he takes more steps forward than I like.

I follow anyway.

"How are you feeling?" he asks.

"Like I want to punch you in the dick."

My head spins again, and I feel my stomach lurch, but I keep my eyes on the slowly disappearing horizon. I panic at the thought of it vanishing. Before I comment, the horizon reappears.

"What do I do when night falls?"

Jesmir turns to me with a smile. "Guess we'll have to find out, won't we?"

I display my displeasure with a snarl.

"Relax. When Ezra sleeps, you'll still see the horizon. It's actually spectacular." He points east. "See the twin moons? They are nearly half full." His arm swings across the sky. "And you think the stars are a sight from Gal-Danang or in the Killinshire plains? Wait till you see them reflected off the water. Trust me. You'll have plenty to look at, and the horizon will make itself apparent."

I swallow a little bile and grimace.

"Come on," he says. "Let's move to the bow."

"I don't think I'm ready for that," I say.

"You'll be fine. Trust me," he says.

We walk onto the bow pulpit. Jesmir peers over the wale. White-knuckled, I grasp the short barrier that is my only protection from a drop into the cold water below. Along the darkened horizon, bright ambers and reds sink into deep purples and finally fade to black. Jesmir was right. The streak of stars across the sky reflects off the ocean waters. I've never been this far from shore before. Water stretches as far as the eye can see, even at night.

My imagination takes hold, and I wonder what awaits over the western horizon. I've met very few people from lands outside of

Conishant. Col-Amot, the angry warrior in Rogue's Pointe, is the only person I know by name. I wonder if we sailed westward, would we find his home? How far would we have to go?

"Hey," Jesmir says. "Have a look at this."

He points to a spot off the bow, directly beneath us. Just under the surface of the water, a woman stares at us. She swims on her back, her hips pumping her legs.

"Ahoy!" Jesmir calls to the rear. "We have a visitor here!"

A deckhand comes running to look and, with immediate panic, yells at the top of his lungs, "Siren!"

He runs to the center of the ship, repeating the word.

"Siren! Siren!"

"What's a Siren?" I ask Jesmir, who grabs my cloak in panic and yanks me with him. "So, it's a bad thing?"

"Yes! Very bad!" Jesmir yells. "I've never seen one, but I've read about them. Fucking run!"

A roar like a crashing wave against rocks shakes the ship. I turn to look behind me, and the most beautiful woman I've ever seen stands where Jesmir and I once were. A wave of water rolls across the deck and disperses at my feet. Her hair flows in the breeze. Her curves, like the waves, shift with hints of sensual pleasure. She smiles with subtle promises of pleasures I can only imagine.

Jesmir yanks me back. "We have to get to the midships."

Jesmir vanishes and reappears, huddled with the rest of the deck crew at the very center mast of the ship. I turn and face the Siren.

"Don't look at her!" Jesmir yells.

"You don't wish to run?" the beautiful Siren says. Her sultry timbre hints at a melody in the background.

How does she do that with her voice?

Scales on her neck flex as she speaks. Her eyes shine, filled with the secrets deep in the ocean. She extends her hand toward me in invitation. Her fingers, webbed and covered in beautiful scales, beckon me closer. The curves of her body move with the ocean's motion. My seasickness fades, and my confidence returns. Her presence soothes my spirit. She reminds me of a more svelte version of Kara.

"Come with me," the Siren says.

Enthralled with her beauty, I take a step toward her.

"Shen!" a voice calls to me. "Don't listen to her!"

But her voice is a melody unlike any I've ever heard.

"Shen? Is that your name?"

I nod to her and step closer.

"You are such a powerful man," she says. "Many have been my lovers, but you outshine them all."

Her full lips, luscious and glistening, draw my eyes to her tongue. Her tongue licks the edge of her top lip. I'm so close I can almost reach out and touch her hand. Our fingertips are so close. Just one more step and she's mine.

A vice grip wraps around my chest so hard it takes my breath away. The air around me swirls in a strange absence of pressure, brief but noticeable. Darkness engulfs me, and the world fades into a black tunnel, darker than any night I've ever experienced. The Siren's voice fades along with the wind and the ocean, replaced with something sinister. Gnashing and wailing surround me, above me, below me, from all points within the darkness. Heavy breath blows against my ear with grunts of effort. An unseen force pulls me backward, and the darkness engulfs me. Beyond the darkness, I sense things, vile and scary. They linger above me, around me, below me. They claw to get at me, held back by something I can't see but can sense. New terror takes hold.

I try to scream, but nothing comes out. My chest constricted, and I fight against whatever restrains me, but I'm locked tight.

The backward pull relents, and for a moment, I am suspended, like there's no force anywhere. The world before me fades out of existence. My eyes adjust to the darkness. Darker shadows of monstrous forms, menacing and evil, held back by an unseen force, lurk in the darkness. Faceless, they huddle out of reach. A menacing hunger lingers too close for comfort, and it chills me to my core.

Time loses relevance. Days could have passed, and I'd never know. The force against my body shifts. The pull transitions into a push. Still, I move backward, the direction out of my control. The air around me increases in pressure, and the darkness vanishes with a bright light that grows from behind.

Jesmir releases his grip on my chest and moves to stand before me. Our eyes lock.

"I can't believe that worked!" he exclaims. The oppressive hunger is replaced with claustrophobia as I find myself huddled with the rest of the crew on the deck. Jesmir's so close I can smell the Rot Root poison in his still-damaged ear.

My chest expands with a violent gasp for breath.

"What the hell did you do?" I gasp.

"I snatched you and brought you back to the midship inside the sigils."

"What sigils?"

He points to a ring of symbols carved into the deck that I somehow hadn't noticed.

"The midship is the safe place from Sirens," a deckhand says. "Listen."

I listen for the beautiful voice, the yearning to be with her still lingering.

"Where did you go, my beautiful man?" she says. Her voice is harsh, and the melody is gone. She sounds like gravel tumbling together under water.

I push my way to the point in the midship closest to the bow to see her, careful to stay within the boundaries of the sigil. She approaches until she's only a few feet away, her hand still out. Her teeth are sharp like tiny needles, and her beautiful scales appear dull. Flecks of flesh molt off her cheeks. Her lips are no longer luscious, but thin like a fish. Her song is dark and unpleasant.

I shiver at the thought of my earlier perception versus this new one.

"I think you should maybe get off the ship," I say to her.

"Yes, let us go together," she says.

"Not if you were the last thing left in Conishant," I say.

"Why would you say such a thing? You are not so sweet. Where is the nice, beautiful man you were?" she says.

Jesmir steps forward, his crossbow aimed at her. My hands go to my knives. Her face contorts with rage at the realization that her spell is broken.

"Disappointing," she says. "You could have a good life with me. Short though it may have been."

A large plume of water rises over the port wale and lands atop her. It recedes into the ocean, and she is gone. The entire crew breathes a sigh of relief, and the captain barks orders for everyone to man their stations. He posts lookouts at points along the deck, each with a crossbow from the ship's armory in case of another visit.

"What *was* that?" I ask Jesmir.

"You've never heard of Sirens?" the prince says.

"No."

"Their voice lulls you into a dream. It's irresistible outside of the sigils. If I hadn't pulled you away, you'd have followed her into the ocean, where she'd drown you and absorb your life energy."

I shudder at the thought.

"I'm rather tired of the dangers that Conishant throws at us," I say. "I'd give almost anything to go back to the RhineWoods where all I had to worry about were netherstacks, bandits, and Cuska safely contained in the valley."

"Don't forget spiderlyches," he says.

I close my eyes in disdain. "Okay, so maybe it wasn't so safe. But at least I knew what I was up against. Kirwaq, Jandu, Sirens? What's next?"

"Best not to ask," Jesmir says. "You may find out."

I shudder again. We can't get to Coraside Bay fast enough as far as I'm concerned.

Chapter Twenty-Five

Journal Entry: 142

Jesma's mental state ebbs and flows. I empathize with her turmoil. Being betrayed by someone you love and admire hurts. She and her brother didn't need more hurt in their lives. I spent my life drowning in that same betrayal. I thought my mother and father had betrayed me. Krin most definitely betrayed me.

At least my betrayals happened early in life. Jesma's come after decades of safety and trust. All destroyed overnight. I know how I reacted to my betrayal. It's not hard to imagine I'd be a pile of bakru shit if I went through what Jesma and Jesmir suffer.

This would send me on a murderous rampage. I don't understand how she isn't ready to rip the queen's skin off.

I struggle to hide my frustration.

Fight or flight, Jez.

Why so much compassion for your grandmother when she had your father killed?

Then again, you love a murderer. Why wouldn't you still love your grandmother?

—

I wrestle with these thoughts as much as she does.

Then there's this new Jez. The fighter. If this were anyone else…she killed without hesitation under the acacia tree. If she doesn't agree to kill her grandmother, we will forever look over our shoulders.

Mutually assured destruction is the only chip we have with which to bargain. There is no way we can trust the bitch queen to live up to any negotiation. Queen Shamna, the Killer Grandma.

There's no chance she lets the twins live their lives in peace with what they know now.

I've been so busy wondering who set up the kidnapping, I've forgotten to ask the fundamental question.

Why?

Slippin' Into Coraside Bay

The air out in the open ocean is much colder than it is inland this time of year. Even with my new cloak, I'm almost frozen solid on the deck. It doesn't help that my cloak is full of holes thanks to the sudden proliferation of magic users in the world.

The temperatures dropped below freezing the last three nights and have been plain cold during the day. The only place to warm myself against the winter freeze is near the cast-iron oven on the lower crew deck. When I'm not topside spilling my guts into the ocean, I'm below deck next to the warm stove that puts out enough heat to keep the crew cabin warm and toasty. Just my luck, as the air grows colder, the winds pick up, so too the waves. The Famoza pitches and rolls with the waves, and the severity of the motion makes it unsafe to keep a fire lit. The captain commanded the fire-watch to close the damper on the chimney flue.

I stand close to the unlit stove until the metal no longer offers heat.

The farther north we sail, the stronger the winds become and the more the sea kicks up. The ship rocks, and only an iron grip on the wale keeps me from sliding along the deck. No matter how hard I try to keep my eyes on the horizon, I can't, so my sea sickness returns with a vengeance. It's been two days since I've taken food.

Tamrin, Kara, Jesma, and Jesmir take to the ocean like it is their home. They each found ways to be useful to the crew, and their friendships with my Picaroon family blossomed through the week.

Be an asset, not a liability. Kiss my ass.

Meanwhile, I've become the butt of more than a few jokes, a point that Jesmir rubs in my face every chance he can.

"Shen, why don't you make yourself useful and get out of the way?"

"Hey, I know something else you're the Harbinger of…hurling."

"See, Shen, there is a job you can do. Look at all that chum. If we want to fish, it'll be so much easier now."

If Jesmir opens his mouth one more time, I plan to aim my next bout of vomit right into his gaping maw.

I head below deck to escape and be out of the way. It takes only a couple of hours for the cabin to feel claustrophobic, so I climb the ladder back to the upper deck. The ship pitches again. My foot slips from the rung, and I fall backward into the crew cabin and land on my ass. With a loud curse about Jesmir's lineage, I stand only to find myself lurched into the ladder face-first by another wave. I raise my hands fast enough to prevent my teeth from a direct strike on a rung, but not my forehead. I fall and drift into unconsciousness.

My last thought is that I can't wait for this trip to be over.

On the eighth day, the sky clears, and the winds die down. Our trip took a little longer because of Captain's insistence that we track more westward to avoid the waves from capsizing the ship. Whether this is true or not, I don't know. Nor do I care because we didn't find ourselves lost at sea, and today we are alive.

Last night's seas were the worst, and the sea spray froze on contact with the ship's surfaces. Sideways icicles decorate the ship on every vertical edge. The top of the main mast has a stunning set that Captain said required removal before they set off back south again. He asked if I'd like the job, and I told him I wouldn't stay on the Famoza one minute longer than necessary. He laughed and went on his way to bark orders at the crew.

While it is the coldest day yet, today the seas are calm, and Ezra doesn't hide behind clouds. A flock of seajays fly overhead, their blue feathers and loud, high-pitched calls a sign that shore is nearby.

On our starboard side, the last stretch of the northern coast of Gal-Danang passes by, and the Toerge Mountain chain appears. It's a slow, steady climb into snow-packed peaks, a welcome sight. I long for the familiarity of solid ground.

Any time now, Coraside Bay should appear, and I'll be off this death trap, just a few more miles around the last turn of the peninsula.

Outside of the awful waves and the Siren, the trip was uneventful. We encountered no pirates, were attacked by no enemies, and we didn't capsize. Nobody went overboard, and I was the only one who got sick.

The few ships we crossed paths with were merchant ships or naval battle vessels from either Teshket or Killinshire. In either event, the presence of the emperor's flag on the main mast was deterrent enough to allow us to sail in relative peace.

Not that a Siren would have cared about that.

The best part about the trip is that I could find my sea legs last night, in the midst of the storm. Also, I finally stopped vomiting midway through the day. I even learned a few sailor's knots today.

The Picaroon sailors have been professional, rowdy, and encouraging, despite my failure to live up to the Picaroon reputation. Jesmir thrives on the sea. I'm amazed at how skillful a sailor he is.

Tamrin and Kara stand at the pulpit, lost in some inane discussion. Kara has proven to be an easy fit with my ever-growing band of adventurers. Alongside Tamrin, the fast friends discovered they shared much in common ground on this trip, from skills in hunting to struggles in finding comfortable places to sleep on the Formoza due to their size.

More important to me is how much Tamrin appears to have healed over his loss of connection to Fildeus. While I know he still suffers from the betrayal, Kara's similar experience appears to be a source of bonding between the two. It's one place I can never help the big guy. I have to admit to a twinge of jealousy over their connection. But I'll never let it show. It's a me problem, not a them one.

Jesma, on the other hand, has been hard to pin down. I don't know where she is at the moment, and I've only seen her in passing for the last two days. The closer we are to Coraside Bay, the more distant she grows.

The seajays dip below the starboard side wale and skim the ocean's surface. An arm slips into mine, and a head leans against my shoulder.

"Hey," I say, "I was looking for you earlier."

"I needed some time alone," Jesma says.

"You okay?"

"No. Nothing about what we are about to do is okay with me. I've been trying to find a way to stop all of this. Jesmir and I both. We've been through every scenario, and none are good."

She pulls away from my arm and leans back against the wale, her eyes intense.

"There has to be another way," she says. "Killing my grandmother cannot be the only answer."

We talked about this ad nauseam at the beginning of the trip. Our connection to one another ebbs and flows with her indecision on the matter. The harder I push, the more distant she becomes. The more I let her talk it out, the closer she draws.

I only hope she can come to the correct conclusion.

The Inspector General's liaison approaches as we tie off the Famoza. I've never dealt with the Inspector General's office. This is my first time entering any city by ship. The woman, with her chin pointed high, carries a ledger nearly as big as the chip on her shoulder. The light-haired, portly woman reeks of self-importance. I have half a mind to throttle her. With her nose and chin still pointed to the sky, she purses her lips.

"Killinshire vessel?" she asks in a haughty tone. "I hope you aren't here to cause trouble."

The captain steps forward. "I assure you not, madam," he says with Picaroon flair. She eyes him with surprise.

"You aren't the Captain of the Famoza," she says. "Where is Captain Samuels?"

"I assure you, my beautiful lady," he says, his tone laced with charm, "that I am the Captain of the Famoza. Captain Pertanian, at your service." He removes his hat and bows with obvious Picaroon flair. He rises, replaces his hat, and smiles. "I've been assigned charge of my ship by the new Emperor himself, Ajuu Patrin of Ariki."

Her face registers surprise at the news of a new emperor in Killinshire. Captain Pertanian sidles up to the woman and puts his arm around her ample waist. She gasps in surprise at Pertanian's flirtatious vigor and laughs with glee. He spins her to face us like she's a belle at a dance.

"Allow me to introduce my passengers," he says with a smile, his perfect white teeth bared for her to see.

"I'd like you to take your hands off me," she says, but softens and adds "Captain" after a brief pause.

"Well, I certainly meant no harm," he replies and slides his hand from behind her back. "I merely wished to introduce you to…"

"Prince Jesmir! Oh my! Have you been hurt?" she exclaims.

"No, he's on his way to a vagabond's ball. He dressed as a wounded drunk," I reply.

The woman gives me a nasty look and then notices Jesma on my arm.

"And Princess Jesma!" The woman's face drains of all color. "Please let me apologize. I did not see you there. You travel on a Killinshire vessel?"

The liaison eyes Captain Pertanian with suspicion.

"Are you alright? Do you need to be rescued?" she whispers.

I snicker.

"Do you really think I can't hear you?" Pertanian asks with feigned shock.

"I don't care if you can hear me," she replies over her shoulder. "Your Highnesses," she bows, "I received notice from the queen herself to be on the lookout for you. My explicit instructions are that you were in danger and may be kidnapped by a Killinshire assassin and a Haabrestand tracker.

I raise my hand. "Well, that apparently is me," I say.

The woman gasps and prepares to call the guards.

Tamrin steps forward. "And I guess that includes me, too."

"Guards!" the woman cries.

"Now stop!" Jesma yells.

Her voice is so loud, it carries across the entire port. Activity everywhere comes to a halt. Even the guards who approach after the liaison's scream feel inclined to obey.

"Listen here, Harbor Inspector…" Jesma starts.

"Sheeley," the woman offers.

"Right, Harbor Inspector Sheeley. This is my soon-to-be husband." Jesma grabs my arm. "And this," she says, her other arm slid through Tamrin's, "is my Maid of Honor. We ran away for one final adventure before our wedding. The queen, though well-intentioned, is misinformed. She's mad that I don't want chiffon at my wedding. I mean, seriously, chiffon? Can you imagine *anything* more hideous?"

"Oh my, no, your Highness. Chiffon won't do!"

"Thank you," Jesma says. "Anyway, we were waylaid in Killinshire, and Captain Pertanian here was kind enough to escort us home before the Killinfolk got wind of our presence there. At substantial risk to his crew and his ship, I might add. He battled a Siren and braved a massive storm to bring us home safely."

"You mean this Killinshire Captain rescued you?" Inspector Sheeley asks, shocked.

"Oh, did he ever! Now, if you will excuse us, we are in a hurry to get home to the queen and finalize our wedding plans."

I bare my teeth in a sinister smile. Tamrin nods with enthusiasm, smiling like a fool.

Harbor Inspector Sheeley sputters.

"I apologize for my brash behavior, Your Highness." She then turns to Pertanian. "New Emperor, you say?"

"Yes, my dear," Pertanian says as Inspector Sheeley steps closer.

She blushes and bats her eyes at him. He grins at me. This poor woman has no idea what hit her.

"Well," she says, "let's get your boat moored and allow you and your crew to gather supplies. Welcome to Coraside Bay."

"Why, thank you," Pertanian says. "Would you be so kind as to escort me to the best tavern nearby? Let me buy you a drink."

She giggles like a teenager and walks off with the captain.

"Picaroons have a way," Kara replies.

I laugh and reply, "That they do."

"Now what?" Jesmir says. "It's only a matter of time before Grandmother knows we are here."

"I say we go in the front door," I reply. "Succeed or fail, we won't get to her by sneaking in."

"Great idea," Jesmir says. "Inspector Sheeley!" he calls out before she's too far away. "I wonder if I might have a quick word. Is there a shipment of goods heading to Kerakot soon?"

"Oh, certainly, Your Highness. The caravan is at the end of the pier." She looks to the sky. "It's scheduled to head out the day after tomorrow. But if you're looking to travel to Kerakot, I'd be happy to arrange a Royal Coach. It will get you there three days faster."

"No, I want to go with the barge," he says and turns to us with two thumbs up.

Captain Pertanian and Inspector Sheeley wander off the pier, the latter clearly enthralled by the Picaroon's charms, and I wonder what Patrin's ascension to the imperial throne means for relations across Conishant.

It's not until this moment that it occurs to me that Patrin must be of Killinshire descent and can prove it, or he would never have been allowed to challenge the emperor.

The Frozen Mast is a sailor's tavern close to the docks. Its proximity to ships moored for the day means we're less likely to stand out as strangers. As luck had it, we found an empty table in the back corner.

The twins hide under their hoods, their disguises long faded. This tavern may be the only place in Teshket where they won't be recognized. I scan the room for prying eyes, but other than the curious glances at Jesmir's bandages when we entered, nobody pays much attention to us.

Jesma hunches, shoulders slouched. I can't see her face, but I can imagine the turmoil that plays out there.

"I can't bring myself to do this," she says.

"Jez," Jesmir says, "I know this is not an easy decision for you. It's not easy for me either."

"So, you agree?"

"No," Jesmir replies.

Tamrin, Kara, and I remain silent on the matter. The twins need to resolve this conflict on their own.

"You'd do this without a second thought?" Jesma whispers.

A server approaches, and I signal with a light cough. We order pints of ale and a platter of eggs, bread, and meat. The waitress walks off, and Jesmir continues.

"Without second thoughts? I've had second thoughts, third thoughts, and a hundred thoughts," Jesmir says.

"So how can you be sure?" Jesma asks.

"It comes down to the facts. Father is dead. We should be dead, but aren't. And regardless of what we've done since that day, we'd be dead if Shen hadn't randomly stumbled onto us in Rhinestab. We would have died that day," he says. "Jez, look at me."

She refuses.

"Jez."

She looks up, and I fight the urge to move to her side of the table and comfort her. Distraught, cheeks wet with tears, jaw clenched as she fights with herself, she's on the edge of a total breakdown. Jesmir holds her gaze and her hands.

"Jez, I hurt as much as you do. But *she* did this to us. *She* is the villain in *our* story," he says. "I don't see 'Grandmother' anymore when I think about her."

"I wish I didn't," she says. "When she's gone, it's just you and me."

"I'm okay with that. You're my best friend. My favorite person. I'll always be here. And we have new friends. Unlike any we've had before. Hell, it's strange, but I don't miss the friends I partied with all the time. I miss Mom. I miss Dad. But I don't miss anything else. Not even our privilege. This is my family now. And I'm at peace with that."

The food and ale arrive, and everyone but Jesma digs in. I make a plate and place it in front of her.

"Eat," I say. "At least a little. We have a long journey still to go."

She ignores me. I hate seeing her like this. This is much harder on her than I gave credence.

Tamrin leans into me and whispers in my ear.

"Imagine if today, you found out that I was the one who put the bounty on your head."

"I'd kill you," I say.

Tamrin leans back and looks at me with a raised eyebrow.

"It'd be that easy for you?" he asks.

The doubtful expression on his face is enough to force me to be less flippant with my answer. And he's right. I'd be devastated. But I could no more exact my revenge on him than I could harm Jesma. It would devastate me. No, it would push me over the edge. I'd finish the job I never seem able to accomplish. I'd rather die than hurt him.

And that's where Jesma is.

"Okay, Jez," I say, my hand on hers. "If you want to try to ask her first, try to reason with her first. Then that's what we do. I won't push you into something you don't want to do. None of us will."

She looks at me, and when our eyes lock, I realize I'd die for her to be happy. I'd give up every part of myself to ensure she has what she needs. But I won't let her just die.

"I only have one condition," I say.

She nods.

"The moment I think you are in danger, I will not hesitate to take her life. Fair enough?"

She nods, and the relief on her face, though minor, relieves the tension. Jesmir disagrees, but he acquiesces.

"Good," I say. "Now about this plan of yours, my playboy Prince."

He sighs with frustration, but changes the conversation with me.

"I'll send word today that Jez and I chose to travel by barge out of fear for our lives. I'll mention Krin's betrayal in the letter. Grandmother can't possibly know that we know the truth. If she is who we think she is, she may suspect we are up to something, but she can't possibly suspect we know the actual truth."

"I never work from a perspective of hope," I say. "Assume your enemy knows everything you know. And dear old granny will operate from that perspective. She's not stupid. We ran. We didn't return to her after what Krin did," I say.

Besides, I left a note. Shit. Why did I leave a note?

Kara raises a finger and says, "You can also assume she asked Ezra and Fildeus for your whereabouts. Our princess and tracker are known for their faith. If the periapts work as we believe, they know you've severed ties."

Jesmir considers this and replies, "So then we assume she knows we know everything. What does she do?"

I answer. "She'll most certainly have spies in every city and every town. She'll have trackers on our asses like a gambling junky on a Shamna Rocks table."

"We split up," Jesmir says.

"I'm sorry?" I respond.

"Not for real. Jesma and I take the barge. The word will reach Kerakot that we're on the barge. Alone."

"Alone?" Kara asks with uncharacteristic concern.

"Only for a short time," Jesmir says. "You'll be there. But no one will know."

He lays out his plan for travel to Kerakot and how we manage the queen's expectations for our arrival. It's not a bad plan. It's not perfect, but it should at least give us the element of surprise and allow us to catch the queen flat-footed.

Once the plan is hashed out, Jesmir says, "Okay, now we need a place to sleep for the night."

"This is a bad idea," I say.

Tamrin, Kara, and I sit at a table outside a small bread shop with coffee and pastries. Dock workers shore the last of the crates onto the barge to Kerakot. The Kerakot barge is less than one hundred yards from where we sit. Jesma and Jesmir stand on the bridge with the barge captain, deep in conversation. The captain laughs at something one of them said.

"You think they'll be safe?" Tamrin asks.

"No. But I think Jesmir has sufficient control of his magic. They can get away a lot easier than they could seven weeks ago. I also think we've been less than fair about that pair's survival instincts. They escaped Brogen before either of them had the strength they do now. If Brogen had encountered these two as they are now, they would never have needed us. And that gives me peace of mind."

"Our babies have grown up," Tamrin says with a sigh.

I punch him on the arm. "That's disturbing."

Kara says, "You two are a strange duo."

"He's the love of my life," Tamrin says without irony.

"How unfortunate for you," Kara says.

"Hey," I reply.

"There are better choices out there than you. Even you'd agree," Kara replies.

"I hadn't thought of it that way," Tamrin says. "I'm in love with him. He's in love with her. And this walking pile of bakru shit doesn't seem to care how much it hurts. Thanks, Kara. It seems I've fallen in love with a narcissist."

"How are you two amenable to such awkwardness?" Kara asks.

"Impressed?" I say.

"It's very Korund of you," Kara replies, genuinely surprised.

I put my hand on Tamrin's shoulder. "I love him more than any other person. Anywhere. Ever."

"Except Jesma," Kara says.

Tamrin scoffs, "True. But still, our little one-man killing crew will do anything for me." He winks at Kara. "Except *that*."

Tamrin sips his coffee, the mug almost a toy in his massive hand. We sit in the comfortable familiarity that is our friendship.

"I see it," Kara says. "You two are quite the pair. But I've never met two people so at ease in one another's presence. I'm glad to be a witness to it."

Tamrin tips his coffee mug in salute.

"Welcome to the family, Kara."

"It's an honor," Kara replies.

The dock crew removes the mooring lines from the cleats and throws them onto the barge, and the barge slips from the dock.

"I'm pretty sure I have separation anxiety," I say, my voice shaking.

"Hey, hey," Tamrin says. "It'll be okay. It's only a few hours and we will be back together. Jes laid out a solid plan."

"Still. It makes my chest ache," I reply. "Hey, what do we do if we encounter Kirwaq? I don't want to do that again."

Tamrin says. "We ride the northern bank this time. Aren't they on the southern banks?"

"I've seen one too many nightmares come to life to fall for that again," I jest.

"Well, then, I guess you'd better hope they don't cross to the northern bank," Kara says.

"Have you ever encountered those things?" Tamrin asks.

"Are they worse than the Jandu?" Kara asks.

"Nothing is worse than the Jandu," Tamrin mumbles.

"Cuska are worse than the Jandu," I retort.

Kara shakes her head. "I chased you through Conishant for over a month, Harbinger. You are the most formidable threat I've seen anywhere. I like our chances."

"You didn't get lost in the frozen wilderness for five days walking in circles," Tamrin says. "Maybe pray to Krikhi that you don't."

"Krikhi is a lie, like the others," Kara says.

The barge floats beyond a row of warehouses, and the twins disappear beyond the trees. Their lives are their responsibility now.

I stand.

"Well, looks like it's up to us now," I say.

I'll be there soon, Jez. Don't worry. I won't let you go through this shit alone.

Tamrin procures horses from the stables on the outskirts of town. Kara and I gather supplies to cover seven days in case we find ourselves lost in the snow again. Tamrin sits with his face nuzzled against a heavy warhorse's face. He hands the reins to Kara and points to a standard quarter horse.

"That one is for you, Buddy," he says.

"This is a nice horse," Kara replies.

"Yeah, well, we're broke now," Tamrin says. "I spent the last of the gold we had. But I figure you and I need larger horses, and these two can bear the added weight of our friends when we catch up to them."

Tamrin hops into the saddle of another heavy warhorse.

"Wait, so Jesma's riding with you?" I say.

"Shut up and ride," Tamrin replies. He spurs his horse forward, and we leave Coraside Bay behind, our path directed toward Kerakot Stream. We reach the northern bank about a mile outside of town. Behind us, the last of Coraside Bay's farmlands vanishes around the bend. Ahead of us, an empty stream and woods call.

I can't help myself, and I stare across the water to the southern bank, and a shiver runs through my body.

"You do remember the Kirwaq helped us last time, right?" Tamrin says.

"I don't care," I say.

"I don't understand," Kara says.

Tamrin fills Kara in on our plight and confusion with the Kirwaq. Kara listens, intent on the details, which Tamrin embellishes a bit. After a few questionable embellishments, I quickly realized the Korund can spot a lie with near-perfect accuracy. Tamrin eventually realizes it, too, and the embellishments grow less frequent and less embellished.

When he finishes, I can't help but tease him.

"That is the most honest story you've ever told, Tam," I laugh.

"And the least interesting," he grumbles.

"I thought it was a great story," Kara says.

"It would have been better if you had allowed me to tell it my way," he replies.

"'Better a tale told truthfully, than a lie left lingering,' as my baba always says," Kara admonishes.

"'Embellishment flavors the tale with one's soul,' my grandma always said," Tamrin counters. "She was a masterful story-teller."

"Then how do you know what's true?" Kara asks.

"The embellishments in Tamrin's stories are always obvious. But they make the stories fun," I say.

"See? Shen gets it," Tamrin says with a smile.

Kara ponders his words before speaking again.

"It seems I owe you an apology, Tam," Kara says. "I didn't understand your intent. Please retell the story."

He shakes his head. "No. That one is done."

We settle into silence, and Tamrin leads us deeper into the woods, away from any unwanted surveillance.

Incapable of silence for long, Tamrin pipes up again.

"How about I tell you about the time Shen and I rescued a bookshop owner from a band of book thieves?"

I groan.

"Book thieves?" Kara asks.

"Book thieves," Tamrin says.

He then falls into a long story about how I stopped a shoplifter as if it were some great caper. While he talks, I drift into my thoughts about my mom and whether I'll ever see her again.

The barge travels at a lumbering pace via a series of warps along the stream's northern bank. The journey is slow and laborious. Loud voices carry over the water. The coxswain calls the cadence.

I hide in the shadows, waiting for Jesmir to jump the gap with Jesma. Tamrin and Kara are well out of sight, deep in the tree line with our horses. Even with the knowledge of where they are, I struggle to see five massive bodies. Satisfied that they won't be spotted, I inch further out toward the bank.

The bow of the barge appears around the bend. When we last saw the cargo vessel, Jesma and Jesmir were safe aboard. As much as it pains me, we left this part of our journey to fate and faith in the twins' abilities to protect themselves.

The barge rolls upriver at a turtle's pace. The crew pulls the ropes on the warp as fast as they can to the rhythm of the coxswain's call. The long, narrow bow turns around the bend. The duration of the turn is excruciating. I can't make out whether the twins are safe on board. The coxswain's voice calls out the cadence, and the deckhands turn the warp pulleys in time. The bow passes, and the crew focuses on their tasks. Jesmir and I make eye contact, and I slip back into the shadows and wait. A full minute goes by. A breeze brushes my ear, and I almost jump out of my skin.

"Boo," Jesmir whispers from behind.

"What the fuck is wrong with you? I almost screamed."

Jesmir shrugs with a sly smile.

"Sorry. I couldn't resist. Are you going to hang out here all night?"

"You could have given a signal."

"Like what? Yell out that I'd like to get off the boat now?"

His quick retort makes me snort, and I search for Jesma.

"Where's your sister?"

"With the others."

"Already?"

"I put us so far in the woods I almost couldn't see the stream, then came to get you."

Let's get out of here and get to Kerakot before that barge," I say.

"That won't be a problem. That's not the best crew. They're slow. No chance they get to Kerakot before us."

"Wow. I thought they were pretty efficient from here. You sure no one saw you bug out?" I ask.

"Please," he replies.

"Jez okay?" I ask.

He doesn't answer right away. "I don't know if she can do this, Shen. I'm not sure she has the resolve."

"And you do?" I counter.

His expression removes any doubt before he even speaks.

"Father is dead. Mother is dead. Jez was almost raped. I almost died." He points to his bandage. "I don't know if this will ever heal. All of it, the terror, the bad dreams, the tears, the pain...is *her* doing. Not to mention that her real name is Shamna, not Grandma."

He looks away and bites his cheek.

"As far as I am concerned, Grandmother died. Whatever the queen is, she is not my grandmother anymore. She's a cancer. Fuck her. Either she dies, or we do. Jez will do the right thing."

"I hope you are right, my friend," I say.

Chapter Twenty-Six

Journal Entry: 143

I find myself buried inside my head in search of memories about my mother. For so long, all I thought about was that bell, or the hardships she placed on us, me specifically. I focused more on my anger. I've buried the good memories for a long time. Now, they aren't available to me anymore.

It's that 'remembering the remembrance' concept again. Because I didn't recreate the good memories by rehashing them, they could be gone forever.

But that means if I do remember one, it will be pure and untainted.

I hope I remember a good day with my mother.

She deserves that.

Sorry, Mom. I'm a bit of a mess, so I hope you'll understand.

I write this here in case someday it comes to you. Should I not return, I want you to know that I understand now. And I do love you.

I don't know if I'll see you again.

In This Corner

The twins' time on the barge served its purpose. The crew will eventually panic, search for the twins, and realize they'd fallen into the stream at some point. I feel bad about the trauma this may cause the crew, but they'll be fine. At least they won't be held responsible for the twins' disappearance. The message will reach the Port Master that the barge passengers were lost "somewhere". There may be accusations thrown at first, but that matter will be resolved before it blows out of proportion.

None of it matters.

By the time the news reaches Kerakot that the twins weren't on the barge, the queen will already know. Because I'll look her in the eyes when I slit her throat long before they deliver the news.

The tree line thins out, and we break out onto the frozen plains. I kick my horse into a gallop, and the others follow suit. Kerakot lies ahead in the distance. The lights of the suburbs beckon.

We covered the distance more quickly than I thought we would. Seven hours after Jesmir performed his vanishing act from the barge, we stand at the edge of Kerakot's city proper. We find a hitch post and tie our horses off.

"I've never wasted more money on anything like I have on horses since I met you two," I say.

"We could keep them," Jesma says.

"I admire your optimism," Kara replies. "Unfounded as it may be."

"Talk about a mood killer," Tamrin says.

"Are we really going to pretend that we don't walk to our deaths right now?" Kara asks.

"Look," I say, and make a circle with my finger. "We, as a team, killed Brogen. And that was before we had your lovely and powerful presence, or their magic." I point to the twins. "Brogen, I might remind you, turned out to be Hakaka, God of War. Let's face it. We're god killers."

"I've been thinking about that a lot," Tamrin says. "Are we sure he was Hakaka?" He addresses Kara. "I mean, how do you know? If he was, then that sure was an anti-climactic way for a god to die. None of us should have survived, yet we all did."

"He did kinda go down like a chump," Jesmir says.

"Most deaths are sudden. They always come by surprise for the dead," I say. "Drawn-out fights are embellishments by bards, minstrels, and playwrights. Epic battles are for entertainment." I clap him on the shoulder. "Kinda like your stories, big guy."

Jesmir laughs heartily. "Don't listen to him. I like your stories, Tam."

"Yeah," I say and point ahead. "Why don't you tell us another one on our walk to our apparent preordained deaths?"

"Lick Nadur's nuts," Tamrin says.

"Oh, that's my favorite story," Jesmir says.

Tamrin, Jesmir, and I burst out in giggles.

Neither Jesma nor Kara so much as smiles, each for very different reasons.

"Still," Tamrin says. "That seemed too easy."

"He's dead, Tam. We saw it. He underestimated Jes. Plain and simple."

"God killers or no," Kara says, unamused by our banter, "You were lucky against Brogen. Unless there's more to the story, I don't think you'll find this time to be as anti-climactic."

"Regardless, we killed him. Luck or no."

"You do realize we are going after the Goddess of Luck, right?" Tamrin says.

"Luck schmuck," I say. "I'll roll her rocks right up her ass. Lucky twenty-three for me, cursed five for her. Either way, I'm done playing games, lucky ones or otherwise."

"Just stop!" Jesma yells.

We all flinch. Folks still out on the street stare at us. A few seem to recognize the twins and mumble.

"Just stop," she whispers, tears in her eyes. "I can't do this. I can't pretend to be so flippant about this. Do you not realize that she's our grandmother?"

She turns to Jesmir.

"She's our *grandmother*. And you're caught in this wave of solidarity with a killer." She flips her hand at me. She turns to me. Her expression is one of hurt.

"Do you even care?" she asks, tears staining her cheeks.

I feel myself shrinking under her scrutiny.

"Of course, I…"

She shakes her head. "No. No, you don't. I came to you several times with my fears, confusion…angst. You said you'd give her a chance, and now you act like we are on some noble mission to glory!"

I clam up, the right words escaping me.

"Are you going to stand there with your mouth shut and not help me through this? Is that it? Your solution is to kill her and move on. Right, *Harbinger*?"

"Jez, listen," I say, but she stops me again.

"No. It's too late. You all can stay here, and I'll go speak to her on my own."

She eyes each of us with anger.

"If one of you touches her, I promise…I will fucking *touch* you."

She walks past us without another word.

The queen's mansion looms at the end of the street. I stare after Jesma, dumbfounded and clueless.

The steps to the large double doors into the great hall of the mansion feel much larger today. Two guards on either side acknowledge our presence with nervous glances. Their discomfort in our presence makes the hair on the back of my neck stand on end.

"What is it, Guardsman?" Jesma asks.

"Your…Your Highness," one says. "The queen has search parties all over Conishant. You've been missing for a little over a month. Our orders are to notify Her Majesty immediately upon any sign of you."

The guard who spoke turns to the other and says, "I will go notify Corvan."

Jesma stops him.

"First, I am entirely capable of announcing myself. Second, our departure was last-minute and unavoidable." Jesma says. "I'll make it up to Her Majesty when I see her. For now, we'll go inside and make our presence known."

The guard swallows hard and looks nervously at the other.

"I am sure you would rather I tell the queen you were helpful and respectful on our return, and not the opposite. Correct?" Jesma says.

They both nod with vigorous enthusiasm. It's only now that I realize the guards do not love their queen. They are terrified of her.

Each grabs a door handle and pushes the large doors open to reveal the grand foyer. The giant chandelier inside illuminates the stairs and us. Once again, I'm struck by the stark differences between the Citadel in Killinshire and Queen's Mansion. In a very literal sense, the difference is night versus day.

Very different tactics to achieve the same result. Intimidation by wealth and power.

I really want to kill this bitch.

The butler, Corvan, approaches, his eyes dark. He waves away the night staff, who stand frozen in surprise at our sudden appearance. Corvan is agitated. If I didn't know better, I'd say he looked downright exhausted. He seems to have aged in the weeks we've been away.

"Your Highnesses," he says, his voice deep but less controlled. "Where have you been?"

"That doesn't matter," Jesma replies. "I keep my own counsel. Where is Grandmother?"

"She is asleep in her chambers, Your Highness," he replies.

"I'd like to speak with her," I say. "But not here."

"I'm sorry, Your Highness?" he questions.

"Corvan," Jesma says, her posture erect, commanding. "Have Grandmother meet us at Shamna's Temple within the hour. Tell her that she should be prepared to learn some bad news about my father's death. Tell her we go to pray to Shamna and demand the goddess give us divine retribution for the crimes committed against us, and we expect her support. Tell my grandmother, she is expected to join us in this effort, and that if she doesn't arrive, we will leave and take matters into our own hands."

Jesma glances at her brother and then at me before she returns to Corvan.

"Regardless of any relationships involved."

Jesma looks back at us.

"One hour, Corvan. The very throne depends on it."

Jesma reaches into her purse and hands something to the butler. He gasps.

"Your Highness…," he begins in a hushed tone.

"Now, Corvan. Tell her she has one hour. We can't be responsible for anything that happens if she arrives late."

Jesma turns and walks out the door.

"Jez," Jesmir says, hurrying after her, "what the hell are you doing?"

"I'm giving her a choice, Jes. She can come talk to us…" She turns and stares at us. "Or she can come kill us." Jesma storms out of the mansion. "Either way, we'll know the truth."

Shamna, the Goddess of Luck, stands before us, thirty feet tall, her massive hands held cupped as she offers her followers a chance to win her favor. Her face bears a smile, a pleasant image of benevolence, captured in bronze, weathered and discolored.

She looks nothing like the Queen. It's been a while since I've seen her likeness up close, and it occurs to me how much this statue resembles Jesma.

Jesmir and I stand before the statue.

"Do you see it?" I ask.

"I do now," he whispers.

He stands, stunned.

"It just became real," he says, a crack in his voice.

I turn to Jesma. She stares at the statue. Tamrin and Kara flank her on either side. I lock eyes with the woman I love, and I know she's come face to face with the truth she'd been denying.

"How did we never notice this?" Jesma asks. "That's the same woman we saw in Grankin's dream."

If there was any doubt, it's gone now.

We stand in the center of the stone courtyard in front of Shamna's Temple. It's too tall to see inside the statue's cupped hands, but I've seen enough of the miniatures sold in shops to know what she offers. Five odd-shaped dice called 'Shamna's Rocks'—two five-sided, two six-sided, and one seven-sided—the drug of her followers, gambling disguised as blessings.

Jesma walks past the statue, her eyes on the enormous bronze doors that lead into Shamna's Temple. Crowds of people wait to enter. A steady flow of folks makes their exit, some with faces filled with joy after rolling the blessed twenty-three. Most, however, leave dejected, likely in the firm belief that they've rolled the dreaded five ones called "Shamna's Curse" and must pay penance to remove it.

The entire system is a poverty tax.

Of all the gods, I've always hated Shamna the most.

"If ever a game was meant to sucker poor bastards out of their money," I said, "Shamna's Rocks is number one on that list."

"I've never played," Tamrin says.

"It's a fool's bet. Costs money to play, eighteen ways to lose, five to win, one to win big, and one to lose everything you own," I reply. "Jez, what's the plan here?"

"We go inside and send everyone out. These people are innocent." She turns to address us. Her eyes smolder. "Scare everyone into a fast exit. But not one acolyte leaves."

"I'll guard the front door and make sure that doesn't happen," Kara says.

"Good," Jesma replies. "Once the crowd is safe, we question the acolytes inside." She points at Tamrin. "Destroy every table, every symbol. If Shamna and Grandmother are one and the same," she closes her eyes and takes a deep breath. "She'll come ready to kill. If they aren't, Grandmother will come angry, admonish our behavior, and demand we fix everything."

"That's not a very good measure of her intent," Kara says. "Logic dictates she'll do the latter, regardless. You'll need to push her with more than Temple desecration."

"If she really is Shamna, she's seen more of human nature than you can imagine," I say.

Jesma says nothing and storms up the steps. Two acolytes in light green robes of Shamna's devout, heavy wool with symbols of dice embroidered in gold, inspect the offerings of those who wish to enter. They admit only those whose offerings they deem sufficient. Those they turn away are told to come back with the minimum required tribute or are sent to one of the lesser temples in the slums.

When Jesma and Jesmir approach, the acolytes are surprised to see the royal twins and make every effort to push the crowd back. They use a little too much force for Jesma and Jesmir's liking, and Jesmir grabs one by the robes.

"Is this how we treat our people?" he growls.

"I…I…only meant to pay proper respect to you, Your Highness."

Jesmir says nothing and shoves the acolyte toward the door.

The acolytes eye Kara, Tamrin, and me with suspicion, but are too startled by the presence of the twin royals to address us or deny us entry. Both men's faces tighten with fear as they look up at Tamrin and then at the taller Kara.

"My bodyguards," Jesmir says with a smirk.

They look at my cloak with its holes and tears with distaste. When I catch their eyes, they divert their gazes to avoid mine.

"You should see the other guy," I say, smirking too.

The temple sanctuary is filled with people. Loud chatter, cheers, and cries of disappointment mix with Shamna Rocks dropping against fifty stone tables. There is only one game in the temple, Shamna Rocks. But there are many variations to offer variety to those who wish to take bigger risks.

The main sanctuary is filled with the lower classes of worshipers. Or as Teshken calls them, 'the Livery'. What the rich and middle classes really mean is those folks relegated to the labor class, a commodity from whom profits can be extracted. The lowest class of citizens has the least amount of money to lose and is the most in need of luck.

The stench of sweat, bad breath, and booze fills the room, tinged with the spicy aroma of incense.

"Someone should tell the acolytes the incense doesn't work," I say, scrunching my nose.

At the far end of the room, two marble doors lead to the antechamber. Inside, the wealthier followers curry favor with Shamna with a more private experience with the acolyte leadership.

Two guards stand before the doors in the silver and gold armor of Temple Salvationists.

"Salvationists. What a stupid name," I say. Tamrin giggles.

An elderly follower approaches the doors and requests entry into the antechamber. The guard on the left stops him with a scowl and a hand on the old man's chest. They exchange words, and one of the guards, a female with her hair in a high ponytail, spins the old man around and pushes him back into the sanctuary.

Tamrin growls under his breath at the treatment of the older gentleman. We approach the doors, and Jesma turns to the angry hunter.

"Tam? I don't feel like being nice today. Get the doors for me?"

Tamrin smiles at her and nods. He approaches the doors, and his enormous frame rises over the guards.

The male guard steps forward, clearly not intimidated by Tamrin's size.

"Sorry, you'll have to use the tables behind you," he says.

The other guard leans over and whispers in the first guard's ear. The male guard peeks around Tamrin, catches sight of the twins, and his eyes bug out.

He clears his throat and says, "We will address Their Highnesses."

"No, you won't," Tamrin said. "If they wanted to speak with you, they would have. They sent me. I'm going through those doors."

The other guard steps forward and says, "Excuse me. But only followers of Shamna are allowed through these doors. It is well known that her Highness is an acolyte of Ezra and that his Highness is *not* an acolyte of Shamna, though it is unknown who he follows this week."

I snicker at that and lean toward Jesmir. "Sounds like they got you pegged."

"What can I say? I wanted to play the field," he whispers back.

"Catch any diseases in the process?" I retort.

"Just a really acute case of atheism," he says.

"You're screwed. There's no cure, I'm afraid."

"Damn, guess I'm going to have to live with it then."

Tamrin smiles and says, "Well, do I have news for you? The Princess has renounced Ezra. She's found a new path. So," he points at the doors, "she will enter that room."

The guards shift in place, uncertain. They exchange glances and shake their heads at Tamrin. Tamrin looks back at Jesma, and she nods.

"Well, you saw. Lady Jesma wants in. She goes in."

Tamrin smirks at the guards. From my vantage point behind him, he shakes with violent tremors. His back muscles bulge and grow. A loud growl rumbles through the room and pulses against my eardrums. Tamrin's body doubles in size. All around us, the sanctuary turns silent.

A lone set of dice clanks on the table, and someone yells, "Twenty-Three!"

Tamrin, now over twelve feet tall, stands before the guards, who look up at his massive head. His legs are as wide as my waist.

He smiles back at me, and the massive fangs in his mouth cause me to burst out in laughter. Even in his transformed visage, his grin is doofy to me.

"Don't smile at me like that, big guy. You're making me horny."

"You lost your chance," he growls. His deep bass voice shakes the air in vibratory concussions.

The quiet sanctuary rumbles with nervous chatter. The guards take a couple of steps back and draw their swords. The silence of the crowd shatters, and screams echo off the marble and stone surfaces. Tamrin slaps the male guard in the jaw and sends him flying across the sanctuary.

I'm not sure if the guard is still alive.

A chaotic ruckus of activity breaks loose as everyone, including the acolytes, attempts to run out the enormous front doors. Screams of panic and shouts of frustration fill the space with too much sound. I cover my ears as the stampede of people grows to a crescendo.

Kara's voice booms from the front door, "Not you, Sweetheart. You get to stay. If I see one of you acolytes try to leave or pray, my blades will behead you before you get the first word out."

The chaos fades into the distance outside, and the temple doors slam shut.

I welcome the silence.

Tamrin grabs the other guard and tosses her to the side. She screams as she flies through the air and lands on her back, unconscious. Tamrin draws back his fist and slams it into the door of the temple antechamber. Both doors give way, and screams of shock, anger, and dismay echo inside the next room.

Jesma walks past Tamrin and through the doors. Jesmir and I follow her. I slap Tamrin on the ass as I pass, and he laughs when I shake my hand in pain.

"Damn," I say, "That stings."

Inside, half a dozen acolytes of Shamna gather their wits and raise their periapts forward. Their mouths move in prayer. Five followers of Shamna turn and face us. Their clothes and jewelry identify them as folks with wealth. Their periapts of Shamna hang from their necks, adorned with intricate materials and designs. Most of them are gold or other precious metals.

"No killing," Jesma demands.

"Well, I'm sure as hell not going to let them kill us," I say.

"No killing," she yells.

"Fine," I grumble.

"You five," I say to the wealthy congregants of Shamna's temple, "go now or suffer the consequences."

Panicked, they run from the room, arms in the air. I turn to the acolytes with their periapts up. The fire in me ignites, and I jump over a table and throw my feet forward. My heels catch the one closest to me in the chest, and his breath explodes from him in a high-pitched wheeze. I land on my feet while he flies backward into a stone pillar. His head hits the pillar with enough force to cause his eyes to roll back. I grab the hand with the periapt, break his fingers, and shatter his access to Shamna. He falls to the floor, writhing in pain. I fling the pieces of stone through a stained-glass window behind him.

Tamrin moves with a fluid grace that defies his massive size. He grabs two acolytes at once and lifts them into the air, slamming them together like cymbals. They're unconscious by the time he lays them on the ground, careful not to do more harm.

"Sorry," he growls at them.

"Tam! Stop being so nice!" I yell.

A gust of wind catches me off guard, and I'm thrown through the same glass window that I just launched the periapt through. I tumble through the air and out into the temple gardens.

"Shen!" I hear Jesmir cry out as I impact the ground.

With a tremendous thud, I land on my back. The same sound that my victim made escapes from my lips. I roll to my side and fight for breath.

"I'm…gonna…definitely…kill…whoever…that…was…" I say as I gasp for air. My chest is on fire.

"Hey, mister," a kid playing in the garden asked, "are you okay?"

"No," I gasp.

"You know Shamna's going to be mad you broke her window," he says.

"Kid…she's…already mad…now…I…am…too."

I catch my breath and tear off back into the temple with a hurdle over the windowsill. When I land, I recognize Jesma's voice. She yells at someone, her tone commanding.

"Put the periapt down, acolyte!" Jesma yells.

"You let her go!" the last acolyte standing says. The acolyte stands at the back of the room, her periapt held forward.

Jesma holds another acolyte by the neck, one hand on the side of the woman's face. The woman trembles, but I can't tell if it's fear or if it's Jesma causing pain. I step to Kara.

"Where have you been, Harbinger?" Kara asks.

"I needed coffee," I reply.

"Hardly seems the time," Kara replies.

"I thought you were watching the kids in the nursery?" I say.

"They're napping," Kara replies with a smirk that gives me the shivers.

"It's less fun when you play along," I say.

"I've learned your methods, Harbinger."

"What are we doing here, Jez?" I ask, addressing the woman I love. Her behavior frightens me, and I don't like where this is headed.

"He's tried to cast three times. Jesma hurts the other acolyte every time he tries," Kara says.

I approach Jesma, the death of the mage in Killinshire fresh in my mind. This isn't who she is. Jesma is kind, compassionate, and gentle. Not this cold killer, all too willing to torture.

Or maybe it is. You've only known her for a couple of months.

"Jez?" I call to her. "What are we doing here? You said not to kill anyone."

She doesn't respond.

"Drop the periapt, acolyte," Jesma repeats.

The acolyte's mouth moves again, and Jesma's hostage screams in pain.

"Jez, stop," I say.

Kara whispers to Jesmir, "Can you do what you did with the Harbinger and your sister with me?"

Jesmir takes Kara's hand, and the two vanish. The air pressure around me drops so low that it threatens to pull the air out of my lungs again. Kara and Jesmir reappear behind the acolyte, who jumps, startled. Kara grabs the woman by her ankle and lifts her from the ground. With a twisted smile I've never seen on any Korund, Kara floats into the air. The acolyte dangles upside-down and screams. Her periapt falls to the floor with the ring of solid gold against marble. Kara hovers fifteen feet in the air, and the acolyte cries out.

"Don't drop me! Please!"

"Okay," Jesma says. "Now that we've got your attention, we can sit and wait for the queen in peace."

"Wait for me? In peace?" The queen's voice echoes through the chamber. "What is the meaning of this, young lady?"

"Hello, Grandmother," Jesma says and turns with the acolyte to face the queen. "We need to talk."

"That, my dear, is an understatement."

"Young lady," the queen says, stepping into the antechamber. "Take your hands off Acolyte Dora."

A contingent of twenty guards stands behind the monarch, beyond the doors into the sanctuary. Armed to the teeth, more than one with a periapt held forward, they file in and surround us. The Queen glares at Kara, who still hovers in the air.

"A Korund? A Chieftain's Child, no less," the queen says, pointing to the earrings in Kara's ears. "How unbecoming of your parents. They'd be disappointed in your brash behavior. What led my peaceful granddaughter to such an act of violence, I wonder? You had better come on down and explain why you'd risk an inter-realm incident, Child of Friends."

The menace in the queen's tone leaves little room for doubt in her intent should Kara disobey. Kara slowly settles to the ground and carefully sets the acolyte upright. The acolyte wobbles, hand to her head, before she gathers herself and runs toward the queen.

"Bless Shamna, Your Majesty," the acolyte cries. "Look what they've done to the temple! They killed everyone!"

"Nobody is dead, you dolt," I say. "Not that I'd care either way."

The queen looks at me with distaste.

"And you want to marry *my* granddaughter?" she scorns. She raises her open palm to Jesma. "See what happens when you choose to consort with the livery, Granddaughter?"

My blades release, and the queen raises her eyebrow.

"If that one moves a muscle, put him down," she orders. Then she turns to Jesma. "What is the meaning of this?" She extends her hand. In her palm rests a broken stone on a gold chain.

It's Jesma's periapt of Ezra, shattered into pieces. At this moment, I understand what she gave to the butler. And with slow realization, I understand her plan.

Jesma steps forward. "I think you know, Grandmother."

"You've renounced your faith in Ezra, at last? Good. But why this behavior in Shamna's Temple? Why not Ezra's if you're so disenfranchised?"

"Come on, Grandmother! Why play coy? You know exactly what is going on here."

Clever, my love.

Jesma, the insolent child, throws no accusations. Instead, she throws a tantrum.

"I assure you, young lady, I do not. Now. First, you will clean this mess you and your…*friends*," she says that last word with distaste, "…made. Then every single one of you, that includes you, Chieftain's Child, will come to the mansion and explain yourselves."

The queen looks at me and then Tamrin. "You two had better pray the explanation is good enough to keep you out of prison."

I snicker.

"Something funny, Harbinger?"

I shrug like a child.

"This charade is," I say.

She scowls at me, and the flash in her eyes tells me she got my note. "Now, fix this place and bring yourselves back to the mansion," she says.

The queen turns to leave.

"I did not dismiss you," Jesma says

The queen turns back.

"Excuse me?" she demands.

"I want to know why I should clean this mess when the gods left the world a mess."

"Now is not the time for existential tantrums, Jesma," the queen snaps. "There are more important matters in this world than your inability to handle the loss of your father. More important than this childish behavior. We will address your actions later."

The queen shifts to an air of concern and compassion.

"I know you hurt, Darling. I know that the loss of your father is devastating. Believe me, I am as sad and angry and shocked as you."

"Are you?" Jesma asks.

"Of course, I am. What is that supposed to mean?"

"Doesn't his death fit beautifully with Mom's? Aren't we too liberal for you, Grandmother? You say it all the time."

The queen steps closer to Jesma.

"You watch your tone, young lady. The loss of my only son is not a matter I will discuss with you here. You two are all I have left of him. He'd be ashamed of your behavior."

"I think he'd be proud," Jesmir says.

"That goes for you as well, young man."

"Or what? You'll have us killed like you did Father?" Jesmir says.

The queen's gaze bounces between the two siblings without a word.

"Answer me this," Jesmir continues. "Do you not see the bandage on my head, or is this temple business here today too much distraction for you to notice?"

She flips his concerns away with a wave. "You're always into something. I assume you got into another fight. It's hardly a surprise."

"Or maybe, you didn't ask because you already knew," Jesma counters.

"Knew what?" the queen asks, her tone glib.

"Knew that Emissary Krin kidnapped and tortured me," Jesmir says.

"She what?" the queen asks, surprised.

I'll give this to the bitch, she plays the role. If I didn't know better, I'd assume she didn't know. But I do know better. And I'm bored.

"Your Majesty," I say. "Let's dispense with the lies so we can all finish our tasks and get on with our lives…or our deaths?"

"What truth, Harbinger? What tasks?"

"I hope you did what my note instructed, Your Majesty," I reply. I pause, but not long enough to let her speak. "Or should I call you Shamna?"

The acolytes gasp in horror.

"Blasphemy," the female acolyte whispers, shocked by my display of disrespect.

"What note?" Jesma asks.

The queen's glare flashes and fades again.

Damn…she's not giving in.

"Harbinger, I know you mean well to protect my grandchildren." She turns to Jesma. "You and your brother have been through a lot with little time to grieve your father. What you've been through since hasn't helped matters." Her eyes fall on me. "And while I recognize the trauma bond you've developed with this man, I assure you it's a fleeting bond. When the trauma ends, this will end. And the trauma ends here." She points her finger at the ground for emphasis.

"Tell me it's not true, Grandmother," Jesmir says, his voice like ice.

"Tell you what isn't true, *Grandson*?" Her emphasis on the last word signals her displeasure with Jesmir's tone.

"Tell me this was not all your doing," he replies. "Tell me you didn't have Father killed. Tell me you didn't conspire with Hakaka to have us kidnapped. Tell me you didn't order Krin to kill us all."

The queen releases a disgruntled sigh. She waves the captain of the guard forward. He approaches without a word. The queen points to the acolytes.

"Escort these two out of here. Take them to the mansion and have Corvan give them rooms for the night. You and your men leave us. This is a family matter, and I need privacy. Have your men set a perimeter at the front of the courtyard away from earshot. No one in or out without my permission."

"Yes, Your Majesty," the captain replies.

The acolytes protest, but the queen stops them.

"I understand your concern, Acolyte Teegle. But this is my realm. I rule it as I see fit. We will repair the damage to the temple. But your services are not required here tonight."

The acolyte bows her head in servitude, and she signals Acolyte Dora to follow the guards out. When the last guard exits and the door slams shut, the queen points to Tamrin and Kara.

"You two, out. It's time my grandchildren and the Harbinger all had a nice private chat."

"Hell, you say," Tamrin's voice booms. "We aren't leaving."

The queen's scream rages so loudly it echoes throughout the temple chamber. Tamrin turns, his eyes glowing a light tint of orange. Kara leans against a pillar, hands on sword hilts. Jesma stands a few feet from her grandmother, shoulders held back, chin raised.

"Answer the question, Grandmother," Jesma says. Her voice cracks and betrays her brave mask.

"No, Jesma!" the queen yells. "I will not answer you. I don't answer *to* you. *I* am Queen. I do as *I* see fit. Now, let's sit, and you can tell me why you think you're entitled to question me."

"No," Jesma replies.

"No?" The queen places her head in her hands and rubs her eyes. "You seem to think you have a choice in these matters." With a flick of her hand, Jesma is lifted off her feet and thrown back toward the altar that sits on the dais.

I sprint to reach Jesma before she slams against the stone slab. I extend my hand to grab her, but the room spins. I tumble through the air as the ceiling and ground blur into one object. My arms and legs flail in a desperate attempt to steady myself.

Tamrin's loud growl shakes the pillars that hold the ornate ceiling in place, and dust falls from above. In mid-air, I rotate my body into a tucked roll and right myself before I hit the ground. My feet touch the floor, my knees buckle underneath me, and I slide to a stop.

I search for Jesma. She struggles to rise from her hands and knees. Stone pews explode from the ground and slam into Tamrin. He cries out in pain, and the resultant crash shakes more dust from the rafters.

"Tam!" Jesma screams.

Jesmir is nowhere to be seen.

Tamrin lies under the pile of stone pews, his eyes closed. Kara rushes to free him.

The queen stalks toward Jesma's position. "Well, how did we end up here, I wonder?" she says. "Krin wasn't lying, was she, Jesmir? You've discovered something. Would you like to tell me what you've learned?"

Jesmir doesn't speak.

I lunge toward the queen, but before I take a step, I'm knocked through the air again by a massive weight.

She wasn't even looking at me!

I realize my mistake when I land, and Krin's face is pressed against mine, arms wrapped around my ribcage. The impact with the ground breaks her grip, and she rolls away with a grunt. A sharp pain in my side reminds me of another time back in Rhinestab. I glance at the blood that pours down my side. Krin's blade once again protrudes from my body. She grins at me, her teeth bared.

"You cunt!" I growl.

"You can't live without me inside you, can you, Babe?" she jests.

"You're like a bad case of diarrhea," I say. "You linger too long and make everything stink."

"Aww, don't you love me anymore?"

I slip her knife out of my side and smell it.

Rot Root. I really fucking hate this woman.

"Looks like that's gonna take some time to heal," she quips.

"Kinda like the venereal diseases you passed around when we were kids," I retort.

"You say the sweetest things."

"I'm full of quips for you, Darling. Come closer so I can just give you the tip," I say.

"That little thing? I never felt it the first time. What makes you think it's bigger now?" she says.

"Let me put it in your ear, you'll feel it," I grin.

"Kinky," she smirks.

"Why are you following this charlatan?" I ask.

"The queen? She's a means to an end. I'm one of Shamna's favored," she says. "Someday, Shamna will make me queen. Want to be my king?"

"I think I'd rather be Cuska," I say.

"Too bad. I rather like our talks." She vanishes, like on the docks. I search for her. The air surrounding me thickens, triggering a memory. The familiar sensation reminds me of Jesmir.

Oh, now isn't that a lovely tell.

I dive at the spot from where Krin vanished as she appears in my previous place. Her other knife swipes at empty air. She spins in a panic to locate me. I wave, and she vanishes again.

The air pressure around me increases once more, and I sprint across the room and throw a knife behind me. Krin reappears, and the knife hits her right quadriceps. I smile with satisfaction when she screams and grabs the knife.

Her leg buckles underneath her, and she drops to one knee, her face contorted with rage.

"Oh look," I say, "Sorry! That appears to be a little more than the tip this time! Is it as good as the last time?"

She rips the knife out, and blood splatters on the ground. She disappears again. I wait, my attention on the air around me, but I can't feel the change in air pressure this time. Wherever she intends to re-appear, it isn't close by. Adrenaline causes my skin to clam up. She's in possession of one of my knives. Rather than dive out of the way, I spin my tattered cloak like a shield, remembering the Korund steel fibers woven into it. The surge of speed creates a cloud of dust that fills the air, obscuring my vision. I only hope it also makes me more difficult to target with a thrown knife.

I tuck myself low inside the blanket of protection my cloak creates—my body partially hidden. Metal clangs against a solid surface and onto the ground–the distinct sound of a knife that has been knocked away, harmless. A momentary sigh of relief escapes my lips.

When the dust settles, Krin is gone once again.

Jesma, Tamrin, and Kara have their hands full with the queen and another assassin. Jesmir slams against the wall on the other side of me, a third assassin's leg lowering from what was obviously a kick into the prince. Jesmir looks like he's in trouble, but vanishes before I can assist him.

The air pressure builds again, and considering the prince had just disappeared into the nether, I am unsure who is about to invade my personal space. Cautious, I hop backward and time my fist for Krin's reappearance and hope it's not Jesmir. I aim at where I suspect her torso will appear.

Please don't be Jes.

My knuckles collide with Krin's breast. The loud pop inside her chest and the way it caves under my fist provide satisfactory feedback that I cracked her ribcage. Krin stumbles back, clutching herself, and her wounded leg once again betrays her. She falls to one knee.

I follow the first strike with a kick in the sternum as she gasps for air. I catch her fingers between my boot and her breastbone, and she screams out in pain. At least two of her digits broke from the impact.

Her diaphragm spasms, and her eyes bulge with panic as she fights to take in air. Angry, bitter, and vengeful, I kick her between her legs and catch her lady parts with the toe of my boot. Her body lifts into the air, and she lands face-first.

I don't know why I didn't extend my blades while I fought her. I do so now, their motion silent. I stand over her.

"I'm going to piss on your grave for the rest of time," I say.

I pull my fists back and prepare to finish the job I should have completed back at the docks.

"Goodbye, Krin. It was never fun while it lasted."

"Harbinger!" the queen calls. The sheer power of her voice causes me to pause. I turn toward her.

Oh no.

Eight more assassins stand around the room. I have no idea when they arrived. Tamrin, Jesma, and Kara are restrained in shackles—a metal collar around their necks. Their heads are hooded. Jesmir is nowhere in sight.

"Jes?" I call out.

"Yes, grandson, come out now," Shamna calls.

I point at the bitch who set these events in motion.

"I *will* kill you."

"No, Harbinger. You will listen. Then we shall come to an agreement."

"Why should I trust a word you say?"

"Because if you don't, I will kill Master Tamrin here. Then Chieftain's Child. Then I will send my assassins to Winding Run and have them kill Mistras and his daughter, and anyone related to them, in case there are others you care about. More importantly, Harbinger, because you have no choice."

"Why are you doing this?" I say and I step forward, my blades ready.

"No, Harbinger. Why are *you* doing this? Why come back to Teshket? What is driving this desire to destroy everything? Who sent you?"

"You did."

"How did I send you?"

"I overheard your conversation with Krin. In your chambers. The morning after we arrived."

The queen closes her eyes. She knows she's exposed now.

"Now I understand your note. I should have trusted my instincts. How unfortunate," she says. "You wander around with only half the information. Too bad you won't live to learn the real truth. But what little you do know can't become public knowledge."

Jesma struggles in her restraints.

"What are you saying?" she demands.

"Oh, dear granddaughter. I do love you. How does the saying go? The jig is up."

I prepare to rush Shamna. A heavy object slams against the back of my head. My vision blurs, and my ears ring. My knees buckle, and I fall to the ground.

"You always liked it when we played rough," Krin says, her voice distant.

"Fuck you, Bitch," I mumble.

"Where's that prince?" Krin says.

"Oh, I'm afraid my dear grandson's streak of cowardice got the better of him."

Krin's boot connects with my jaw. The world goes black.

My head pounds with the noise of a ceremonial parade filled with drummers who never learned to play. Armies march on my skull, their boots out of sync, the sound unpleasant and painful. I have no idea where I am, but wherever it is, I'm uncomfortable. Several grunts escape my lips while I roll over and almost fall from a ledge. Hands press against my chest, gentle, small, firm.

"Easy, there," Jesma says.

"Ow." I grab my head with both hands.

"Take a second, Pal," Tamrin's voice echoes from further away.

I open my eyes, but the world is blurry and dark. Dim yellow light flickers against wet stone, the shimmer a blur. Shadows dance off the uneven stones overhead. The scent of burning oil mixed with musty, sour air tingles my nose. From several directions, rhythmic drips ring off hard surfaces.

I try to sit up, but my side hurts. My clothes stick to my skin, and I wince in pain. The coppery smell of blood reaches my nostrils. I place my hand against the source of pain and find it covered with a heavy cloth. Blood-soaked, the fabric is wet and tacky. I'm in trouble. It hurts as badly as Krin's previous attack that left me in the hands of Cuska.

"That bitch stabbed me again," I groan.

"Yes, she did," Jesma says.

She's a blurry dark shadow surrounded by a halo of yellow light. I try to focus, but it's difficult. My eyelids are heavy, and sleep seems easier. Jesma shakes me, careful not to damage me further. It takes several minutes for my eyes to focus.

I turn my head and spot iron bars,

Shit.

"Help me sit," I mumble.

"That's not a good idea," Jesma says.

"I don't have a lot of time, Jez," I say, aware I'm bleeding out. "You can't heal this. It's like Jes's ear and Tam's finger. Krin used Rot Root on me. If we don't stop the bleeding, I'm dead. I have maybe a few hours, at best a day. Now, help me sit."

She nods and cradles my shoulder. Tamrin takes my legs and helps me swing them onto the floor. He sits next to me. I look around the cell for a source of flame. But we are in a dungeon. The only source of light is the gas lamps outside the cells.

"Where's Jes?" I ask.

Tamrin, Jesma, and Kara exchange glances.

"He vanished," Kara says. Her voice is laced with disappointment. "The queen overpowered us, and he vanished. And never came back."

I turn to Jesma, "He'd never leave you."

Her gaze falls to the floor, and I know she's worried.

I try to get a sense of what we are working with. The constant drip of water plays havoc with the pounding in my head. I touch the back of my skull and wince. Krin left a lump behind. Across the way, haggard faces stare at us with curious interest. Filthy and rail-thin from starvation, I know they've been here a while.

I realize there's something around my neck. When I try to look around, my range of motion is limited. Cold iron rubs my jawline with every twist. I tug at the thick metal collar. When I shift to adjust myself, I'm surprised that my motions make noise.

"What the fu…" I start. "That was loud."

"Our magic is blocked," Jesma says.

"What? How?" I ask.

"It's these collars," Kara says. "We've failed. The gods have won."

A closer examination of Jesma's collar reveals an engraved symbol I know well. Five dice, whose top faces add up to twenty-three. Shamna Rocks. The sigil of the goddess of luck.

A frustrated groan rumbles in my throat at the memory of Grankin's display of control over my magic. It all makes sense now.

We're defeated. All my time as the Harbinger, and this is how I go down. Jesma avoids eye contact with me. Kara stares ahead, unblinking. Tamrin holds his head in his hands, mumbling to himself.

How has it come to this? This can't be how this ends.

I dig in to feel the well of magic and find nothing there but a wall. I can sense it, but I cannot draw from it. I adjust my position and wince in pain.

"If you were any louder, champ," Tamrin grumbles, "the guards would come in here and crack your skull for disturbing their party."

I move, and the noise is so loud I wince.

"Quiet in there," a guard yells from a dark hallway.

"See?" Tamrin says.

"It's these collars," Jesma says. "The sigil of Shamna keeps us from tapping our power freely."

"Damnit," I say. I try to move fast. All I accomplish is more pain in my gut.

"Stop," Jesma demands, her hand on my shoulder. "Tam's fur barely clings to the wound. If you move too much, it won't stay."

"What do we do now?" I ask.

"We die," Kara replies.

I've never seen a defeated Korund. I don't like it one bit. *Where's our gear? Shit, they have my journal.*

Chapter Twenty-Seven

Journal Entry:

Luxury Accommodations

I stress over the idea that Shamna has my journal. I can't record my thoughts, and they're free to taunt me with self-recrimination and an endless cycle of beratements stuck in a swirl in my mind. It's a bit of a shock to the system. That little book has been a constant companion, and I feel lost without it.

Stuck inside my head, I obsess over how badly I've failed everyone this time. Reliance on others has weakened my fortitude and mental acuity. I should have killed the queen the moment I heard Krin's voice. If I'd taken care of business and escaped back into the RhineWoods, none of this would have happened.

The walls close in, and the cell shrinks with every passing minute. Time drags, and the physical prison manifests itself in my mind. The musty air and scent of my own blood start to get to me. Every motion hurts. The lack of connection to magic, as constant in my life as my angst, hurts.

Fever hasn't set in yet, and I'm still conscious, the only positive light I can cling to. My blood loss hasn't reached a critical point, though I'm tired. Pain or not, I can't sit here and allow us all to die.

No one has spoken since Kara announced our imminent deaths.

I'm surprised that Shamna hasn't appeared to gloat.

Jesma sleeps on a cot in the corner, fatigued after caring for me while I was unconscious.

Fruitless attempts to discover a way to break free resulted in uncovering anguish, frustration, and despair. The bars are solidly in place, and the guards are well away from us with the keys. Our weapons are gone, and we have no magic.

Tamrin tried to rip my collar off with brute strength. He twisted at the lock. He pried at the hinge. Kara failed, too. All they accomplished was to apply uncomfortable pressure on my neck. The bruises formed almost instantly.

Tamrin sits against the wall with his knees to his chest, his head bowed, defeated. I've never seen the big guy so morose.

"Hey, Tam," I say. "We'll find a way out."

He doesn't acknowledge my words.

"Jez," I whisper.

"Let her sleep, Harbinger," Kara says.

I try to stand, but the pain is too much, and I grunt in anger. It takes all my strength to rise. Though I try to make as little noise as possible, I sound like a herd of cattle on gravel.

"I can't believe how hard it is to move in silence," I mumble.

"Yeah, you've been spoiled," Tamrin says. "It's annoying. You never actually had to learn how to *be* quiet. You've never had to think about motion the way the rest of the world does."

I turn to Tamrin to say something snarky. My words are strangled in my throat when I notice his physical appearance. He looks exhausted and…old. The stress of the last month has aged him. He looks sickly.

Why haven't I noticed before?

"Tam? Are you alright?" I ask.

"Do I look alright? Do any of us look alright to you?" he growls.

I limp over and squat before him, my hand on his knee for stability. My side protests with a twinge of real pain. He glances at me, apologetic.

"No, Tam. You look unwell," Kara confirms.

"When did you turn grey?" I ask.

"What?" he replies.

I point to his beard.

"Grey. A big 'ole streak of it, right down the center," I say.

"What are you on about?" he growls. "I'm not grey. It's the light in here. Messes with your eyes. And what does that have to do with any of this?" He throws his hands out to show our environment.

I yank a hair out of his beard.

"Ow, you prick!"

I hold it for him to see.

"Your entire chin is like this," I say.

He rips the hair out of my hand, glances at it, and drops it on the ground.

"What do you want me to say? We're getting old, Shen. In case you haven't noticed, we aren't kids anymore. We're both in our fifties. Too old to be putting ourselves through the last two months of shit."

He stands and pushes past me. I stumble, and Kara catches me before I fall to the ground. The pain is so intense I almost vomit.

Kara looks at Tamrin with curiosity.

"No, tracker. He's right. You look ill. And that streak of grey wasn't there yesterday. And your face has new wrinkles."

Tamrin hurls curses at us, grabs the iron bars of the gate, and tries to shake it loose. I wobble over to him and pull him into the brighter light. He scowls. I grab his beard gently and pull his face to mine. Crow's feet appeared at the corners of his eyes, which I had never recognized before. New wrinkles line his forehead and jowls, and the hair at his temples is grey.

"Wow. Have we aged this much?" I say.

He squints at me. "I don't know what you mean? You don't really seem to age much." He slaps my hand. "Now are we done talking about how old I am?"

Kara leans over my shoulder.

"No, Tam. This isn't normal. You look much older than you did hours ago," Kara says.

"In case you haven't noticed, a lot has happened in the last few hours," he retorts.

Jesma wakes, our conversation too loud.

"What are you doing over there?" she demands.

"Come look at this," I say.

Jesma rolls out of her cot and stomps over to us in frustration.

"What?" she demands.

I point to Tamrin. Jesmir turns to him and gasps.

"Tam? You look ten years older."

Metal creaks and clangs are accompanied by voices. Boots scrape against the stone floor, the beats louder and closer with each step. Shamna appears around the corner, flanked by Krin and another assassin.

"Well," the bitch who plays god says. "It's good to see everyone's awake." She looks at Tamrin. "Oh my. It seems you don't have much time left, Tamrin Salzar. I suggest you take what I'm about to offer you seriously."

"What are you doing to him?" I demand.

"You'll learn soon enough," she replies. "Much like your father did. Now, what I really want to know is who sent you after me?"

None of us speaks.

"I have to hand it to you, Shen-Zarl, *of Ditherun*." She waits for me to catch her meaning. "I first suspected that the Harbinger was the son of Hakaka's long-time friend about a decade ago, but couldn't find any records to prove it."

"I've got to hand it to you. You've eluded the best Conishant has to offer. You forced me to rethink my plans. It's been a very long time since someone has made me work for a creative solution to my problems. But the mark of a great ruler, and let's face it, I am one of the best, is adaptation."

"The only reason I haven't killed you is because you have information I need. And let me tell you something almost no one believes. Torture works. It *always* works. But I've been at this for a long time. I know when direct torture won't work on someone. You are the type of person who will take the pain and give me all types of false information. You'd only frustrate me into killing you, and that just won't do."

She holds my journal in her hand and taps her other palm with it.

"Delicious reading. So much self-hatred. So much love. And so many secrets." She smiles with her mouth, but her eyes smolder with sinister intent.

A gust of wind pushes us backward. I grit my teeth against the force that presses against my wound and pins me to the back wall. A guard unlocks the cell with a key, and the queen steps in. She points at Jesma. Krin, who appears to be healed from her wounds, along with the other assassin, grabs Jesma. I try to fight back, but the force of the queen's magic holds me in place.

Jesma struggles against the hands that hold her.

The queen points at Tamrin.

"He has so little time left," she says. "I'll prolong his decline to give you some time together. You'll be witness to his rapid progression toward the ailments of a long life. It won't be pretty as his mind succumbs to forgetfulness and confusion, or I can make it quick. Just tell me what I want to know."

"What do you want?" I ask through gritted teeth.

"I want to know who leads this little rebellion of yours. And don't say Grankin. That fool is stuck at the bottom of the river. He can do little from there. Someone, somewhere in Conishant, pulls the strings that make you dance. Someone encourages unbelievers to spread their lies and filth. No matter how many times we wipe them out, they reappear. There's a puppet master out there. I want *that* person."

"I don't know what you are talking about."

She waves my journal in front of my face.

"You really reveal yourself in this, even name names. I can use that to find what I want. But that takes time, which you can save me if you talk. Thanks to your little neurosis, I think I found a way to make you talk."

"Did it never occur to you that you might be captured? Were you so confident in yourself that you never thought this little book of secrets could be useful to your enemies? Never considered it would end up in the wrong person's hands?"

I try to lunge at her, but it's no use. I'm held fast.

"Come now, Shen-Zarl," she says with disappointment. "Tell me what I want to know, and this all ends. Jesma need not suffer."

"I don't know what you want."

"Simple, really. Where is your mother?"

"Rogue's Pointe. She fights in the ring tonight. I have ten gold, the bitch loses."

The queen digs her thumb into my wound, and I cry out. My vision flashes white, and I gasp for breath.

"Always quick with the snark," she says.

"You think that was quick?" I say through my teeth. "Wait till I stick my cock in your dead eye socket. I'm a premature ejaculator."

She punches me in the stomach. I gasp for air. Her punch is incredible for a thirty-thousand-year-old.

"Whoa!" I say through gritted teeth. "That only hurt because someone stabbed me. I can do this all night."

She purses her lips.

"I don't doubt it," she says. "I have a different plan. Let's see how long you hold out."

Krin and the other assassin grab Jesma. Helpless, I watch as she fights against her assailants. They carry her out of the cage, her body flailing against them.

"Tell them nothing!" Jesma cries as her voice grows distant, echoes the only remnant of her. "No matter what!"

"Jesma!" I scream back.

"Jez!"

I stare out at the long path out of the dungeon.

"Jez!"

The prisoners across the way watch, most out of boredom, their fates sealed. I ignore them.

"Jez!"

I scream her name in vain for hours. My cries go unanswered. My voice grows hoarse and my throat sore. Her name comes out as little more than a cracked whisper. She doesn't answer. No one answers. I shake the cage with everything I have. Warm blood flows from my wound, the dried blood no longer sufficient to hold Tamrin's furs in place.

I'm increasingly light-headed. Jesma's screams are the most terrifying sound I've ever heard. They come from somewhere deep in the dungeon, guttural and filled with fear. I don't know how long it's been. It doesn't take me long to break. I yell out to the guards, offering to tell the queen what she wants to know. But no one comes to tell me Jesma's pain will stop.

She continues to scream, and I fall to my knees.

Tamrin sits with his hands over his ears, his face covered in tears. The lines in his skin deepen, and the grey covers half his beard. Kara shakes the bars in a futile attempt to help me break the gate free.

I'm the Harbinger of Death, Karsija, D'aonar, Shen-Zarl of Ditherun. This is all my fault. I caused this.

I run out of anger. The pressure cooker that kept me sharp is spent. All the hurt and anger at my parents, at the gods, at the world did nothing to empower me to save my soul's mate. I scream again, but my voice is broken. I shake the door, but I have no energy. It barely moves.

Jesma's screams echo through the dungeon and reverberate off the walls. They die out every few minutes, only to begin anew.

I cry.

I don't know how long.

My knees hurt. I have no energy left to care. My arms hang dead at my sides. My chest heaves with silent sobs. Jesma's screams begin again, and I don't even flinch. I never notice the yells and frantic commotion in the guards' room. Loud thumps and grunts don't register. Only Jesma's screams register.

Boots appear on the floor outside the cage. Motion inside the cell makes me aware of the world again, and I recognize the boots. Their familiar shape points in my direction. Keys jingle against each other. The lock on the cell door scrapes and clicks.

"Ezra's Light," Tamrin whispers.

"Quietius' Ghost. Jesmir," Kara says, relieved.

The Korund rushes past me. Kara stands in an embrace with a smaller person.

"Jes?" I question, too stunned to trust myself.

Jesmir stands in the open cell doorway, his finger to his lips. He smirks and extends both hands to me. I grab them, and he helps me rise.

"Never thought you'd kneel before me," he says with no snark. "I'm not sure I like it. How about you get the fuck up and help me kill these assholes? Huh?"

"How?"

He holds his finger to his mouth to silence us and points at the collars on our necks.

"Where have you been?" Kara demands.

"Communing with our gnome friend," he whispers, and lifts his shirt. His chest is emblazoned with a handprint exactly like the one I used to have. Before any of us can speak, he holds his fingers to his lips again.

I pull him close and kiss him on the lips.

You beautiful son-of-a-bitch, I say, mouthing the words.

Grandson-of-a-bitch. My mother was a saint, he returns. In silence, we leave the cell and follow Jesmir out of the dungeon.

Two guards, their bodies in heaps, lay on the ground, their throats slit. Blood pools on the stone floor around them. One has a knife stuck in his ear, buried to the hilt.

"Krikhi's tits," Kara says through tight lips.

Jesmir glares at the Korund, his finger to his lips again. Kara winces. The prince went on a rampage here. Blood splatter on the walls forces me to look at the bodies again. Each bears multiple stab wounds, which causes me to stare at Jesmir slack-jawed.

A pitcher of water sits on the table, reminding me how dehydrated I am. I drink straight from the vessel, my throat dry from my screams. It hurts initially, but the water slowly soothes my throat. It does little for my larynx, but that will recover over time.

Jesmir points to our weapons stacked against the wall and scattered on the table. We gather our belongings, and Jesmir takes Jesma's rapier and small pack of healing supplies. Tamrin points at me and then at the table. He clasps his hands together and points to my injury.

On the table now, Tamrin mouths.

I limp to the table and sit. Kara and Tamrin help me lie down and remove the cloth from my wound. Tamrin points to an oil lamp, and Jesmir brings it over. Jesmir sets it next to Tamrin and pulls one of my knives from my harness. Tamrin shakes his head when Jesmir offers the knife.

Tamrin points at me and then at Jesmir's ear.

Jesmir smirks, and a wicked grin forms on his face.

"Please don't enjoy this too much," I growl.

Tamrin clamps my mouth shut, a finger over his own.

Oh, I'm going to enjoy this a lot, Jesmir mouths, my knife held in the flame. He points at my face and then holds his finger to his lips.

I nod vigorously, mouthing, *I got it, Asshole. Get it fucking over with.*

Tamrin stuffs a piece of dirty cloth in my mouth, and I bite down.

Kara and Tamrin hold me fast to the table. Jesmir pulls out the glowing knife, his hand wrapped in one of Tamrin's smaller furs, skin side out. He slaps the hot metal onto my wound without hesitation. My body goes rigid from the shock, and my eyes bulge in pain, my jaw clenches tight.

I make no sound, but I glare at Jesmir while he smirks. If not for the cloth, my screams would shake every stone loose on top of us.

It hurts unlike anything I've ever felt.

The smell of burning flesh and blood fills the air. When the ordeal is done and I'm back on my feet, I look at Jesmir with an apologetic smile. I point to his ear and clasp my hands, a silent apology for my callousness back at the Teshket docks.

"Wow. I'm really sorry about that ear," I whisper.

Jesmir smacks my arm, and Tamrin whaps me upside the head.

I make fists ready to punch them both.

I'm going to make you both pay for this, I mime.

Jesmir returns my knife. It's cool enough for me to handle. I inspect it. Blood, black from the heat, covers one side. The once sharp edge is dulled, too.

Jesmir rummages through Jesma's pack and pulls out a wad of cloth. Unwrapping it carefully, he withdraws a mushroom. I recognize it from the ones Jesma harvested a few weeks ago in Sanctum Mountain.

It's mostly dry, its texture mildly rubbery. I raise an eyebrow, and Jesmir shrugs. He points at my mouth and makes an exaggerated chewing motion.

Let's kill some shit, I snarl silently and pop the mushroom in my mouth. Jesmir continues pantomiming, and I chew the mushroom until it's minced. It tastes like sweaty ass, but I chew until Jesmir nods.

I swallow it and rush back to the water jug, desperately trying to rinse the taste away.

Bleh. I make a vomit face.

Jesmir smirks and waves for us to follow him toward Jesma's cries.

With my eyes on Tamrin, I notice the grey at his temples spreads. He ages before our eyes, and I don't understand why. Jesma's screams begin anew from beyond a bend in the hall.

Jesmir points to his ear and stops.

Our movement travels too, he says.

Shamna's voice replaces Jesma's screams as they fade into sobs.

"I wish I could tell you how much this pains me." Shamna's voice carries down the hall. Her tone is almost sincere. "You, your brother, and your father were only meant to draw out the Harbinger. Brogen allowed your escape into Rhinestab, hoping the Harbinger would find you. We sent teams to lead him your way."

"Why?" Jesma asks, crying. "Why harm your own family to get to him?"

"Sacrifices are required from each of us when the world is threatened, Darling."

Jesma's screams begin anew. Tamrin grips my shoulder, preventing me from charging forward. Jesmir places his hand on my chest, and we lock eyes. He holds up a finger.

Wait.

I clench my jaw and my fists. I know he's right, and instinct tells me to trust him. Jesmir holds a key in his hand and signals for each of us to turn around. He unlocks my collar but warns me not to remove it.

If you remove it, she'll know.

We continue along the hall, our sound camouflaged by Jesma's screams. We round the corner into another long hall. Midway along the right side, light shines from a large opening. Shadows stretch from an archway on the right. Flames from gas lamps flicker. The shadows cross the stone hallway floor and climb the opposite wall.

One shadow in particular, shortens and elongates as Shamna's voice changes proximity to the entryway. Between the flutter of the gas lamps and the constant change in the shadow, I grow woozy. My vision blurs, and I stumble backward into Tamrin. He catches me and holds me upright.

Everyone freezes in place, listening for an alarm. Jesmir glances back at me. I must look bad, because he waves a hand in front of my face, face twisted with concern. His hand moves in front of me, stops, and moves again, like it is leaving a trail in the air.

How does he do that?

I smile, enjoying the trick. I move to clap, and he grips my arms. Tamrin covers my mouth for some reason. I lick his hand like I used to when my brother clamped his hand over my mouth. Jesmir's panicked and disgusted expression—eyes wide, jaw clenched— makes me giggle, but he doesn't remove his hand. His eyes look like they might fly from their sockets. My skin tingles, and it reminds me of that feeling right before lightning strikes nearby. I glance upward for a thunderstorm.

That's odd.

Down the hall, Shamna's voice drops a full octave, and I struggle to understand her words.

I get a sensation that I'm not really in my body, or like I'm sinking into it. Jesmir grabs my face with both hands and shakes his head. The touch of his skin against mine is pleasant and relaxing. I grip his hands with mine and hold them there, savoring the sensation.

I listen to the conversation in the other room. It's less pleasant than the sensations out here.

"You don't understand the danger his existence poses. Ever since the Guild fire, we've searched for him. Only an unbeliever was capable of such power. The Guild's inability to catch him all these years and Hakaka's death confirmed my suspicions."

"Please stop," Jesma begs. Her voice rings like crystalline shards pouring on the ground. I crinkle my nose, displeased by the sound. "There has to be a better way."

"Your bleeding heart is so much like your mother's," Shamna says. "Time and again, this rebellious wave rises, and we crush it before it goes too far. It's exhausting. We need to know who leads it. Cut the head off the snake."

Shamna's shadow shifts across the stone floor. It grows monstrous, spreading up the wall, the shoulders broadening, legs elongating, the head swelling. I imagine popping that head with my new blades. Jesma's cries ring out again, and the sound hurts my eardrums.

I look back at Tamrin, and his face is bulbous. The lines in his face grow deeper. But his lower lip puffs out. His nose looks much bigger than it used to. I bop it with my finger.

Tamrin grips my wrist, and his brow furrows, his expression stern.

What the hell is wrong with you?

A sudden surge of energy comes over me, and I grow antsy. I want to *do* something. I twist my hips out of boredom and notice my pain is gone. I glance at my wound, and it's still there, but I almost can't feel it.

Jesma screams again, and this time it hurts my soul. Something inside me snaps, and I spring into action. Jesmir tries to stop me, but I shove him out of my way. Halfway to the entry, the collar falls from my shoulders. New energy fills me like a dam burst. Everything around me moves slower than before, much slower.

Then I remember that I have magic.

Oh, do I ever have magic!

"While this pains me, your screams serve a purpose. It's time to break your lover…"

The surge of energy inside is like a new life. Gone is the pain of Krin's blade. Gone is the self-recrimination. Gone is my fear of Jesma's wrath when I kill her grandmother. Wonderous power returns to me. And I use it.

Krikhi's ass, the mushroom! It's magic too!

Filled with raw power and might, I rush into the room to rescue Jesma. Goosebumps cover my entire body. The energy burns like an engine inside me. Its absence under the prison of Shamna's collar offered more knowledge than Grankin's lesson. I know what it feels like to be denied my own power now. The null reference awakens my mind.

Or it could be the mushroom.

The world blurs as my eyes readjust to the burst of speed. I'm through the archway before the collar hits the floor. Strange beings, vaguely resembling people I know, spring into action.

Flicking my wrists, my blades extend as a humanoid being rushes the entryway. His distorted features snarl.

"You have a weird face. Were your parents blood kin?" I say.

I laugh at the sound he makes. Unsure what I'm looking at, but certain I want it to pay for Jesma's pain, I strike. The being never sees death come.

"I am vapor in the wind, a stitch in time, too fast for your mind to interpret," I sing.

Korund steel pierces his wild eyes. With a swift boot to his chest, I send his body over Jesma and back into the room. His corpse flies through the air, taking forever to land. I don't wait for time to catch up.

"I have people to be and places to kill," I say.

No, that's not right.

Motion to my right moves so slow it's like I'm the god of time. I lunge at the source. It's another human type thing. Colors swirl around me like an artist's swirl of paints. Footsteps echo amongst low-pitched cries that I think are calls of alarm.

"What strange magic is this?" I whisper.

It turns out my current target isn't Shamna. Whoever it is, they'll do. I recognize them as one of the ones who took Jesma earlier. He attacks, and his eyes glow bright green. He has a connection to magic, like a tether. I want to sever that line. The easiest way is through one of the many orifices in his body.

Nadur's nutsack, am *I fast!*

Arms like springs, the assailant swipes at me. I dodge left, then right, as he tries to land two knife swipes. I spin behind him, drop to my knee, and shove my blade straight up his ass.

"Taint that a bitch?" I ask.

He screams, and oddly, it sounds like a tuba, low and slow. I push my blade through his body and press down. His insides fall to the ground in a nasty pool of organs. He collapses with a thud.

"Two down and Krin to go," I say.

I spot my ex-lover on the other side of the room. She stares dumbfounded, her face wobbly like gelatin. I shake my head at the sight, too freaked out by her appearance. I turn toward Shamna, who stands between me and Jesma. Shamna looks so much like Jesma, I almost run to hug her. But Jesma's on the table, eyes swollen and bloodshot. Her face glistens with tears. She looks haggard, but her eyes ignite with relief at the sight of me.

Literal fire burns in her eyes.

"Oh, that's hot," I smirk.

She looks at me like I'm insane.

Jesmir appears next to Krin, his new magic on display, every bit the hero. I wave at him, and both he and Krin frown. She swipes at him with her knife. He vanishes and reappears behind her. She vanishes and appears next to me. I roll from her attack as Jesmir appears next to her again. Krin appears on the other side of the room, panic in her eyes. Jesmir reappears near his grandmother. Shamna swings her hand in a circle, and a gust of wind pushes him backward onto his ass. Krin vanishes. Jesmir follows suit. The air pressure increases around me. It feels like I'm underwater.

The lamps dance, and the shadows remind me of my first encounter with Grankin.

Shamna's hands flutter in the air, and rather than worry about who's coming from the black place, I sprint at the goddess who hurt my friends, my blades poised. Gale-force winds slam into me.

The wind resistance increases against my body, my cloak creating drag. I slow to a crawl but match the energy speed for speed. My body is on fire. Inertia is my ally. Shamna's eyes narrow in determination, but all she does is slow my momentum.

I persist, the fire in my body hotter than it's ever been. She increases the wind. Still, I advance—albeit inches at a time. She scowls, and I sense trepidation in her. I feel the air pressure behind me increase. Certain it's Krin, I drop to my hands and crawl toward Shamna, my speed still gaining on her.

I'm rewarded with a scream as Krin appears inside the gale and is thrown across the room.

I push against Shamna's efforts. She growls in frustration. I growl back.

Tamrin and Kara appear in the archway. Their collective presence is a barrier of scales and fur—Tamrin now in beastly form, claws and fangs ready.

"Where have you two been?" I call out.

"What in the *hell*, Shen? You've been in here less than ten seconds!" Tamrin exclaims.

The wind stops.

I release the energy inside, stand erect, and stare at Tamrin. His fur glows like glitter while Kara looks like a kaleidoscope.

"Say that again?" I ask, stunned, how my sense of time and theirs differ greatly.

"Look out!" Tamrin calls. Too late to react, I'm hit with a massive force, my feet lifted from the ground. A tornado surrounds Shamna, its circular winds sweeping me from the side.

I fly through the air.

"Weeee!" I cry, giggling.

Where the hell did that come from?

Too distracted by my confusion, I forgot about my enemy. Shamna pressed the advantage. Everyone and everything that wasn't secure slams into the walls. Tamrin and Kara grip the edges of the archway. Tamrin's claws dig into the stone. Kara's Korund hand seizes the other side. He and Kara lock arms and together fight to remain in the room.

Jesma cries in pain again. I grit my teeth against an impact with the wall. Warm fluid spreads on my side, my wound bleeding freely once again.

The winds cease to blow, and I slide down the wall. When my feet touch the ground, I'm no longer laughing. I'm angry.

"Enough!" Shamna yells. Krin and Jesmir fall to the floor, breathless. Tamrin and Kara stand erect, their muscles no longer under the strain of their fight to remain in the room.

"I've wasted enough time on this," Shamna says. She points at me. "Tell me where your mother hides, or I'll kill you all where you stand. Last chance."

The silent stalemate lasts for only a moment, but my mind begins to process what just happened. The intensity of the strange colors and odd perceptions lessens. My mind shifts from hallucinations to singular focus.

"Fucking mushroom," I say.

"Sorry," Jes says from across the room.

"No, before was crazy, but *this* is great," I reply. I'm overcome with a sense of hyper vigilance. Krin stands behind Shamna. Jes stands on the opposite end with me, his sister between him and me.

Shamna releases a heavy sigh.

"Dynorphus Silas," I mumble.

Shamna shoots Jesmir a look, and, for a moment, his grandmother returns. He averts his eyes. Shamna bows her head.

"Let's work something out," Shamna offers.

"I have no intention of anyone I care for dying here today, *Shamna*," I say.

Krin's head snaps to the woman who has played goddess for so many years, confusion on her face. Shamna doesn't like my tone. For the first time, I see fear in her. She knows this only ends when one of us succumbs to death.

"We know what it took to stop Grankin. None of you could stop him single-handedly. Look around, *Gram*. You're alone here. No other members of the Great Eight come to help you. Or should I say seven? One-on-one, Grankin ends your reign ten thousand years ago. It's just you and Krin here today. Do you believe the four of us are here, without a plan?"

She narrows her eyes.

"So that's where we are now," Shamna says. "You know the truth?"

I ignore her. "Krin?"

My onetime friend turns to me, but her eyes remain on Shamna. Krin's face contorts in confusion and betrayal.

"Krin!" I call again. She looks at me. "You could be free." I point at the queen. "She blocks you from the source of your powers." I touch my chest. "Our powers are in here. Your periapt and belief in her benevolence grant her the ability to imprison you, not empower you. Each of the gods uses us. Look at us," I indicate my friends. "We stand before a god without fear. We exercise our skills without restriction. Denounce your faith and abandon this witch. Fight *with* us, not against us."

Krin stares at me with hatred. "You lie."

"Do I?" I retort. "You've known me since we were kids, Krin. Do I lie?"

She wrestles between doubt and faith. Her scowl falters. She turns to Shamna.

"Is this true?" Krin asks.

Shamna focuses on me and Jesmir. Tamrin steps forward, and Jesma cries out in pain before his foot touches the floor.

"One more step, beast, and I'll kill her," Shamna says.

Krin flexes, ready to strike if one of us moves, but indecision keeps her rooted in place.

"Is it true, your Majesty?" Krin asks, her voice unsure.

"It is true, faithful servant. But not without purpose. Remember, you are favored. I grant you more power than any in my realm." Shamna addresses me. "I know better how to distribute power than you do. Mine is a rightful place of rule. Power in the hands of the many is chaos. We restore power to the worthy, the faithful, those who will do the most good with it. We take it from the less worthy. And with that power, we keep the world safe."

Kara sidesteps into the room and moves to flank the Queen.

Jesma screams in pain again.

Kara freezes, uncertain.

The queen appears to consider a thought. "*I* have the power to make *you* one of *us*, Harbinger," Shamna says.

"I have no desire to be one of you," I snarl. "I aim to kill every fucking last god on this continent."

"That's unfortunate. You'd make a great replacement for Hakaka," she says. "You are so much like he was when he was younger. Since you killed him, I'd say maybe even better."

"I'd tell you to fuck yourself, but since you're my girl's family, I'll say lick Nadur's Nuts."

She snickers.

"I have. They're salty. But I *do* admire your incorrigible nature. It's so appropriate for a child. Useless in the real world, however. Maybe Krin would like the title then?"

Silence falls over the room. The only sounds are the heavy breathing of every person and soft whimpers from Jesma. I can't take my eyes off Shamna, but I long to run to Jesma and comfort her—to ease her pain. I yearn to comfort her. There's only one way.

"To save the world, Shen, I must rid it of you. You are the cancer that will sicken us all. It's not even your fault. It's natural." She looks at Jesma, and in her expression, I see sorrow.

"*You* made all of this necessary, Harbinger. Until I read your diary, I had no idea how little of a threat you posed. I miscalculated. But the die has been cast. I've inadvertently made you into the threat I thought you were. So here we are."

"We work for the good of those who seek us," Shamna says. "We hold the darkness locked away, so it doesn't rip the world to shreds. You have no idea what the world was like before us. We bring order and peace."

"Peace? You murdered your own son! There's no peace in that. You sent the world's worst killer after your grandchildren."

"I hear hypocrisy, *Harbinger of Death*," she says.

"Except I do not claim to bring *peace*. I come to rip you into pieces."

"You aren't the first. You won't be the last."

"Was my father a cancer?" Jesmir asks through gritted teeth.

"No, child. He was a true and devout believer. Your mother was the cancer. She poisoned you to believe you owed the lower classes. Without a class structure, there is undisciplined chaos. Equality breeds infighting. Equality and disbelief always coincide. The two are rarely independent."

Jesmir stands dumbstruck by Shamna's words.

"You killed our mother…" Jesma whispers from her place at the table.

"Cancer must be stopped at its source," Shamna says.

Shamna's lack of compassion for her grandchildren rips at my heart. The pain is excruciating. Her fingers on her right hand twitch. It's a tell I hadn't noticed before. The well of energy inside reveals itself to me. It churns inside. I stoke it, nurture it, building the conflagration. I realize I can store it, prepare it for effortless use, like I always have

"I have no idea how you've extended your life for so long, but it ends today," I say with a growl.

"You can do no more than I allow," she says. "I can kill my granddaughter with a thought. You aren't that fast, Harbinger."

Wanna bet?

I set my feet, ready to attack. To my right, Jesmir fidgets with something behind his back. Krin stands locked in indecision. Her eyes dart back and forth between me and Shamna.

I can take her.

The epiphany arrives without emotion. Shamna isn't as powerful as we've been led to believe. Not in the sense that gods *should* be. Belief is the only reason the gods maintain any control.

Nothing will satisfy me more than my blades taking her life. I knew I was angry, but I didn't realize I'm fucking livid. My visceral need for vengeance is overwhelming. I want her to pay for what she's done to Tamrin, the twins, and Kara's friends.

I want all of them to pay.

Jesmir twitches. Shamna glowers at him, his hesitation obvious. He's projected his intentions already.

Again, clarity slows the events around me, the clarity induced by Jesma's mushroom lays out the events in my mind like they've already happened. My path is clear. The look of determination on Jesmir's face, his eyes intent on his grandmother, and the smirk on hers, force me into action.

I lunge. This time, muscles don't snap. *I'm* in control. Magic ignites inside, a fireball of rage-fueled vengeance. The world blurs, the details lost in a streak of motion. Jesmir is there, hands behind his back. Krin stands frozen, still unsure. Shamna notices my movement and shifts to attack me instead, three thousand lifetimes of experience telling her I'm the greater threat.

You die today. Shamna.

She knows I'm unstoppable. The fear in her eyes evolves into resignation over her fate. Krin vanishes, and I suspect she'll appear between me and her queen.

It doesn't matter. I have two blades. I'll kill them both at once. Shamna's clothes billow, wind energy building around her. Krin can't stop me now. Shamna is almost within my reach.

Air pressure increases, the wind builds within Shamna's imminent gusts, but she's too late. I'm already here. I punch my blades forward, seven inches of Korund steel on each. Shamna cries out, aware she's lost.

My momentum is committed. I'm so close, I can't stop myself.

Krin appears directly behind Shamna, and her arms wrap around the queen's waist.

Jesmir appears before his grandmother, holding a collar like the one on Jesma's neck.

No!

My blades pierce flesh.

The collar snaps with a loud click.

Krin and Shamna vanish.

Jesmir grunts.

It all happens too fast.

I happen too fast.

One blade passes into Jesmir's back. The other into the back of his neck.

The fall to the ground takes an eternity. Clarity shatters. My blades retract.

Jesmir and I fall to the ground, his body cradled in my arms. "Help!" I scream.

There's so much blood. Jesmir smiles, his eyes manic.

"I did it. Grandmother can't take it off. She has no power anymore." Jesmir's voice is strained and fades away. He stares off into a place only he can see.

I scream till my body shakes.

Jesma's cries will haunt me for eternity.

Shamna got away.

And I killed my friend.

Jesma, covered in her brother's blood, cradles his head in her lap, rocking back and forth. Desperate to heal him, her screams rattle the stone walls. Stunned, I sit in the middle of the room, Jesmir's blood still wet on my own body. Jesma presses Jesmir's head to her bosom.

"Come back. Please! Come back!" she cries.

Her eyes glow, the bright blue energy in them reflecting off her tears. No amount of healing can repair what I've done. No magic can raise the dead. He's gone. Helpless, I can only bear witness to the damage I've inflicted.

Death comes suddenly. I am Death.

Jesma straightens Jesmir's limp head and rests her chin on his forehead. Her tears soak into his hair, mingling with the crimson flow. My tears are hollow.

Jesmir, Prince of Tal, grandson of the queen of Teshket, twin brother to Princess Jesma, Warrior, Rogue, and friend, is gone.

Why, Jes? Why didn't you tell us?

No. You did this, Shen. This is all on you.

Calls of alarm resonate through the halls, punctuated by the stomp of boots. I can't move. I don't want to move.

Let them take me. Let them execute me, please.

The others don't seem to care about the approaching guards either. Tamrin's tears travel the new lines in his face. His body is back to its human form. Kara stands beside him, a hand on his shoulder, jaw clenched.

I stare at my blood-stained hands.

Jesmir's blood.

Why didn't you kill yourself when you had the chance, Shen?

If I had, Jesmir would still be alive. This is my fault. I had to be the savior—the hero.

But I'm no hero.

You're the villain.

"Don't move!" a loud voice booms. We don't react when the guard steps in. "What is going on here?" he demands.

The guardsmen on his heels gasp. Two assassins lie dead on the ground. The table where Jesma was chained is covered in urine from Jesma's time under torture. The prince lies in the princess's lap, the last of his blood long since spilled in a wide puddle on the floor.

"Princess?" the guard gasps. "Oh, gods, Prince Jesmir? Who did this?"

I raise my hand. The guards rush in. I don't resist their handling as they yank me to my feet. Tamrin cries in dismay.

"What are you doing?"

I can't tell if the question is directed at me or the guards. I don't really care. The guards spin me to the table and slam my face onto the piss covered surface. Overcome with numbness, I don't even wince when they yank my arms behind me.

"Unhand him this minute!" Tamrin yells.

Jesma stares at me, confused by the activity.

"No! What are you doing?" she cries.

Again, I don't know to whom she speaks.

Tamrin rushes over, and a guard holds his sword up, threatening Tamrin. The big man slaps the sword aside like it's a toy. The guard looks back at the captain.

"If he interferes again, arrest him, too," the captain orders.

"But this is not his doing. This was an accident," Kara interjects.

"I see two dead assassins and one dead prince. This man confessed already," the captain replies.

"That will be enough, Captain."

I recognize the voice. Corvan enters. Jesma and I still look in each other's eyes. All I see is her anger and sorrow. I refuse to look away, forcing myself to feel her pain. Corvan walks over to me and places his hand on my shoulder.

"This man is not the murderer." He points at the dead assassins. "These men are. Release him."

The guards are reluctant to obey. Slowly, they release my arms and step back. I don't move, still looking at Jesma. She looks confused.

"Why is he under arrest?" she asks, her voice barely above a whisper. Corvan kneels before Jesma.

"Your Highness," he begins. "Apparently, he says he killed Prince Jesmir."

She shakes her head.

"No. He didn't." She looks back at me. "You didn't confess to anything, did you?"

I don't respond but blink slowly.

"No! That's not true! The queen did this!" Jesma screams.

"What?" the captain exclaims.

"Tell them, Shen," she pleads. "Tell them the truth."

But I can't speak. Tears flow from my eyes again. I cry out in anguish. Shock releases and uncontrollable shakes take over, and Tamrin rushes to grab me as I slide to the floor.

The guard signals for his colleagues to lower their weapons. Swords clang, armor creaks, and boots scrape as the contingent of guards stands down.

Corvan waits for the commotion to settle.

"Your Highness," Corvan begins again, his voice gentle, "I know this tragedy is hard. You cannot stay here. You must leave this place. Please, allow the guards to take Prince Jesmir to the mortuary. I will tend to him."

Jesma, eyes on Jesmir, speaks softly, confused.

"Why are you here, Corvan?" she asks.

He signals the guards to leave. Another round of loud and clumsy motion ensues before the room clears. Corvan waits until the last set of steps fades into the distance before he speaks.

He clears his throat, and when he speaks again, his voice changes. The rumble is rough with age and exhaustion. "It's time for the Great Eight to pass from this world," he says.

He stands and surveys the room.

"My heart breaks for your loss." He looks at me. "I can't imagine the pain *you* feel or the burden this will be to carry. But all of you have started something. You must, as all do when war comes, bottle your pain and finish the fight."

I've waited for your kind to succeed where your predecessors failed. If you allow me, I'll guide you to answers, maybe even some you didn't know you were looking for."

Corvan turns to me. "I'm so tired, Shen. Before I die, I'd like to make things right." He extends his hand to me. "Will you allow me to help you?"

I look at Jesma. She's as confused and lost as I am.

"Why would you help us, Corvan?" Jesma asks.

He kneels next to Jesma and places his hand on Jesmir's forehead.

"Sweet Prince," he says, "May your journey to the next realm be joyous." He turns to Jesma, "Please allow me to carry this burden for you, Your Highness."

Corvan, Butler to Shamna, Queen of Teshket, rises with Jesmir cradled in his arms. Jesma, too stunned to resist, looks up at the butler, immobile.

"Corvan, why are you here?" Jesma asks again, her voice shaky.

The image of Corvan shimmers like a reflection on water. The butler's uniform glistens in a wave of black. His face sinks into itself. His once dignified appearance grows gaunt, lines of age forming on his skin. His pallor turns grey, and his close-cut hair grows into wispy white strands, long and dry and thin with age. Dark spots appear on his hands, and the veins turn varicose. His teeth turn yellow, and some disappear entirely.

"You may call me Quietius. It's time for my kind to die," Corvan says.

Chapter Twenty-Eight

Journal Entry:

Death Unleashed

"**S**hen, don't."

I approach Quietius with malice.

"Shen," Jesma whispers. "Please."

The fire inside burns until I feel I might combust. I shake with every negative raw emotion, anger, sorrow, guilt, despair. The help-lessness to repair the damage I caused threatens to spill into violent destruction of everything. I know I should listen, but no part of me wants to hear anything except the tortured screams of the gods.

The sooner you finish the job, the sooner you can leave.

Jesma stands before me, her hands on my chest. Her words are lost in the hollow throbbing of my ears.

"I'm going to kill you," I say.

Quietius doesn't respond, nonplussed.

"Shen, hear him out," Tamrin says.

"He's a liar like the rest of them," I say.

"I don't think that's true," Jesma says softly.

She repeats my name in a mantra, like the sound of it means something to her, even though I murdered her brother.

"I'm going to kill him and all the others."

"Shen, my brother is dead." I look over her head, and she rests her palm on my cheek. "It happened to me. And I want to hear what this…," she looks back over her shoulder, "person…has to say."

I close my eyes, and more tears fall.

"We will deal with our emotions later," she whispers. "All of them."

Quietius stands with Jesmir in his arms, his ancient face twisted in sorrow. How can any of us trust him? All *I* see is one more reason we are in this well of destruction.

I am Death.

Though I'm the reason her brother is dead, Jesma swallows her emotions and prepares to move forward with killing her grand- . mother.

If I'm honest, killing Shamna is the only thing that will keep me going.

That only makes me feel worse.

Quietius carries Jesmir in his arms. The dungeon tunnel exits through a door into a study. Jesma gasps.

"That dungeon is under the mansion?" she asks.

"It is," Corvan replies.

The discovery that Shamna has a hidden dungeon with cells full of elderly people only increases our resolve to see her dead.

"Who are those prisoners?" Tamrin asks.

"They are not prisoners," Quietius replies. "They are hostages. Your grandmother takes from the prison population and brings them here. She then steals their magic from them."

"Then we must free them," Jesma demands.

Quietius faces us.

"It has to be done delicately. They have suffered worse than your large friend here has. I assure you, I will see to it that they are freed. But we must hurry if you are to catch your prey."

Quietius' image shimmers and returns to his role as Corvan.

"Please, hand the Prince to me," Kara says.

Kara's words are more emotional than I expected. There must have been a deeper connection between the Korund and the prince than I realized.

How didn't I see it?

Jesma inclines her head to Kara, eyes on Corvan. The butler-god gently passes Jesmir over. Kara cradles him close, his blood staining the Korund's scales.

"Where is the mortuary?" Kara asks.

"I will arrange transport for you," Corvan says.

"No. I will carry him. Just guide me," Kara replies.

If my heart could break further, the pain would kill me.

Corvan replies, "I will lead you there."

"No. I know the way," Jesma says. "You free the hostages."

"I will give the order. Then we go," Corvan replies.

Tamrin sits beside me. Jesmir's body lies on an ornate altar reserved for royals.

"What will they do with him?" he asks.

"They will embalm him today. Then prepare him for the royal ceremony," Jesma replies, her voice cracking.

Corvan approaches.

"We will wait for your return to hold the funeral. He is a Prince of the Realm," Corvan said. "We will honor him."

Jesma thanks Corvan for his help and collapses into a chair. A small fireplace heats the room. I stare into the flames, unable to pull away.

The fire pops, and Jesma and I both flinch at the loud sound. We exchange glances, and she laughs a tiny laugh. Overwhelmed by guilt, I lower my eyes. Her smile fades, and she turns back to the fire.

Tamrin places his hand on my leg. "Shen?" he says.

I don't answer.

"Don't speak. Don't argue. Just listen," he says. His deep baritone rumbles on my eardrums. He pauses and takes a deep breath. "This is very important, Shen. You need to hear it."

He squeezes my leg to get my attention. I turn my head to him.

"I know what's going on in that head of yours. Nobody knows you like I do. You shut down, brother. Don't get trapped in there. This was not your fault."

I look away.

"Do you hear me?"

"No, Tam, it is my fault," I reply. "I knew he was about to do something stupid. I thought I could keep him safe. I didn't believe in him, so I acted."

"This," Tamrin counters, "is Shamna's fault. She set these events in motion. You are as much a victim as Jesmir. Jesmir made his choice. You made yours. Within those choices, a tragedy happened. You each made your decisions with the right intentions. What happened was an accident. He'd no more blame you than you would him if the roles were reversed. There is no blame for you or Jesmir to carry."

"Easy for you to say," I reply.

Jesma stands over me.

Her slap comes as a shock. My head rocks sideways. Her hand cups my ear, and it rings from the impact. Heat rises to the surface of my cheek. Before I can recover, she slaps the other side of my face. Tamrin jumps to grab her, but Kara pulls Tamrin away.

"Leave them be," Kara says.

Another slap sends my head spinning. Jesma unleashes a series of slaps while she yells at me, enraged.

"Is this what you want! You wish to be punished! Is this what you deserve?"

Another slap cups my ear, and all sound becomes muted. Her words become distant and dull.

This is less than I deserve! Can't you see that?

Her balled fist slams into my nose, and the cartilage dislocates. That catches my attention. I'm surprised at how quickly the blood flows. She falls to her knees before me, streaks of tears flowing. Her face is still covered in Jesmir's blood.

"Does that make you feel better?" she whispers.

I shake my head, eyes watering.

No, now everything is worse.

"Do you want me to take your knife and slit your wrists for you?" she asks. "Would you put that on me?"

She stares at me, pleading.

"I lost my brother today. Don't make me lose you, too. I can't promise I won't blame you later. But right now, I don't. My grandmother did this. We must find her." Jesma grabs my hands. "I need *you* to *find* her, Shen."

She kisses my blood-stained hands. "We have to kill her." My hands still held in hers, she kisses my red cheek where her handprint burns. Her tears mix with mine as he holds our faces close.

"I can help you with the first part," Corvan interrupts, entering the altar room. "I know where she is headed."

"Why are you helping us?" I ask Corvan.

Jesma tends to my broken nose. The whites of her eyes turn a soft blue. The cartilage resets, and the pain ebbs into a dull ache.

Corvan doesn't answer right away, and I sense he's reticent. We wait for him to speak, too exhausted to push. When he does, it's two sentences.

"In our hubris, we've killed the world. Now, only you can return it to life." He points to each of us.

"I don't understand," Jesma says.

"You will, soon enough. But first, let me show you where Shamna is going. Follow me."

Corvan takes us to the roof of the mortuary. Kerakot spreads out around us for miles. We huddle around him. He points to the Assassin's Guild tower.

"She heads to the Guild Tower?" I ask, dubious. "You could have said so instead of lugging us up here in the cold."

"No. See the small tower to the right of the Guild Tower?" he asks.

"That's the Engineer's Guild," Jesma replies.

"Now come toward us from there. You'll see a building with a gold roof," he says.

"I recognize the roof, but I've never asked what's in there," Jesma says.

"It used to be the Rhinestab Embassy back in the day," I reply. "But that relocated behind us now on the other side of Kerakot. It's abandoned or was when I lived here."

"You're part right," Corvan says. "That building is now a secret laboratory for new magic. Shamna performs her crazy experiments there. She searches for powers that will resolve unique problems. The lab used to be where the secret dungeon is. A few thousand years ago, she developed those collars in her lab."

He turns and faces us. "The Great Eight are connected. We've been together for so long, used magic for so long, we can track known connections to it." He looks at me. "We can also sometimes trace unique connections. That's how bounty hunters found you over the years. Every time you push yourself, it sends a tiny beacon, a surge in the magical connection between everything. But you always disappear before the others can pinpoint your exact location. Worse, there's nary a place in the RhineWoods you haven't touched, so trackers struggle to follow you. It's been impossible to determine who you had close relationships with, if any."

The Tillions.

Bile rises in my throat.

No time for that.

"If I understand it now, I'm always connected. Magic has made me soundless for all my life," I say, setting aside the quilt.

"That could also explain why we didn't notice you. It's possible your continuous connection appears as a natural life energy. If we had known more about you, we might have found you more easily. You were a great mystery that Shamna couldn't let go."

"The closeness of the relationships between the Great Eight makes our familiarity easy to identify. We are always connected. At any moment, I can find my colleagues simply by looking."

He points southwest. "Morze is out that way somewhere, swimming the oceans."

He points south. "Nadur locks himself away in his lab at Rhinestab Castle. He doesn't get out much except to retreat to his other lab further south. He has some interesting maps on this topic. You may find them useful."

"Ezra wanders Conishant," he says. "In the winter, she is in Killinshire. In the summer, she wanders north all the way here."

He points toward Haabrestand. "Fildeus is there. Currently in her little shack in the woods."

"Krikhi is there," he points west to Gal-Danang. "She walks among her people. Though they don't recognize her. She's one of the only ones who cares for every one of her people." He looks at Kara. "She loves you all very much. Her commitment to you is great. There is a reason you outlive your human counterparts by twice, sometimes three times as long."

"Why?" Kara asks.

"You will learn the truth soon enough, I think," he says.

"I'm sick of the secrets," I say. "Grankin said the same thing. Just tell us what we don't know."

Corvan ignores me and continues his thought path.

"Our connections never end. They know I am here. That is how we knew Hakaka died. His connection was snuffed out. Shamna's is vanishing as we speak. It didn't go out, yet, but it dimmed greatly about the time your friend died. Someone places a veil, much like the veil our periapts place over believers."

"I don't know who. I don't recognize the source. But whoever it is wants Shamna weakened. Her first priority will be to remove that veil." Corvan points at the gold roof again. "That's the queen's destination."

"Catch her before she finds help and removes that veil. While Shamna's trapped in it, she has no power. You can kill her."

"Again," I say. "Why help us?"

"We've made a horrible mess of things. All through the world, magic lives. We've taken a lot from this world. I can't stomach it anymore. We were never worthy."

Corvan flitters his body in urgency. "You don't have much time. Get to Shamna before she finds a way to remove that veil."

Corvan orders a royal coach to take us to the secret lab. He instructs the driver to stop for no one, under any orders. He hands the driver five sealed notes.

"This should be plenty. If anyone stops you, hand them one and continue on your way. These notes will see you through any barriers Shamna may have placed. She wouldn't know I helped you."

We climb into the coach, and I wince in pain. He hands Jesma a pouch.

"In here is an antidote to the Rot Root poison in the Harbinger's wounds. There are five vials. It's all I could ever make. It takes a day to cleanse the system. Tomorrow or the day after, your magic should work on him."

"Thank you, Corvan."

The butler, who is a god, smiles a sad smile. "Your mother was something special. You're a lot like her. She'd be proud of you. Someday, I hope you will be Queen. Conishant will be much better for it."

"I appreciate that. But I have no intention of taking a crown," she says. She hops into the coach and hands me one of the vials. "Drink up, Buttercup."

I don't argue for once. I just do as she asks.

Corvan says, "One more thing. Once you are done with your task, you should look for her portal. You'll know it when you see it. Worth a look."

Jesma leans back in her seat. Corvan slaps the side of the carriage. The driver flicks the reins, and the coach lurches toward the mansion gates. Jesma stares out the window, shoulders heaving as she weeps. I place a hand on her back, and she pulls away.

I wouldn't want to be touched by me either.

Hand in my lap, I sit and stare straight ahead. Tamrin pats my leg and leans back into his seat. Kara stares straight ahead. Jesma closes her eyes.

Jesmir's face comes into my mind.

I miss him already.

Jesma's sobs continue until we arrive at our destination.

Chapter Twenty-Nine

Journal Entry:

Shamna Lamna Ding-Dong

From the outside, Shamna's laboratory looks abandoned and is in disrepair. If not for the gold roof, it would be unremarkable. Once ornate windows that lined the walls are now filled with mismatched stone. The older stone of the original design hasn't been cleaned in decades. If not for the group of guards who appear to loiter outside, this building might be inhabited by squatters.

Eight guards, dressed in what appears to be the oldest armor of the entire guard corps, look as bored and uninspired as a desk clerk. Since we know what lies inside these walls, I suspect their appearance to be a ruse. Quality weapons and the hard look in their eyes say these guards are killers, likely members of the elite guard disguised as low-foot soldiers. They congregate before a worn, solid oak door.

One notices us right away, and the killers split into four pairs.

"Well, that was quicker than expected," the forward guard says. She wears bronze shoulder plates on her armor.

"Captain," Jesma says, "I'm Princess Jesma. The queen is expecting me?"

"Your Highness," the captain says, the words laced with disrespect. "The queen specifically mentioned that you were not to enter. Nor your brother."

My eyes water at the mention of Jesmir. Jesma flinches, too.

I reply, "Captain, we're not here to argue. We will enter that building. You can try to stop us, but it won't end well for you."

Even I am surprised by their response. All eight rush. It's a well-thought-out tactic, each of us beset by a pair. Two rise into the air, and Kara answers the challenge, dual swords clashing in a contest with the guards overhead. By the exclamations from the guards, they didn't expect Kara's magic.

"Uh oh," I say, "looks like we can fly too."

Two guards vanish, and the air pressure rises so quickly I almost miss it. I drop low and spin, my blades extended, their legs my target when they appear.

Elite guards, my ass.

They are smart enough to reappear within the range of their swords. Both guards wince in pain as my blade tips slice their legs, one in the quadriceps, the other in the hip. They disappear again, and I leap into the air, pulling my knees to my chin. They reappear, and both swords stab downward in expectation that I'd try the same trick again. I land in the middle of them as their swords impact the cobblestone street. This time, they are too close. I come down on the captain with both blades.

Caught unaware, she collapses to the ground, both clavicles severed by my blades. Without hesitation, I roll over her body, away from the other guard. When I rise, the other guard appears before me, and I raise forearms just in time to block her sword against my bracers.

Tamrin's guards lay dead, his hammer resting on his shoulder.

"I thought these were elites," he says.

"You noticed that too?" I call back and punch my guard in the face, my blade exiting the back of his head.

A loud thud sounds behind me, and I flinch. I turn to the source. Kara kneels on the ground, one sword impaled into a guard.

"Nadur's nuts!" Tamrin says in awe.

I look for Jesma, and she sits on the steps to the doors like a spectator. I search for her guards and find them on the ground. Their bodies look broken and decayed, their skin grey.

"What the hell?" I gasp, appalled by the sight.

"I know what happened to Tam," Jesma says, her voice quaking with anger. "And to the hostages. I understand what Quietius meant about the prisoners. It's worse than you can imagine. Let's go ask Shamna some questions."

Jesma stands and pushes open the door. "If I'm right, these gods are evil. I hope I'm wrong. But if I'm not, we don't leave here until she's dead."

Shamna's laboratory is disappointing. The main entry is abandoned and unkempt. An old reception area, covered in dust and the carcasses of mice and rats, sits just inside the doors. Cobwebs fill every corner. Roaches scatter from the light that shines in behind us.

The stale air reeks of dead things.

"Disgusting," Kara says.

Kara's voice echoes to the left and right along two hallways. The one on the left ends at a door hanging by one hinge, blocking entry. The one on the right turns left at the end.

"Which way?" I ask.

Tamrin's eyes glow, and he points to the right.

"Tracks go that way. Two sets. Female, by the size and shape."

We follow the longer hallway on the right. Empty rooms with old tables and chairs line the left wall, likely meeting rooms for Rhinestab visitors to meet with embassy staff.

Further down, the conference rooms become offices, equally disheveled and infested. Tamrin leads us to the end of the hall, where two sets of stairs rest—one up and one down. He points to the one that leads down.

"They went that way," he says.

"Back underground we go," I say.

The stairs end at a landing that turns and continues into another long hallway. This hall splits into three. Tamrin points straight ahead. Orbs light the way with a blue glow. The hall ends at a stone wall. A single door on either side appears to be our only options.

"Door on the left," Tamrin whispers.

I take the lead. If there's any sort of trap, I intend to be the one who suffers the consequences this time. I stop everyone and advance the last ten feet on my own. I stand before the door.

"I don't give a damn what you say! Get this thing off me!" Shamna's voice rings out.

"It's not pickable, *your Majesty…*" Krin says, her tone venomous.

"Oh, cut that 'your Majesty' crap out, Krin," Shamna says.

I turn to my friends and nod. I kick the door open.

I'm not prepared for what I find.

Shamna is bent over a table, and Krin is behind her, lock-pick tools in her hand, her hips pressed against Shamna's ass.

"Am I interrupting something?" I ask.

Krin rises slowly. Shamna stands and faces me.

"If you value your lives," Shamna says, "then leave. And don't return. I've been merciful so far. I will not be merciful again."

"I've had enough of the games, Shamna," Jesma says as she steps around me. "Nothing you say now matters, *Grandmother*."

"Get over yourself, girl. Grow up. The world is dangerous. You have no clue what it takes to keep millions of people safe from the whims and selfishness of the entire human race," Shamna spits, all pretense gone.

"No amount of safety justifies your actions," Jesma spits.

"I am your grandmother, young lady."

"No. You're a tyrant. A thief. And a murderer. How many millions died for you to extend your own magic?" Jesma demands.

Shamna's expression surprises me. I don't know what it is, but it looks an awful lot like fear.

"Yes," Jesma says. "I figured it out."

Shamna recovers and stands defiant. "I don't know what you're talking about."

Krin drops her tools and draws her knives.

I extend my blades and step forward. Jesma blocks my way with her arm.

"Krin," she says, "If you want to learn the truth, stay your hand. Shen, stay put."

Jesma fills the room with her presence. The power of her personality overpowers Shamna's and makes the queen look small, almost frail. I step back, awed by the force of Jesma's will. Krin cowers back, shrinking against the wall.

Jesma tilts her head. "I couldn't figure out how you lived so long. If you aren't really a god, then you must be mortal. It was the last piece of the puzzle. I almost doubted that Shen had it right."

She smiles at me. "I suspected that maybe 'Shamna' was just a name passed to each new queen. Took on the mantle, so to speak."

She stands before her grandmothers, almost nose to nose.

"I discovered I can kill as easily as I can heal. Healing requires me to put my own life into the patient. If I keep doing that, I'll die. Won't I?"

Shamna nods. "Jesma…"

"Shut up!" Jesma commands. "Killing just required me to *take* from the patient. My patients can just as easily become my victims."

Jesma's eyes darken, absorbing light from around them. "The surge of energy is such a rush. I was ashamed at how good it felt."

Shamna, horrified, says, "*Was*?"

Jesma takes a step closer to Shamna.

"Jesma," Shamna says. "You don't understand the dangers that magic poses. Of all of magic, yours is the most dangerous."

I grab Jesma's arm. Shamna's tone worries me. Jesma pulls her arm from my grip. She places a finger against her grandmother's temple. Shamna cries out in pain, her knees buckling. Wrinkles around her eyes deepen, her skin loosens around her muscles, and the hair around her temples turns grey. When Jesma removes her finger, Shamna looks ten years older. Jesma sighs with pleasure. She drops her hand. I glance back at Tamrin. His face is crestfallen.

"Big mistake putting the collars on us. You should have killed us when you had the chance. When you pulled my life from me, I knew. Look at what you did to Tamrin. Same as all those hostages under the mansion."

Jesma looks to Krin.

"Magic lives inside us, ever present. Prayers don't grant us power *from* the gods. They remove the veil placed *by* the gods." Jesma put her finger on Shamna's forehead. "She picks and chooses who can pierce the veil to the magic that is rightfully ours at birth. Magic tied to our own lifespans."

Shamna's screams are high-pitched and pierce my eardrums. Her legs buckle, and she leans on the table for support. Before our eyes, she ages another decade. The once beautiful queen looks one hundred years old. And it only took seconds. Krin steps forward but stops herself. Jesma turns her back on both women and walks toward me.

"You were the danger, my love. You've always accessed your own power. You threaten their reign."

Jesma looks back over her shoulder.

"Isn't that right, Shamna?"

Shamna shakes her head. "Your bleeding heart will be the world's undoing. Before us, the world was chaotic. Humans tore each other apart. We created a new world of societies, realms, and cultures. Teshket thrives because everyone knows their place."

"You created a society where most suffer and a few rule," Jesma counters.

"A necessary structure to maintain a workforce and order. I provided a sense of belonging."

"Krikhi's tits. It's all true," Krin gasps.

"Oh, come off it, Krin. You've benefited from this more than anyone. This collar blocks me from any magic. I can't even block you for yours. Go ahead. Kill them all. You have all the power you need."

Krin stands frozen.

"Are you taking from me?" Krin asks.

"Don't be naive, Woman. What we do, we do for the good of all," Shamna says.

"But…I loved you," Krin says. "I've always loved you."

Shamna sneers at Krin. "Means to an end for both of us. You used me, I used you. Our relationship was merely transactional. Don't pretend otherwise. Shamna addresses me. "I curse the day you were born, Shen-Zarl. Your father couldn't see the value in his talent. Too good to follow the rules. He could have been Emperor."

"Don't talk about my father," I say. "Or I'll kill you right now."

"Don't be melodramatic. It's beneath you," she replies. "If you kill me, you doom the world. Someone wants us *all* dead, the entirety of the Great Eight. I notice your necklace. I recognize that symbol." She smirks. "You have no idea who you are working for, do you? And you think you operate under free will. You're a foolish child. A pawn…like the rest of the livery."

"Krin! No!" Jesma cries out.

"You're noth…" Shamna's voice is lost in a gurgle of blood. She grips her own throat, red liquid spewing between her fingers.

Krin holds her knife, wet with Shamna's blood, tears in her eyes. Shamna falls to the ground face-first. Jesma rolls her grandmother onto her back and stares into the dying woman's eyes.

"This is for my mother, my father, and Jes," she says. "I watched him die today. Now you can watch me watch *you* die."

Krin drops her knives and walks past me, eyes downcast. Tamrin and Kara step aside and allow her to pass, both in shock.

I step next to Jesma and look down at the dying god. Shamna, truly afraid, gasps for breath. And I couldn't care less if I tried. Shamna reaches toward Jesma for a last bit of comfort, and Jesma slaps her hand away.

The callousness of Jesma's action hurts in my chest. I fear a coming callousness. Hardness is forming, and I worry if it's her actions more than the loss of Jesmir.

I hope for the latter because that will heal someday.

"Now what?" Jesma asks from her position in front of her grandmother as Shamna closes her eyes for the last time.

"Apparently, there's a portal somewhere in this place. I say we find it and get the rest of them," Tamrin says.

I walk over to Jesma and place a hand on her shoulder. She grips it. Once again, she cries. I can only offer my support. Inside, I feel relief over her tears.

"This has to end," she says. She rises and turns to leave. As she passes, she lays her head on my arm. "None of this is your fault. Please don't shun me. You're all I have now."

Without another word, Jesma leaves the room. I stare at Shamna's lifeless body with a sense of empty satisfaction. This time, revenge seems hollow, the cost too high.

Death comes suddenly.

The collar on Shamna's neck catches my eye. The symbol of a hand slowly fades away.

Grankin, you wily bastard.

I turn to leave and notice a familiar book on the table. I grab my journal and follow my friends to find the mysterious portal. When I reach the door, I stop and turn back to the dead goddess that caused so much trouble. The pressure in my bladder makes me smile.

"This is definitely going in the journal," I say as I untie the fly on my trousers and glance behind me to make sure the others are far ahead.

Tamrin leads the way out of the building. A contingent of guards intercepts us at the entrance. I sigh in relief at their dress, light blue uniforms of heavy wool and yellow overcoats, the standard dress of Teshket patrols. They aren't members of the queen's elite, which bodes well for us.

"Halt!" the guard captain calls. "Put your hands up, all of you."

"I most certainly will not," Jesma says, pushing her way in front of Tamrin.

"Your Highness," the captain stammers, surprised. "I didn't see you. My lady, the entire battalion is on alert searching for you and your brother," he says.

"Well, you've found me," she replies.

His eyes dart over Tamrin, Kara, and me. "Are you in need of assistance, Your Highness?"

"I assure you I am not," she says and bows her head. "I'm afraid, however, we were not in time to save the queen."

The captain's face falls at the news.

"What do you mean, my lady?" he asks.

Jesma informs the guard of Krin's murder of the queen. She leaves out our involvement and any reference to 'Shamna'.

"Krin's a member of the Guild," Jesma offers.

"The Guild murdered the queen?" the captain exclaims.

"Hard to say," Jesma replies. "I only know she's a member."

"Your Highness, please, take me to her," the captain requests.

On the way, the captain and Jesma speak in hushed tones. We arrive back in the queen's lab, and the scent of ammonia overwhelms the smell of blood.

"I'll have this Krin hanged for this," the captain says.

Tamrin turns to me and raises an eyebrow.

I manage a halfhearted shrug.

The captain waves over one of his crew. He instructs the guard to have a royal coach summoned. The guard, eyes on the queen's body, tears in his eyes, salutes and runs out of the room.

"When the carriage arrives, we will place her inside discreetly. No one should see her like this," he says.

"They can place her next to my brother's body," Jesma tells the guard.

"Gods!" the captain exclaims. "Prince Jesmir is dead as well?"

"He died this morning. Also murdered by Krin."

"I'll find her, Your Highness. Her death will be slow."

When the captain leaves, Jesma looks at me and says, "Could you please drink some water? You're clearly dehydrated."

"How…" I start.

"The day we met."

That actually makes me smile. For a moment, we forget everything else and stare at each other.

"Oi!" Tamrin exclaims. "Have a look."

Jesma and I break eye contact, and sadness falls over me.

Tamrin points to a stone block that sits slightly higher than the rest of the floor. The mortar around the stone is chipped and, in some places, worn away. He steps on the stone and sinks level with the rest of the floor. Mechanical clicks and grinds, deep under the stone floor, rumble beneath us. A portion of the wall at the back of the room swings open. We hurry over to the opening and find a hidden chamber. Well-lit, the room is furnished with a desk, a table, a long couch, shelves filled with books, and odd metal pieces. On a far shelf, jars filled with fluid, herbs, and dead things crowd the flat surface. In the far corner, oval and mounted on two bird claws, a black mirror rests. In its center, a strange cloud swirls, and I'm reminded of the orb in the queen's armoire.

"Wanna bet that's the portal?" I ask.

Jesma approaches the black surface with the grey mist, and the cloud clears, replaced with the image of a room none of us recognize. Stone walls with large windows surround other mirrors similar to the one before us. Jesma touches the surface of the mirror, and her hand passes through. She follows her hand by stepping over the mirror's frame and the place beyond. We watch as she looks around. She beckons to follow her. Kara shrugs at Tamrin and me.

"Might as well follow her," Kara says.

Tamrin waves me forward.

"After you," he says, his voice cracking.

"The world gets stranger every day," I say.

"At least we'll always have Mistras' Tavern," he smiles.

I snort and step into the mirror. A familiar drop in air pressure surrounds me, much like when Jesmir disappeared. The sensation is immediately followed by a sort of push to the other side. I look back, suspecting Tamrin shoved me, but he stands back with his hands on his knees, anxious. I 'pop' out on the other side of wherever we are. Jesma meanders around the room, inspecting the other mirrors, remaining far enough away not to activate them.

Kara steps out of the mirror. "Whoa! Krikhi's wisdom, what is this place?"

"I think it's a way for them to get to each other quickly," I say.

She points at the top of the mirrors.

"Each bears a symbol of one of the gods," she says. "There's Ezra. Fildeus. Hakaka. Krikhi. Quietius. Morze. Shamna. And Nadur." She looks at me. "Didn't Quietius say we should find Nadur's map?"

"Yeah, he made it sound important," I reply.

"Where's Tamrin?" Jesma asks.

"He's afraid to walk into the portal," Kara says.

I stand before Shamna's portal and glower at Tamrin, who waits on the other side. I wave him over, and he shakes his head, unwilling to move.

"Get over here, big baby," I say, though I'm sure he can't hear me.

He shakes his head again, and I walk away. The air here is damp. Through the windows, waves roar and crash far below. The call of seajays, their song high-pitched and short, accompanies the waves. Jesma and Kara stand at the portal with Nadur's sigil on it.

"Easiest thing to do is walk through," I say.

"I'm not sure we should," Jesma says.

"Well, we can't stay here forever," I reply. "And going back isn't the best choice either."

I step to the mirror, and it responds to my presence.

"Shen?" Jesma starts.

I look back at Shamna's mirror and wave goodbye to Tamrin before I rush through the mirror, my blades ready.

Chapter Thirty

Journal Entry: 146

How will Jez and I ever work? Our strength is our differences. What if we become the same? Where's the strength in that?

Netherwhere We Go, We'll Follow It Now

Nadur's decor is that of a scholar. Dark wood shelves line every wall. Two chandeliers hang from the rafters, powered by fuel lamps. Their flames burn with a steady light, without a flicker.

The shelves, perfectly organized, are filled with books and scrolls. Three large, tilted desks sit facing each other in the middle of the room, set in a triangle. A large, ornate wooden door, curved at the top, is the only way in or out that we see.

Jesma and Kara step through the strange mirror and crowd me, shoving me forward.

"This is a scholar's room," Kara whispers.

"Nadur must be a wealth of knowledge," I whisper back.

We spread out and inspect the extensive study. High above the shelves, on the wall furthest from the door, a large circular window sits under the peak of a high-pitched roof. The windows are so clean and clear, we can see the night stars.

The scent of old paper, contained within books produced long ago and coated with oils from years of human hands, fills the air. I approach the first desk and find rough sketches that look a lot like netherstacks stacked in a haphazard array. Many different styles, shapes, and sizes fill the pages. I flip through the stack. Some sketches depict netherstacks in clusters, their signature black plumes flowing upward.

Some sketches are adorned with a strange series of numbers and symbols in the top left corner of the page. Black dust rubs off on my hand, and I realize they are drawn with charcoal. An enormous book with a ribbon draped out of the bottom of the binding sits next to the stack of pages. I grab the ribbon and use it to flip open the book.

Inside are handwritten notes. It's a journal. Much larger than mine. Its last entry looks like it was entered today.

"The netherstack in the highway north of Valshannon appeared two weeks ago. It is the first to form in a well-populated area. All the witnesses died, so it is impossible to ascertain the direct cause.

Until now, they've only formed in remote locales. Some appeared in small towns, rendering them uninhabitable. But none like this.

This latest appearance is the final proof that Quietius' and my theory is valid. I located the new netherstack on the map. It's within twenty feet of the intersection between two major ley-lines: the line from Shamna's mansion and my own, and the one from Krikhi's adobe in Gal-Daro to Fildeus' cabin west of Charger's Wharf.

This can't be a coincidence.

Today, I pick up the larger map from the cartographer. The current one is too small to trace this properly."

I whistle to get the others' attention.

"Look at this," I say. "Remember the netherstack on the King's Regal we ran into?"

"Of course," Jesma replies.

I locate the spot on the map. "It was right about here, correct?"

"Near where those lines intersect," Kara says.

"So read this," I say and hand the journal to Jesma. Kara reads over her shoulder.

"What's a ley-line?" Tamrin asks.

"Glad you could make it, big guy," I say. "Get scared all by yourself?"

"Didn't want you guys to get into trouble without me," he mumbles. "What's a ley-line?"

I shrug. "Never heard of it."

Jesma shakes her head.

Kara shrugs. "No clue."

I search the map and find Sanctum Mountain. With my finger, I make a line to Galbring.

"Look. Galbring. How far from Galbring is that netherstack field?" I ask Kara.

"About four miles, center to center," Kara says.

I rip a piece of paper from the back of Nadur's journal and grab a quill from an ink bottle. I find the legend on the map and mark the legend's length for four miles with two ticks on the paper. With one line at the center of Galbring, I spin the paper. The other line passes through where I know the field of poison plumes sits in the real world. About half a mile inside the circle, six ley-lines intersect.

"It's not quite four miles, but it's close," I say.

"I'd say that qualifies as *about* four miles," Kara replies.

"There's merit to Nadur's theory," I say.

The door into the room opens. There's no time for us to hide. We freeze like a deer just after it hears a noise. A man about my height, dressed in a drab green vest, loose white blouse, and brown pants, enters the room, hands full, struggling with his belongings. Quite put together, the gentleman's hair is manicured, beard trimmed, skin lightly tanned with few wrinkles, except the crow's feet around his deep-set eyes, and he enters. He balances a cup and saucer in one hand, a large scroll under his arm, and a plate with a sandwich in the other. He is unfazed by our presence.

"Didn't expect to see you here so soon," he says, his posture nonchalant.

His eyes fall on Jesma.

"Oh my," he says. "You're the spitting image of your mother. Last time I saw you, you couldn't have been more than three feet tall."

"I'm sorry?" Jesma says.

The man closes the door, his back toward us. The giant scroll threatens to slip from its position.

"Could one of you grab this scroll for me? I'm afraid my hands are rather full," he says.

Jesma and I exchange glances, unsure what is happening.

"Why not?" Jesma replies and hurries to remove the scroll.

"Oh, thank you, granddaughter," the man says.

A stunned silence falls over the room as the man walks over to the group of chairs. The teacup nearly slides from the saucer as he sets it atop the small table. His mouth opens in an 'O' shape, and his eyebrows climb nearly into his hairline. He steadies his hand and adjusts the cup to the center of the saucer.

The man stands erect, sandwich plate in his hand, and takes half the sandwich and bites into it. He chews while he looks around the room. Pointing with the sandwich at a table next to a large corkboard, he smiles at Jesma.

"Please set that map on that table for me?"

Jesma giggles softly and does as he asks, her eyes wary.

"As I was saying, if you'll at least allow me to eat my sandwich before we fight, I'd be forever grateful."

"That's *not* what you were saying," Kara replies.

"What was I saying?"

"You *were* saying I'm your granddaughter," Jesma whispers.

Instinctively, we slowly spread ourselves throughout the room, our motion deliberate. Jesma steps closer to the gentleman, a curious expression on her face. Her eyes wander over the man's face.

"You look like my father," she whispers.

"I should hope so," he says. "He is my son."

"I don't understand," Jesma says.

"Ask your grandmother about that," he says. "Wasn't my decision." His expression falls into one of pity. "Oh, a bit too late for that now, isn't it. Pity."

He sets his sandwich plate down, places the partially eaten half between his teeth, and gestures for Jesma to hand him the scroll. Sandwich still in his mouth, he walks to the large pegboard and unrolls the map. With another gesture of his arm, Nadur requests Jesma's help. Jesma glances at us, uncertain. Her eyebrows furrowed, she helps pin the map in place.

With fluid grace, he places pins on the map. He points to a spool of string on the table. Jesma hands it to him. Enthralled, we watch as the man, who I'm certain is known to the world as Nadur, runs the string, connecting pins in straight lines to each other.

When he's finished, he steps back, crosses his arms, and finishes his half sandwich while admiring his work. The map is covered in a spiderweb of string, crossing itself in several places.

"Ah, yes, this is much easier to follow," he says, as much to himself as to us.

"That's where you were born," he says, pointing to a small dot in Killinshire. He glances over his shoulder at me. When I don't respond, he walks over to the table and places the other half of his sandwich in his mouth.

"Are you Nadur?" I ask.

"Mmhmm," he confirms.

Chewing, he picks up his tea and washes the bite down. He sets the cup back on the saucer and wanders back to the map.

"That's Rhinestab Tower." He points to the pin in Valshannon. "I used to live there, right at the very top, long before the current King attained the throne. Ezra lives there now, when she lives anywhere that is. It's better suited for her."

He points to another pin in the northeast corner of Teshket.

"That's the Teshken Royal Mansion," he says, mouth full of food. He turns to Jesma. "Now only Quietius lives there. Well, let's not call what he does living."

He continues, pointing to pins as he talks.

"Krikhi and her little stone cottage are here in Gal-Daro. She always was a minimalist," he says to Kara. Then turns to Tamrin, his finger on the pin in Haabrestand, "Fildeus. I believe you've been to her cottage. It's where the Wild Hunt starts every year, no?"

Tamrin nods, dumbfounded by the absurd situation.

"The Citadel," he says, finger on the pin in Renshmere. "Hakaka's home."

He points to one out in the middle of the large ocean, far west of Gal-Danang.

"The underwater city of Xenia." He turns to me. "Did you know there was an underwater city there? Fish people, mostly Sirens and merfolk and selkies. Morze lives there."

"Now pay attention because this is important," he says. He points to a pin on a small island I've never seen on any map, far out in the eastern sea beyond Haabrestand.

"This is the Isle of Tunia," he says, like an instructor at a university. "Everything you know started here." He traces the strings with a light touch. "These are ley-lines. They connect powerful wells of magic. I believe that every netherstack forms at an intersection of these lines. I just can't determine why."

Nadur stares at the map for a while. When he turns to face us, his eyes glow bright yellow.

"Okay, now," he says, "What's the plan here? One at a time? Or all at once. It makes no difference to me. You've killed two of us already, so I doubt you intend to leave me here alive. Before we commence with violence, I'd appreciate it if you'd at least tell me why."

"You seem surprised that I know who you are." He points at me. "You've lurked in my realm for decades. I've enjoyed watching you evade capture, bring justice to the wicked, and sneak around the map of magic. Quite the busy beaver, Shen-Zarl."

I blink in surprise, and he taps the side of his nose.

"Tell me, do you really sneak coins *into* the pockets of the needy? I'm fascinated by how you've eluded the bounty on your head—impressive indeed. You're an interesting fellow. Much smaller than I expected, however."

He turns to Tamrin. "And you, my gargantuan beast master, are Tamrin Salzar. Fildeus speaks very highly of you. Says you're delightful. 'A solid good time on the wild hunts,' I believe, were her exact words. She doesn't speak about many of her subjects, but the few she does are with fondness. You're high on her list of favorites."

"She does?" Tamrin says, his face reddened in embarrassment.

"She does. You should know she's saddened by your recent rejection. Perhaps you'd rethink that decision?"

"Chieftain's Child, I am not familiar with you," Nadur says to Kara.

"I am Kara-Kar."

"Pleased to meet you. I'd be very interested to hear what brings a Korund into companionship with this lot."

He turns to Jesma.

"My dear Jesma, Princess of Pal, heiress to the throne. Teshket does love its female rulers." He looks around the room as if he's missing some detail. "Where is your brother? You two are never far apart."

The mention of Jesmir crashes over us in a tidal wave of sadness and anger. I swallow back guilt, almost retching.

There will be time for that later, Shen. Don't let him trick you.

Nadur balks at the sudden shift in mood amongst the group. "Such sadness. Was it something I said?" Nadur says.

Jesma chokes back a sob. I clench my fists. Kara grips both sword hilts. Tamrin's shoulders slump, and tears roll into his beard. Nadur's calm expression changes into a deep frown.

"Has he passed?" Nadur asks, a deep sorrow clouding his face. He approaches Jesma, his eyes returning to normal.

I move to protect her, but Nadur waves me back, patting the air. He stands before Jesma and wraps his arm around her shoulders. Tenderly, he pulls her into a hug.

My mouth falls agape.

"Oh, dear child. Tell me what happened."

Jesma's head falls onto Nadur's shoulder, and she wails in lament.

"He was murdered," Tamrin says.

Nadur flashes his eyes and turns to Tamrin.

"By whom?" he demands.

"By his own grandmother," Kara replies, her expression dark, darker than I've ever witnessed on a Korund. In that single look, I realize that if Korund ever wanted to control Conishant, it would be impossible to stop them.

"I don't understand," Nadur says, still embracing Jesma.

Jesma pulls away, confused.

"She wants us dead, just like my father."

Nadur's arms drop, and he steps back. He falls back into the corkboard and steadies himself.

"Oh, Shamna, no," he whispers. He glances around the room. "That is why you killed her?"

"You already know she's dead?" Tamrin asks.

"I was aware the moment she took her last breath," Nadur replies. "And Hakaka?"

"Dead because of his hand in your wife's plan. His sword took your son's life," I say.

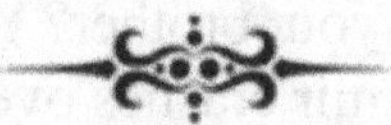

Nadur's hands sparkle with lightning, blue arcs passing between his fingertips. The air in the room crackles with tension. The warm glow of the chandelier overhead against the dark woods of the room belies the cold intensity of those illuminated within its warm reach.

His hand lashes out, and a bolt of electricity, its jagged path too fast to follow, travels over my head into the large circular window. Unsure of his intent, I throw a knife, my body burning with energy while ducking away from his hot blue ray.

He curses in pain.

"What the hell did you do *that* for?" he yells, genuine surprise in his voice.

"You attacked me!" I yell back, rising from behind the desk.

"I attacked my own window," he says, indicating with his head. He yanks my knife from his hand and throws it at the desk in front of me. Pointing to a cloth napkin next to his tea, he says to Tamrin, "Please hand me that napkin."

Tamrin does as Nadur asks, shaking his head in confusion.

"Damn that woman's obsession with unbelievers," Nadur curses.

Wrapping the napkin around his hand, he walks over to Jesma.

"Would you please?"

Jesma looks at me, unsure what to do. Just as clueless, I shrug. Jesma touches his hand. Nadur's wound seals, stopping the flow of blood.

"Thank you," he says, a gentle hand on her shoulder. He walks to the desk where his drawings and journal reside. He flips through the pages and taps the stack of sketches.

"You saw this?" he asks.

Jesma replies, "Yes."

He nods toward the giant map. "These things are related." His head down, lost in thought, he pounds his hands onto the desk. Collectively, we flinch.

"Your grandmother was always hot-headed. It's why she and Hakaka could never make it work. Two hotheads make for a volatile pair. One party must maintain an even keel, or the relationship cannot last. I knew those two were up to something."

He paces the room, his hands clasped behind his back.

"Honestly, I thought they were having an affair. It wouldn't be the first time. Hell, we never expected an eternity of fidelity. That would be absurd." He sighs, resigned to some thought. "No matter how well you know someone, you can still misread them if you're distracted. And these netherstacks have me distracted."

He strides back to the map and toys with the intersection of four lines within the Valley of Cusk.

"This one was the first from what we know." He points to one between Valshannon and Rogue's Pointe in Rhinestab. "This was the second. Spiderlyche country." He touches the big knot of crossing lines in Gal-Danang, where the largest known field of netherstacks exists. "The third. Jandu." He points at a remote area of Haabrestand, "Fourth."

"Peltersnipes," Tamrin says.

"Nasty little bastards," Nadur says. "Hiding inside trees, bringing them to life. I've pelted with splinters, acorns, and blacknots on more than one occasion. But that's just their distraction, those noodle-like arms and razor teeth, are the real danger."

He points at Renshmere, "First one in Killinshire. No telling what happens there yet." He taps Teshket. "None here that we've discovered. Notice anything?"

"The lack of any apparent pattern to their location or timing made them seem unimportant. But over the last forty or so years, the pace accelerated. Ten years ago, I stumbled onto a theory."

"Ley-lines," I say.

"Ley-lines," he confirms. "Specifically, where they intersect. Every point of intersection creates an energy hotspot. Again, notice anything?"

Jesma steps to the map and points to Teshket.

"All the lines only intersect in Kerakot," she observes.

"Very good."

He taps all the capital cities of the Five Realms. "Until this one in Renshmere, none of the seats of the Great Eight contained a netherstack. Odd coincidence, don't you think?"

He points at a pin midway between the Great Rankin River and Winding Run.

"We are here," he says. "This is my home. Moved here about one hundred years ago."

Nadur scratches his chin. "Magic yearns to be connected to other magic. But it must be connected *through* something. Earth is the best conductor. Even as gods, we don't know why. We do know that magic will always take the path of least resistance. This path is a ley-line."

"What happens when they cross?" Jesma asks.

"Yes!" Nadur exclaims with enthusiasm. "What happens indeed?" He walks over to her. "The more ley-lines that cross at a point, the greater the power potential in that place."

"For one reason or another, netherstacks are always located at one of these wells. When the netherstacks form, they shatter the connection, and ley-lines die like withered roots. The ley-lines protect Conishant. We need them. The netherstacks are killing the ley-lines. New hot spots are required to replace them. Unfortunately, there are no longer enough gods to facilitate the creation of new hotspots."

He waves his hands to the outer edges of the map and turns to us.

"What we do, we do for the greater good. There was no other way to keep the darker parts of the world at bay. Without the magic power we syphon from you, we can't maintain the prisons that contain the Baa'n. You see, the tenets of faith ensure we maintain a safe Conishant."

"Baa'n?" Kara and I say in unison.

"Inhabitants of Baa. There's so much to this world you don't know," Nadur says. He walks over to a shelf and removes a wooden ball. "The world is shaped like this. We live on a mass of land that covers here." He holds four fingers against the ball, then spins the ball to the other side and places four fingers almost opposite, but over a larger area.

"Baa is here. And it is a dark and evil place. They want the entire world for themselves. And the Great Eight have kept them contained there, within Baa for thousands of years."

"You take from us without our knowledge?" I say. "All because you believe we can't protect ourselves?"

"You don't know how to," he replies.

"That's your fault," I say.

He stares at me. I don't back down. He takes a while to respond.

"It *is* our fault. We interfered with the natural order in an effort to save human life. But not without reason. Humans are violent and naturally uncivilized. Yet every one of us desires to live in safety. People have always warred amongst themselves. It's our nature. Limited resources, competing interests, opposing political views, and animosity among religions. We almost destroyed ourselves when I was a child."

He points to the Isle of Tunia.

"A great man brought us all here. Long lost to history, Juu was the father of the Great Eight."

"Juu?" I ask.

"Our teacher. Together, we hatched a plan to save the world. Thus, the Great Eight were born. It started slowly at first, but eventually there were temples erected in our honor."

"You must understand human nature to understand our choices. Most won't admit to themselves how they yearn to be led; they beg for someone to bear the mantle of leadership. Their cry for freedom is at odds with that. Given safety versus freedom, people choose safety every time. Religion gives them that very leadership they crave while providing the *illusion* of freedom. It gives them a sense of purpose."

"Don't you see? We need the masses to give something they wouldn't give on their own as individuals. We've kept humanity safe for thirty thousand years."

"At what cost?" Jesma demands.

Nadur nods. "Sometimes we must make sacrifices for the greater good."

"So, you get to live on forever while the rest of us toil our short lives away? At. What. Cost?" Tamrin growls.

"Your lives are just a little shorter. We take a little of your life energy to power the magic that keeps the world safe."

"Define a little," Kara says.

Nadur doesn't answer right away. I step forward, and Nadur's eyes narrow. "Think carefully before you lie," I say.

"Very well," he replies, "At first, we took a few years. Over time, as the population grew, the world changed, needs changed. Natural human life is nearly one thousand years. Too long for a species that procreates like bakru."

"Ezra's tits!" Jesma cries. "You've convinced yourselves that you are benevolent saviors, yet you steal nine hundred years from every human in the world? You're *murderers*," she says.

Nadur looks at Jesma with sorrow. "I hope to rectify that someday to reduce the need for such efforts. I'm so very close to finding the solution to these netherstacks," he says. "I need more time. Time you can give me. Stop your vendetta against us. Together, we can save this world. That requires the continued sacrifice of the people. The faith and belief of the people allow us to consolidate the magical energy for the greater good."

He smiles at Jesma.

"It's why your grandmother did what she did. If I'd paid more attention, I'd have seen she was right. Unbelievers pose a danger to the world. You'll take away the magic that keeps everyone safe and unleash unspeakable horrors. Don't you see?"

"Then what?" Jesma says. Her eyes turn black. "How many years do each of us lose to your *benevolence*?"

Nadur backs away from Jesma, horror in his eyes.

"Jesma, what have you done?" he asks, horrified.

Jesma smiles in euphoric pleasure and stands before Nadur.

"You'll *never* stop," she says. "For the greater good, *Grandfather*."

Nadur pleads to Jesma. "You've taken her power. So much power, child. The world needs a new Shamna." He glances at me. "And a new Hakaka."

"You'd have us take their place?" I ask, aghast.

"Who better than you two? Shamna and Hakaka loved each other," Nadur says. "As it's clear you love each other. Same story, new faces."

"And what of our friends? Do they become gods?" I ask.

"You'll have to kill them. Unfortunately, they'll never allow themselves to be subjugated now."

"Do you hear yourself?" Jesma asks within arm's reach of him.

Nadur's hands crackle with lightning. "Please, consider it. Don't make me do this. I won't let you doom the world."

Jesma relaxes back a step. She looks at Nadur, eyes still black. "Okay," she says, "make me a god."

Nadur relaxes and places his hand on her shoulder. "Just assume the title and it's yours," he says.

Jesma nods and offers to hug him, tears in her eyes. They hold each other, and my heart sinks.

She's not the person I thought.

A pit forms in my stomach, and the loss of Jesmir builds like a fire inside. Anger at how these gods have changed the woman I love in such a short time grows into a growl that burns deep in my soul. A heavy hand grips my shoulder, and I yank myself from Tamrin's grip. He nods to Jesma with a knowing look.

Ready to lunge and kill Nadur while he's distracted, I pause. Jesma releases Nadur and caresses his cheeks. Too late, Nadur realizes his miscalculation. Lightning crackles, and he tries to strike Jesma, but the euphoria returns to Jesma's face. Nadur contorts in pain, a slow wail breaking free from his throat. Lighting pops inside his mouth, his teeth glowing a bright blue. Jesma's solid black eyes observe her grandfather with cold curiosity. Nadur screams, and the remnants of lightning vanish. He grips her wrists in vain, pulling against them, muscles atrophied. His skin shrivels, and he ages rapidly.

The joy on Jesma's face frightens me. She closes her eyes and experiences an ecstasy that I fear she may grow addicted to. My stomach lurches in revulsion.

Unable to allow Jesma to fall victim to her new power, I leap over the desk and stab him through the side of his head. His body collapses to the floor and out of Jesma's hands.

She opens her eyes; a flash of fury reflects in them. When our eyes lock and she sees the horror in my face, her fury fades into despair as her eyes return to their normal blue. Jesma buries her face in her hands and screams with the same lament as her grandfather.

I reach over to pull her close, but she recoils.

"Don't touch me!" she screams.

I drop my arms. She falls to her knees and sobs.

"I don't want this power. Please don't make me keep this power."

I ignore her plea to stay away and pull her into my arms. Tamrin and Kara watch on in silence.

Nadur's body lies in a heap on the floor, blood in a pool on the rug. We wait to see if Nadur's screams carried far enough to alarm anyone. It's unclear how big the house is, but the silence indicates it's either a large home and any staff are far away, or it's a small home and he lives alone.

Unsure if we'll ever return here, we begin a thorough search of the volumes of books and scrolls. Nadur's collection goes back centuries, maybe even millennia. Some materials crumble with the slightest touch, their pages old and brittle.

"How do we know what's of value?" I say.

"It's all of value," Kara replies. "But your point is valid."

"Thanks. Glad you approve," I say.

"I don't. But I wanted you to feel smart," Kara says.

I turn to give the Korund a dirty look. Kara just smirks at me.

"Is that a smile, Chieftain's Child? What would your baba say?"

"Baba would say, 'A smile a day keeps death at bay, but a calm face is a warm embrace.'"

Tamrin slams a book in frustration and says, "What does that even mean?"

Kara pulls a book and instead replies with, "Here's something interesting."

"What did you find?" Jesma asks, her voice hollow.

Kara reads the title page.

"Periapts—How to Power a Faith."

"That could be of use," I say. "Good find."

I locate a book of maps and pull it from the shelf. Inside is a collection of maps of Conishant through time.

While the information is interesting, I don't see much value in a historical map lesson. Midway through the book, I find a map with three land masses. One covers the northeastern portion of the map. I recognize its shape as Conishant. A long landmass nearly splits the map in two, its tips at the north and south white. I don't recognize it. The third landmass, twice as large as Conishant, is black and covers most of the southwest portion of the map. My skin tingles.

"Guys, look at this."

I carry the book to Kara and Tamrin, who stand at one of the desks, and lay it in front of them.

I lean over to point at the black land mass. My necklace with Patrin's family crest dangles free.

Kara reaches over and snaps it from my neck.

"Harbinger," she whispers. "What is this?"

"Nadur's nuts, Kara," I exclaim, rubbing my neck.

"Harbinger, I've seen this symbol somewhere."

"Yes, on my necklace. It's the symbol of my Picaroon family."

Kara rushes to a series of shelves. With frenetic energy, the Korund yanks books off the shelf, inspects them, and drops them to the floor.

"Have you ever seen a Korund lose its shit?" I ask Tamrin.

"Nope. It's kinda frightening."

Kara rises from a crouch near the lower shelves and shakes the necklace. "I'm telling you. I saw this somewhere." Kara's face scrunches another exasperated headshake, tossing another book to the ground.

The Korund comes to a stop, arm extended toward a group of books on the top shelf, and extracts one. With my necklace held to the spine, Kara shakes the book at me.

Jesma appears by my side. "What sent Kara off the cliff?"

"My necklace," I say, still confused.

"I never thought I'd witness a Korund panic," Jesma says.

"Me neither," Tamrin adds.

Kara brings the book over with a look of triumph. The symbol on the cover, embossed in gold, is identical to Patrin's emblem.

"What the fuck does this mean?" I ask, confused.

"Well, hello, everyone," a familiar voice says from behind.

I open the book and read the title.

Fathering Gods.

But it's the author's name I'm most interested in.

"Allow me to finally introduce myself."

I recognize the voice, and my adrenaline surges. I turn to face the source. There, standing in front of the portal mirror, is Patrin. "My name is Juu. You may call me Father."

Chapter Thirty-One

Journal Entry: 149

How can I ever look her in the face again? She stands by me, and all I can feel is the tension between us.
I can't get her scream out of my head.
This is our lives now, mine and hers.

Juu Hear Me?

Patrin, my friend for over twenty years, stands in Nadur's study. Instead of the Emperor's crown from the other night, he wears his signature purple hat adorned with a long yellow feather. He twists the ends of his waxed mustache while he dances on his toes over to Nadur's body. He lifts Nadur with surprising ease and begins to dance with his body before setting the dead man into a chair. Patrin leans into the dead god's ear.

"Something tells me you didn't see this coming, ole boy, did you? Haha!" Patrin slaps Nadur's shoulder and glances at me with a smile. "Kinda like your prince friend didn't, huh? I'm terribly sorry to hear about your brother, Princess. And you, D'aonar. It's most unfortunate that your blades took his life. But look at all you've accomplished!"

He spreads his arms to encompass the entire world.

"How the hell do you know that?"

"Oh, my dear son, don't look so angry. I never lied to you. I just never told you all my secrets. Picaroon, remember?" He holds his hands out to me and waves me forward. "Come, let's hug it out and move on."

When I don't move, he snaps his fingers and smiles.

"Right. You're still in shock. We'll get there." He clenches his fists and dances with glee, shaking his hips and pumping his arms. "Dear Shen, what a consummate overachiever you are. Simply stunning."

Patrin dances around Nadur's chair and massages the dead man's shoulders as if Nadur were still alive.

"Oooh, the Harbinger really stuck it to you, didn't he? I mean, look at you now." He observes the lifeless form and clicks his tongue. "Come on. Don't be a deadbeat. Tell us how it feels to be…dead!"

With a laugh, Patrin slips a hand under Nadur's chin and moves it like the dead man can talk. He imitates Nadur's voice.

"Well, it's kinda dark in here. Gotta say, it came as one hell of a surprise."

Patrin laughs at himself. "I bet it did, you nasty old goat." To me, he asks, "Did you know this is…was…the most powerful of the Great Eight? Smartest too. Emotional intelligence of a turnip, though."

He walks around the cluster of chairs, plops into one next to Nadur, and pats the corpse's knee. Light reflects off his earrings when they sway with the energy of his movement. His fingers, covered with gem-studded rings, form a steeple at his chin while he talks.

"In less than three weeks, you've accomplished what I've waited thirty thousand years to bring to fruition. Think about that. The Harbinger of Death killed three of the Great Eight in as many weeks!"

He looks at Jesma. "You should be proud. Granted, he killed your brother, but as I hear, *that* was an accident. Tell me, Princess. Is he as good in bed as he is in combat? I've often wondered. Too bad he isn't more like our friend Tamrin here. Maybe I could have had a go." He smirks, causing his mustache to lift on one side. "I know Reena would love to find out. I'd be lying if I denied I'm a bit curious myself. How about it, Shen? You and me, a romp in the sack? Little rumble tumble between friends?"

Jesma steps forward, her face shaking with rage.

"Oh, don't try to take a bite of this pie, honey, you'll choke on it. You keep your grubby little hands away from me. My word, how you remind me of Shamna. She's dead now. But you and she would have been great partners."

"Now, back to that question. How about it, D'aonar? You and me. We're all friends here. Tamrin here would love to join in, now wouldn't you, beast master?"

Tamrin grips his hammer until his knuckles crack.

"Shen," Patrin says, "All jokes aside, it only gets easier from here. You're on the downhill run now with the wind at your back. Fildeus will give you some fits, but look at all you've accomplished. After Fildeus, the others don't stand a chance against you. I mean, good luck drawing out Morze. The fishy-smelling dolt will have to wait till the next council meeting in ten months. She never leaves the ocean. And Quietius? That crybaby? Well, he'll probably 'pull a Shen' and off himself by the time this is all done. I'd save him for last. He never wanted any of this life anyway. I was rather surprised by how he helped you. He was too afraid to be left behind, but never had the stomach for the work. That's why we gave him such a tiny role."

"Lord of the Final Slumber. God of Death. There is no final slumber. We simply cease to exist." He leans forward. "You know, I still don't know how Quietius held on to enough followers to maintain his life. I thought he'd die off centuries ago. But he still lingers. Like herpes, that one."

Patrin pinches his fingers together and pretends to look through the gap. "He's this close to death, always." He claps his hands together and stomps his feet on the ground like a herd of horses.

"Now, since we are all friends," Patrin says, "I'll assume you can set aside your shock and sinister 'I'm gonna kill you now' vibes so that we can find a way to work together? Hash out a plan? Who are we gonna kill next?"

I'm still stunned, but I scrape up the will to move toward Patrin.

"Shen, come on, stud. You're better than this. Who's next?"

"You…fucking…cunt," I manage to say.

He smiles with that big grin, and it infuriates me further.

"Picaroon. Picaroon King, actually! Come now. Haven't I always looked after you? I've never done anything against my nature. A nature you know perfectly well, Shen-Zarl of Ditherun." He stands.

"Look, I want you to come by my side willingly. Ever since that first day we met, I knew you'd be the key. I like you. Always have. No, I love you, like a son. After all, a part of me is inside you. Or would like to be, if you know what I mean." He winks with exaggerated flair.

When we don't respond, he says, "Nothing? Not even a giggle?"

He sighs.

"Fine. Like it or not, we're kindred souls—deeply connected since you were a child. Let's say we work together and finish what we've started."

"No. I'm done with this," I say.

I actually mean it. Vengeance isn't worth all this. No part of my life is real. My friend is dead. My girl is shattered. The bloodshed never ends, and every move brings more danger.

And the people I most trust betray me at every turn.

"I'm tired," I whisper. "Everything I do only makes matters worse. You want the other gods dead, do it yourself."

Patrin clicks his tongue in rapid succession.

"Looks like we have to do this the hard way. So be it. Remember, D'aonar, this, like Prince Jesmir, is *your* doing."

He walks over to the portal, and the grey cloud grows and dissipates. Anastaja stands, a knife to her throat. My hearts accelerate. Reena sneers from behind.

Patrin makes a sad face. "I hoped it wouldn't have to go this way. But you leave me little choice."

My mother speaks, but Reena tightens her grip on my mother's neck.

"What's that, Anastaja?" Patrin mocks. "Okay, I'll tell him. Your mother says, 'Don't dilly-dally.' She'd like to go home soon. The sooner you get the job done, the sooner she can go home. I ask again. Who's next?"

You are, Dickhead.

The fire inside builds, and I lunge at him.

He catches me by my throat, mid-air, my feet several inches off the ground. His grip is intense. The blood flow to my head stops immediately. Pressure builds inside my skull. My body goes rigid as my brain malfunctions. Pressure builds in my ears. Conservation of energy dictates he should have at least stumbled. But he didn't even sway.

I kick, but the motions are little more than involuntary spasms, and my body goes limp. My vision blurs.

"Release him," Jesma warns.

Tamrin growls. My ears ring. My vision fades.

"You will finish the job." He shakes me like a rag doll, and my joints hurt from the force. "Or Anastaja dies. Juu hear me? Ah, I always liked that joke."

"D'aonar, I wish you had come and just been a part of my family. This would have gone so much easier. But you always resisted your true calling."

I fight to stay conscious, but it's no use. My legs spasm underneath me, and I go still.

The world fades into darkness.

I wander in the woods. Home brings me peace. Fall colors are not quite at their peak. In a week, they'll be perfect. It's my favorite time of year. Mom's too. She gathers branches from the trees, her little saw in her hand. Her hand is like milk chocolate against my darker skin. It reminds me of when she and my father used to hold hands. Only his were so much bigger, strong like iron. Mom and I walk side by side while she sings.

It's a ballad of loss and sorrow, but she sings it with such a beautiful voice that I never find sadness in it, even though I know she is sad.

"This one. Don't you think it's perfect?" she says to me.

"It's perfect, ma," I reply.

She cuts a branch and lays it on the stack already cradled in my arms.

"Can you still carry that?" she asks. "I can take some."

I shake my head. I want to show I'm strong enough. She rubs the back of my head.

"What about that one?" I point to a thin branch covered in leaves that are the palest of yellow.

"That is perfect, Shen! My favorite color. Everyone loves the bright reds and oranges. But this is my favorite time. The light yellows remind me of the sands on the beaches back home."

She cuts the branch and lays it in my arms.

I grunt under the strain.

"Okay," she says. "I think we're good. Let's go decorate the house now."

We make our way through the woods toward our home in the slums of Kerakot. She sings her song while we walk. Lost in her melody, she doesn't realize her pace is too fast for me to keep up.

I move my feet as best as I can. But she moves faster with each step.

The ground around me softens, and my feet stick in the forest floor—each step requires more effort than the last. I call out to her, but she doesn't seem to hear me. I try to move faster, but the harder I fight, the more resistant the earth becomes.

I'm up to my neck now. The branches are scattered all around me. I cry out.

"Mom! Don't go!"

But she's gone.

I'm all alone.

I'm trapped.

I open my eyes. My face is stuck to the rug; coarse fibers dig into my cheek. Tingles brought on by oxygen deprivation feel like pins in my skin. The metallic earthiness of blood fills the air. Voices call out, their sound muted. Heavy hands shake me.

How did it get on the floor?

Memories rush back. Patrin. Mom. Reena. Anger fuels my limbs to regain connection to my brain.

With frustration, I struggle to pull my limbs toward my body. I struggle to push my shoulders off the floor. My neck is incapable of supporting my head.

I groan with the effort. My vision clears enough to let in light. My stomach protests, and I fight back nausea.

"Let him get himself up," a female says. I recognize Jesma's voice.

On all fours, I cough, the urge uncontrollable. My throat hurts once more. But this time on the outside too. Jesma, Tamrin, and Kara kneel next to me.

"Shen," Tamrin says. "You've got to get up."

"Ugh," I groan. I push myself onto my knees and extend an arm to Tamrin. He assists my effort, and I stand. Dizzy and disoriented, the room spins. I lose my footing and stumble. Tamrin steadies me. I nod a thank you, my voice stuck.

"You okay?" he asks.

I take a deep breath and catch the worried glances from Jesma and Kara.

"I'm good," I say, voice scratchy. I search for Patrin. "Where did he go?"

"Back through the portal. We wanted to follow, but we couldn't leave you behind."

"No, it's good you didn't. He'd have killed you."

I bend over, hands on my knees, still a bit woozy.

"What do we do now?" Jesma asks, fear in her voice.

Nadur's dead eye stares at me.

Is it my imagination, or did he wink?

"I don't know," I reply.

"We should rescue your mother," Tamrin says.

I wave him off while I try to gather my thoughts.

"Patrin has my mom," I say.

"I know, buddy," Tamrin says. "Wherever he took her, he won't kill her. At least not yet. He'll hold her life over you to ensure we do what he wants. She's safe. For now."

I pace to relieve the stiffness and fog. "How long was I out?"

"Five minutes, tops," Tamrin says.

"Seemed longer," I reply.

I stop at the map on the board and trace one string.

"Why do you suppose Patrin doesn't kill the other gods himself?" I ask.

"I don't know," Jesma says. "Probably because he can't."

"No. He handled me like I was nothing. He said Nadur was the most powerful of them. He lied. Patrin's power runs deep. It's extraordinary. There's a reason behind his madness. And I aim to discover it."

"We could ask Quietius," Tamrin says.

"Enlist his help for real?" I ask.

"Why not? He seems to want us to succeed," Jesma says.

"Yes, but to what end?" Kara asks. "I don't think we can trust any of them after this. And let's face it, Harbinger. You are good at killing, but you are a horrible judge of character."

"I let you stick around," I say with a smile. "And apparently I'm not as good at killing as we all once thought."

"Yes, but that is because I am charming and beautiful, my character is unimpugnable, and you've begun to hunt bigger game. Besides," Kara waves a hand at Jesma and Tamrin. "They are here to help you judge properly. On your own, you make horrible friend choices."

"Hey," Tamrin says.

"You chose him," Kara replies. "You're a much better read of character."

"Are we done here?" I ask.

"Yes," Kara replies. "We are done."

"Let's grab the books and head out. Make sure you grab that one Juu wrote."

Everyone avoids eye contact with me.

"He took it, didn't he?" I ask.

"Yeah."

"Something in that book is of value to us then," I say.

"Who knows?"

"Maybe Quietius?" Jesma replies.

"Put it on the list," I say.

Chapter Thirty-Two

Journal Entry: 150

F*uck!*

> *I want Jesmir back.*
> *How do I get Jesmir back?*
> *Someone, please, tell me this is only a nightmare. Please tell me I did not kill my friend. Please. I can't live with this guilt.*

Some Assembly Required

"**W**hat next?" I ask.

"Tamrin places his finger on the pin in the middle of the map, northeast of Winding Run, south of the river. The smirk on his face tells me he has an idea.

"What if the death of the gods frees Grankin? If eight gods couldn't stop him, who's to say Patrin can?"

"Right," I say. "We're a half-day journey to the Great Rankin River."

"Good idea, Shen," Kara says. "Glad you thought of it."

"Oh, come on!" Tamrin says.

Kara laughs that windchime laugh of hers, and regardless of the doom and sadness we feel, it lifts our spirits.

Once outside, I look back at the house and freeze. "Nadur's balls," I say.

"You think it's wise to use the name of the god you killed in vain?" Kara asks.

"He's more than a god," I say.

Tamrin takes a step forward to stand beside me.

"Oh shit. How didn't I recognize him?" Tamrin says, stunned.

"I've never met him in person," I reply.

"I have. Shit, Shen, this is worse than killing a god," Tamrin says.

"What are you two on about?" Jesma asks.

Tamrin and I look at each other, then back at Jesma and Kara.

"We killed the Tinkerer," Tamrin says.

"Who's the Tinkerer?" Jesma asks.

"The Fireworks maker for Winding Run's End of Year Festival. He's a legend. And beloved."

"Would that have changed anything?" Kara asks.

"Not for me," Jesma says. "Though he was actually pretty nice. I don't know why I couldn't stop myself." She shudders with revulsion at herself.

"If I had known Patrin was the puppet master all this time, I don't know that I would have pushed Nadur so hard...or killed Shamna. I'm sick of acting on missing information," I reply.

"Let's go talk to Grankin. We need answers," Tamrin says.

I point north.

"River's a five-hour hike that way," I say.

"I don't want to do this again," Jesma says. "Neither time was pleasant."

"He knows we're here," Kara says. "My handprint is warm."

"Well, let's get it over with," I say and prepare to jump in.

Kara grabs my shoulder and points across the river. The short, stubby gnome waves at us and hops into the river. He swims across the rushing water, unaffected by it. He leaps out, arms and legs stiff, and lands on the grassy bank like a lawn ornament.

Tamrin's eyes twinkle with delight.

"Well, met, friends," Grankin says, and he walks over to us. He takes Jesma's hand in his and pulls her to his height, leans in, and hugs her. It's a genuine embrace. Jesma bursts into tears the moment her head hits his shoulder.

"I really liked the young lad. Loss is always hard. Especially when it's this close to the heart." He strokes her hair. "It's all right, little one. Love finds a way to heal the broken. And you are sur-rounded by a lot of love. Even if you have a hard time seeing it right now."

He releases her and grabs her arms.

"Buck up. There will be time for mourning. For now, there is work. Come. Closer to the river," he says. "It's better to talk by the water."

He extends his hand to me. "Take my hand, young man."

I reach over, and he squeezes it with such care that my eyes well up. "You will take extra work to heal. But don't lose hope. You are the good man you *wish* yourself to be. But for now, you must put those thoughts away. Now is the time for your specific brand of ac-tion."

"I don't have your book," I say.

"Oh, I know. And I know who has it. Most unfortunate. But also, beyond your control. I want to show you something. But this is only for you."

He turns to the others.

"I ask you not to follow this time. I will bring him back shortly. You will be safe here."

With his stubby finger, he traces a large arc around where we all stand, starting from the bank, around us, and back to the bank some distance away. A trail of river water follows the path and surrounds us. Then he points at the new trail of water and draws an arc overhead. The water forms a dome over everyone that shimmers in Ezra's light.

"My associates will be along shortly with food, some ale, and cots. This dome will keep everything and everyone out unless I let them in. Rest in safety."

Grankin pulls me into the river, and I glance back at my friends and shrug, clueless about the journey I'm about to take.

Grankin and I float through the water.

"The time has come, as recent deeds, to pull your memories from the weeds." He giggles at his rhyme.

"About?"

"As much as I enjoy a story," he says, "remembering is greater glory."

"Where are we going?" I ask, already over his games.

"Memory Lake, of course."

"Another memory of yours?" I ask.

He smiles a sad smile. "Tell me what happened to Jesmir."

My jaw locks. My throat tightens as I fight the urge to cry. I shake my head.

"Now listen. I know it's not easy to talk about it. You feel responsible."

"I am responsible," I interrupt.

"You were involved," he says. "There's a difference."

A school of salmon swims up to us. Grankin pets one absently. It rubs its cheek against his, and he giggles. The salmon continue on their way.

"Not from where I stand," I say.

"It's all about perspective, dear boy. From your perspective, you killed him. From his perspective, he jumped in front of your blades. From Shamna's perspective, he shielded her."

"That's quite the reach," I mumble.

"No more than you walking around acting like you killed him with intent."

"I'd rather not talk about this."

"Maybe not. But you know what your friends aren't going to want to talk about?"

I don't answer.

"Your death by your own hand."

My stomach flips as we change direction in the water, and I realize we ascend the waterrise.

"Because I'm here to tell you, it's no picnic for them if you take your own life, especially when they'd carry your burdens with love and compassion."

We crest the waterrise and slide along the plateau and into the cave at the top of Sanctum Mountain. The stars fade into the background, and we descend into Memory Lake.

"I want you to think about this," he says as we fall. "You were a boy once. A child. You lived in Killinshire, and your parents fled their home. You didn't want to leave. So, one night, on the journey to Teshket, you ran away. Not far from here. Do you remember that?"

I try to remember, but I'm not sure.

"No, I don't."

"Do you remember you couldn't swim? You struggled."

A distant memory tugs at the back of my mind.

I remember falling.

Wait, I am falling.

I remember a splash.

The dark waters of Memory Lake engulf me.

"Help!" I scream, my little arms slapping at the water. The river's current takes me under. Water fills my mouth. The surface of the water shimmers overhead as I sink further under the surface. My feet touch the bottom, and I push up, but the current tumbles me.

My head pops out of the water, and I spit out what's in my mouth. I catch the tiniest of breaths before I'm pulled under again. My arms flail as the river spins me like a pinwheel.

My head hits the rocky bottom, and my air escapes. My chest hurts and tries to force me to breathe in. My head bobs up again. I take a deep breath and yell.

"Mommy!"

I'm back underwater again. My back bounces off a rock, and again, air escapes. I want to cry, but if I do, I'll drown. I try to reach and pull like my dad taught me, but it's no use.

My chest hits a rock, and my hand finds a hold. I grab it with every ounce of strength I have. But it's slippery. My grip slips, but I reestablish my hold. I find a grip with my other hand and pull with everything I have. The water presses me against the rock and tries to push me to the side. I get my head above water and take a deep breath.

Spray fills the air. The noise makes my ears hurt. The river flows around my head and over it. Tired and scared, I pull myself higher and lay my head on the top of the rock. I take a deep breath and cry.

"Mommy!" I yell. "Daddy!"

A shadow appears over me.

"What's this?" a strange man says. He is short. Almost as short as I am. His fingers are stubby.

A goldfish swims in his beard made of water.

"I'm Grankin," he says. "Would you like some help?"

I nod, tears flowing.

"Well, let's see if we can get your god to answer. Which one do you follow?"

I shake my head.

"Please. I want my mommy," I cry.

"I'm sure you do. Now, which god did you say?"

I shake my head again.

"Hold on. I can't understand you. Let's get you on this rock."

He takes my hands and pulls me onto the rock. I stand bent over, and cough as my lungs expand fully for the first time since I fell in the river.

"How old are you?" Grankin asks.

I hold up four fingers.

"Four? That's awfully young to swim this river. And awfully old to not know your god."

"Gods aren't weal," I say.

"Gods aren't real?" he asks.

I shake my head. "No."

"And how do you know that?"

"B'cawse daddy said so," I reply.

"Tell me, do you know magic?"

I shake my head.

"Well now," he says, tapping his thumb.

Grankin holds his hand out to me. "Come with me," he says.

I take his hand.

"Don't let go. No matter what."

I nod.

He jumps into the water, and I scream.

"No!"

But when we land, there's no water. We drift in the air, floating past fish, grass, and frogs. We drift a long way. He takes me up a long wall and into a cave. We land in a lake and float to a little house made of stone.

Little flowers with pretty blue and green lights that sway around us.

He lifts me and plops me onto a table.

"Now this won't hurt a bit. But I need you to lie back."

He's so nice. He saved me, so I listen.

"I want my mommy."

"I promise. I will take you to her as soon as we are done here. Now, lie back, please."

I do as he asks. He turns my head, and I stare into eyes that swirl like stars in the night sky. They glow with the light of many stars before they turn black.

His hand moves to his chest, but I can't look away from his eyes. They are so black. A squishy sound makes me want to look, but I can't look away from his eyes. He looks at my chest. I follow his gaze.

His hand holds a squishy thing covered in blood that moves. He places it near my chest.

"I don't want it," I yell. "What is it? I don't want it. Mommy!"

"Shh," he says. "It's okay. You'll be glad someday that you have it."

"I don't want it!" I scream, tears stinging my eyes.

"I'm stuck here. It does me no good to have it. The world needs you, child, and you'll need this to help them. Someday you'll understand."

My chest opens like a hungry mouth, and the blood-soaked thing sinks in. There's no pain. My chest closes, and the blood vanishes.

"Close your eyes," Grankin says.

I shake my head. I don't want to close my eyes. I'm so scared.

"Close your eyes and listen with your ears."

He places his fingers on my eyes and whispers, "Listen."

I'm afraid. I don't know what to listen for. The loud roar of rushing water fades away until all I hear is his breath and mine alternating in a slow rhythmic pattern. Our breaths fade away as my heartbeat pushes itself until it's all I can hear.

Bump-bump-bump

Bump-bump-bump.

Not bump-bump like it always was.

I listen.

Bump-bump-bump.

It's not the same.

"You hear it?" he asks.

I nod.

"Good. You have the heart of a fighter." He helps me sit. He places his hand on my cheek. "And now you have the heart of a god. I only hope it's not misplaced. But something tells me, you are a good boy."

He helps me off the table.

"Now, let's go find that mother of yours."

He leads me back into the water, and we float in the air again. Up we go. Down we go. Ezra's light is bright as she says, "Hi." A dark shadow passes overhead. It's a bridge.

The small man stops and helps me onto the riverbank.

"Have a good life, Shen-Zarl. May you never find faith in gods. Your father is right. They aren't real."

He disappears into the water, and I'm alone. I crawl from under the bridge, crying.

"Shen!" a voice cries out. It's my mom's.

"Mommy!" I scream and run onto the road.

"Shen!" she calls again.

"Mommy!" I cry, dragging out the end.

"Oh, my word!" she cries behind me. I turn around. She runs to me, arms wide. "Where have you been? And why are you all wet?"

I point at the river. "A man helped me. He had a fish in his beard."

"Now is not the time for stories, young man. Your brother and father are worried sick. I thought the bad men stole you. No more running away, understand?"

I start crying. "I'm sorry, mommy."

She holds me close.

"It's okay. You're safe now."

She picks me up, and I hold on tight, my face in her neck.

"I don't know what I'd do if I ever lost you, Shen-Zarl. You're my special baby."

We bob to the surface of the lake. Grankin wades through the water in front of me. It's the first time the lake feels like water.

I have two hearts because of this gnome!

"You put your heart inside me?" I ask.

I'm surprised at how unfazed I am with this new revelation. He did this to me without my permission, but oddly, I'm not mad.

"Not mine," he says.

"Then whose?"

Grankin doesn't answer right away. He opens his mouth to speak, but stops himself several times.

"Umm…" I say, "Why do I get the feeling I'm not going to like this answer?"

When he finally speaks, my scalp tingles, and a sense of dread builds.

"If I had known, I never would have done what I did."

"I really wish you'd say what's on your mind," I say.

"Ten thousand years ago, I fought the gods, much like you do. But I had help. If not for Kara carrying my symbol, I wouldn't have realized *his* help was much less benevolent than it appeared. A man came to me. He knew I didn't follow the gods. I was damn vocal about what I knew. By then, my ability to control my magic had grown. I understood its source, and I discovered why the Great Eight seemed to have such unlimited resources."

"This man made me an offer. In exchange for unimaginable power, I only had to agree to kill the gods. End their reign."

"That was why they couldn't kill me. The Great Eight did what they do when they can't eliminate an enemy. They find a way to imprison them. For me, it's this river and mountain."

"I pushed and pushed against the barrier, seeking all manner of escape. But their magic is powerful and forever unlimited. More powerful than I could ever have imagined."

"Then *you* fell in the river that day. I can sense every rock, insect, fish, and person that touches these waters. The river transfers more than memories. It reveals their character. When you fell into these waters, your spirit called me. It revealed everything."

"I saw a chance to break a piece of me free, to send that extra power out into the world and someday break the prison we all live in."

He pleads with me to understand.

"I'm sorry. I acted without your permission. You have every right to be angry."

Part of me *is* angry. Every time I turn around, I discover that one more person made decisions for me I would never make for myself. Each time under the guise of some greater good.

I should have the choice!

Everyone rolls Shamna Rocks for me, and I'm left to deal with the consequences. There's no risk to them once they send me on my way.

What good is killing the gods if the end result is just oppression by a different name? Why do I have to be the one to bear the burdens others place on me without my consent?

"Shen-Zarl, I can't express my remorse enough."

He's sincere, and that sincerity is what makes him different. Shamna and Nadur pretended to be sincere. They pretended that what they did was for the greater good.

They plotted and schemed for thousands of years. Grankin made a rash decision in a moment. If anyone can understand, I can. Isn't that what I do? Make decisions that impact others' lives without thinking it through?

Grankin is no different from me in that regard. He's not one of the Great Eight. He hates them as much as I do.

I giggle, and Grankin looks confused.

"It's okay," I finally say.

"Really?" he says, surprised.

"I don't mind, actually. Having two hearts has saved my ass on more than one occasion," I say.

"You have always been a remarkable young man," he says with a smile. "I saw it when you were a child. I truly didn't know what I know now. For that, I am sorry."

"You said that before," I say. That sense of dread returns.

He frowns.

"I don't like it when you frown, Grankin."

"Your conversation with the man who called himself Juu. I only met the man that one time. He never entered the water. He gave me his heart at the edge of my domain, on dry land."

He doesn't need to say it.

"Juu gave you this heart," I say.

My ears ring from the increased blood pressure. My head spins. Multi-colored dots move through the edges of my vision. My body tingles, and I struggle to catch my breath.

"I'm sorry, Shen."

I inhale deeply and release it with a scream. My voice bounces off the void of the cavern walls and repeats forever.

"Why do these gods keep fucking with me?"

Chapter Thirty-Three

Journal Entry: 151

I can rage against the world. Rage against circumstances. Rage against injustice. But no matter how much I rage, the problems never go away.

So, rage is hard to justify.

But rage gives me an excuse to murder. And dear old Patrin is going to get a nasty little surprise. I'm not just going to kill Juu. I'm going to destroy everything he cares about.

Rage may be hard to justify, but it ain't hard to feel.

I'm going to shove one of the Tinkerers' fireworks up Juu's ass and light that bastard up.

Juu and Shen

Grankin and I sit at a picnic table on the shore. My friends sleep, safe from danger. A small fire crackles, keeping the area warm under the dome of water. We each hold our third mug of ale.

"You really are the good boy I thought you to be," he says.

He raises his mug for the third toast of the night.

"To good people and the hard choices they must make."

"To good people," I say.

We drink in silence. The fire snaps, and I stare at a jet of flame that vaporizes the sap pocket released by the fire. The water overhead is like glass, and the stars shine through.

"Will I ever be normal?" I ask. The question is rhetorical, but Grankin answers anyway.

"No," Grankin answers. "You never had a chance. But you can find normalcy."

"When?"

He shrugs. "I can only move short distances in the past and future. The events to come are as much a mystery to me as they are to you."

A twinge of hope forms.

"Can you move us into the past in time to save Jesmir?"

The sadness in his expression shatters my hopes before they can build.

"Death is permanent. It cannot be undone. That is why we must take our moments and live our lives as best we can. Cherish our time. For most of us, it's fleeting. Humans weren't meant to live forever. We're supposed to move on when it's our time. If we went back to save Jesmir, what we'd have wouldn't be Jesmir. Time has a way of evening things out. It'd be an abomination. I learned that the hard way."

I stare into my cup. He touches my hand.

"The Great Eight stole our time for themselves. They've lived too long, while the rest of us live too little. Aside from my time here on the river, I've had a good run. My time should pass too."

"How do I free you?"

"Kill the gods," he says. "But since that seems to be what Juu wants, I'm no longer sure it's the right path."

"So, what am I to do?" I ask.

"If it were me? I'd seek out the other gods and work together to find out what Juu is planning. Whatever he has planned is worse. Stop him."

"Of course, that's what you'd say," I reply with a smirk.

"Never thought the day would come," Grankin says.

I finish the rest of my ale. He refills our mugs and pulls a plate of sliced steak close.

"You like elk, right?" he says.

I nod.

"Try this," he says and throws a slice in his mouth.

I do the same. It melts with the easiest of bites. We scarf the rest of it, groaning in satisfaction.

"Unctuous," he says.

"I hate the day I met you," I laugh.

"Same!" he replies.

We clink mugs and empty them.

"One more and then you need rest," he says.

"One more," I say.

Grankin's ale is strong. I already have a buzz.

"I'm truly sorry for your loss, Shen. Jesmir was really quite remarkable. He had a kind heart."

"He was a fierce warrior, too," I say. "He'd want everyone to know that."

"Make sure they do," Grankin says.

He raises his mug and says, "To fierce warriors."

"To fierce warriors," I say.

I wake with a start, my breath arrested. I remember we are under a dome and panic, my body flailing. A big, toothy, bearded grin hovers over my face. Tamrin pinches my nose and holds his hand over my mouth. I try to punch him, but he pushes my hand away like he's swatting a fly.

"Wakey wakey, sleepy head," Tamrin says and releases my nose. He kicks my cot with relentless rhythm.

"You son-of-a-bitch," I say.

"Keep acting like a baby and I'll drink the last cup of coffee," he says.

"Ugh!" I complain and roll over on my back, flopping my arms on the cot.

The water dome still shimmers overhead. I give Ezra the finger and push my reluctant body into a seated position. Tamrin holds a coffee, and the smell makes me smile.

I reach out for it, and he pulls it away.

"Say you're sorry for calling my mom a bitch," he says.

"No! I'm not going to apologize for insulting the woman who forced you onto the world," I reply and reach for the mug again.

Tamrin holds it to his lips.

"Fine! I'm sorry I called your mom a bitch," I say.

He laughs and passes the mug over. I hold it to my nose and breathe in the nutty aroma. He drips a small amount of whiskey into my mug.

"Hair of the bakru," he says.

"Thanks," I say and take a sip.

He walks back to the table.

"You're mom's still a bitch," I say.

"I heard that!" he replies.

"Good!"

Jesma walks over and strokes my hair. "Tie one on with Grankin, did ya?"

I stare at her, puzzled. "You were asleep. How would you know that?"

She points at the picnic table. A naked gnome snores on top of it. His beard lies in a puddle next to him, the goldfish asleep too.

"Where are his clothes?" I ask.

"Probably the same place your pants are," Jesma says. "Got anything you want to tell me?"

My gaze snaps to my exposed pecker and back over to Grankin.

"Umm."

"Well, your pants are over there," she points at the water.

I force myself to rise and gather my belongings. I stand at the water and drink my coffee, relieve myself, and dress. By the time I return, Grankin is awake and smiling.

"What happened last night?" I ask, terrified of the answer.

"We danced around the fire and chanted to the stars," he says.

"But you're naked," I say.

"You were, too, dear boy. And we had a glorious time."

He hops to the ground, gathers his clothes, dresses, and lowers the dome. The water recedes back into the river. Grankin's family of gnomes emerges from the water and clears the table, cots, and supplies.

Grankin smiles at me and holds out his hand. I shake it.

"Thank you. For everything."

"It's kind of you to be gracious after what I did." He smiles and offers a round of goodbyes to everyone. He stops at Kara. "Good work. You are good for them. Keep them safe as best you can."

"Of course, Friend. I rather like these humans."

"Guys," Tamrin says, a warning in his voice. He points away from the river. A man approaches, his familiar purple hat and yellow feather bouncing in the breeze.

"Juu," Grankin says. "Don't worry. He has no power this close to the river. Only I do."

"I can hear you from here, Grankin, old buddy!" Juu calls out. He stops fifteen feet from us. "Of course, you'd come running here first, D'aonar."

"What do you want, Juu?" I say.

"Oh, come on. Can't we have a chat?" he asks, with a feigned hurt in his tone.

"What do you want?" I repeat.

"Well, I came to see how my heart was doing. After all, I told you a piece of me was in you."

I can sense everyone's eyes on me.

"Don't worry. I can't use it to hurt you. Or track you even. Once I gave it up, it was no longer mine. No, I knew you were here because I marked you." He points to my neck, where my beard is.

I turn to Tamrin, and he hurries over to inspect me. I tilt my head, and he searches through my beard. He pulls back and nods.

I pull a knife out of my belt. I look at Tamrin, and we exchange silent communication.

"This ends here," I say and glance sideways at Jesma. Tamrin stands frozen, and I know he understands what I'm asking him to do. He knows because he's seen the look in my eyes before. His lip twitches with anger. I stare into his eyes, and Tamrin swallows hard, blinking back tears.

"Thank you, Grankin, for telling me the truth. It's mighty useful right now," I say.

I turn to Juu and step within five feet of him.

"You think you can kill me?" he says.

"No," I reply. "Something tells me you'll be no better than herpes. You'll just come back over and over and over again."

"You're right," Juu says.

"It's not worth the effort to kill you. I'm so tired of everyone's games. Here's my offer. Remove this mark and never mark anyone I care about again."

"That sounds more like a demand than an offer, Shen. I thought you were better than that. You know, we Picaroons never succumb to demands."

"Oh, it's an offer. Remove it, now." I hold my knife to my jugular. "Or lose me forever."

"Oh!" he exclaims, hopping and clapping his hands. "I like this game! Here's my counter. If you kill yourself, I'll kill your entire party as soon as they leave the river."

"I like negotiating fine, so here's my counteroffer."

I fuel the fire in my magic so hot my knees almost buckle. My first knife hits Tamrin in the chest. My second hit Jesma in the stomach. When I finish spinning, my third knife is still on my neck.

"Now. You were saying?"

"Are you insane!" Kara screams.

"No, no, no, no!" Grankin exclaims.

Tamrin's collapse to the ground and Jesma's cries of pain send a chill up my spine.

Please don't die.

Juu narrows his eyes.

"Too late," I say.

The slice is so fast I don't even feel it. I'm astonished at how quickly the lightheadedness sets in. I fight to stay standing.

"No!" Juu cries, and he rushes forward to catch me.

"Your move, Patrin," I choke out with a smile, the copper taste of blood in my mouth, and fall to the ground.

"Fine!" I feel his hands touch my neck, and a tingle as he removes his mark. "Damnit. Somebody stop this insanity!" Juu yells.

"Step away from him, Juu," Grankin's voice says. I feel the man I once counted as a friend rise and step back.

"Stay with me, Shen," Jesma says through gritted teeth. Her silhouette, against the blue sky, hovers. She's remarkably beautiful.

"Tam first," I say.

"You stupid man. I already took care of him. Now hush."

A radiant blue light ignites in Jesma's eyes. So bright, I close my eyes. The pain subsides. The lightheadedness passes. I open my eyes, and Jesma's face is filled with equal parts awe, love, and rage.

She slaps my chest with an open palm.

"Don't you *ever* do that again," she cries.

She helps me stand, and I face Juu.

"Well done, D'aonar! You beat me with that one. I might have caught on if you had delayed a moment longer."

The man I once considered a friend turns and walks away. Less than forty feet from us, he stops and inspects the ground. He kneels and touches the grass, petting it with curiosity.

"Well, well, well," Juu says. "What have we here?"

"What is he doing?" Tamrin asks, still holding his chest.

"I don't know," I reply.

Grankin stands next to me.

"Ley-lines," the gnome says. "Four different ones intersect there. One actually goes through the center of the world to the other side. A land called Baa. Powerful magic surges there. Dangerous magic."

"Shen-Zarl of Ditherun!" Juu calls. He stands where he rubbed the ground. "Your move!"

Juu extends his arms, his eyes turn black, and the ground beneath him explodes. A shock wave travels along the ground, and the force throws us backward into the river. I land with a hard slap on my back, and the water pulls me under. Grankin circles and gathers us into his pocket of air.

With uneasy glances, we rise to the surface and climb out of the water.

In place of Juu, a netherstack stands, spewing its black death until it touches just outside Grankin's protection.

"Ezra's ass," Grankin says.

"Where's Juu?" Kara asks.

A yellow feather-adorned purple hat drifts through the air and lands at my feet.

Fuck you, Juu.

Epilogue

Teshket mourned the loss of a Queen, a Duke, a Duchess, and a Prince all at once. For the sake of the people, the truth was kept hidden. Regardless of the crimes she committed behind closed doors, in Teshket, the queen was beloved.

True at least, for the upper class.

The poor turned out in greater numbers for the loss of Jesmir. His legacy as the Playboy Prince with a heart of gold would live on. Stories of how he hung with members of all classes, helped the black market thrive, and gave his time to help those less fortunate could be heard in every tavern and home.

Savis showed up for the funeral, and even I agreed. Now was not the time to kill the bastard. He approached us but quickly withdrew. The cold shoulder he received sent the message.

Throughout Kerakot, tears of sorrow and cheers of pride rang out as the procession passed. Behind the caskets, somber pipes played the funeral dirge.

Jesma was asked to speak at the ceremony. She spoke with the poise of a leader–like a queen.

Jesma neither declined nor accepted the throne. She instead assigned the role of "Queen in Interim" to her Aunt Doris, the Duchess of Horn. Jesma kept the truth of the events that led to the queen and Jesmir's deaths a secret.

The truth would sow too much discord in Teshken society and create too much infighting over rights to rule, fitness of Jesma, and fate of the Temple of Shamna—not to mention the other gods.

Instead, Jesma chose to allow the Teshkens to grieve and ultimately accept the death of the long-standing and beloved monarch, her son, her eldest daughter, and her grandson in such a short time. Jesma chose the merciful path. Another sign she'd make a great queen.

Everyone involved agreed, sharing with the world that Shamna and the queen were one and the same would lead to riots and panic. The right time would come, but her funeral was not that.

Quietius helped by playing the role of a grieving loyal servant, Corvan. Alongside Jesma as they rode in the royal carriage behind the last bit of the long-standing royal family, Corvan remained a steady presence.

Teshken custom prevented me from riding with Jesma since we aren't married. Again, we decided it was for the best.

The solemn parade made the journey throughout the Realm. We visited every city and town, affording every citizen the chance to pay their respects and say goodbye.

The circuitous route took four weeks to complete, including four days aboard ships to visit the isles of Pal and Tal, Jesma's home.

The Queen's body, embalmed and presented in a glass coffin, rode at the top center of the funeral wagon. Jesmir's body lay behind and below the Queen's. Two empty glass caskets rode below and in front of the Queen to symbolize the two siblings, the Duke of Pal and the Duchess of Tal.

Their bodies were never found.

The procession through Hericot gave me a chance to see Baron Bun-Marlon again. It was the only moment of joy I had the entire trip. Solace in a kindred spirit. Tamrin, Kara, the Baron, and I spent the entire day-and-a-half drunk.

I hardly saw Jesma during the cortege, except as a passenger in her carriage. We exchanged glances, light touches, and waves whenever we could–small moments. Her duty to the process kept her busy.

By the time we arrived back in Kerakot, not one of us had the energy to speak. Jesma and I spent our first night alone in her chambers and crashed. Neither wanted to be in the queen's chambers, the wounds still too raw.

The queen's body was placed in stasis in the center of the grand foyer of the Royal Mansion. The indignity of seeing her several times a day made my skin crawl. More than once, I thought of shattering the glass top, dousing her with oil, and setting her ablaze.

Tamrin dared me to open the casket and piss on her again, so she'd have to smell it in whatever hell she was sent.

I considered it more than once when I was drunk.

The last official day of mourning ended, and the first day of normalcy arrived. Together, we faced the gaping hole left by Jesmir's absence. The month-long lack of adrenaline-inducing danger left us preoccupied with that emptiness. The parades over and the noise fading into history, we found solace in one another.

Jesmir's body was placed in the family tomb, where it would sit for a full day before he would be sealed away from us forever.

Jesma never left his side once he was placed in the stone internal prison. I never left hers. We stood with him for almost half the day until Corvan ordered chairs brought in. Then we sat, cried, and exchanged stories. Tamrin finally told us what happened in Garrow's Basin. I wish I'd had a chance to hear Jesmir's version.

Kara remained standing, hands on the glass casket, eyes locked on Jesmir's face. Kar-Kara, Kara's zatia, arrived to console the bereaved Korund.

"I wish I'd had a chance to know him as you did," Kar-Kara says.

There definitely was something between Jesmir and Kara that neither revealed while he was alive. I find joy in knowing Jesmir had someone who thought that highly of him.

The next day, we held a private ceremony for our lost friend. There were only a few hours left before internment.

Jesma spoke.

"From the first time my heart beat, yours was there. We rarely spent a day apart. Except for when you went hunting with Dad. Or when you snuck out to go on one of your stupid bender adventures. I used to get so mad at you for not inviting me to come along. But you needed that time away, and I always understood. Besides, you always said you didn't want me to make the 'Grandma' face. I'd call you a selfish prick, but you always had this way of making it up to me when you returned. And I always forgave you."

"You were there for my first heartache, my first loss in fencing, my debutante ball, that time…well, no one is here now who will remember that story, so it doesn't matter. But you had my back that day. As you did every day."

She chokes on her words, and the tears escape her control.

"You tried so hard to be everything a brother should be. And you did it with joy and pride. That's why I love you. You never let me know if it was a burden. You never refused to support me. You told me when I was being pigheaded. You stole my last bite of cookie every time. You gave me your last bite of ice cream…every time."

She sobs, and my throat constricts again.

"You cared for the poor. That was my favorite thing about you. You loved to argue with Grandmother about it. How much livelier would your arguments have been if you knew what we know now, I wonder."

"I'll never forget how you took my hand when that vile man killed our father and ran us right off the cliff. You showed no fear. When we reached the cliff, you jumped, and I jumped with you. Jez and Jes. The Wonder Twins. You gripped my hand so tight on the way down I thought you broke it, but you wouldn't let me go."

"That was you, dear baby brother. You never let go. You held on to every moment for dear life. Savored it. Even when you knew it would go against you, you stepped into it."

She looks at him.

"You got us through that wilderness, out of Killinshire, and into the arms of a hero, never realizing *you* were my hero."

She turns to me, and our eyes lock. My guilt builds to more than I can bear, but I don't look away. This is about her. Not me.

"You found your inner warrior, Jes. What a fierce warrior you turned out to be."

She turns to his casket and places a hand near his head.

"I have always and will always love you. I'll forever miss the stupid doofy grin. Go with peace. You can let go now. I'll be okay."

She sat next to me and grabbed my hand with all her might. I bore through the discomfort. We sat staring at him until the day ended. The hours passed. Ezra set. The tomb tenders came, lifted him, and placed him in his place in the wall. They installed a headstone.

And they left.

Still, we sat.

Then Kara rose, kissed the wall, and read his stone.

"Jesmir, Prince of Teshket, The Greatest Warrior Who Ever Lived. And The Greatest Lover. There Will Be Songs, Brother."

THE END

Glossary

BABA: Genderless Korund word for parent.

BABA-DI: Genderless Korund word for grandparent.

CHATI: Genderless Korund word for aunt/uncle.

NETHER: Little is known about nether other than it kills everything living form that comes into contact with it. No wells have been discovered or documented, and the only known source is from netherstacks. Any contact with nether is deadly and there is no known cure.

NETHERSTACK: stalagmite type formation that forms unexpectedly and spews deadly nether into the air.

PERIAPT: A holy emblem worn to demonstrate the wearers affiliation with their god. Used in prayer to access magic.

SITI: Genderless Korund word for sibling.

ZATIA: Genderless Korund word for spouse.

Acknowledgments

As always, thank you to the best partner anyone could ask for, my wife Jill. I know it's not easy putting up with "Chuckles". Your continued willingness to laugh and find joy in the trainwreck that is me is the bedrock of my sanity. Thank you for pretending that I'm a professional author alongside me.

To Laura Thompson and RB Michaels at Writer's Journey. Once again, we beat this manuscript into submission. Your efforts to edit me into a better storyteller and writer are much appreciated. No story can reach its full potential without strong editing partners and critical eyes.

To my beta readers, Andrea and Amanda. Once again, your honest feedback set the story along a better path. Thank you for suffering through that first draft. It was rough, but the final version is much better for it.

To the collective of nerds, steeped in fantasy and sci-fi lore, that I am fortunate to call friends: Don, DJ, Luke, Ken, Max, Zoe, Hope, Zach, and my son Patrick, a deep thank you. Your support, encouragement, and friendships mean the world to me! Thanks for putting up with my intermittent presence in our Sunday sessions. Don, take a point of *FLUCK* in Luke's game, just because you're awesome.

Huge thank you to Libby Mussachio for once again creating an extraordinary book cover. We both know the hours you spend painting these. Your attention to detail and grasp of "old school" style continue to amaze me. Time to get started on Book III!

Special thanks to my fellow authors who are also my loudest supporters, especially Arlo Z Grave (author of *Black Rose* and *The Ice Moves For No One*) and J. B. Corvin (author of *Harmony of Storms*). It tickles me how much you love this story and how loudly you share it to the world. I'm honored.

Lastly, thank you, the readers of *The God Killers Trilogy*. Without you, there'd be no books. I hope book two lives up to your expectations and that you find within these pages an adventure worthy of your time.

About the Author

Sean has never been far away from his love of *LOTR,*, *Shannara, Dungeons & Dragons, Star Trek, Star Wars, Buck Rodgers*, and *Battlestar Galactica* (the original). An avid reader at a young age, he always enjoyed wide tastes in books from fantasy to mystery to romance—a range only matched by his musical tastes.

A graduate of The Ohio State University, where he studied Mechanical Engineering, he works as a specialist in space flight controls for rocket propulsion and life support systems.

Darkness Blooms marks his second installment into *The God Killers* Trilogy and is his third published work within that world.

Sean currently lives with his wife, Jill, in Pittsburgh, PA, with their annoyingly cute Puggle, Sweaty Betty the Spaghetti Yeti.

COMING SOON!

Also, From Sean D Gregory:

The God Killers Trilogy

- The Growing Darkness
- Garrow's Basin (A God Killers Story)
- Darkness Blooms
- Decades of Night (coming October 2026)

The Case Files of Miles Ward

- The Ruby Rage (coming Spring 2026)
- The Opal Offering (coming Spring 2027)

Stand-Alones and Anthologies

- Sierra the Cyborg Doesn't Want to Kill Anybody (and Other Oddities of the Multiverse) (coming soon)
- Stop to Smell the Hydrangeas (working title)
- Everybody's Everyplace Every-bar (working title)

For updates, news on the latest releases, merchandise, and more, join our newsletter at www.sean-gregory.com

Follow me on Social Media!
Facebook: https://www.facebook.com/authorseandgregory/
Instagram: https://www.instagram.com/sean_gregory_author/
Threads: https://www.threads.net/@sean_gregory_author
YouTube: https://www.youtube.com/channel/@seangregoryauthor
Goodreads: https://www.goodreads.com/seangregoryauthor

Preview of Ruby Rage:
A Miles Ward Case File

PROLOGUE

*Cleveland National Forest
Orange County, CA
April 18th, 1944*

Miles' blood-stained hands shook as the adrenaline receded, and the reality of his experience took hold. His ears still rang from the successive concussions that echoed through the house as he'd emptied his Colt M1911A1 into the monster that had performed the horrid acts against the young girl. Miles' broke into a cold sweat.

Always steady, calm, and decisive in action, Miles fell apart in the aftermath. His confidence gave way to second guesses, regrets, and "shoulda-couldas". He crashed against the rocks of his own inner dialog, and the emotional tsunami swept him into dispair. Guilt, fear, and doubt threatened to pull him under water as he fought in panicked desperation to cling to a small portion of his sanity.

Across the overgrown lawn, his partner, Detective Thom Perring, spoke with Captain Samuels in hushed tones. A kaleidoscope or blue and red lights bathed the surrounding forest and the dilapidated Queen Anne Victorian home in bright strobing colors. The headlights from the coroner's meat wagon illuminated the house in an erie display of dark shadows from overgrown vines...the only evidence of the ghosts the hid inside.

Though they'd ended nearly an hour ago, Miles could still hear the tiny whimpers of twelve-year-old Katy McCoy. Through the gunshot fueled tinnitus, her cries pummeled his consciousness. He clenched his jaw and squeezed his eyes shut, hoping to push the memories away. But her small voice, frail and frightened, lingered. Their memory overshadowed those of the gunshots that killed her abductor...and of the one that killed her.

Though he knew the decision to end her life would haunt him forever, there was little else Miles could do for Katy McCoy. Too deep in the woods and too late to save her, all Miles could do was watch her die a slow and painful death, her injuries too extensive. Miles wanted to run to the car and call out on the radio for help, to bring emergency services to save her life. That would have required him to leave the poor child alone, frightened and dying, in that place.

Even if he'd attempted to radio for help, she never would have survived long enough for him to return. Worse, she'd have died alone.

Katy's fate was sealed long before Miles arrived. He'd arrived too late, taken too long to find the old house in the middle of the national forest.

Miles made a choice. He held her shattered and broken body close as she cried her last tears. He whispered that everything would be okay—that a better place waited for her—even though, in his heart, he believed no such place existed. Miles held Katy's tiny head in his lap as she bled from her many injuries. He swallowed back his tears and told her how beautiful and loved she was before he placed is pistol to her temple and ended her suffering.

He knew there'd be consequences for his decision. He accepted them. His decorated career was over. But he knew too that he had other problems.

No one was going to believe he saw what he saw.

His worst fears had come true. He'd long since started to feel the genetic erosion of his sanity; his perceptions of the world skewed by the same ailments passed along through his mother's bloodline. Reason said that what he saw wasn't possible. But he had witnessed the impossible, he was certain of what he saw. But the doubt lingered. Had he finally gone insane?

Like his mother.

Reality and fantasy mingled and left behind images that seemed so real he couldn't deny their validity at the time.

Now, in the aftermath, the steady assuredness with which he'd acted was cast in doubt.

He'd finally crashed.

Hard.

If only Thom had arrived sooner. If his partner had finished the search in Hollywood Hills faster, he could have been here to witness what Miles saw. But Thom hadn't seen what Miles saw. His longtime partner arrived too late.

From across the overgrown property where he spoke with Captain Samuels, Thom glanced toward his partner and friend. Miles knew Thom was in a pickle. He'd heard the words come out of Miles' mouth, words so unbelievable that Thom was sure Miles' had finally cracked. If Thom didn't believe Miles, there was little chance Captain Samuels would. They'd most certainly send Miles to the looney bin for this.

Everybody knew Miles had a family history of psychotic breaks that stretched back generations. Miles's tale was the kind of story used to scare children at campfires. The stuff of monsters. Of boogey-men.

"Have him checked out by psych," Captain Samuels said, his commanding voice carrying over the noise of squad cars, chatter, and activity.

"Yes, sir," Thom said and made his way over to Miles who still leaned against his car door, head bowed, arms crossed.

"Hey Ace, how you holding up?" Thom asked.

Miles extinguished a cigarette on the heal of his boot.

"I know what I saw. It's not what you think, Thom."

Thom lowered his voice, compassion and worry evident.

"I know what you believe you saw, but I'm telling you, there's no evidence of it." Thom sighed. "He was just a man who did a horrible thing," Thom said. "Let the delusions go. You got the guy. He hurt little Katy. He was a whack job that needed put down. But he is, or was, as human as you and me. That's all."

"I'm telling you," Miles said through clenched teeth, "I know what I saw."

"Listen, if you continue with this—" Thom stopped. He whispered, "Partner, you sound crazy."

"Like my mother. Right? That's what you're all thinking," Miles said.

The uncertainty in Miles' eyes broke Thom's heart. He didn't want to acknowledge Mile's words, but all the evidence pointed to the fact that he was losing his friend to genetic insanity. Thom looked back at the gurney coming from the house.

"C'mere. Come look at the body. Tell me what you see."

Thom put his hand on Miles' shoulder and nudged him to come along. Miles stood and stared at Thom, his eyes simultaneously defiant and unsure. Thom led Miles to the gurney where the forensics team loaded the perpetrator's body into the coroner's wagon.

"Hold up," Thom said.

The coroner's stopped and glanced at the pair.

"This guy smells like he's been dead for months. I've seen some filthy bodies, but this guy hasn't bathed in months," the coroner said.

Thom didn't acknowledge the coroner's comment. He glanced at Miles and placed a hand on the zipper of the body bag.

Miles was terrified that what Thom said would be true and that what he saw inside the house was all in his head. But he couldn't shake the image: the eyes, the scales, the claws...the oppressive darkness. His memories leapt back to the moments before the darkness cleared, and the monster revealed itself. Miles was certain of what he saw.

Thom pulled the zipper and spread the opening to reveal the body of an elderly man, his face practically unrecognizable from the bullet damage. One hand had a hole in it with a finger blown off.

"Look, Pal. It's just a bad old man. A man you pumped five slugs into. A man who deserved what he got."

Miles resisted looking at first but finally glanced at the body. It was just as Thom said—no scales, no elongated limbs or neck. No tail.

The man's face, obliterated by several rounds of .45 caliber bullets, was still very obviously human. What lay in the body bag told the truth. The 'creature' Miles killed was nothing more than a regular old man.

What the hell is going on? *Miles thought.*

"Hell is. All of it," *the voice in his head said.*

"That's why I told you to kill them both."

Miles shook his head violently.

Thom put a hand on Miles' shoulder, his face grim.

"Buddy, you've got bigger issues," Thom said.

At that moment a second team came out with the body of the young girl. Thom and Miles watched as they loaded Katy's body into a second hearse. Thom studied Miles with sadness.

"Tell me again, why did you shoot Katy McCoy?"

Miles stared at Thom unable to speak.

CHAPTER 1

Hollywood CA
Bradbury Building
October 7th, 1945
11:32 a.m.

"Ooooowww..." Miles groaned.

"That feels exquisite, no?"

Go away.

No sooner had Miles awakened, and the voices started at it again. He wasn't in the mood for voices. Though his head pounded harder than a beating from his stepdad, it clearly wasn't enough to drown *her* out. Nothing hit hard enough to do that. The bitter metallic taste of last night's bender hung in his mouth like dry cotton. He grimaced at the bright light that shined through his eyelids. Without some much as a peek, he knew he'd forgotten to close the blackout shades. The red glow revealing the inner veins inside the flap of skin that struggle to open was already too much to bear.

Damn-it.

The bright had grown to an unbearable red-yellow glow that seared the pattern of his veins through his eyelids and into his retinas. Dawn had long since passed, which meant he'd overslept again.

He opened his eyes a sliver and observed the single pane window that allowed the early morning light to spill into his dreary office. Cold sweat soaked the sheets and his undergarments, his body attempting to cleanse his system of alcohol. His clammy skin stuck to itself, the dirty stickiness in the crooks of his arms a sign he needed a shower. The whole place smelled like a locker room. He knew he probably smelled like a dead animal. Thankfully, it was cooler than normal overnight, and he didn't have to add sweltering heat sweat to the rich tapestry of his odor.

He rolled over on the cot to face away from the sunlight, too tired, too hungover, and too depressed to get up to close the blackout shades. A loud clang of glass on the hardwood floor range out, the empty Jameson bottle from last night, rolling off the cot and down the slope of the worn wooden floor. It hit the ground with a perfect ring, signaling a new day of suffering, adding to the misery of his throbbing head.

"Oh c'mon, man," he grumbled as he squinted his eyes shut tighter. The bottle rolled the full length of his office, announcing its journey with the hollow ring of empty promises of forgotten trauma.

He opened his eyes a sliver and was welcomed by a blurry view of the smoked glass window in the door of his tiny office. He could almost make out the backwards sign on the window: "draW seliM" with "rotagitsevnI etavirP" in smaller letters underneath. Through the blurry haze he couldn't really make out the letters, but he'd read it enough, even his hungover brain could fill in the details. Each reading of the backwards office decal told him what he was…a disgraced hero turned private dick.

Most people left the "private" off that, nowadays.

He lay there and willed himself to fall back asleep, lacking any desire to be awake. Miserably unable to return to the unfeeling bliss of passed out sleep, he groaned again. He wished the day would just pass quickly, desperate for a few more hours of sleep. He'd almost slipped back into unconsciousness when bile rose in his throat, the burn and taste and early warning. He reached under the cot for the little bucket he kept for such emergencies and groaned in useless misery when it wasn't there. Mild panic set in as he sat up in a hurry. Vertigo struck and his head spun. He blinked his eyes open in rapid succession, held a hand over his mouth, and bolted from the bed to the small water closet he was fortunate enough to have in his office.

Shit, he thought, as bile filled his mouth.

He forced his head over the porcelain god just in time to heave a small amount of bile into the mineral stained toilet. He hung there and waited. A slight cramp seized his stomach and signaled another bout of dry heaves was on the way. The pressure in his head grew as his stomach lurched, his abdominal muscles clenching with painful violence. The effort exponentially increased the orchestra's activities behind his eyes and in his temples. It didn't do much for the rancid mouth taste either. His gut convulsed, the sucker punch of another useless heave, but nothing came.

Great.

He laid his head down on the toilet. The cool porcelain soothed his forehead even though he was aware that if someone walked in, they just see a disgusting man with his head against an equally disgusting commode. When the urge to heave finally passed, he rose, hands on either side of the cold throne, just in case. Miles hovered there for a moment, one last acquiescence to the throne of his iniquity.

He took a deep breath and forced his body erect. Wobbling, the room spined, its dim light and dirty walls against the blemished mirror, another metaphor for his shattered life, He steadied himself. "C'mon pal," he coaxed himself to remain upright and reached over to turn on the sink.

The water ran discolored for a moment before it finally cleared, the well water scent of sulfur filling the air. When it cleared, he grabbed the rubber stopper and inserted it into the drain. With hands on both sides of the sink, he squeezed his head under the faucet, his body twisted into an uncomfortable crouch. The cold water ran over his head, down and around his face, falling from his nose, ears, and chin to fill the sink. It felt refreshing, even if he was physically contorted in the effort. Time slipped away and remained there, focused on his breathing as the water cascaded past his vision. He watched the streams of falling water as its path shifted and jumped along his features slowly filling the sink.

On a three count, he took a shallow breath and plunged his face into the water. Holding his breath, he counted to five, then released it slowly, the bubbles in the water travelling up the side of his face. He held his breath on another five count, removed his head from the water, and took in new air, this time counting to thirty as he did. Plunging his face back into the water, Miles held his breath again, also on the thirty count before releasing the breath and holding it one more time, matching the thirty-beat cadence. He stayed there for fifteen more seconds before he removed his face from the water and drawing in one more slow breath.

He thanked his mother for the ritual that had become his first line of defense when he needed to clear his head. A head which still throbbed as if Sid Catlett were beating him with sticks while Benny Goodman orchestrated the assault.

Reaching for the already damp towel that hung from the hook on the wall, he let the water drip from his hair and face into the sing. He draped the over his head and fished in the sink to uncork the stopper. The drain made a sucking sound as the mini whirlpool began for form. The damp towel did little to curb the dripping water, too wet to absorb another drop from his unkept hair and face, but he managed as best he could. The old mirror on the medicine cabinet above the sink reflected his haggard image and he stared at the sunken bloodshot eyes, unshaved face, and crooked nose from one fight too many.

"Miles, you look like the ninth circle of hell."

"Yeah, third day in a row," he replied aloud.

He studied the lines in his face, cracked lips, and bushy eyebrows were a mix of course and fine hairs, some significantly longer than others, started to show signs of aging. Even though he was barely about to turn thirty-one he had the appearance of a homeless mad scientist twenty years older. Grey already touched his temples and spread upward into his light brown hair. On the streets he'd look like a homeless drunkard.

One more missed rent payment on this office and you will be.

"Fuck off," he replied aloud.

The voice was right though. If he didn't find work soon, he'd indeed be out on the street.

He smiled at himself in the mirror even though he didn't feel like it. His one redeeming feature was the dazzling set of perfectly white, perfectly straight teeth. One of two genetic gifts from his mother and the only one that was positive. He'd certainly been blessed with his mother's teeth.

"And her crazies."

Go to hell.

"You first."

He flashed a quick smile at the mirror that was nowhere close to how he felt and reminded himself how little he had to smile about. His permanent scowl returned with ease. The towel fell to his shoulders, drawing his attention to the stained white T-shirt he wore.

"Miles, you really look like shit," he repeated aloud.

He placed the damp towel back on the towel ring next to the sink and sniffed his armpits. He grimaced at the stench.

"And you stink."

Scram.

"You'd miss me if I left."

Try me.

He glanced at his watch.

11:32 am.

"Christ, it's late," he mumbled.

Miles grabbed his toothbrush and a box of *Arm & Hammer* baking soda. He stuck the toothbrush under the faucet, turned the water on for brief moment, shook off as much excess as he could and jammed the toothbrush into the tattered orange box, its edges frayed from excessive handling. He wiggled the brush around inside, extracted it, and stuck the brush in his mouth. He began to gently work the wet baking soda around his teeth and gums, counting twenty seconds before he switched positions: top right, bottom right, top left, bottom left. He repeated the process, over and over again until he was satisfied.

He heard his mother's voice in his head, "Miles, you can have everything in the world, but if you have an ugly smile no one will like you." Or her other famous words, "You'll catch a wonderful wife with that smile."

Apparently, a pretty smile wasn't enough in this world if the world thought you were several sandwiches short of a picnic.

"Loony as a jay bird, you are."

Can we just cool it today?

"Yes mother, I'm crazy as a loon but at least I'm brushing my teeth," he mumbled with the toothbrush at his molars.

He looked at his watch. 11:39. Time's up. He turned the water back on, rinsed his mouth and his toothbrush, placed the items back in the medicine cabinet, closed the cabinet and smiled at the mirror again.

"Yeah, the pearly whites are white. Everyone likes me now."

"You're aces."

"Fuck off," he said to himself and no one before heading back to his desk. The modest office was appointed with a less than modest desk, a desk chair, two client chairs that were one client away from collapse, three filing cabinets that were chipped and rusted, a coat rack that wobbled, and his cot, which thankfully hadn't popped springs yet. The entirety of his life was contained in this small office, and all of it looked like ready for the junk yard. He owned only two items of value.

He tried not to think about the shambles his life had become as he stepped to the desk. The center stationary drawer held the aspirin bottle. He pulled it open, an act that always took effort and made no small amount of screeching as metal ground on metal. The high-pitched squeal bounced around in his head, and he winced in aggravation. His relief at finding the bottle was short lived and he fought back a tantrum.

Empty.

His heart sank. He'd forgotten to refill it from the last bender, the day before. His headache retaliated with ferocity. Too much whiskey and not enough water.

"Nice job, Dick Tracy."

"Damn it all to hell," he groaned.

Miles always talked to himself when he was over stressed, over tired, over hungry, or hung over. Or when that annoying voice seemed particularly out of control, which was pretty much all the time anymore. Today, all those conditions existed simultaneously.

His stomach rumbled.

He didn't have much of an appetite, but he knew he needed water, food, and aspirin if he had any hope of taming this headache. And coffee, a gluttonous amount of coffee. Water, aspirin, coffee, and food.

"A nice plate of bacon, eggs, and toast would be nice right about now.

You really need to take better care of yourself, Miles.

You used to be in much better shape. Now you're a souse."

"Zip it. You're bustin' my chops and I ain't in the mood," he snarled.

His eyes fell on the cot. Not bothering to straighten the sheets he folded the got, stuffed the loose sheets into the folded mattress, and shoved the whole mess into the closet. He fought the metal frame to finagle it in so the door could close. He leaned against the closet door, head bowed and forced the negative thoughts down.

If he didn't land a case soon, he wouldn't even have this shitty office with its shitty heat and shitty water closet.

He missed his little house in Van Nyes. The charming ranch home with its small yard had filled him with pride—his own little chunk of Southern California. He had hoped to eventually save enough to upgrade to a nicer place back then. Now he'd settle for enough cash to get aspirin, coffee, breakfast…and another bottle of whiskey.

But nobody wanted to hire a disgraced LAPD Homicide Detective.

Nearly out of funds, completely out of whiskey, and almost out of time, Miles was desperate. He'd take a sleezy adulterer if it meant he could cover the rent for one more month.

Miles opened a drawer in the metal filing cabinet he used as a dresser, removed his last clean T-shirt along with a clean well-worn blue button down. Never accused of being a traditionalist, Miles had easily transitioned to the newer "post-rationing" changes in men's fashions when he had money. Now he couldn't afford to keep up with the changes in fashion. Before he'd been booted from the Detective Squad, he bought a new slick shirt or pair of slacks every month to stay on trend. His suit, like his chairs, were just one notch up from threadbare.

As with every other aspect of his life, his clothes were a sad reminder of what he'd lost, and they were nearly as tattered as the rope of sanity he clung to.

A year in the loony bin and six months without gainful employment would do that to a man.

He grabbed his briefcase and stuffed the shirts, a clean pair of boxers, a pair of socks, and his shower bag inside. He was in desperate need of a shower and shave. A quick flip of the wrist drove the case shut with a snap that was a little louder than he intended.

"Ugh", he groaned.

He snagged the dirty shirt he wore the night before from the back of a chair, threw it on, tucked it in his trousers, buttoned and zipped himself, and readjusted his suspenders. From the coat rack he grabbed his shoulder holster with his Colt Model 1911, the first of his two items of value, and swung it over his shoulder.

He considered throwing the pistol in the briefcase but didn't feel the need to recreate that sound again. His throbbing head would retaliate. Instead, he grabbed his coat and tie from the rack, threw on his well-worn fedora, checked his pocket for his keys, counted his measly forty-six cents in change, snatched up the briefcase, and headed for the door.

His fingers hadn't quite reached the handle when a shadow appeared in the hallway on the other side of the smoked glass…